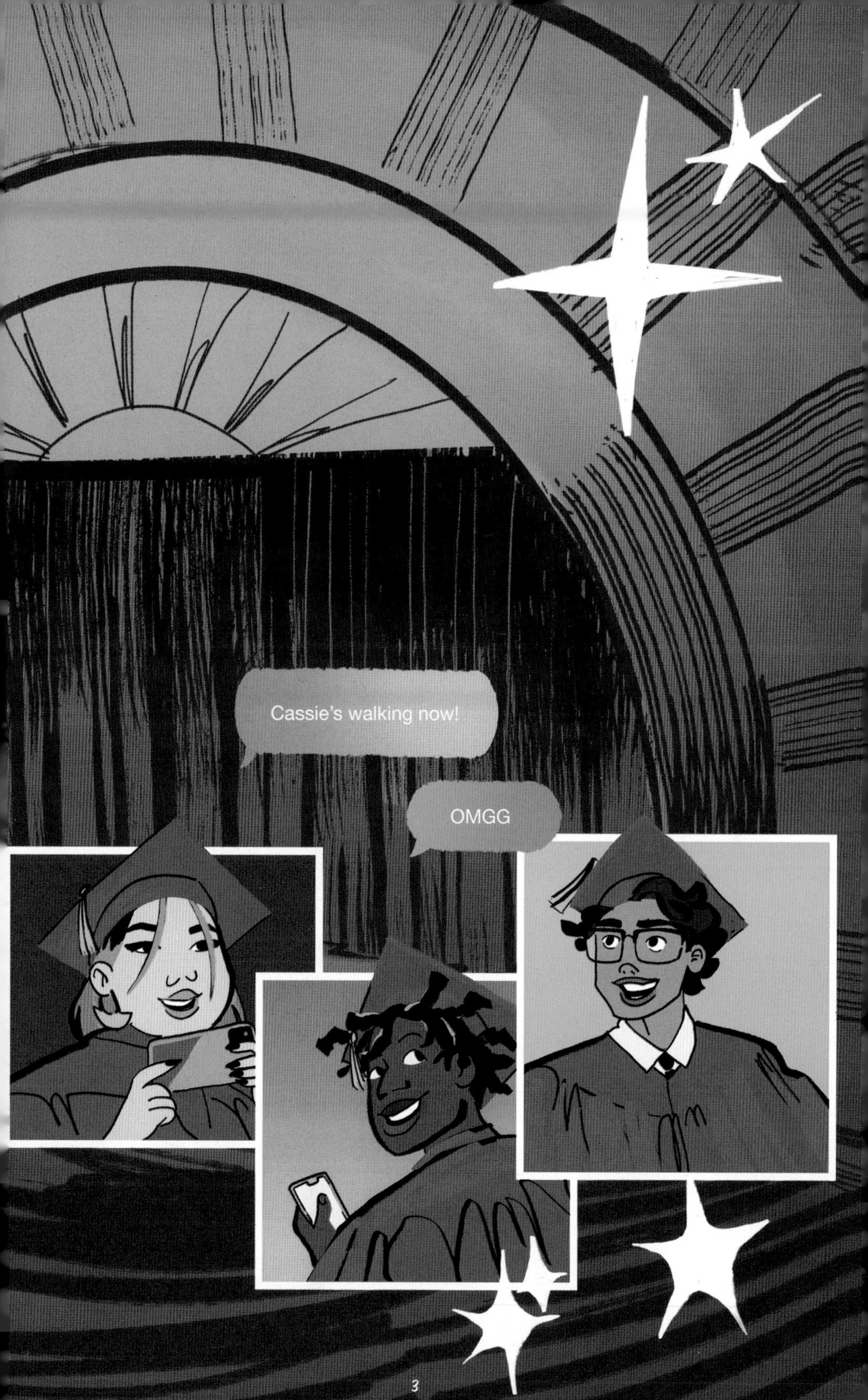
Cassie's walking now!
OMGG

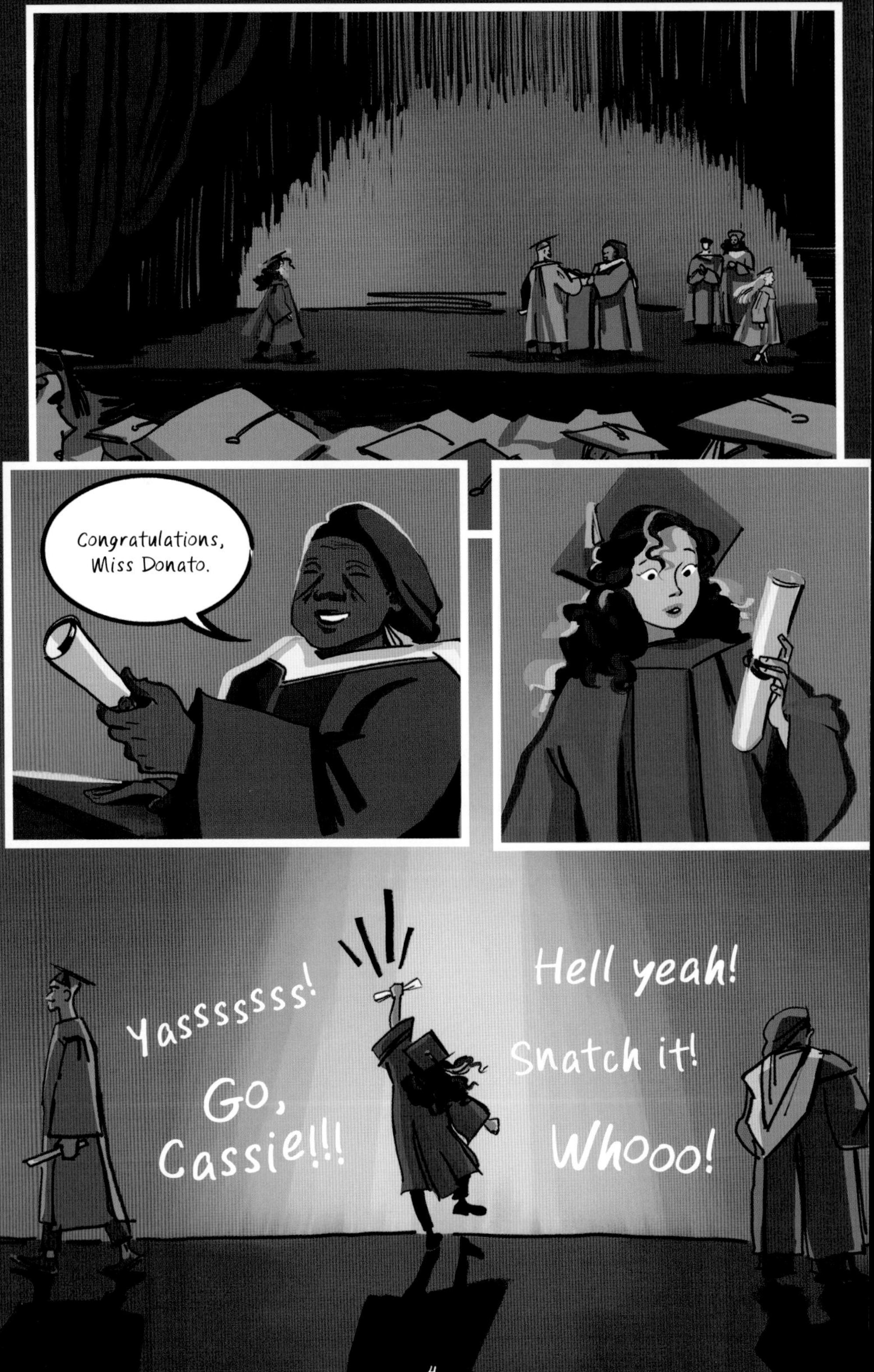

Congratulations, Miss Donato.
Yassssss!
Go, Cassie!!!
Hell yeah!
Snatch it!
Whooo!

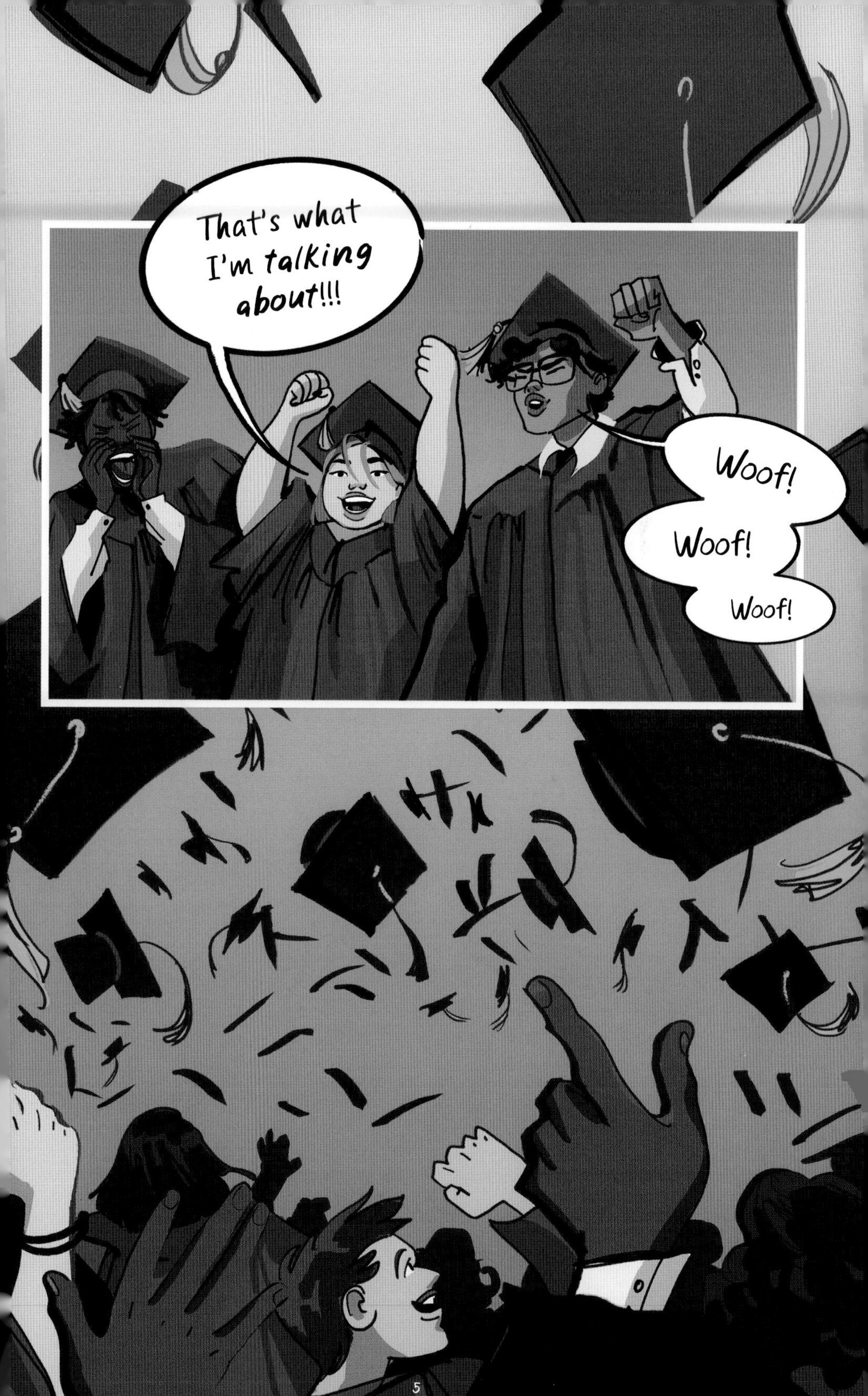
That's what I'm talking about!!!
Woof!
Woof!
Woof!

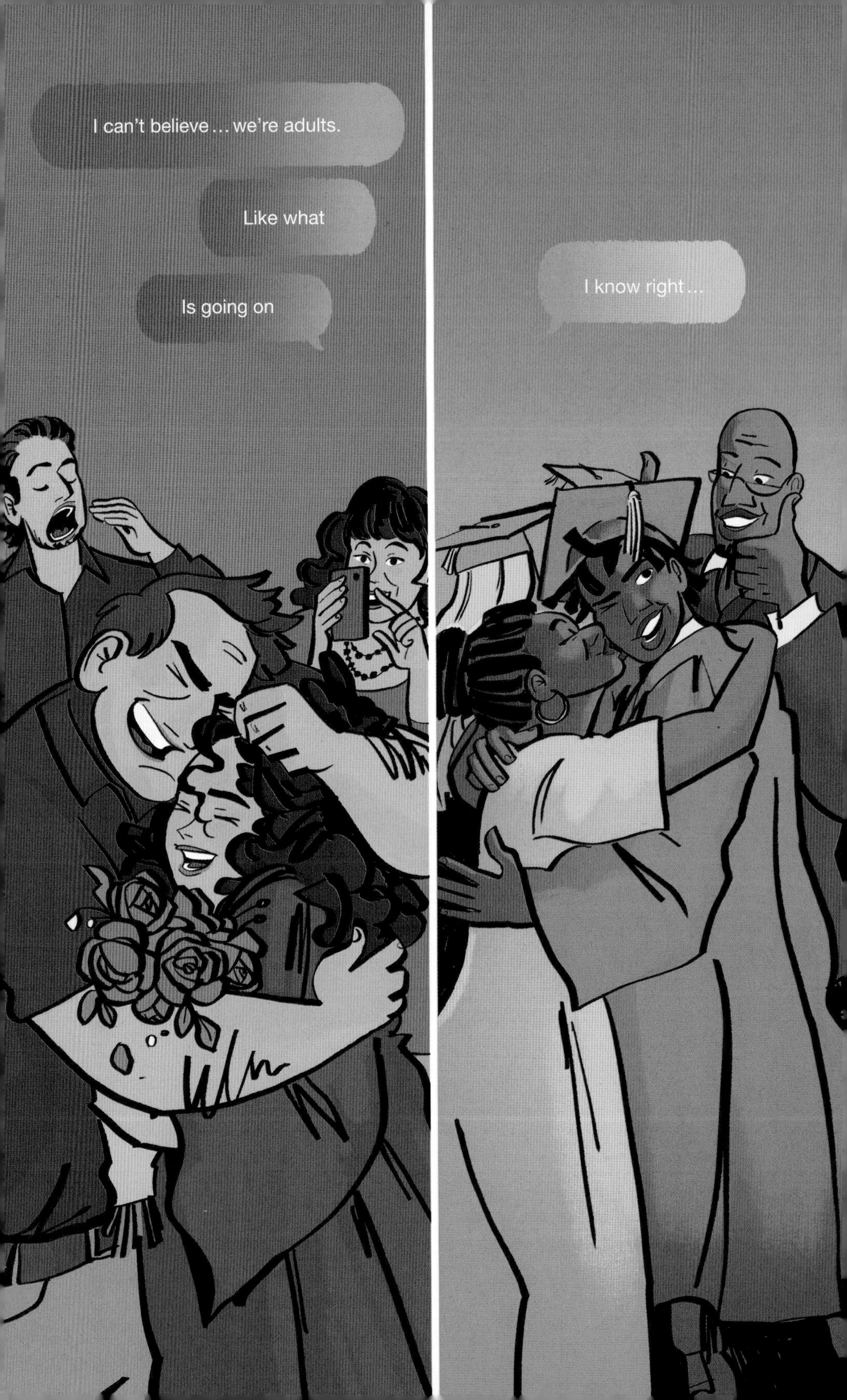
I can't believe… we're adults.
Like what
Is going on
I know right…

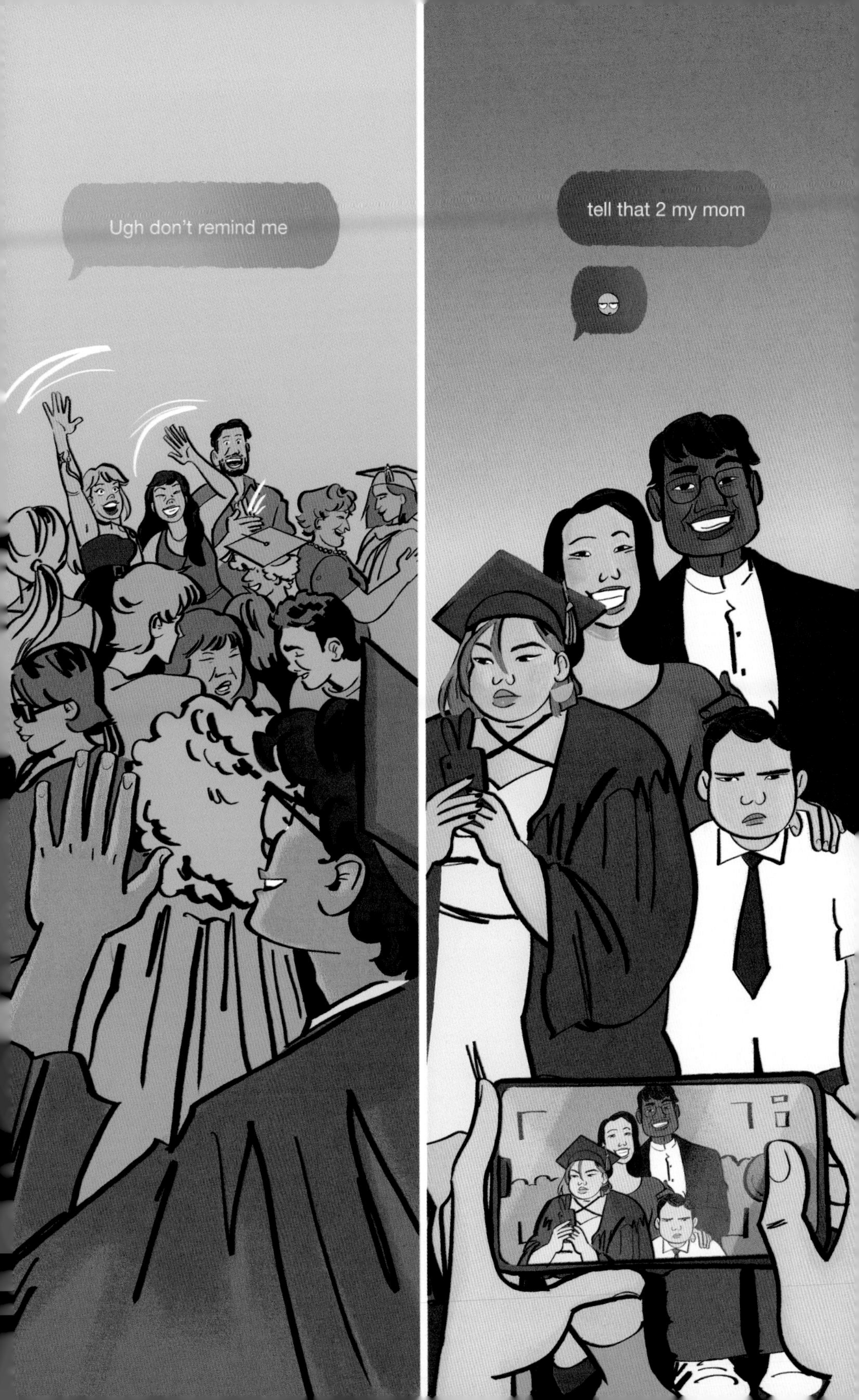
Ugh don't remind me
tell that 2 my mom

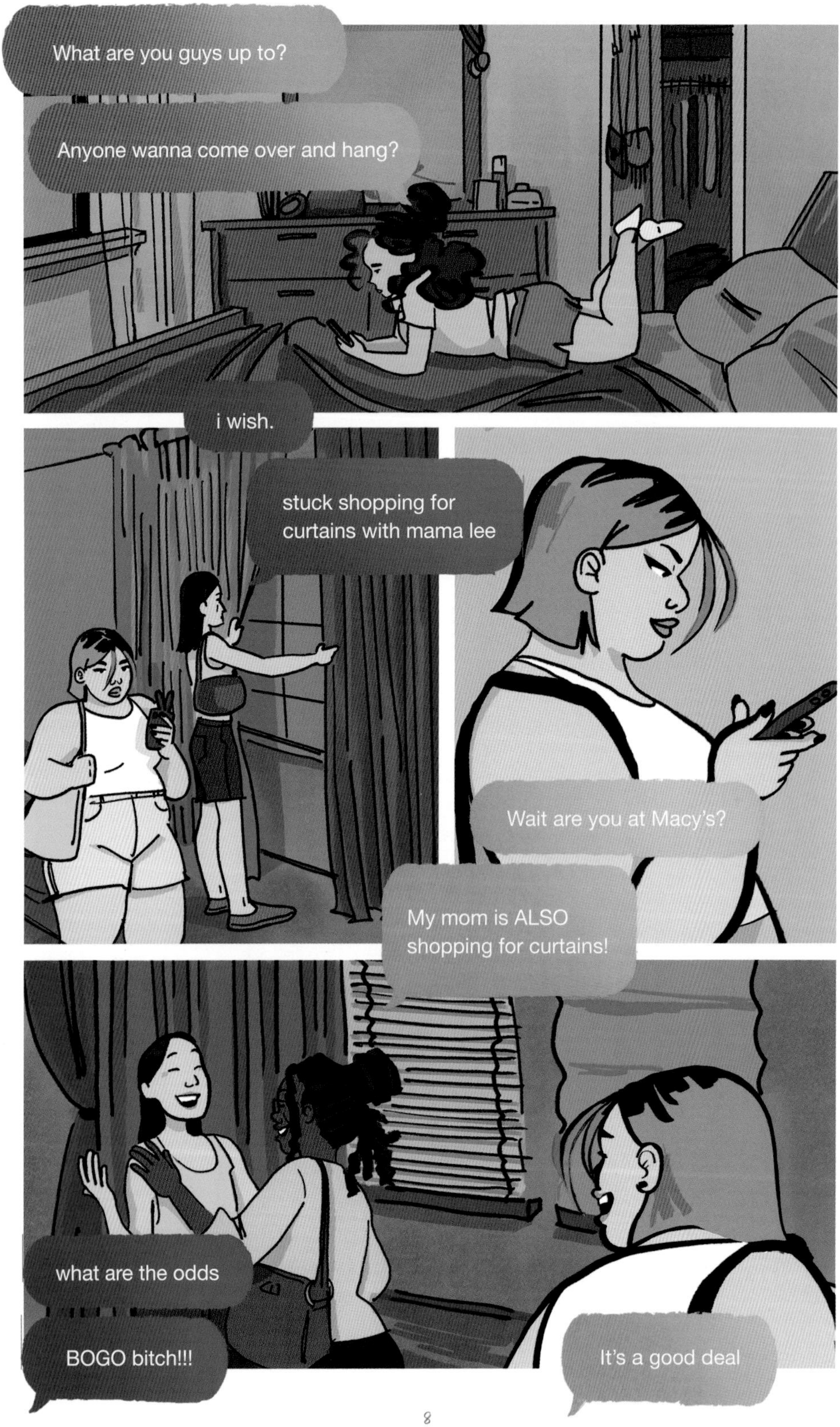
What are you guys up to?
Anyone wanna come over and hang?
i wish.
stuck shopping for curtains with mama lee
Wait are you at Macy's?
My mom is ALSO shopping for curtains!
what are the odds
BOGO bitch!!!
It's a good deal

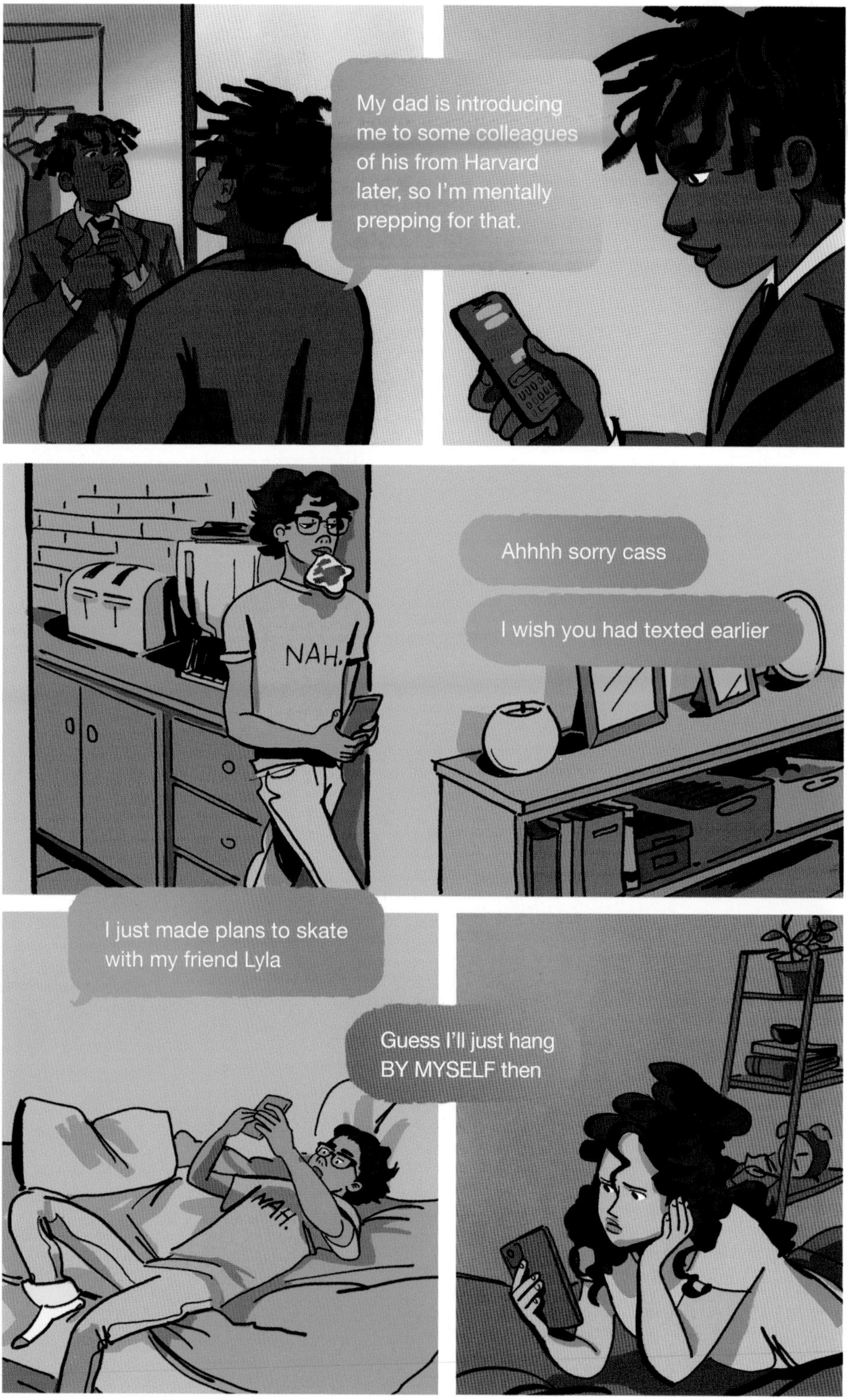
My dad is introducing me to some colleagues of his from Harvard later, so I'm mentally prepping for that.
NAH.
Ahhhh sorry cass
I wish you had texted earlier
I just made plans to skate with my friend Lyla
Guess I'll just hang BY MYSELF then
NAH.

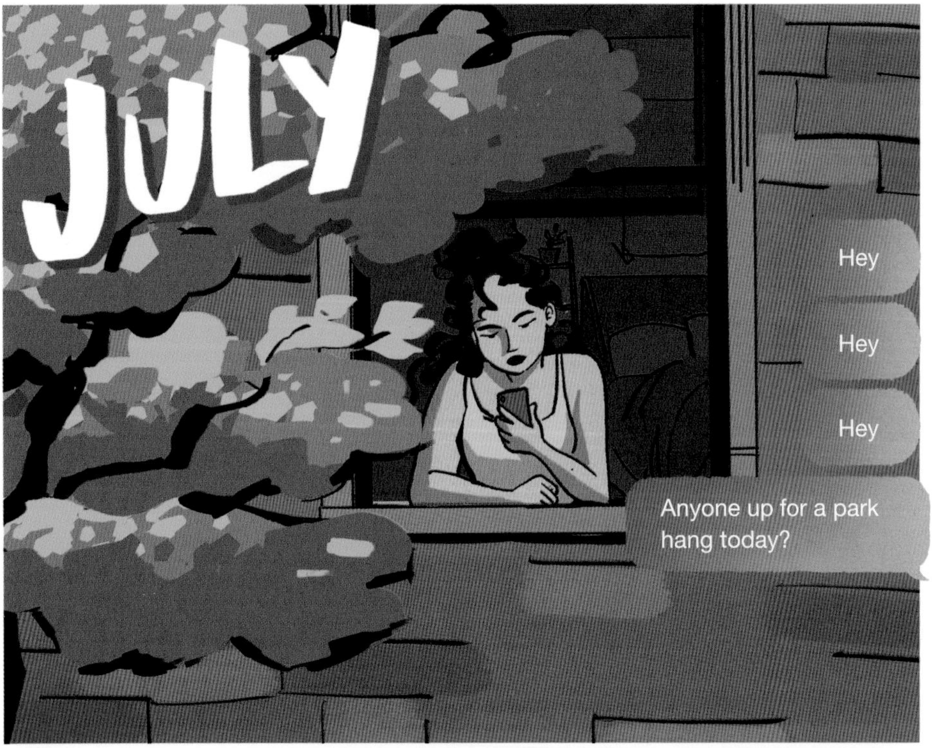
JULY
Hey
Hey
Hey
Anyone up for a park hang today?

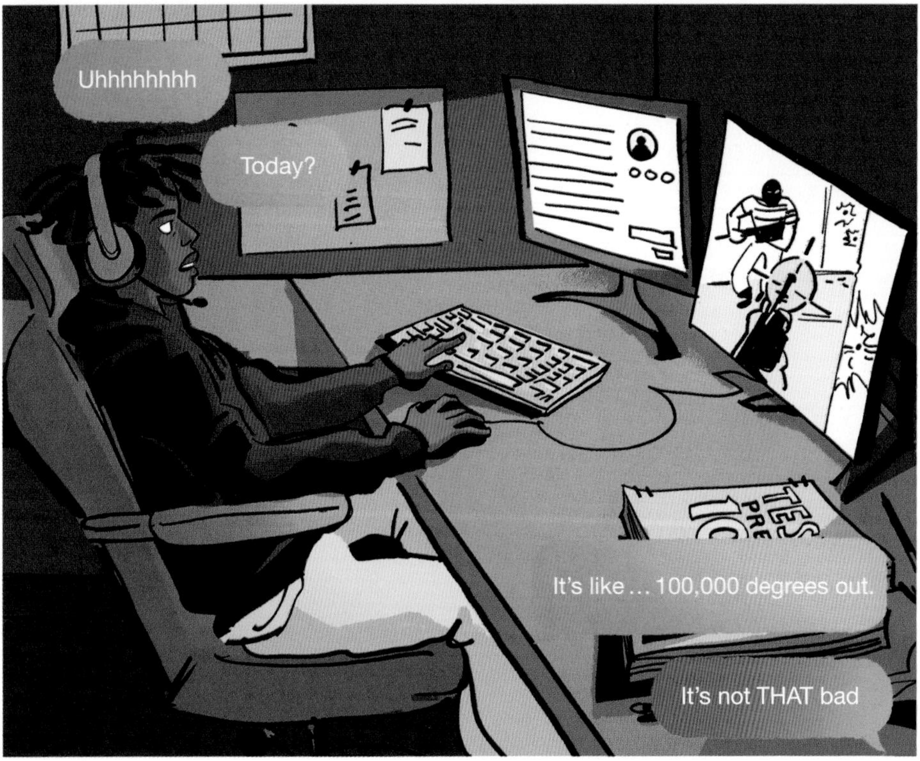
Uhhhhhhh
Today?
It's like... 100,000 degrees out.
It's not THAT bad

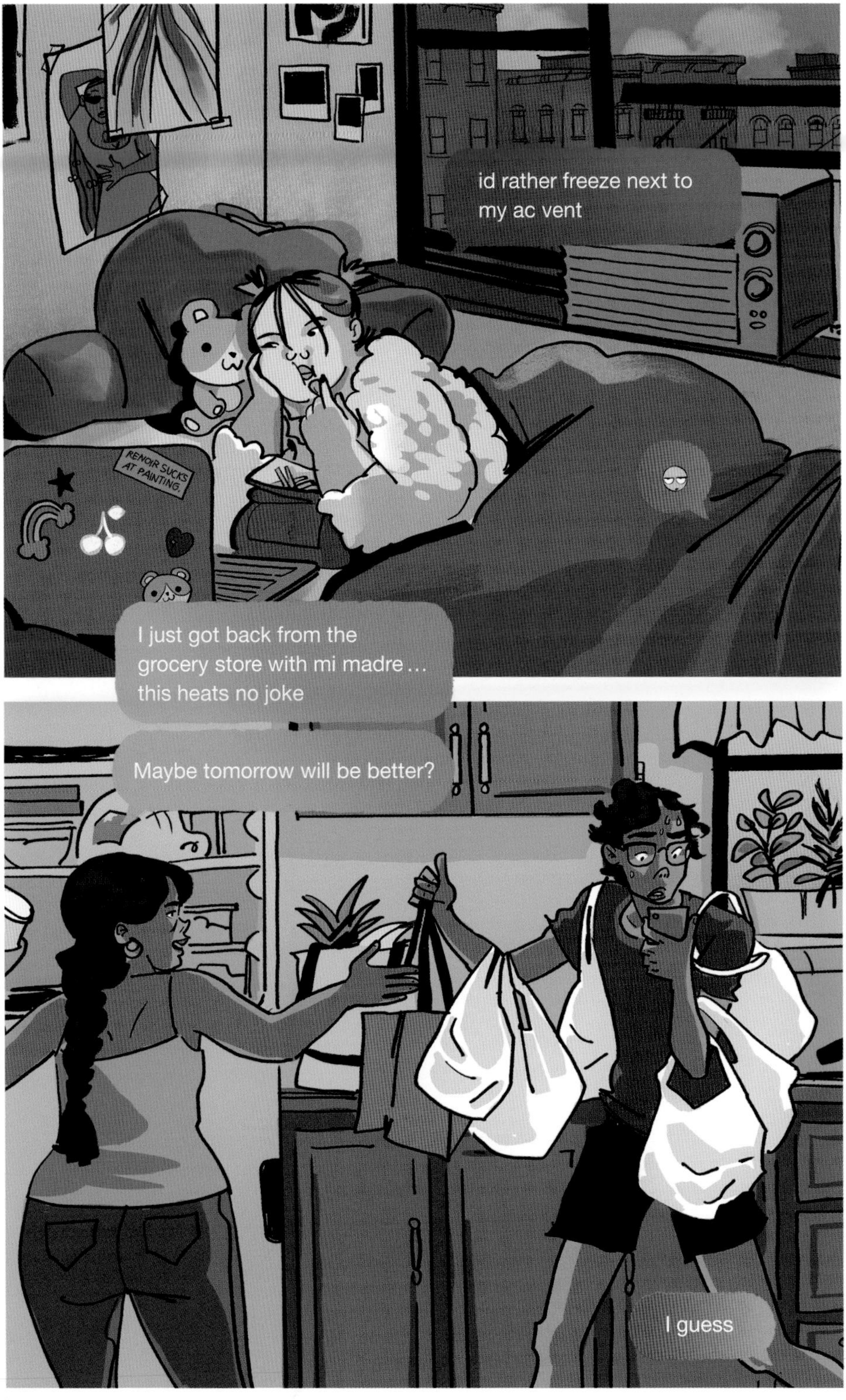
id rather freeze next to
my ac vent
RENOIR SUCKS AT PAINTING.
I just got back from the
grocery store with mi madre…
this heats no joke
Maybe tomorrow will be better?
I guess

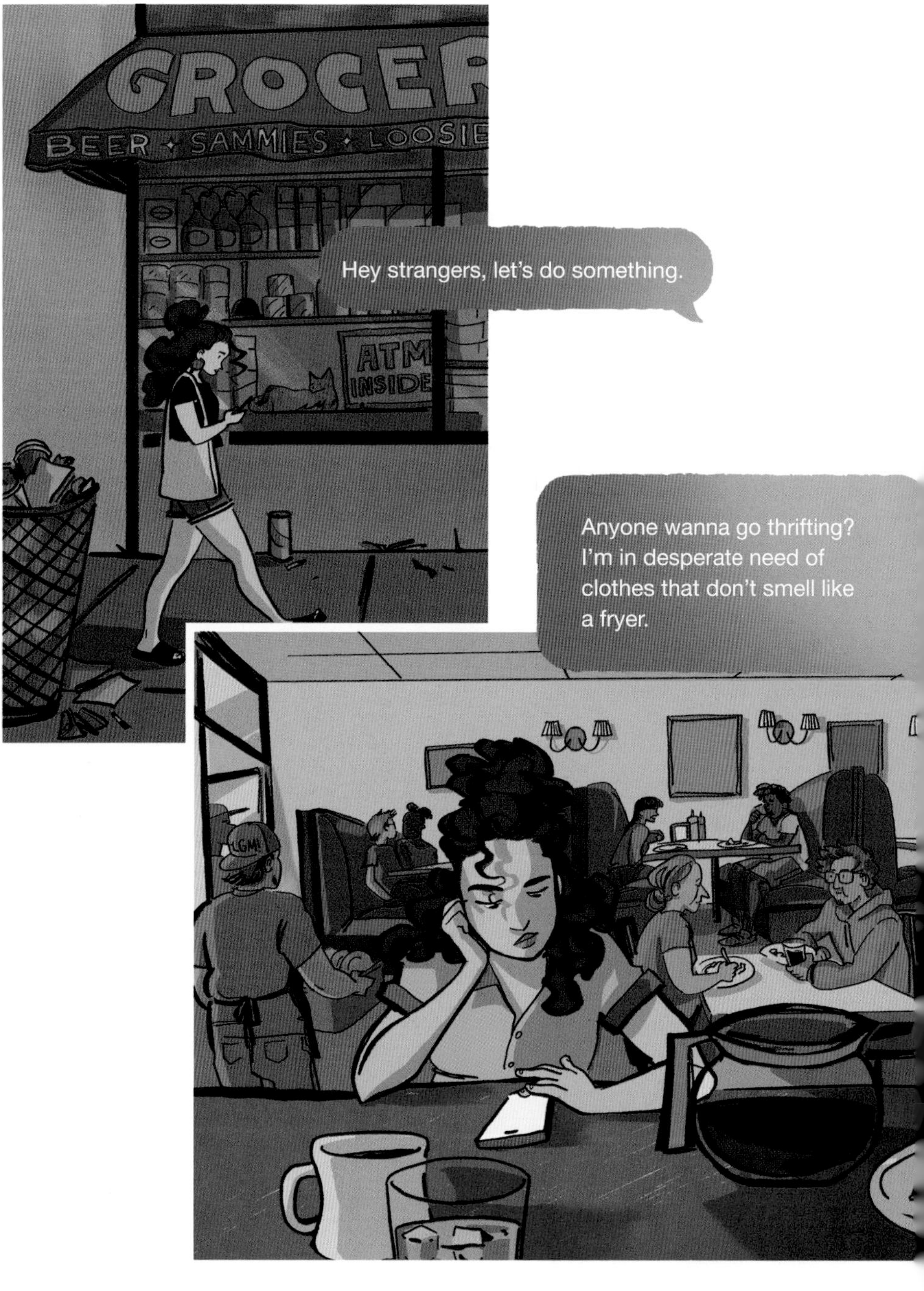
GROCER
BEER ✦ SAMMIES ✦ LOOSIE
ATM INSIDE
Hey strangers, let's do something.
Anyone wanna go thrifting? I'm in desperate need of clothes that don't smell like a fryer.

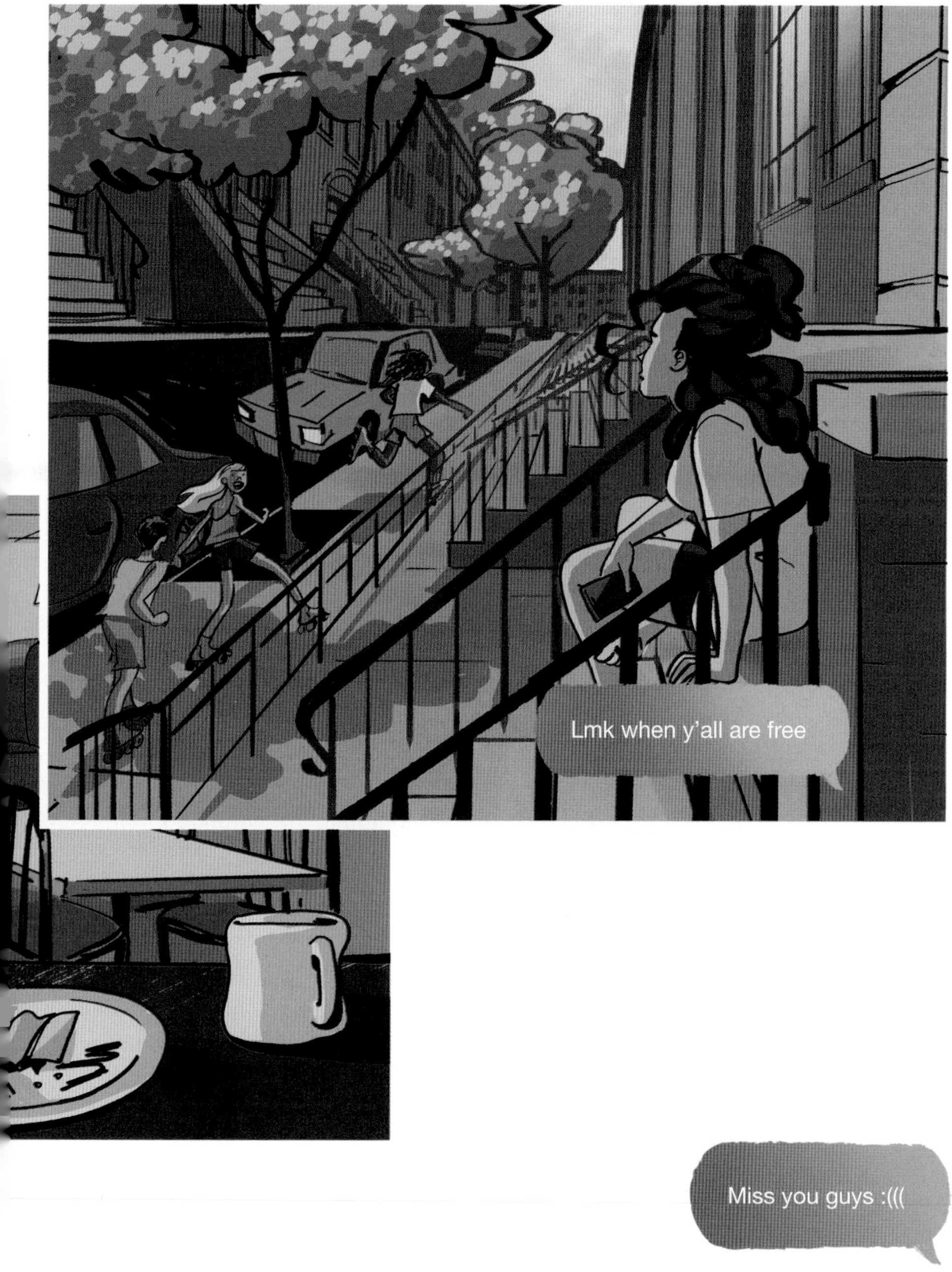
Lmk when y'all are free
Miss you guys :(((

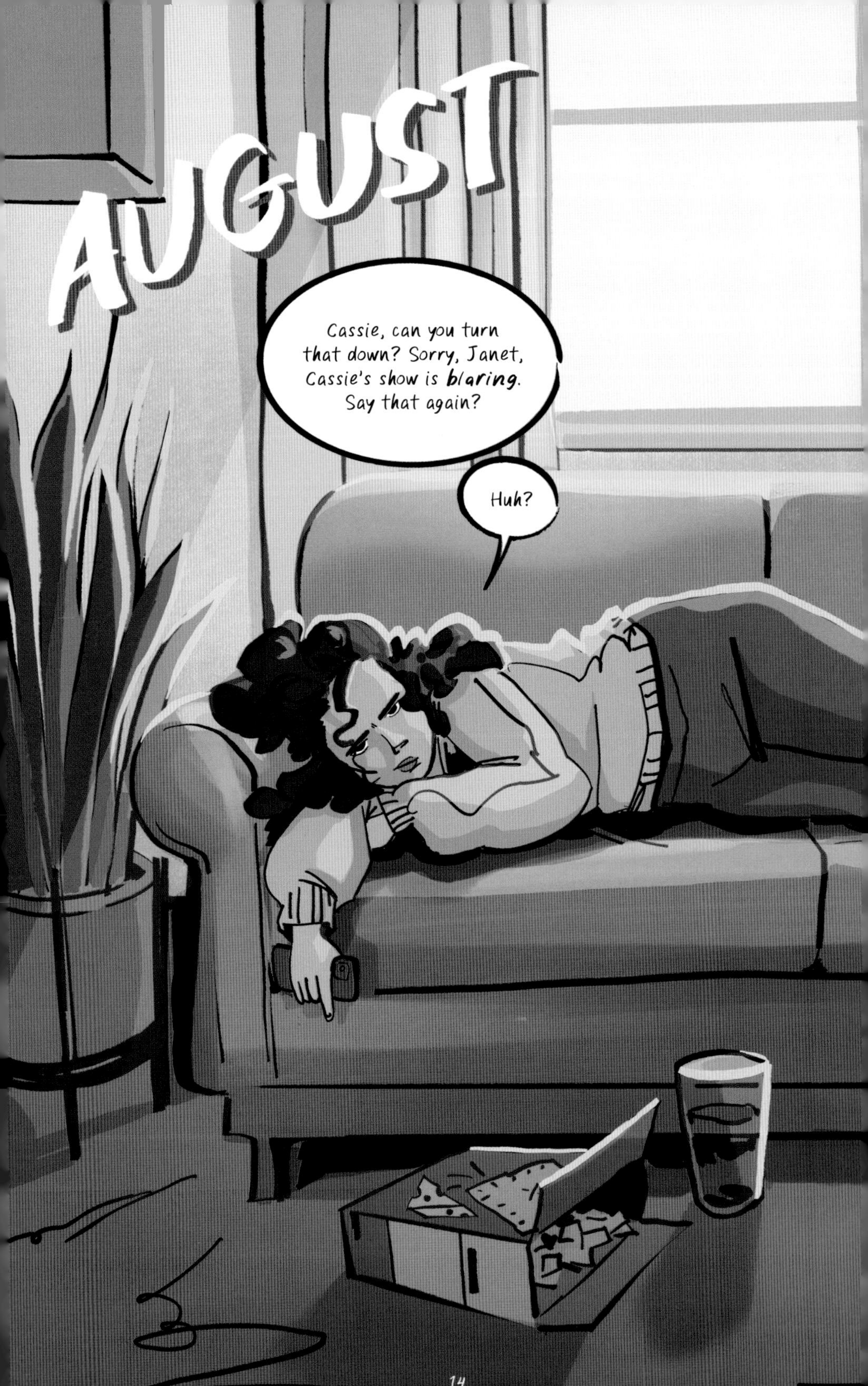
AUGUST
Cassie, can you turn that down? Sorry, Janet, Cassie's show is *blaring*. Say that again?
Huh?

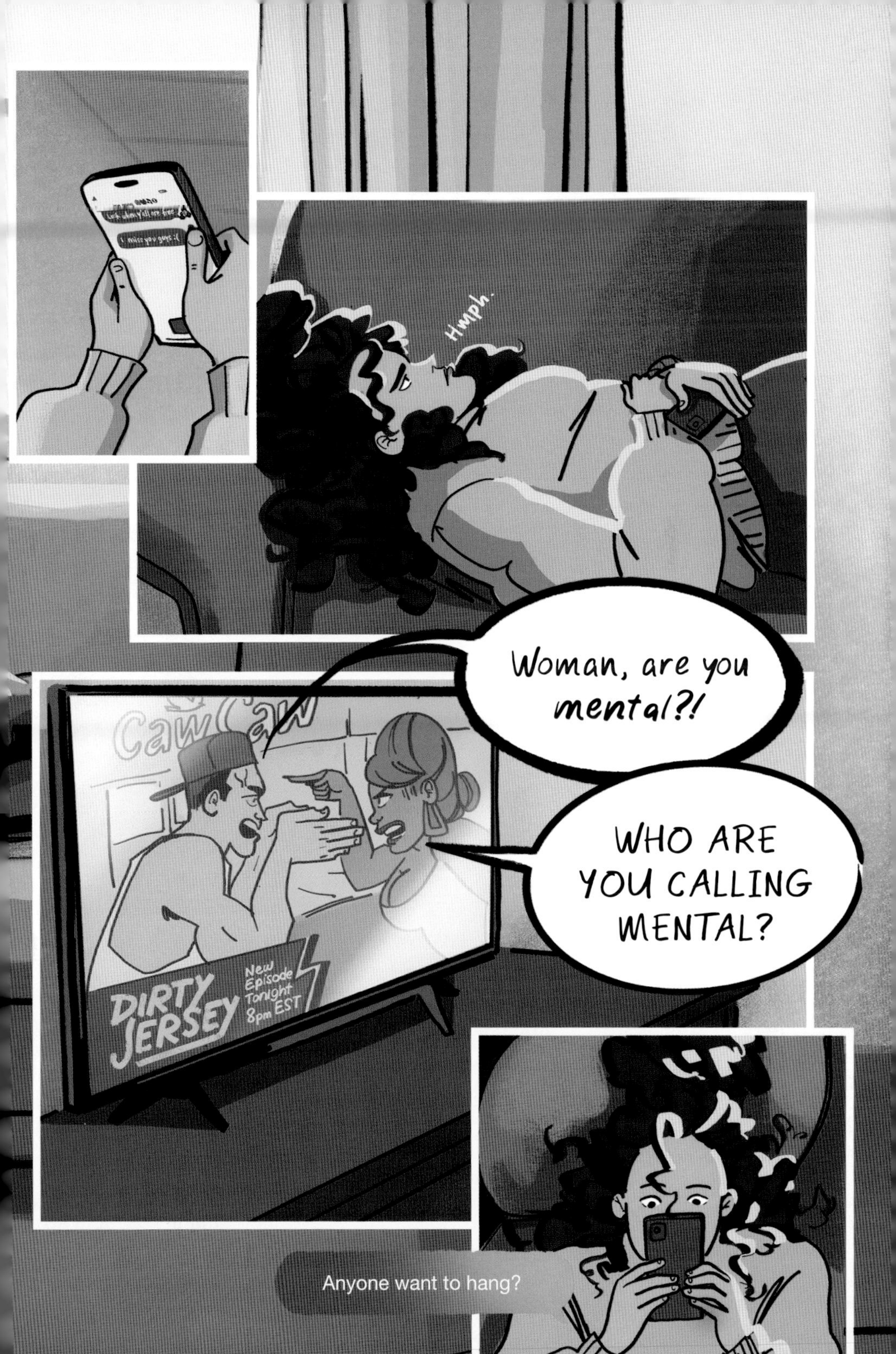
i miss you guys :(
Hmph.
Woman, are you mental?!
WHO ARE YOU CALLING MENTAL?
CawCaw
DIRTY JERSEY
New Episode Tonight 8pm EST
Anyone want to hang?

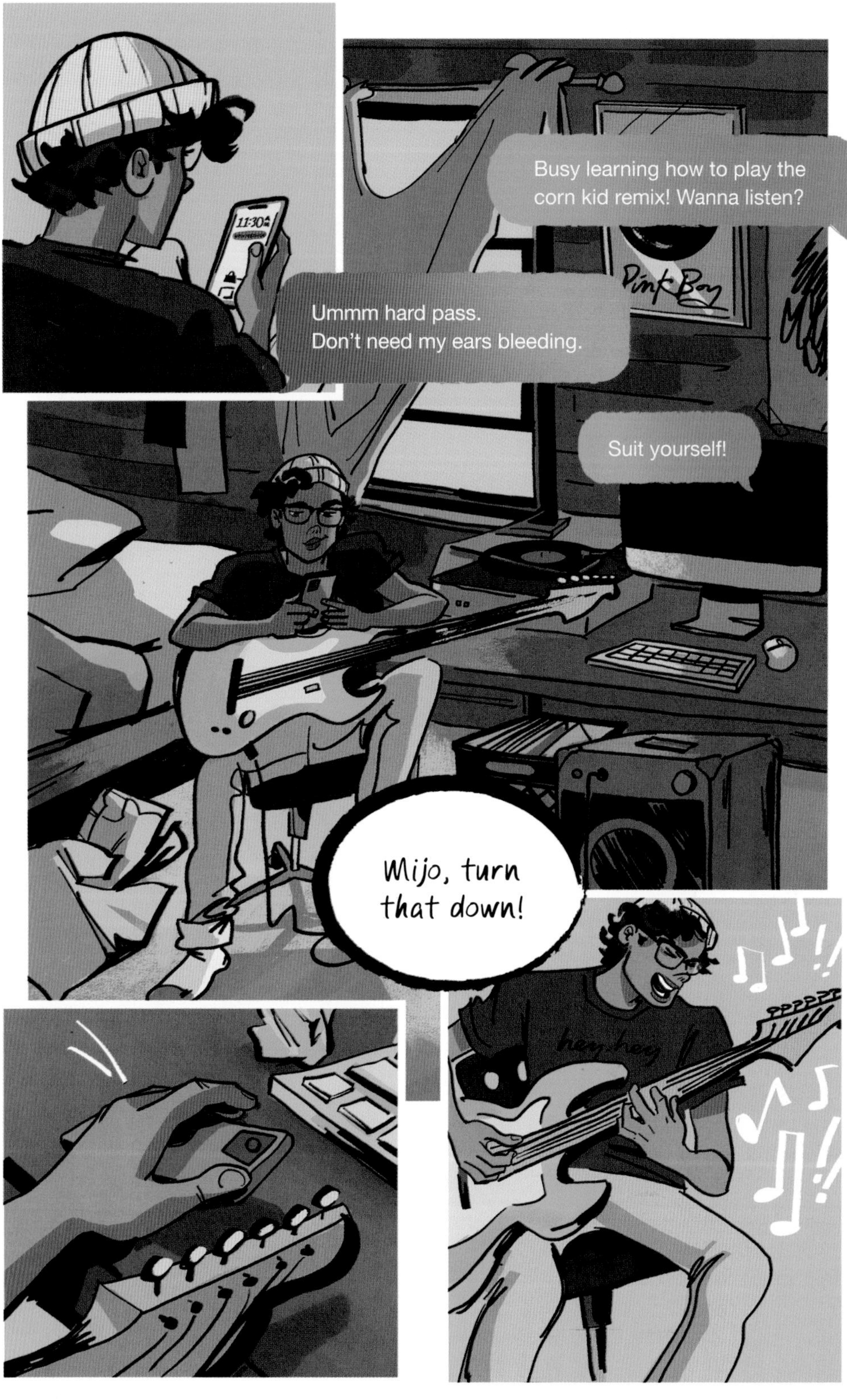
Busy learning how to play the corn kid remix! Wanna listen?
Ummm hard pass. Don't need my ears bleeding.
Suit yourself!
Mijo, turn that down!

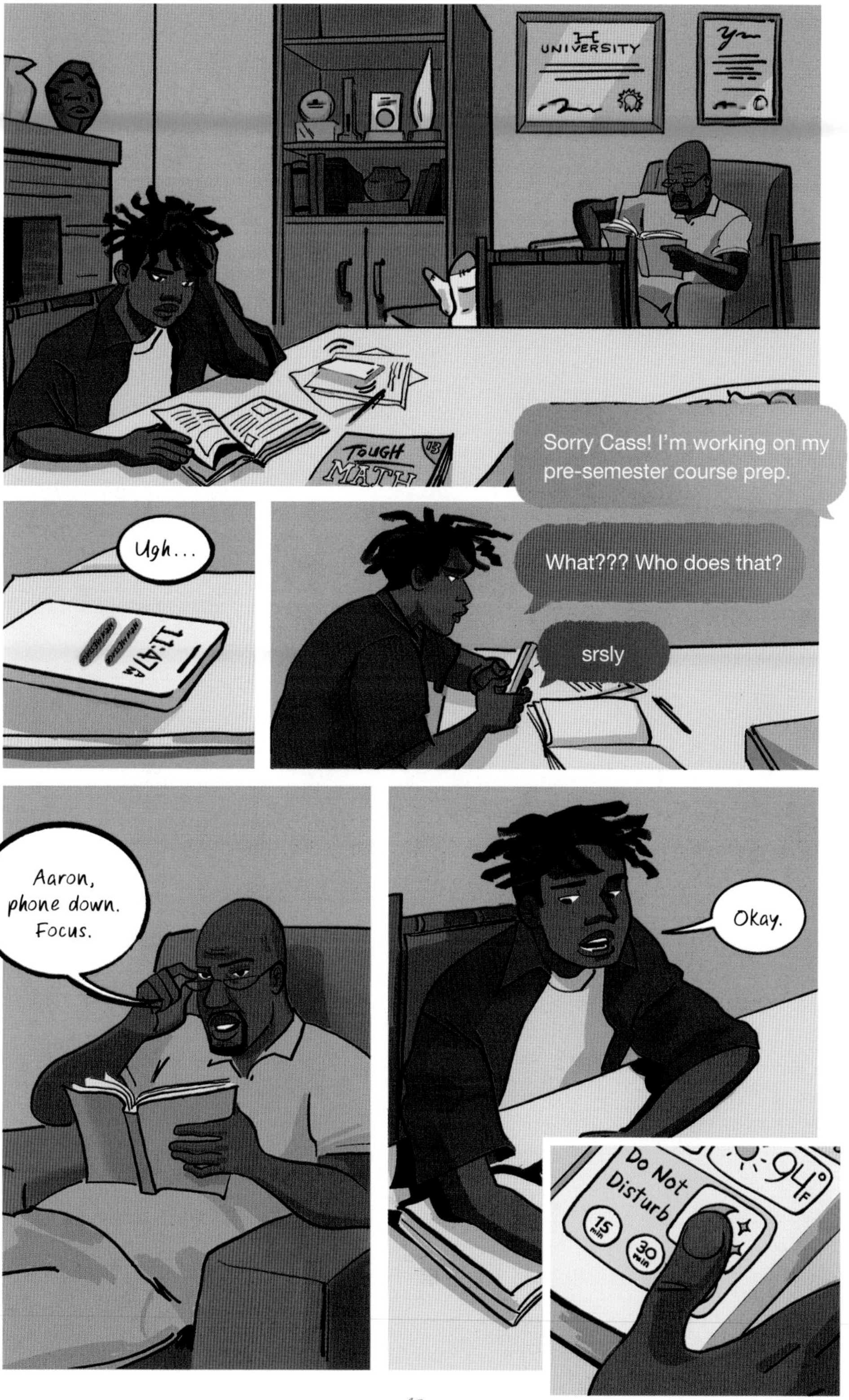
UNIVERSITY
TOUGH MATH
13
Sorry Cass! I'm working on my pre-semester course prep.
Ugh...
11:47
What??? Who does that?
srsly
Aaron, phone down. Focus.
Okay.
Do Not Disturb
94°F
15 min
30 min

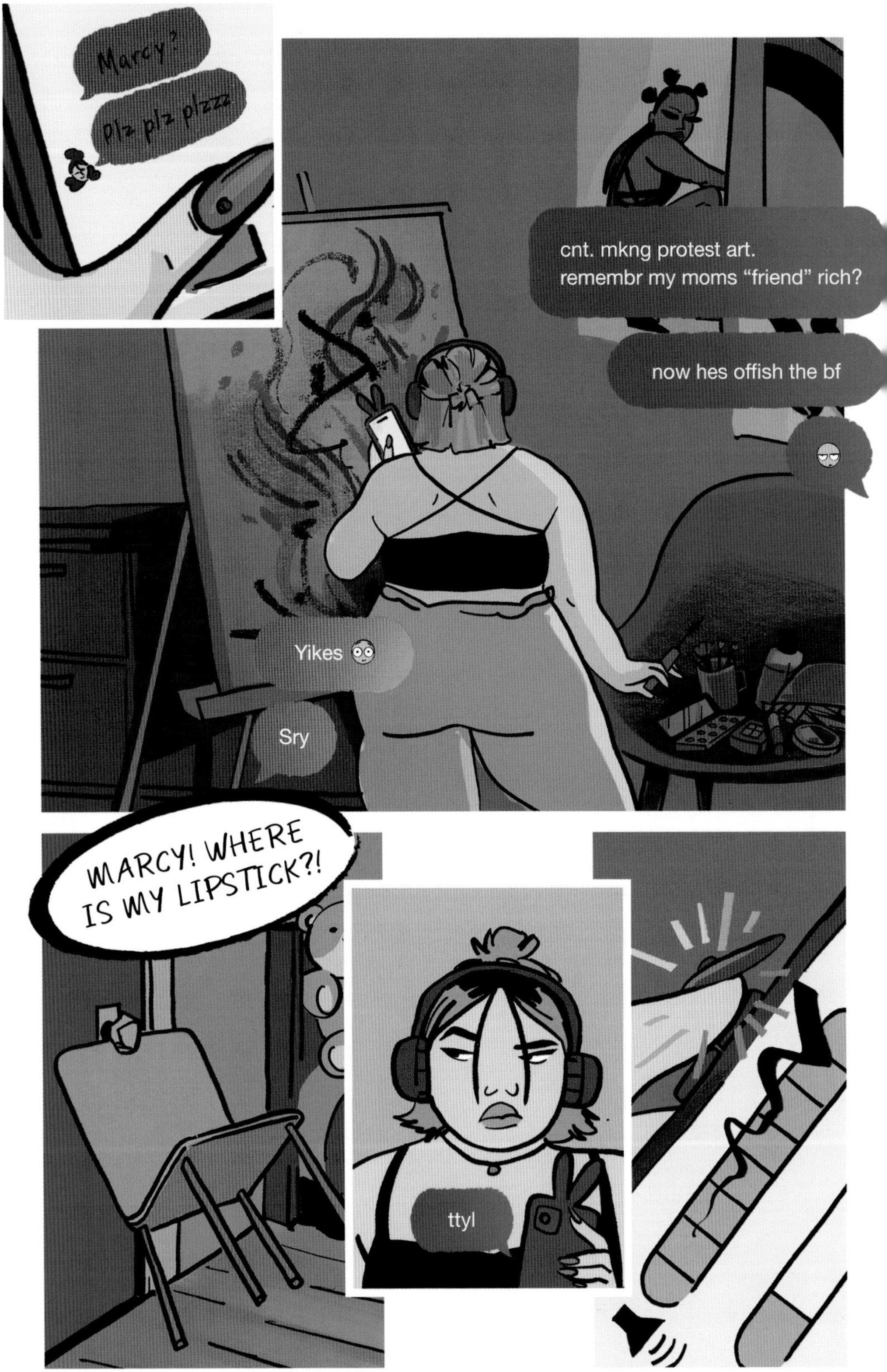

Marcy?
plz plz plzzz
cnt. mkng protest art.
remembr my moms "friend" rich?
now hes offish the bf
Yikes
Sry
MARCY! WHERE IS MY LIPSTICK?!
ttyl

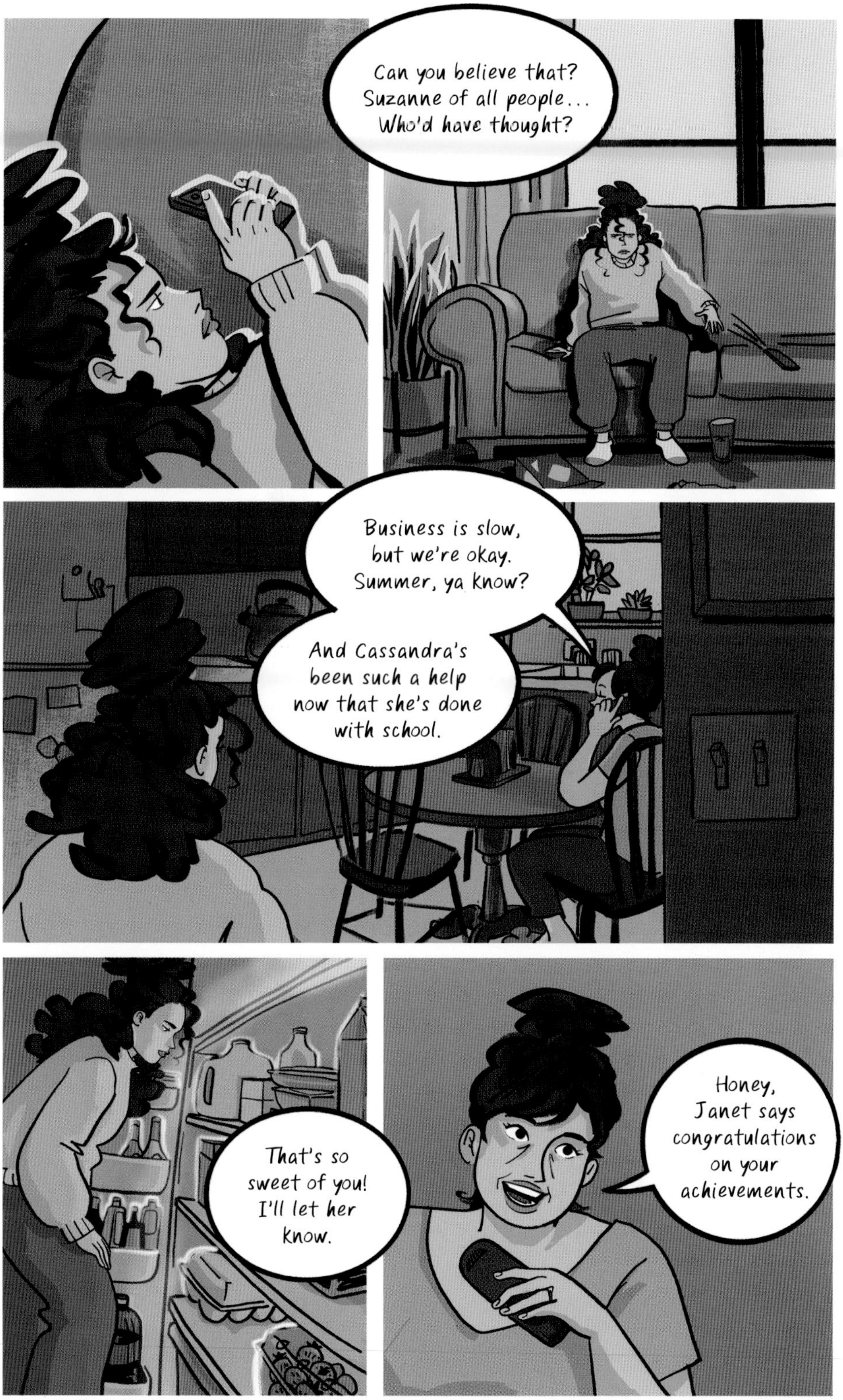

Can you believe that? Suzanne of all people... Who'd have thought?
Business is slow, but we're okay. Summer, ya know?
And Cassandra's been such a help now that she's done with school.
That's so sweet of you! I'll let her know.
Honey, Janet says congratulations on your achievements.

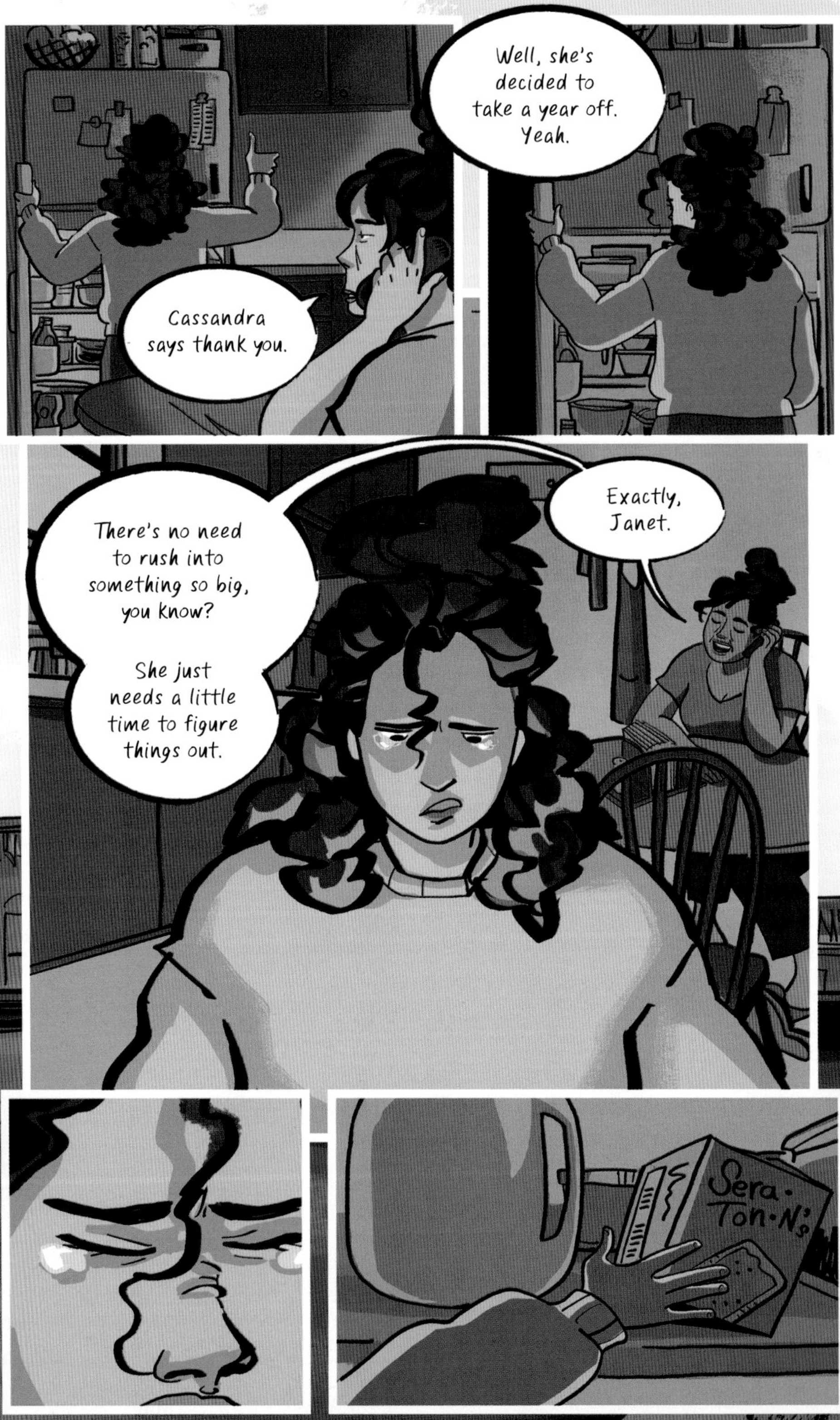
Cassandra says thank you.
Well, she's decided to take a year off. Yeah.
There's no need to rush into something so big, you know?
She just needs a little time to figure things out.
Exactly, Janet.
Sera-Ton-N's

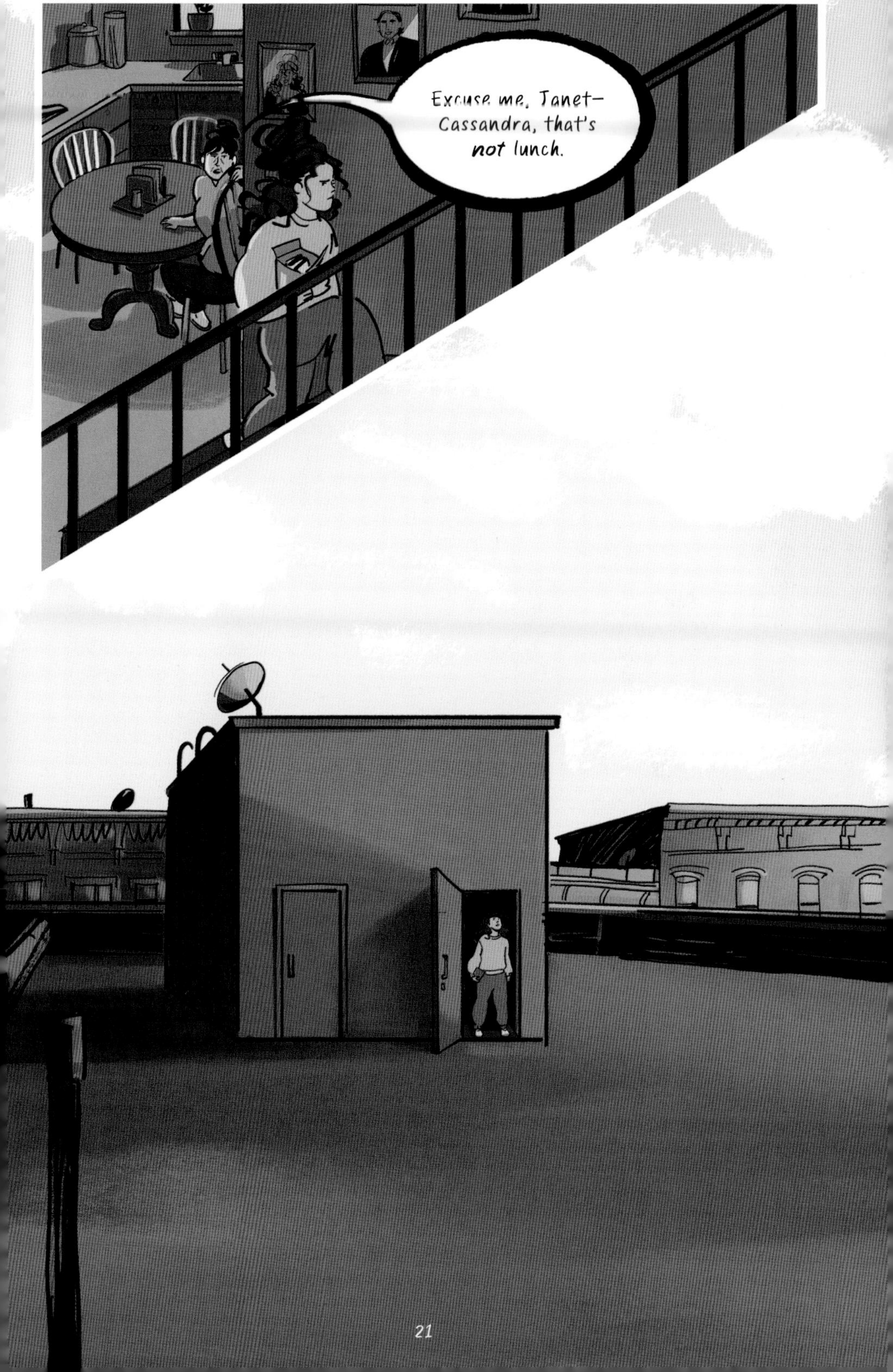
Excuse me, Janet—
Cassandra, that's *not* lunch.

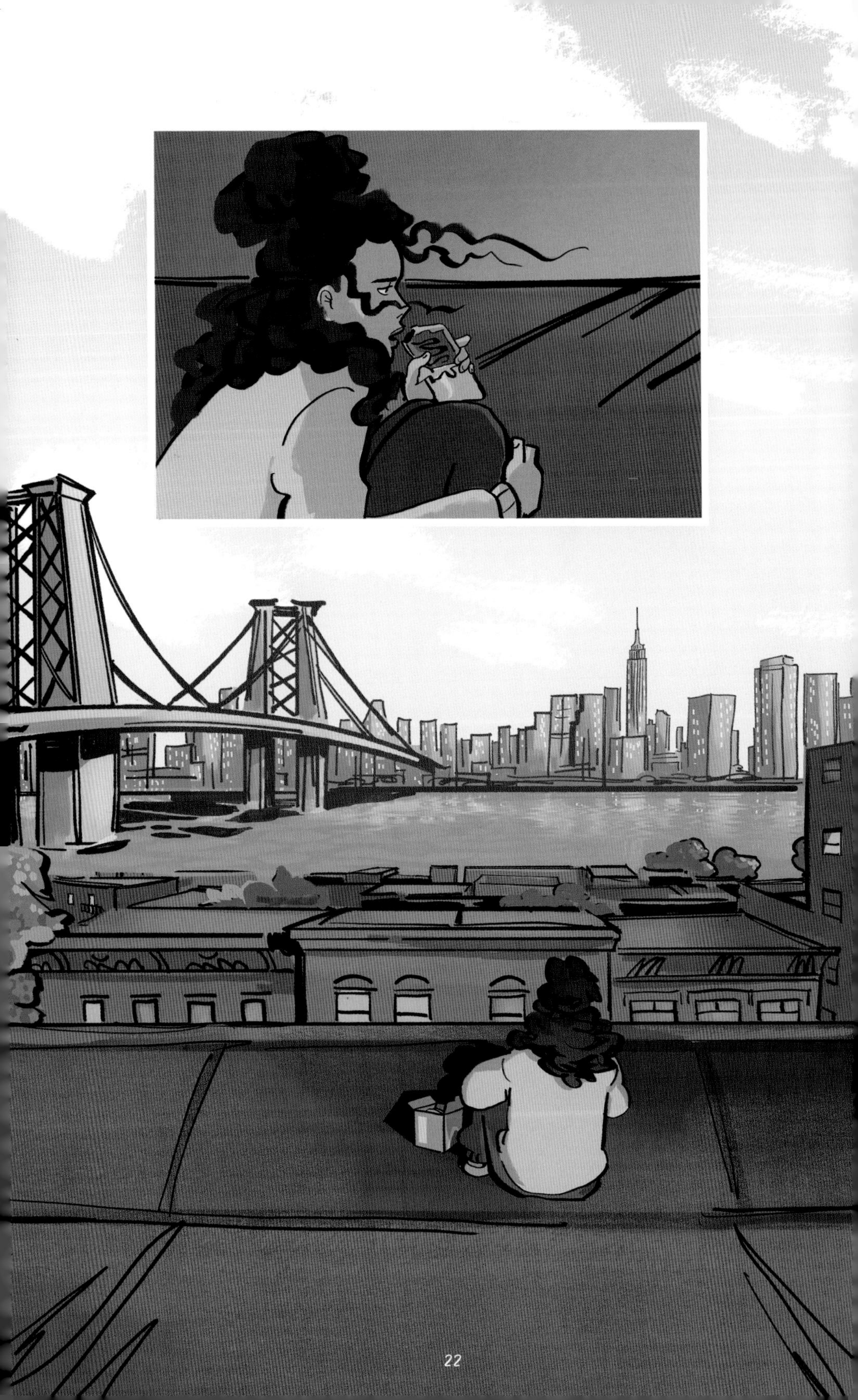

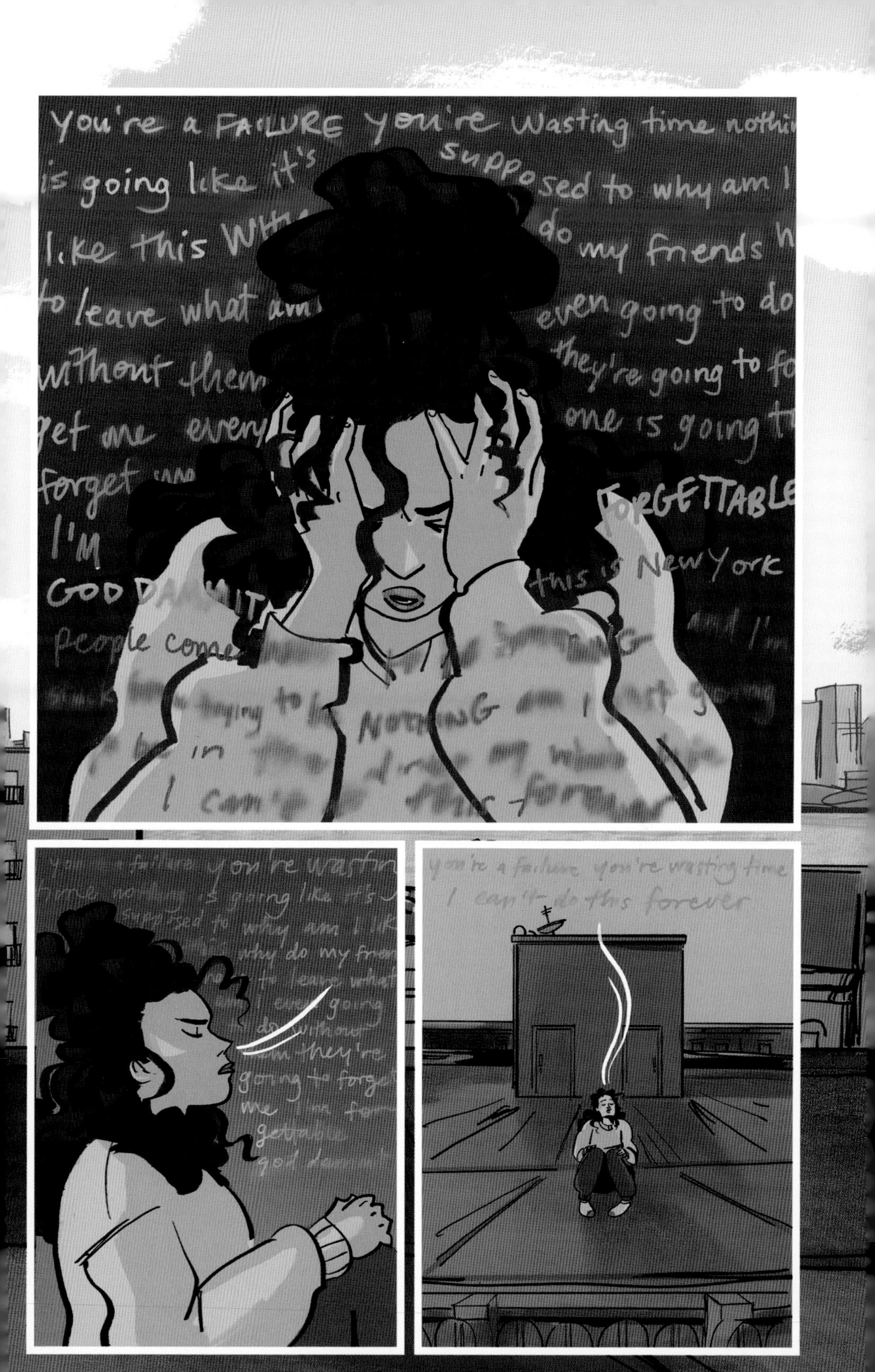
You're a FAILURE you're wasting time
is going like it's supposed to why am I
like this
do my friends
to leave what am
even going to do
without them
they're going to
get me every
one is going
forget
FORGETTABLE
I'M
GOD
this is New York
people come
NOTHING
you're wasting
going like it's
supposed to why am I
why do my
to leave
going
they're
going to forget
me
you're a failure you're wasting time
I can't do this forever

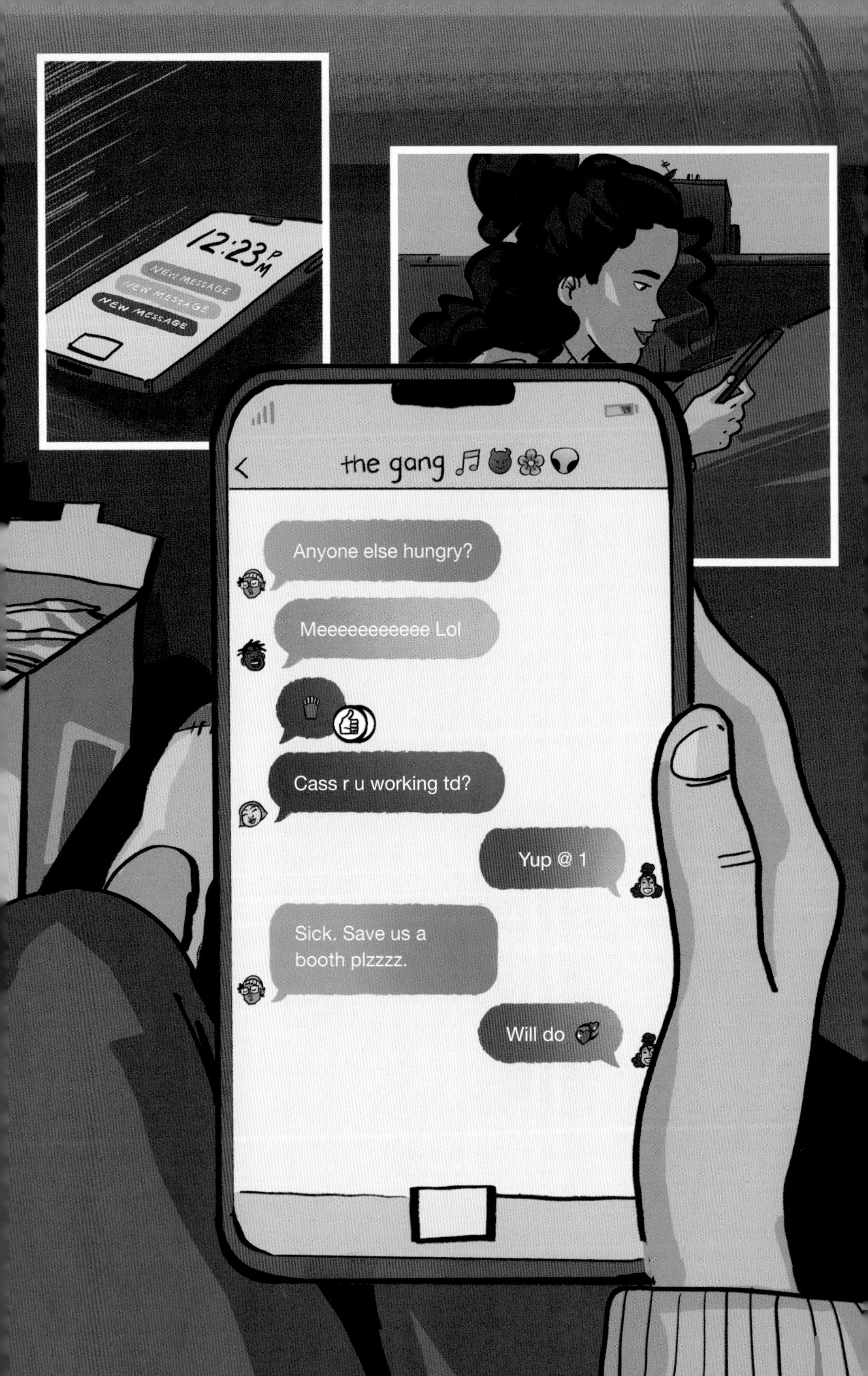
12:23 PM
NEW MESSAGE
NEW MESSAGE
NEW MESSAGE
the gang
Anyone else hungry?
Meeeeeeeeeee Lol
Cass r u working td?
Yup @ 1
Sick. Save us a booth plzzzz.
Will do

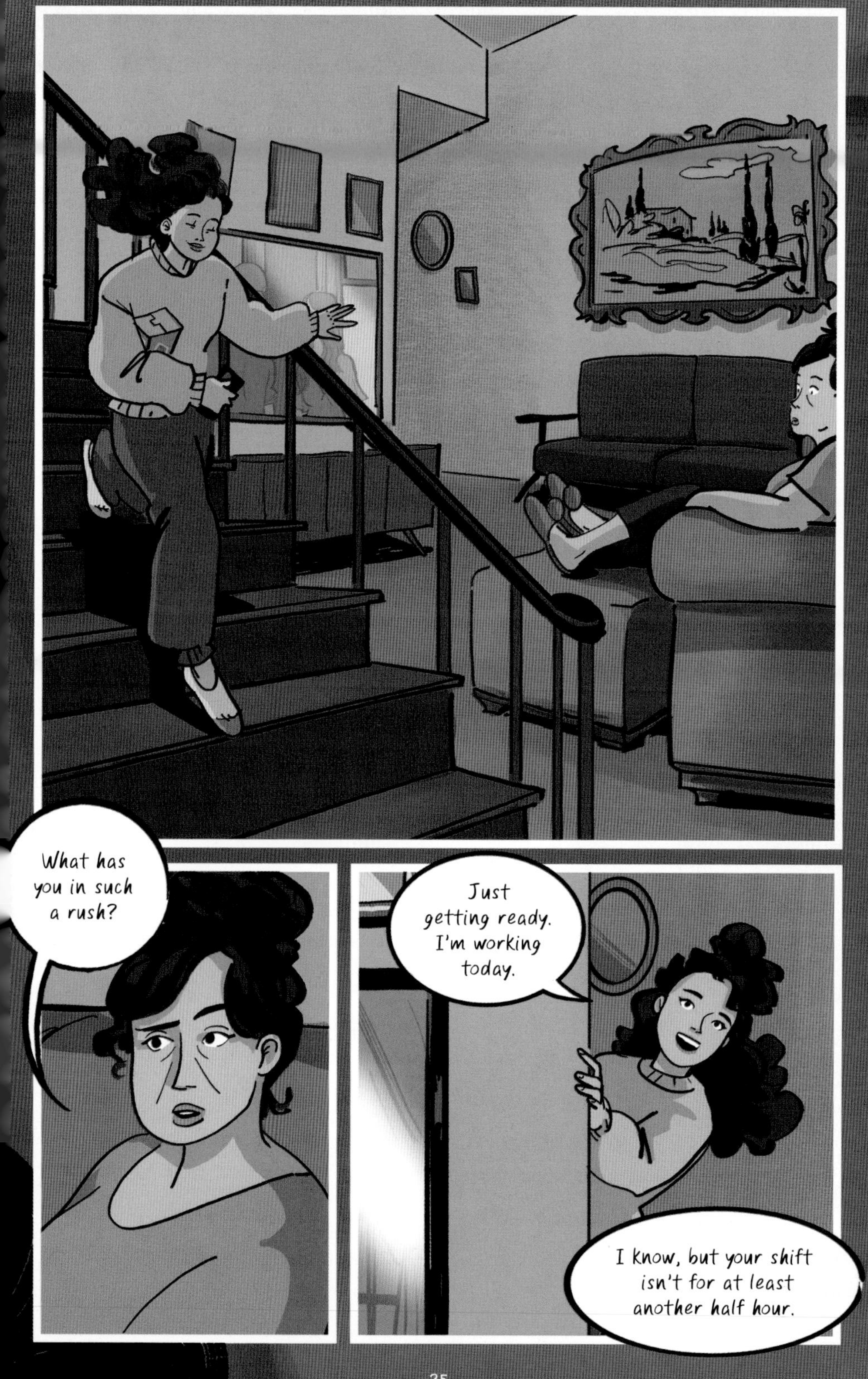
What has you in such a rush?
Just getting ready. I'm working today.
I know, but your shift isn't for at least another half hour.

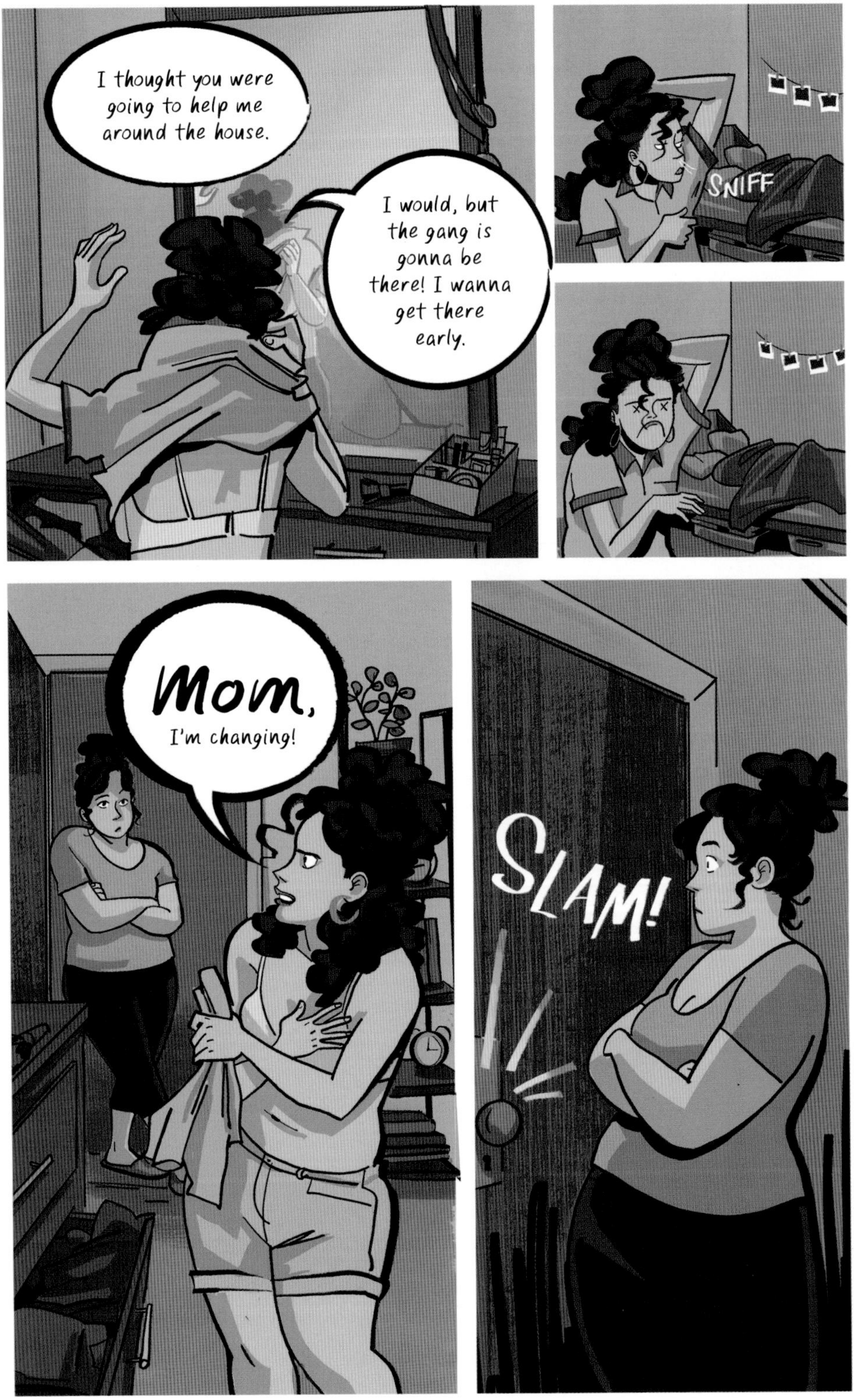
I thought you were going to help me around the house.
I would, but the gang is gonna be there! I wanna get there early.
SNIFF
Mom, I'm changing!
SLAM!

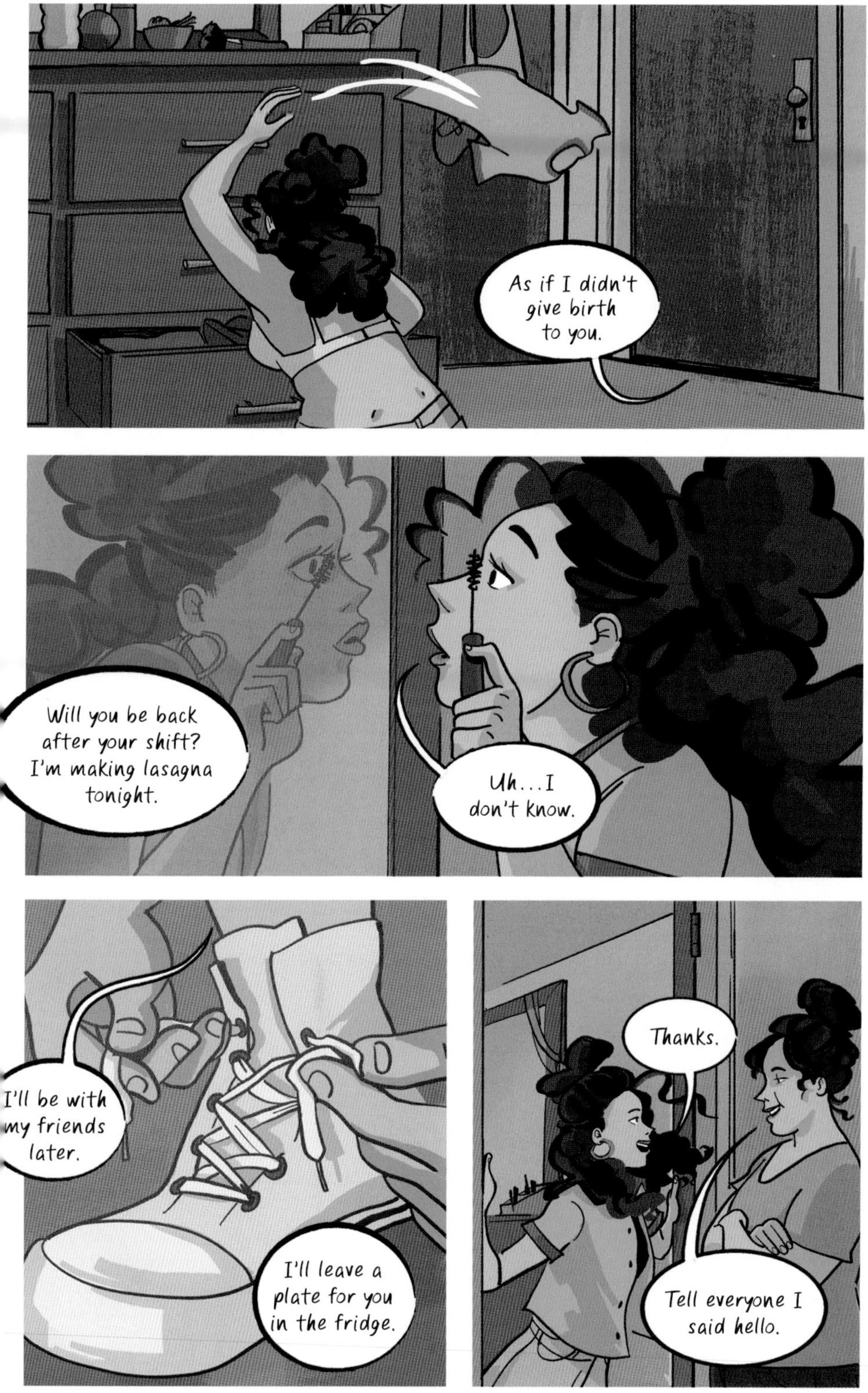
As if I didn't give birth to you.
Will you be back after your shift? I'm making lasagna tonight.
Uh...I don't know.
I'll be with my friends later.
I'll leave a plate for you in the fridge.
Thanks.
Tell everyone I said hello.

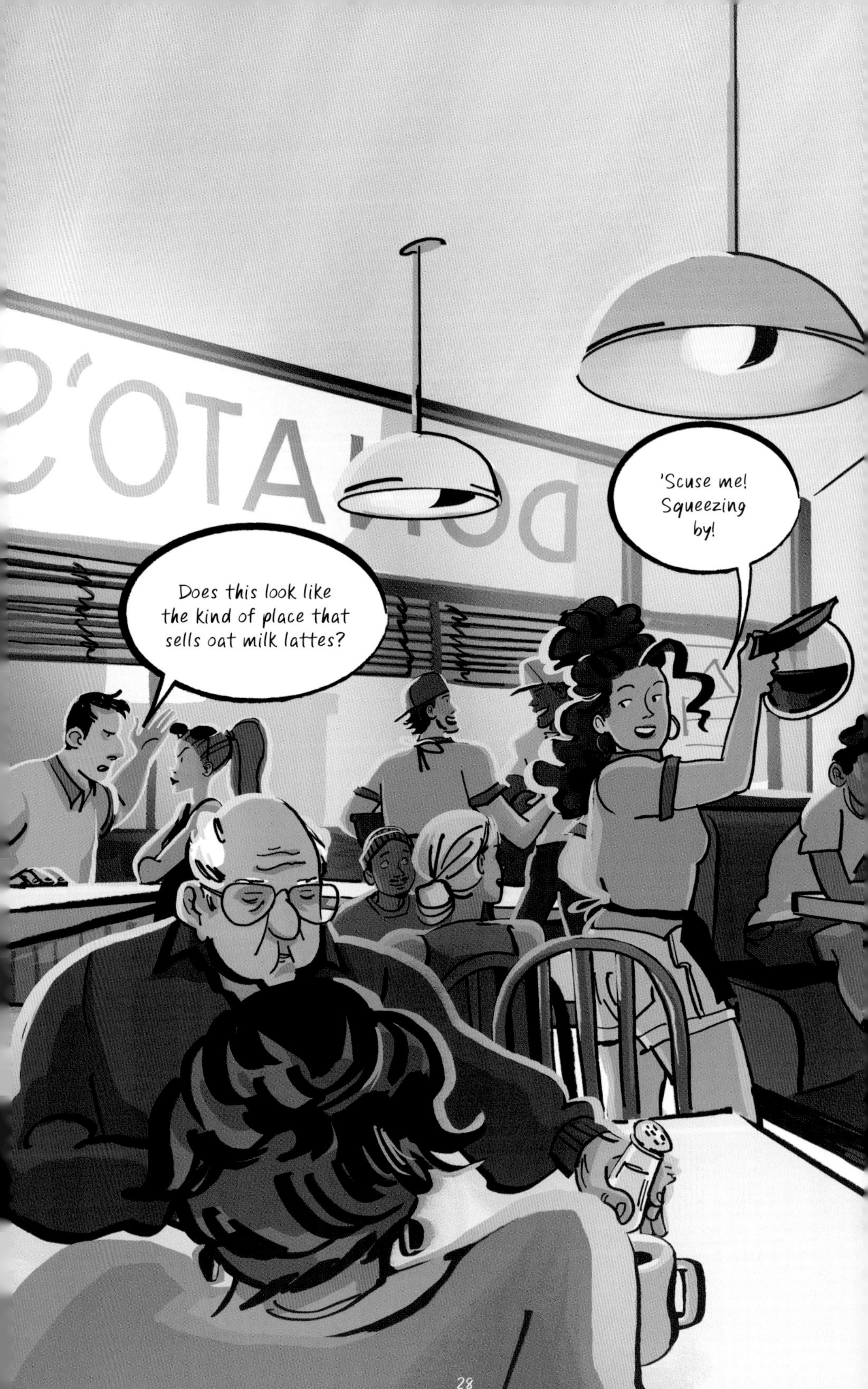
Does this look like the kind of place that sells oat milk lattes?
'Scuse me! Squeezing by!

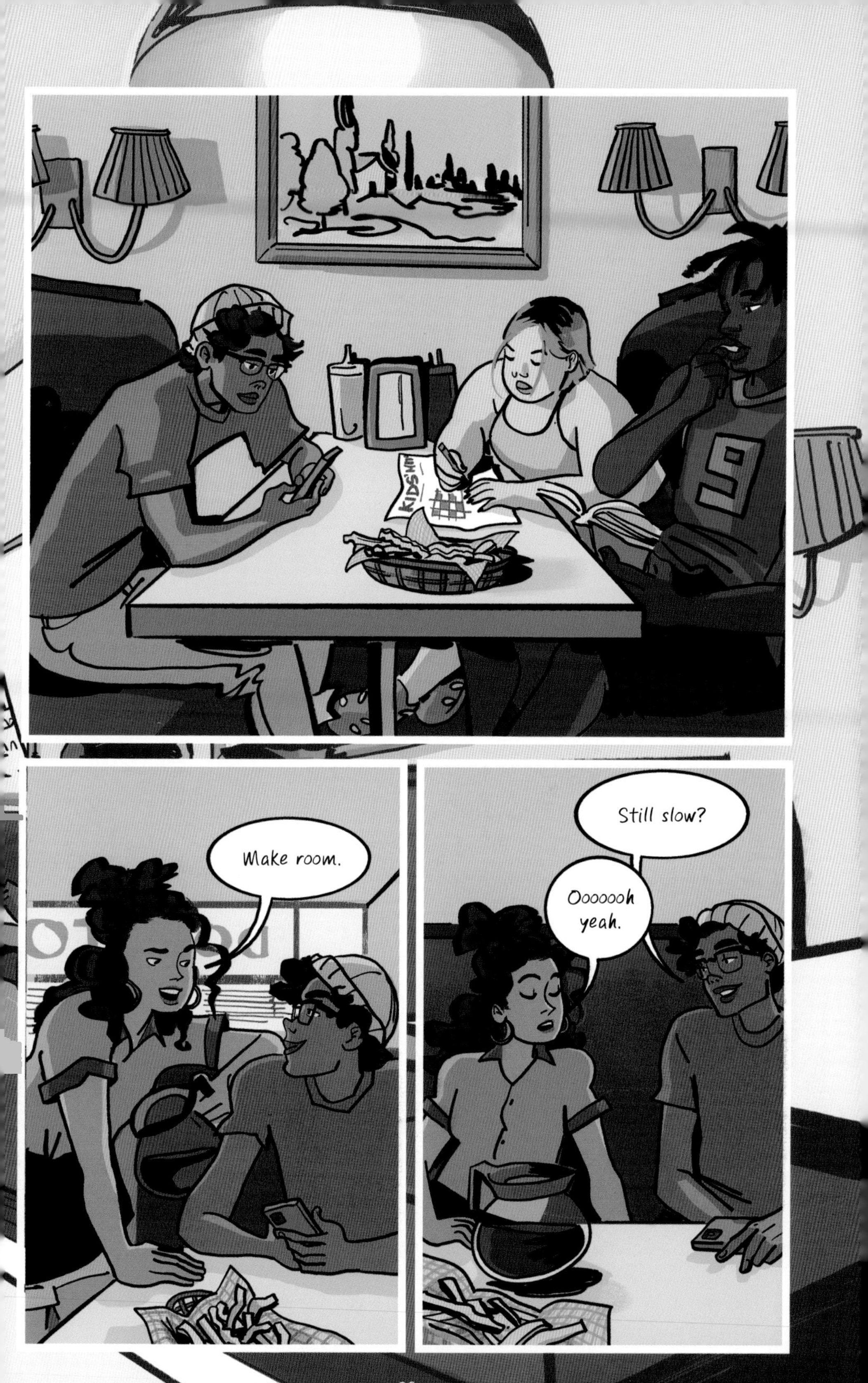
Make room.
Still slow?
Oooooooh
yeah.

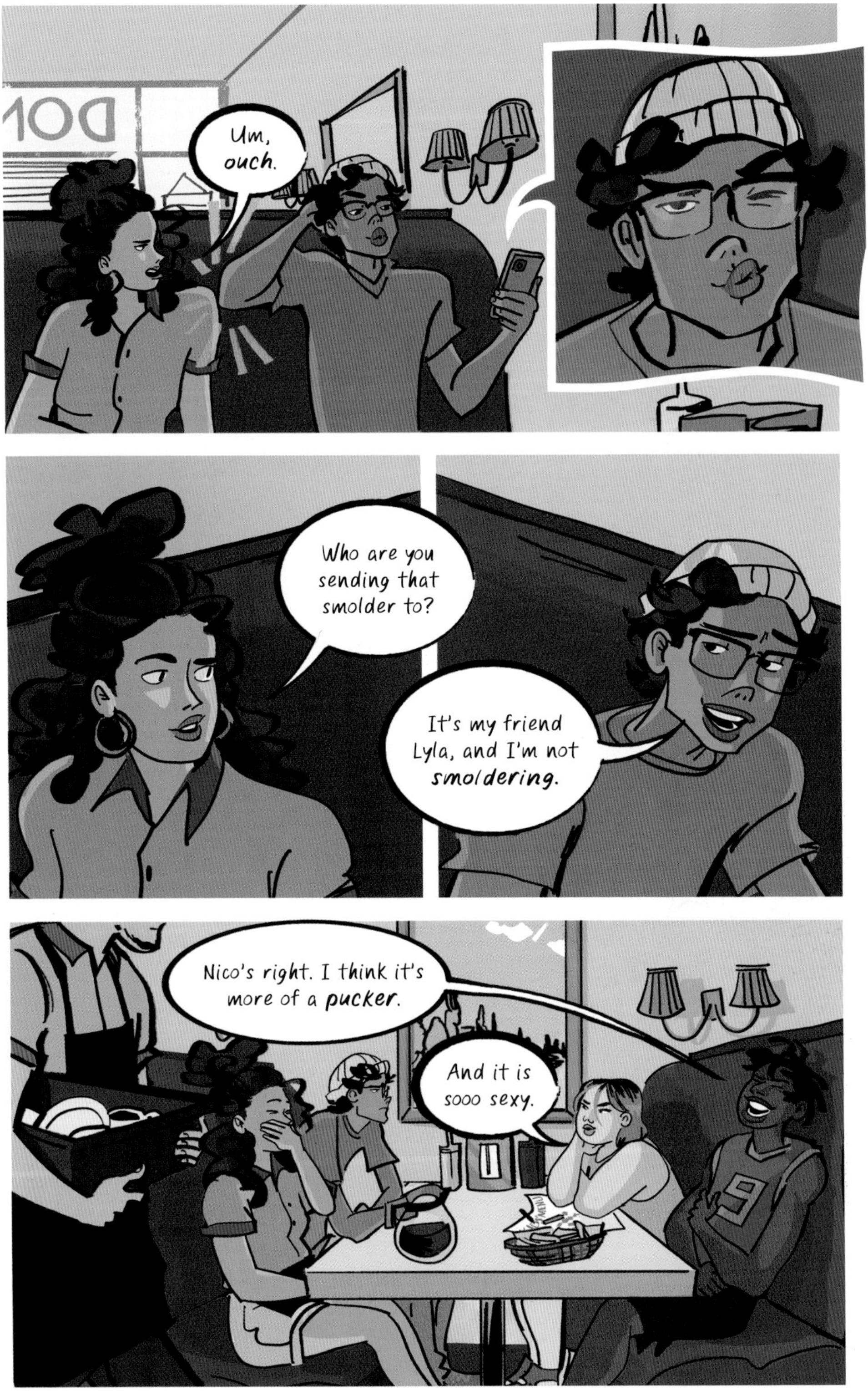
DO
Um, ouch.
Who are you sending that smolder to?
It's my friend Lyla, and I'm not smoldering.
Nico's right. I think it's more of a pucker.
And it is sooo sexy.
MENU

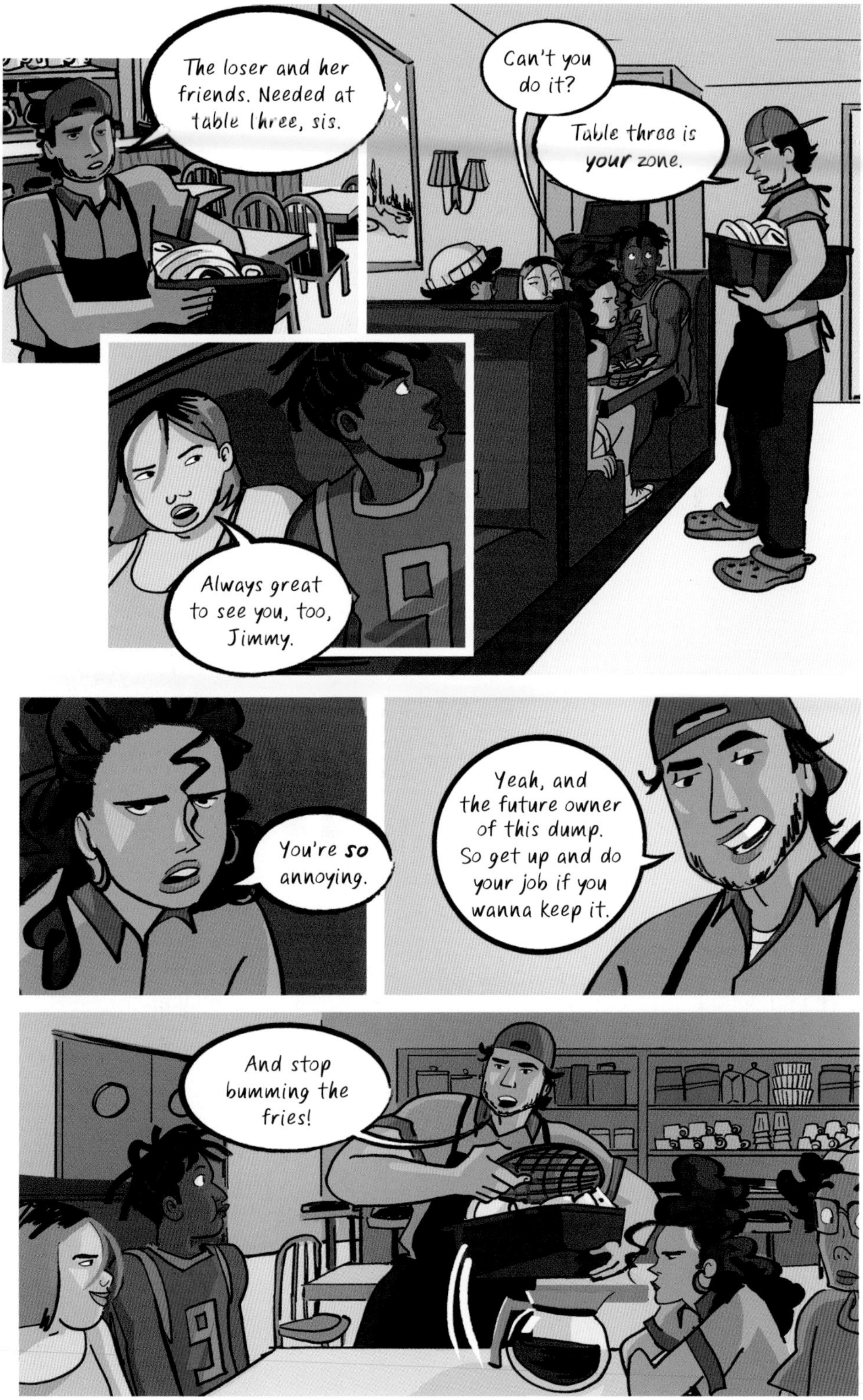
The loser and her friends. Needed at table three, sis.
Can't you do it?
Table three is **your** zone.
Always great to see you, too, Jimmy.
You're **so** annoying.
Yeah, and the future owner of this dump. So get up and do your job if you wanna keep it.
And stop bumming the fries!

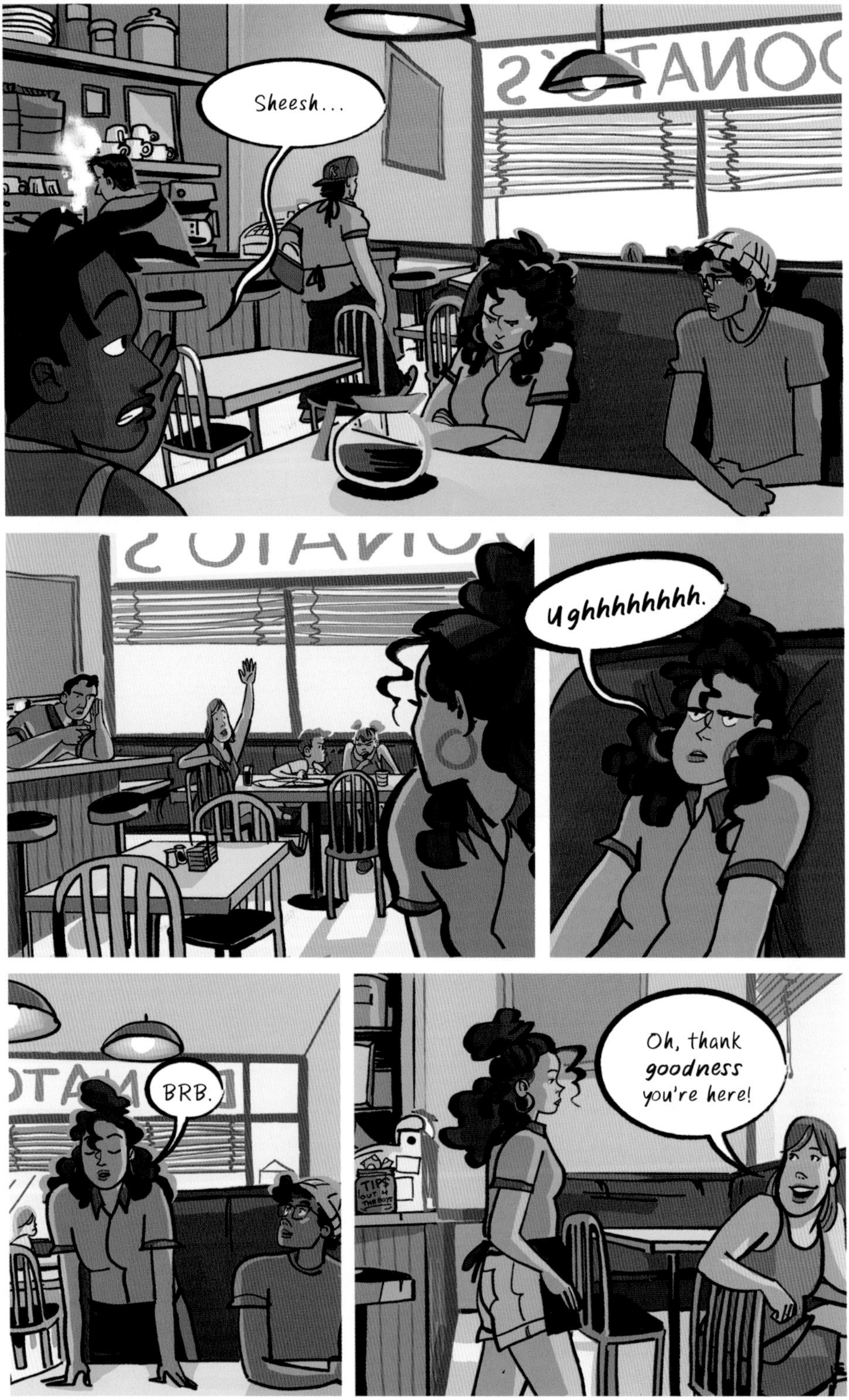
Sheesh...
Ughhhhhhhh.
BRB.
Oh, thank goodness you're here!

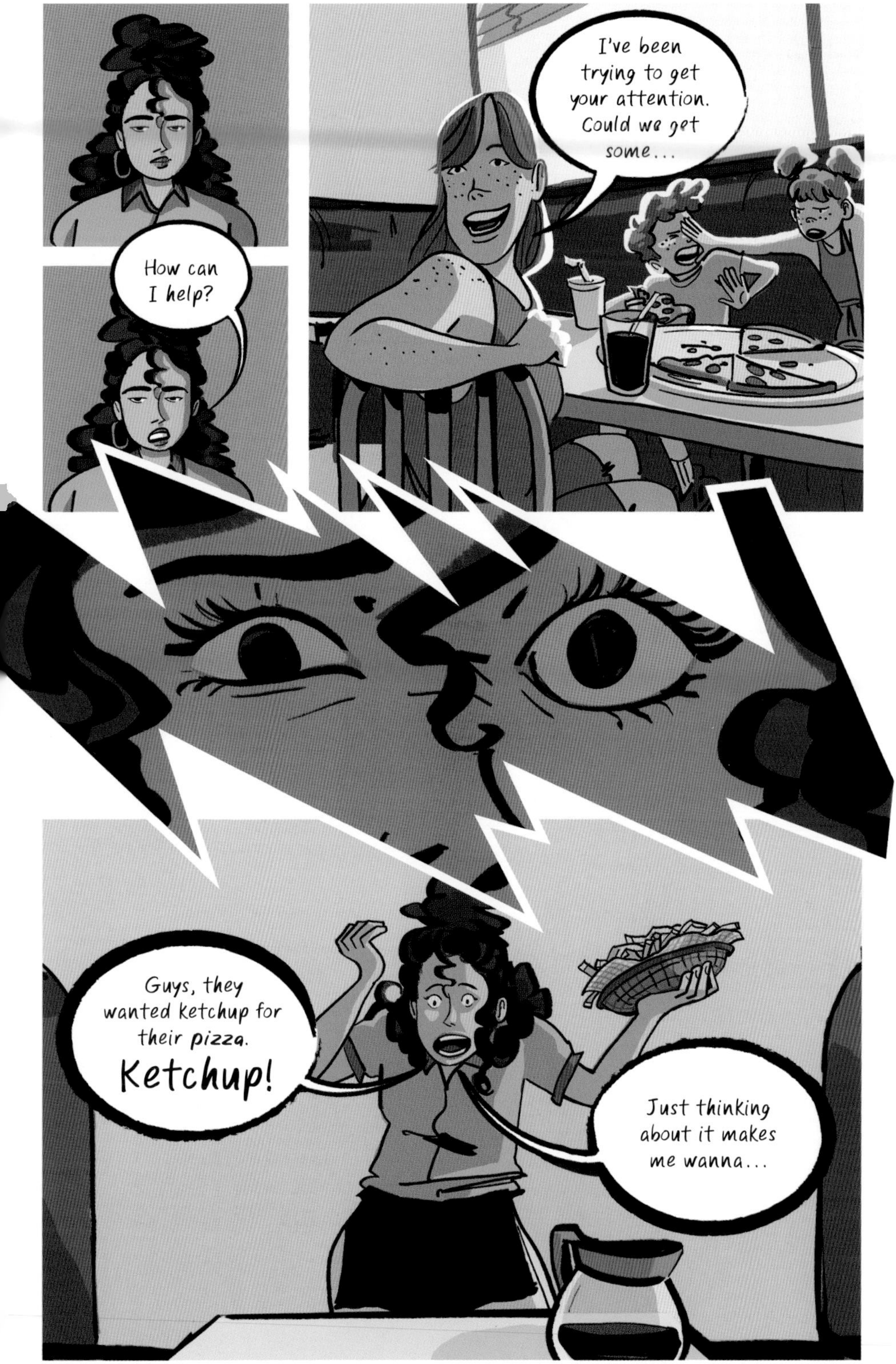

I've been trying to get your attention. Could we get some...
How can I help?
Guys, they wanted ketchup for their *pizza*. Ketchup!
Just thinking about it makes me wanna...

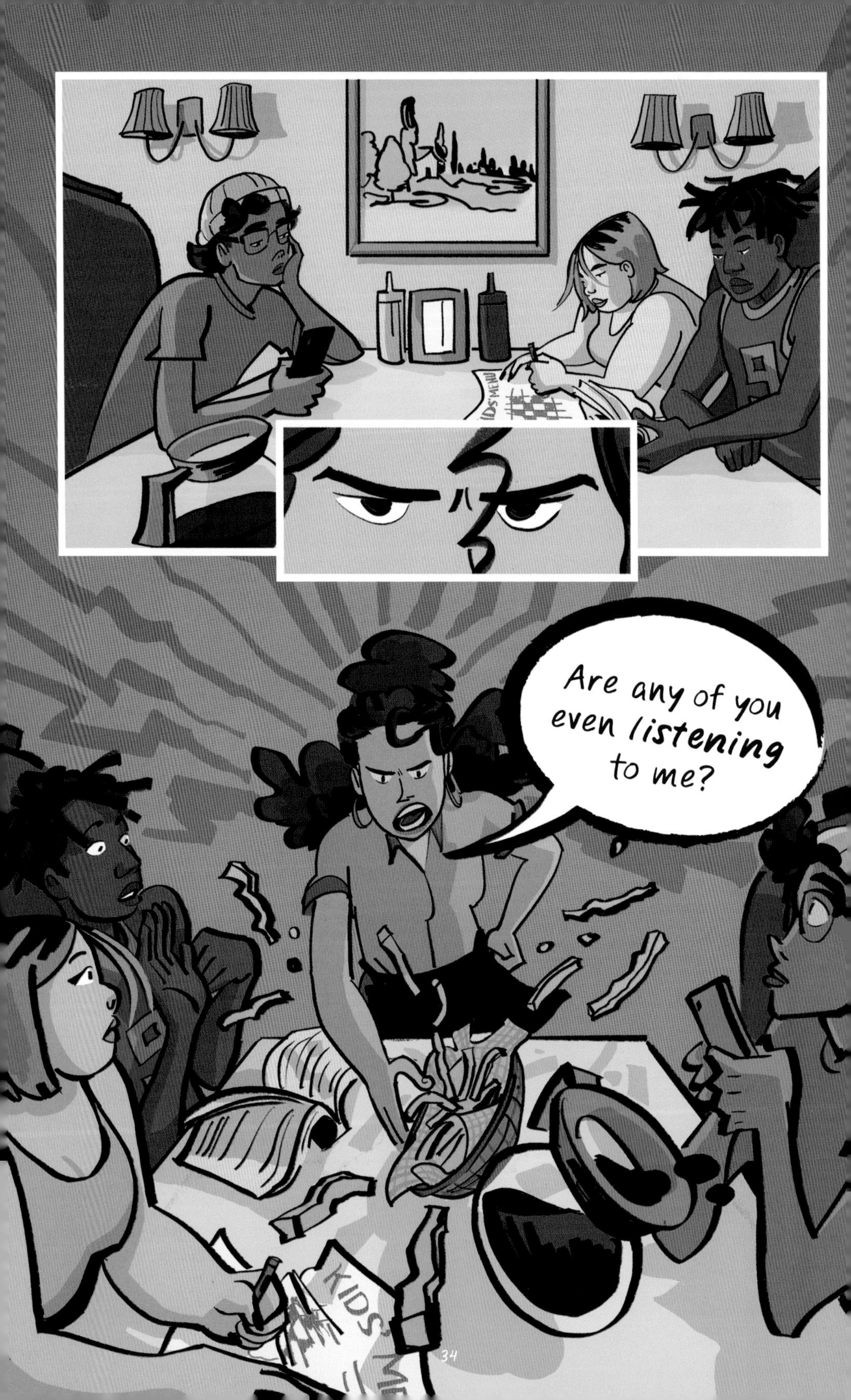
KIDS' MENU
Are any of you even listening to me?
KIDS' ME

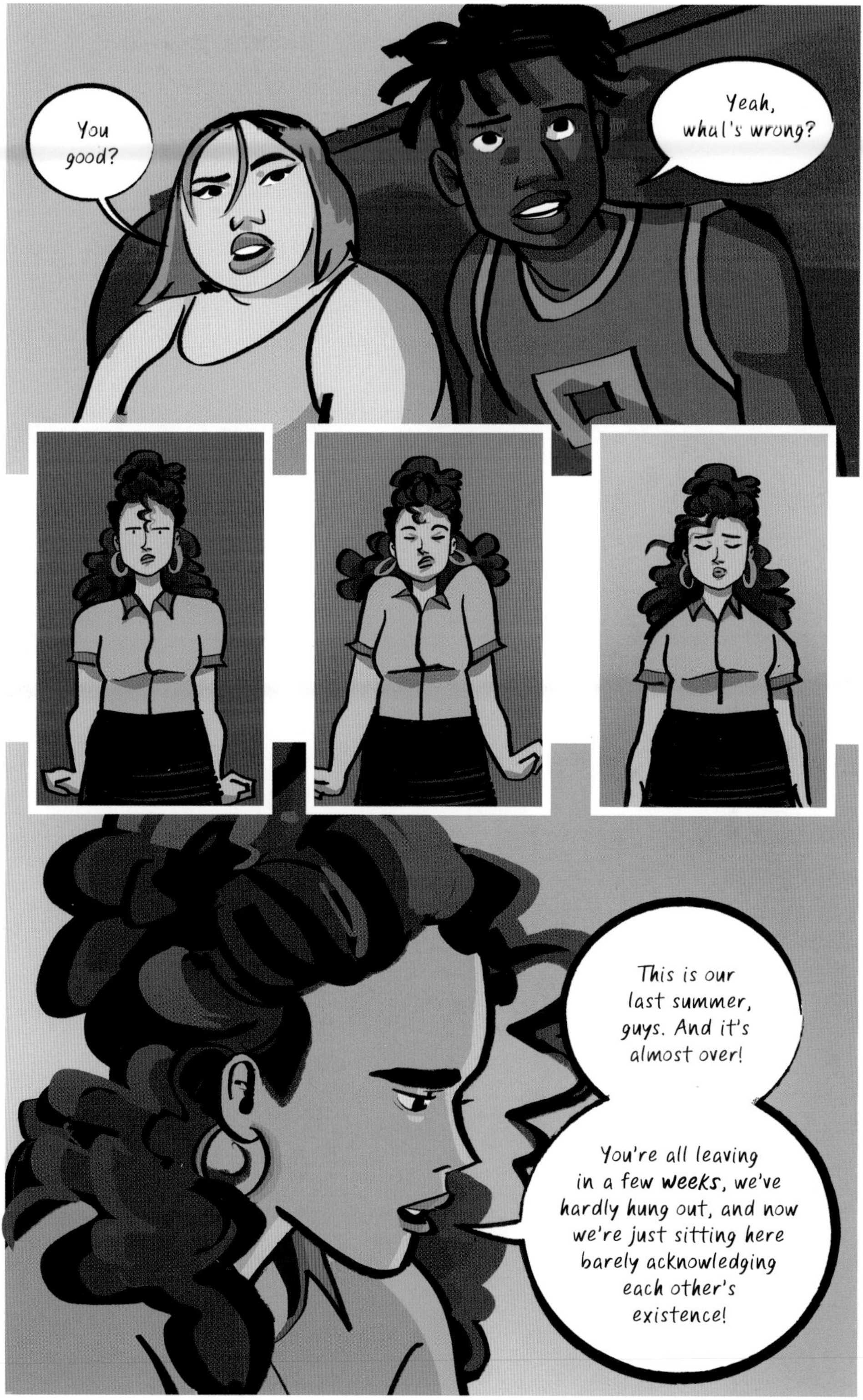

You good?
Yeah, what's wrong?
This is our last summer, guys. And it's almost over!
You're all leaving in a few **weeks**, we've hardly hung out, and now we're just sitting here barely acknowledging each other's existence!

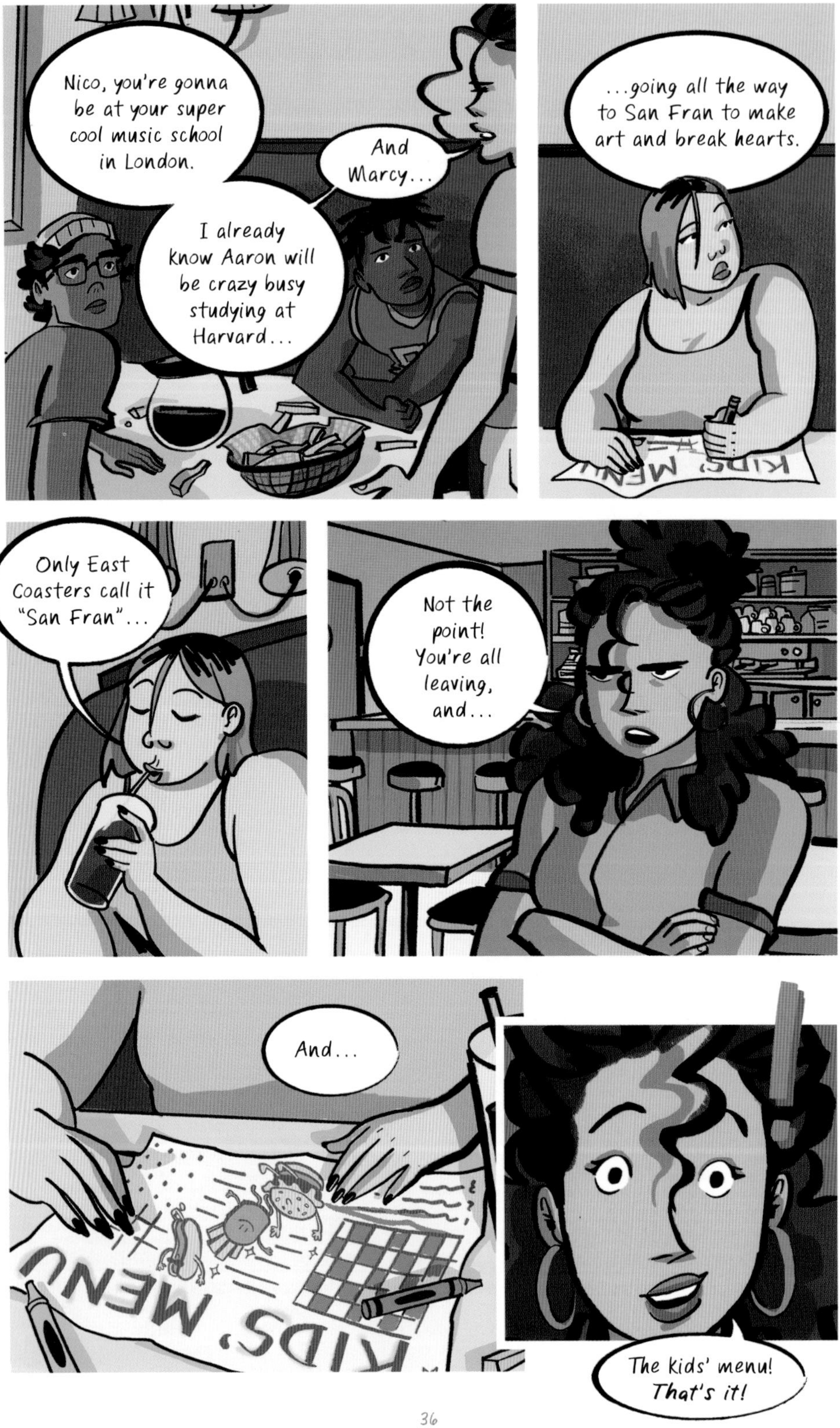
Nico, you're gonna be at your super cool music school in London.
And Marcy...
I already know Aaron will be crazy busy studying at Harvard...
...going all the way to San Fran to make art and break hearts.
KIDS' MENU
Only East Coasters call it "San Fran"...
Not the point! You're all leaving, and...
And...
KIDS' MENU
The kids' menu! That's it!

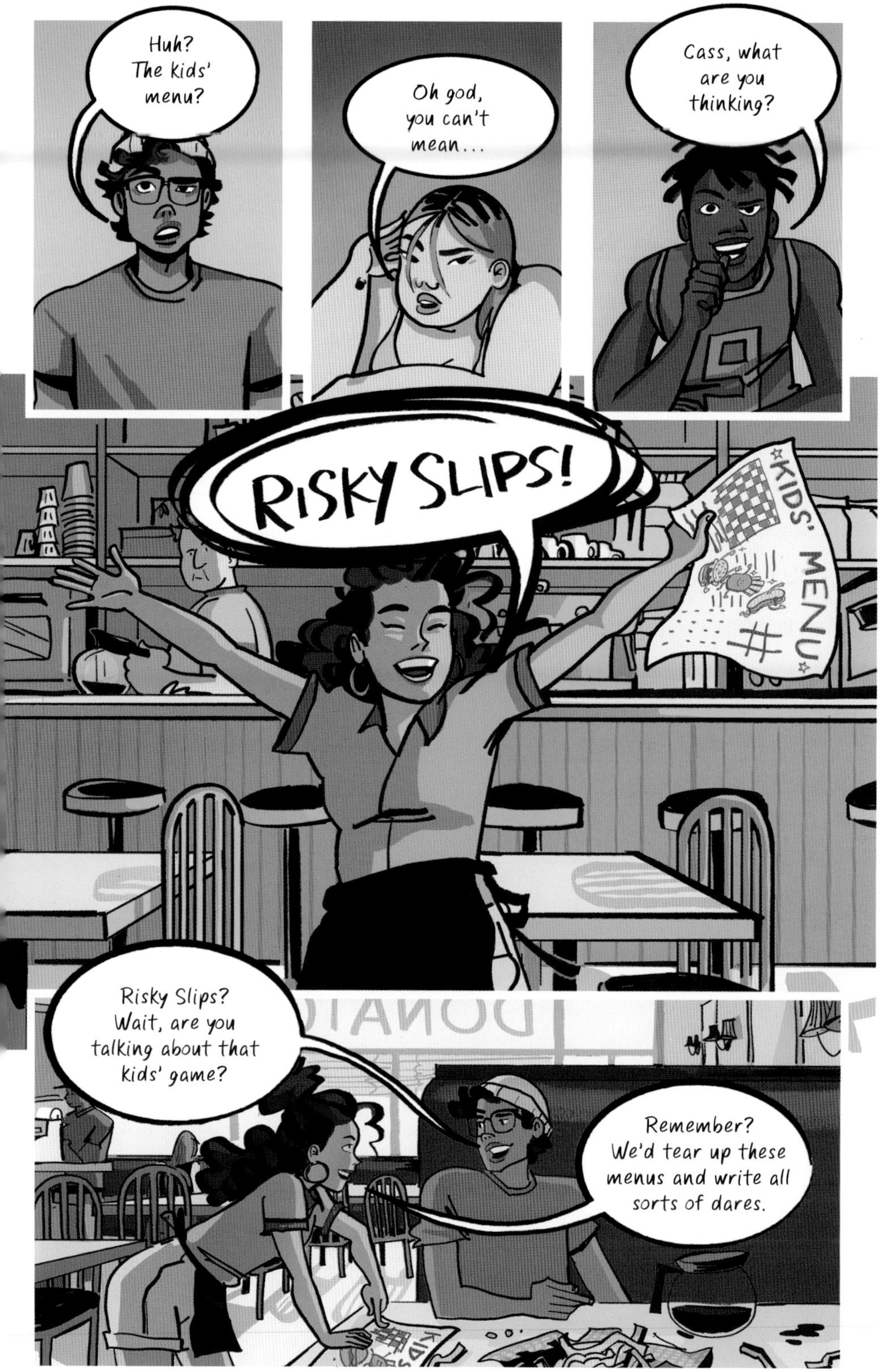

Huh? The kids' menu?
Oh god, you can't mean...
Cass, what are you thinking?
RISKY SLIPS!
KIDS' MENU
Risky Slips? Wait, are you talking about that kids' game?
Remember? We'd tear up these menus and write all sorts of dares.

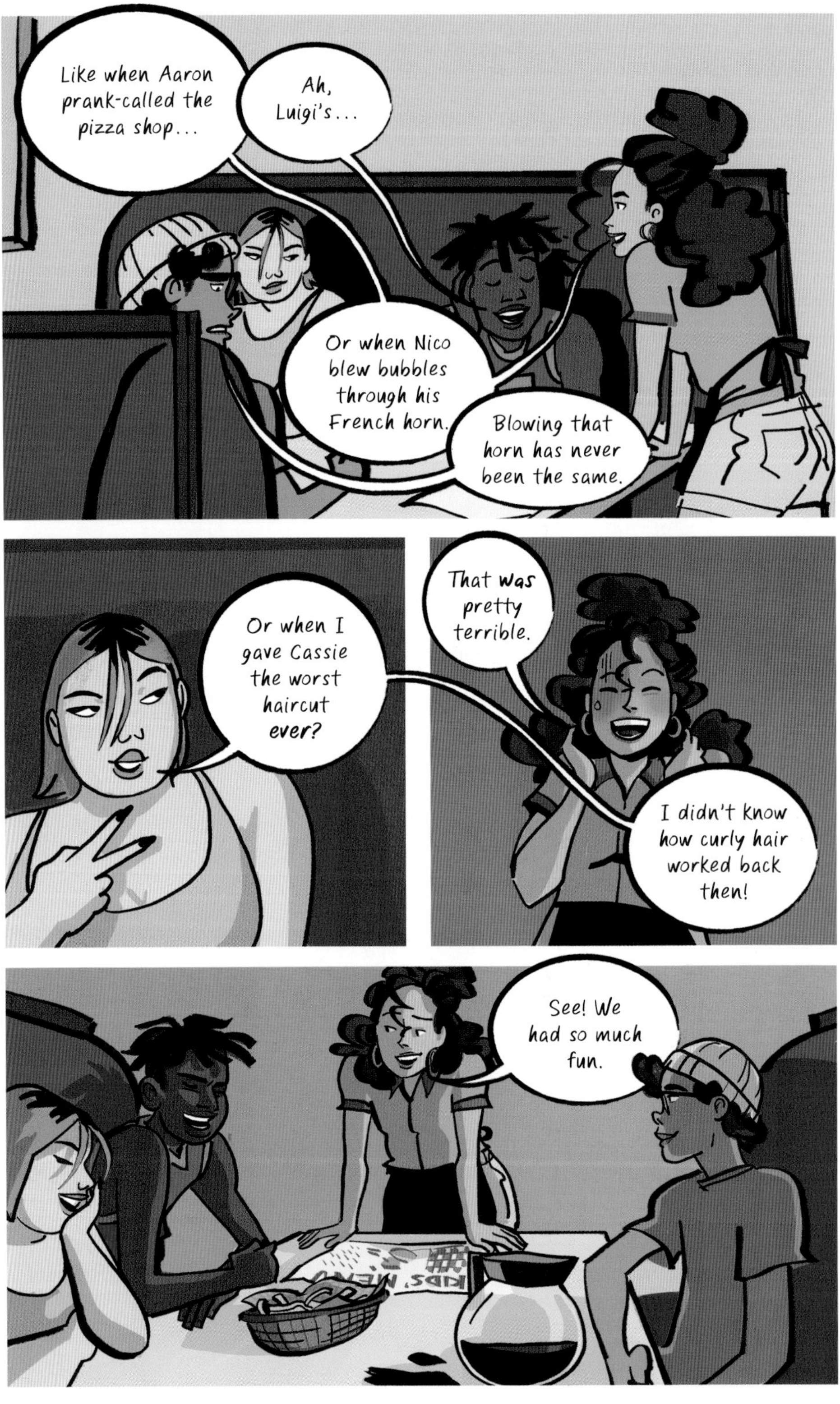
Like when Aaron prank-called the pizza shop...
Ah, Luigi's...
Or when Nico blew bubbles through his French horn.
Blowing that horn has never been the same.
Or when I gave Cassie the worst haircut *ever?*
That **was** pretty terrible.
I didn't know how curly hair worked back then!
See! We had so much fun.
KIDS' MENU

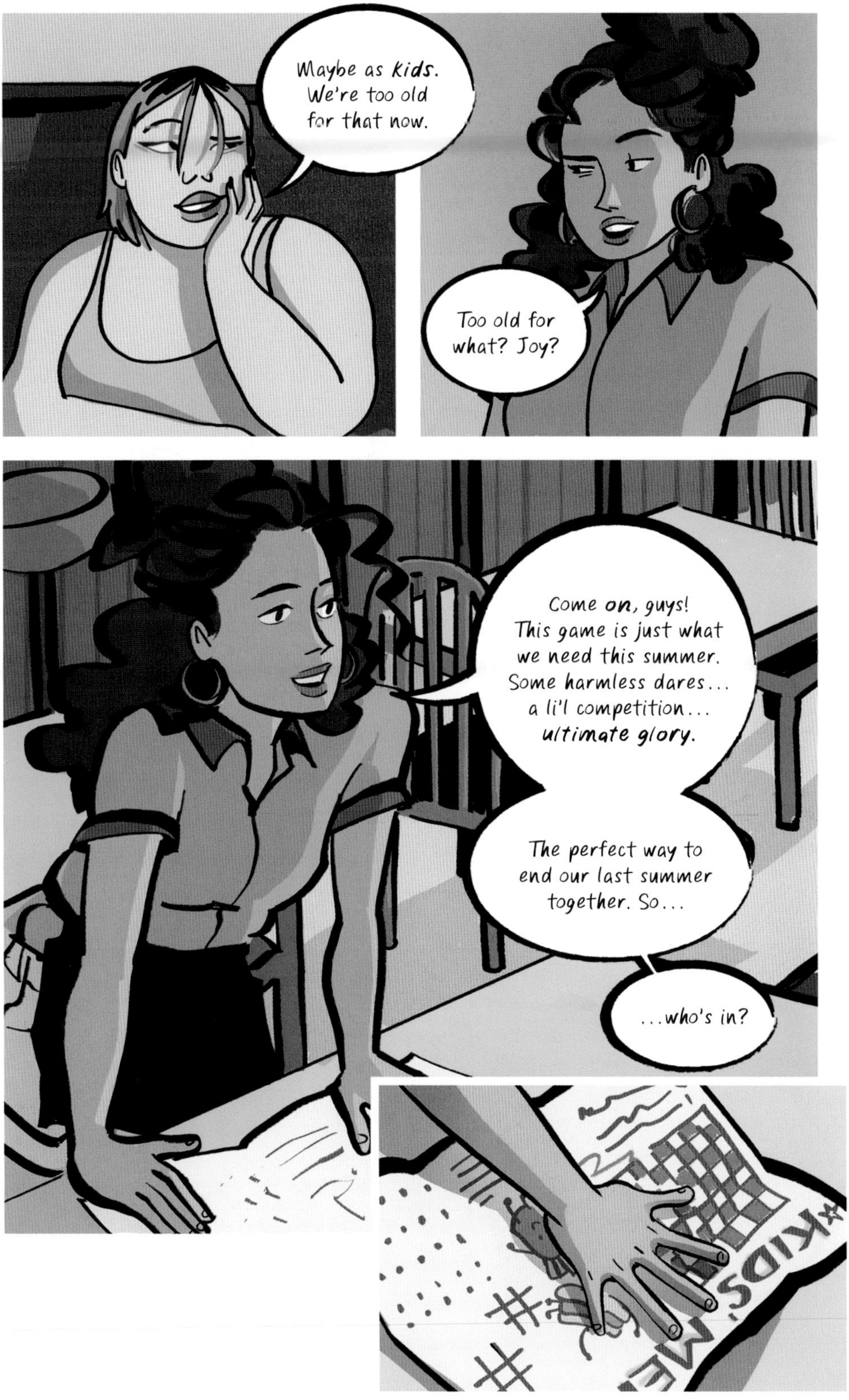
Maybe as kids. We're too old for that now.
Too old for what? Joy?
Come on, guys! This game is just what we need this summer. Some harmless dares... a li'l competition... ultimate glory.
The perfect way to end our last summer together. So...
...who's in?
KIDS' ME

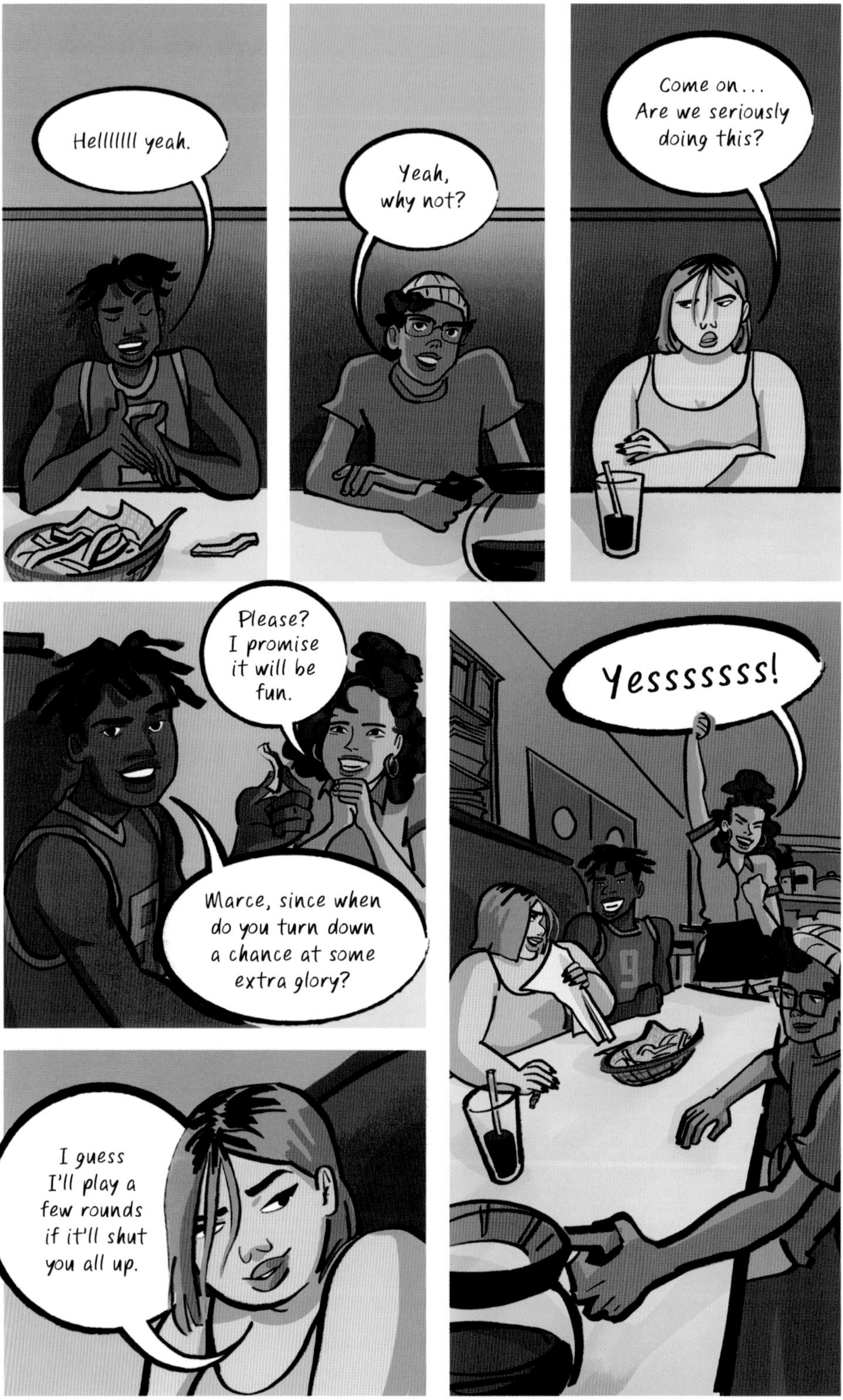
Hellllll yeah.
Yeah, why not?
Come on... Are we seriously doing this?
Please? I promise it will be fun.
Marce, since when do you turn down a chance at some extra glory?
I guess I'll play a few rounds if it'll shut you all up.
Yesssssss!

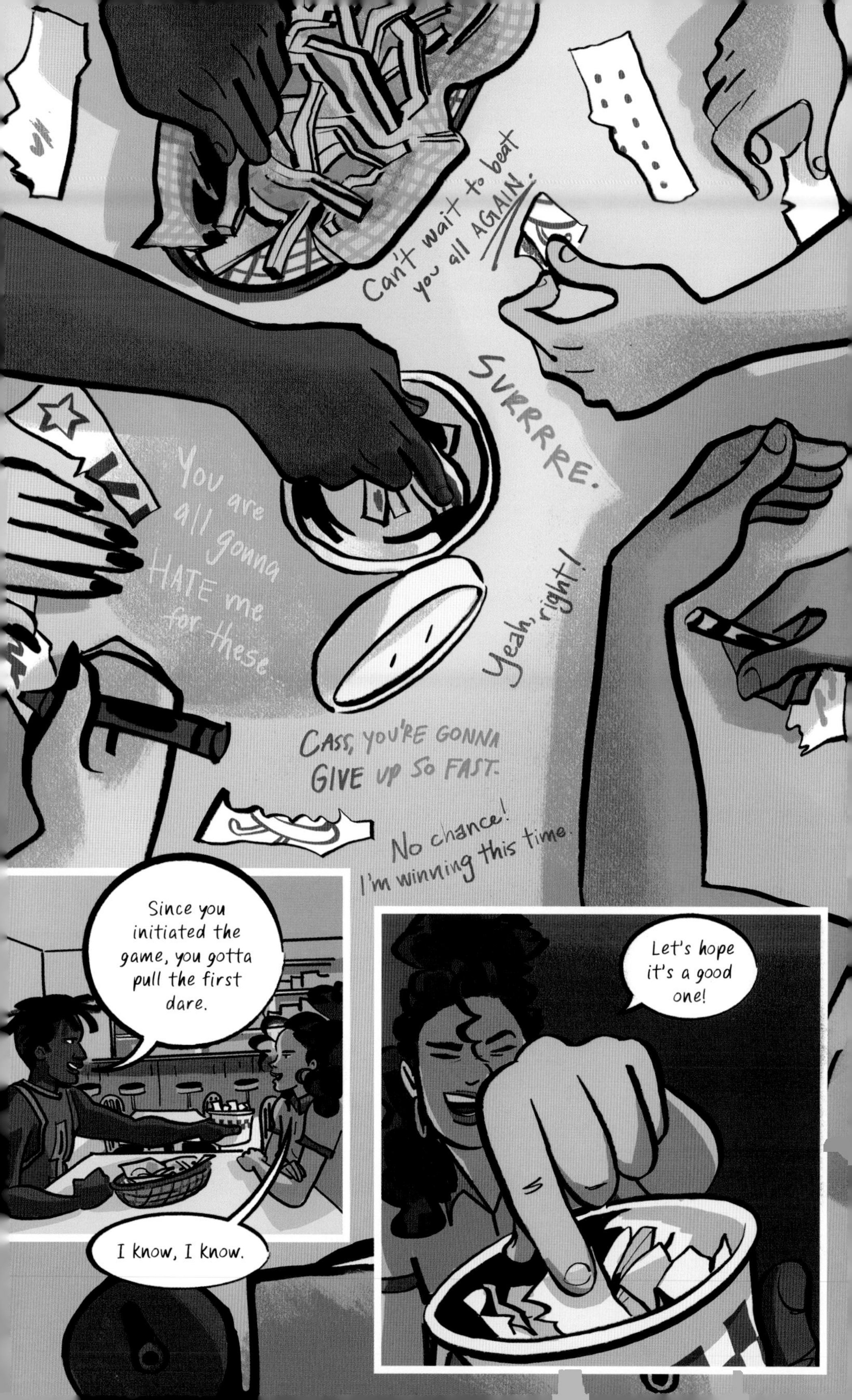

Can't wait to beat you all AGAIN.
SURRRRE.
You are all gonna HATE me for these
Yeah, right!
CASS, YOU'RE GONNA GIVE UP SO FAST.
No chance! I'm winning this time.
Since you initiated the game, you gotta pull the first dare.
I know, I know.
Let's hope it's a good one!

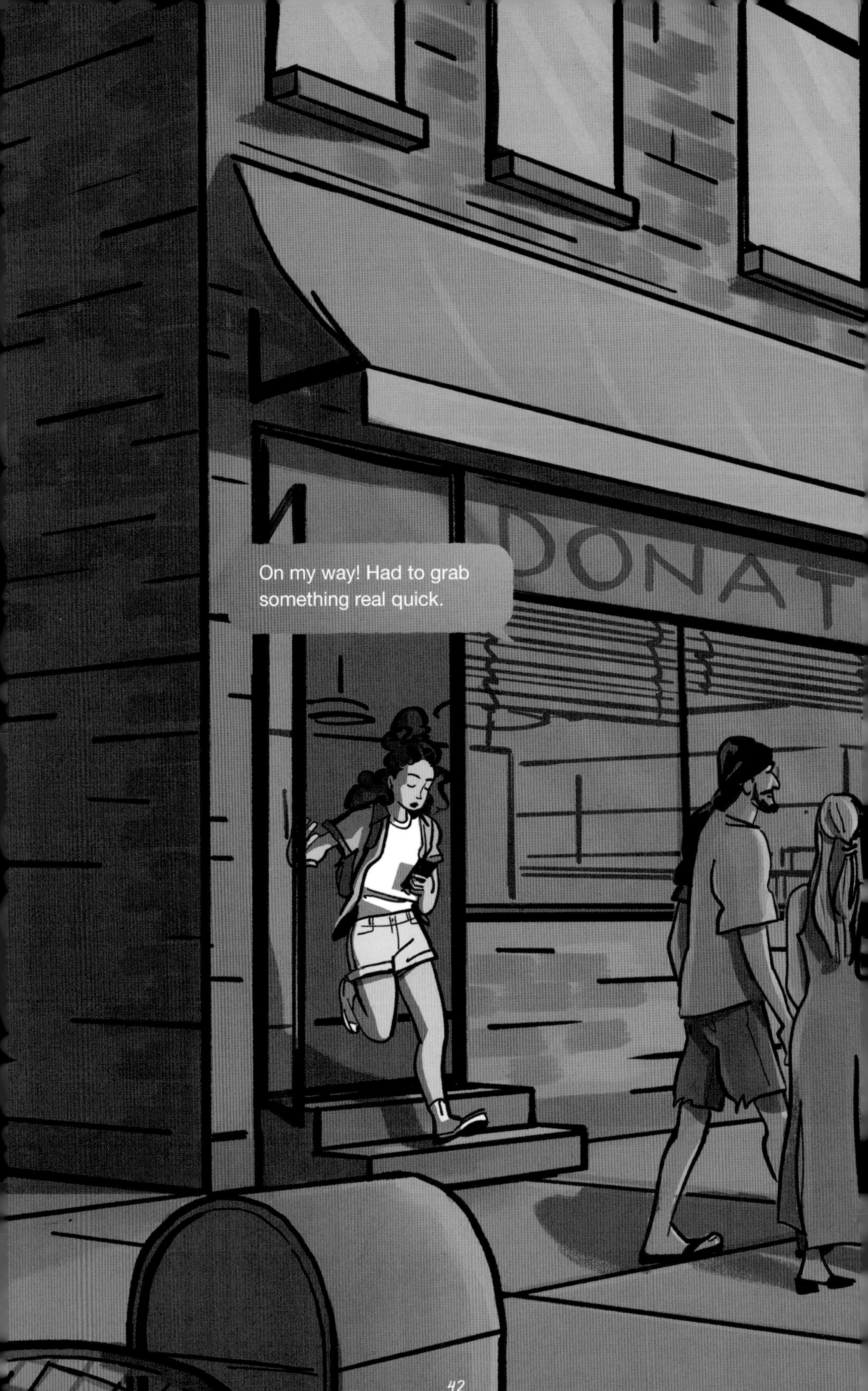
On my way! Had to grab something real quick.
DONAT

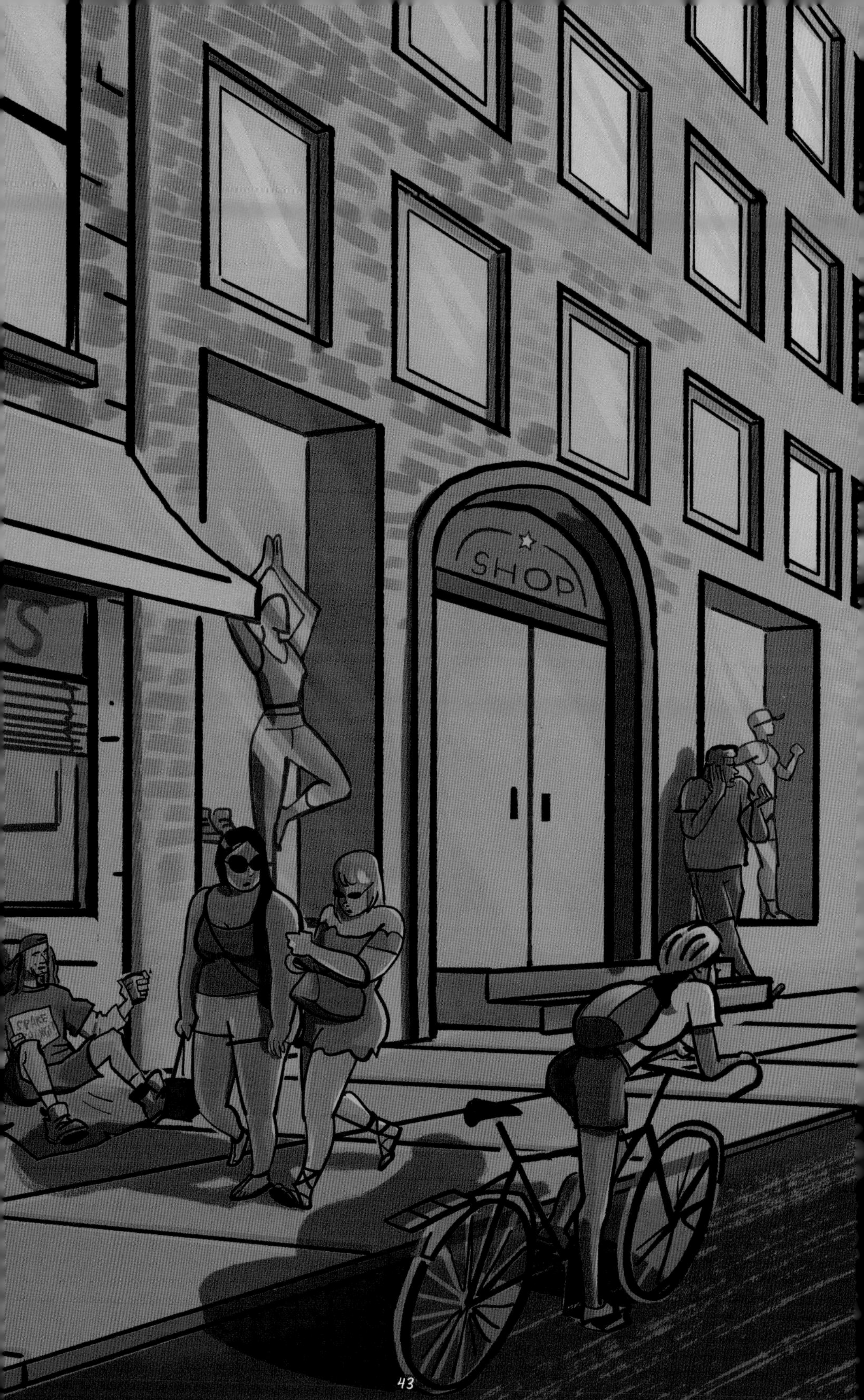
SHOP

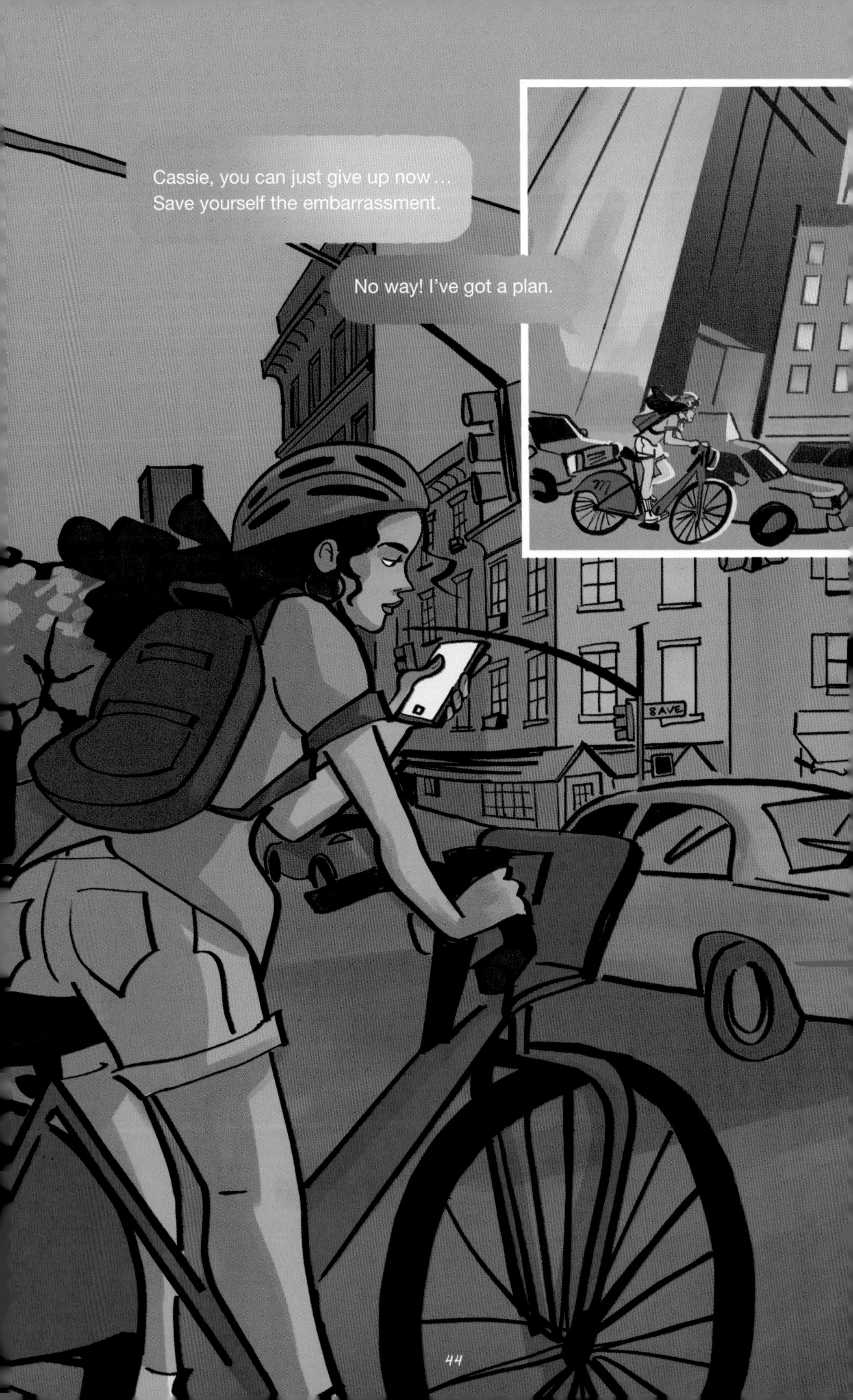
Cassie, you can just give up now . . .
Save yourself the embarrassment.
No way! I've got a plan.
8 AVE

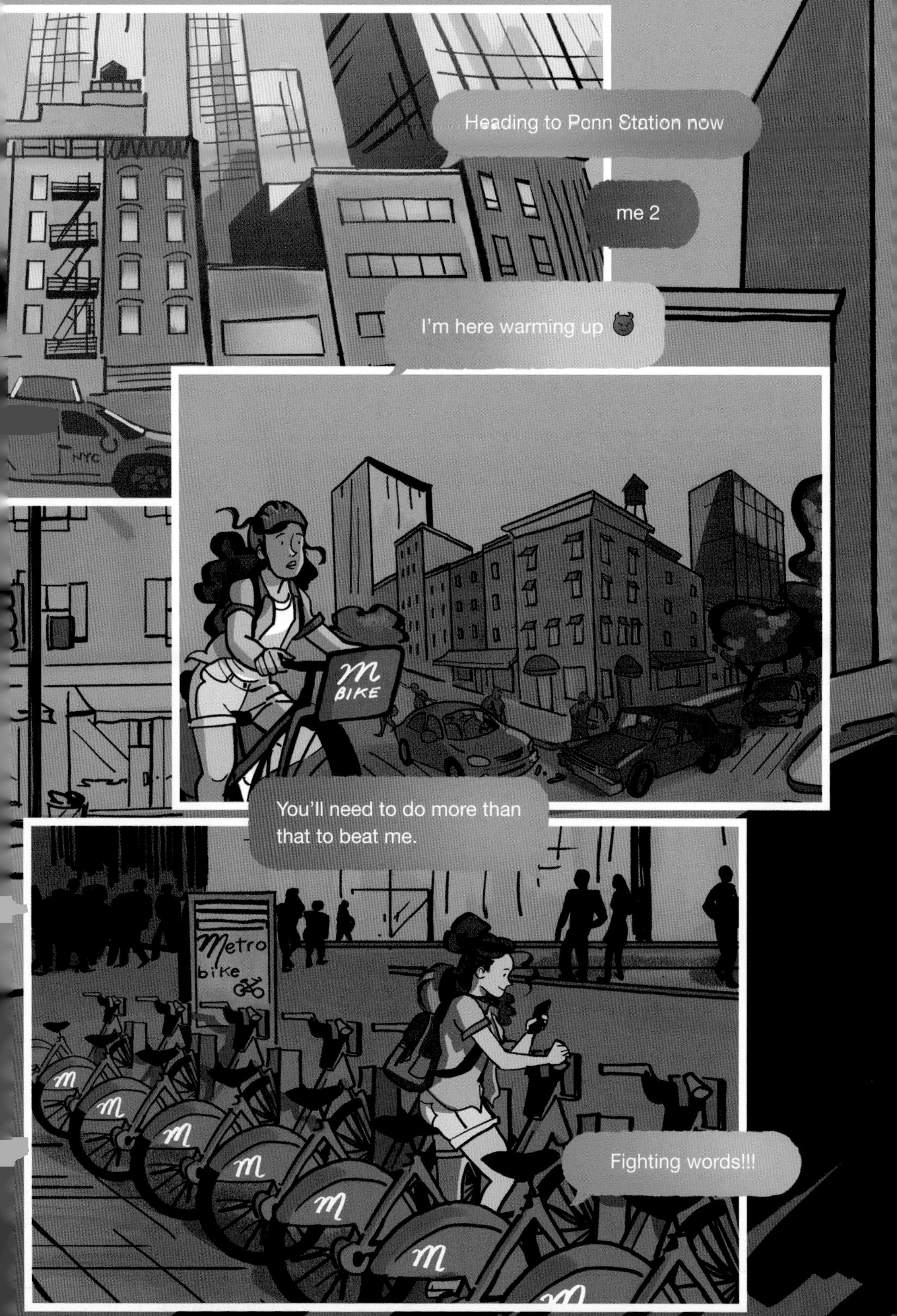
Heading to Penn Station now
me 2
I'm here warming up
NYC
M BIKE
You'll need to do more than that to beat me.
Metro bike
Fighting words!!!

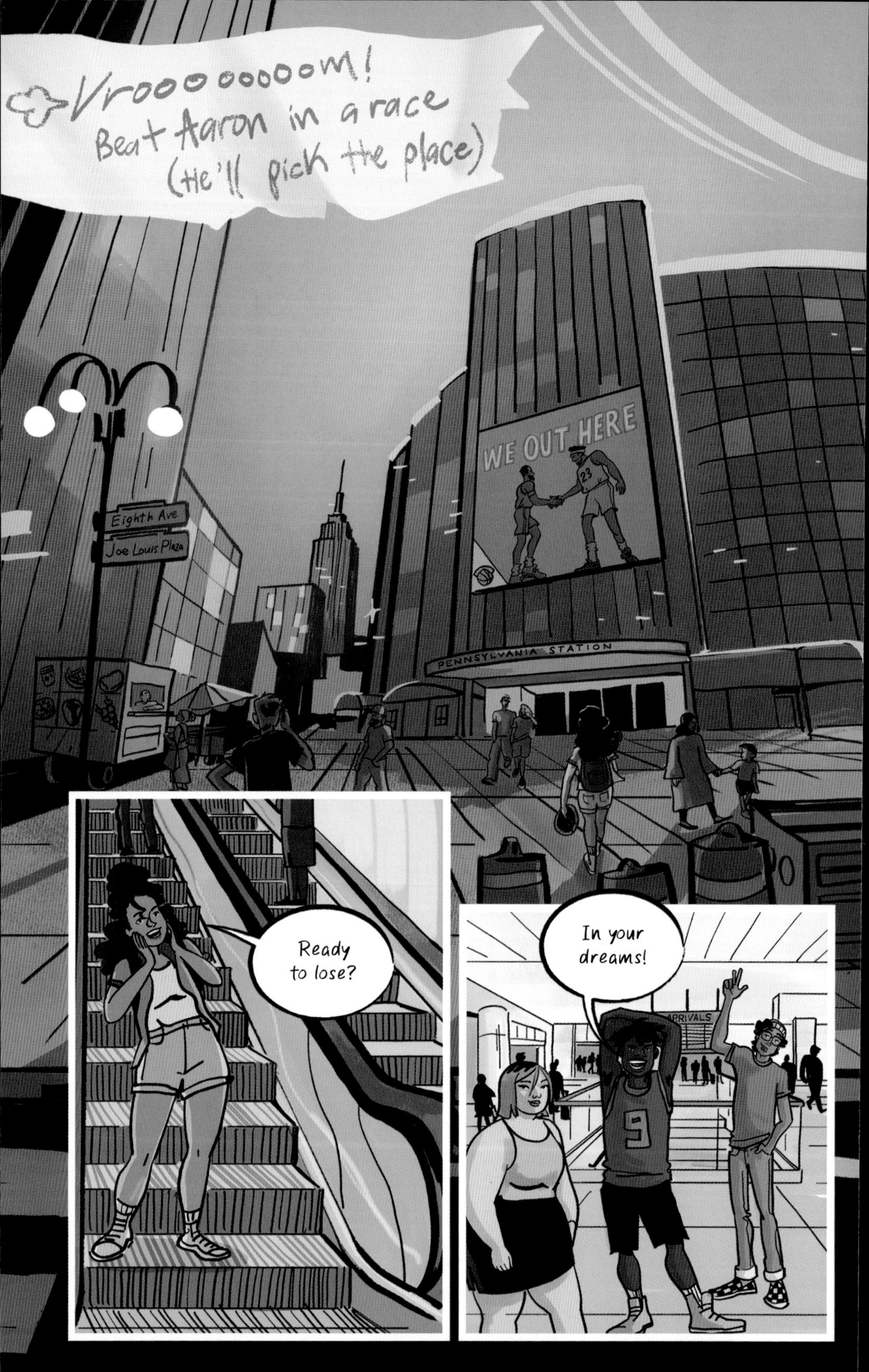
Vroooooooom! Beat Aaron in a race (He'll pick the place)
Eighth Ave
Joe Louis Plaza
WE OUT HERE
23
PENNSYLVANIA STATION
Ready to lose?
In your dreams!
ARRIVALS
9

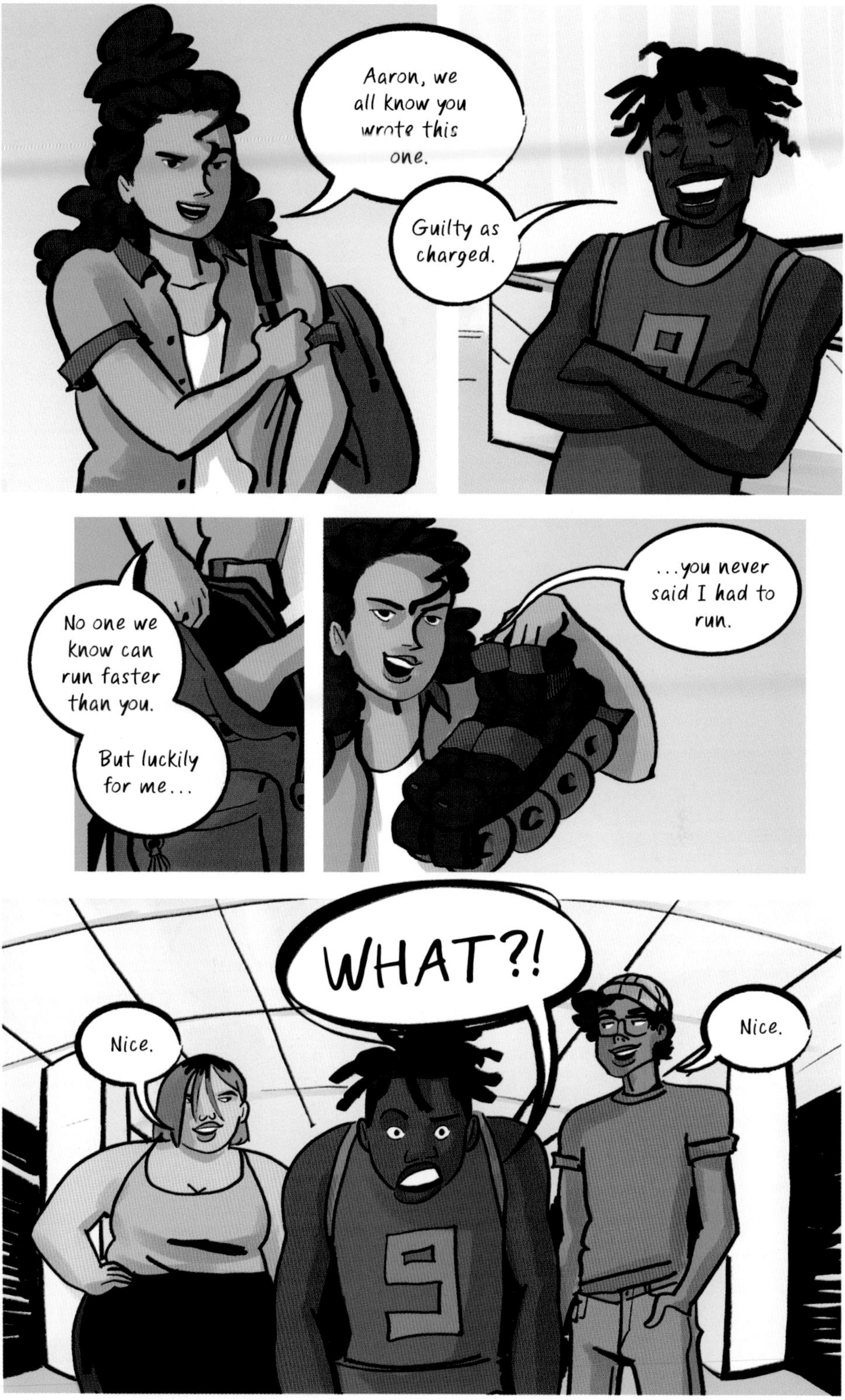
Aaron, we all know you wrote this one.
Guilty as charged.
No one we know can run faster than you.
But luckily for me...
...you never said I had to run.
WHAT?!
Nice.
Nice.

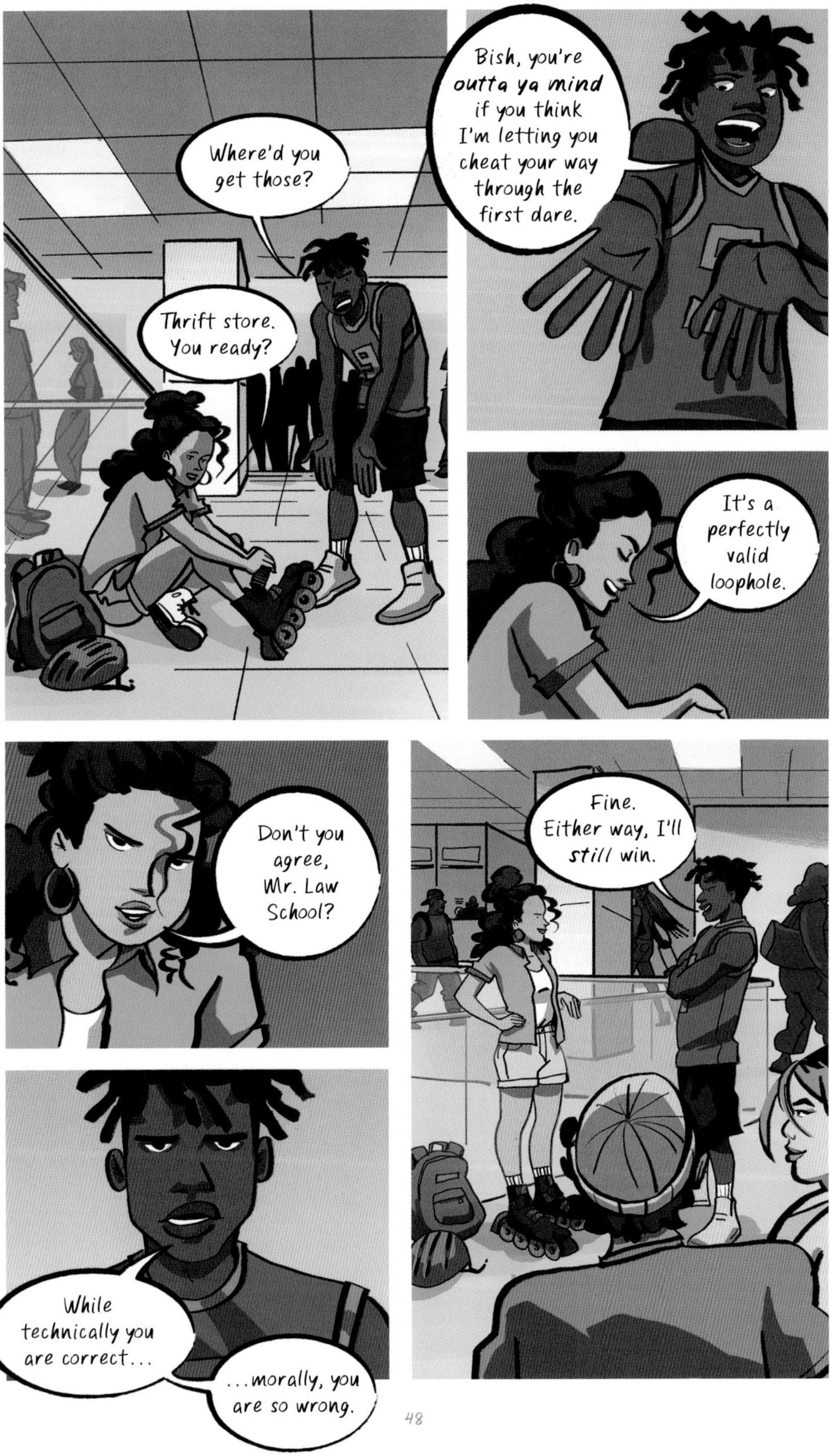
Where'd you get those?
Thrift store. You ready?
Bish, you're *outta ya mind* if you think I'm letting you cheat your way through the first dare.
It's a perfectly valid loophole.
Don't you agree, Mr. Law School?
While technically you are correct...
...morally, you are so wrong.
Fine. Either way, I'll *still* win.

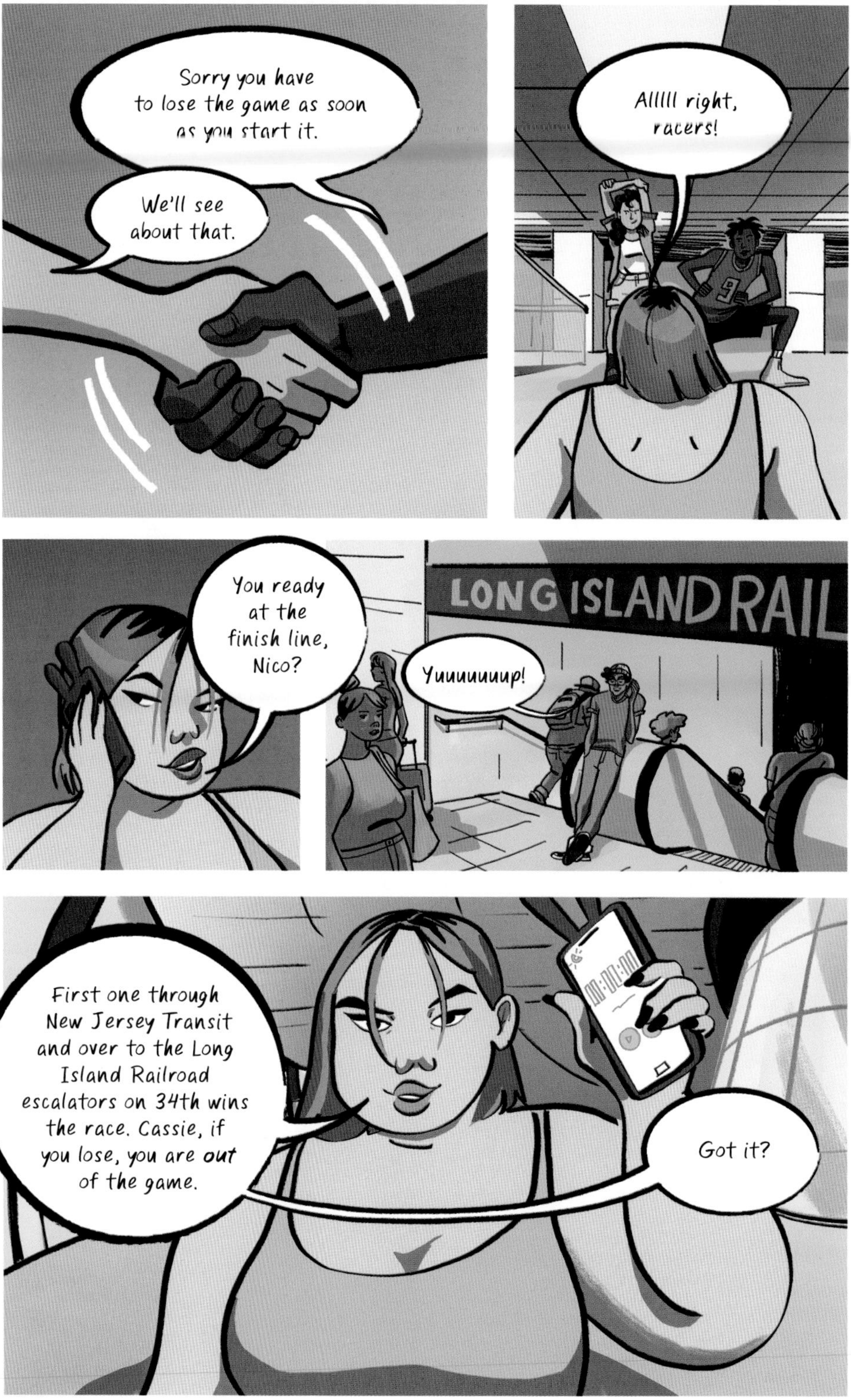
Sorry you have to lose the game as soon as you start it.
We'll see about that.
Alllll right, racers!
You ready at the finish line, Nico?
LONG ISLAND RAIL
Yuuuuuuup!
First one through New Jersey Transit and over to the Long Island Railroad escalators on 34th wins the race. Cassie, if you lose, you are **out** of the game.
Got it?

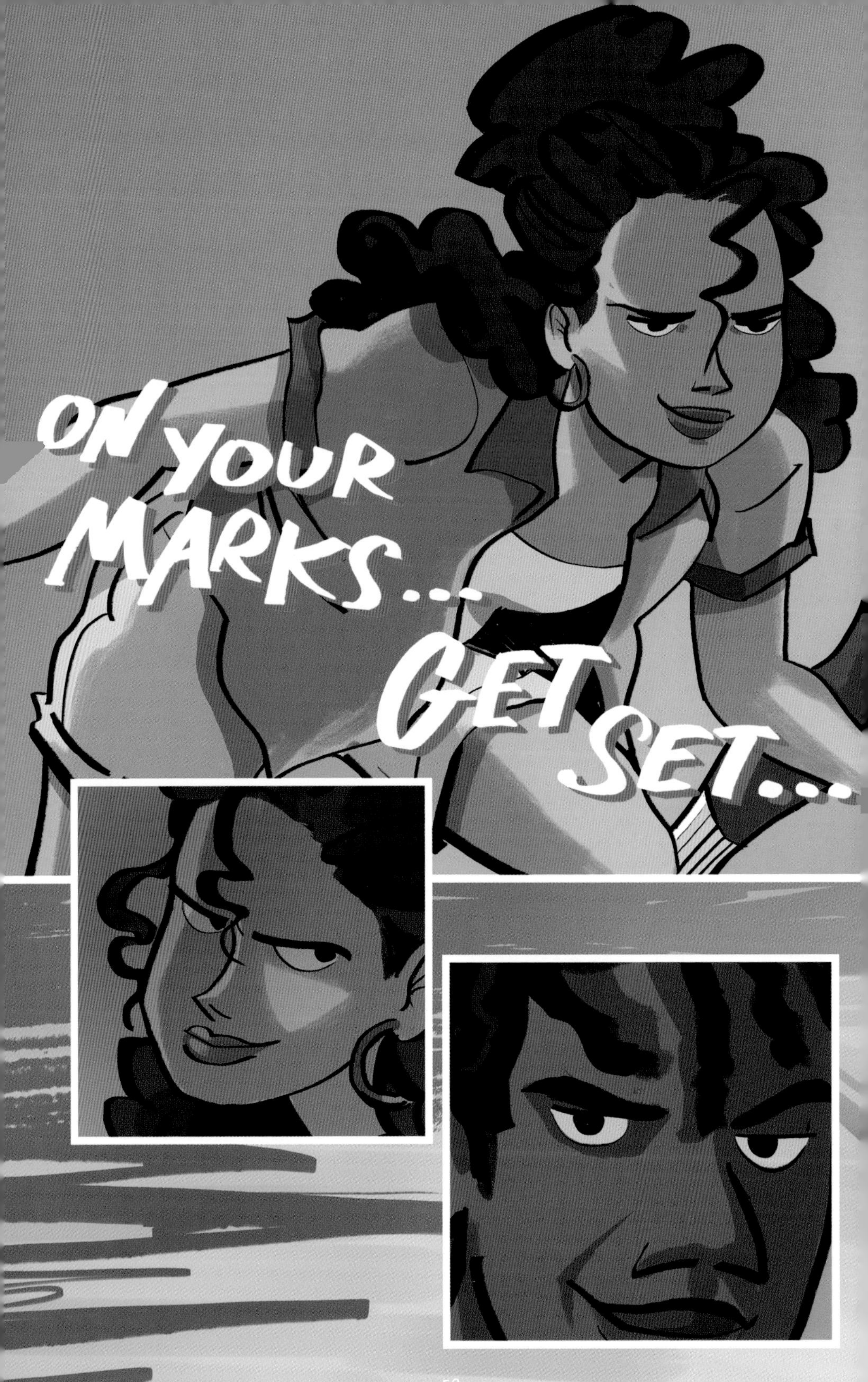
ON YOUR MARKS...
GET SET...

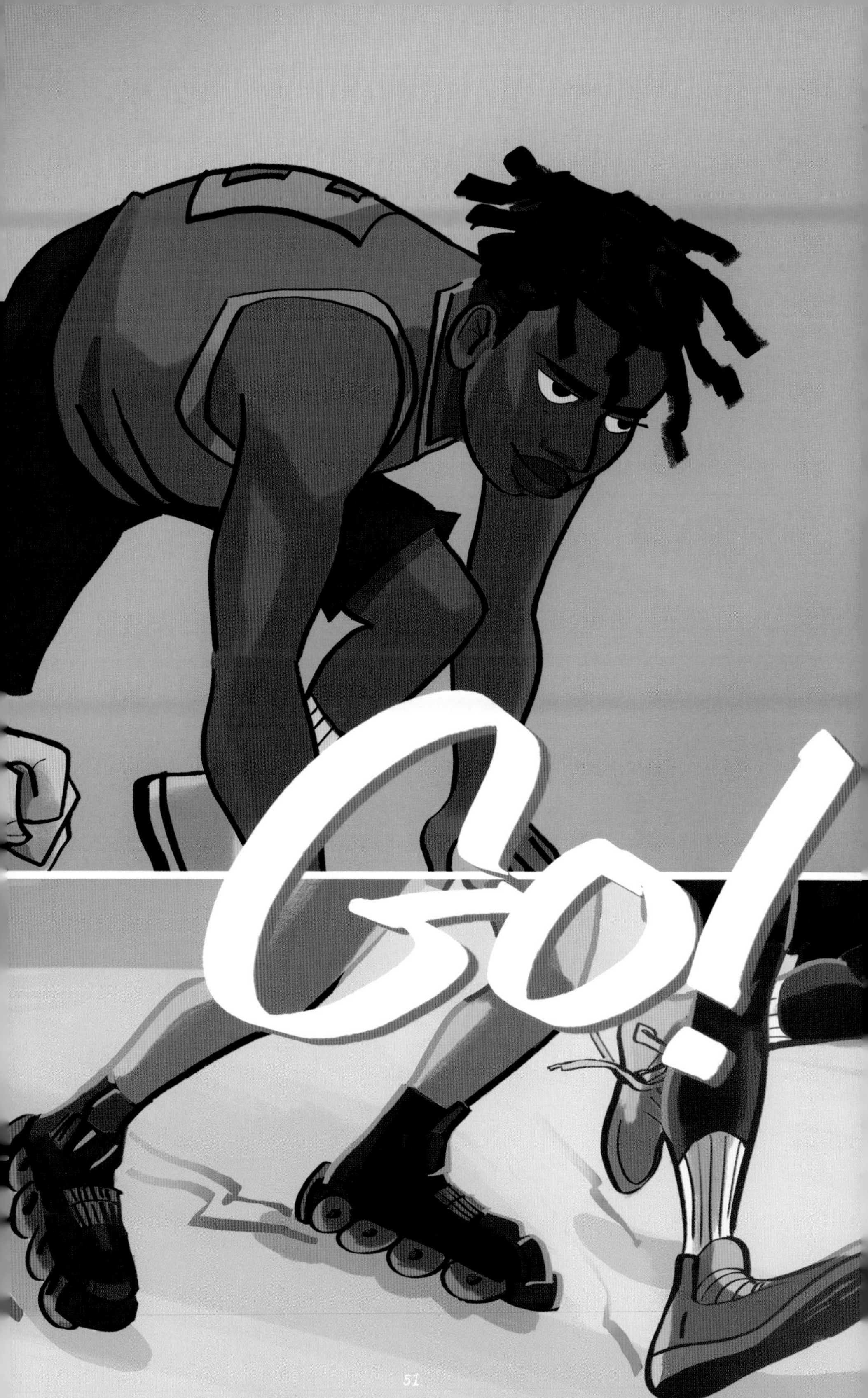
GO!

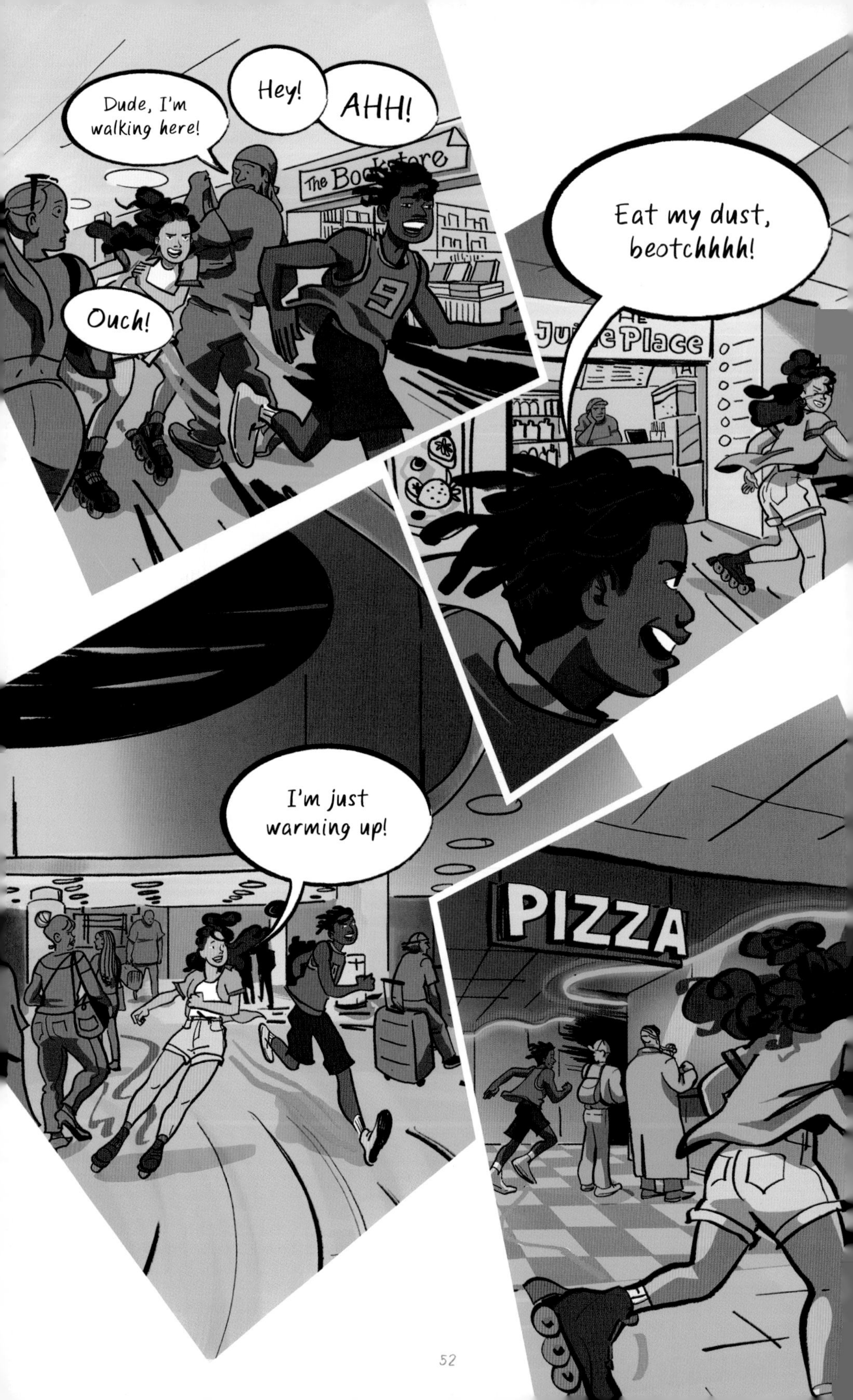
Dude, I'm walking here!
Hey!
AHH!
The Bookstore
Ouch!
Eat my dust, beotchhhh!
Juice Place
I'm just warming up!
PIZZA

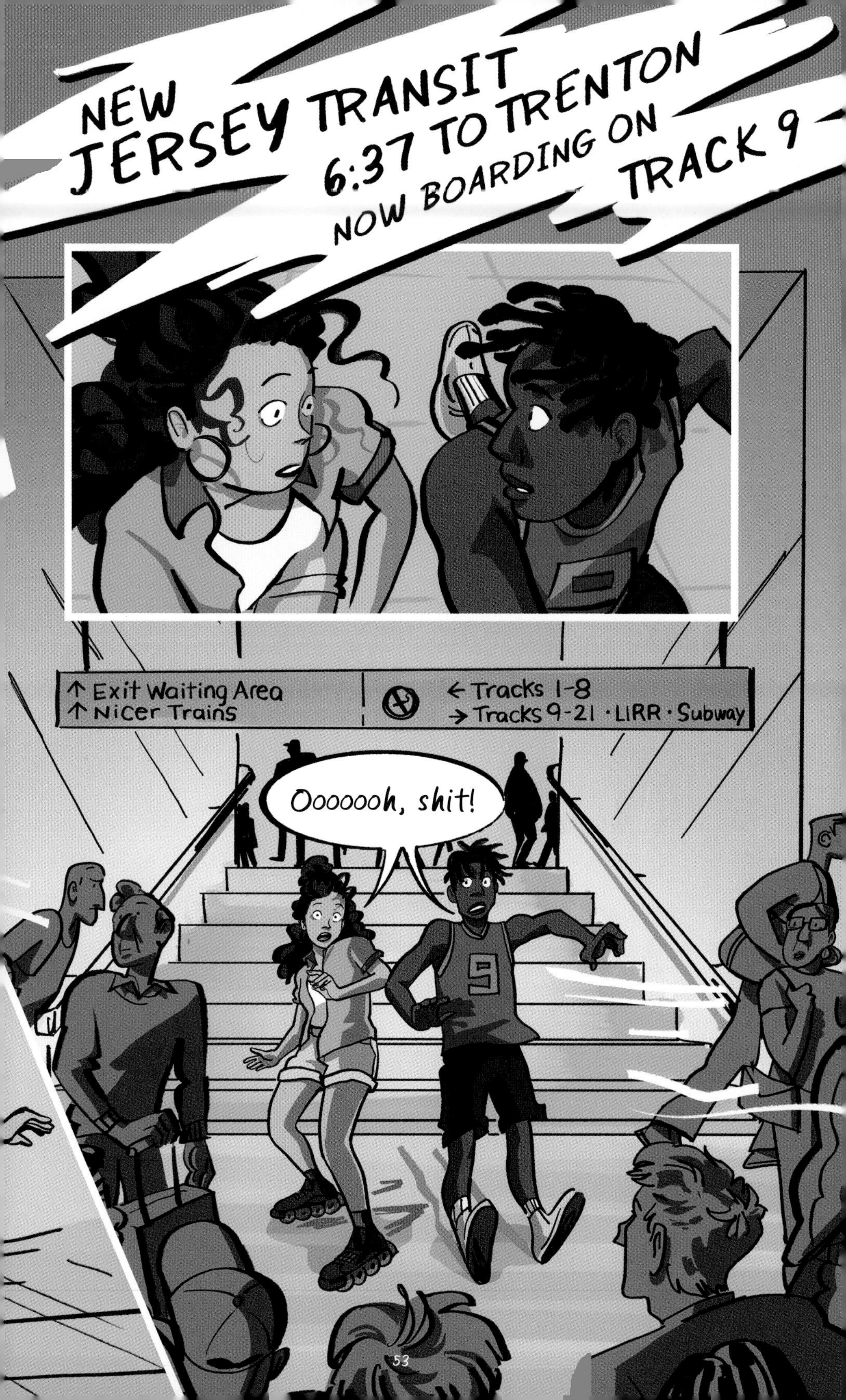
NEW JERSEY TRANSIT
6:37 TO TRENTON
NOW BOARDING ON
TRACK 9
↑ Exit Waiting Area
↑ Nicer Trains
← Tracks 1-8
→ Tracks 9-21 · LIRR · Subway
Ooooooh, shit!

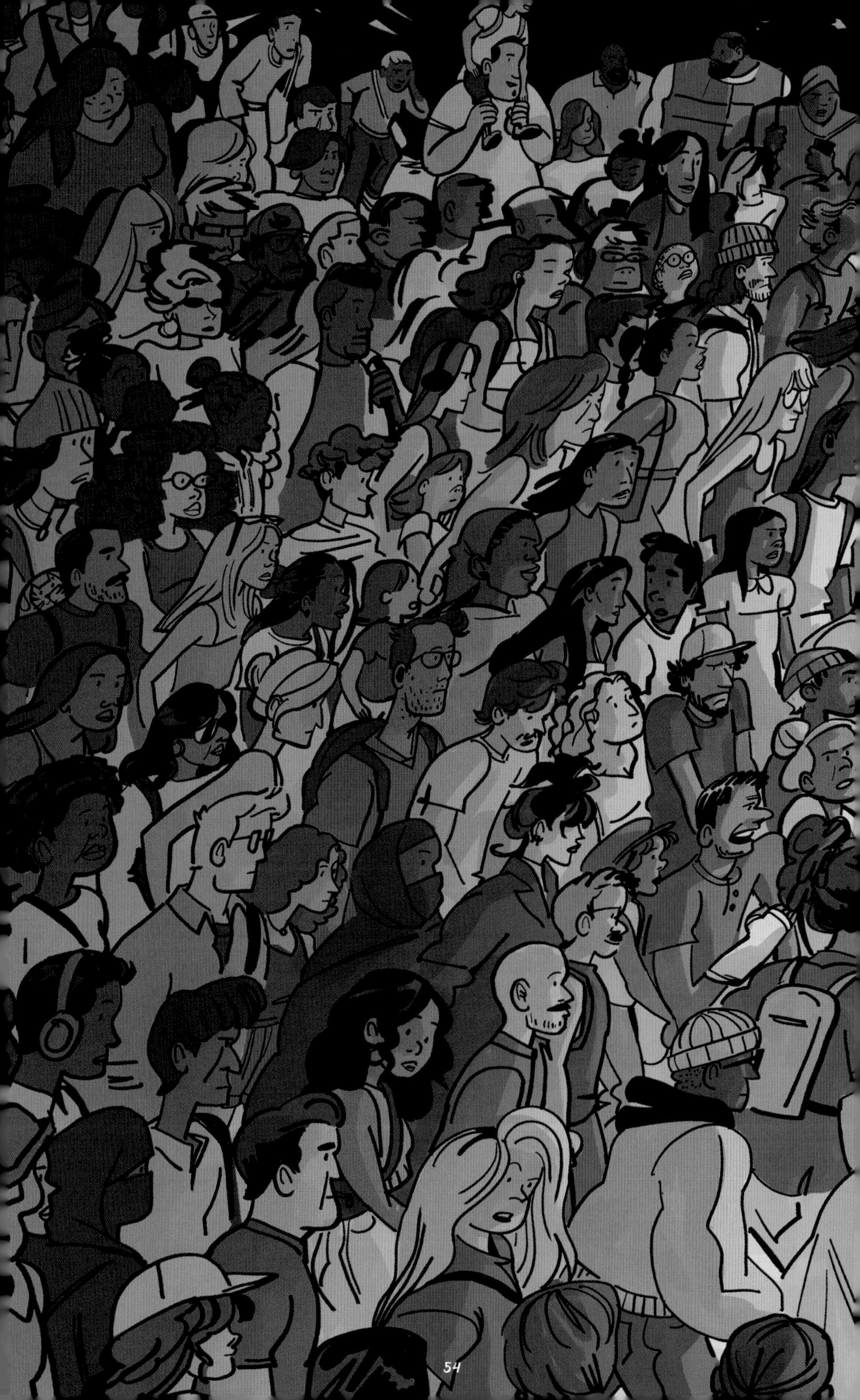

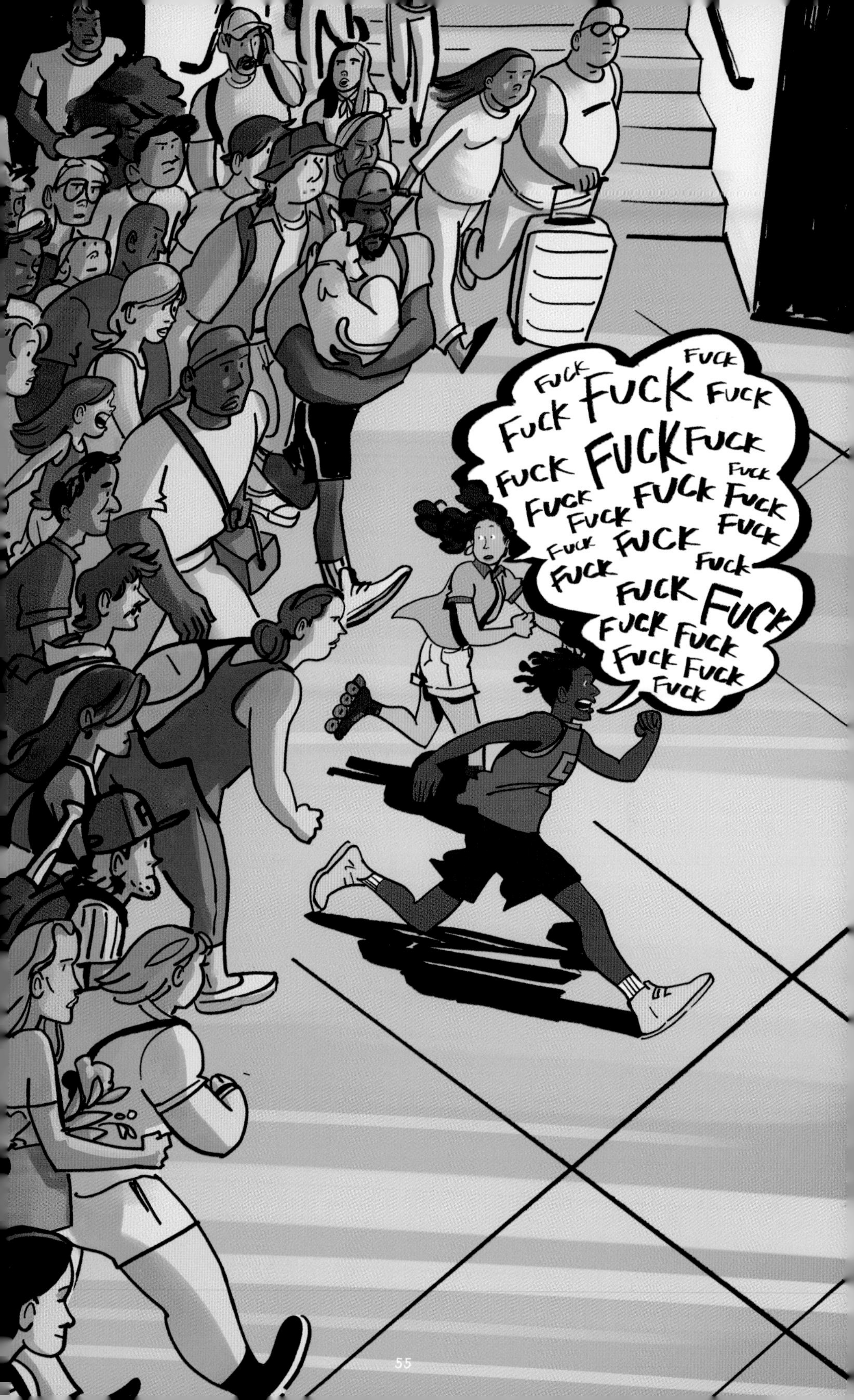
FUCK FUCK FUCK FUCK FUCK FUCK FUCK FUCK FUCK FUCK FUCK FUCK FUCK FUCK FUCK FUCK FUCK FUCK FUCK FUCK FUCK FUCK FUCK FUCK FUCK

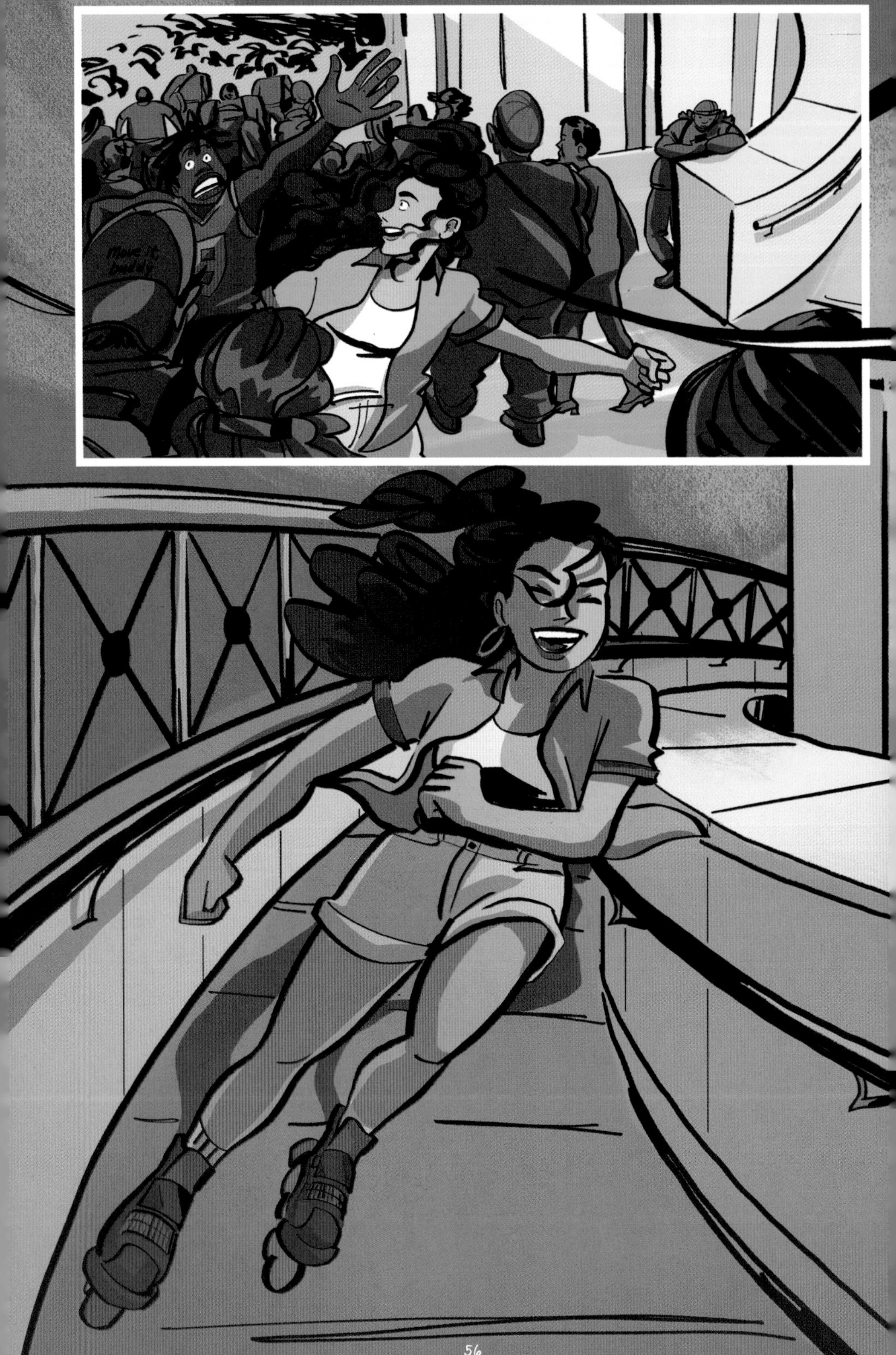

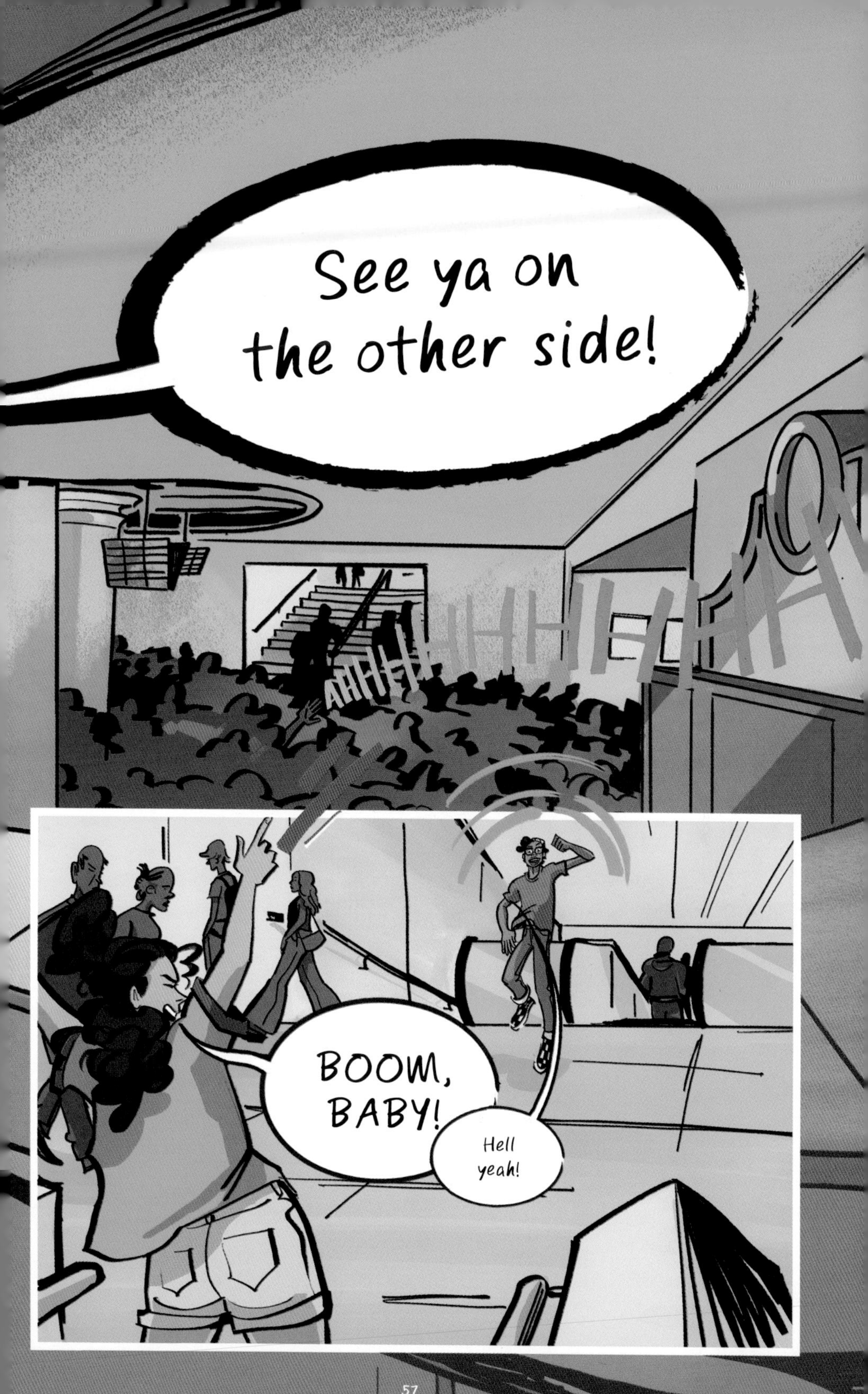
See ya on the other side!
BOOM, BABY!
Hell yeah!

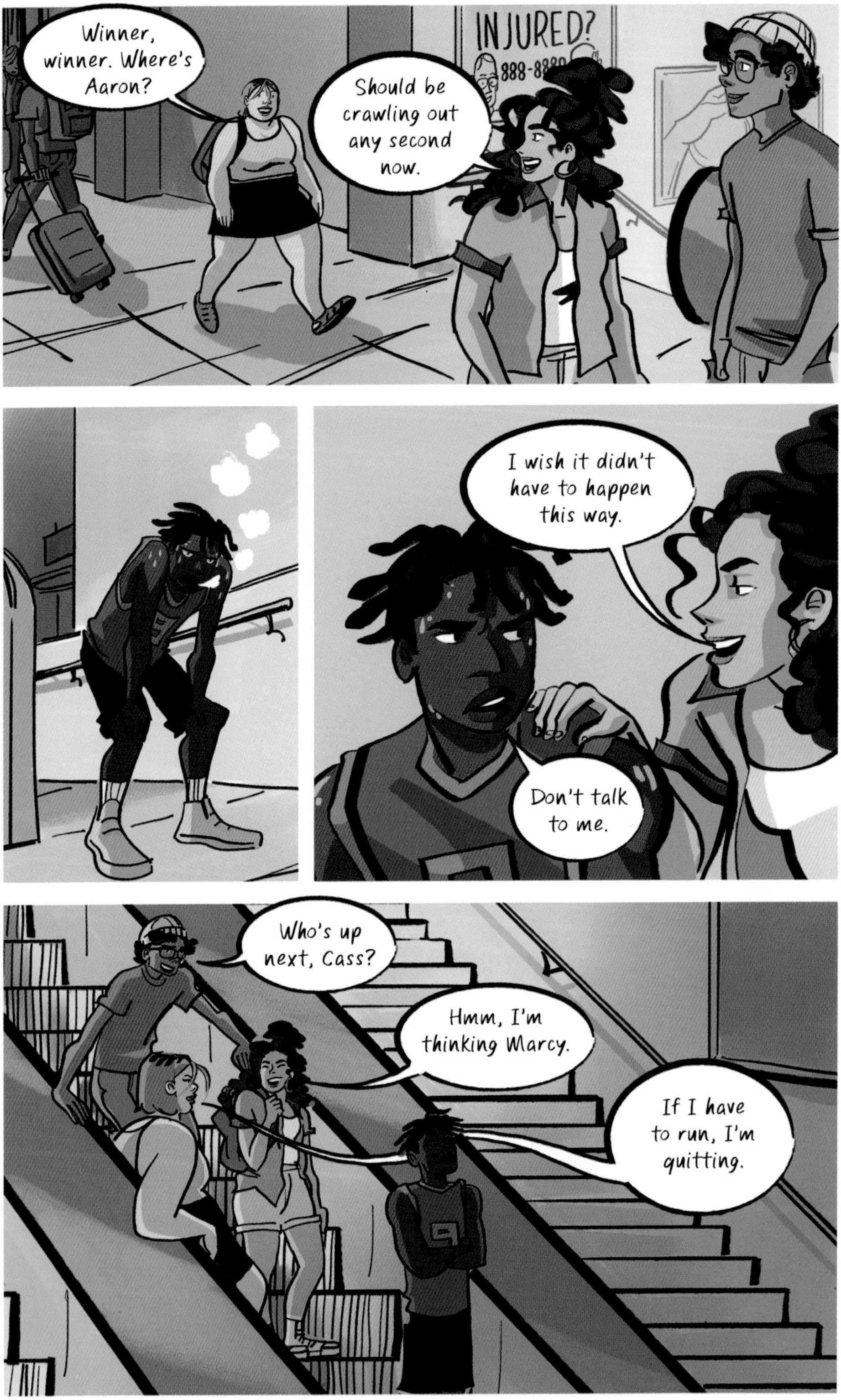
INJURED?
Winner, winner. Where's Aaron?
Should be crawling out any second now.
I wish it didn't have to happen this way.
Don't talk to me.
Who's up next, Cass?
Hmm, I'm thinking Marcy.
If I have to run, I'm quitting.

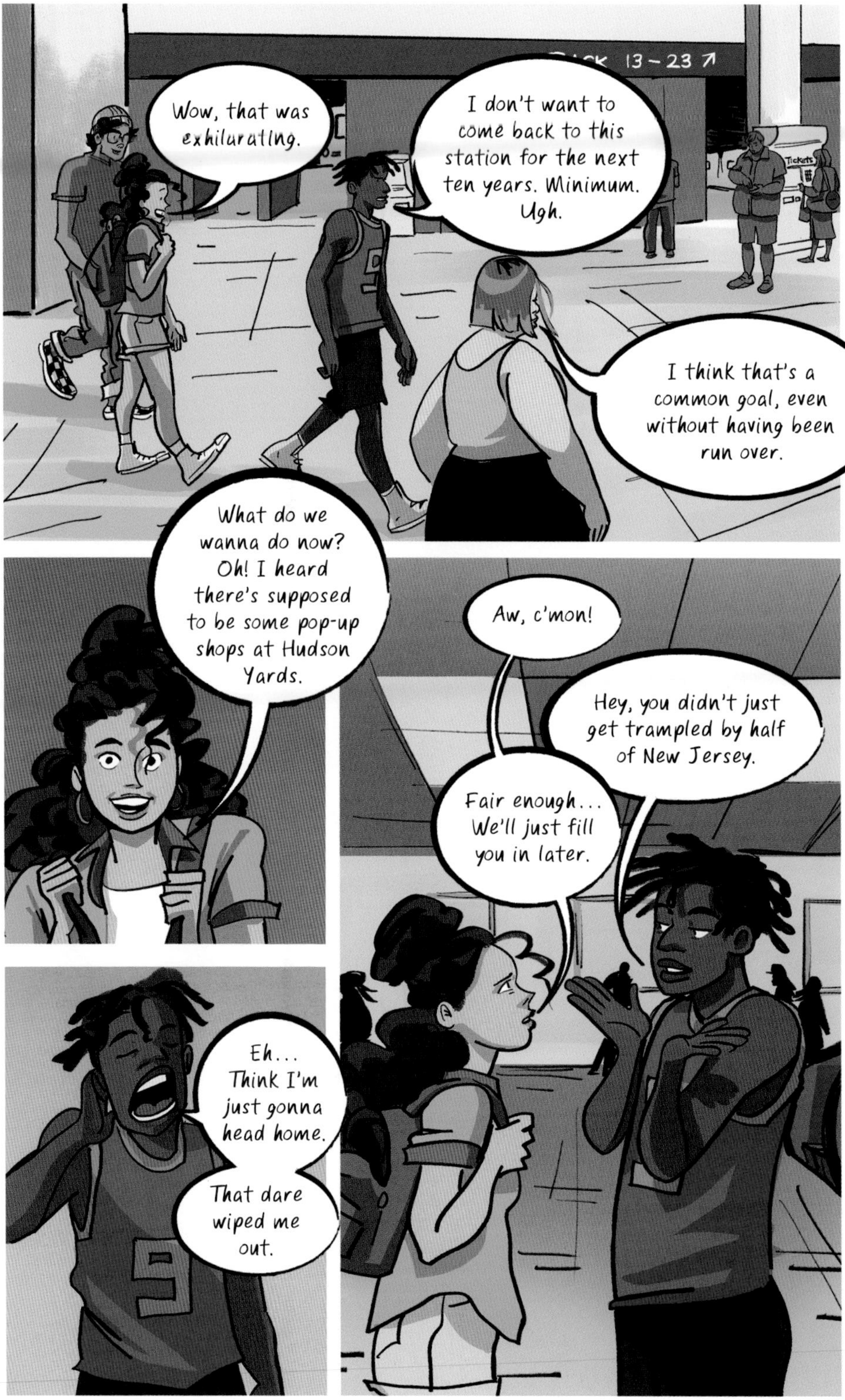
13 – 23
Wow, that was exhilarating.
I don't want to come back to this station for the next ten years. Minimum. Ugh.
I think that's a common goal, even without having been run over.
What do we wanna do now? Oh! I heard there's supposed to be some pop-up shops at Hudson Yards.
Eh... Think I'm just gonna head home.
That dare wiped me out.
Aw, c'mon!
Hey, you didn't just get trampled by half of New Jersey.
Fair enough... We'll just fill you in later.

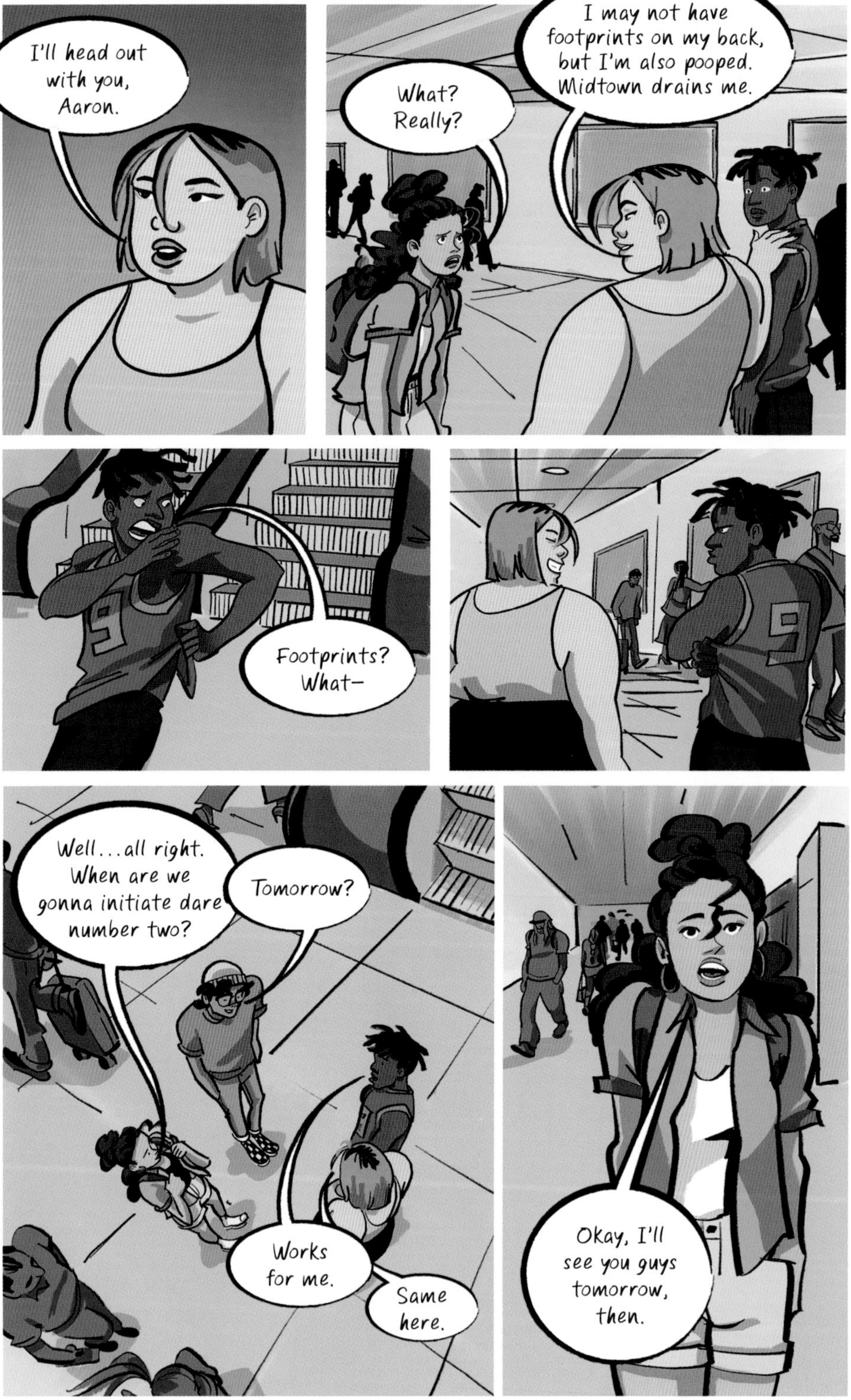
I'll head out with you, Aaron.
What? Really?
I may not have footprints on my back, but I'm also pooped. Midtown drains me.
Footprints? What—
Well...all right. When are we gonna initiate dare number two?
Tomorrow?
Works for me.
Same here.
Okay, I'll see you guys tomorrow, then.

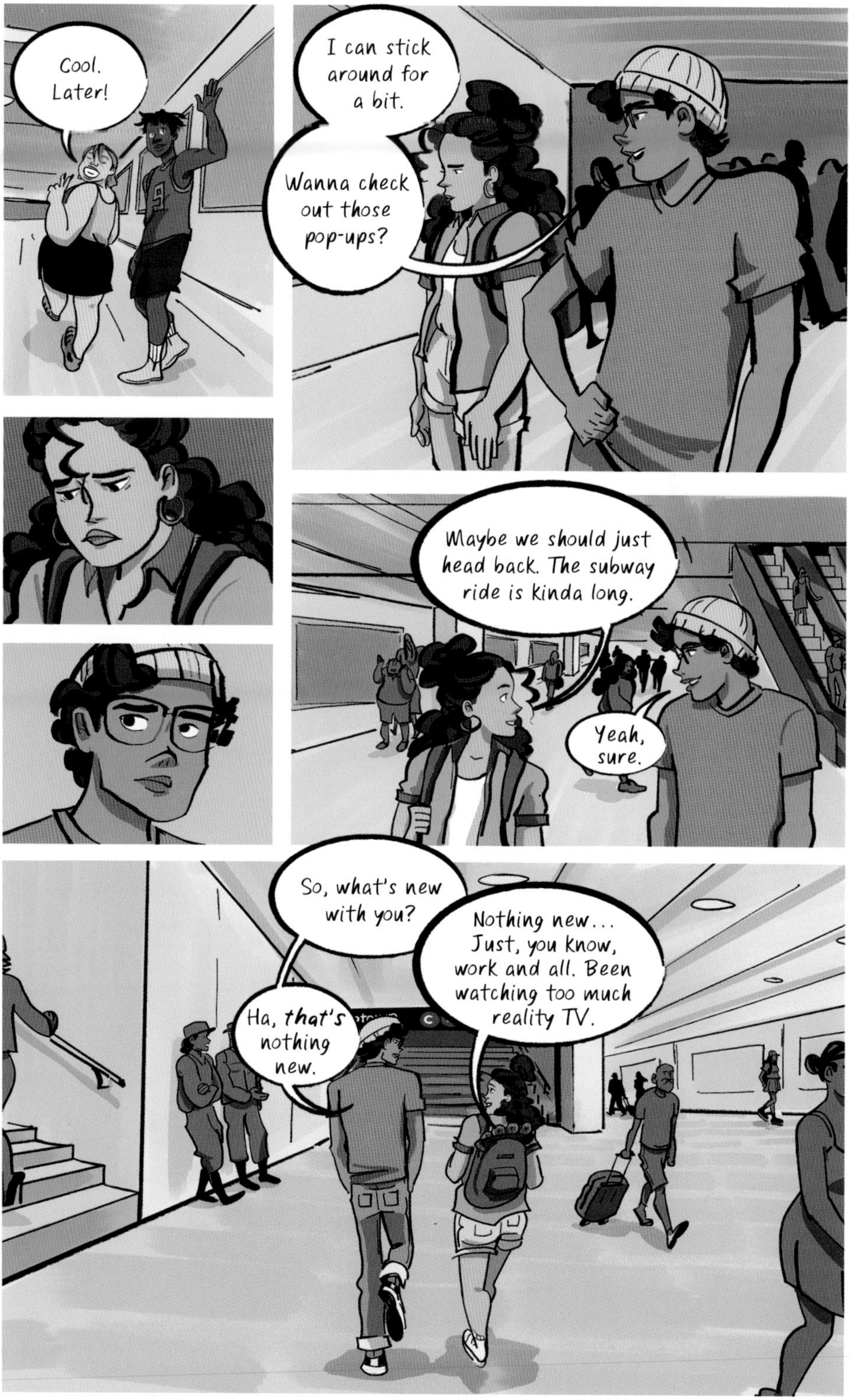
Cool. Later!
I can stick around for a bit.
Wanna check out those pop-ups?
Maybe we should just head back. The subway ride is kinda long.
Yeah, sure.
So, what's new with you?
Nothing new... Just, you know, work and all. Been watching too much reality TV.
Ha, *that's* nothing new.

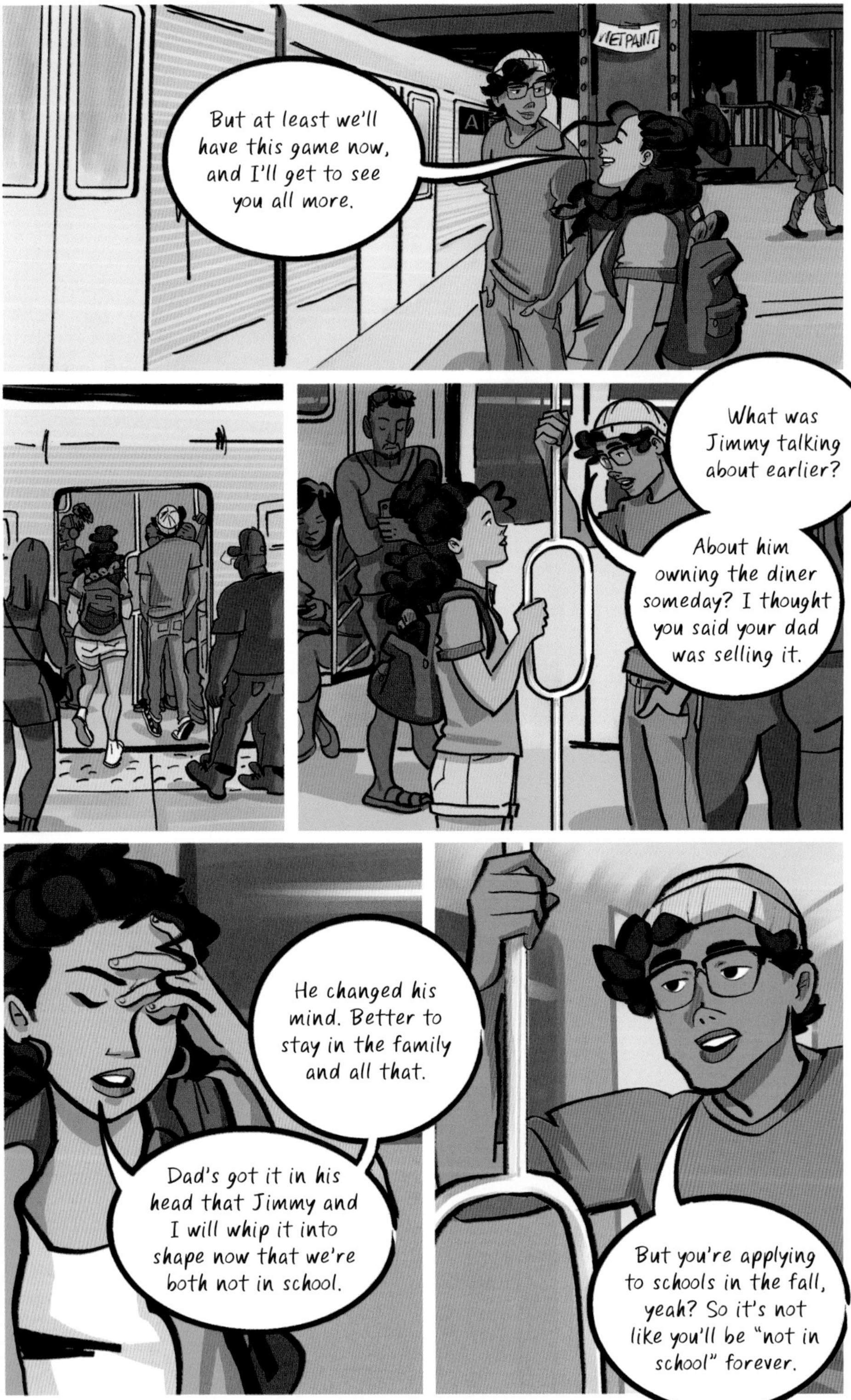
WET PAINT
But at least we'll have this game now, and I'll get to see you all more.
What was Jimmy talking about earlier?
About him owning the diner someday? I thought you said your dad was selling it.
He changed his mind. Better to stay in the family and all that.
Dad's got it in his head that Jimmy and I will whip it into shape now that we're both not in school.
But you're applying to schools in the fall, yeah? So it's not like you'll be "not in school" forever.

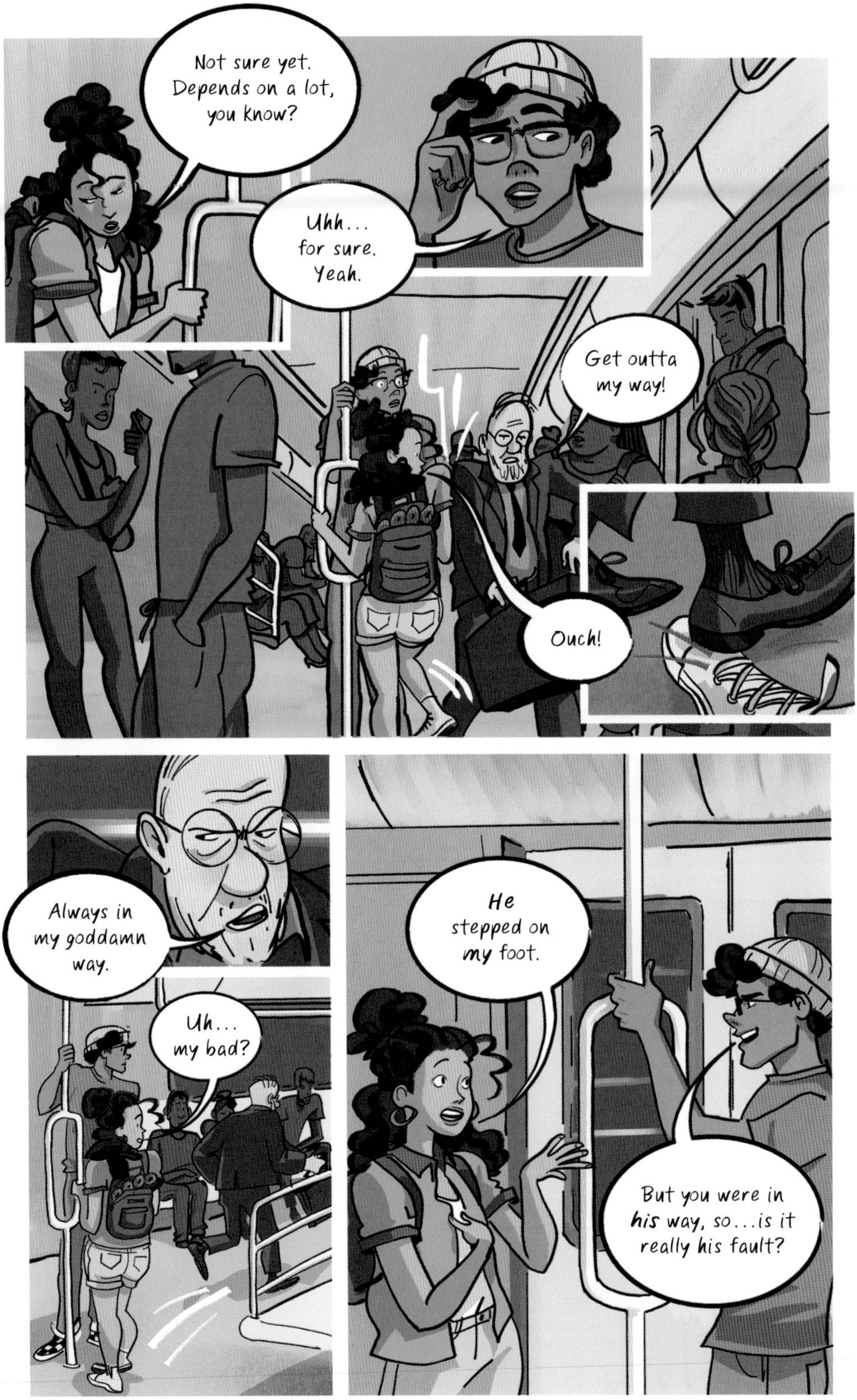
Not sure yet. Depends on a lot, you know?
Uhh... for sure. Yeah.
Get outta my way!
Ouch!
Always in my goddamn way.
Uh... my bad?
He stepped on my foot.
But you were in his way, so...is it really his fault?

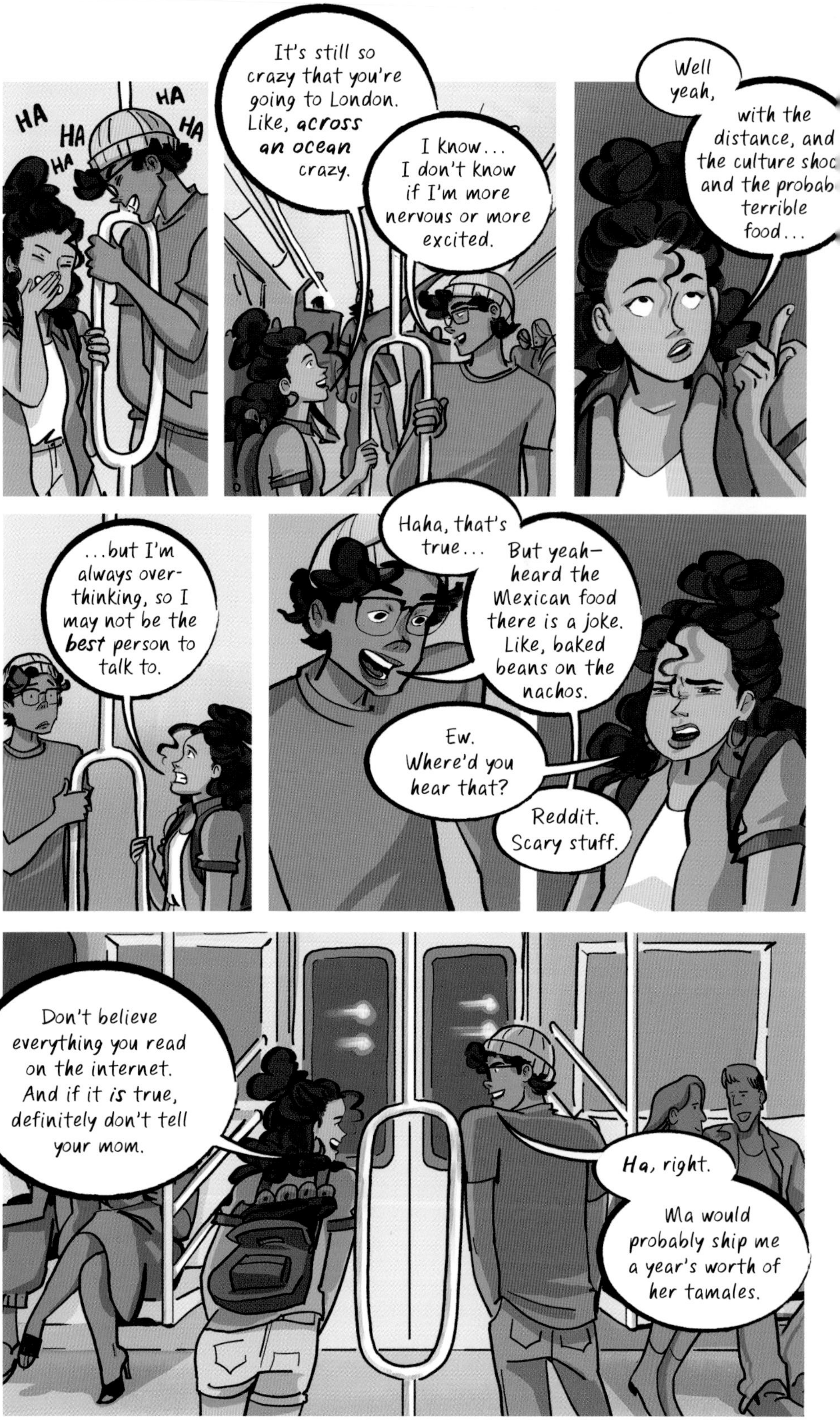
HA
HA
HA
HA
HA
It's still so crazy that you're going to London. Like, across an ocean crazy.
I know... I don't know if I'm more nervous or more excited.
Well yeah,
with the distance, and the culture shoc and the probab terrible food...
...but I'm always over-thinking, so I may not be the best person to talk to.
Haha, that's true...
But yeah— heard the Mexican food there is a joke. Like, baked beans on the nachos.
Ew. Where'd you hear that?
Reddit. Scary stuff.
Don't believe everything you read on the internet. And if it is true, definitely don't tell your mom.
Ha, right.
Ma would probably ship me a year's worth of her tamales.

Well, uh, I'm sure London will still be super cool.

The music scene is gonna be crazy.

Let me know if the subway mariachis are any good.

It's called the tube there. But if Brits really do put baked beans on their nachos, I think the bar is low for mariachi.

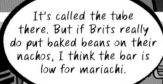

PING

HOY

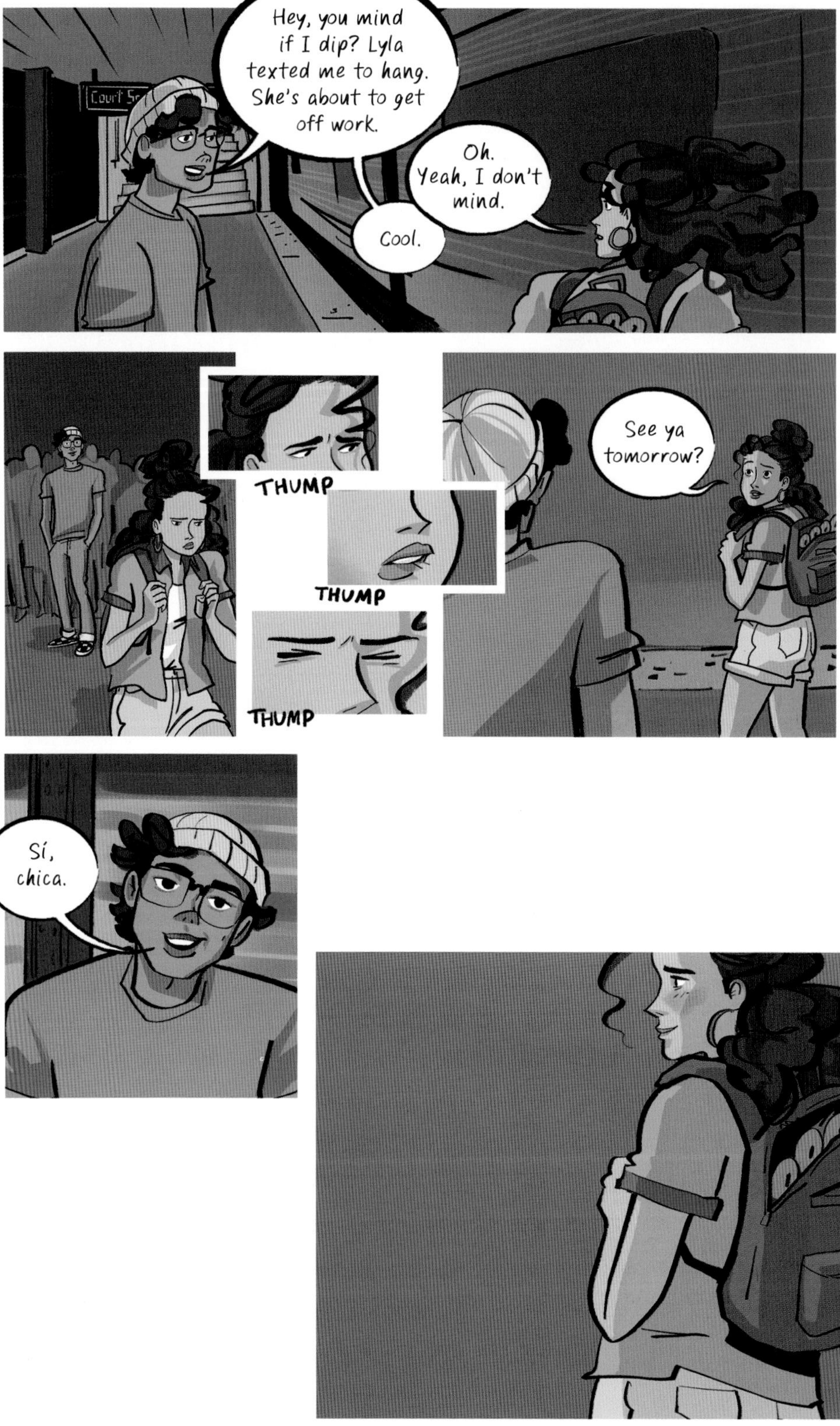
Court Sq
Hey, you mind if I dip? Lyla texted me to hang. She's about to get off work.
Oh. Yeah, I don't mind.
Cool.
THUMP
THUMP
THUMP
See ya tomorrow?
Sí, chica.

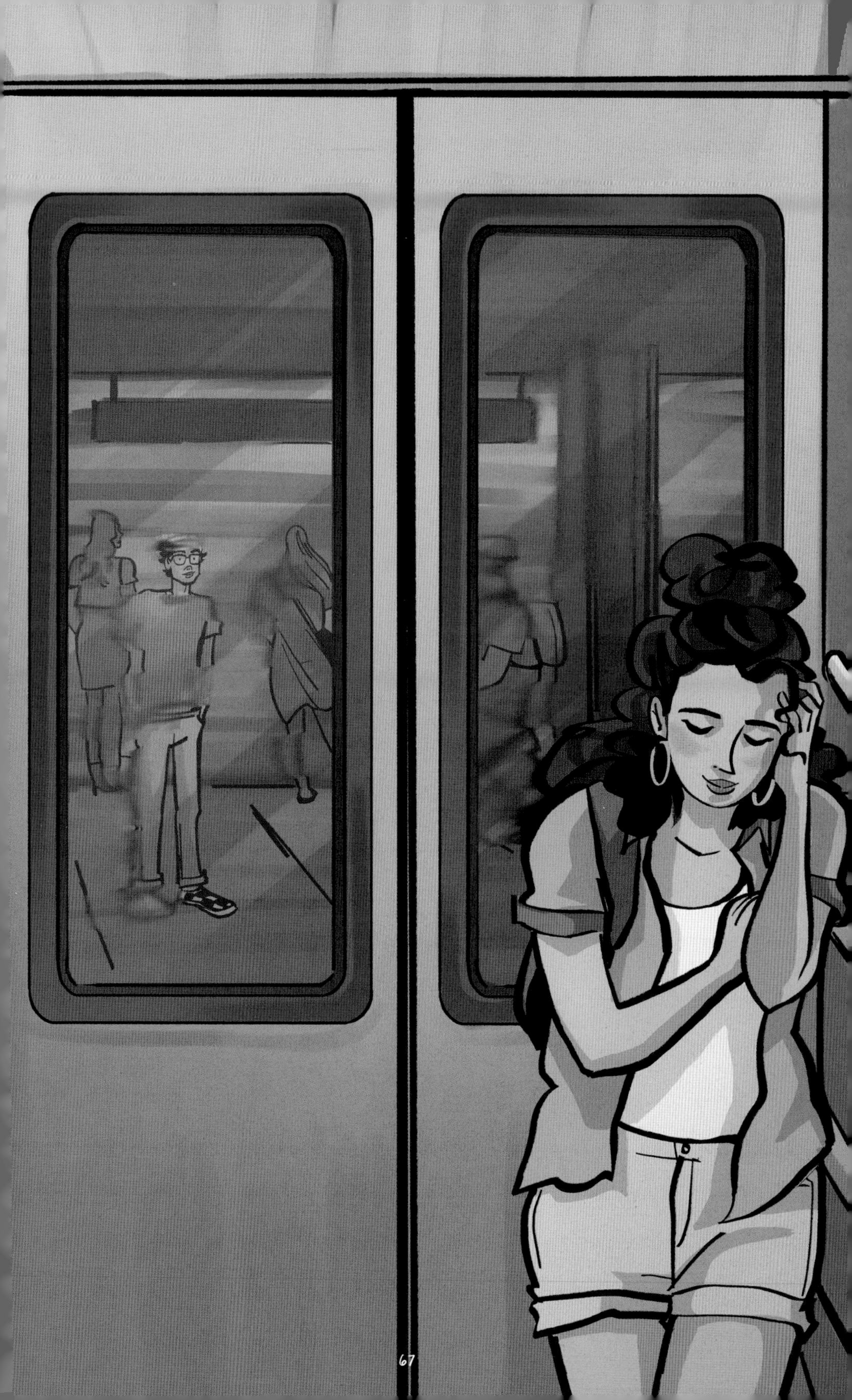

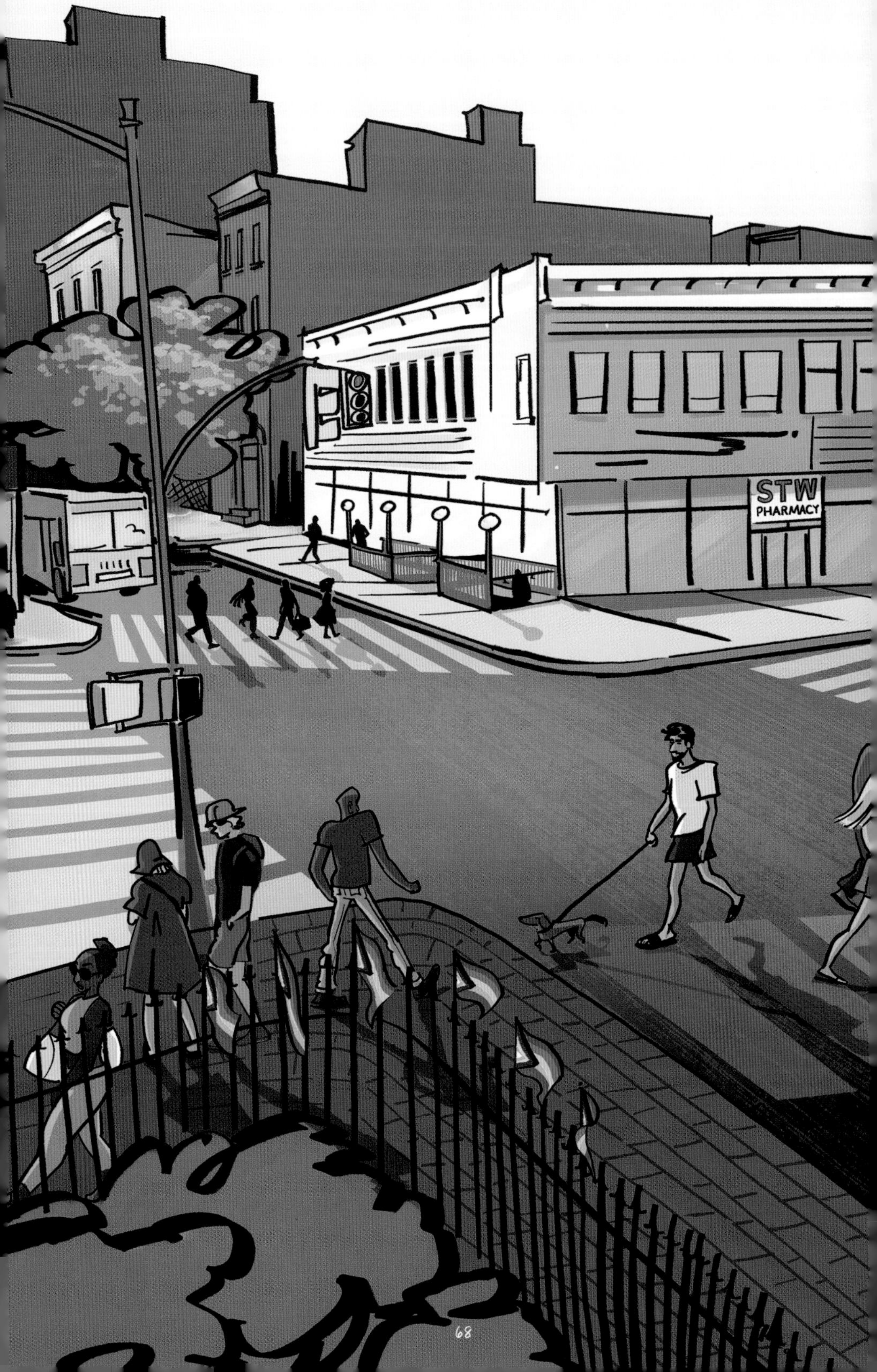
STW
PHARMACY

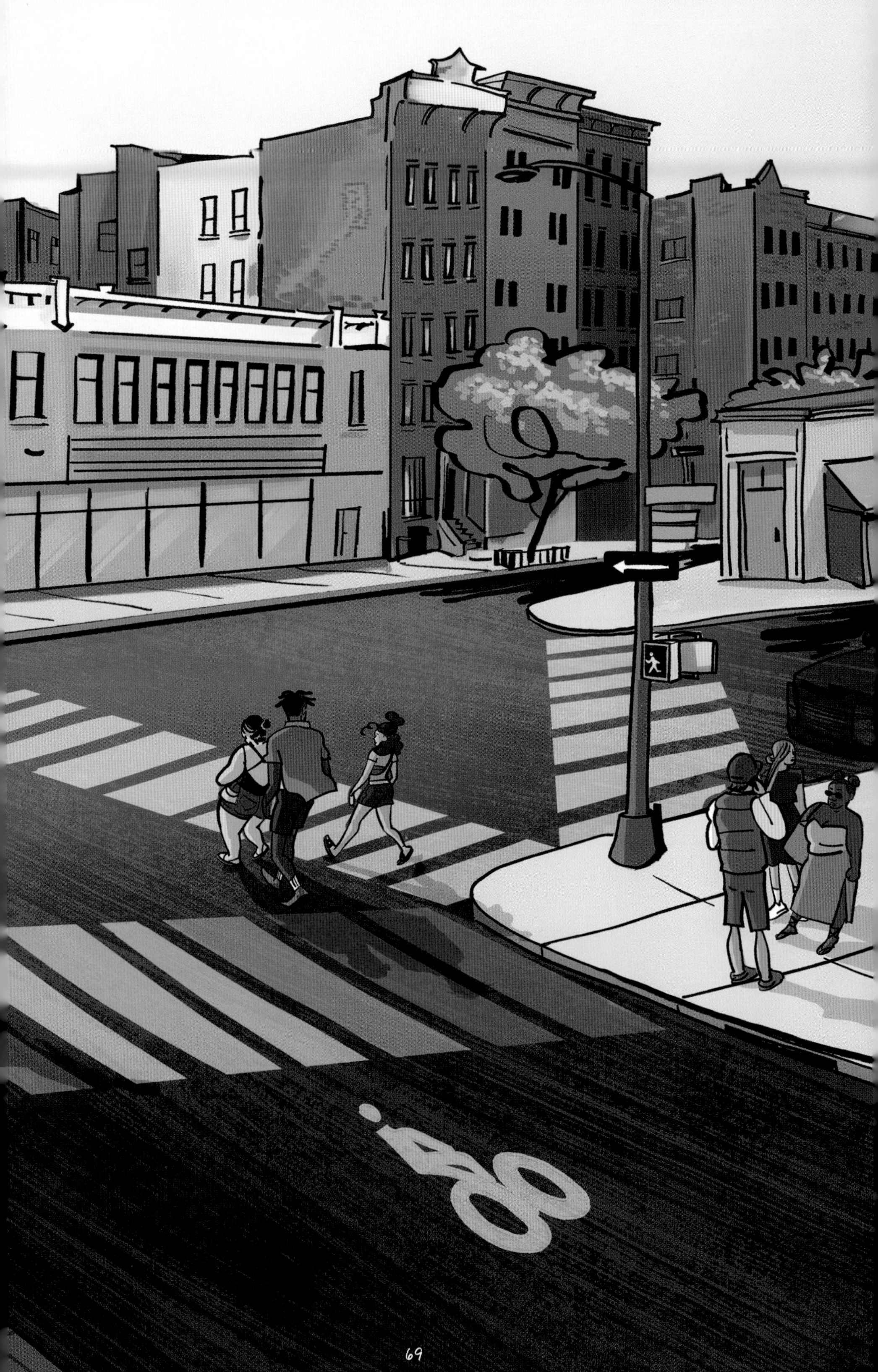

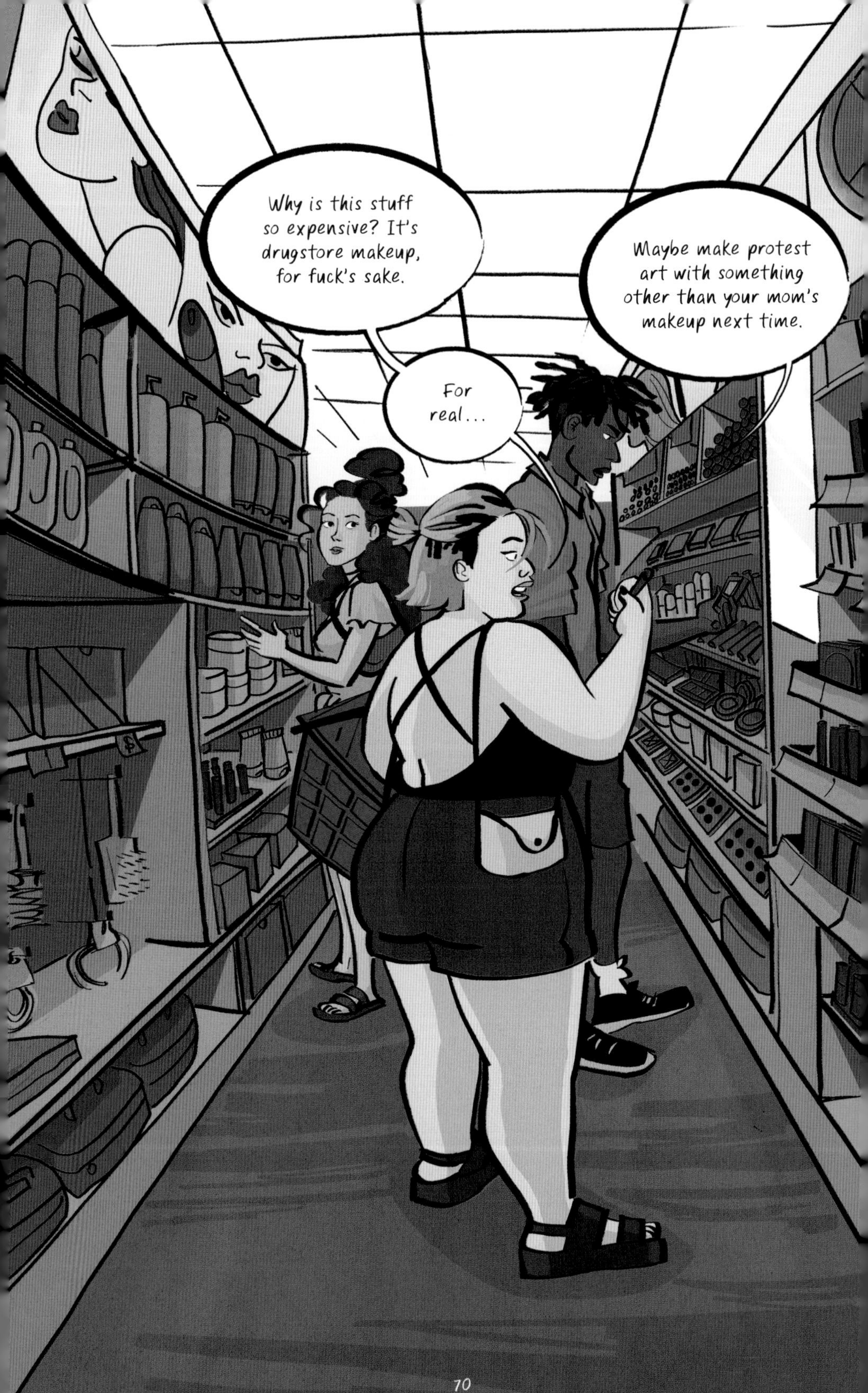
Why is this stuff so expensive? It's drugstore makeup, for fuck's sake.
For real...
Maybe make protest art with something other than your mom's makeup next time.

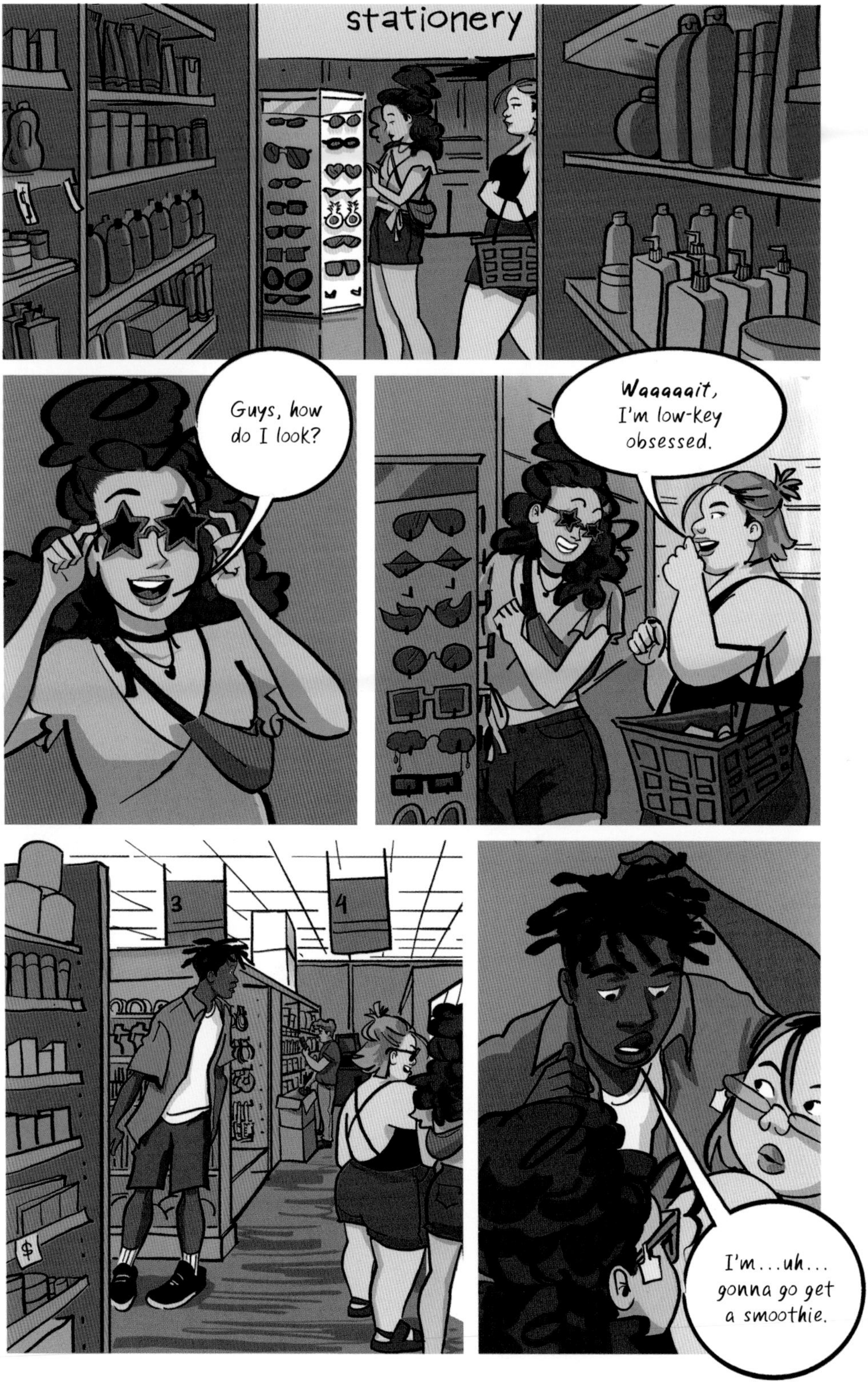
stationery
Guys, how do I look?
Waaaaait, I'm low-key obsessed.
3
4
$
I'm...uh... gonna go get a smoothie.

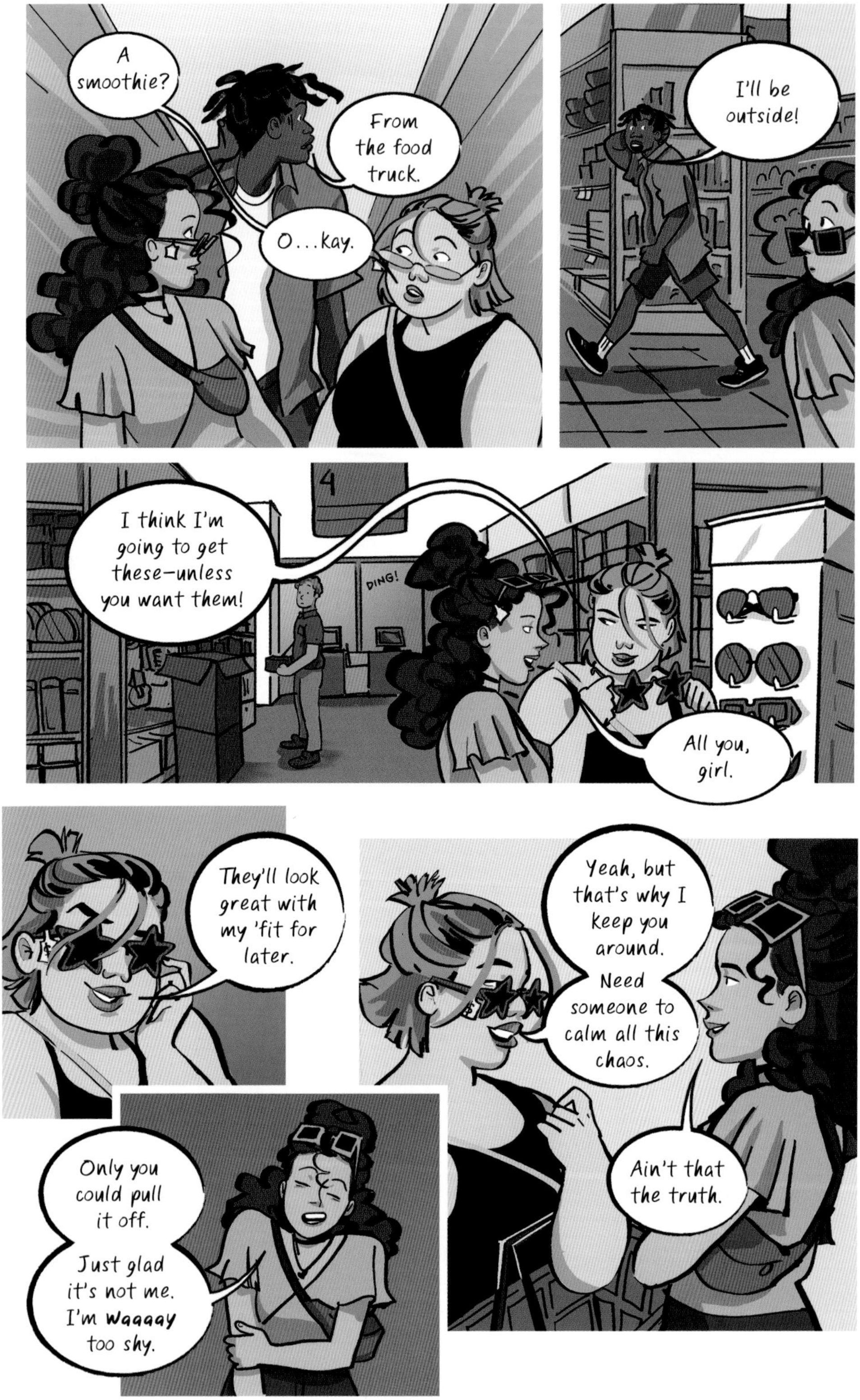
A smoothie?
From the food truck.
O...kay.
I'll be outside!
I think I'm going to get these—unless you want them!
DING!
All you, girl.
They'll look great with my 'fit for later.
Only you could pull it off.
Just glad it's not me. I'm **waaaay** too shy.
Yeah, but that's why I keep you around.
Need someone to calm all this chaos.
Ain't that the truth.

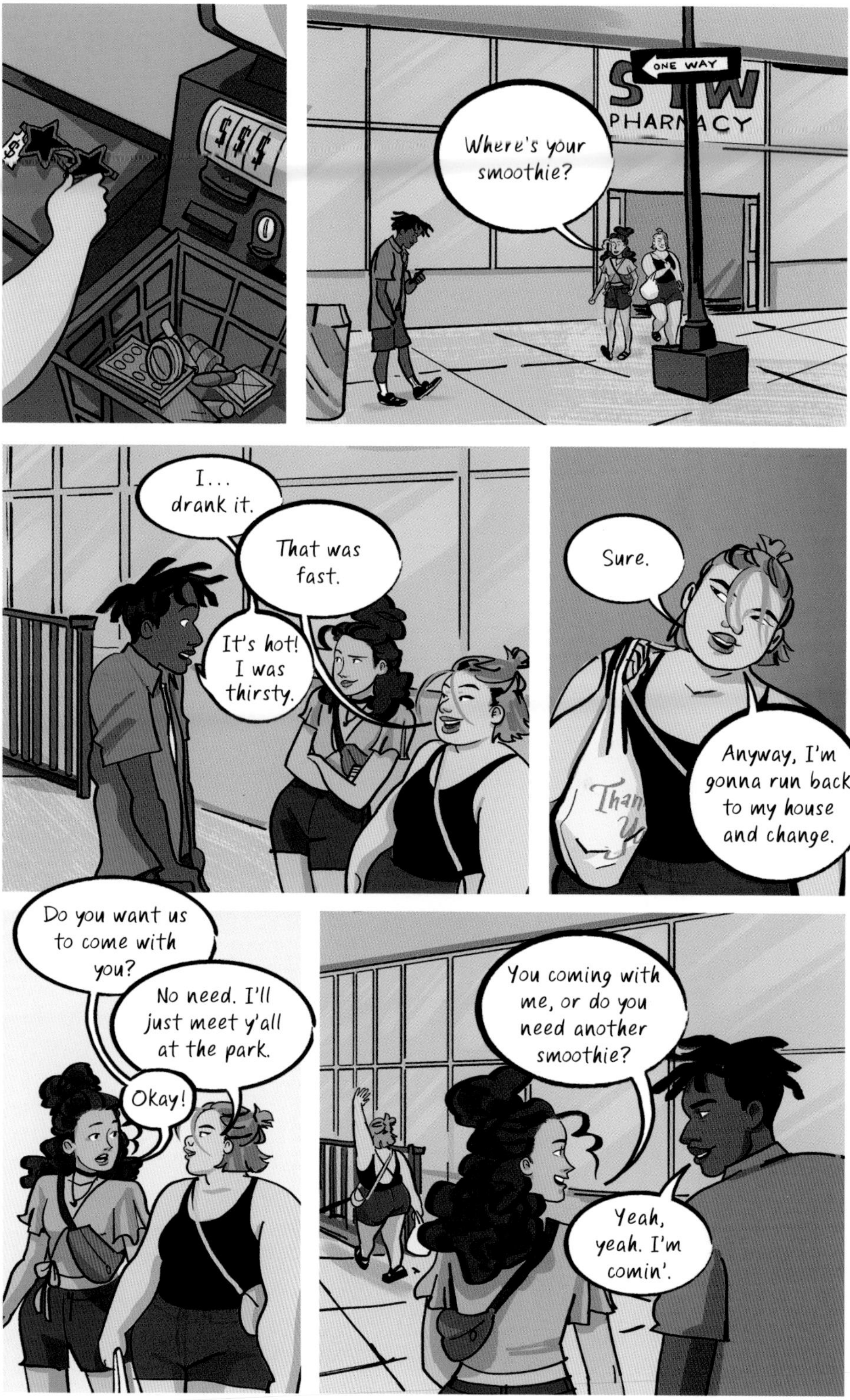
$$$
ONE WAY
S W PHARMACY
Where's your smoothie?
I... drank it.
That was fast.
It's hot! I was thirsty.
Sure.
Anyway, I'm gonna run back to my house and change.
Do you want us to come with you?
No need. I'll just meet y'all at the park.
Okay!
You coming with me, or do you need another smoothie?
Yeah, yeah. I'm comin'.

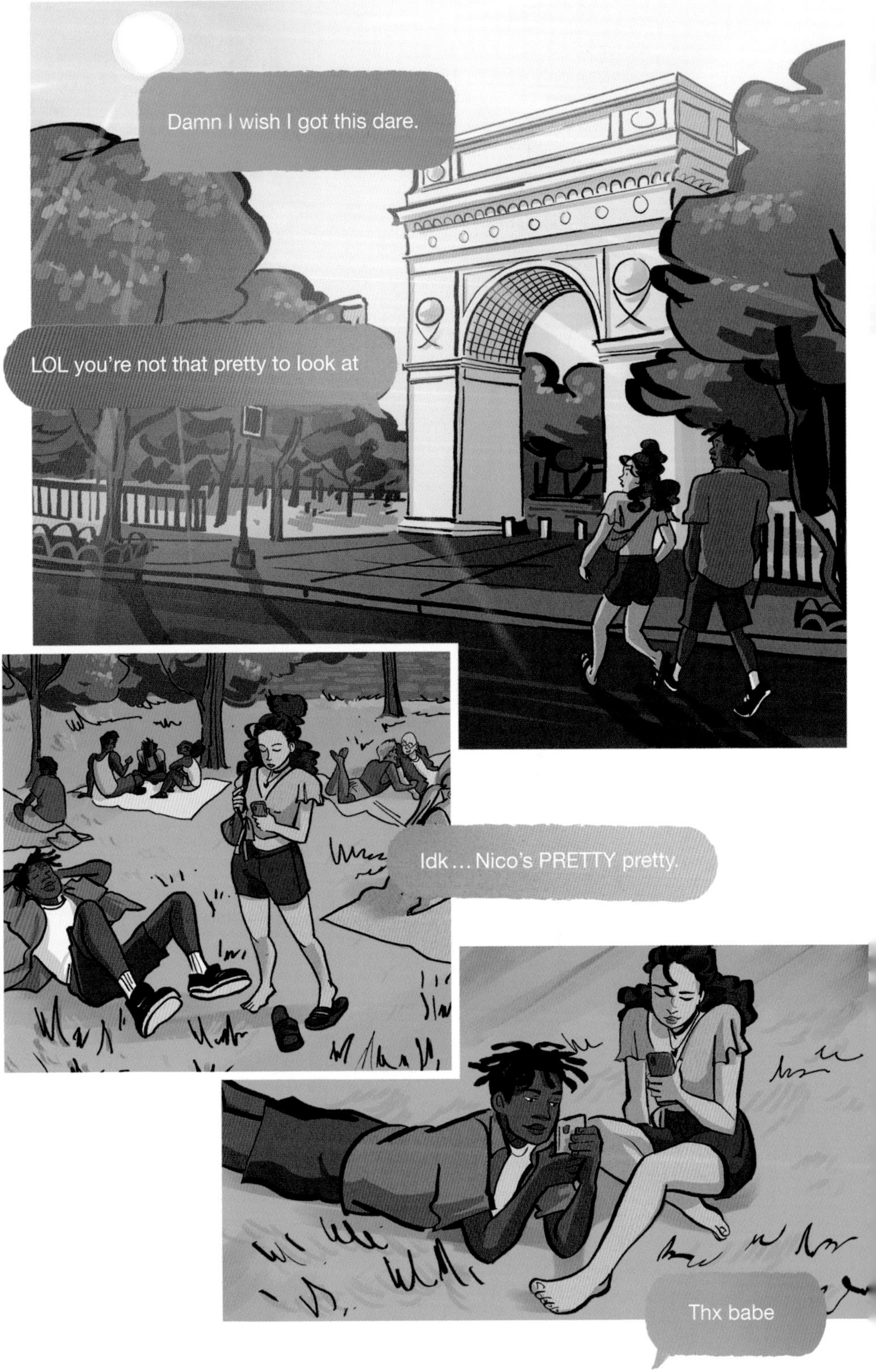
Damn I wish I got this dare.
LOL you're not that pretty to look at
Idk... Nico's PRETTY pretty.
Thx babe

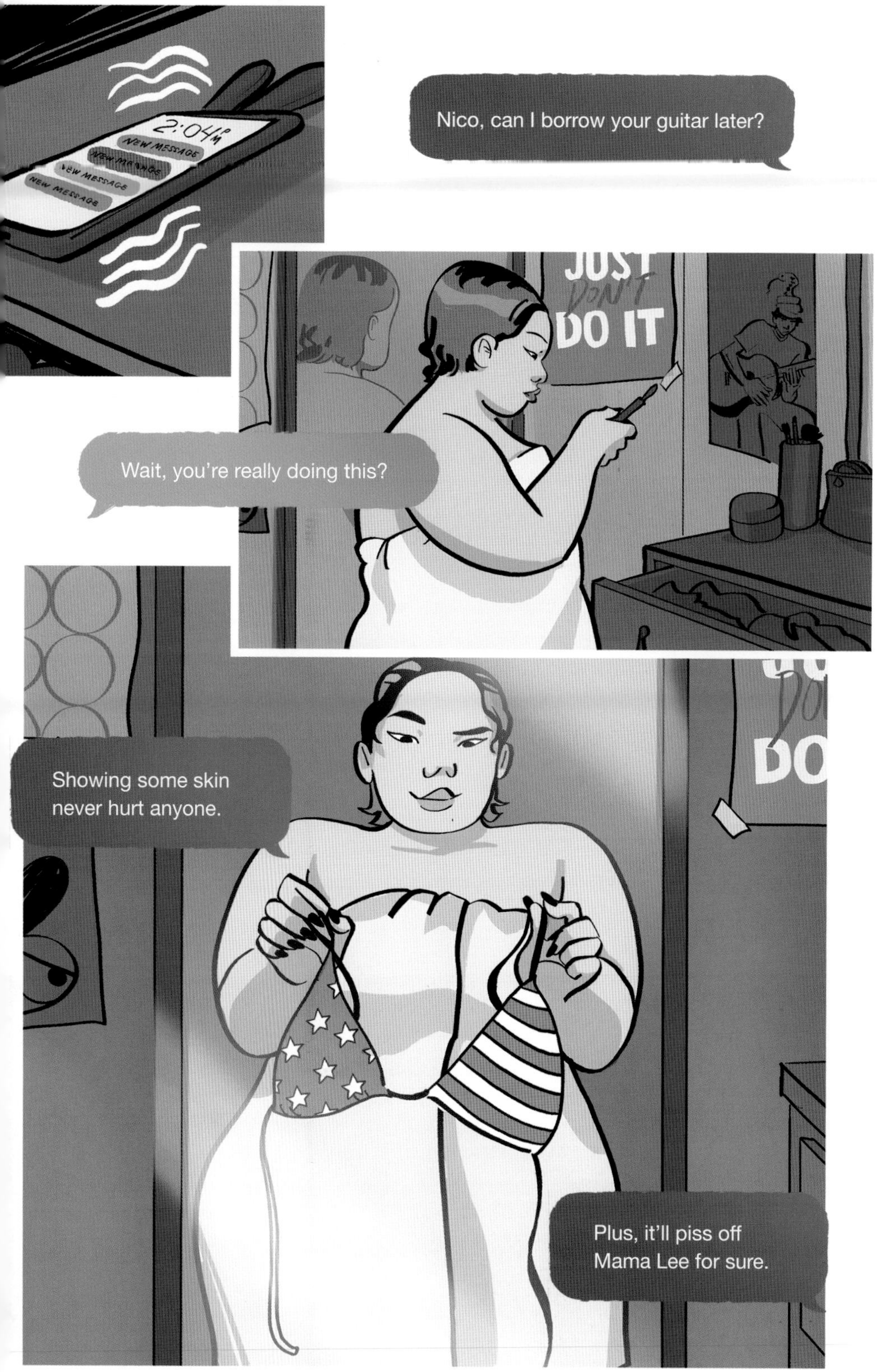
2:04 PM
NEW MESSAGE
NEW MESSAGE
NEW MESSAGE
NEW MESSAGE
Nico, can I borrow your guitar later?
JUST DON'T DO IT
Wait, you're really doing this?
Showing some skin never hurt anyone.
Plus, it'll piss off Mama Lee for sure.

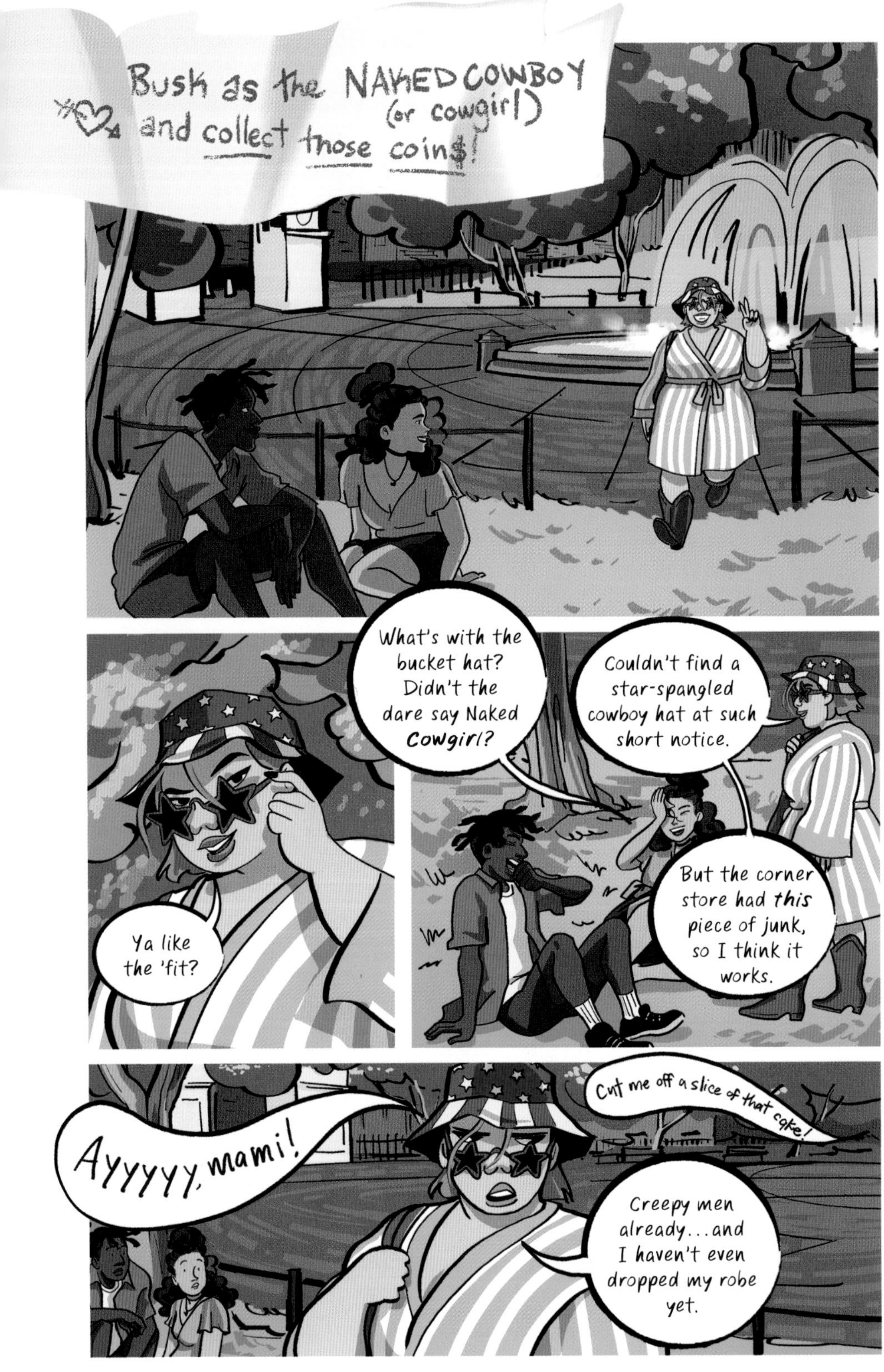
Busk as the NAKED COWBOY (or cowgirl) and collect those coin$!
What's with the bucket hat? Didn't the dare say Naked Cowgirl?
Couldn't find a star-spangled cowboy hat at such short notice.
Ya like the 'fit?
But the corner store had this piece of junk, so I think it works.
Ayyyyy, mami!
Cut me off a slice of that cake!
Creepy men already... and I haven't even dropped my robe yet.

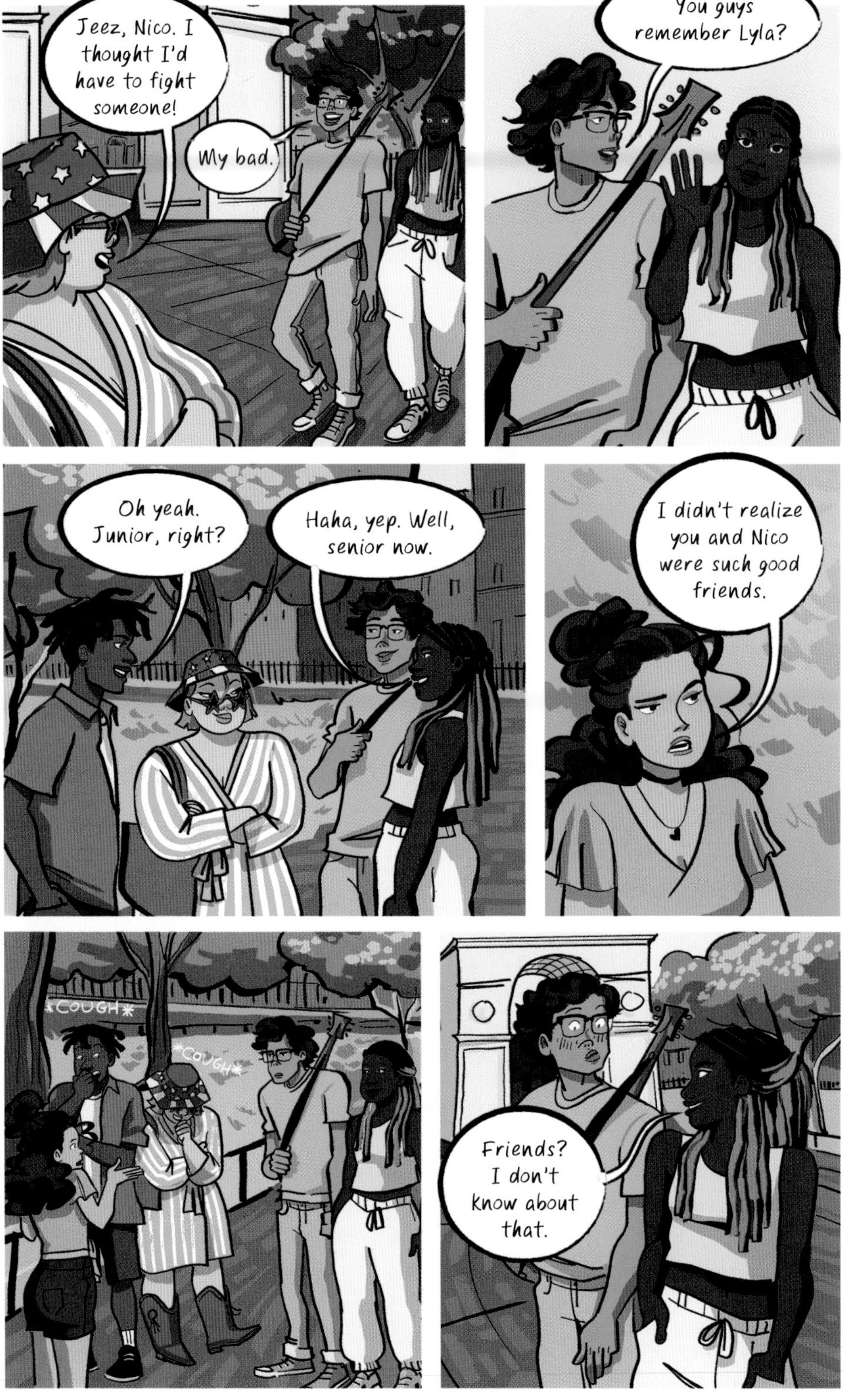
Jeez, Nico. I thought I'd have to fight someone!
My bad.
You guys remember Lyla?
Oh yeah. Junior, right?
Haha, yep. Well, senior now.
I didn't realize you and Nico were such good friends.
COUGH
COUGH
Friends? I don't know about that.

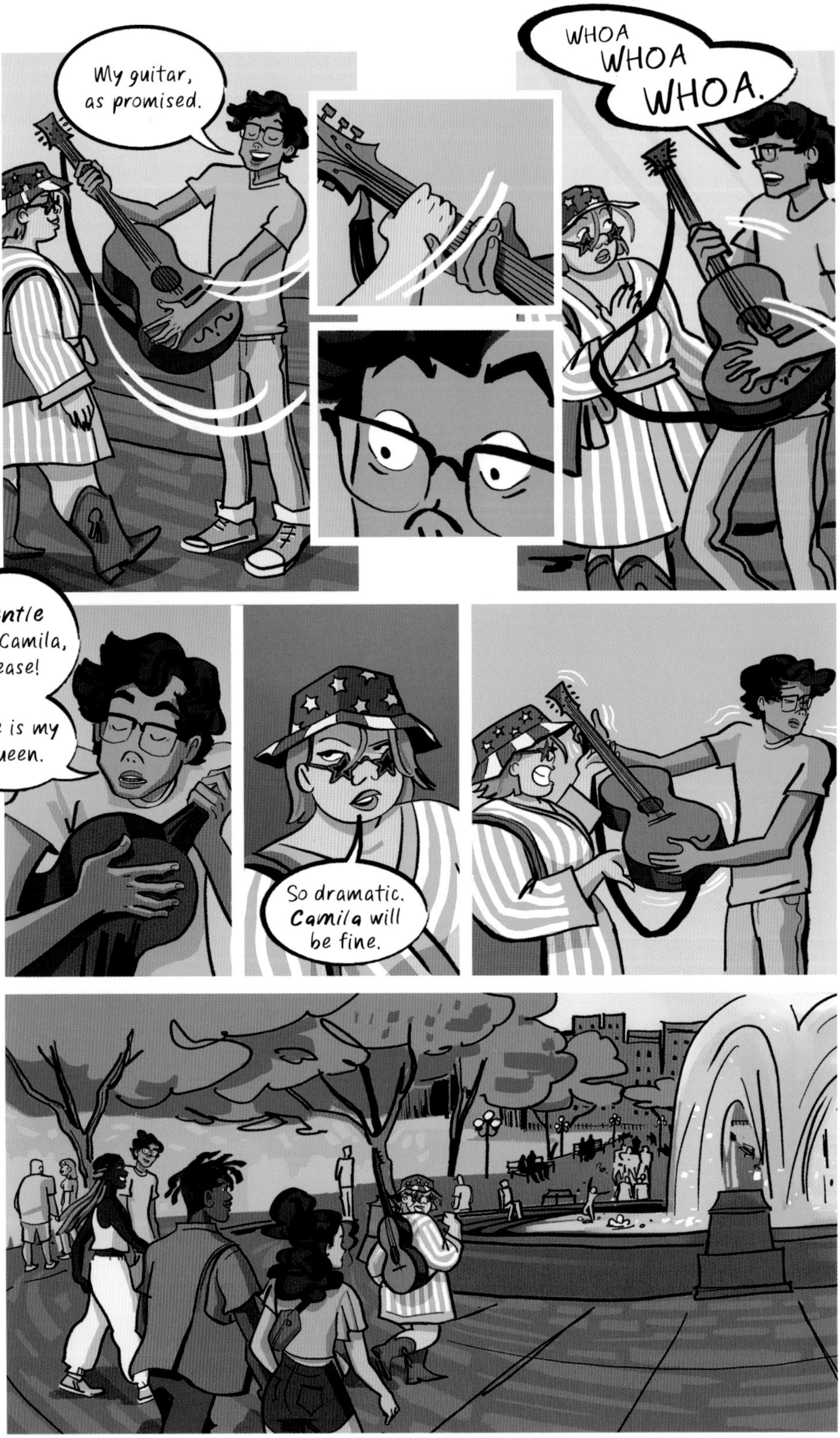
My guitar, as promised.
WHOA WHOA WHOA.
Gentle with Camila, please!
She is my queen.
So dramatic. Camila will be fine.

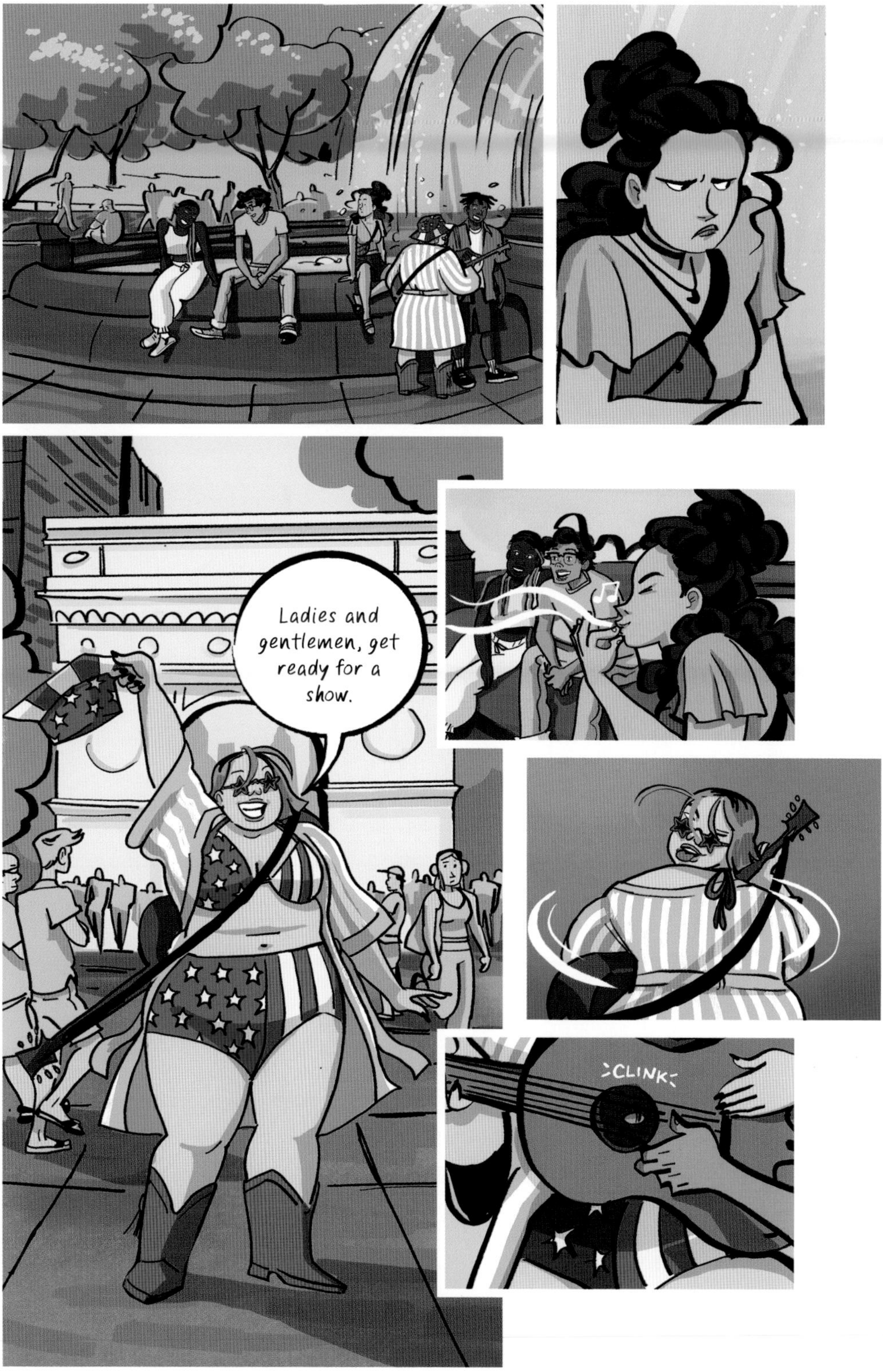

Ladies and gentlemen, get ready for a show.
CLINK

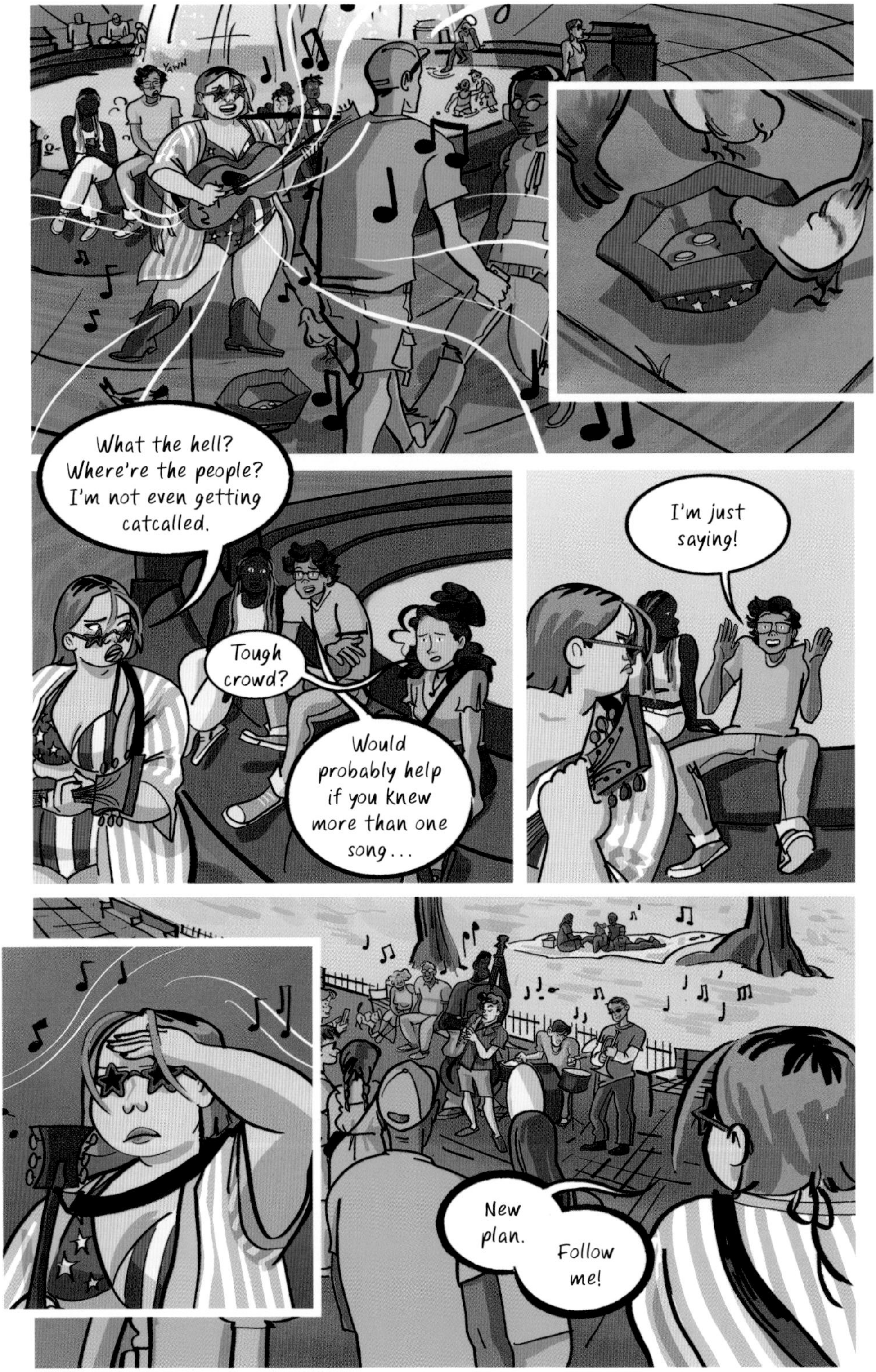
YAWN
What the hell? Where're the people? I'm not even getting catcalled.
Tough crowd?
Would probably help if you knew more than one song...
I'm just saying!
New plan.
Follow me!

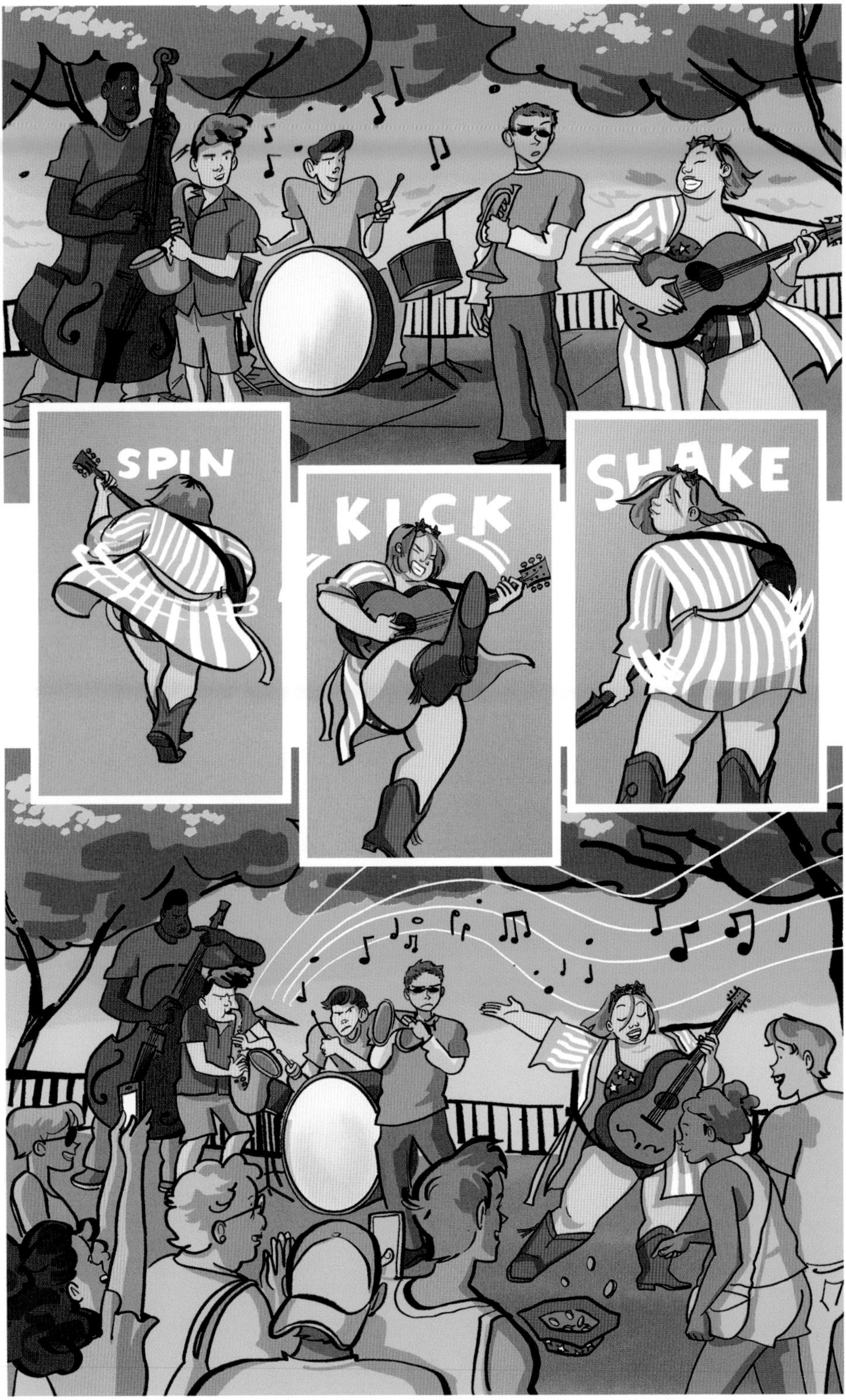
SPIN
KICK
SHAKE

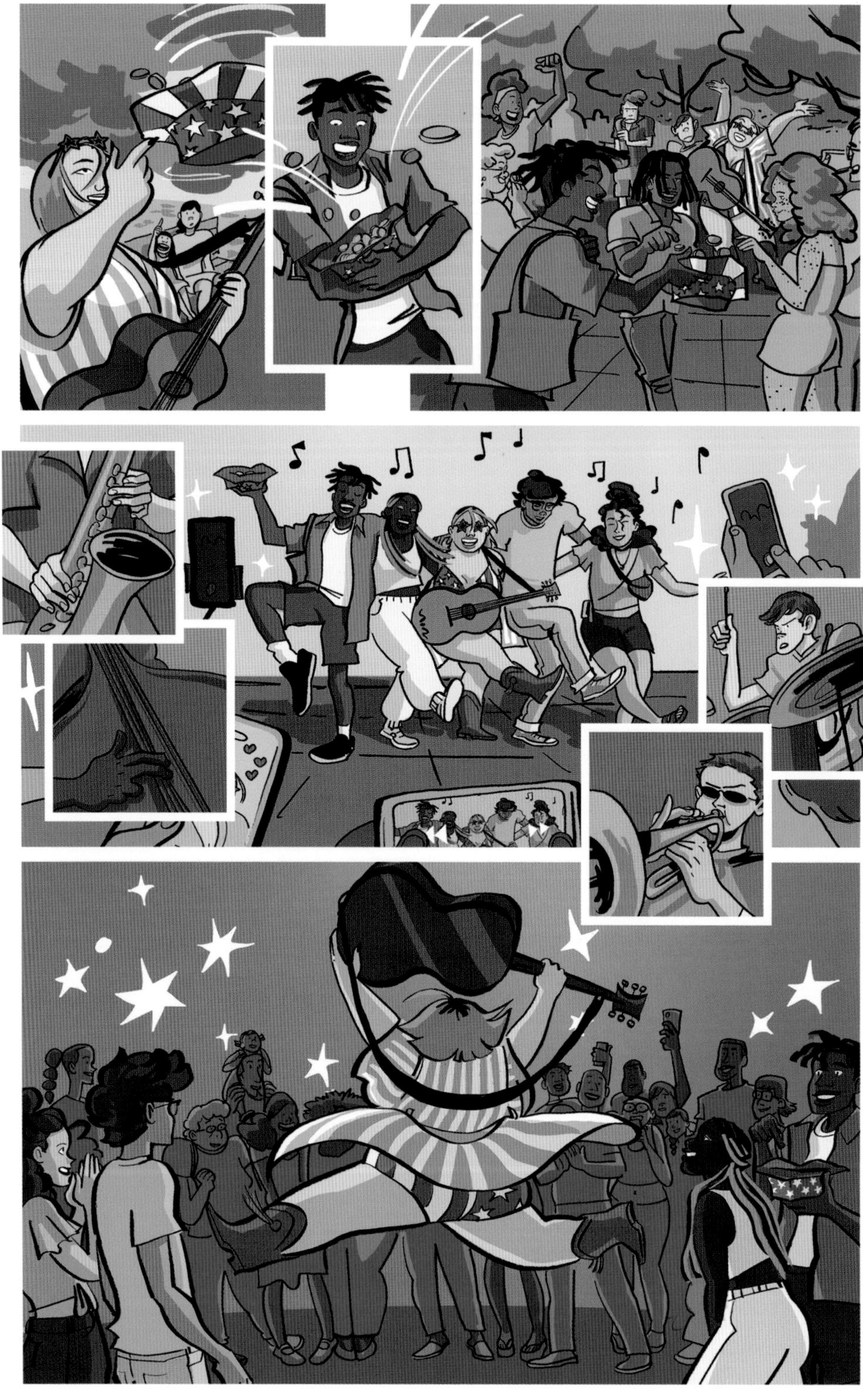

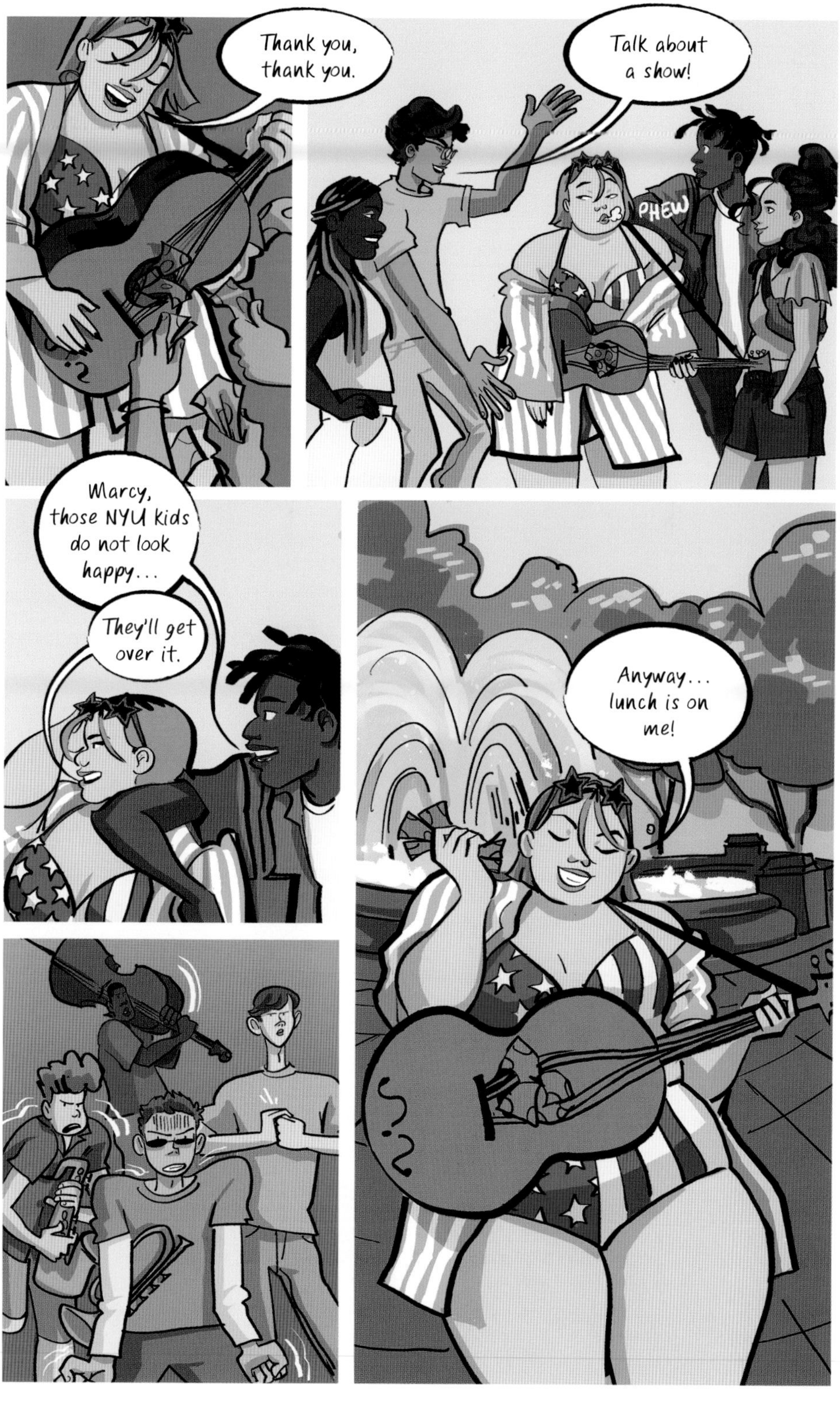
Thank you, thank you.
Talk about a show!
PHEW
Marcy, those NYU kids do not look happy...
They'll get over it.
Anyway... lunch is on me!

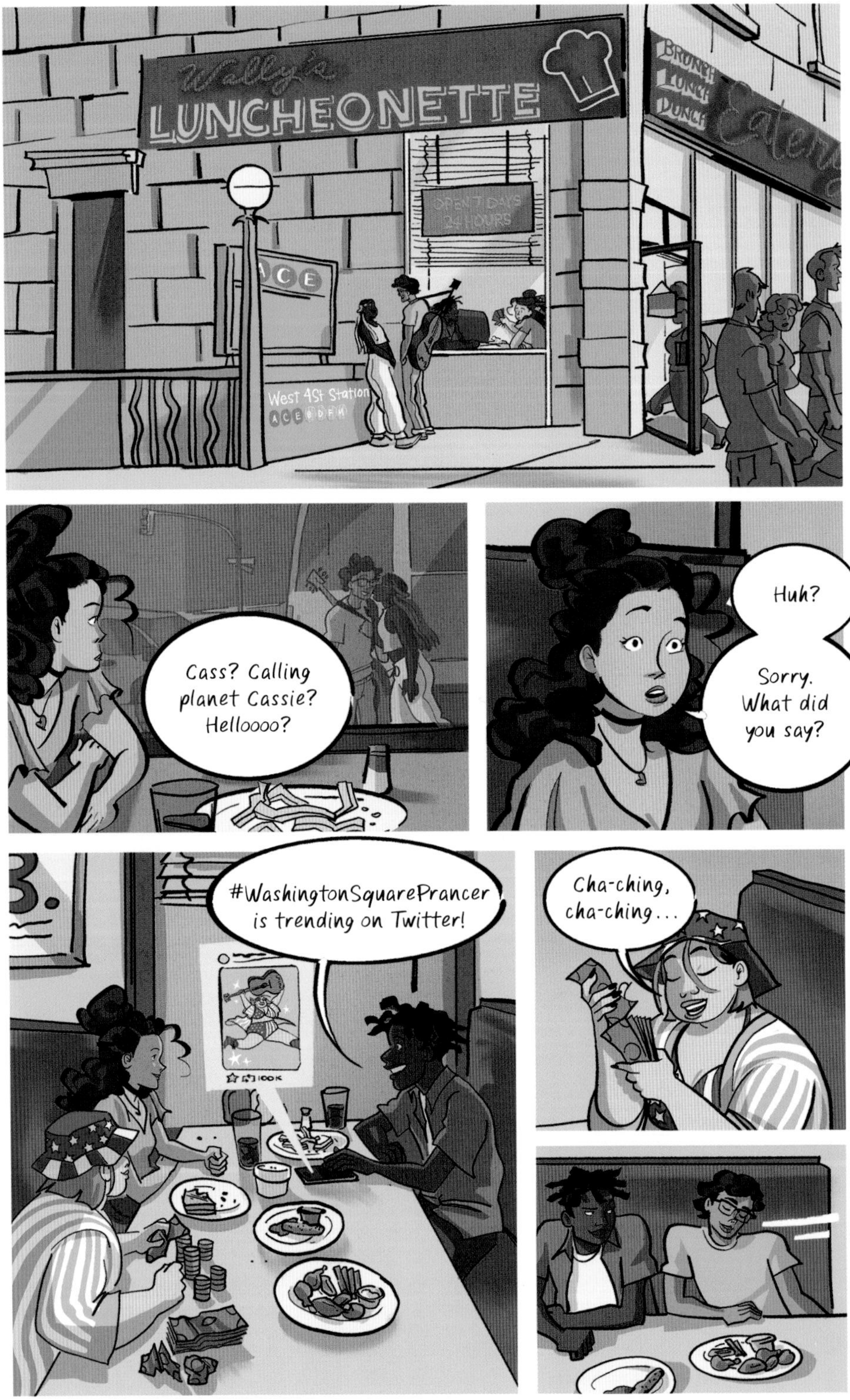
Wally's
LUNCHEONETTE
OPEN 7 DAYS 24 HOURS
BRUNCH LUNCH DUNCH
Eatery
West 4St Station
Cass? Calling planet Cassie? Helloooo?
Huh?
Sorry. What did you say?
#WashingtonSquarePrancer is trending on Twitter!
Cha-ching, cha-ching...

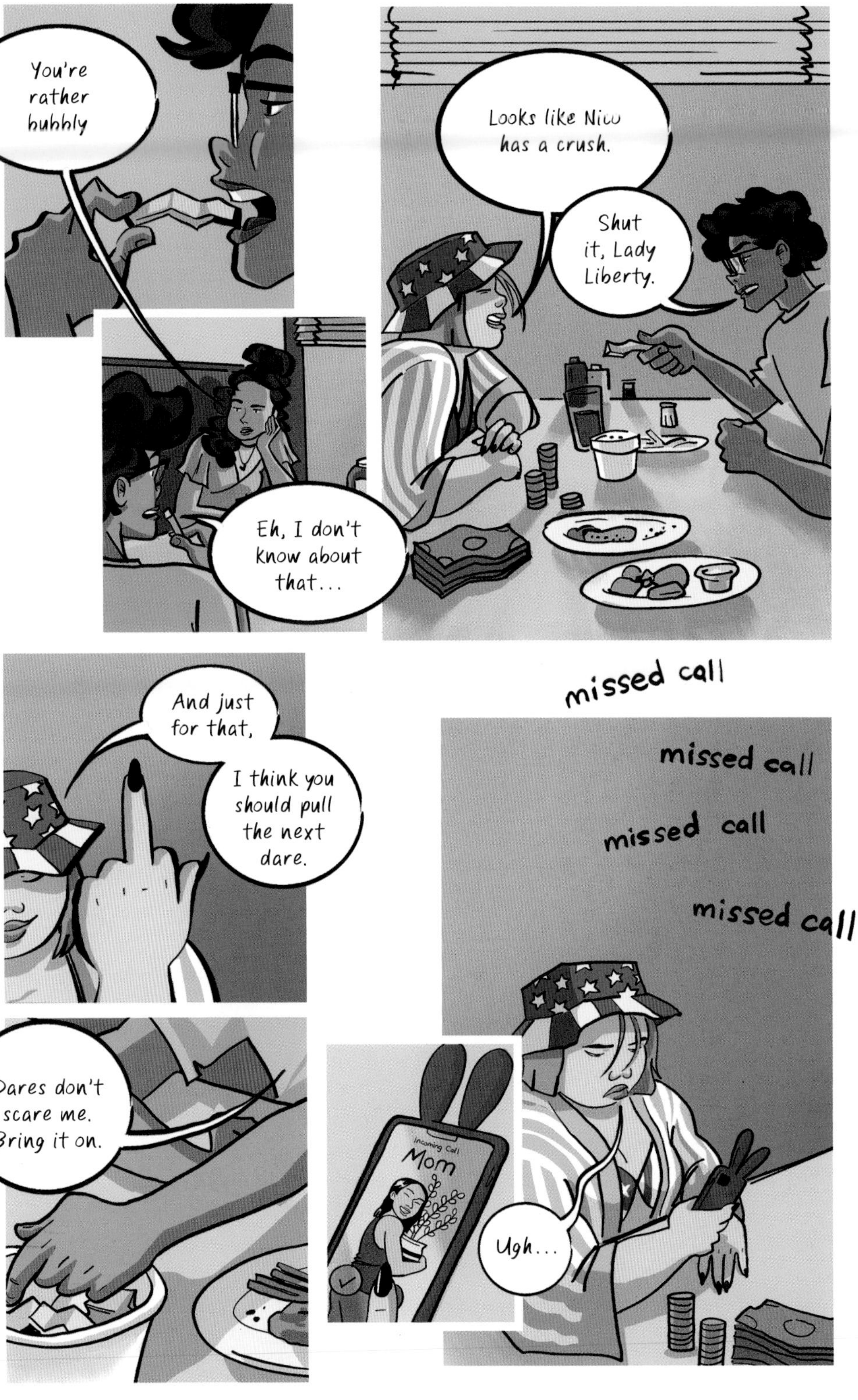
You're rather bubbly
Eh, I don't know about that...
Looks like Nico has a crush.
Shut it, Lady Liberty.
And just for that,
I think you should pull the next dare.
Dares don't scare me. Bring it on.
missed call
missed call
missed call
missed call
Incoming Call
Mom
Ugh...

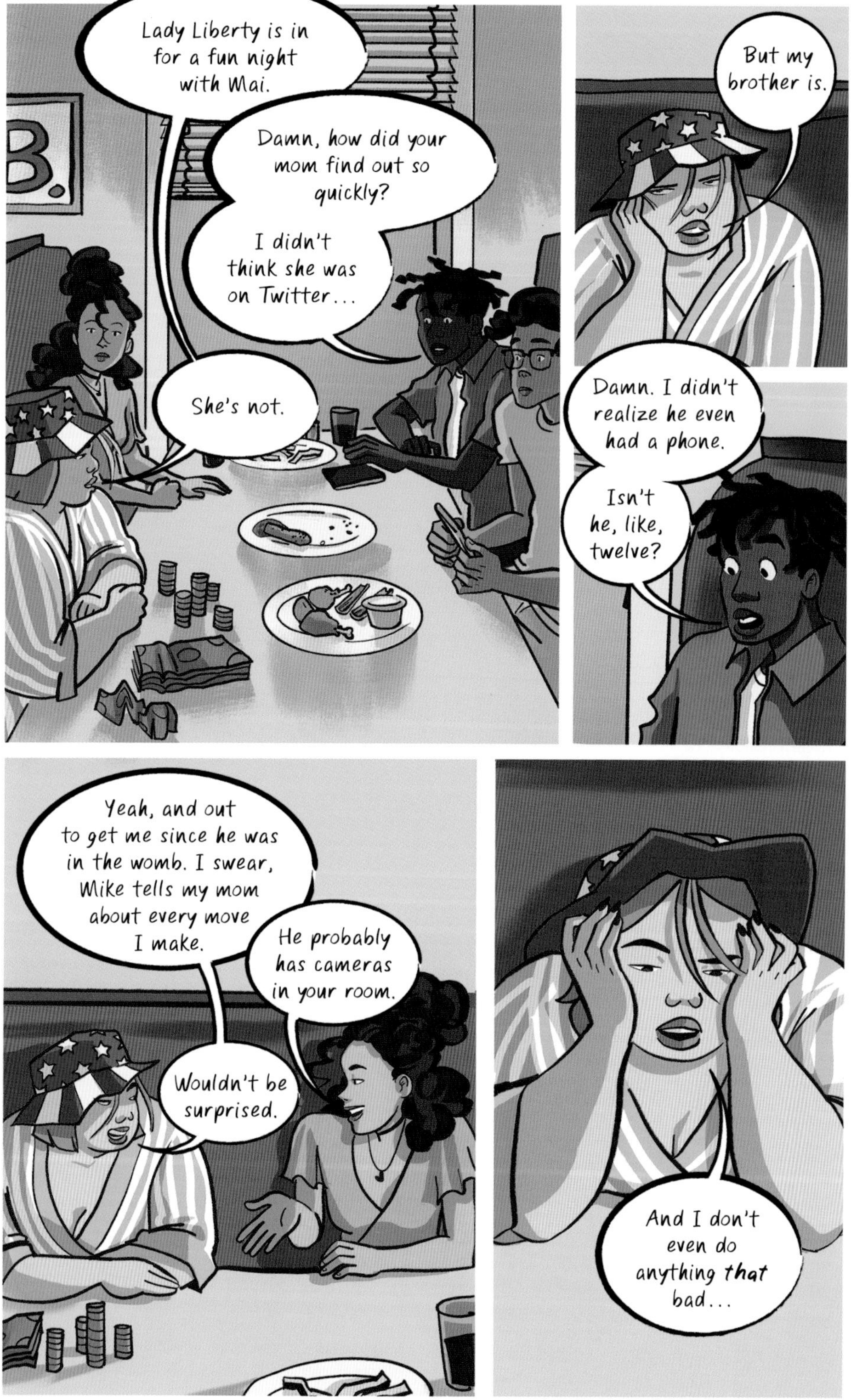
Lady Liberty is in for a fun night with Mai.
Damn, how did your mom find out so quickly?
I didn't think she was on Twitter...
She's not.
But my brother is.
Damn. I didn't realize he even had a phone.
Isn't he, like, twelve?
Yeah, and out to get me since he was in the womb. I swear, Mike tells my mom about every move I make.
He probably has cameras in your room.
Wouldn't be surprised.
And I don't even do anything *that* bad...

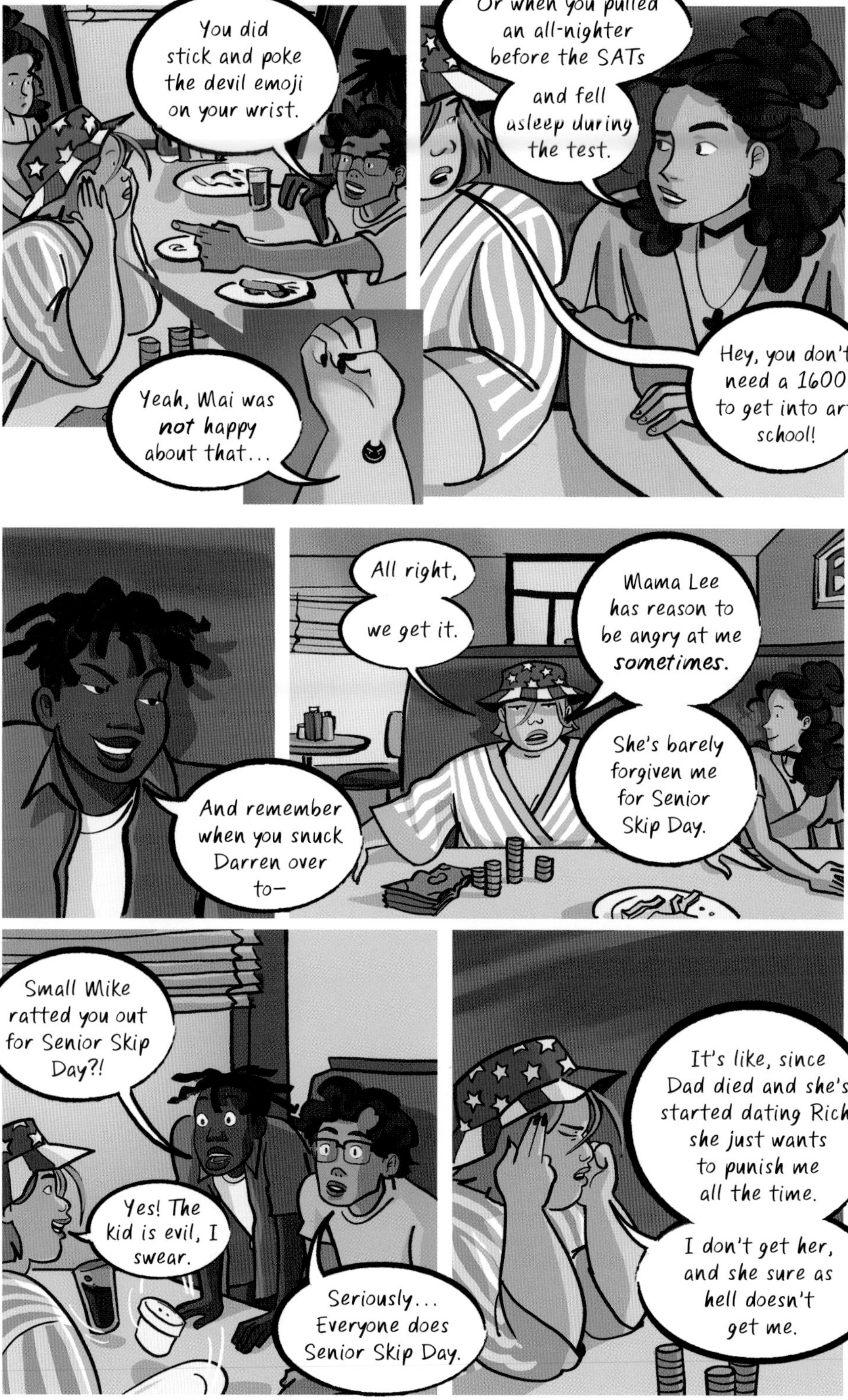
You did stick and poke the devil emoji on your wrist.
Yeah, Mai was not happy about that...
Or when you pulled an all-nighter before the SATs
and fell asleep during the test.
Hey, you don't need a 1600 to get into art school!
And remember when you snuck Darren over to–
All right,
we get it.
Mama Lee has reason to be angry at me sometimes.
She's barely forgiven me for Senior Skip Day.
Small Mike ratted you out for Senior Skip Day?!
Yes! The kid is evil, I swear.
Seriously... Everyone does Senior Skip Day.
It's like, since Dad died and she's started dating Rich, she just wants to punish me all the time.
I don't get her, and she sure as hell doesn't get me.

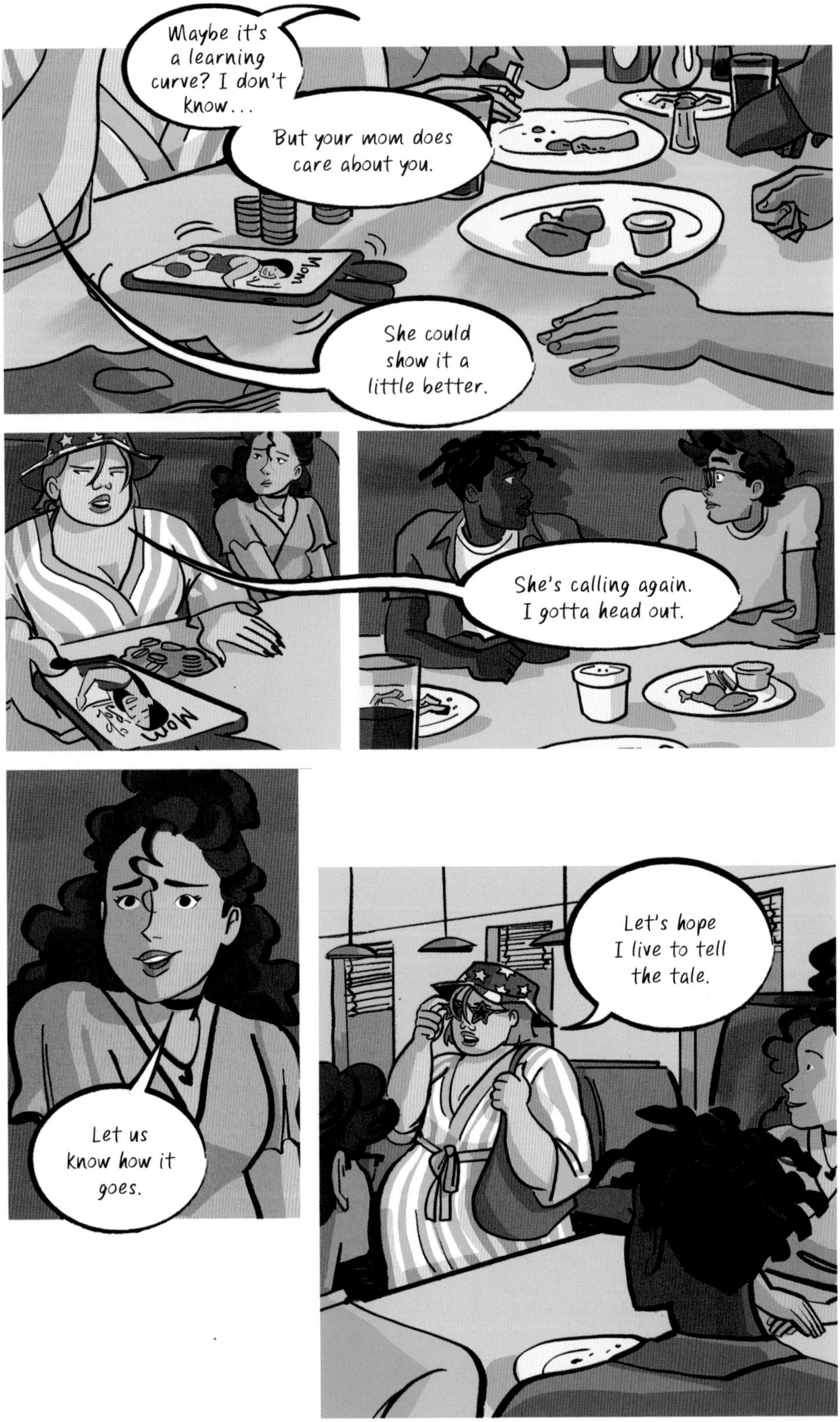
Maybe it's a learning curve? I don't know...
But your mom does care about you.
Mom
She could show it a little better.
Mom
She's calling again. I gotta head out.
Let us know how it goes.
Let's hope I live to tell the tale.

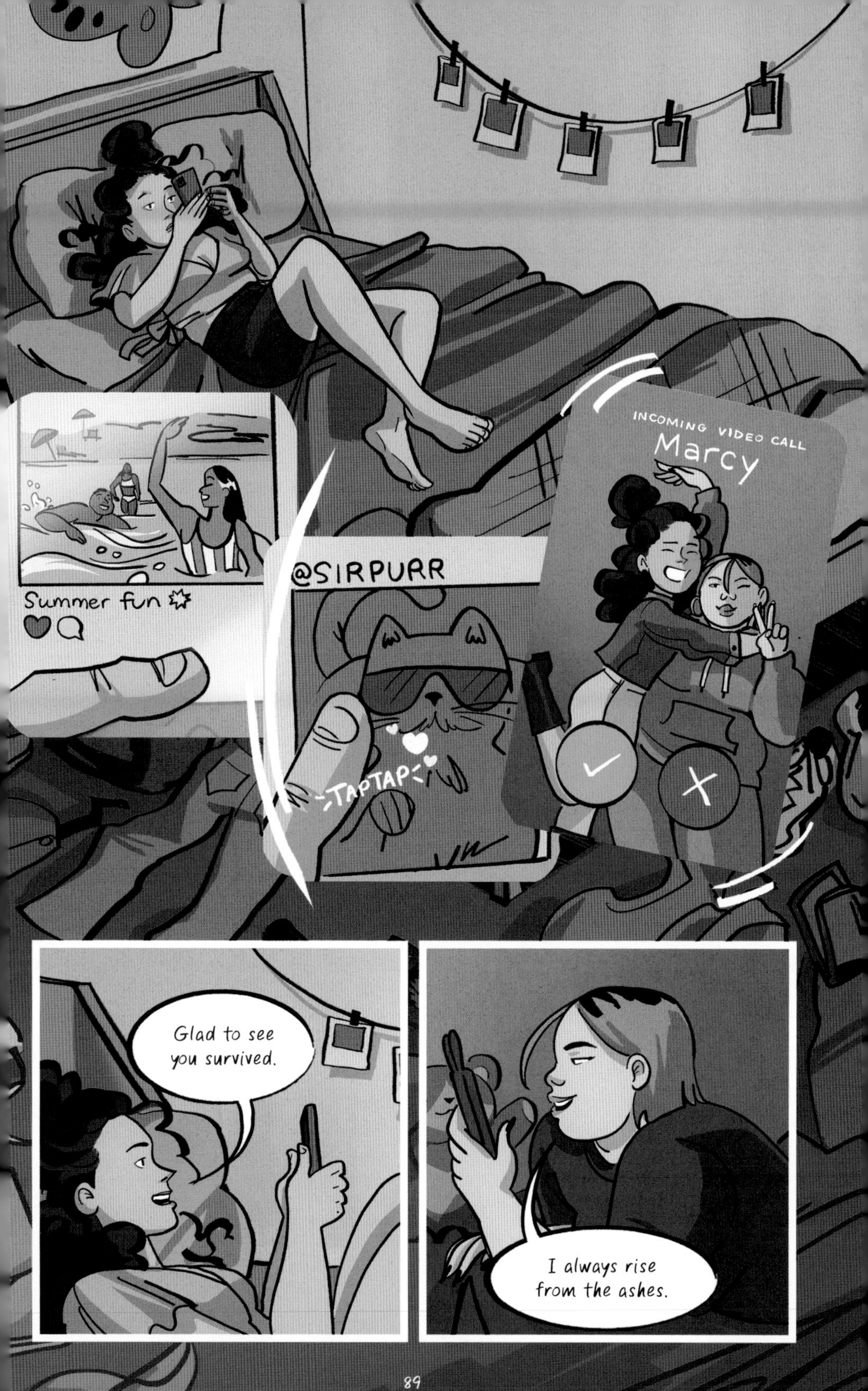
Summer fun
@SIRPURR
TAPTAP
INCOMING VIDEO CALL
Marcy
Glad to see you survived.
I always rise from the ashes.

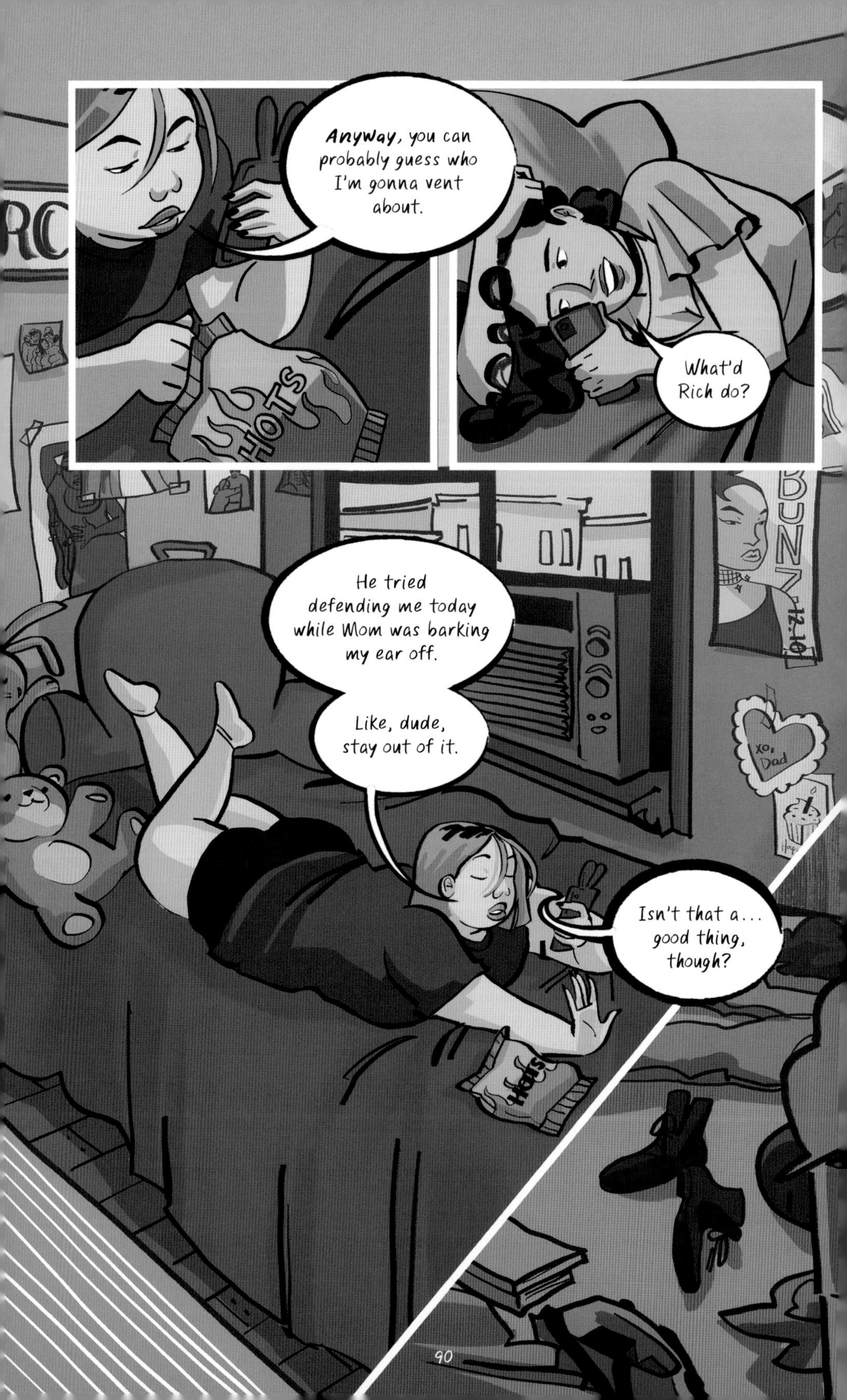
Anyway, you can probably guess who I'm gonna vent about.
What'd Rich do?
He tried defending me today while Mom was barking my ear off.
Like, dude, stay out of it.
Isn't that a... good thing, though?

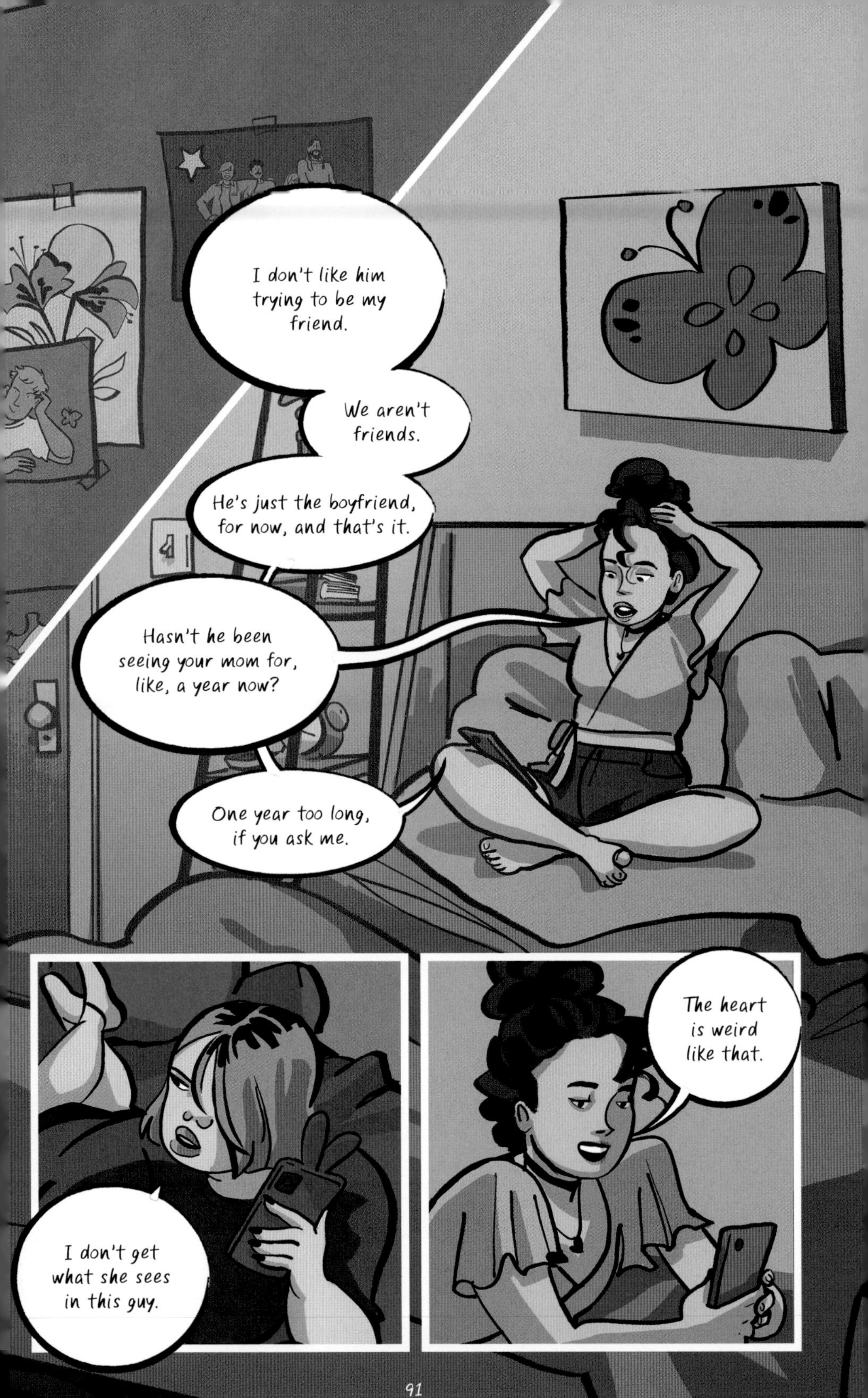
I don't like him trying to be my friend.
We aren't friends.
He's just the boyfriend, for now, and that's it.
Hasn't he been seeing your mom for, like, a year now?
One year too long, if you ask me.
I don't get what she sees in this guy.
The heart is weird like that.

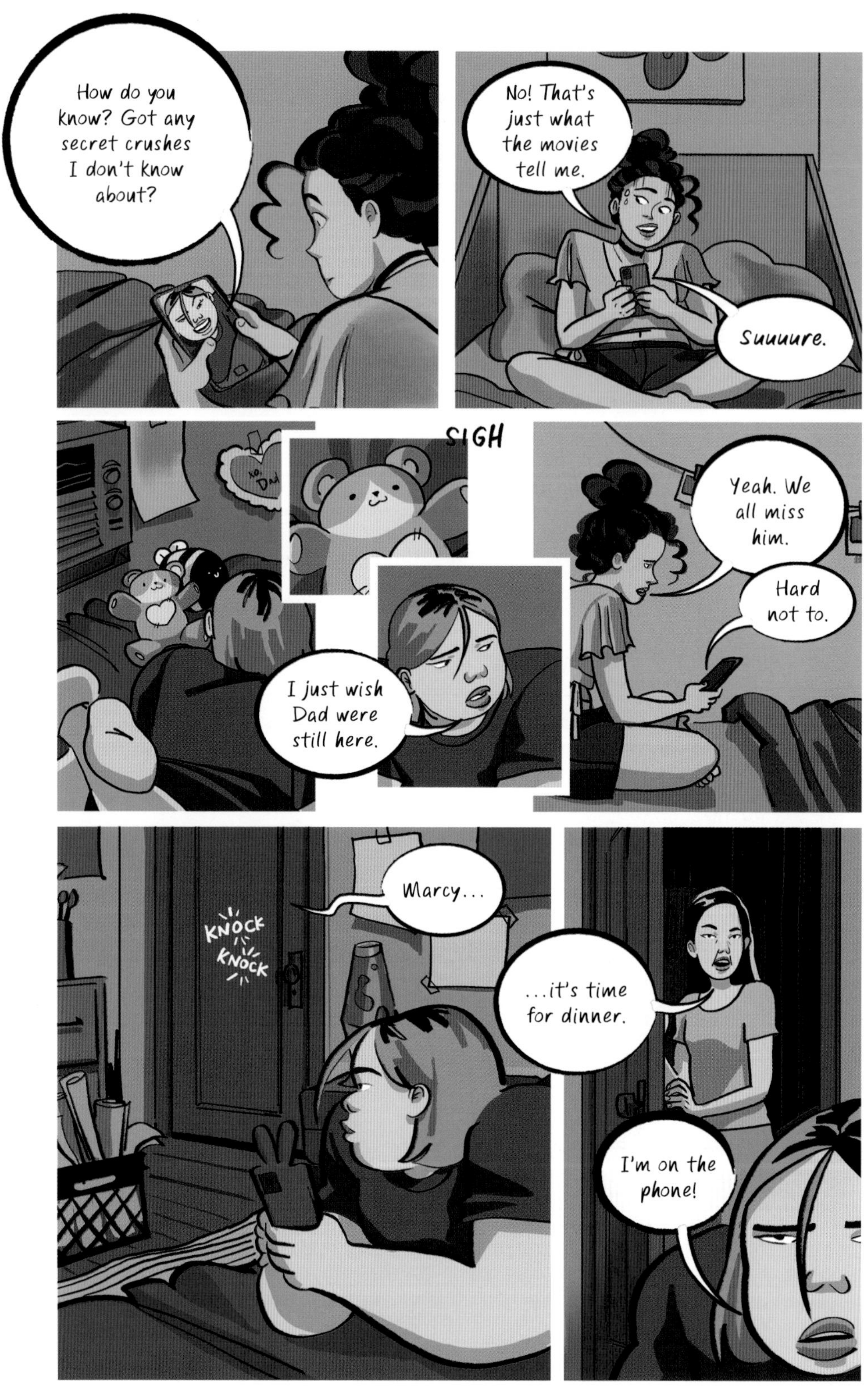
How do you know? Got any secret crushes I don't know about?
No! That's just what the movies tell me.
Suuuure.
SIGH
xo, Dad
I just wish Dad were still here.
Yeah. We all miss him.
Hard not to.
Marcy...
KNOCK KNOCK
...it's time for dinner.
I'm on the phone!

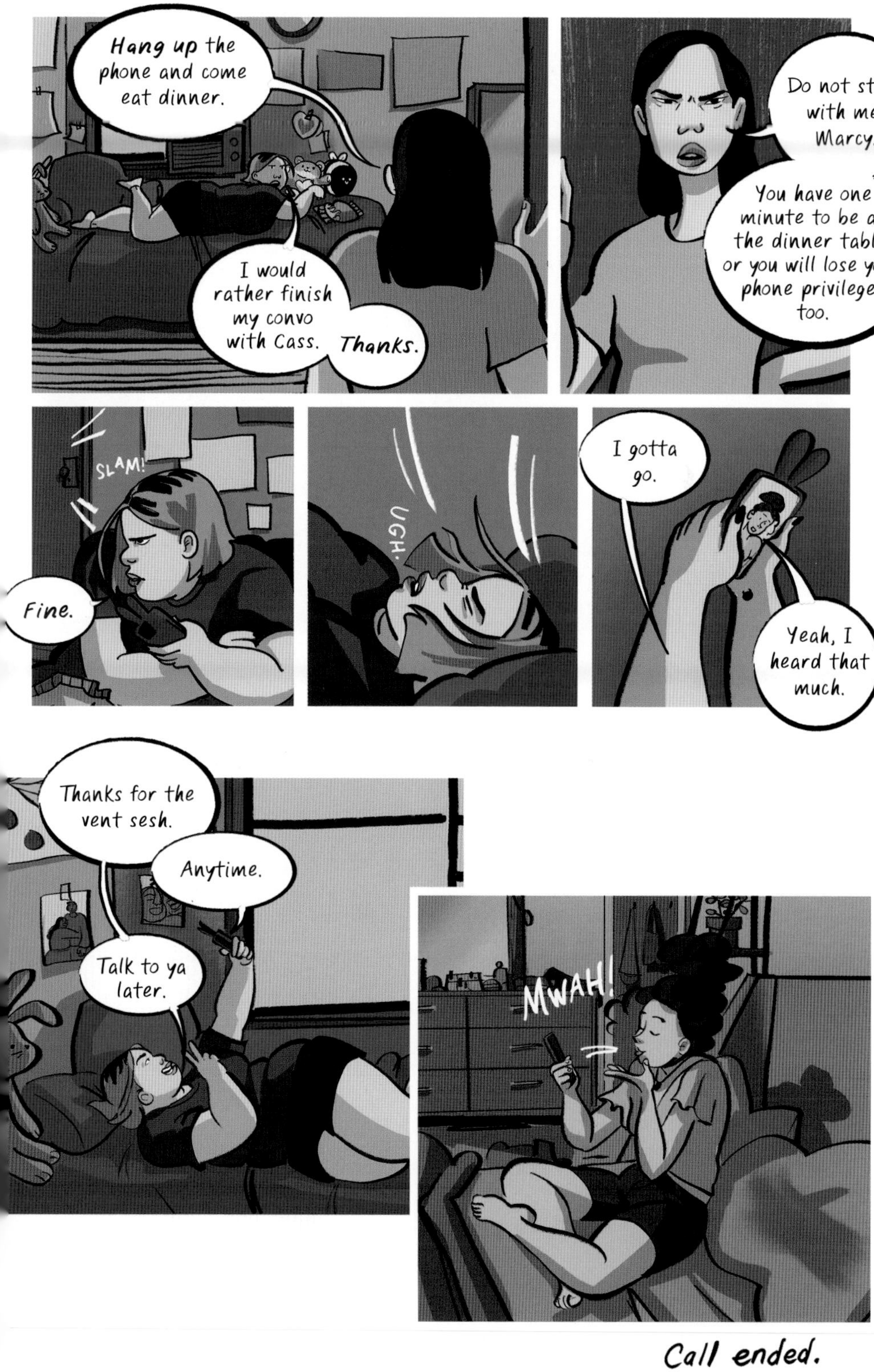
Hang up the phone and come eat dinner.
I would rather finish my convo with Cass.
Thanks.
Do not start with me, Marcy.
You have one minute to be at the dinner table, or you will lose your phone privileges too.
SLAM!
Fine.
UGH.
I gotta go.
Yeah, I heard that much.
Thanks for the vent sesh.
Anytime.
Talk to ya later.
MWAH!
Call ended.

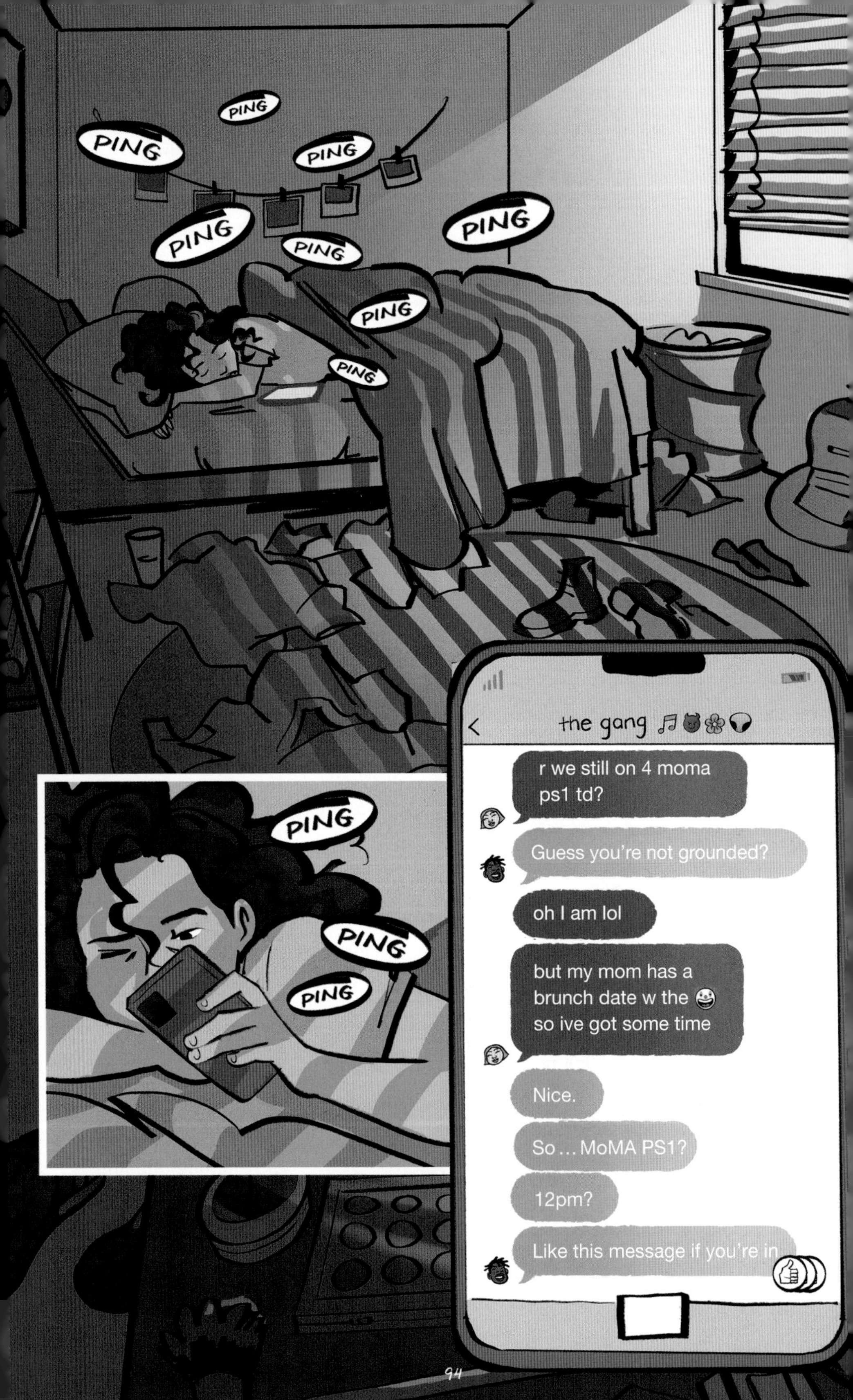
PING
PING
PING
PING
PING
PING
PING
PING
PING
PING
PING
the gang
r we still on 4 moma ps1 td?
Guess you're not grounded?
oh I am lol
but my mom has a brunch date w the 😀 so ive got some time
Nice.
So... MoMA PS1?
12pm?
Like this message if you're in

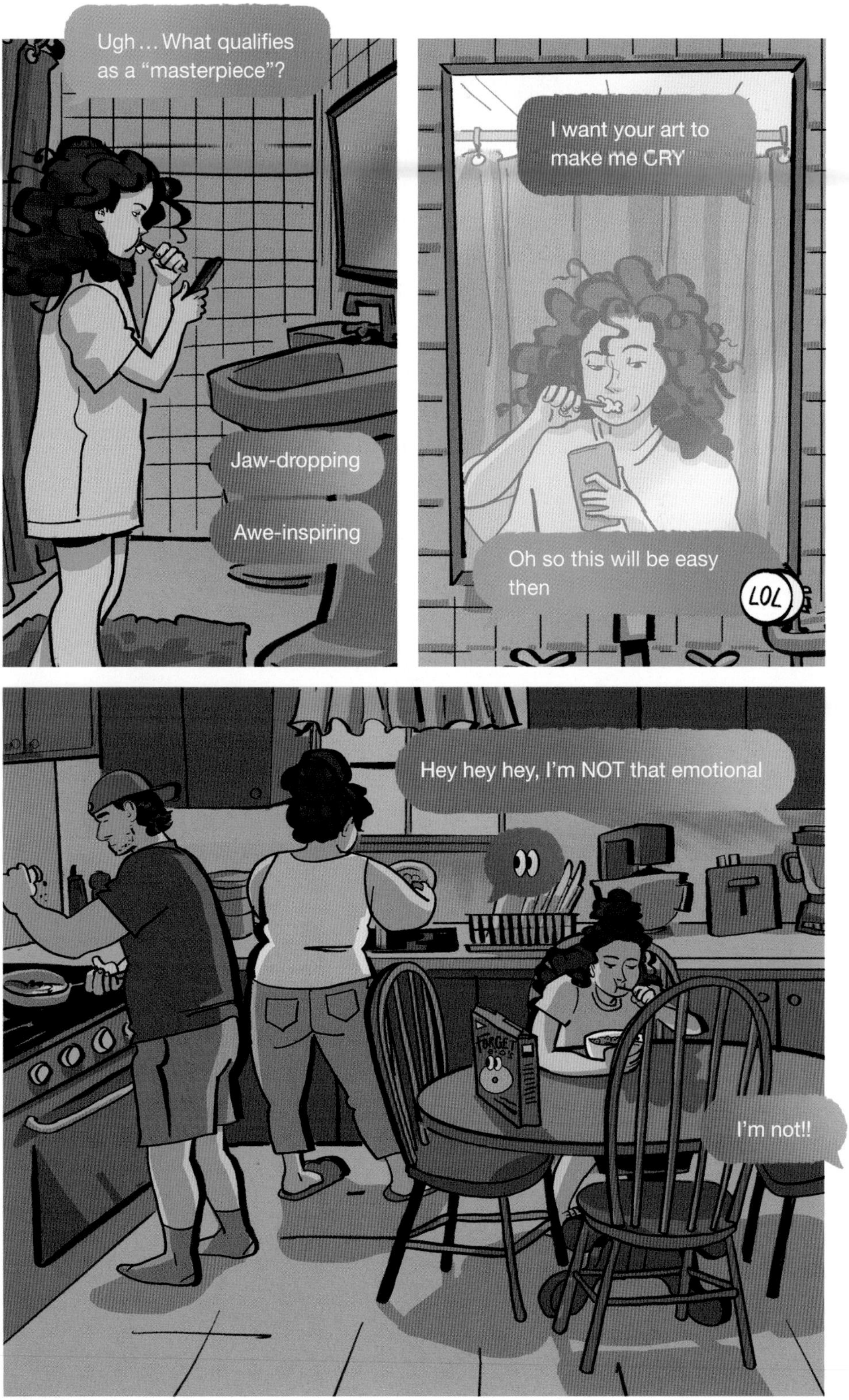
Ugh... What qualifies as a "masterpiece"?
I want your art to make me CRY
Jaw-dropping
Awe-inspiring
Oh so this will be easy then
LOL
Hey hey hey, I'm NOT that emotional
FORGET
I'm not!!

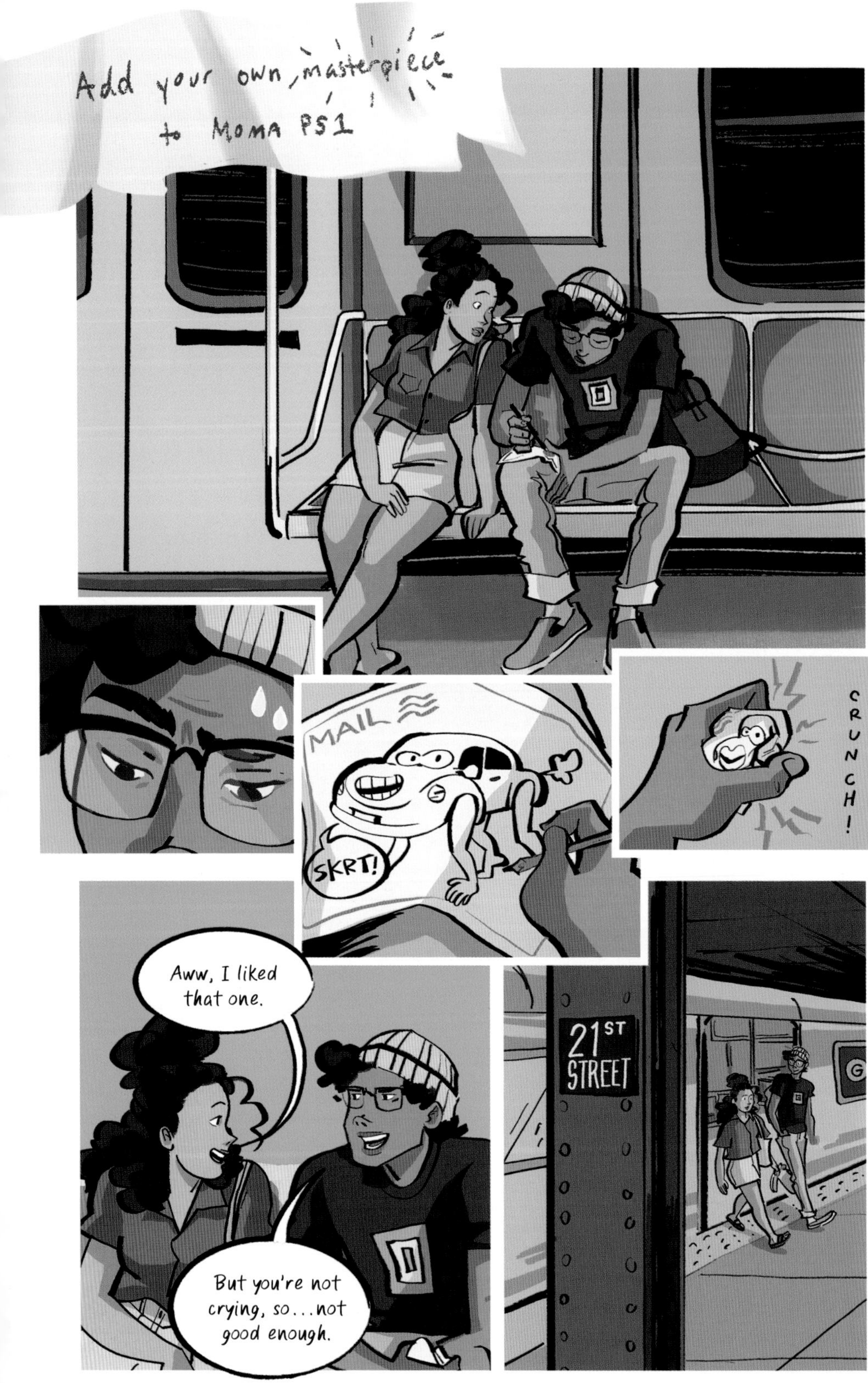
Add your own masterpiece to MoMA PS1
MAIL
SKRT!
CRUNCH!
Aww, I liked that one.
But you're not crying, so...not good enough.
21ST STREET
G

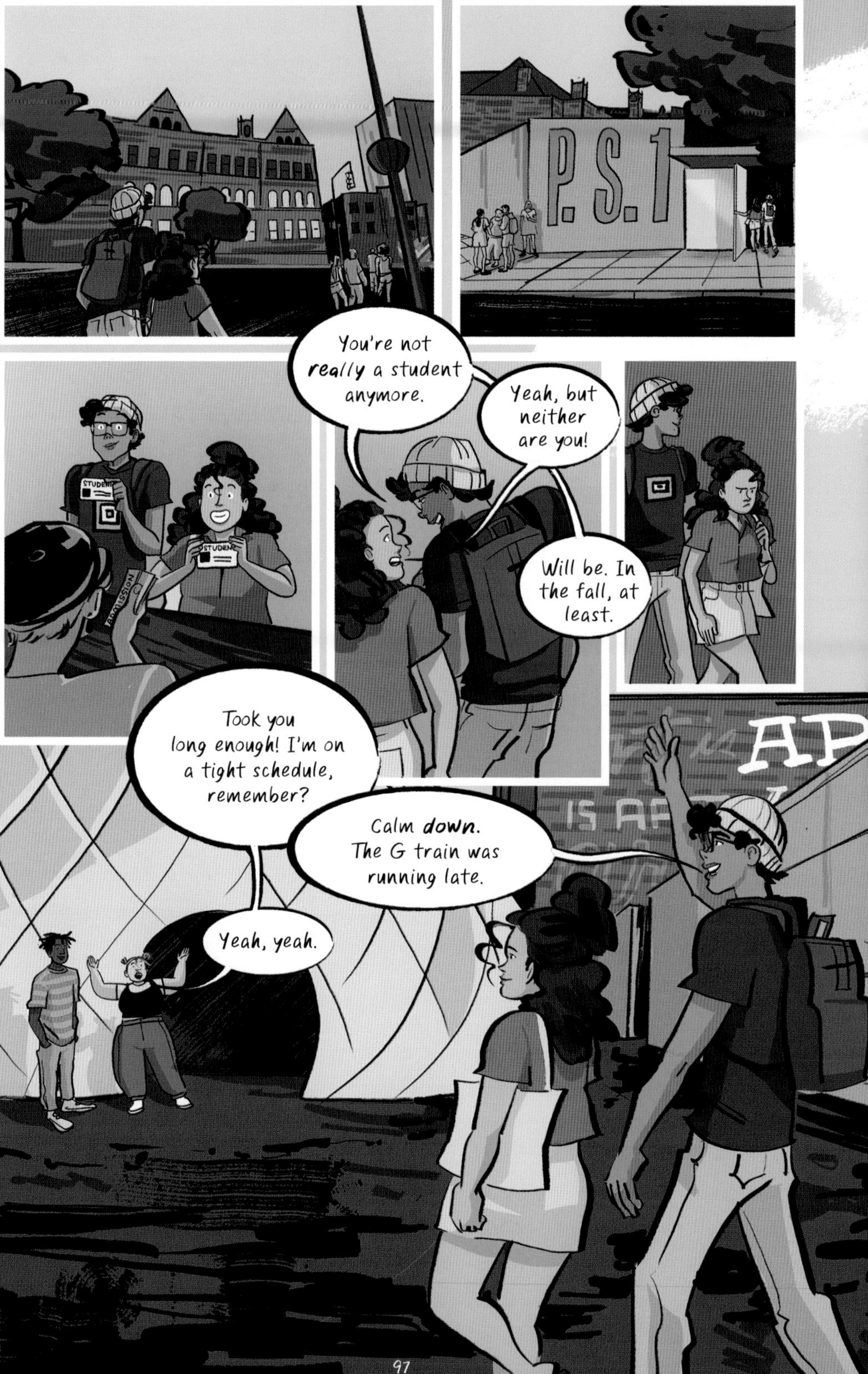
P.S. 1
STUDENT
STUDENT
ADMISSION
You're not *really* a student anymore.
Yeah, but neither are you!
Will be. In the fall, at least.
Took you long enough! I'm on a tight schedule, remember?
Calm **down.** The G train was running late.
Yeah, yeah.

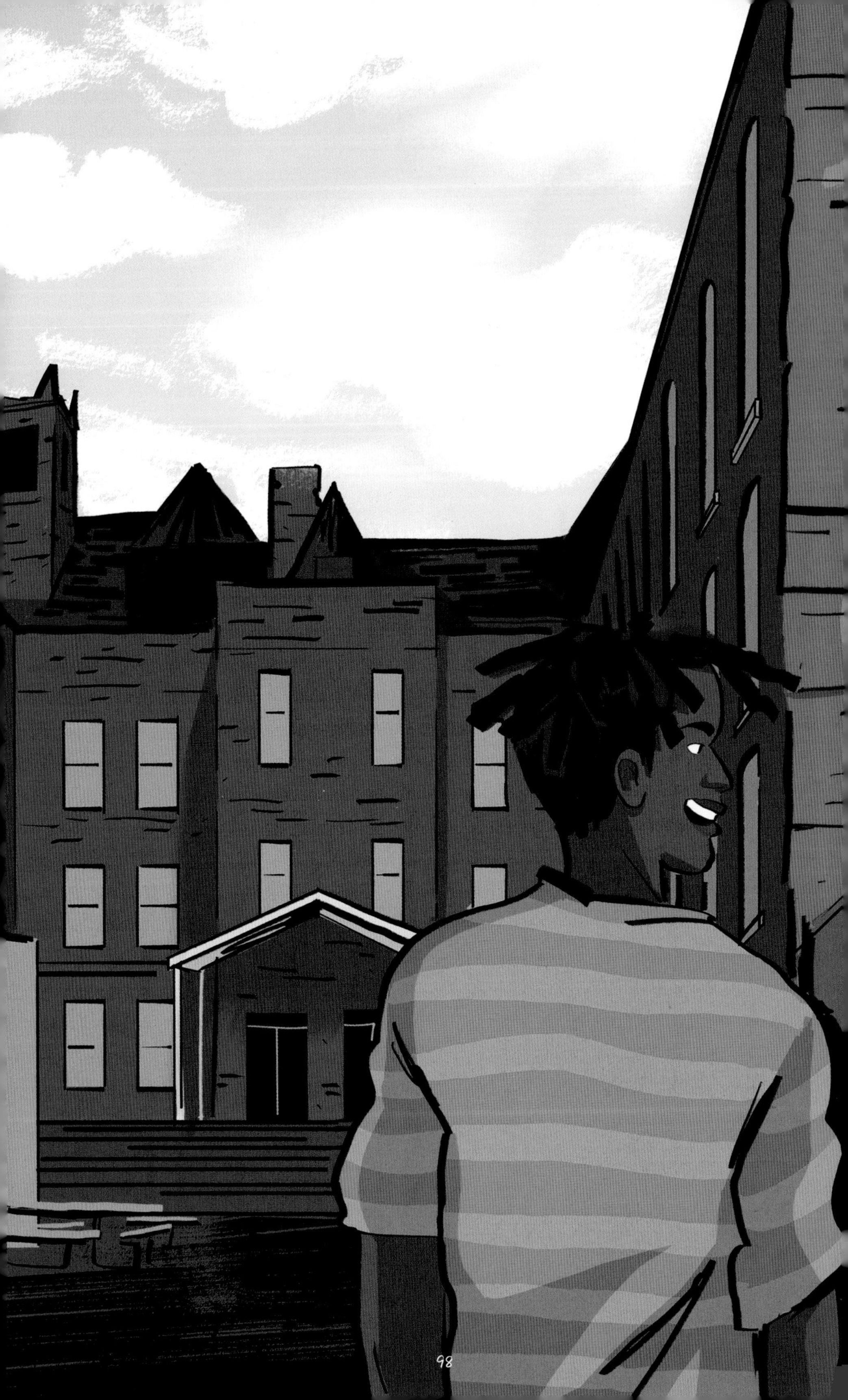

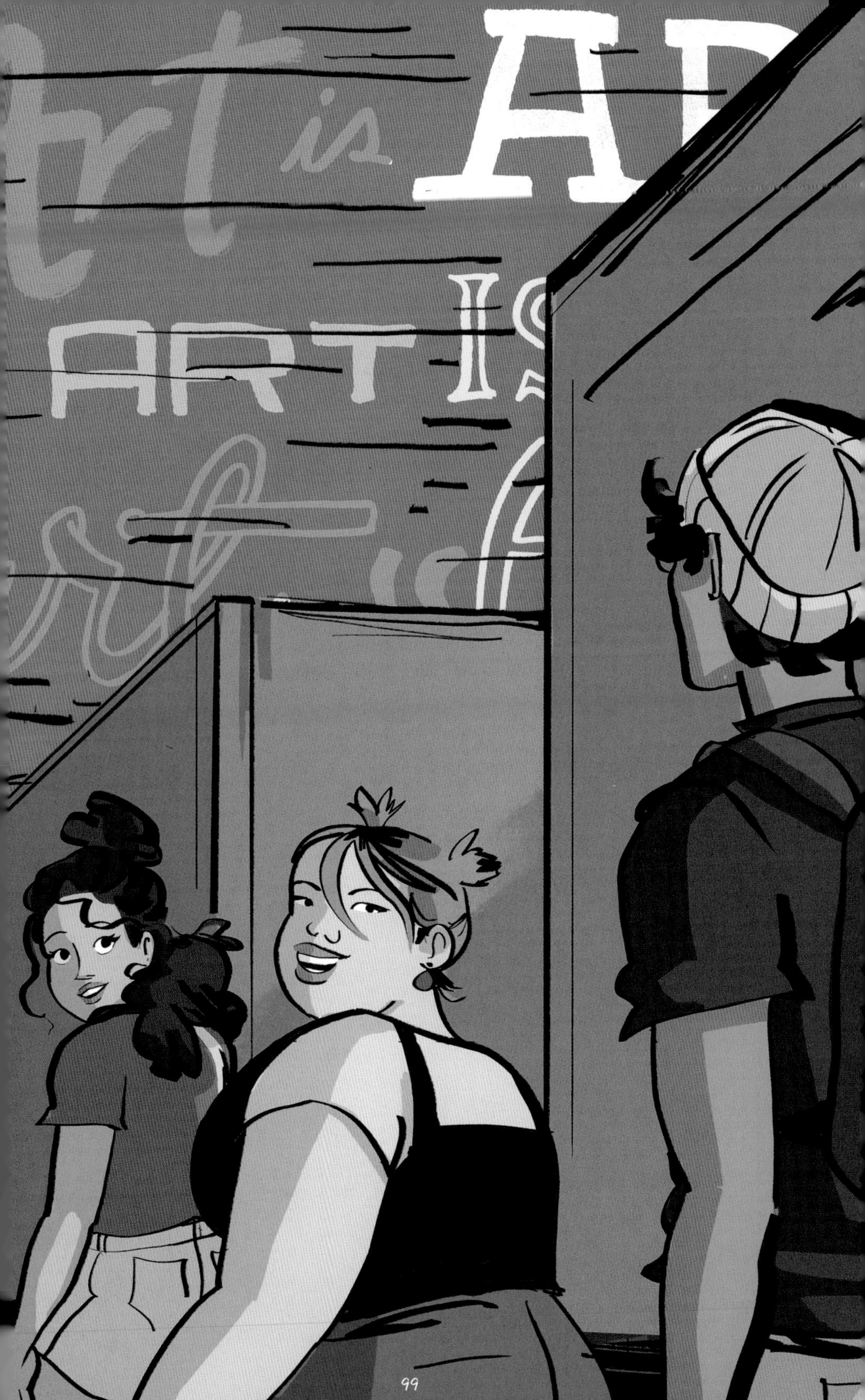
is
ART

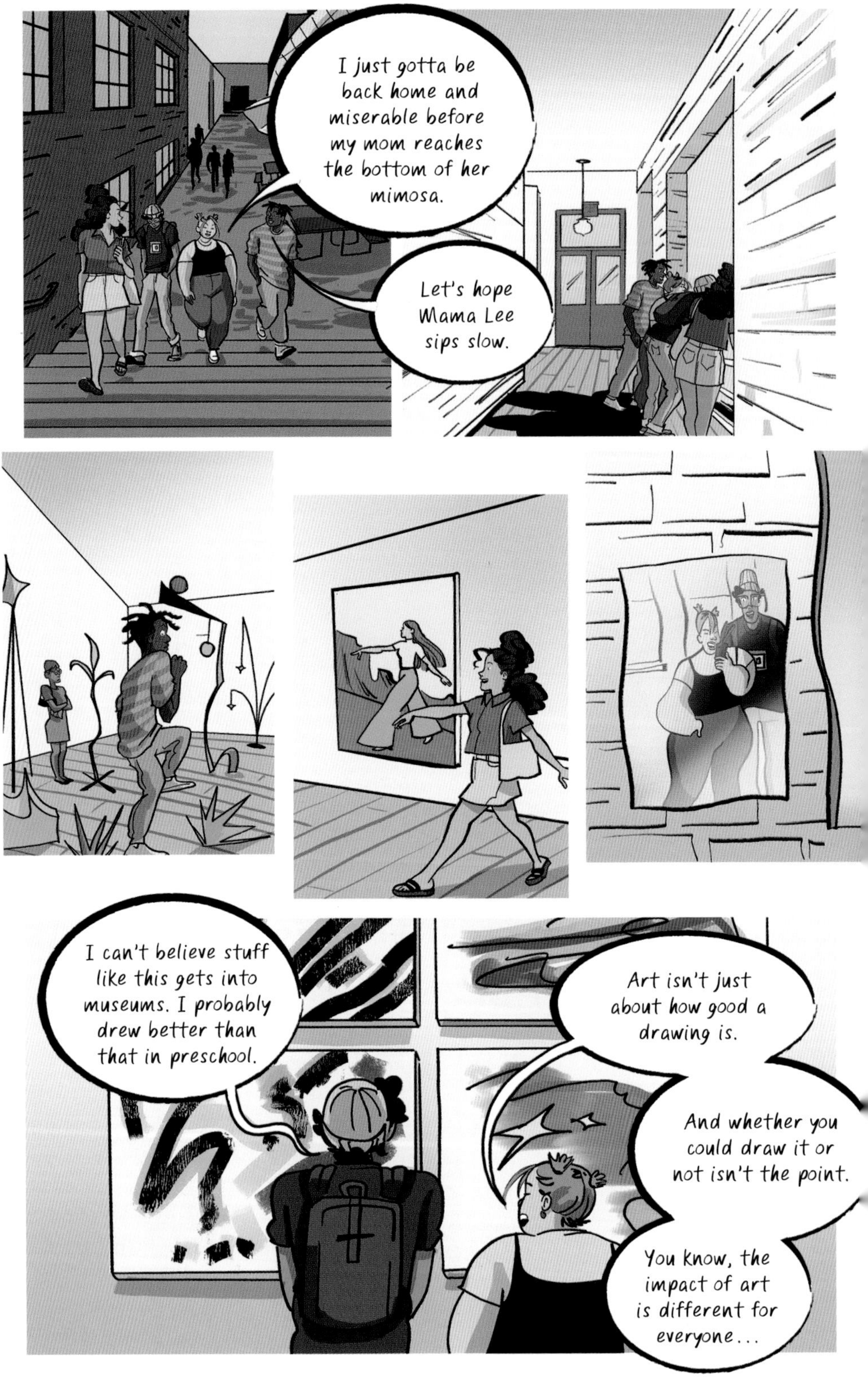
I just gotta be back home and miserable before my mom reaches the bottom of her mimosa.
Let's hope Mama Lee sips slow.
I can't believe stuff like this gets into museums. I probably drew better than that in preschool.
Art isn't just about how good a drawing is.
And whether you could draw it or not isn't the point.
You know, the impact of art is different for everyone...

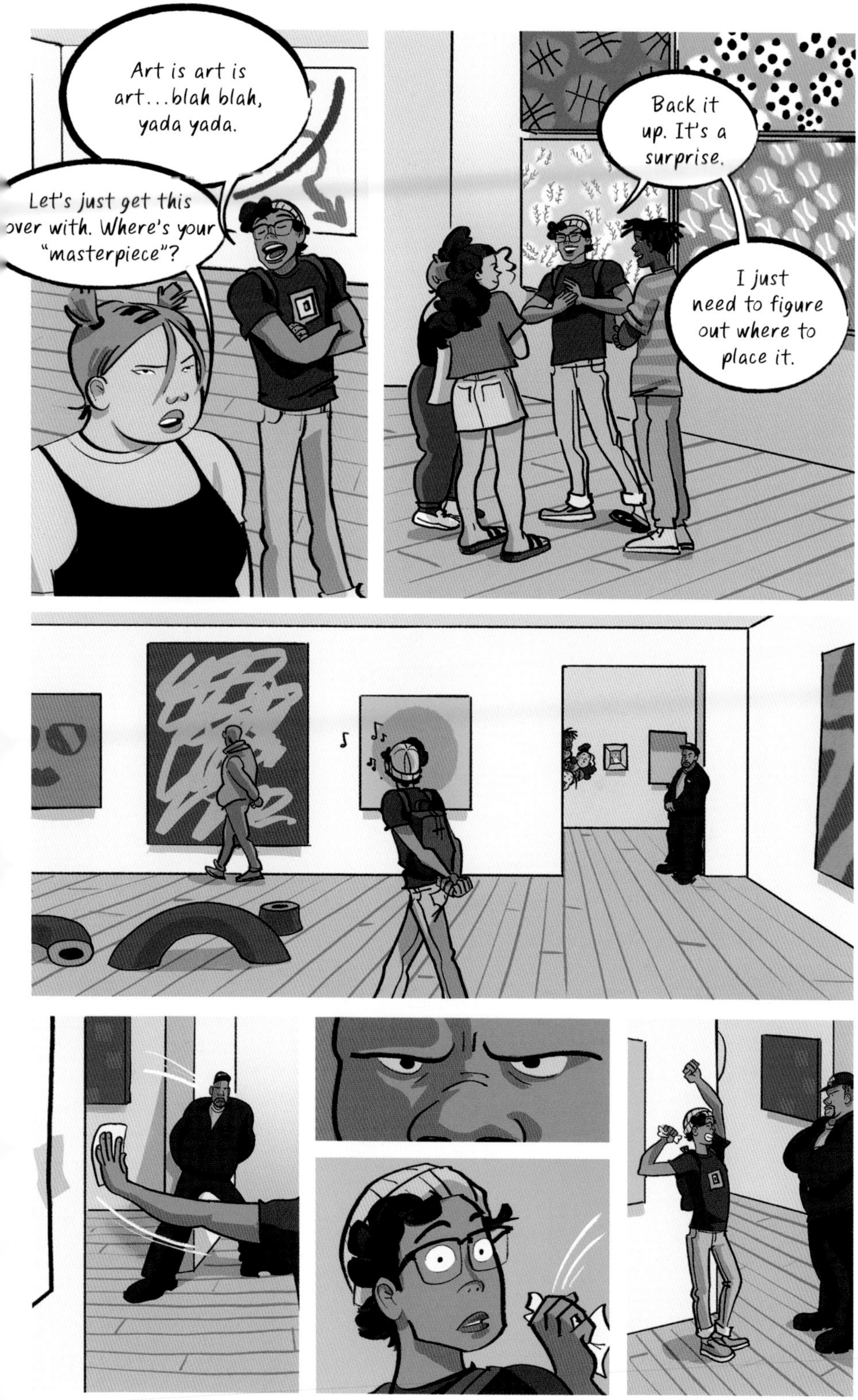
Art is art is art...blah blah, yada yada.
Let's just get this over with. Where's your "masterpiece"?
Back it up. It's a surprise.
I just need to figure out where to place it.

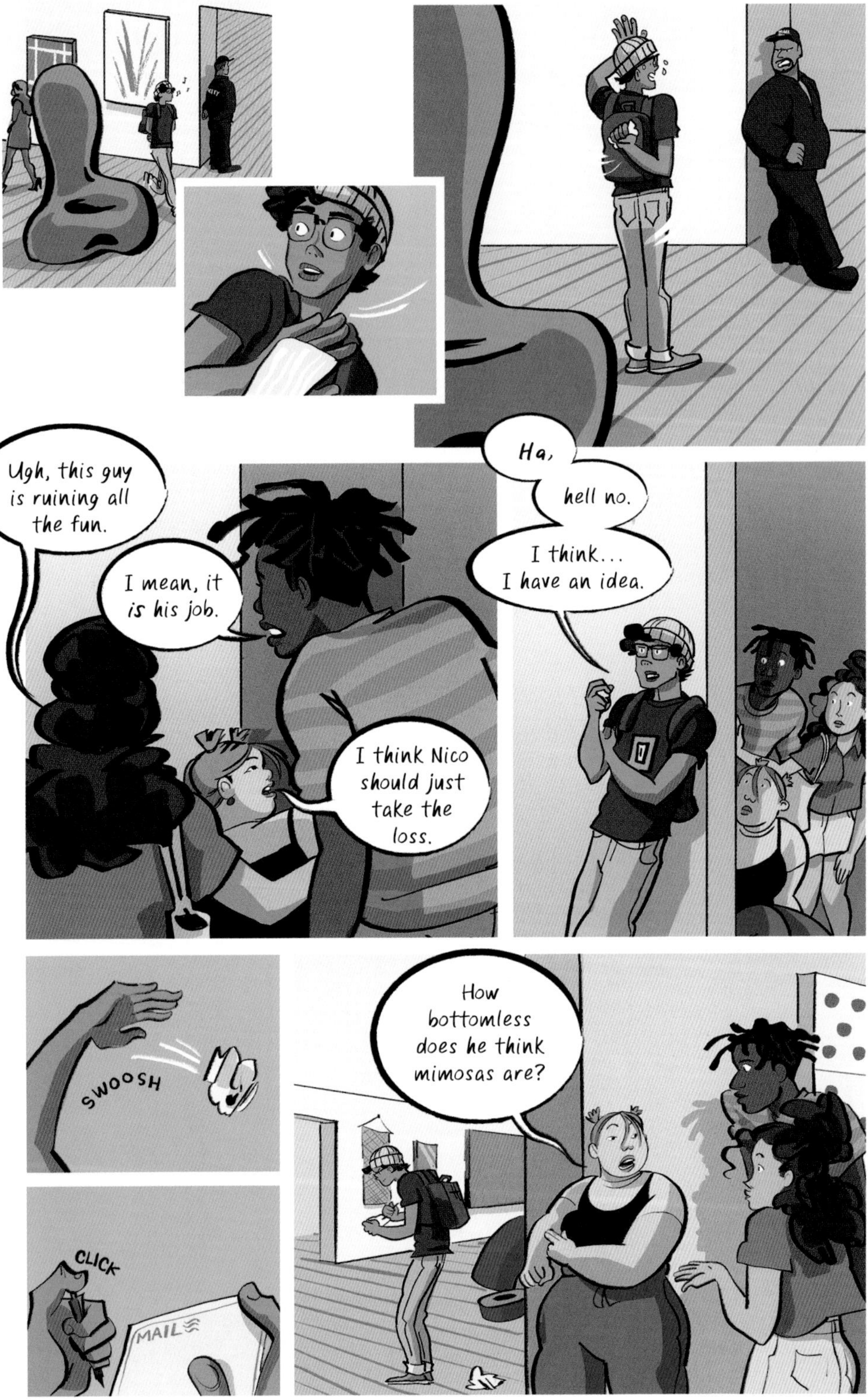

Ugh, this guy is ruining all the fun.
I mean, it *is* his job.
I think Nico should just take the loss.
Ha,
hell no.
I think... I have an idea.
SWOOSH
CLICK
MAIL
How bottomless does he think mimosas are?

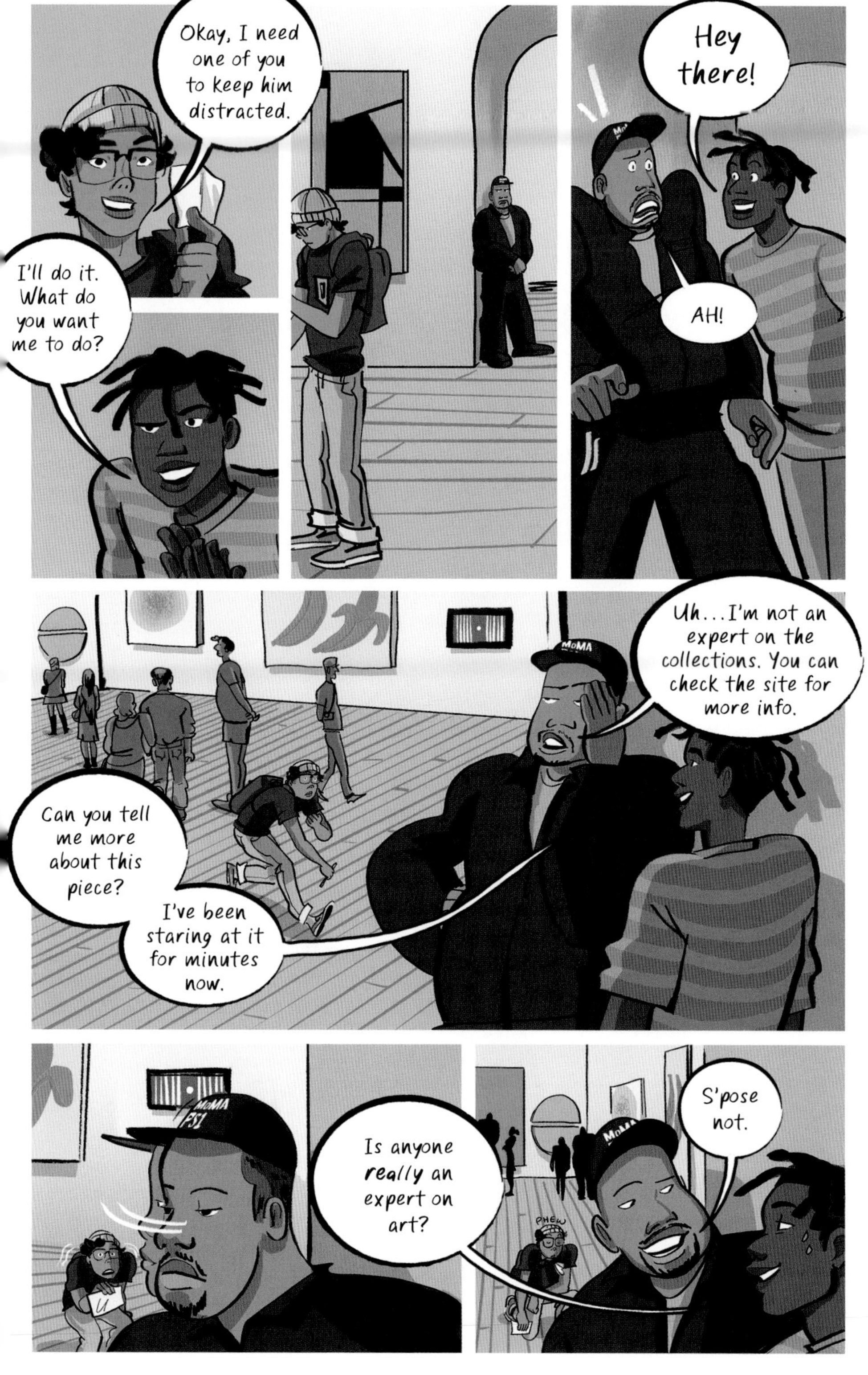
Okay, I need one of you to keep him distracted.
I'll do it. What do you want me to do?
Hey there!
AH!
Can you tell me more about this piece?
I've been staring at it for minutes now.
Uh...I'm not an expert on the collections. You can check the site for more info.
MoMA PS1
Is anyone really an expert on art?
PHEW
S'pose not.

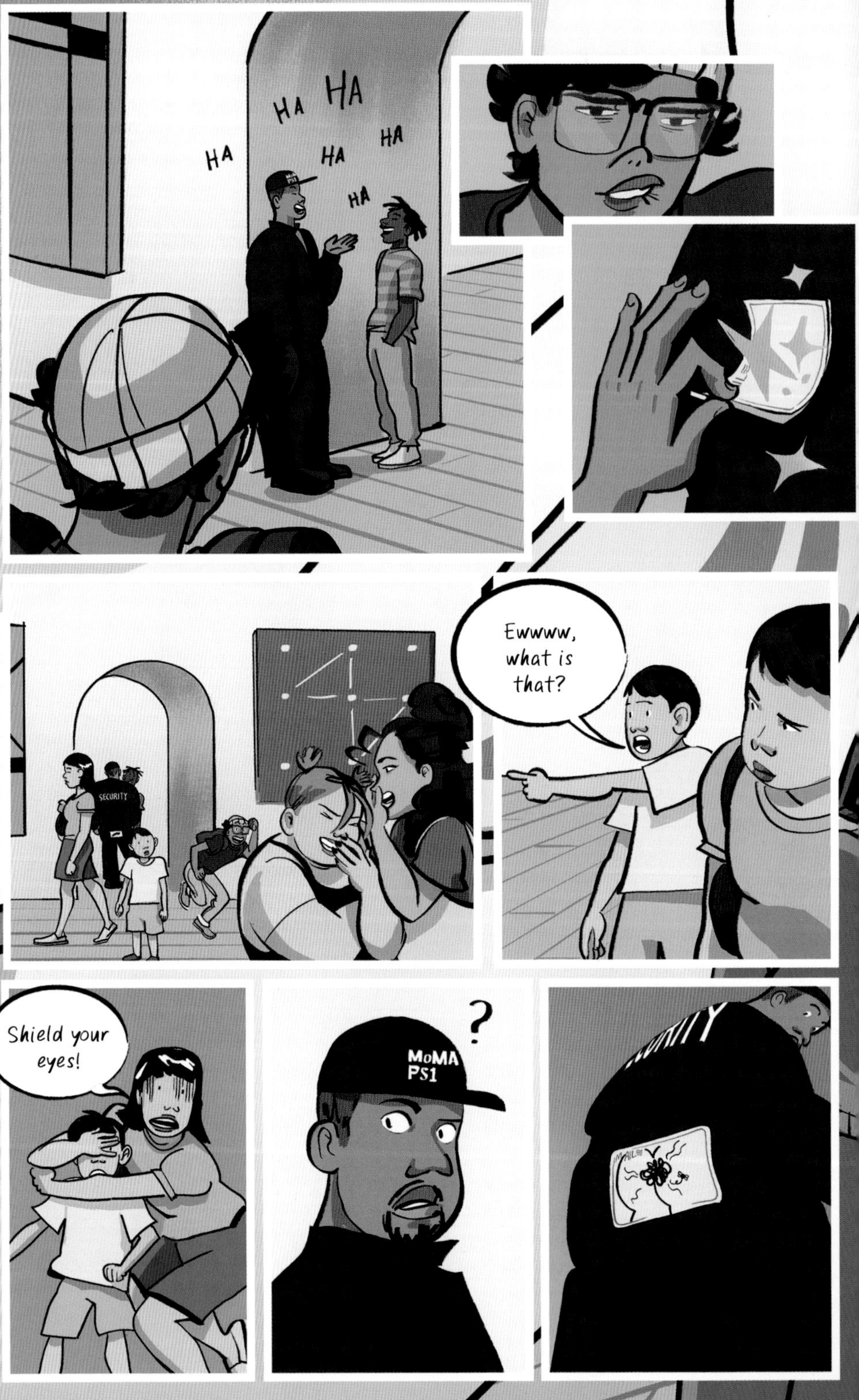
HA HA
HA
HA
HA
HA
MoMA PS1
SECURITY
Ewwww, what is that?
Shield your eyes!
?
MoMA PS1

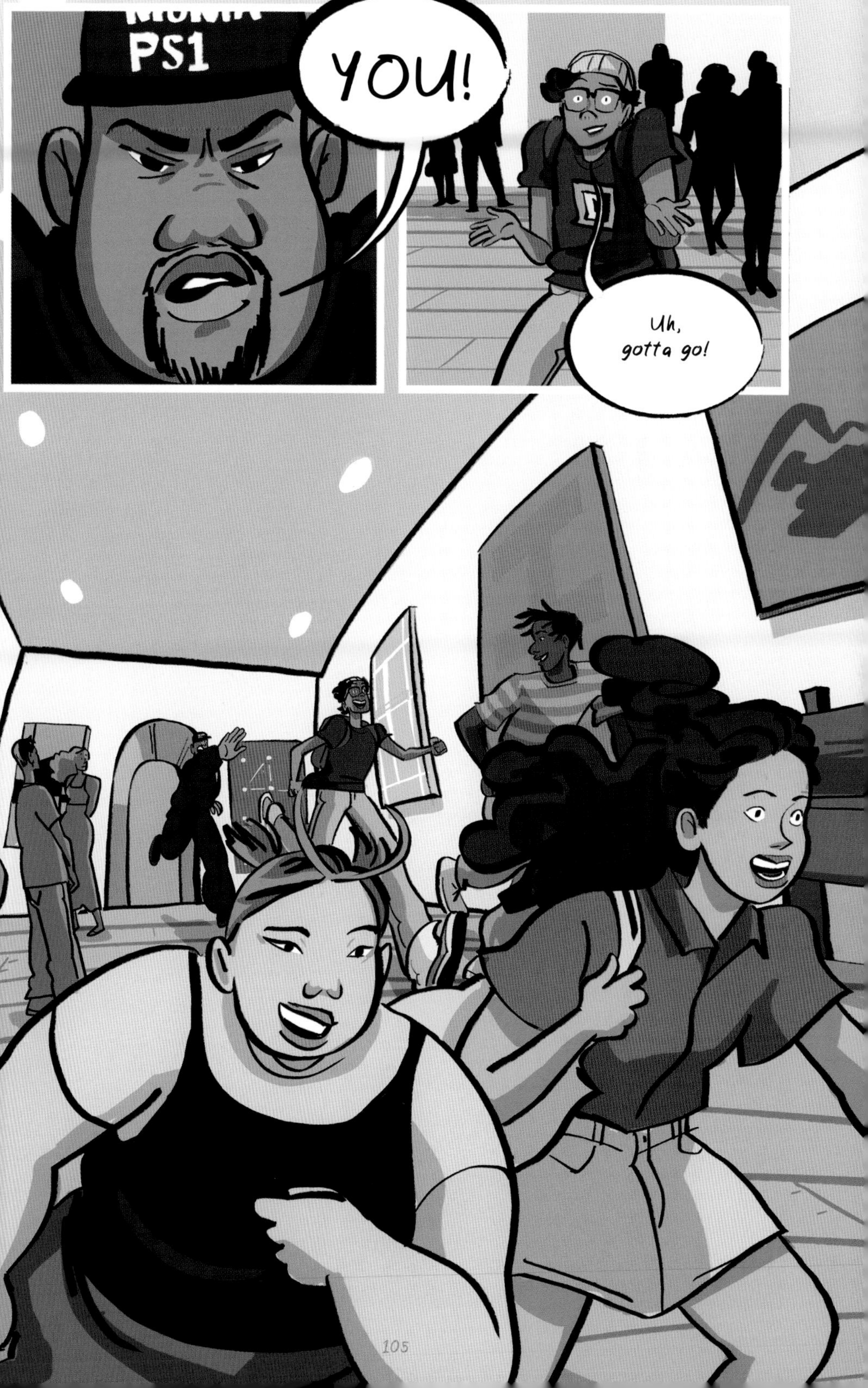
MOMA PS1
YOU!
Uh, gotta go!

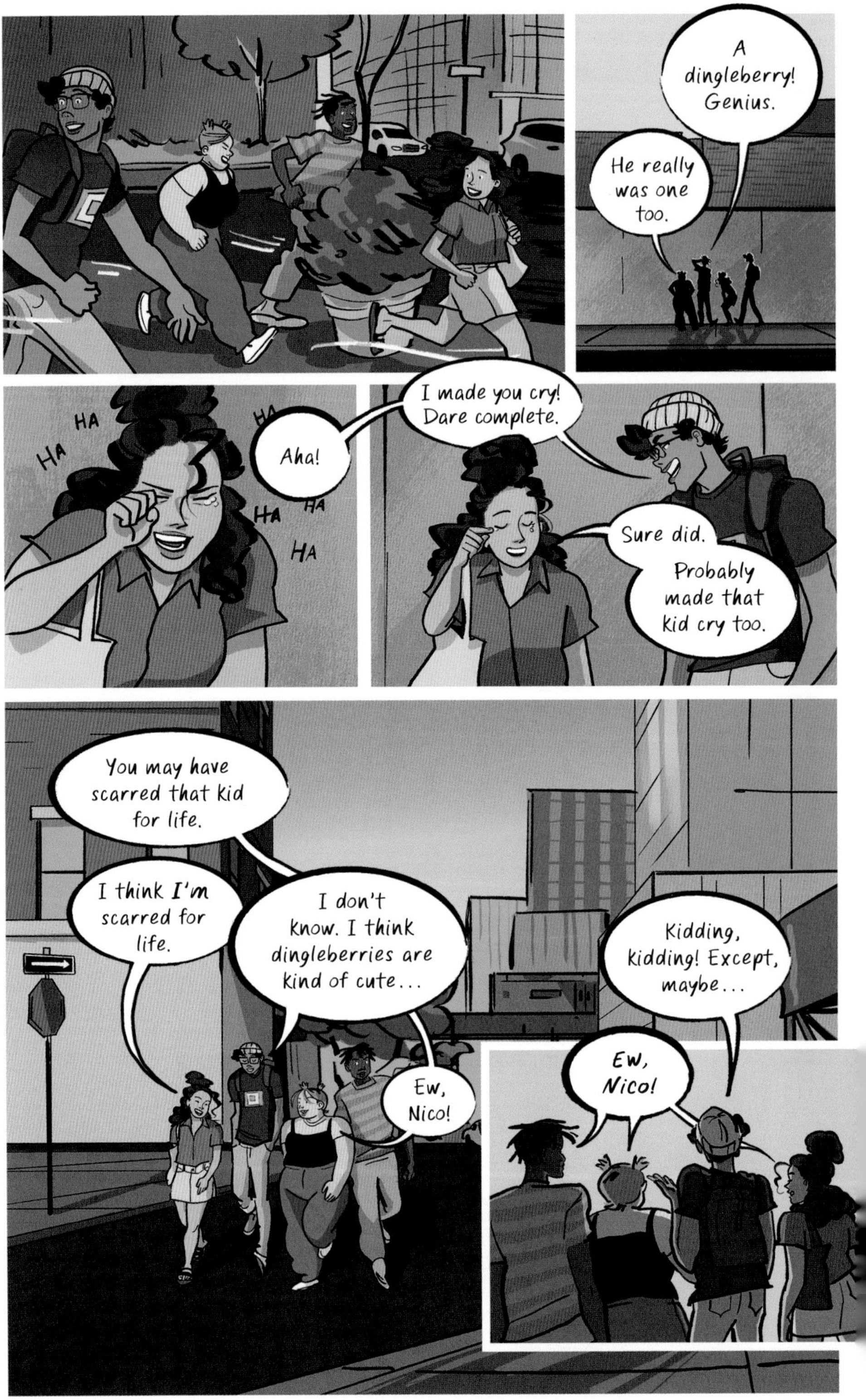
A dingleberry! Genius.
He really was one too.
HA HA HA HA HA HA
Aha!
I made you cry! Dare complete.
Sure did.
Probably made that kid cry too.
You may have scarred that kid for life.
I think I'm scarred for life.
I don't know. I think dingleberries are kind of cute...
Ew, Nico!
Kidding, kidding! Except, maybe...
Ew, Nico!

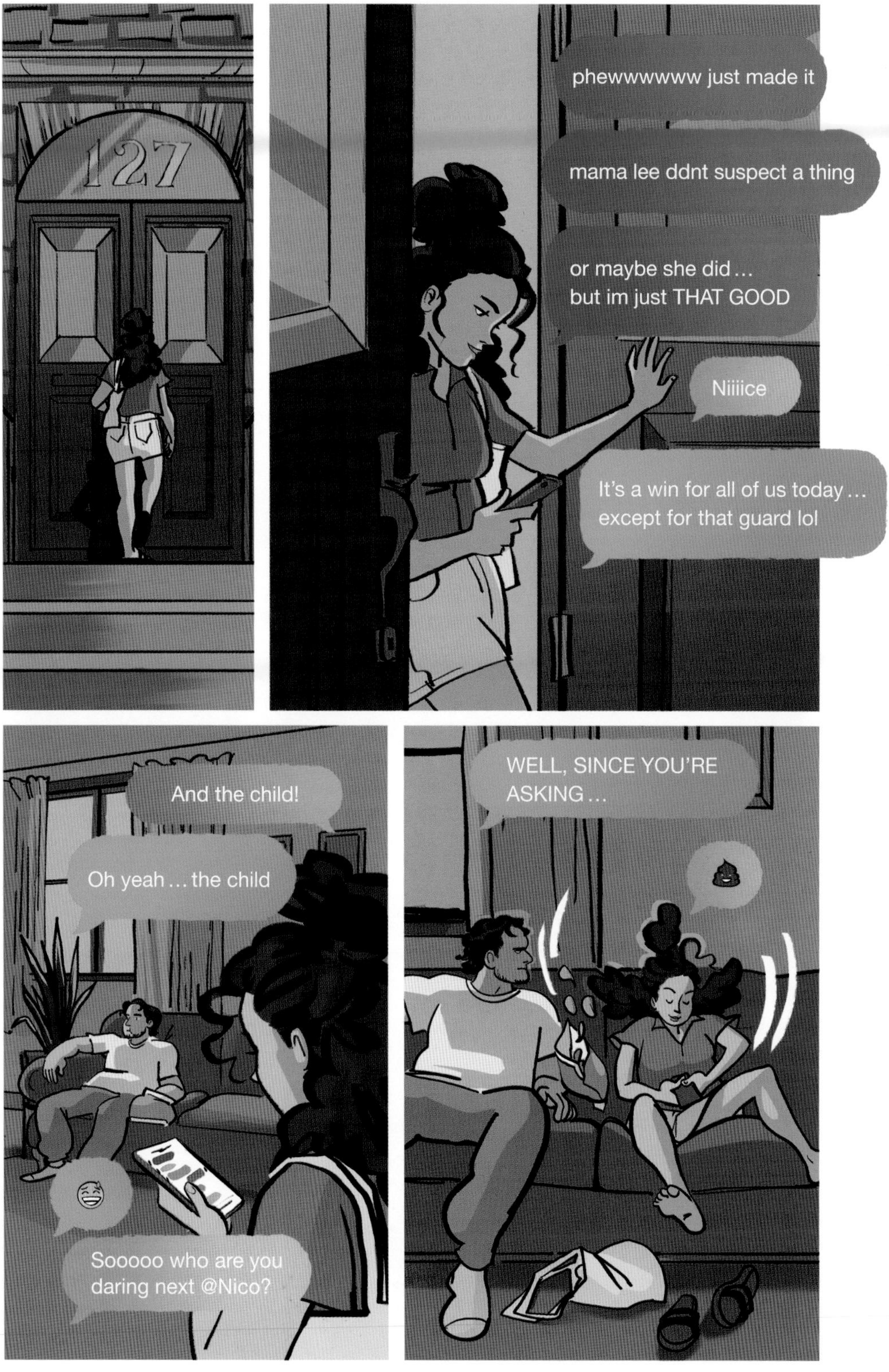

127
phewwwwww just made it
mama lee ddnt suspect a thing
or maybe she did...
but im just THAT GOOD
Niiiice
It's a win for all of us today...
except for that guard lol
And the child!
Oh yeah... the child
Sooooo who are you
daring next @Nico?
WELL, SINCE YOU'RE
ASKING...

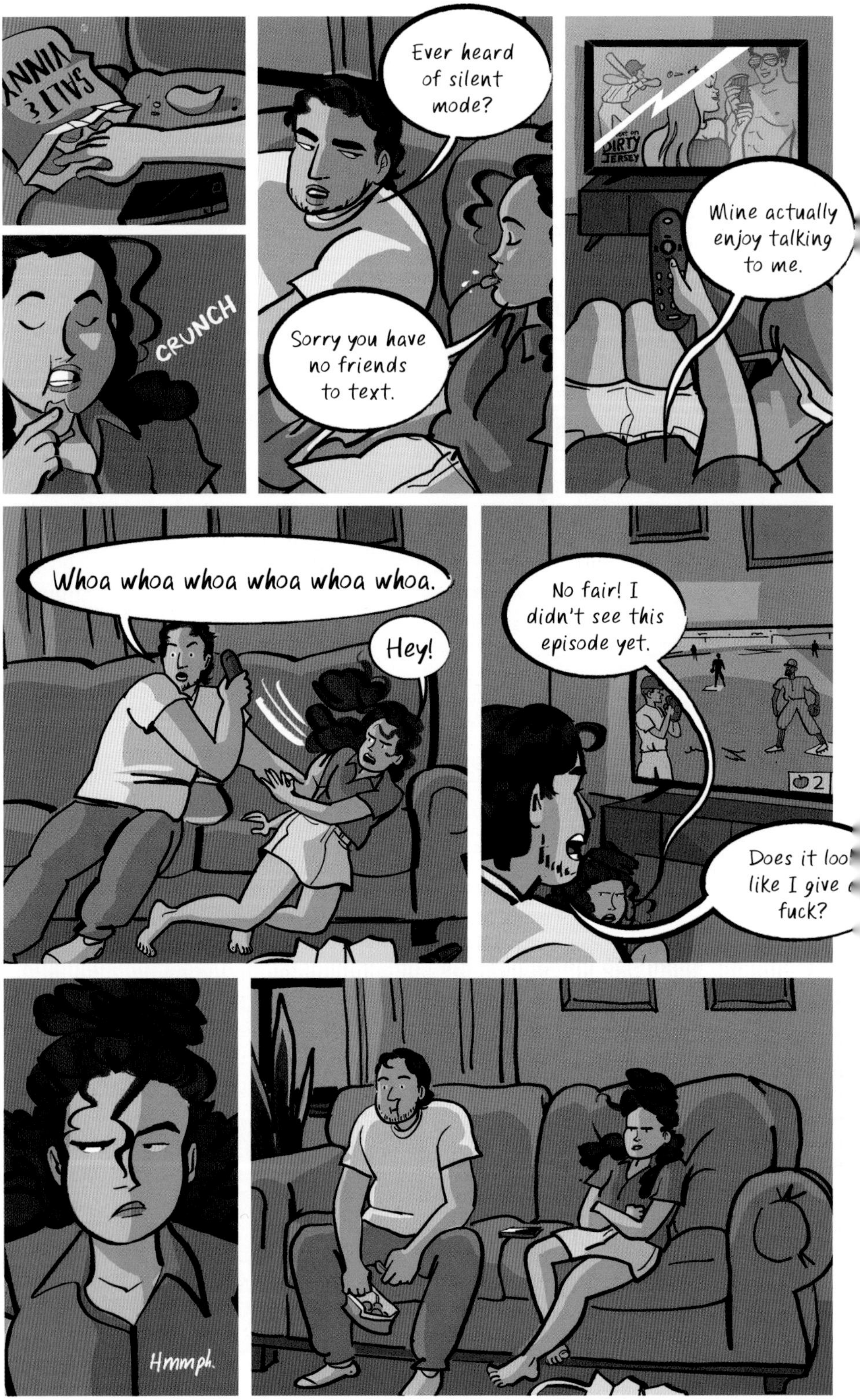
SAL'S & VINNY
CRUNCH
Ever heard of silent mode?
Sorry you have no friends to text.
DIRTY JERSEY
Mine actually enjoy talking to me.
Whoa whoa whoa whoa whoa whoa.
Hey!
No fair! I didn't see this episode yet.
Does it look like I give a fuck?
Hmmph.

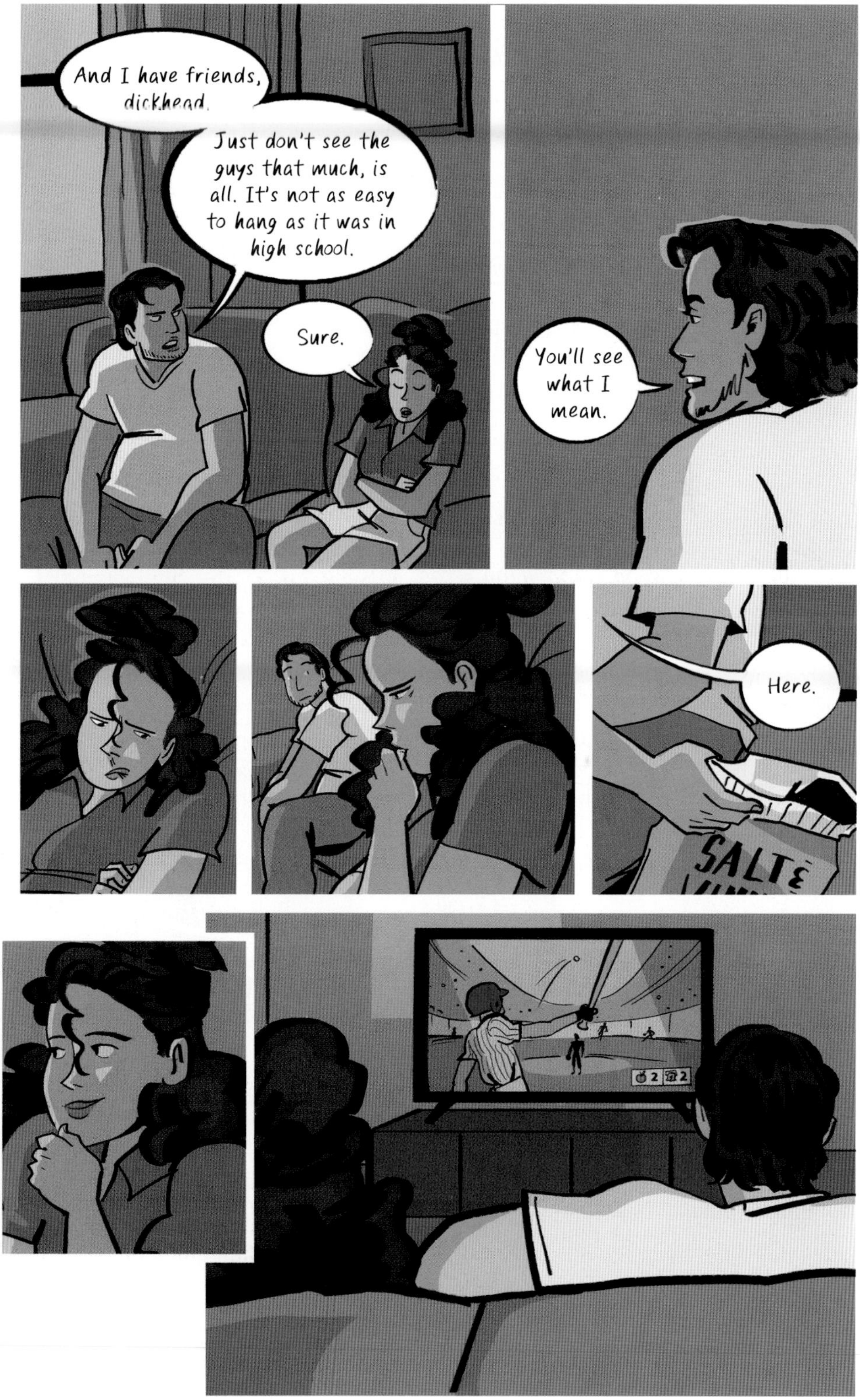
And I have friends, dickhead.
Just don't see the guys that much, is all. It's not as easy to hang as it was in high school.
Sure.
You'll see what I mean.
Here.
SALTE

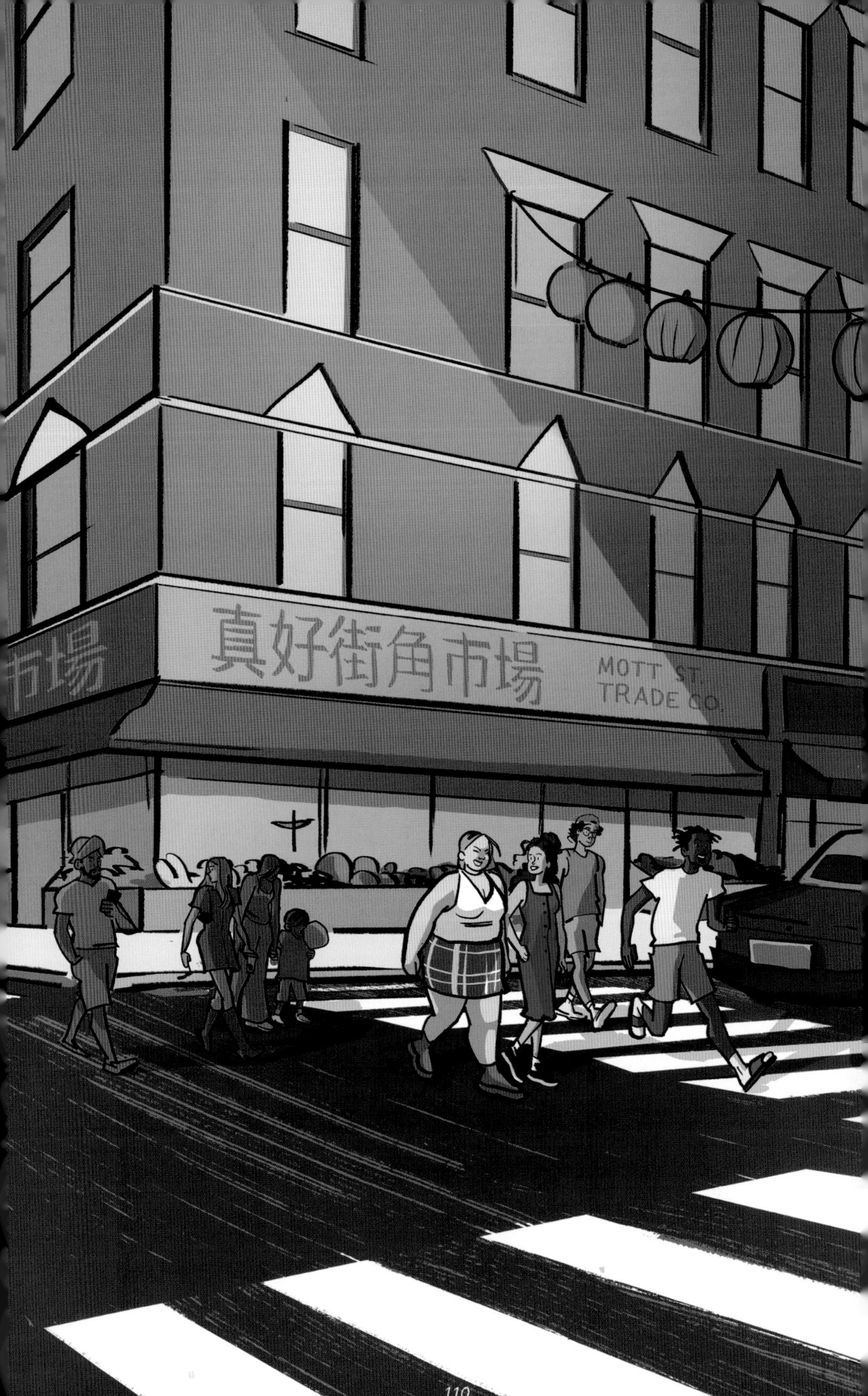
市場
真好街角市場
MOTT ST.
TRADE CO.

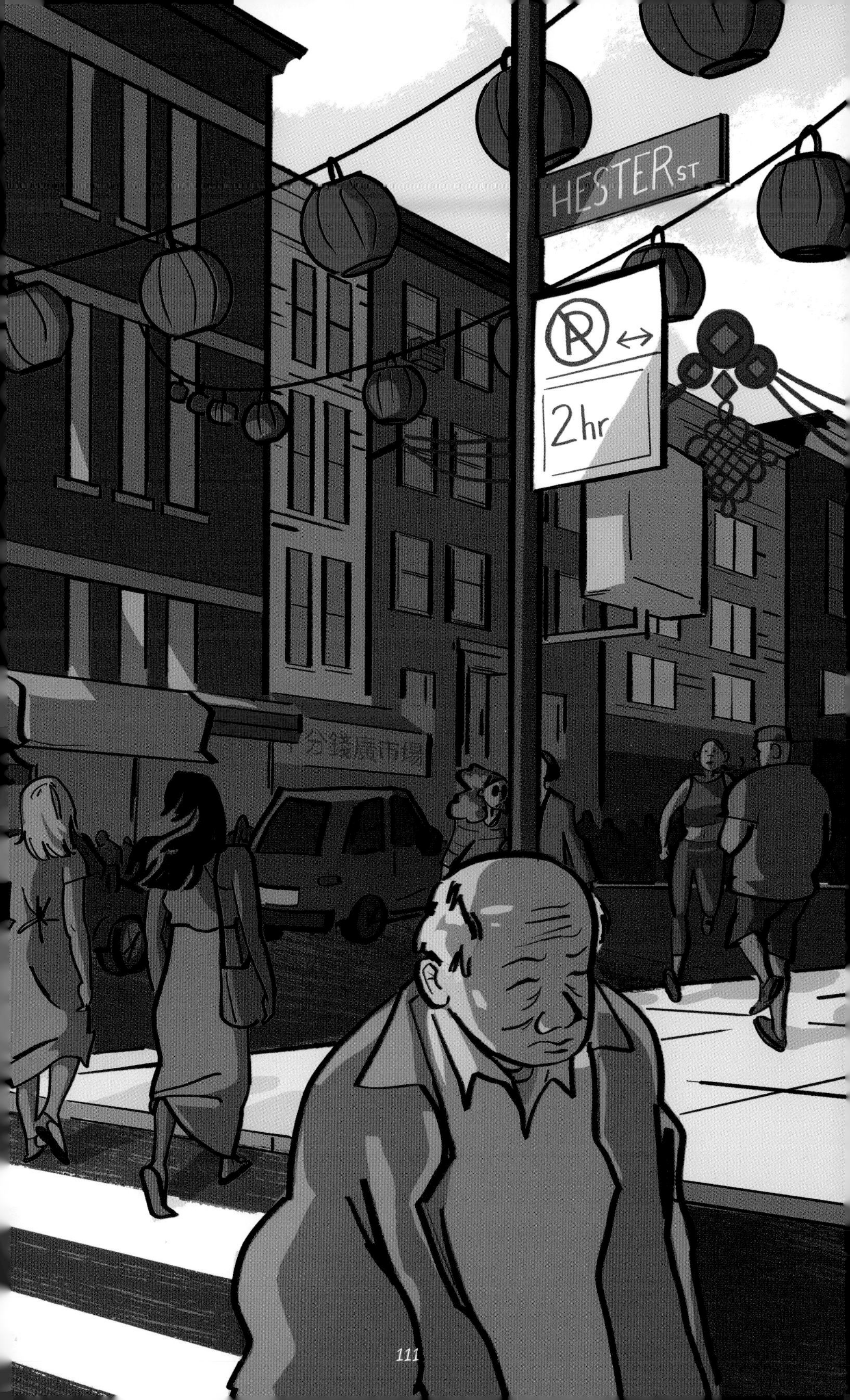
HESTER ST
2hr
分錢廣市場

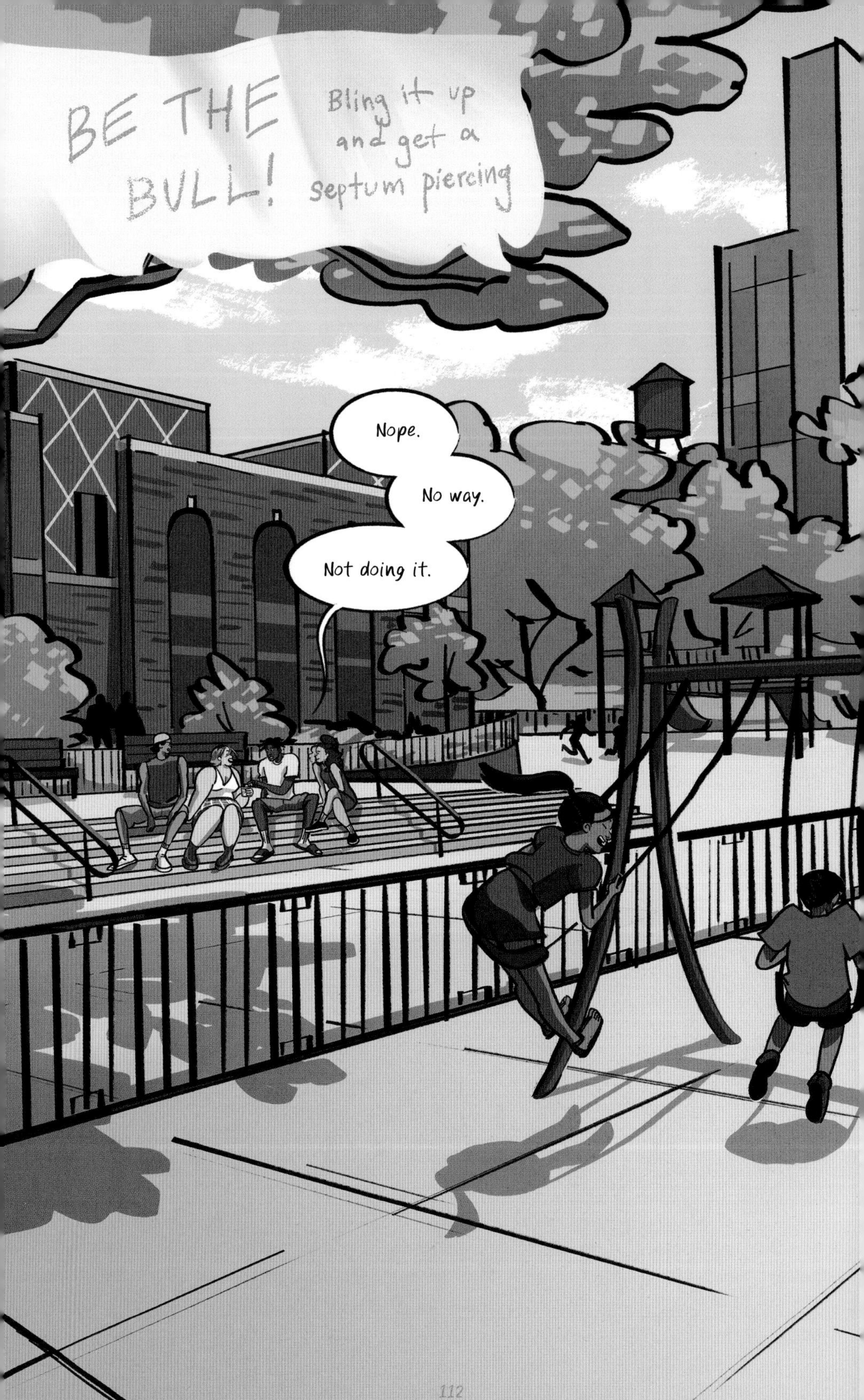
BE THE BULL!
Bling it up and get a septum piercing
Nope.
No way.
Not doing it.

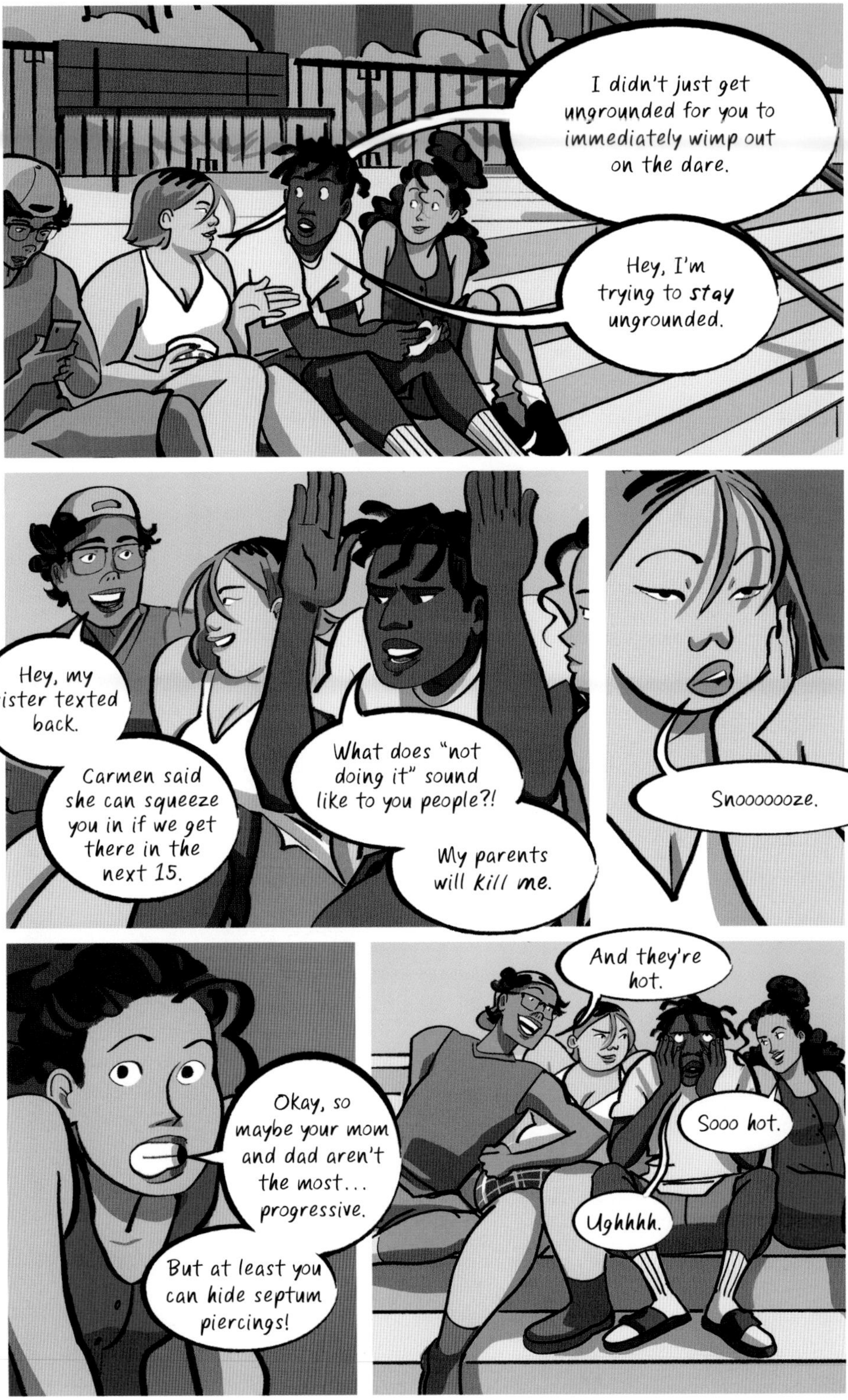
I didn't just get ungrounded for you to immediately wimp out on the dare.
Hey, I'm trying to stay ungrounded.
Hey, my sister texted back.
Carmen said she can squeeze you in if we get there in the next 15.
What does "not doing it" sound like to you people?!
My parents will kill me.
Snooooooze.
Okay, so maybe your mom and dad aren't the most... progressive.
But at least you can hide septum piercings!
And they're hot.
Sooo hot.
Ughhhh.

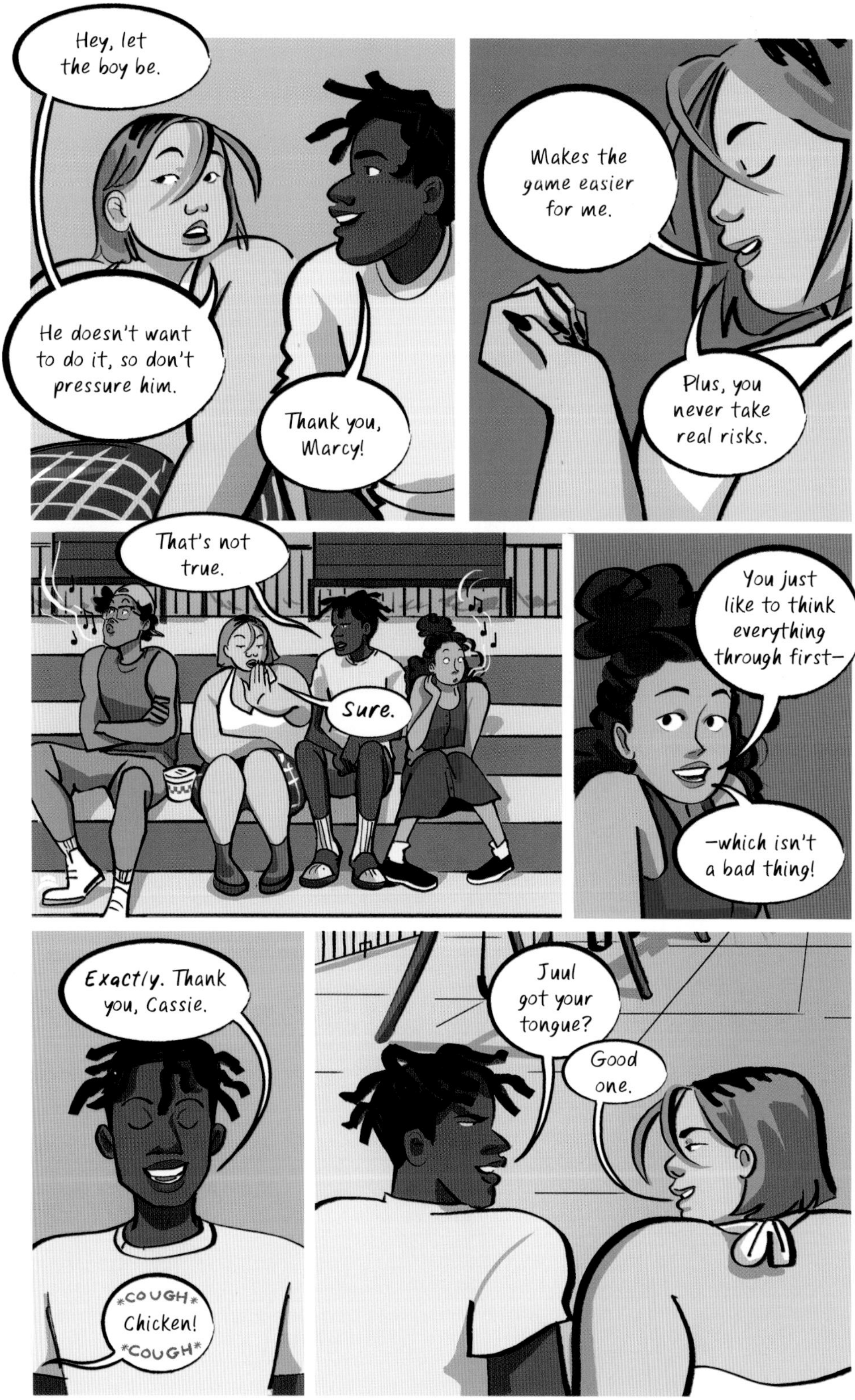
Hey, let the boy be.
He doesn't want to do it, so don't pressure him.
Thank you, Marcy!
Makes the game easier for me.
Plus, you never take real risks.
That's not true.
Sure.
You just like to think everything through first—
—which isn't a bad thing!
Exactly. Thank you, Cassie.
COUGH Chicken! *COUGH*
Juul got your tongue?
Good one.

Nico, I guess you should pick someone else to go.

Get your hand off that cup.

I have a game to win.

That's the spirit!

GULP

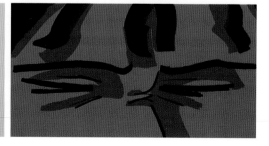

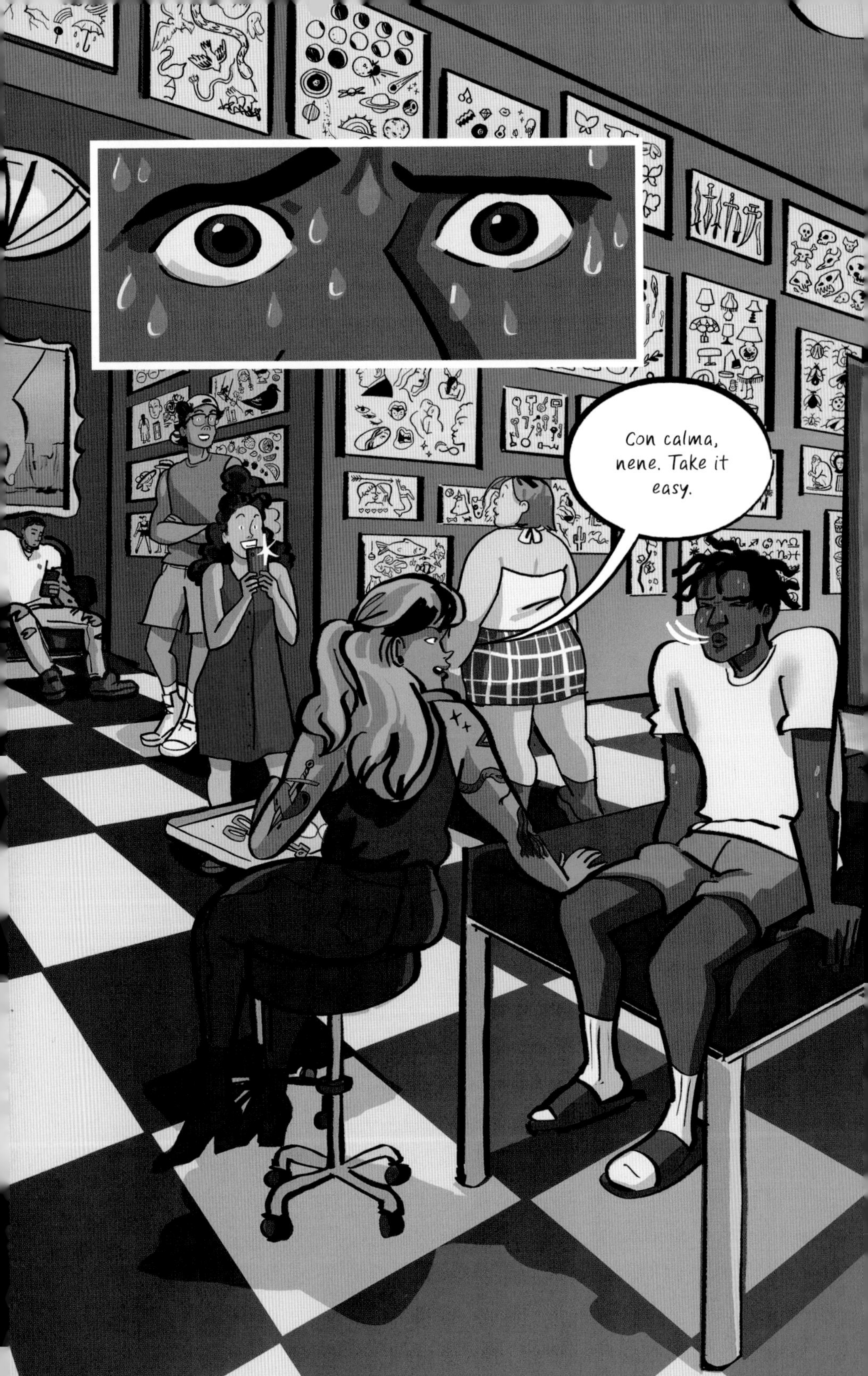
Con calma, nene. Take it easy.

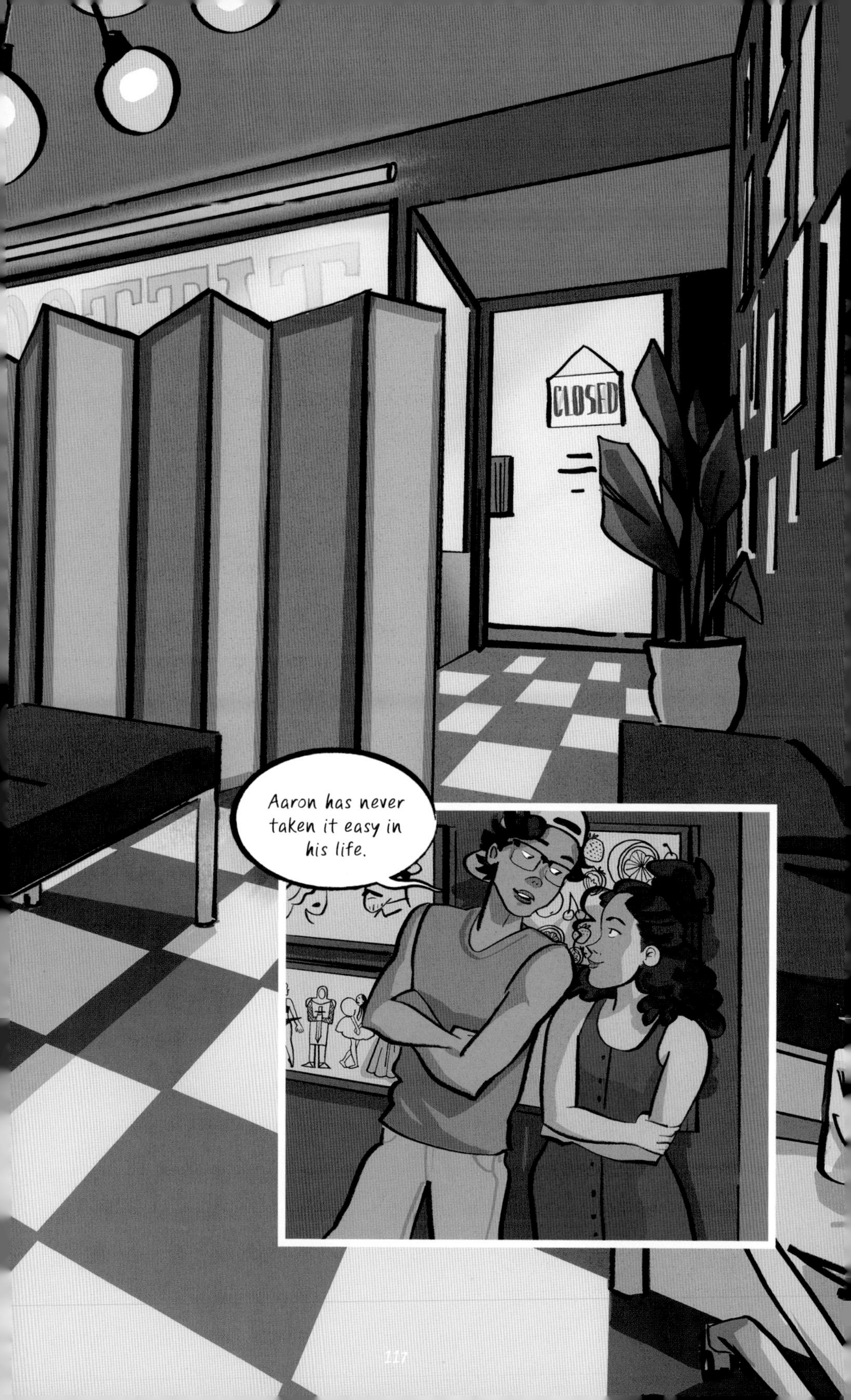
CLOSED
Aaron has never taken it easy in his life.

HA HA HA HA HA

Wow, these designs are *really* sick. Like, so cool.

Uh, thanks.

What medium did you use?

Uh, ink.

Oh, true.

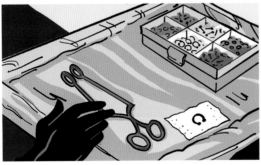

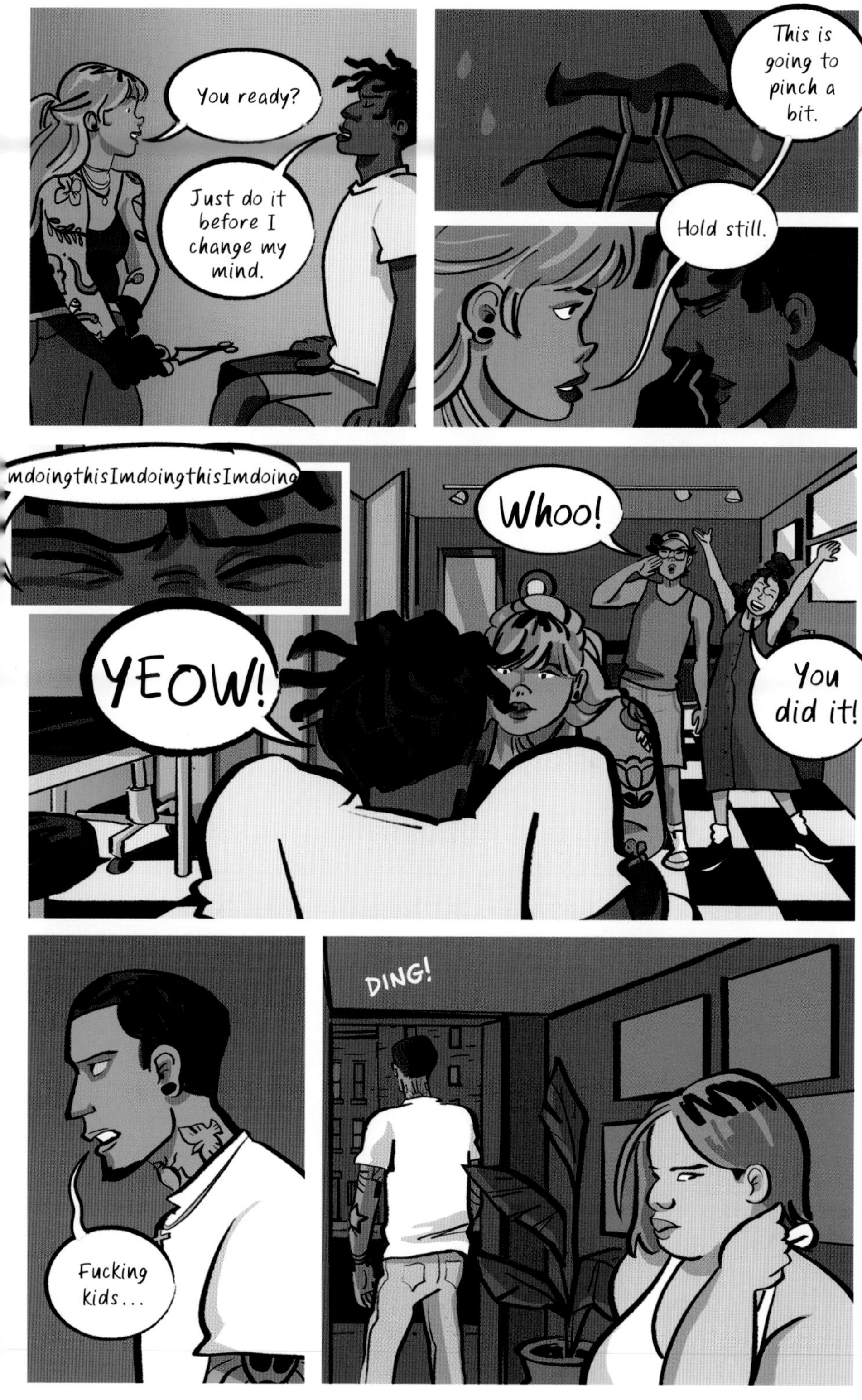
You ready?
Just do it before I change my mind.
This is going to pinch a bit.
Hold still.
ImdoingthisImdoingthisImdoing
Whoo!
YEOW!
You did it!
Fucking kids...
DING!

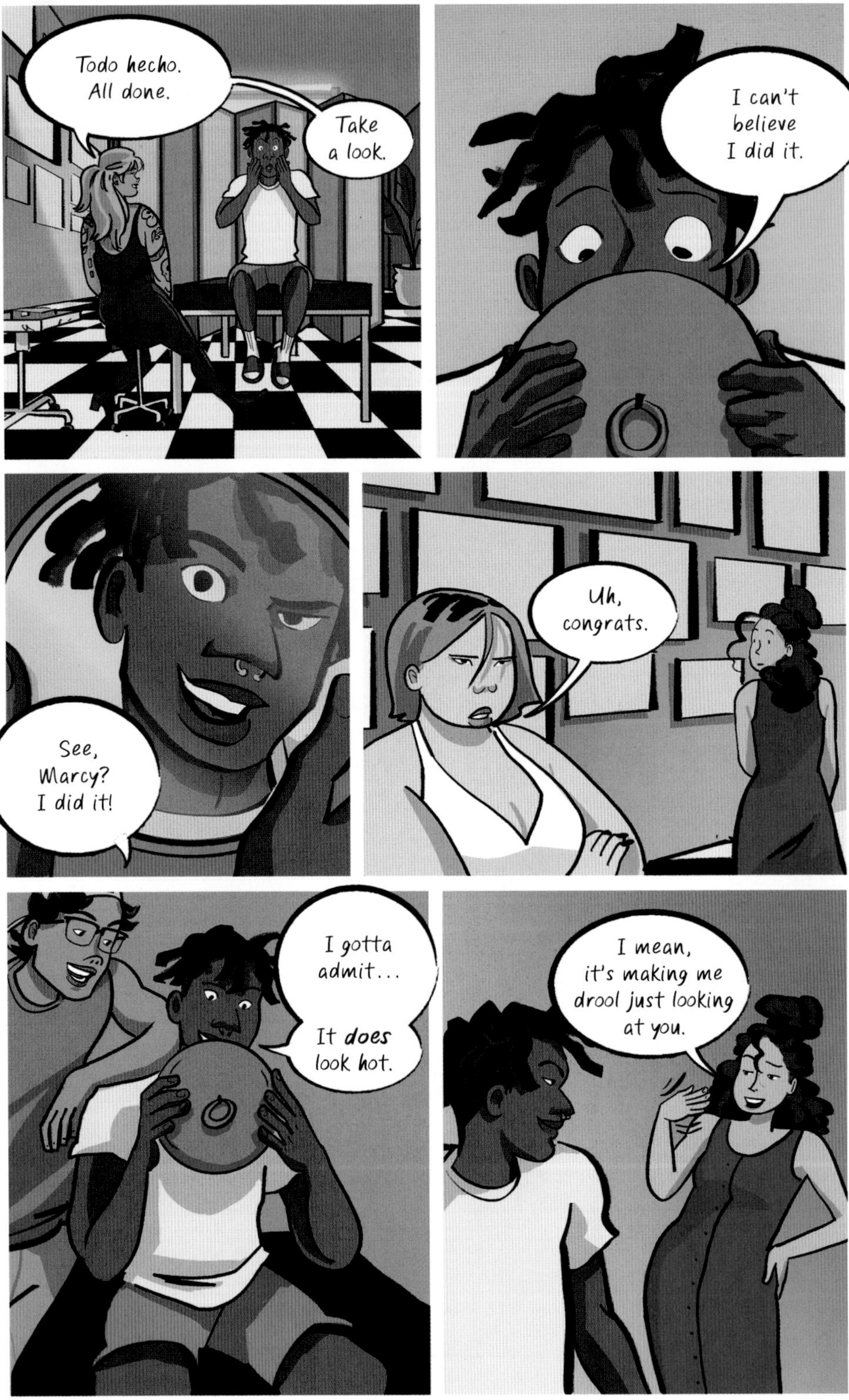
Todo hecho. All done.
Take a look.
I can't believe I did it.
See, Marcy? I did it!
Uh, congrats.
I gotta admit...
It *does* look hot.
I mean, it's making me drool just looking at you.

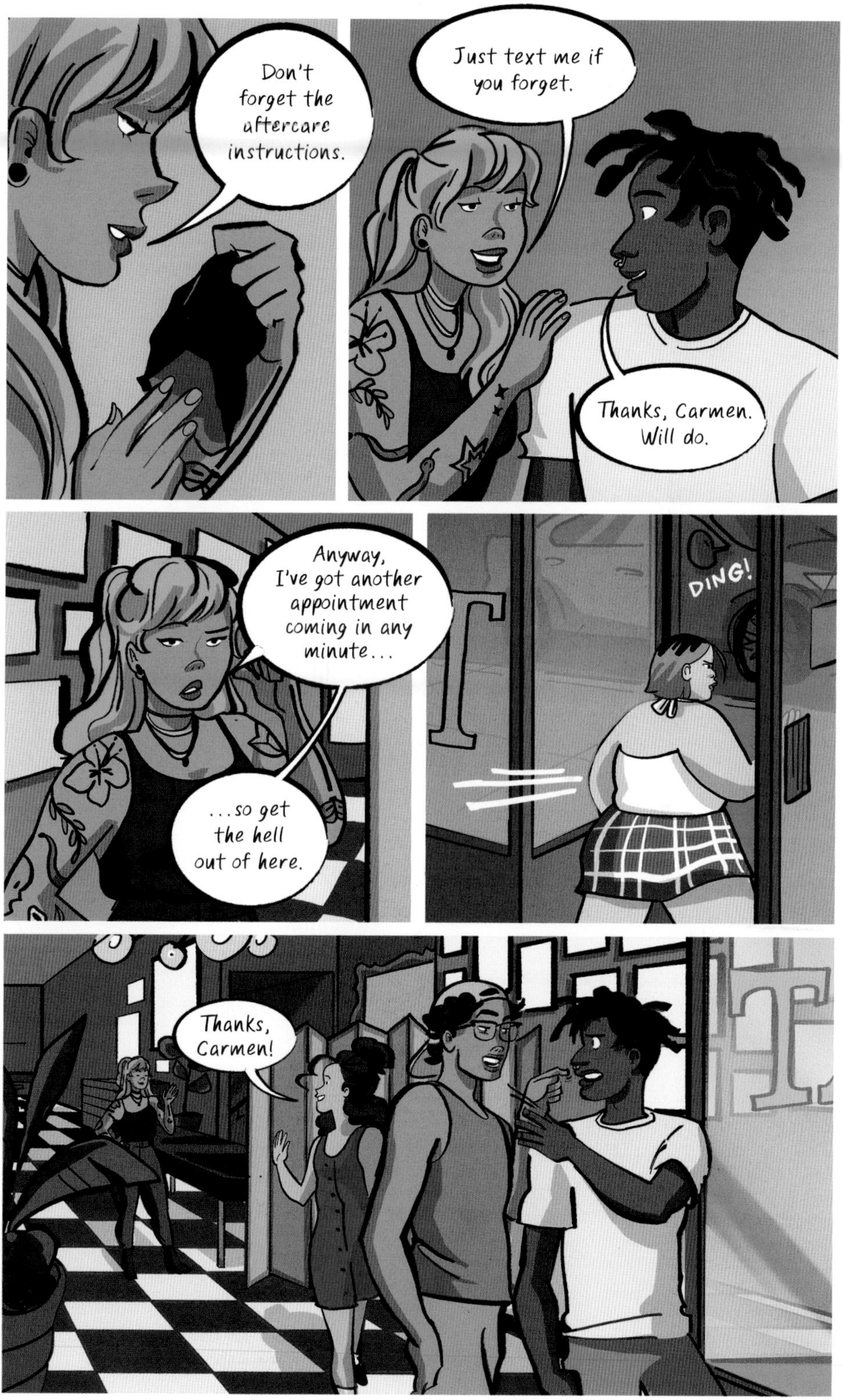
Don't forget the aftercare instructions.
Just text me if you forget.
Thanks, Carmen. Will do.
Anyway, I've got another appointment coming in any minute...
...so get the hell out of here.
DING!
Thanks, Carmen!

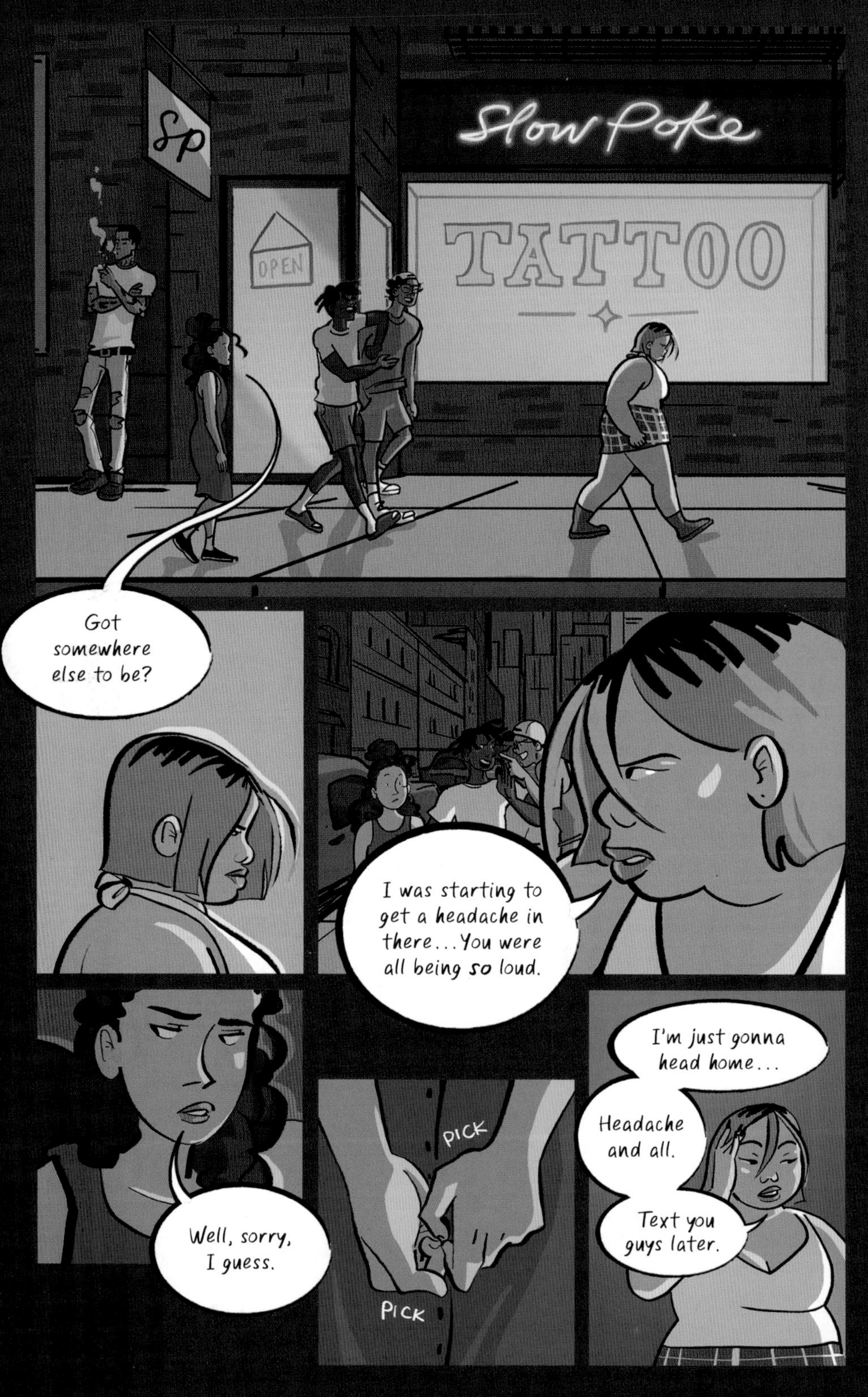
Slow Poke
SP
OPEN
TATTOO
Got somewhere else to be?
I was starting to get a headache in there... You were all being so loud.
Well, sorry, I guess.
PICK
PICK
I'm just gonna head home...
Headache and all.
Text you guys later.

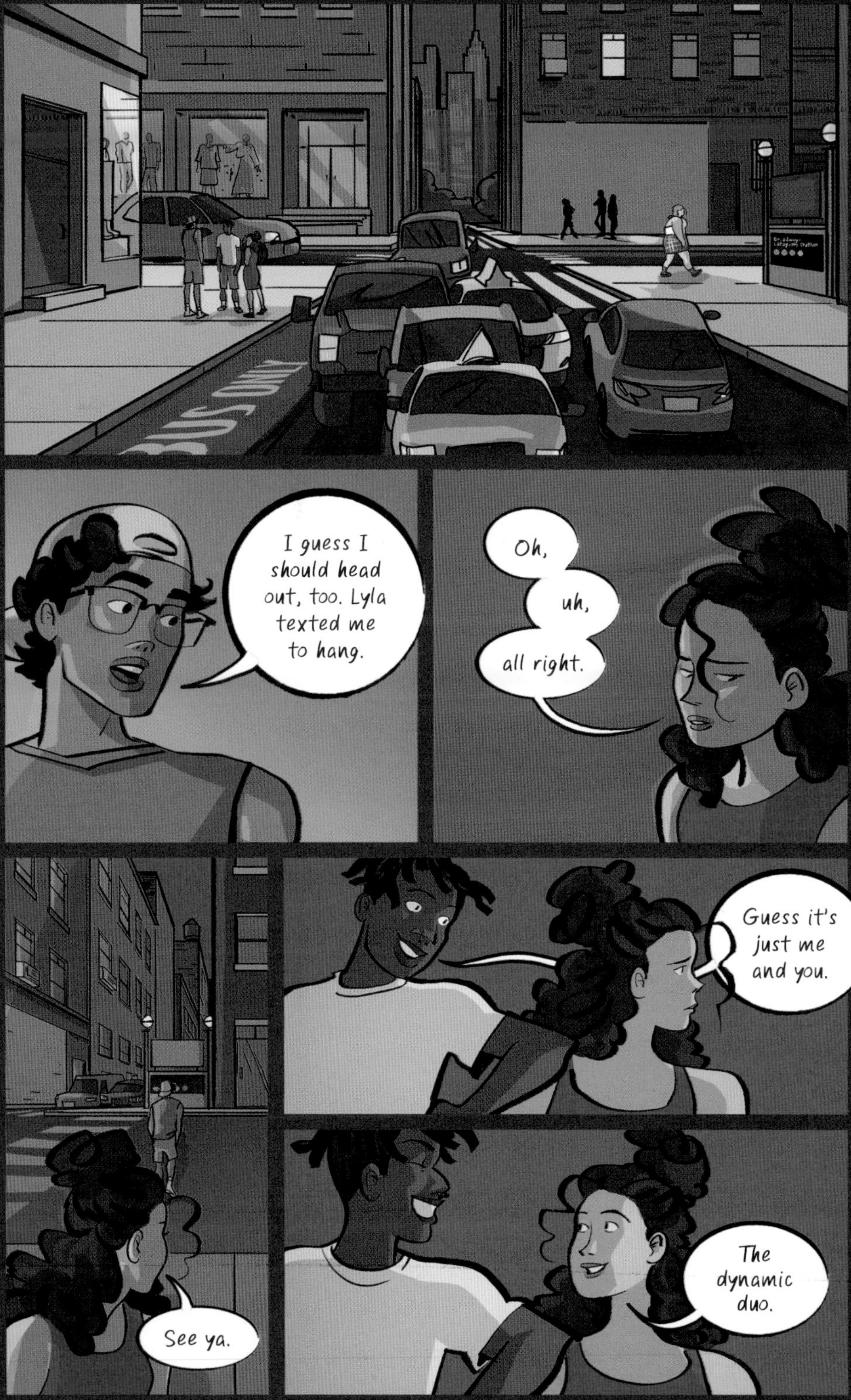
BUS ONLY
I guess I should head out, too. Lyla texted me to hang.
Oh,
uh,
all right.
See ya.
Guess it's just me and you.
The dynamic duo.

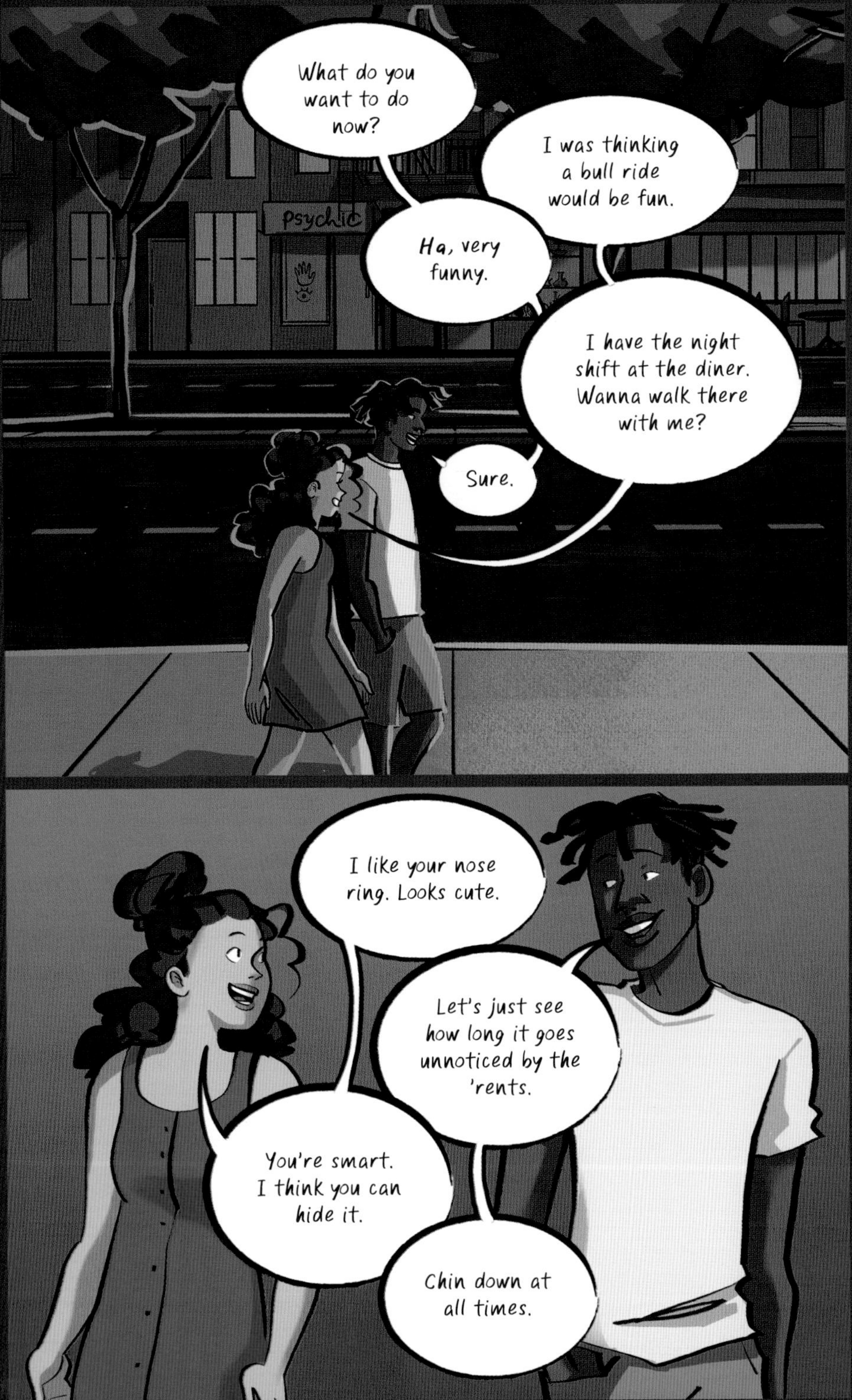
psychic
What do you want to do now?
I was thinking a bull ride would be fun.
Ha, very funny.
I have the night shift at the diner. Wanna walk there with me?
Sure.
I like your nose ring. Looks cute.
Let's just see how long it goes unnoticed by the 'rents.
You're smart. I think you can hide it.
Chin down at all times.

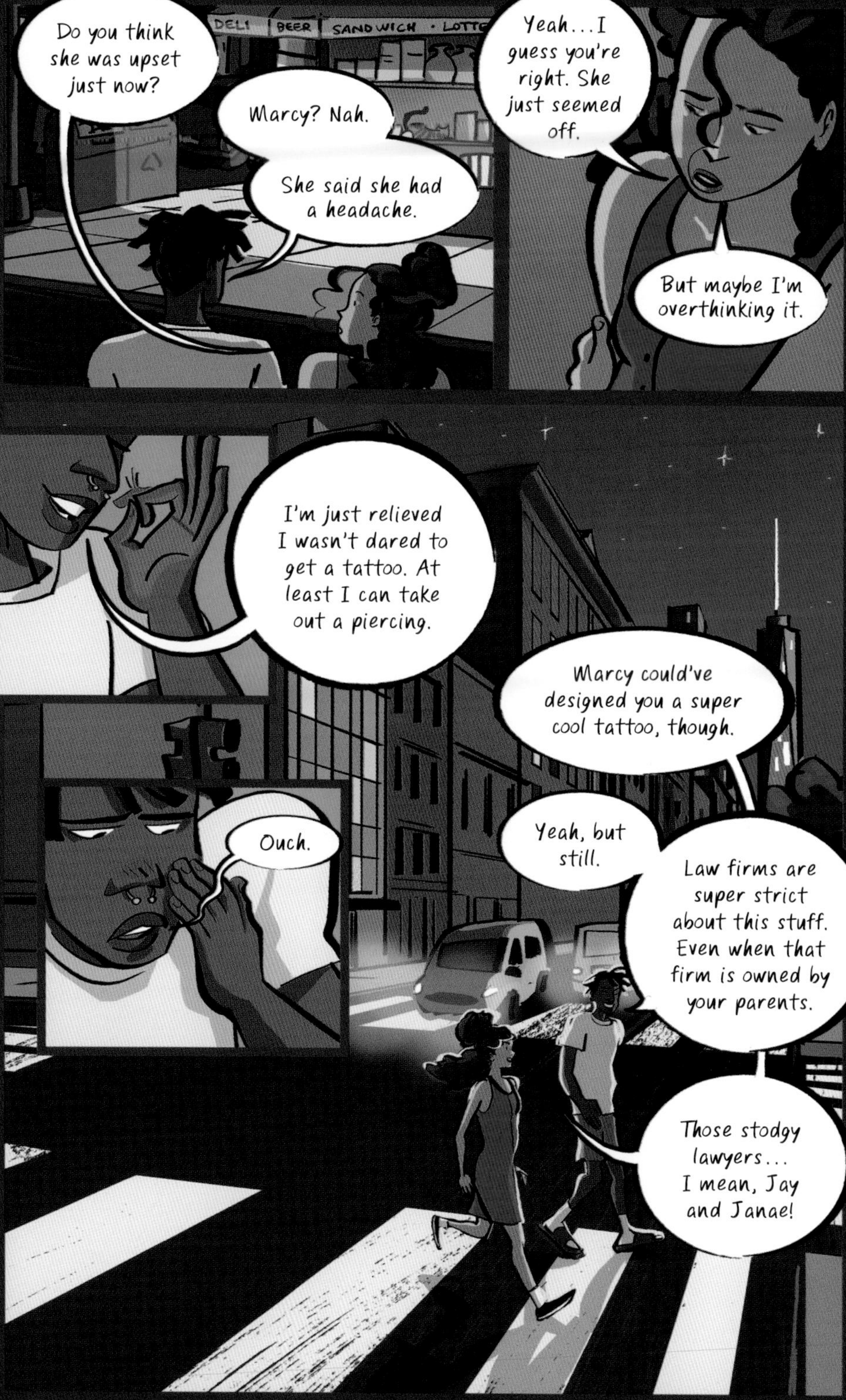

DELI
BEER
SANDWICH
LOTTE
Do you think she was upset just now?
Marcy? Nah.
She said she had a headache.
Yeah... I guess you're right. She just seemed off.
But maybe I'm overthinking it.
I'm just relieved I wasn't dared to get a tattoo. At least I can take out a piercing.
Ouch.
Marcy could've designed you a super cool tattoo, though.
Yeah, but still.
Law firms are super strict about this stuff. Even when that firm is owned by your parents.
Those stodgy lawyers... I mean, Jay and Janae!

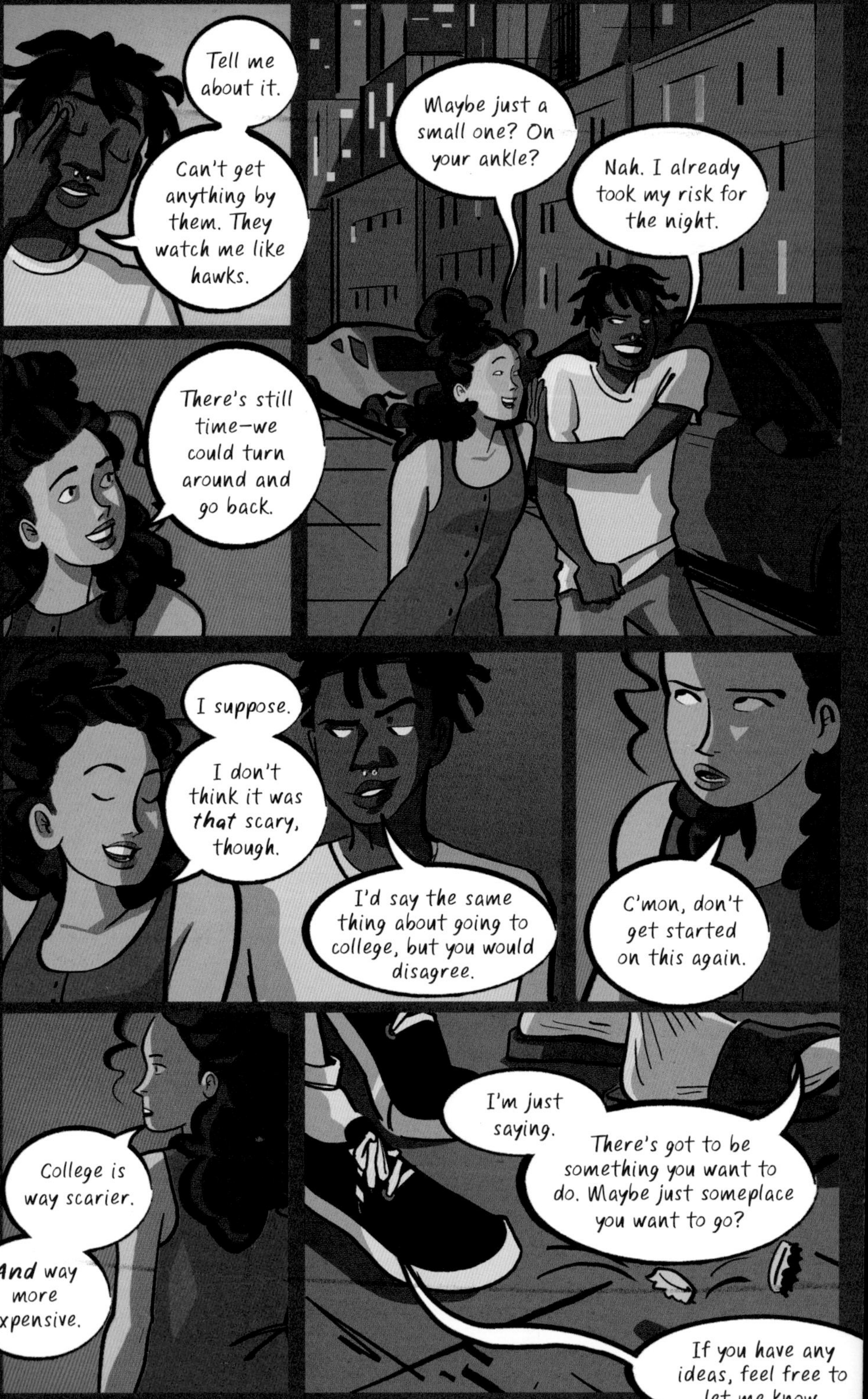
Tell me about it.
Can't get anything by them. They watch me like hawks.
Maybe just a small one? On your ankle?
Nah. I already took my risk for the night.
There's still time—we could turn around and go back.
I suppose.
I don't think it was *that* scary, though.
I'd say the same thing about going to college, but you would disagree.
C'mon, don't get started on this again.
College is way scarier.
And way more expensive.
I'm just saying.
There's got to be something you want to do. Maybe just someplace you want to go?
If you have any ideas, feel free to let me know.

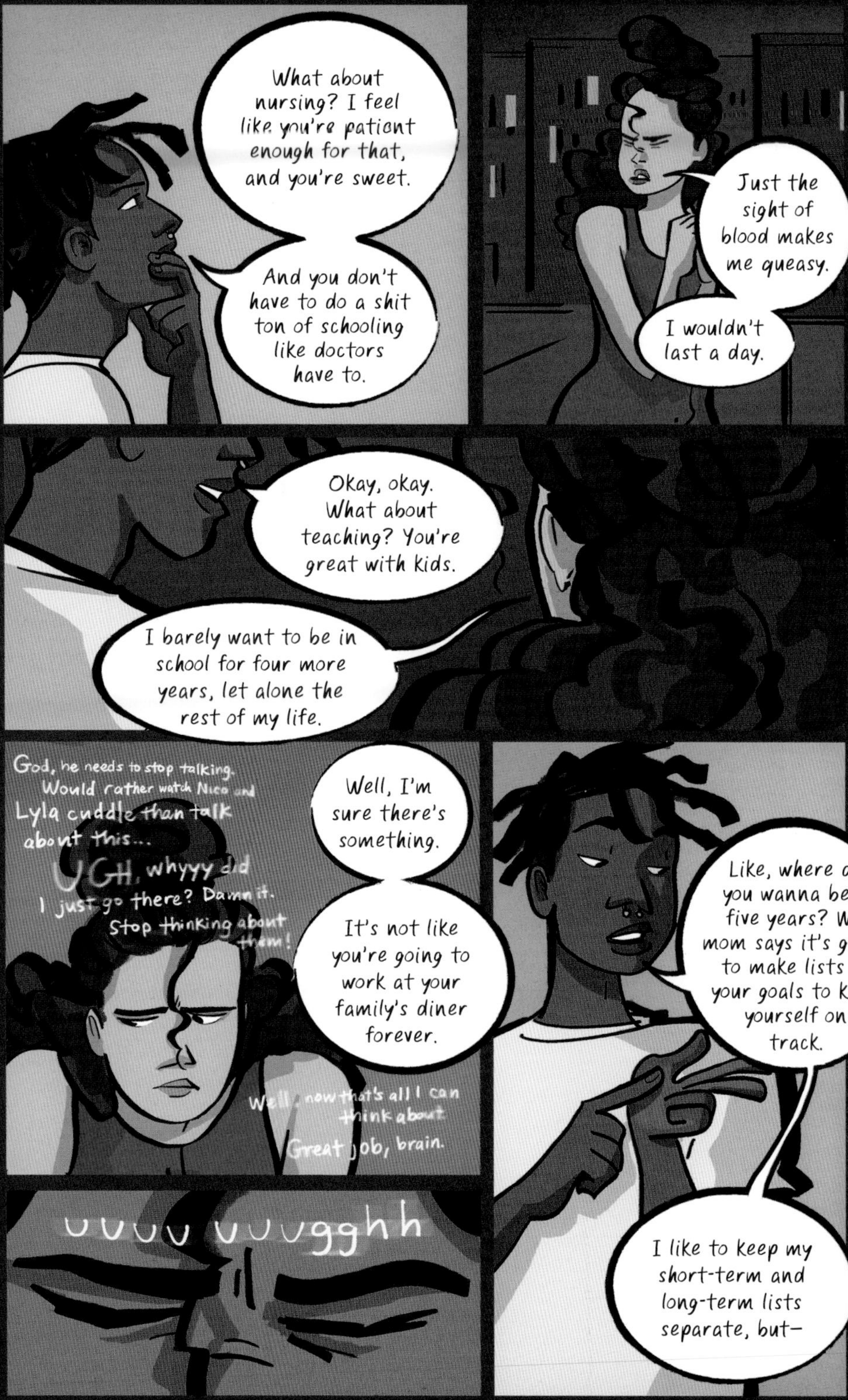
What about nursing? I feel like you're patient enough for that, and you're sweet.
And you don't have to do a shit ton of schooling like doctors have to.
Just the sight of blood makes me queasy.
I wouldn't last a day.
Okay, okay. What about teaching? You're great with kids.
I barely want to be in school for four more years, let alone the rest of my life.
God, he needs to stop talking. Would rather watch Nico and Lyla cuddle than talk about this...
UGH, whyyy did I just go there? Damn it. Stop thinking about them!
Well, I'm sure there's something.
It's not like you're going to work at your family's diner forever.
Well, now that's all I can think about.
Great job, brain.
uuuu uuugghh
Like, where do you wanna be in five years? My mom says it's great to make lists of your goals to keep yourself on track.
I like to keep my short-term and long-term lists separate, but—

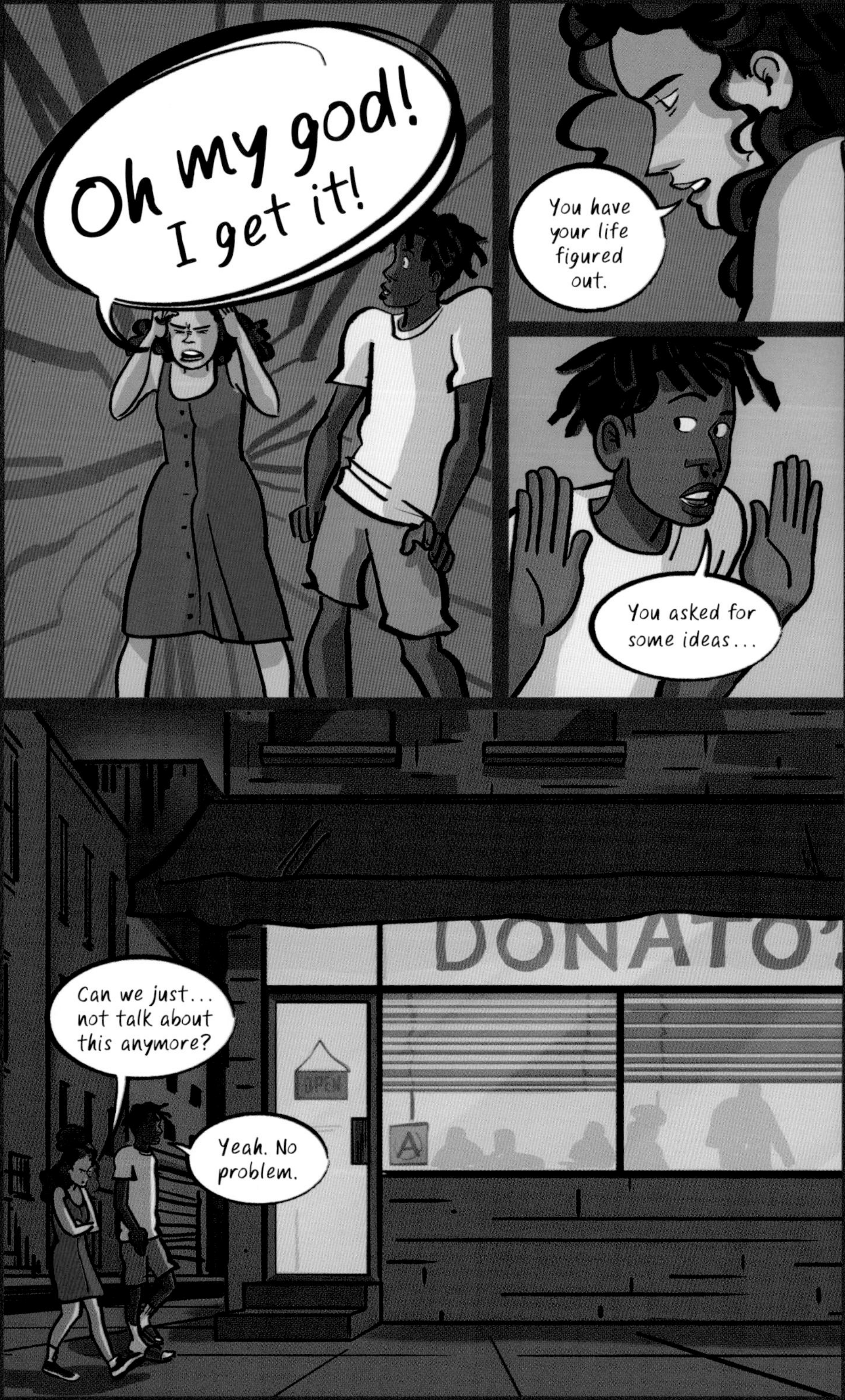
Oh my god! I get it!
You have your life figured out.
You asked for some ideas...
DONATO'
OPEN
A
Can we just... not talk about this anymore?
Yeah. No problem.

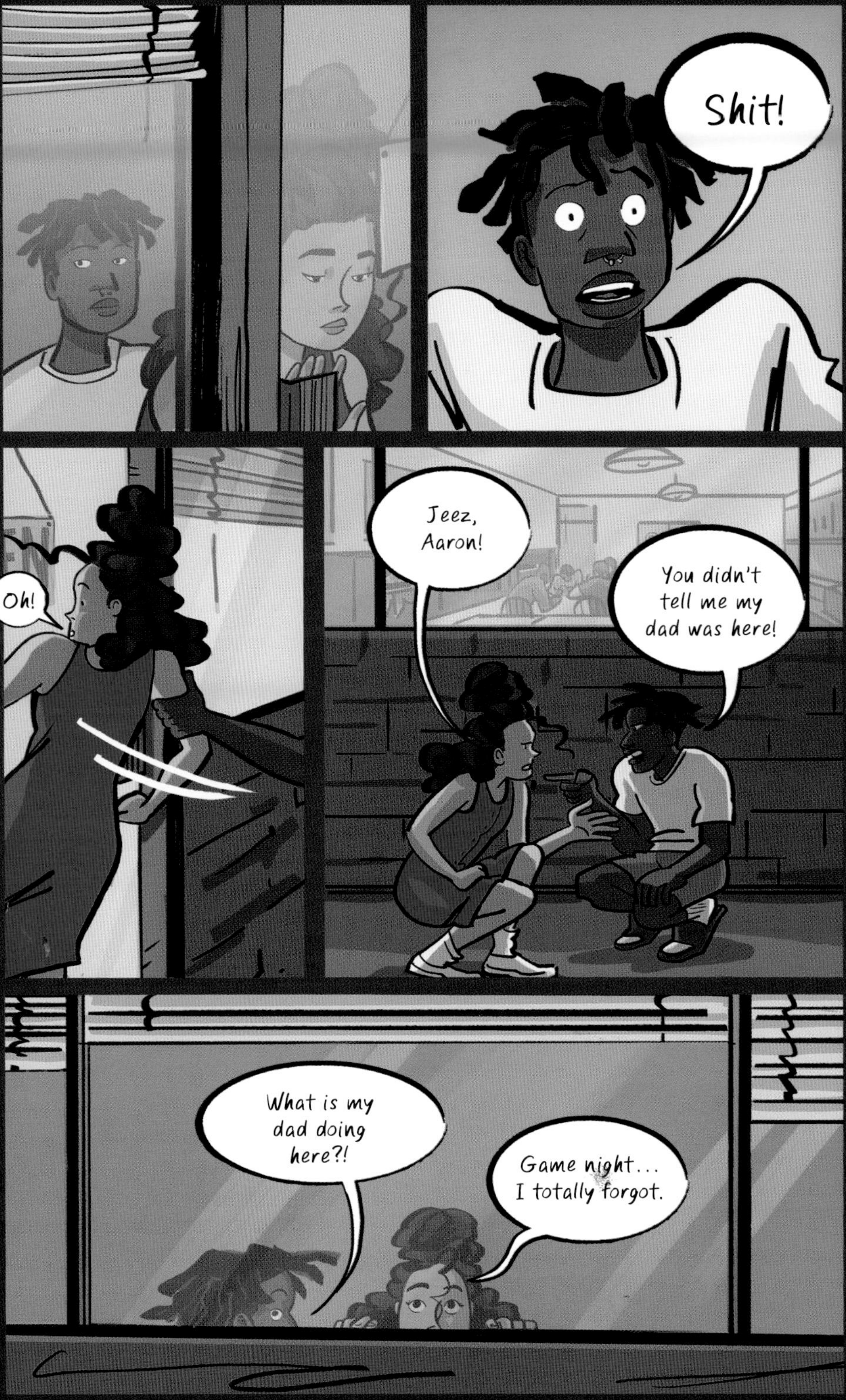
Shit!
Oh!
Jeez, Aaron!
You didn't tell me my dad was here!
What is my dad doing here?!
Game night... I totally forgot.

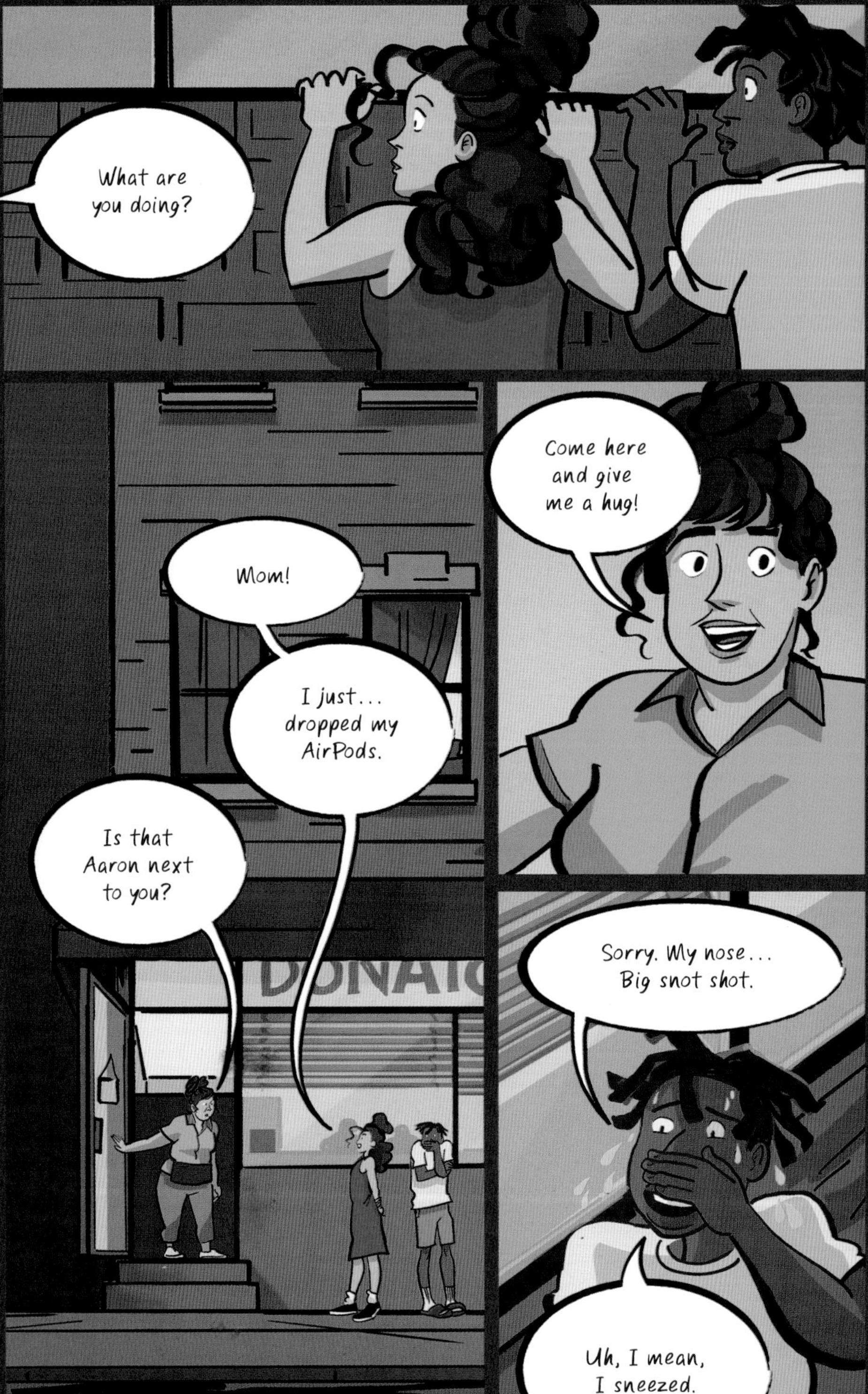
What are you doing?
Come here and give me a hug!
Mom!
I just... dropped my AirPods.
Is that Aaron next to you?
DONAT
Sorry. My nose... Big snot shot.
Uh, I mean, I sneezed.

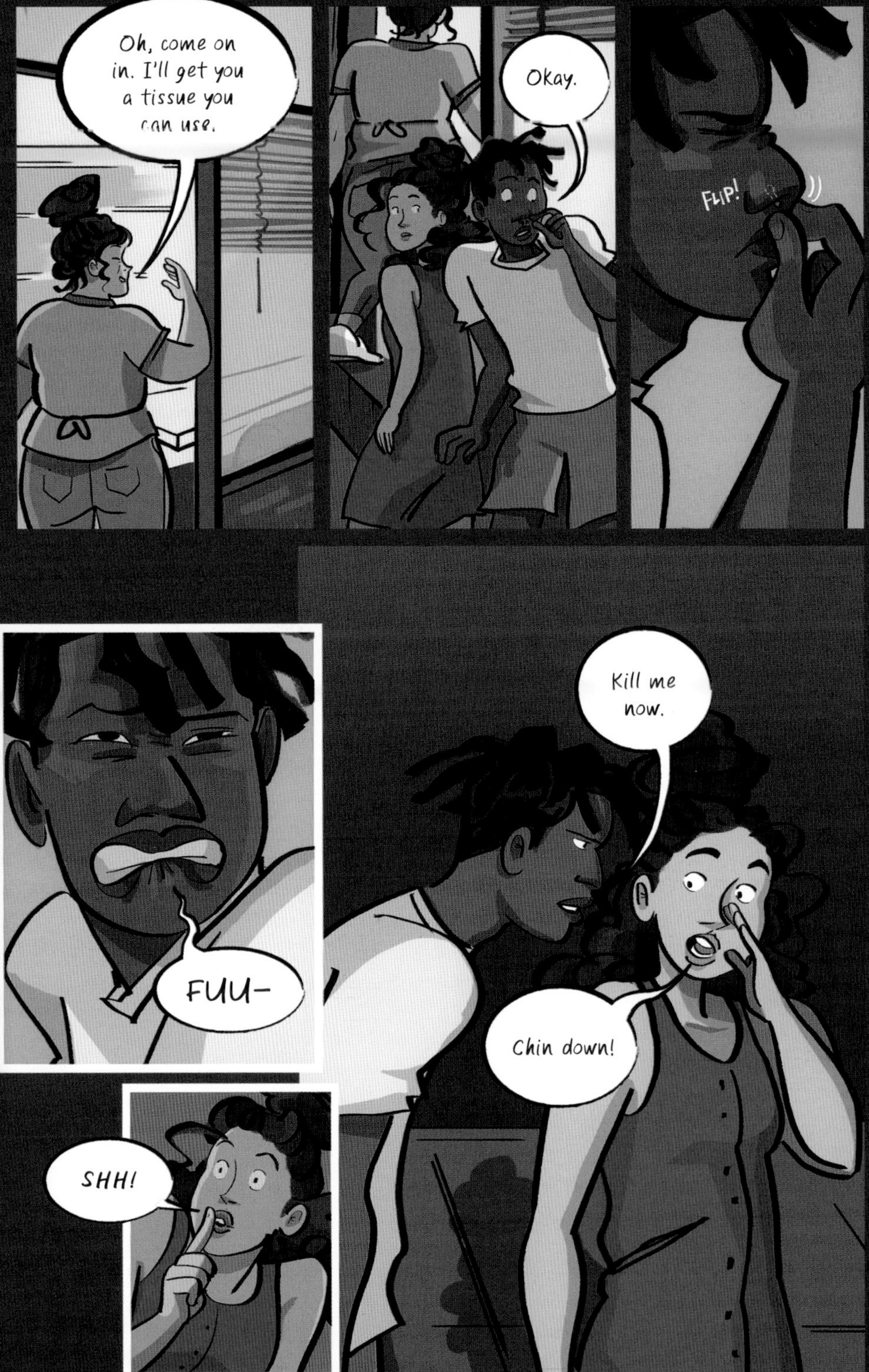

Oh, come on in. I'll get you a tissue you can use.
Okay.
FLIP!
FUU-
Kill me now.
Chin down!
SHH!

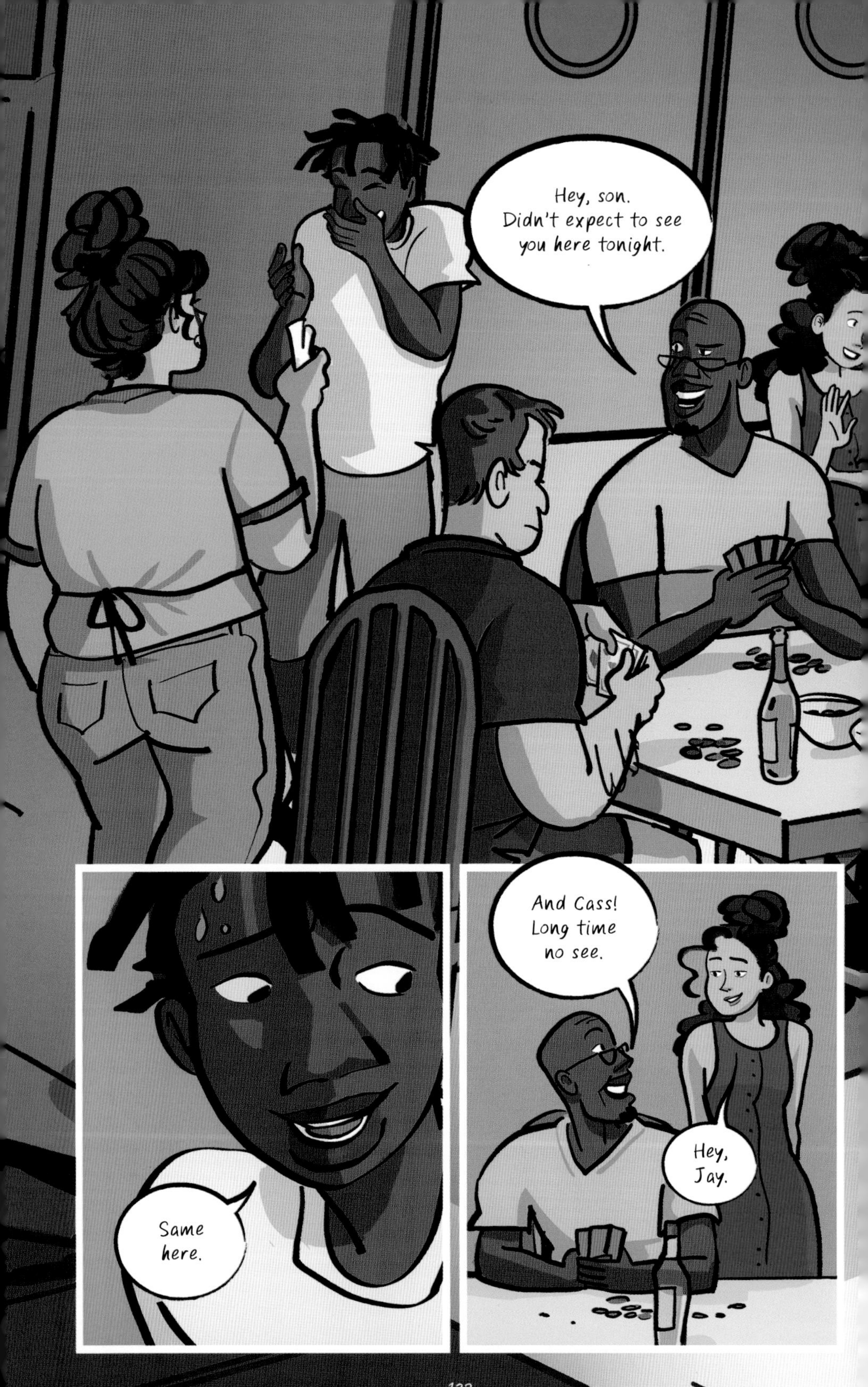
Hey, son.
Didn't expect to see
you here tonight.
Same
here.
And Cass!
Long time
no see.
Hey,
Jay.

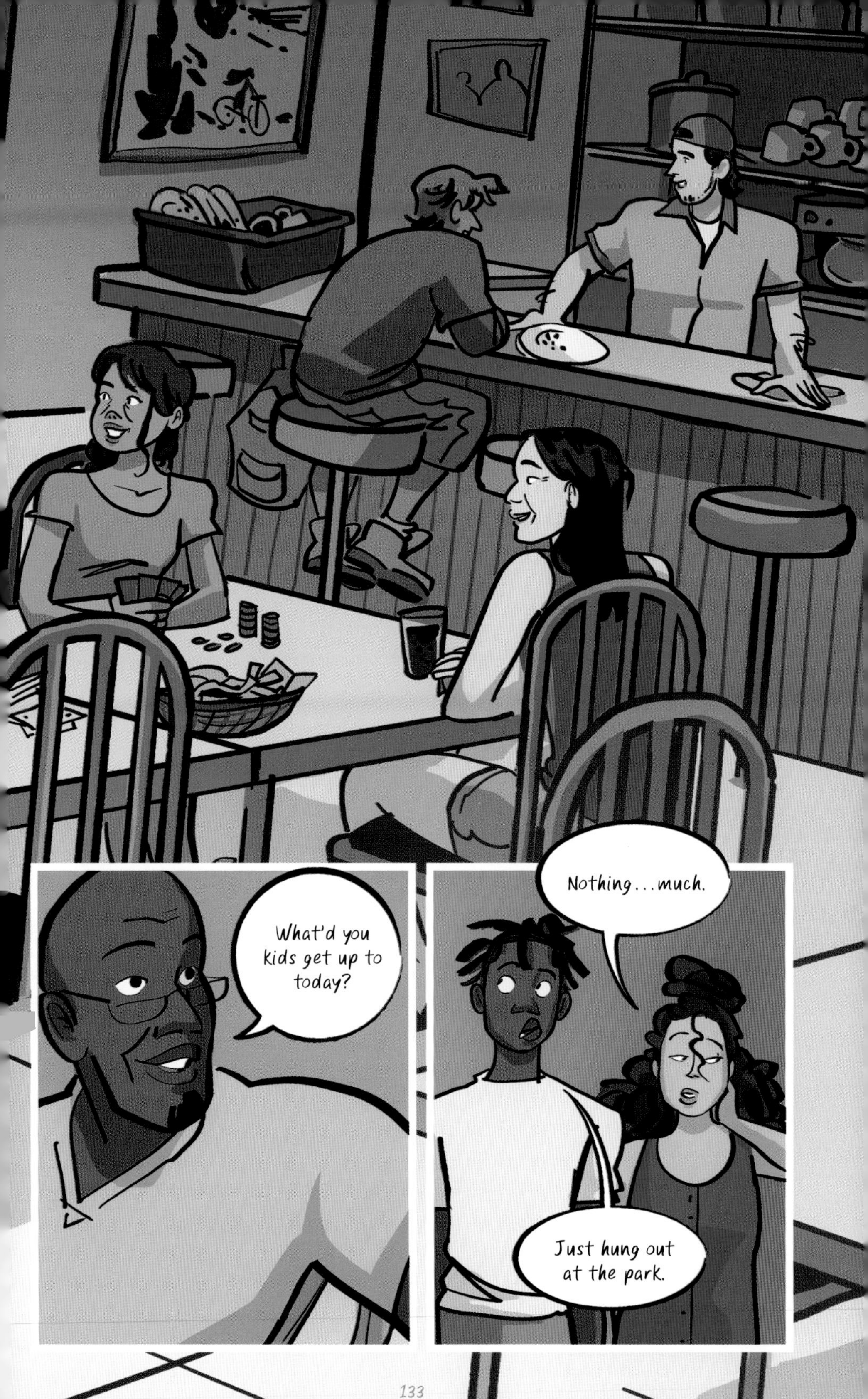
What'd you kids get up to today?
Nothing...much.
Just hung out at the park.

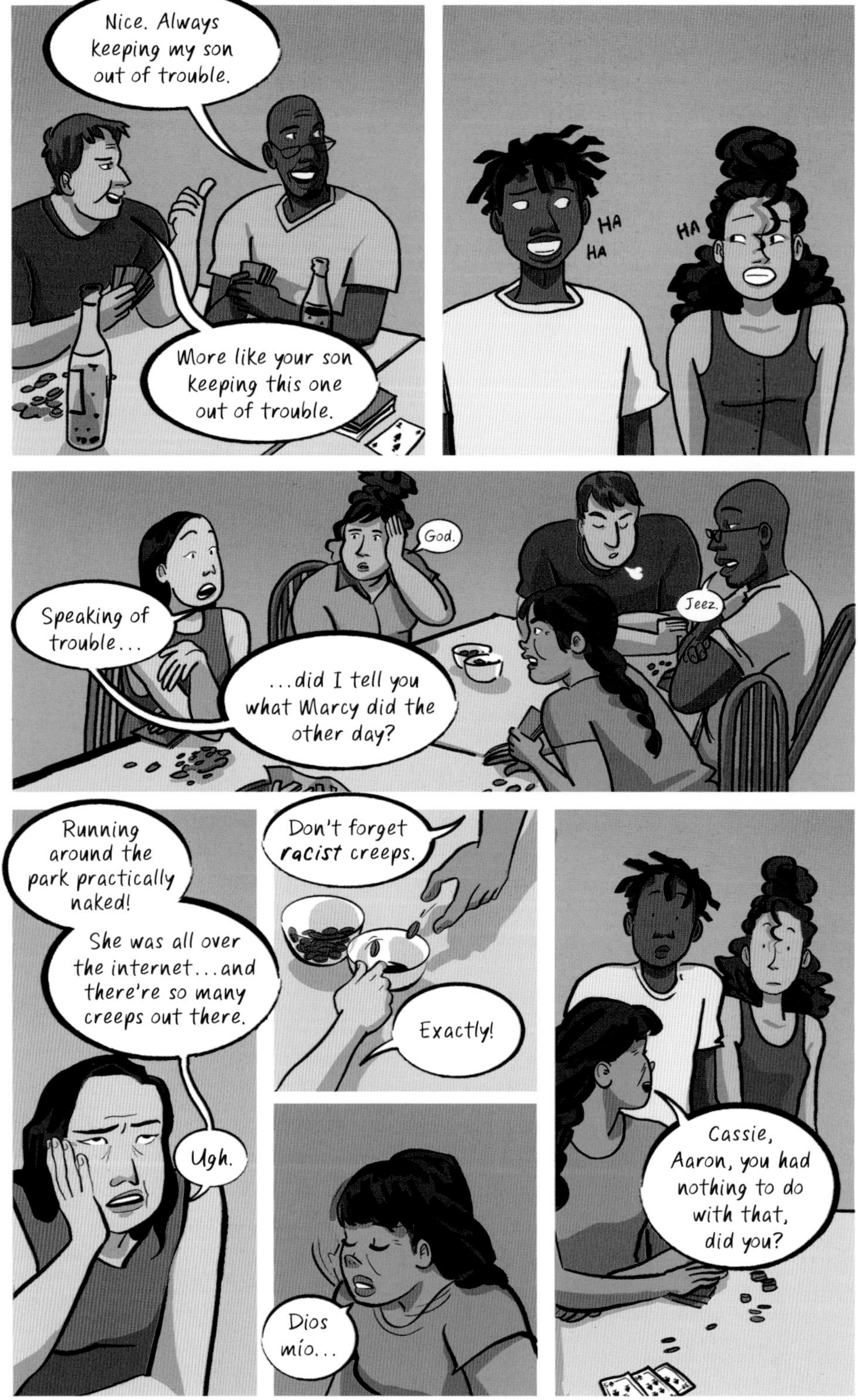
Nice. Always keeping my son out of trouble.
More like your son keeping this one out of trouble.
HA
HA
HA
Speaking of trouble...
God.
Jeez.
...did I tell you what Marcy did the other day?
Running around the park practically naked!
She was all over the internet...and there're so many creeps out there.
Ugh.
Don't forget *racist* creeps.
Exactly!
Dios mío...
Cassie, Aaron, you had nothing to do with that, did you?

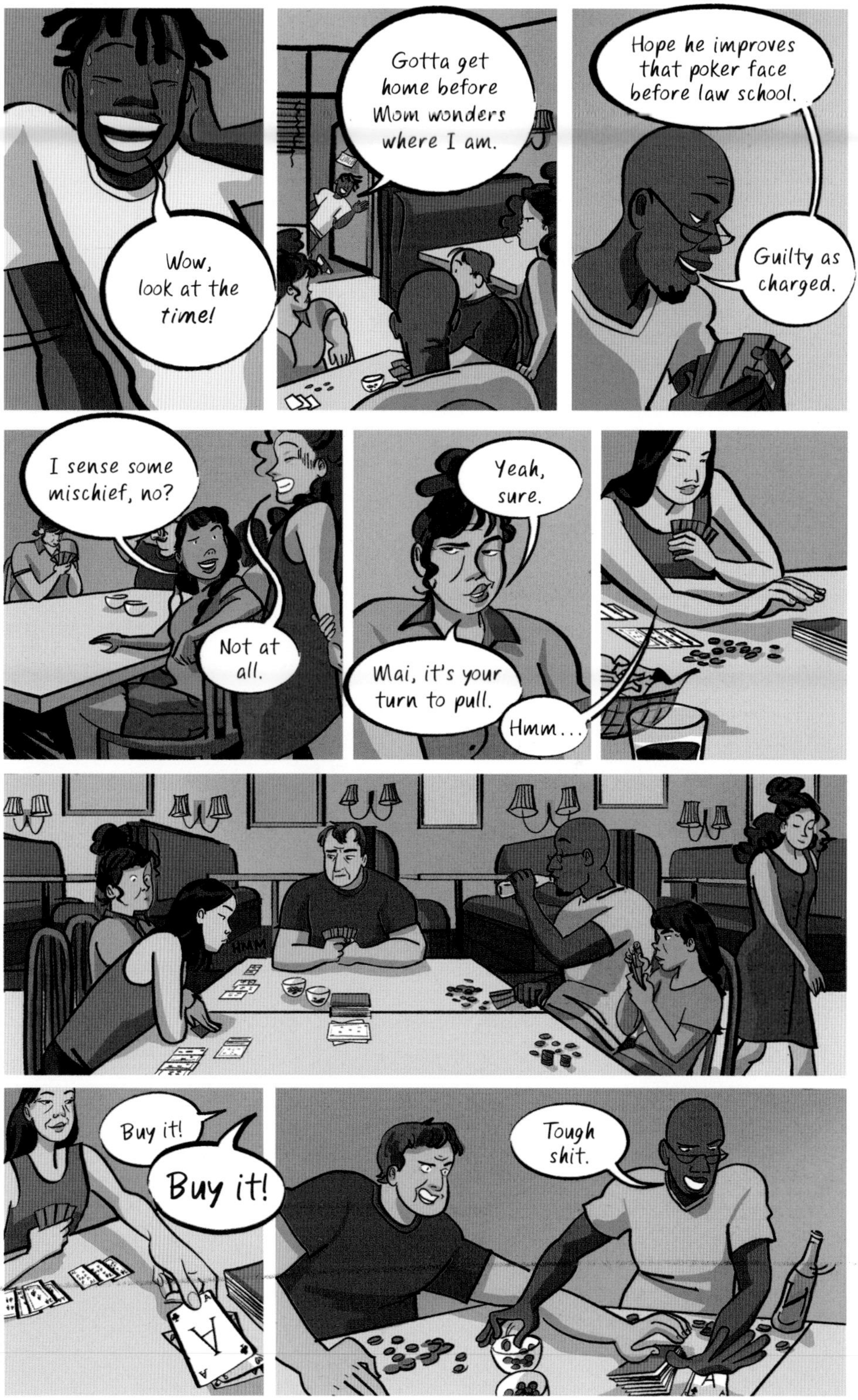
Wow, look at the *time!*
Gotta get home before Mom wonders where I am.
Hope he improves that poker face before law school.
Guilty as charged.
I sense some mischief, no?
Not at all.
Yeah, sure.
Mai, it's your turn to pull.
Hmm...
HMM
Buy it!
Buy it!
Tough shit.

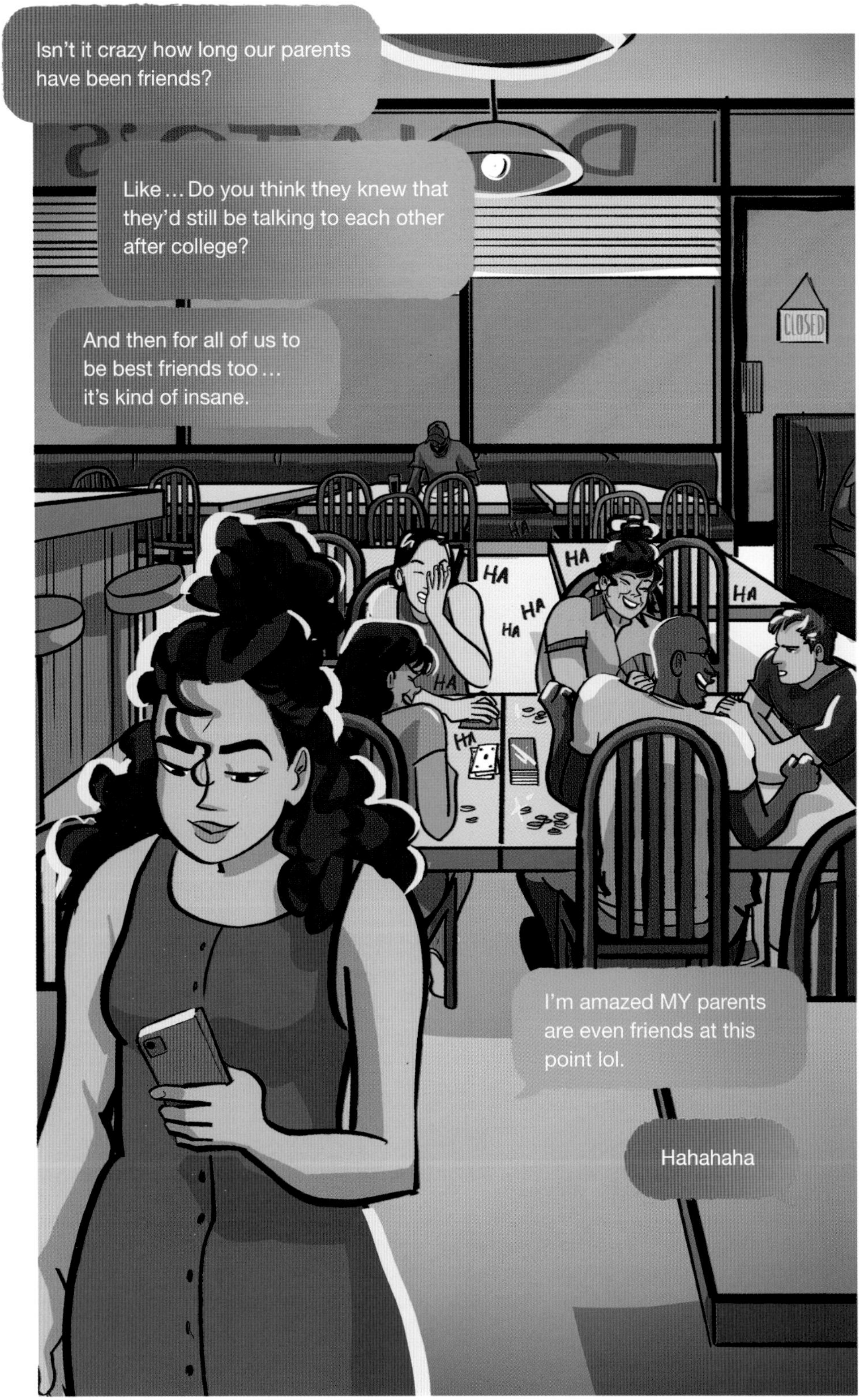
Isn't it crazy how long our parents have been friends?
Like … Do you think they knew that they'd still be talking to each other after college?
And then for all of us to be best friends too … it's kind of insane.
CLOSED
HA
HA
HA
HA
HA
HA
HA
I'm amazed MY parents are even friends at this point lol.
Hahahaha

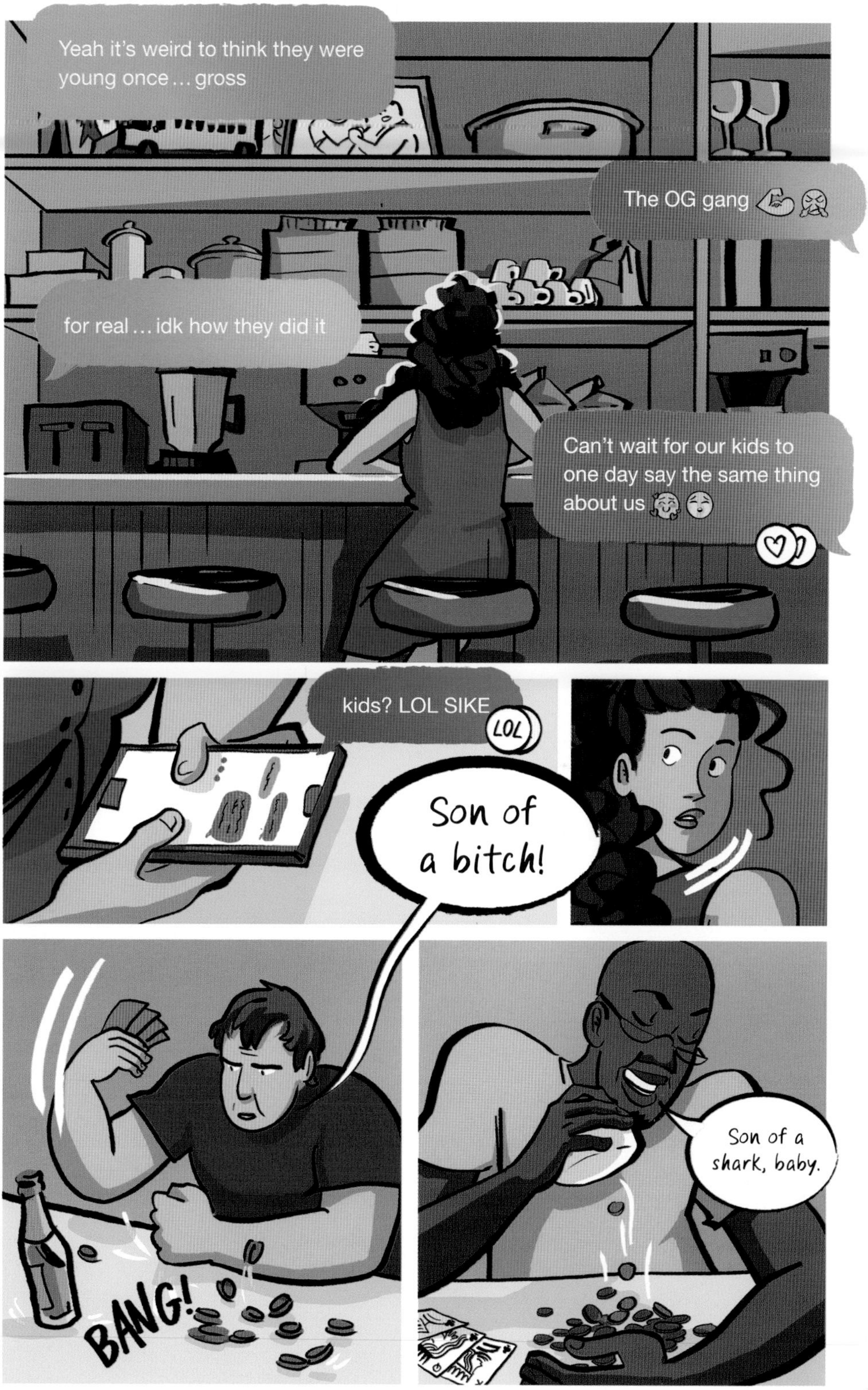
Yeah it's weird to think they were young once... gross
The OG gang
for real... idk how they did it
Can't wait for our kids to one day say the same thing about us
kids? LOL SIKE
LOL
Son of a bitch!
BANG!
Son of a shark, baby.

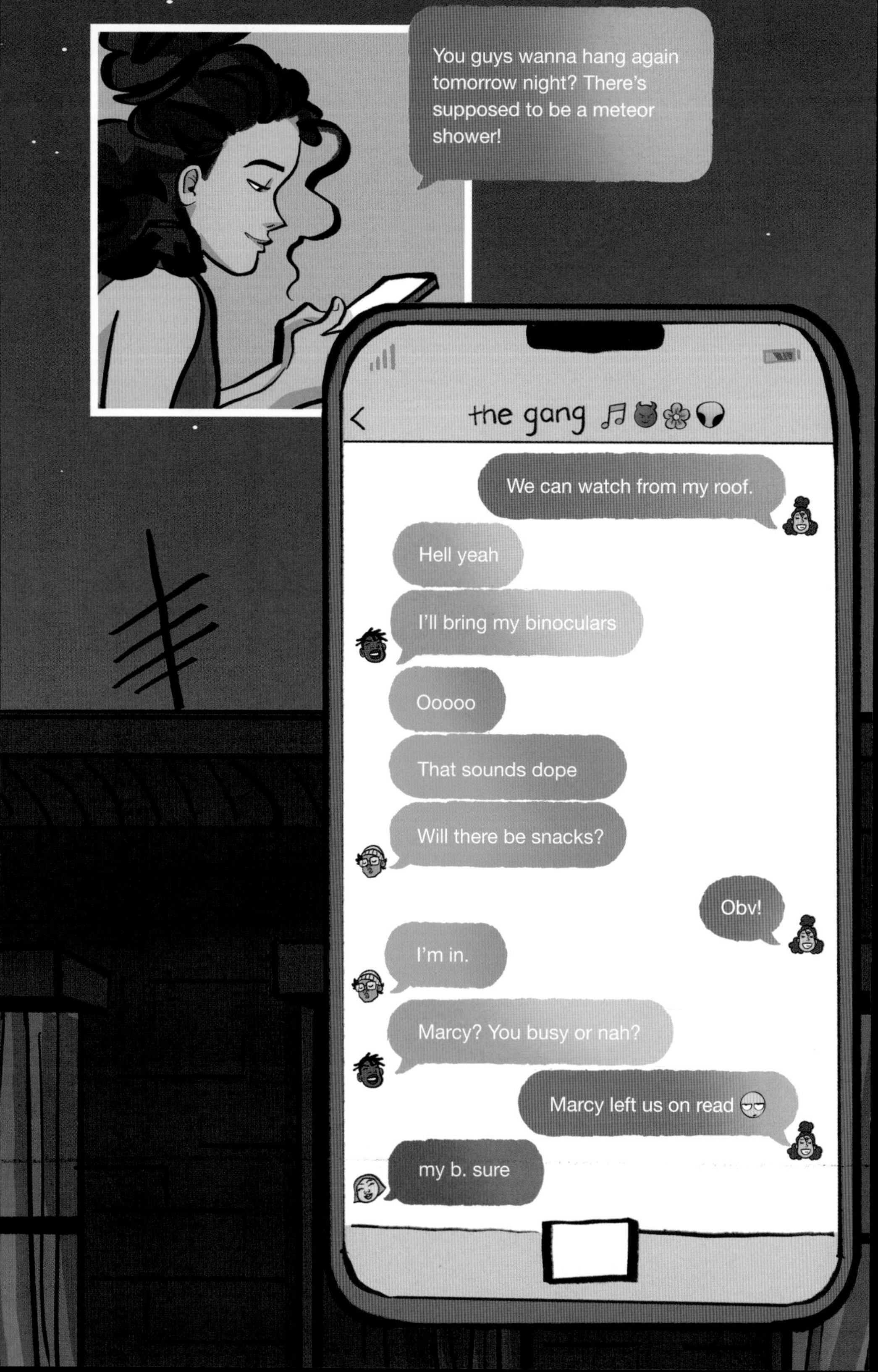
You guys wanna hang again tomorrow night? There's supposed to be a meteor shower!
the gang
We can watch from my roof.
Hell yeah
I'll bring my binoculars
Ooooo
That sounds dope
Will there be snacks?
Obv!
I'm in.
Marcy? You busy or nah?
Marcy left us on read
my b. sure

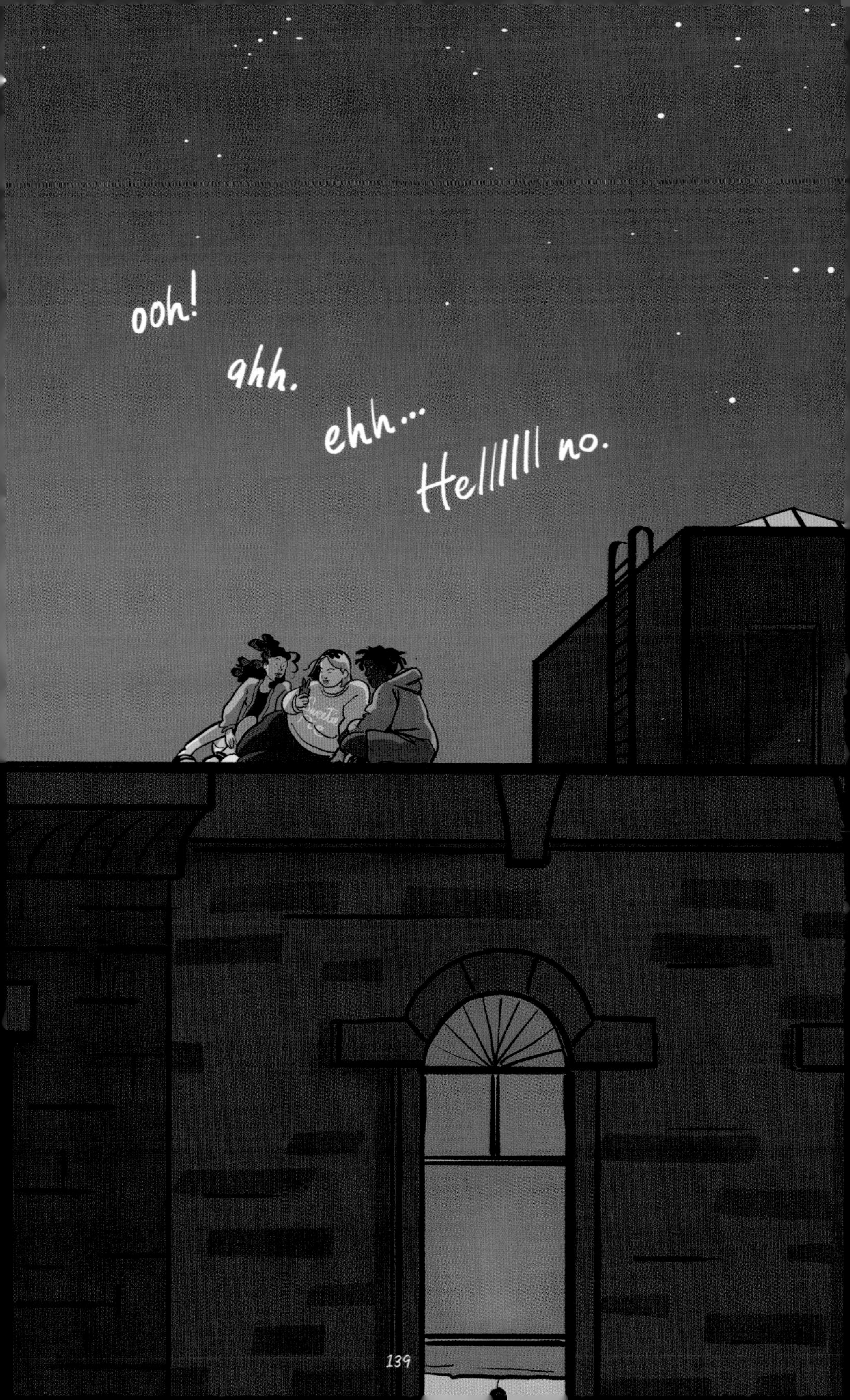
ooh!
ahh.
ehh...
Hellllll no.

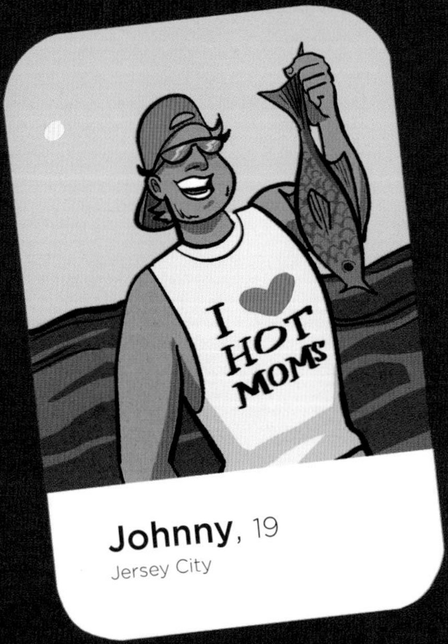
I ♥ HOT MOMS
Johnny, 19
Jersey City

He seems kind of cool.

I'm a little offended that you think he and I are of the same caliber.

Don't judge a book by its cover!

You know what they say about small fish...

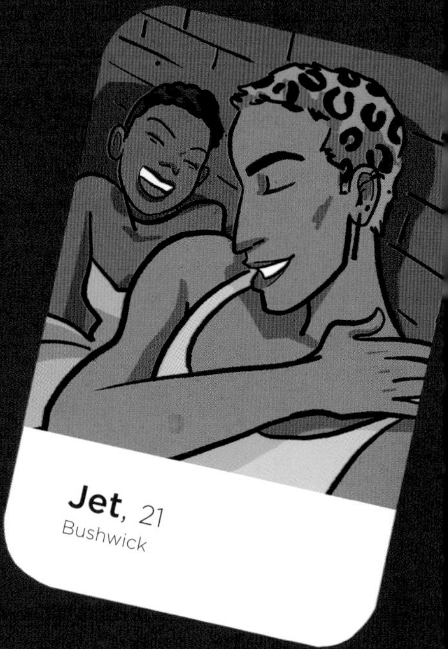
Jet, 21
Bushwick

Ooo, I like this one. How about him?

Ehhh, I don't know. I think he's a li'l too femme for me.

What's wrong with femme men?

Nothing! Just not my type.

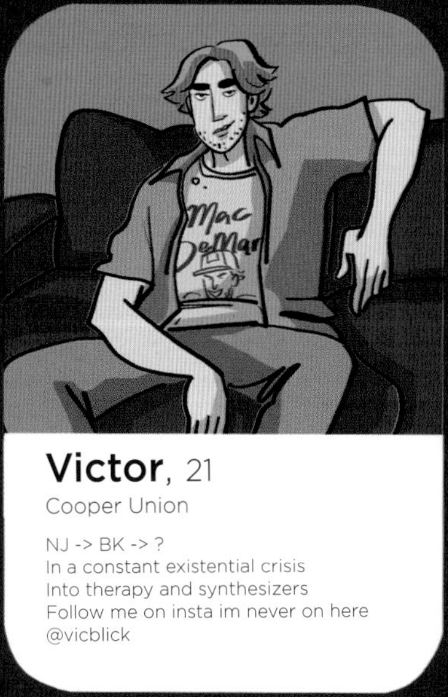
Mac DeMarco
Victor, 21
Cooper Union
NJ -> BK -> ?
In a constant existential crisis
Into therapy and synthesizers
Follow me on insta im never on here
@vicblick

Hmmm.

Are you serious? *That* is doing it for you?

Maybe it is.

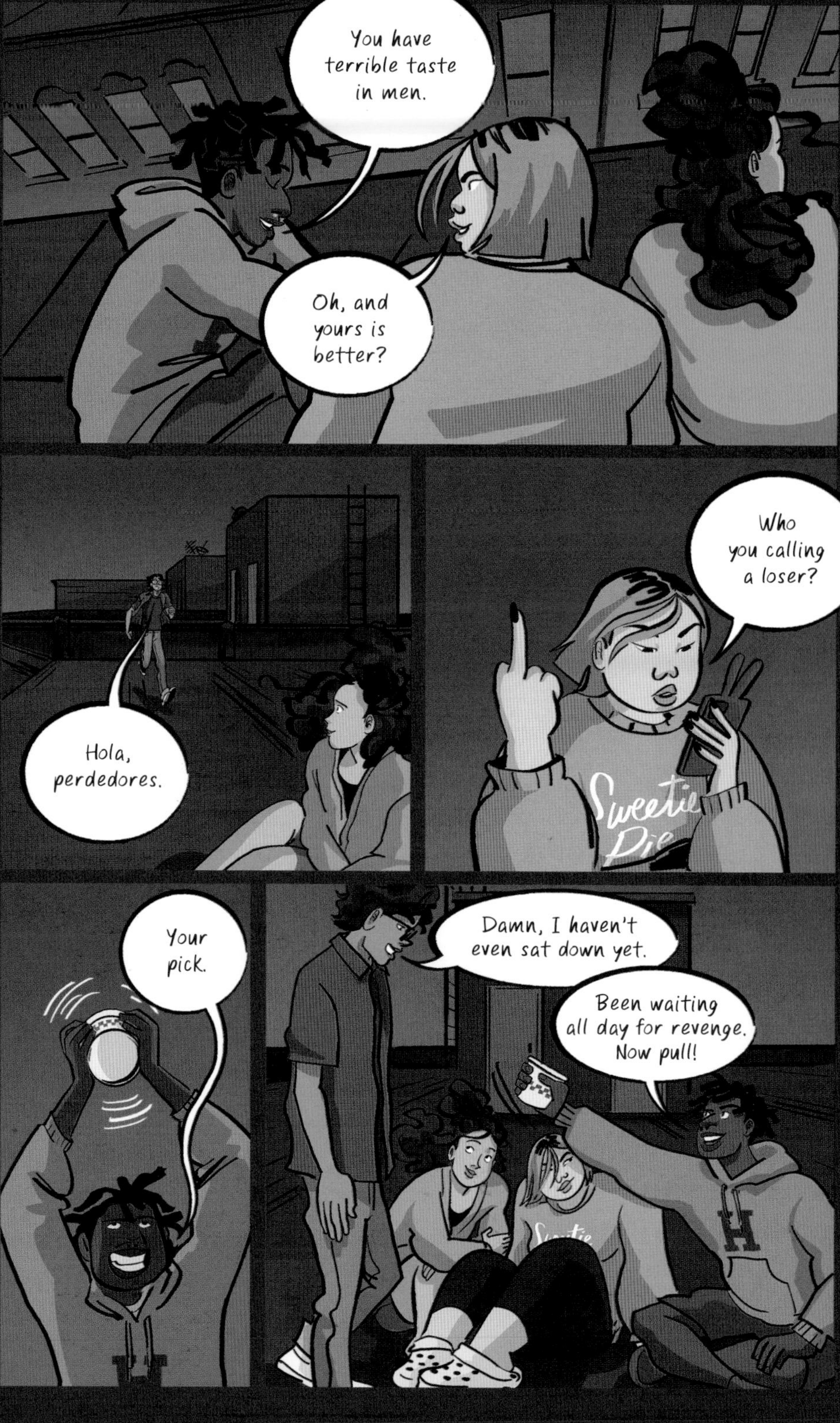
You have terrible taste in men.
Oh, and yours is better?
Hola, perdedores.
Who you calling a loser?
Sweetie Pie
Your pick.
Damn, I haven't even sat down yet.
Been waiting all day for revenge. Now pull!

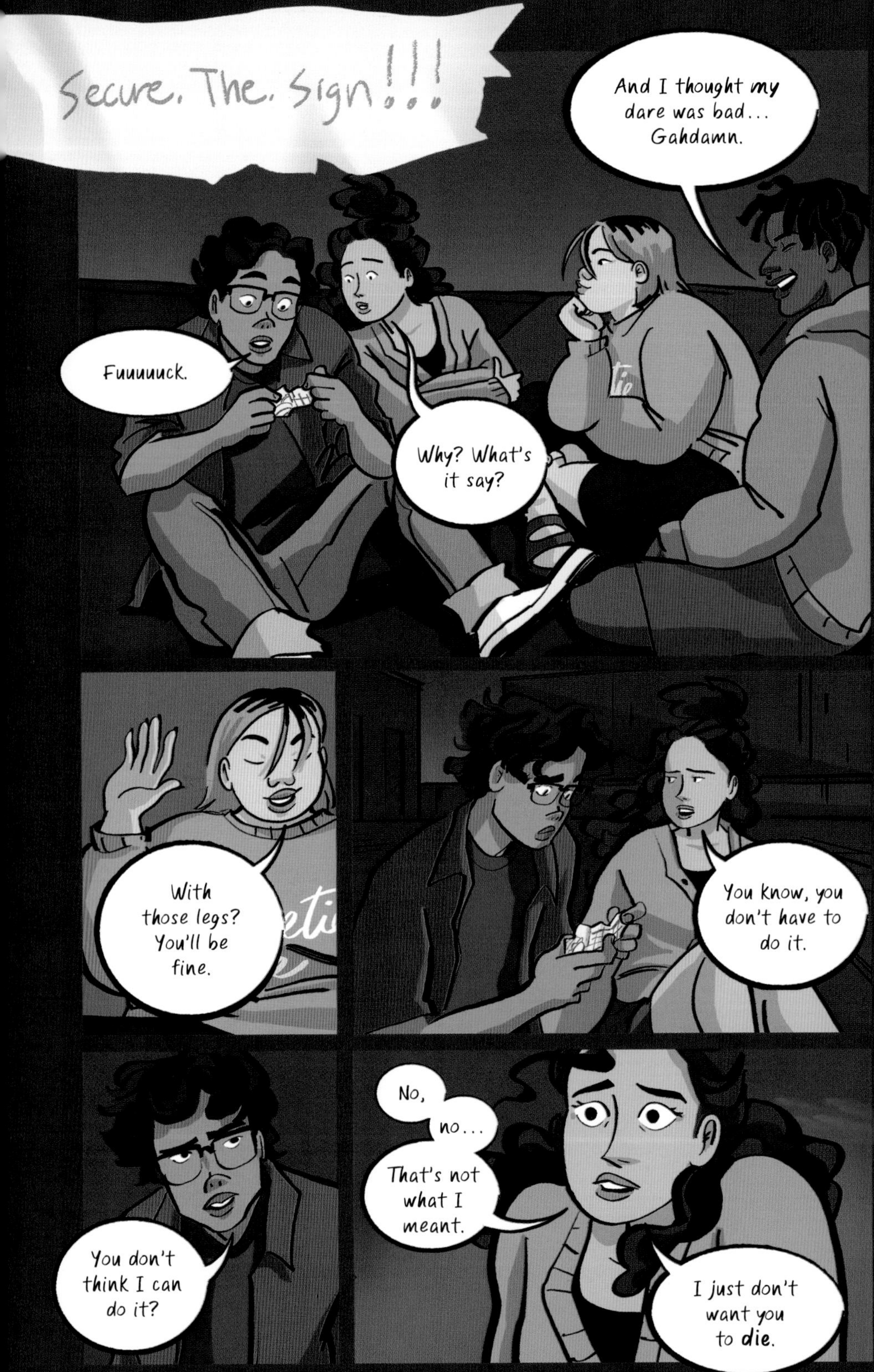
Secure. The. Sign!!!
And I thought my dare was bad... Gahdamn.
Fuuuuuck.
Why? What's it say?
With those legs? You'll be fine.
You know, you don't have to do it.
You don't think I can do it?
No,
no...
That's not what I meant.
I just don't want you to die.

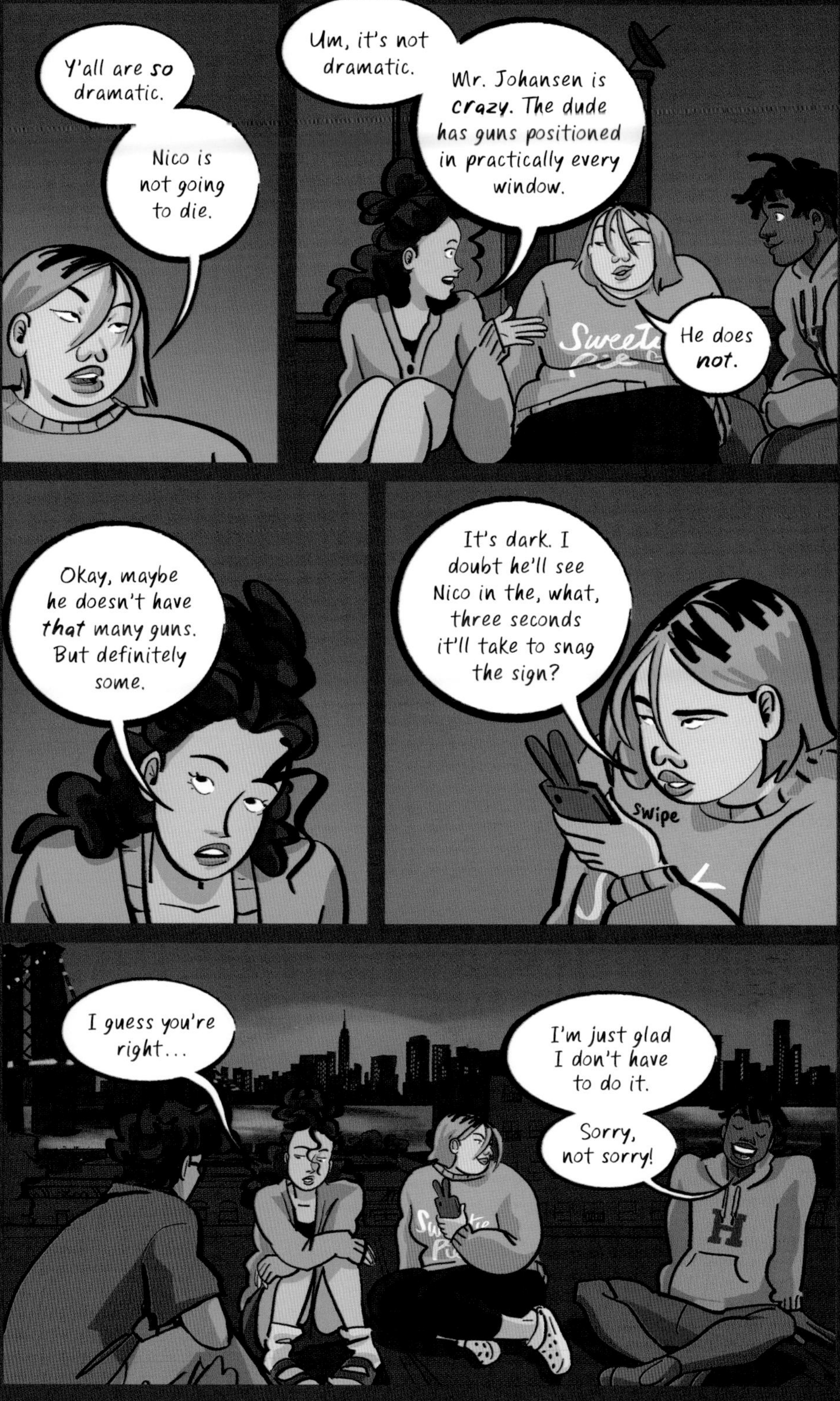
Y'all are so dramatic.
Nico is not going to die.
Um, it's not dramatic.
Mr. Johansen is crazy. The dude has guns positioned in practically every window.
He does not.
Okay, maybe he doesn't have that many guns. But definitely some.
It's dark. I doubt he'll see Nico in the, what, three seconds it'll take to snag the sign?
SWIPE
I guess you're right...
I'm just glad I don't have to do it.
Sorry, not sorry!

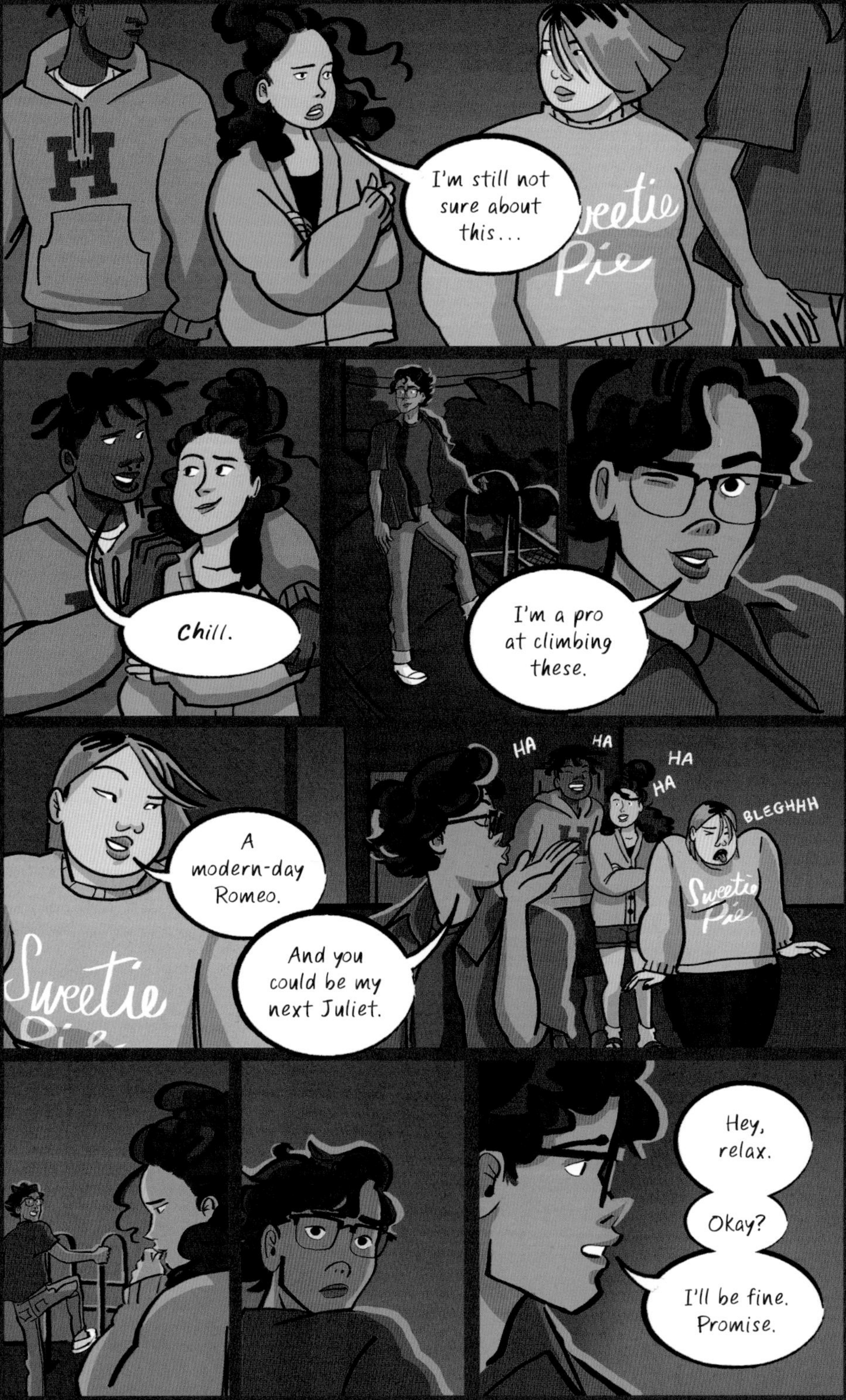
I'm still not sure about this...
Chill.
I'm a pro at climbing these.
A modern-day Romeo.
And you could be my next Juliet.
HA
HA
HA
HA
BLEGHHH
Hey, relax.
Okay?
I'll be fine. Promise.

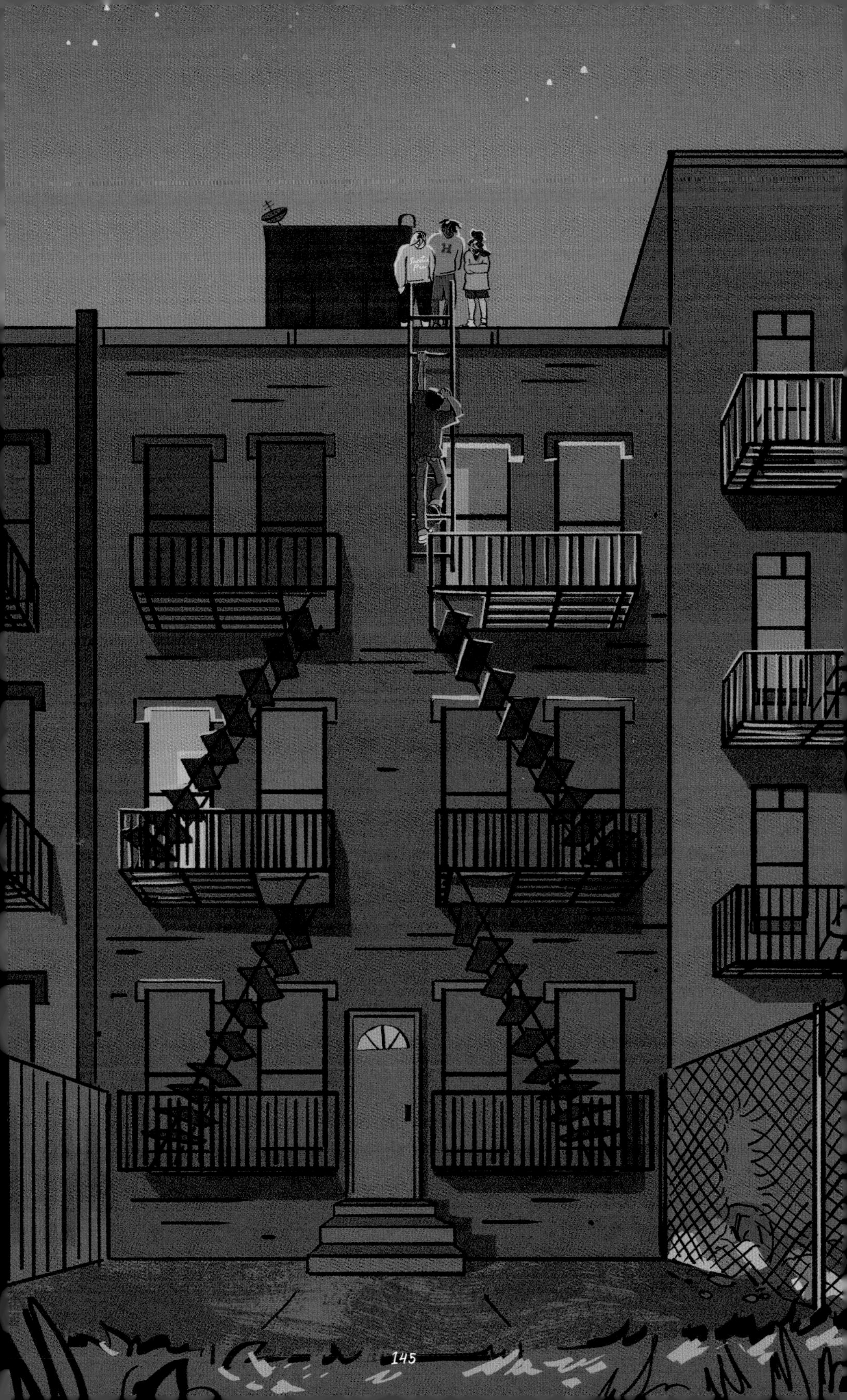

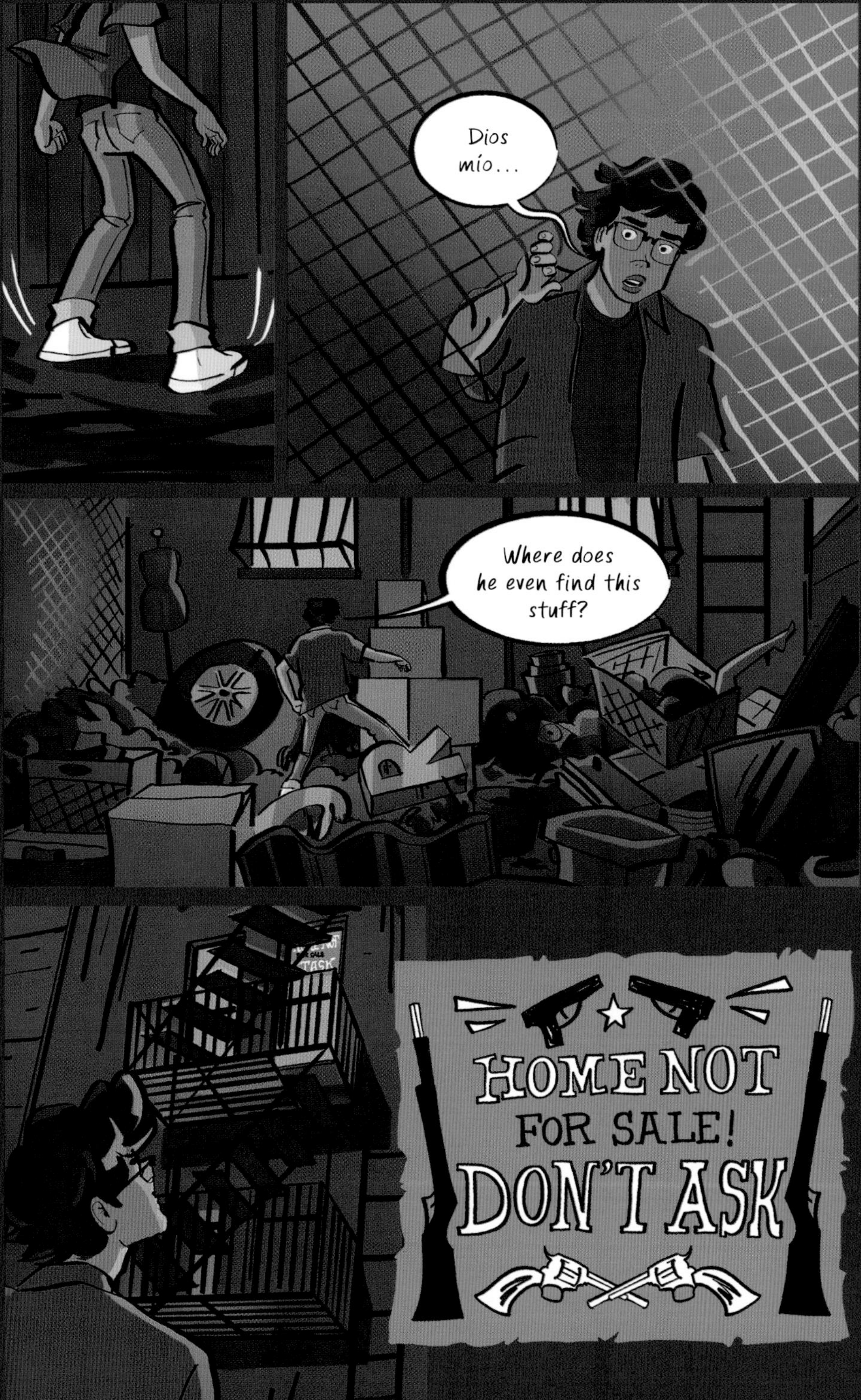
Dios mío...
Where does he even find this stuff?
HOME NOT FOR SALE! DON'T ASK

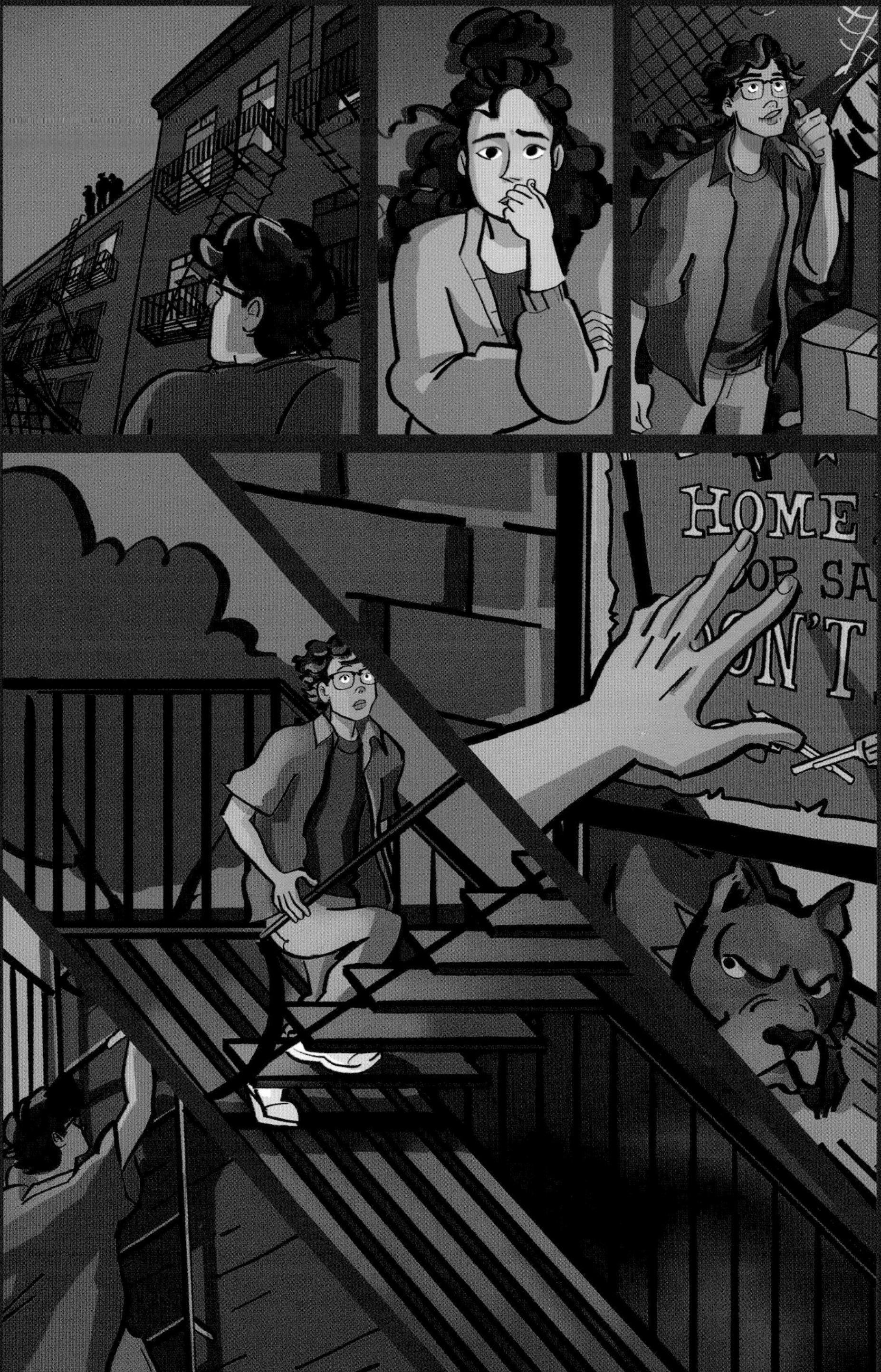
HOME

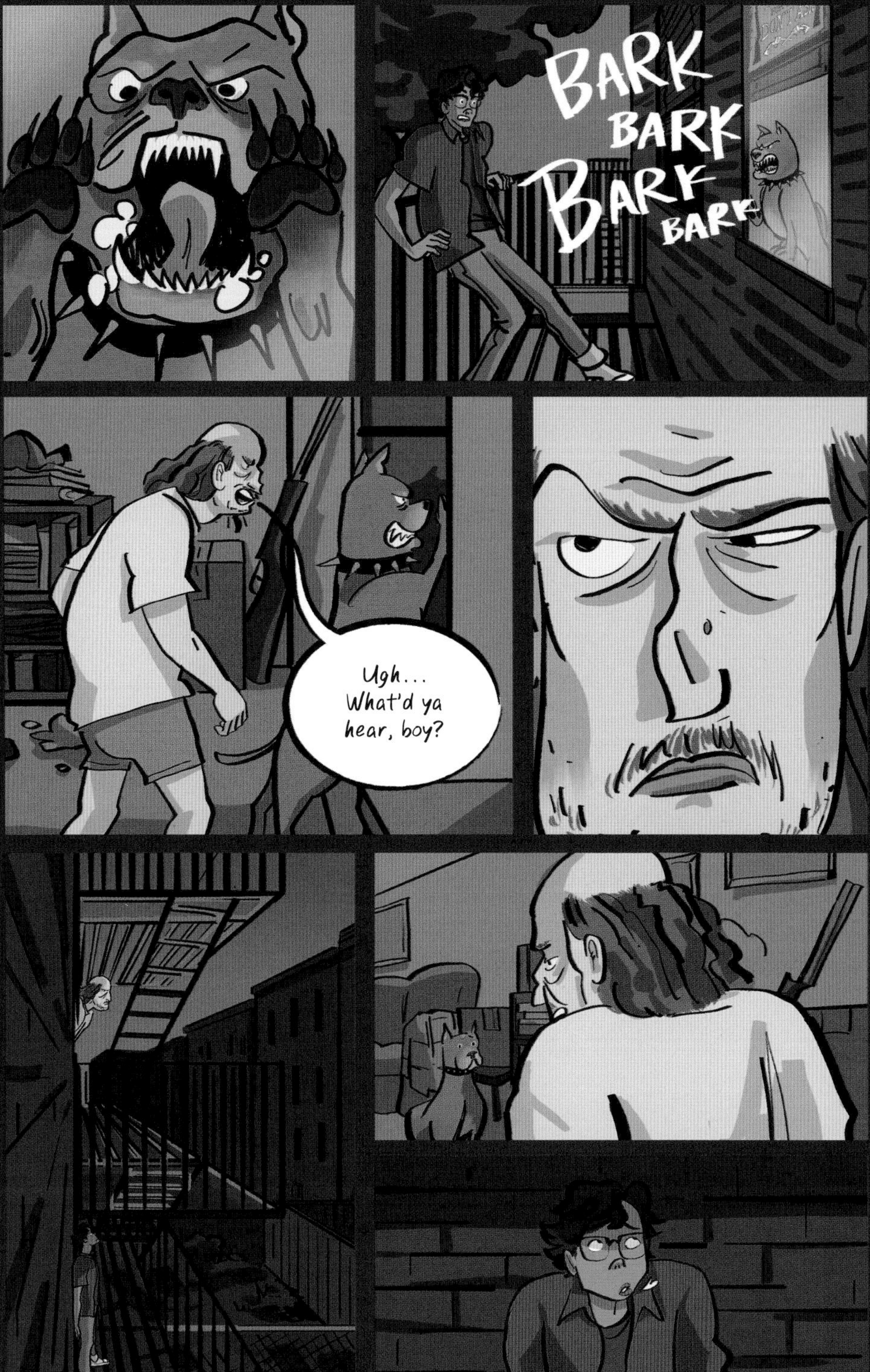
BARK
BARK
BARK
BARK
Ugh... What'd ya hear, boy?

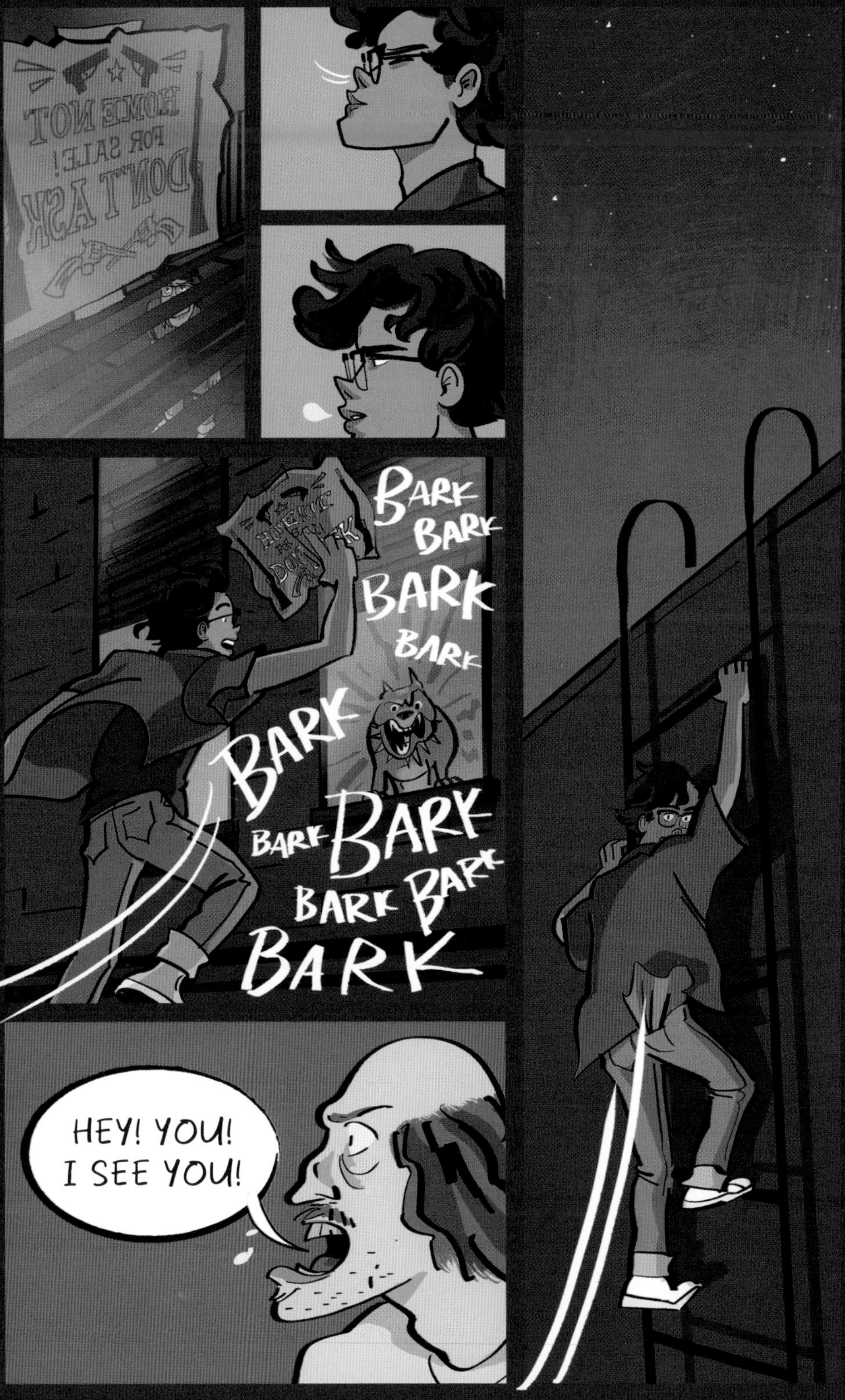
BARK
BARK
BARK
BARK
BARK
BARK BARK
BARK BARK
BARK
HEY! YOU!
I SEE YOU!

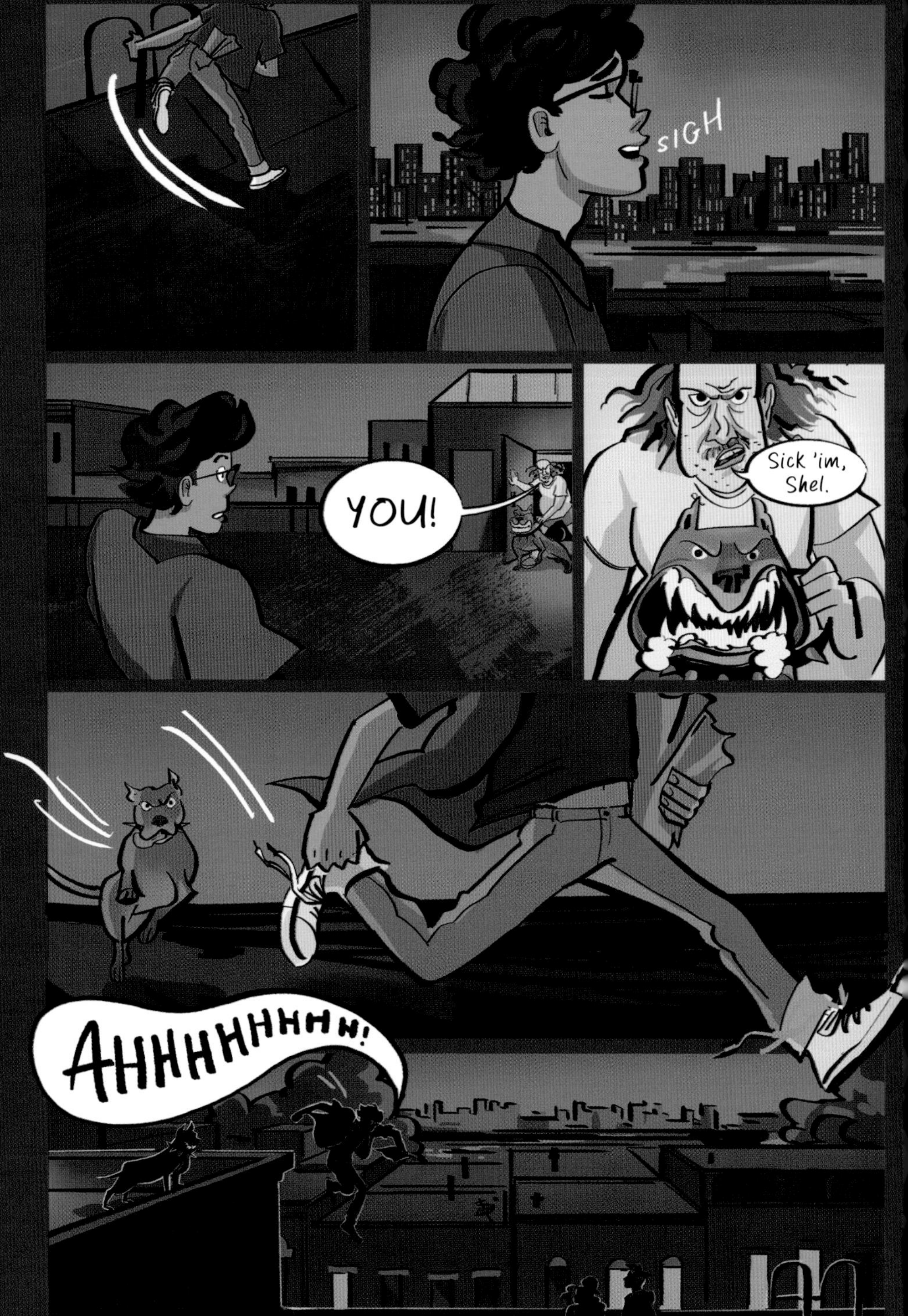
SIGH
YOU!
Sick 'im, Shel.
AHHHHHHHHH!

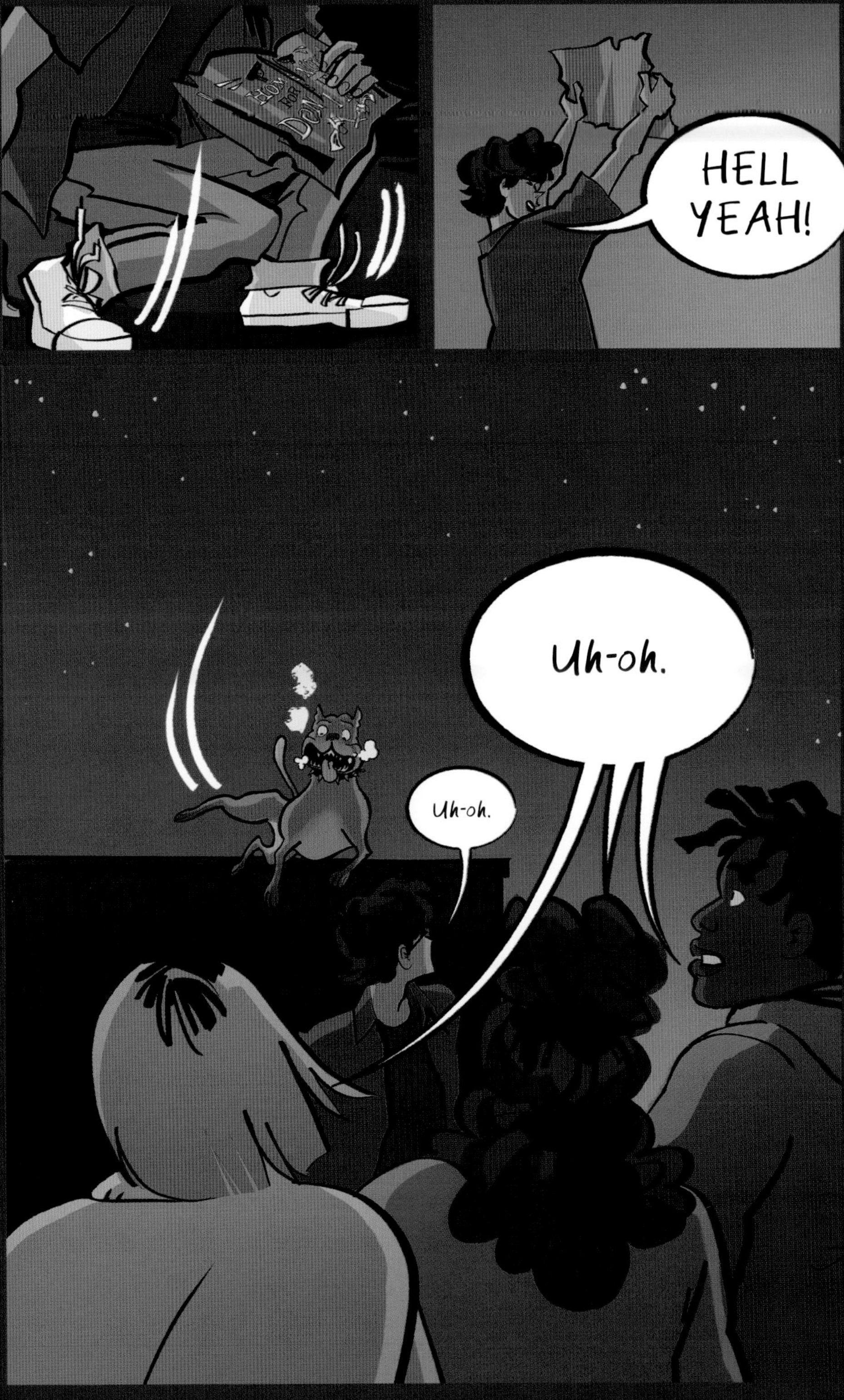
HELL YEAH!
Uh-oh.
Uh-oh.

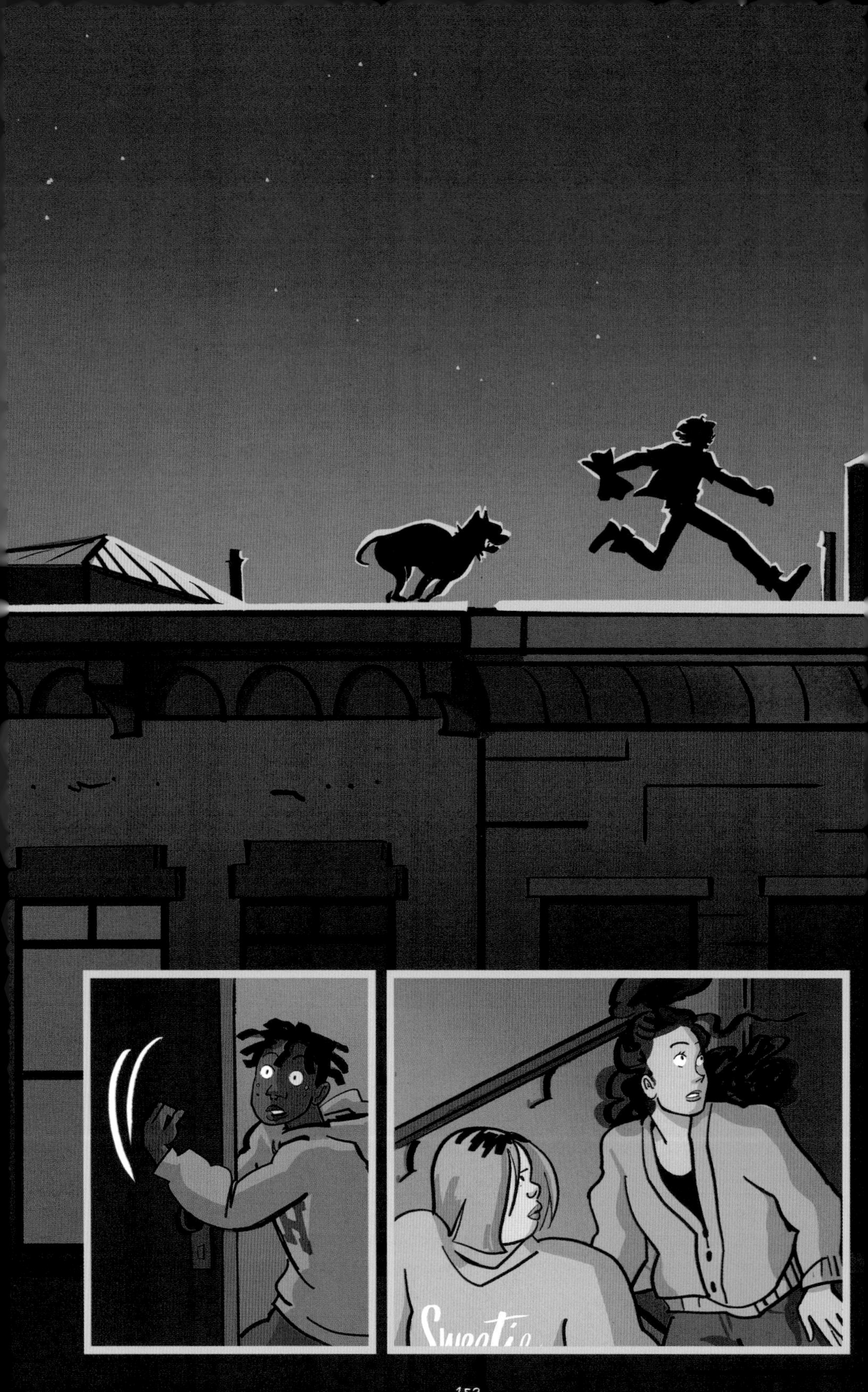

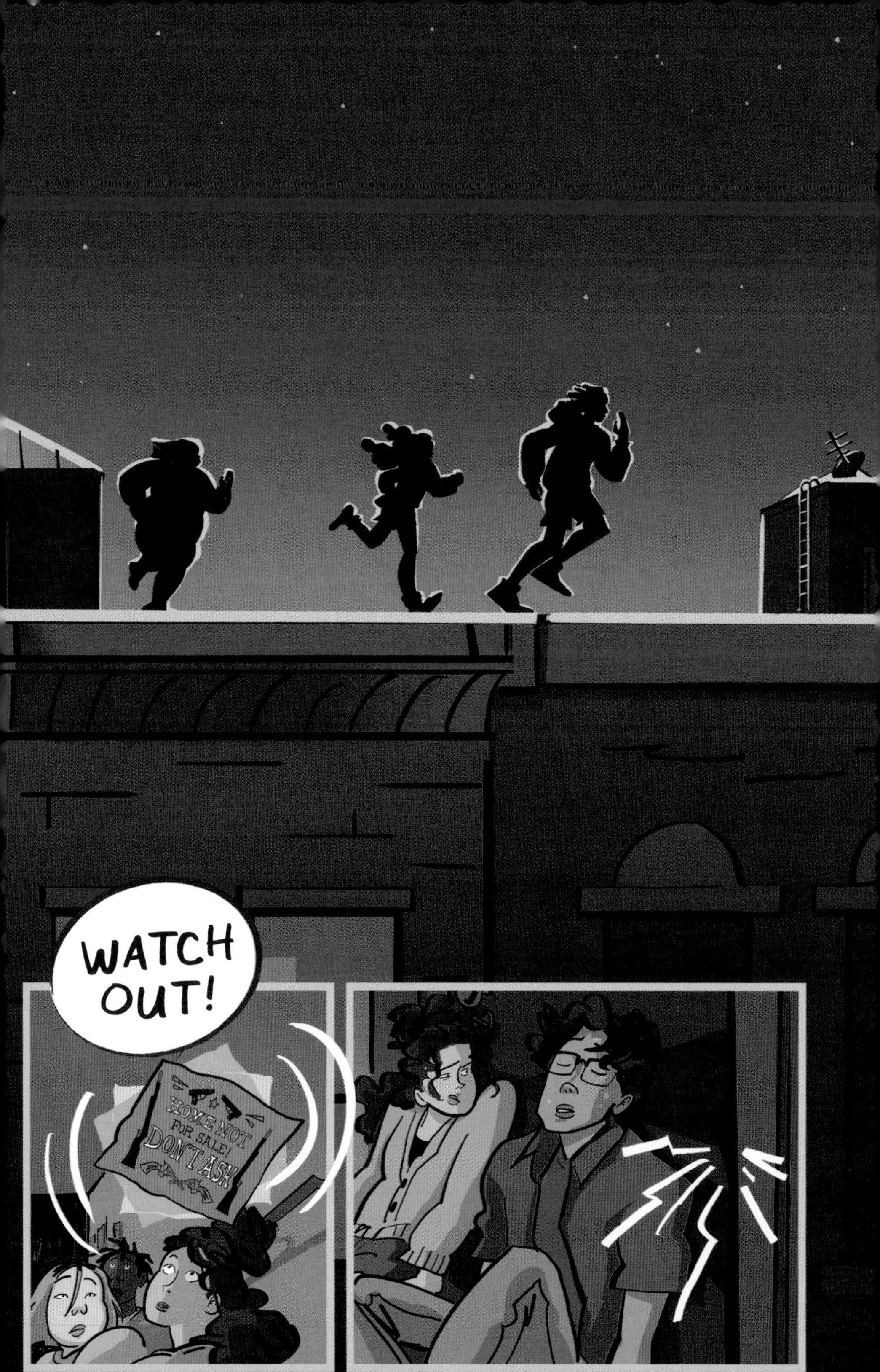
WATCH OUT!
HOME NOT FOR SALE! DON'T ASK

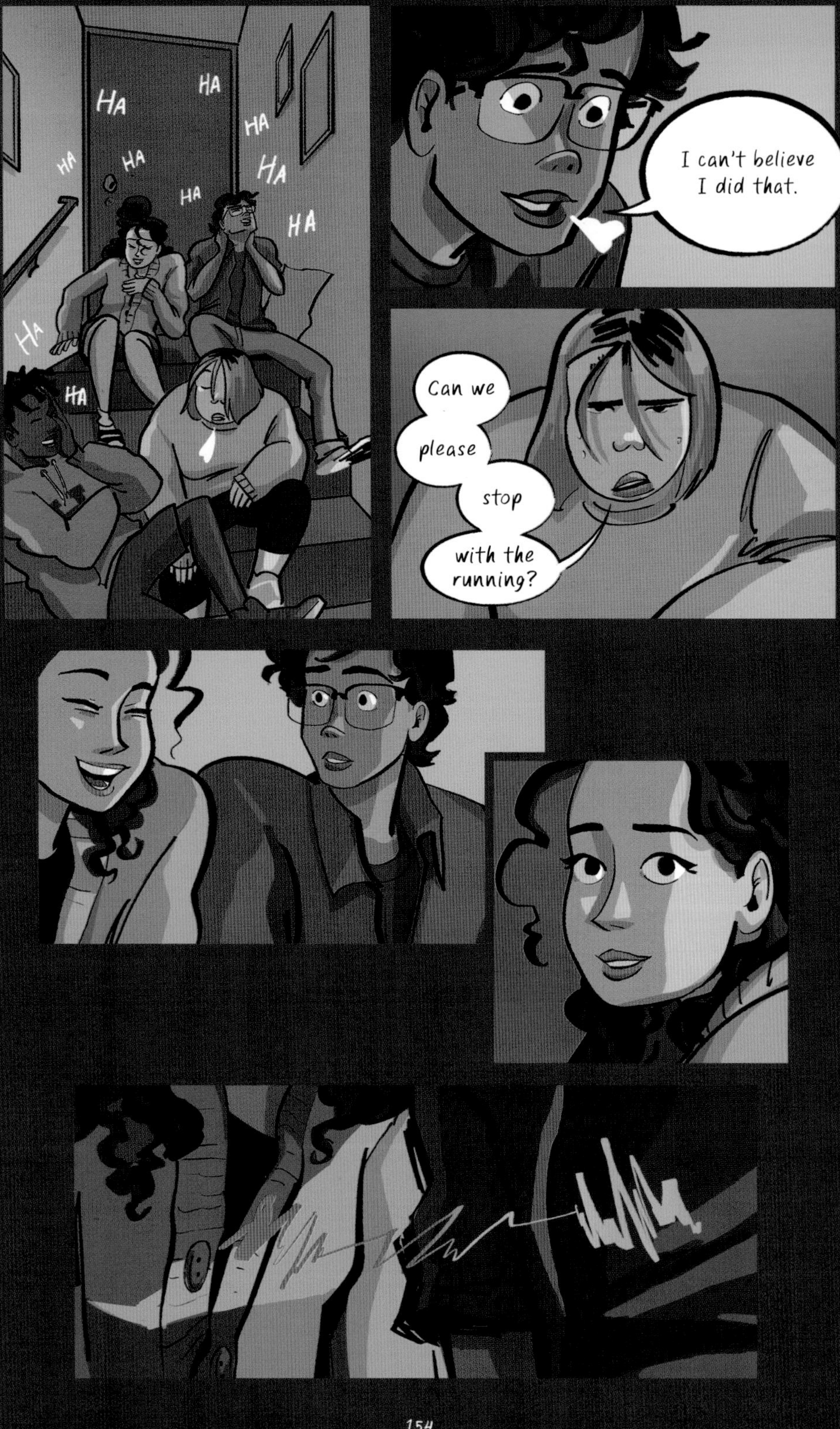
HA
HA
HA
HA
HA
HA
HA
HA
HA
HA
HA
I can't believe I did that.
Can we
please
stop
with the running?

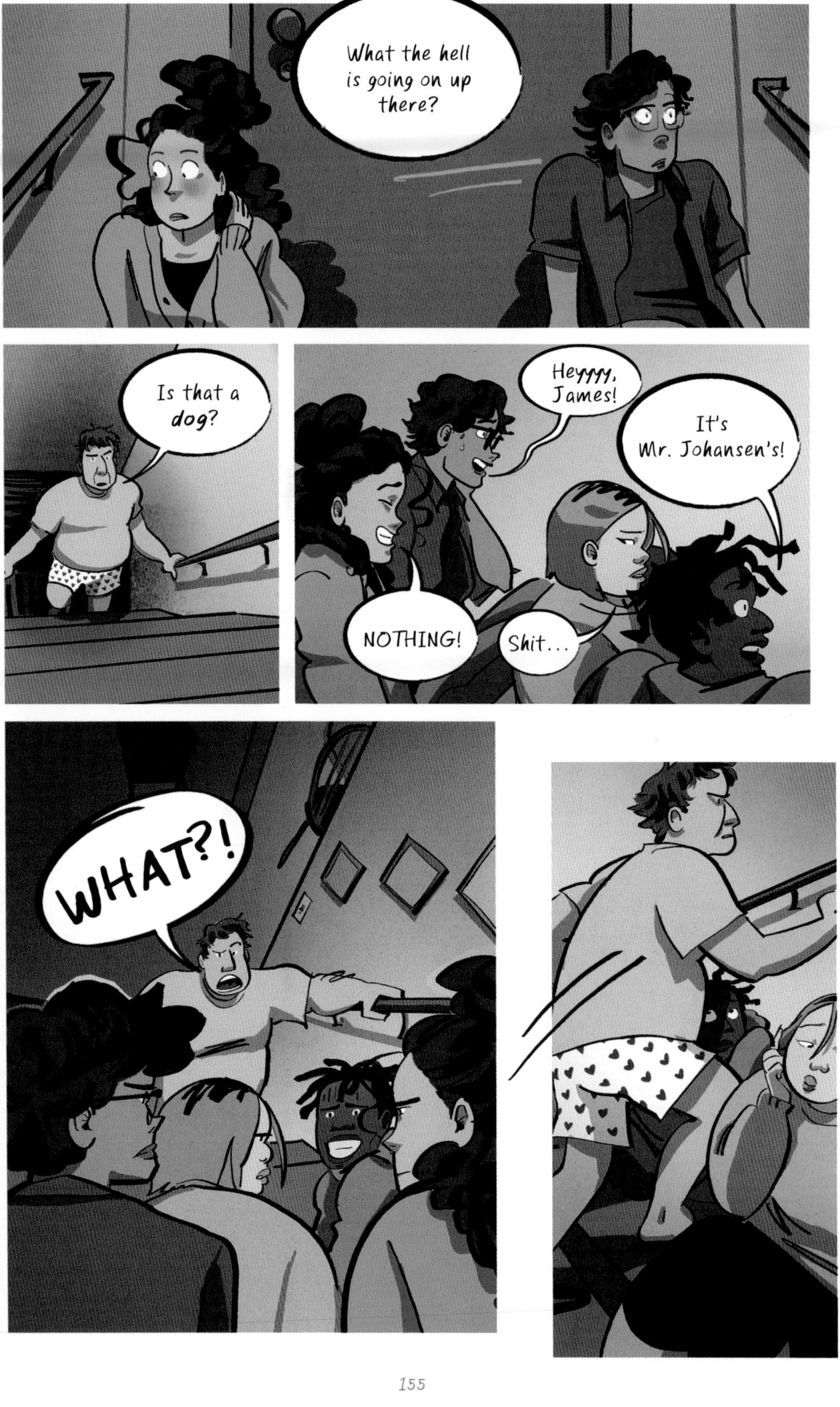

What the hell is going on up there?
Is that a dog?
Heyyyy, James!
It's Mr. Johansen's!
NOTHING!
Shit...
WHAT?!

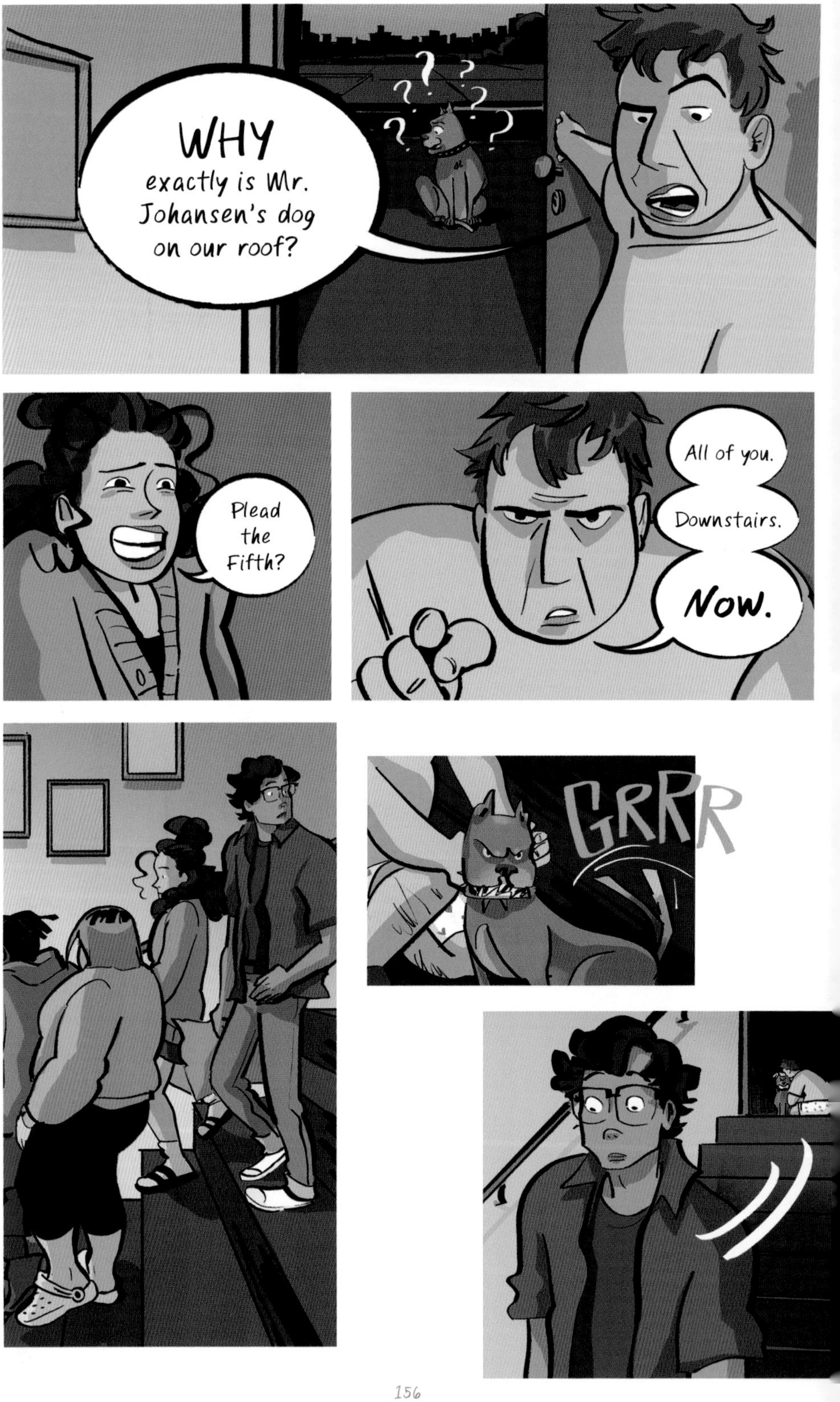
WHY exactly is Mr. Johansen's dog on our roof?
Plead the Fifth?
All of you.
Downstairs.
Now.
GRRR

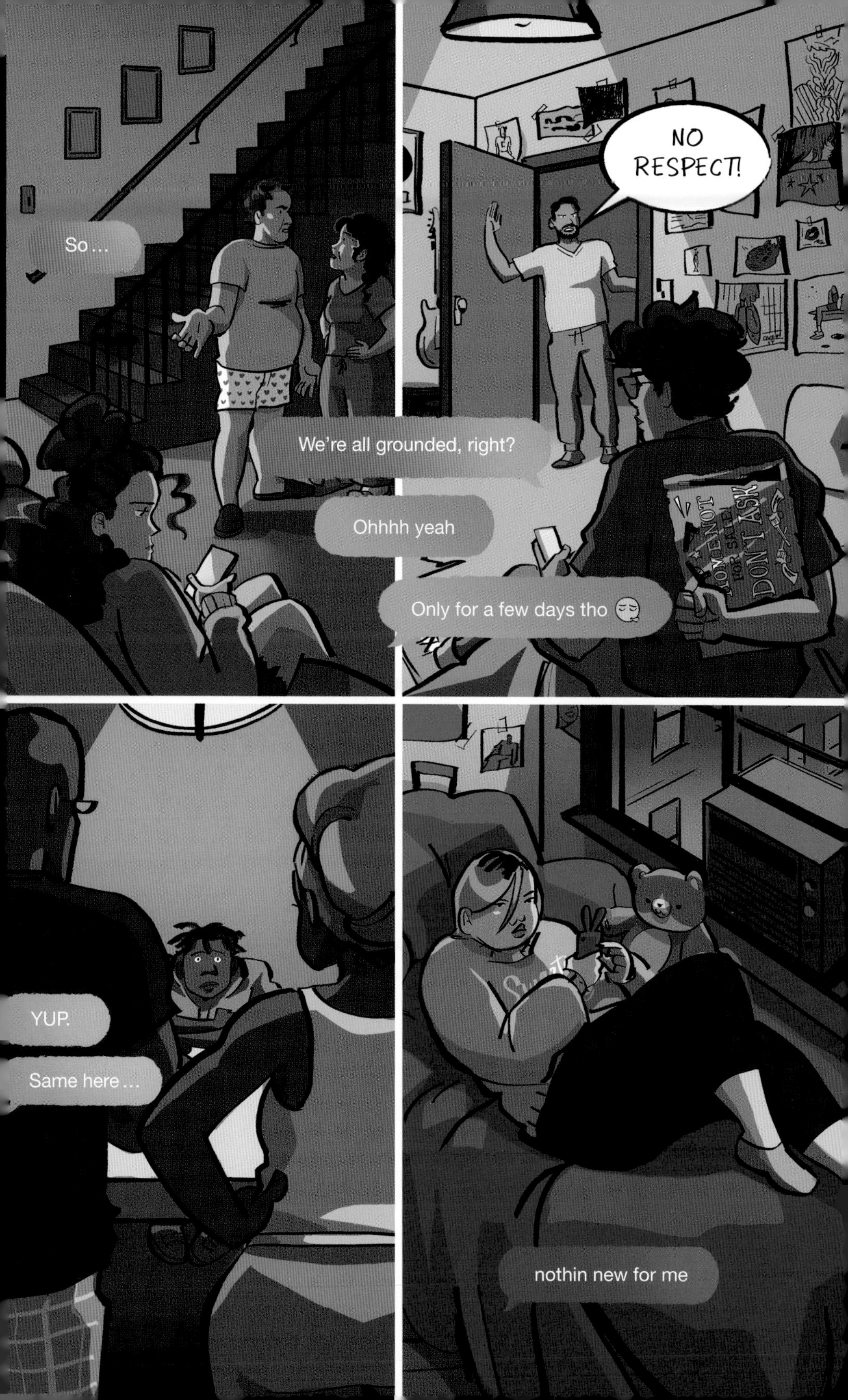
So …
NO RESPECT!
We're all grounded, right?
Ohhhh yeah
Only for a few days tho
HOME NOT FOR SALE DON'T ASK
YUP.
Same here …
nothin new for me

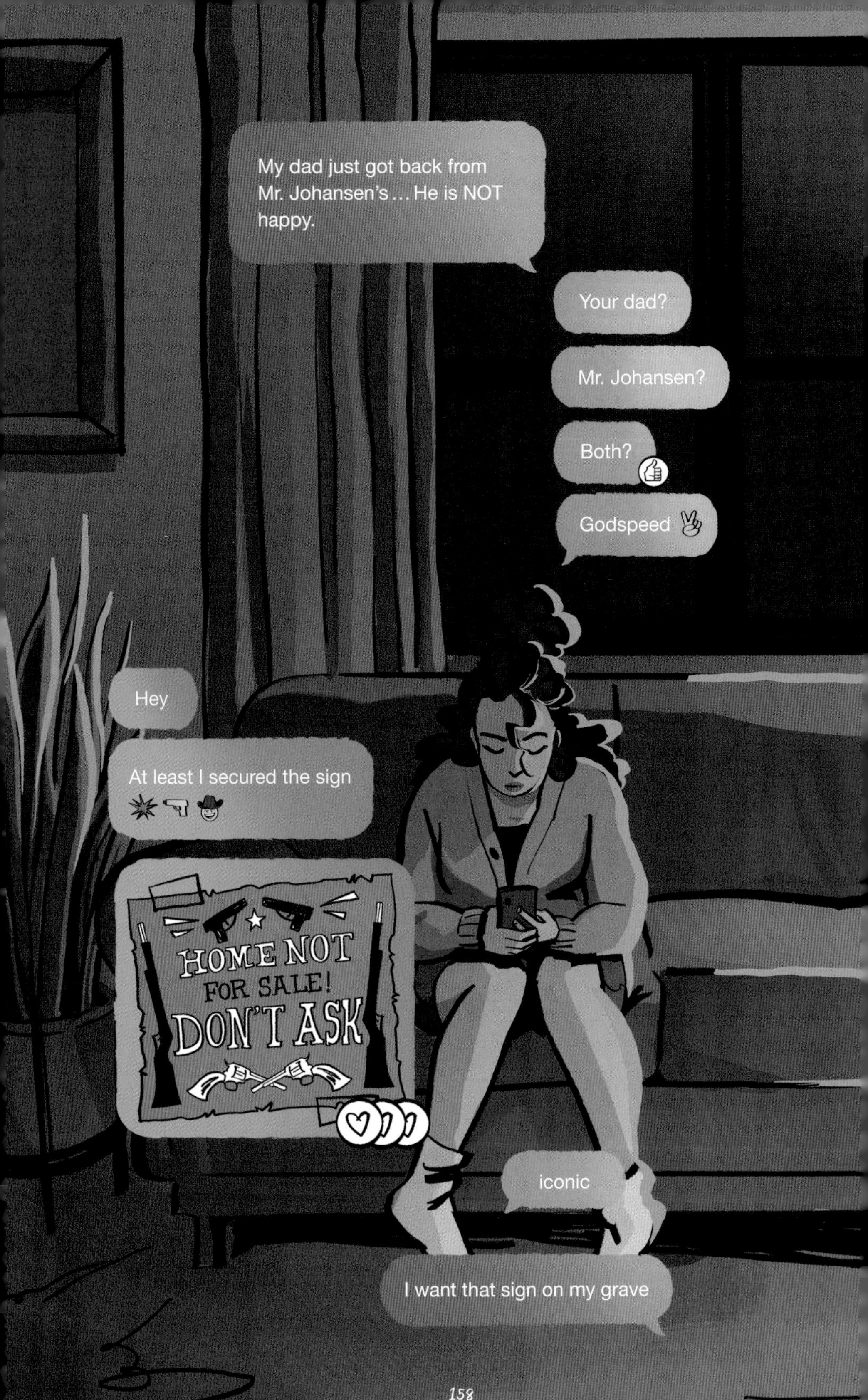

My dad just got back from Mr. Johansen's... He is NOT happy.
Your dad?
Mr. Johansen?
Both?
Godspeed
Hey
At least I secured the sign
HOME NOT FOR SALE! DON'T ASK
iconic
I want that sign on my grave

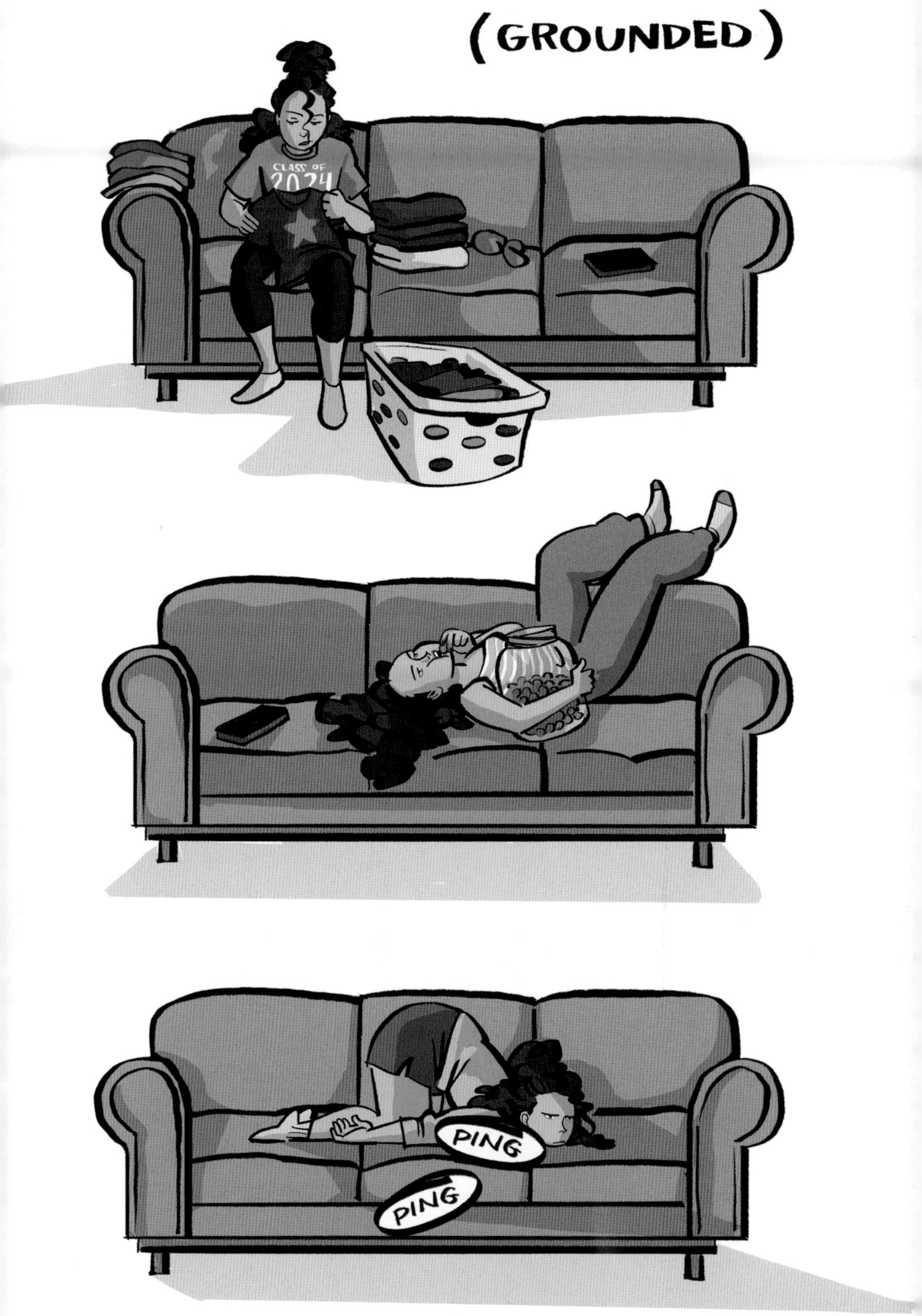
(GROUNDED)
CLASS OF 2024
PING
PING

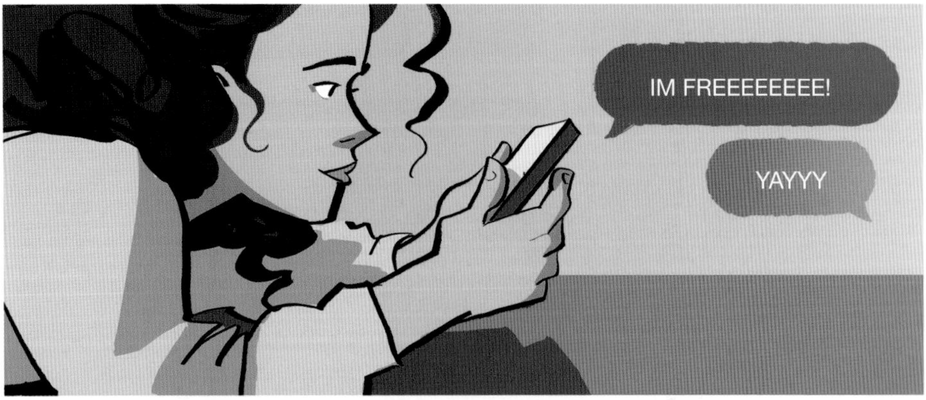
IM FREEEEEEEE!
YAYYY

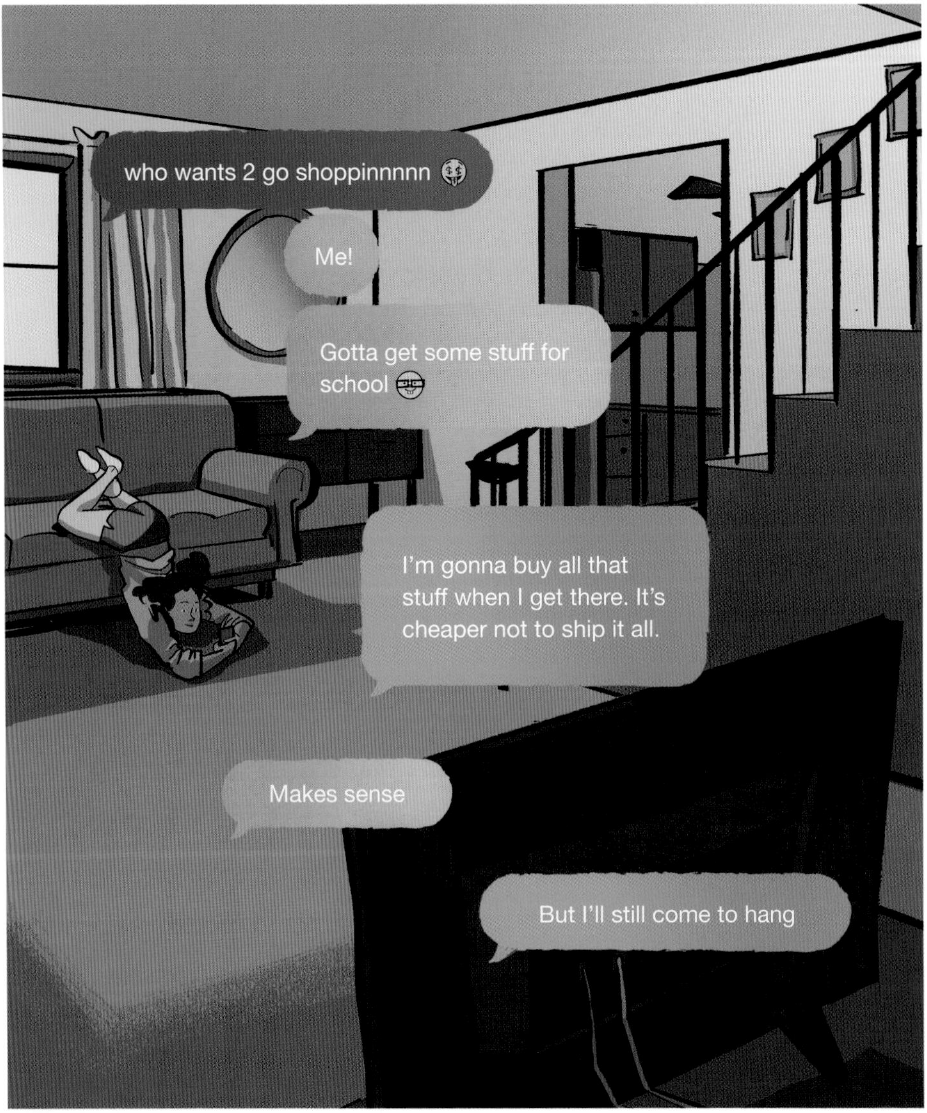
who wants 2 go shoppinnnnn
Me!
Gotta get some stuff for school
I'm gonna buy all that stuff when I get there. It's cheaper not to ship it all.
Makes sense
But I'll still come to hang

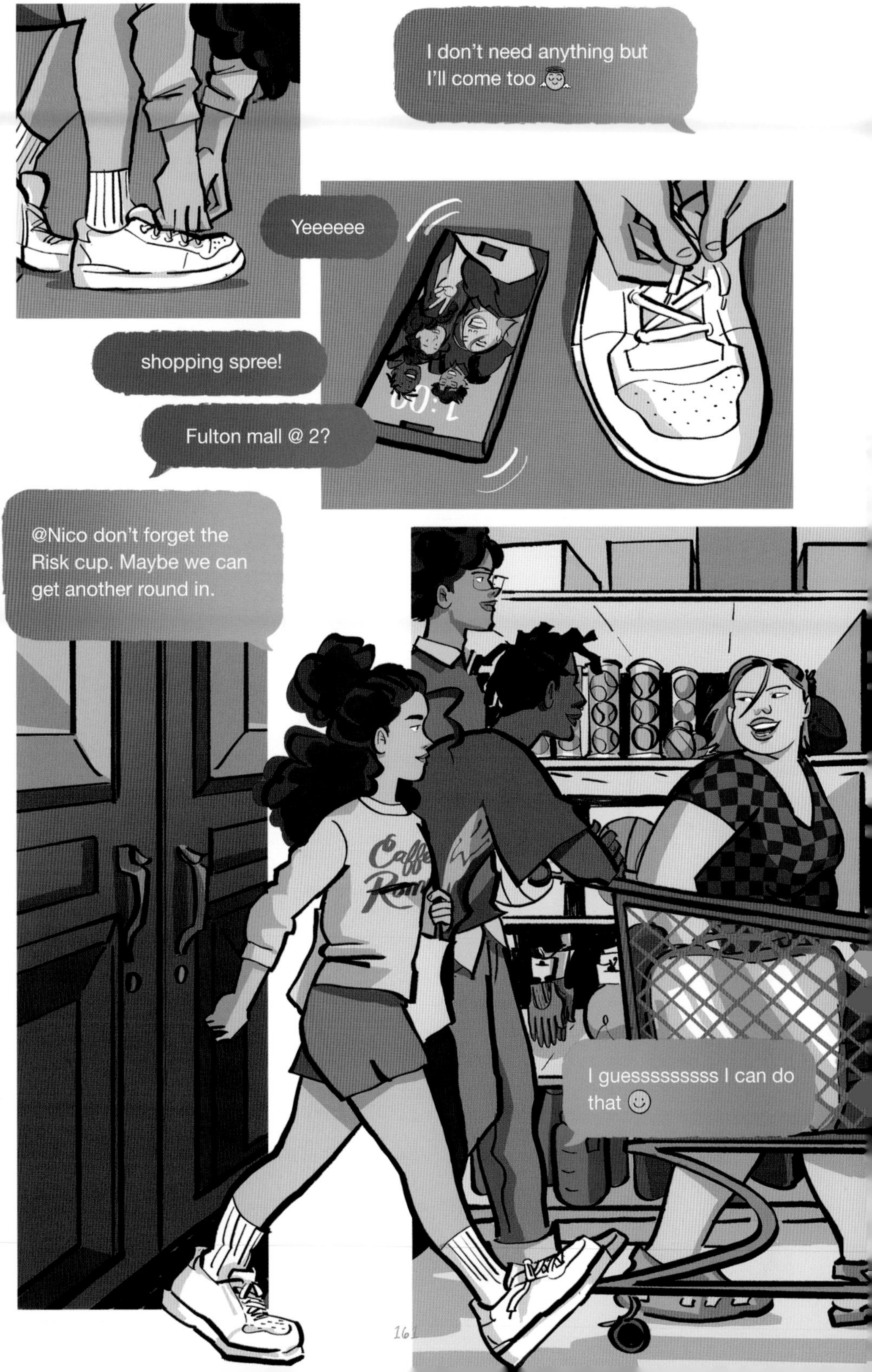
I don't need anything but I'll come too
Yeeeeee
shopping spree!
Fulton mall @ 2?
@Nico don't forget the Risk cup. Maybe we can get another round in.
I guesssssssss I can do that

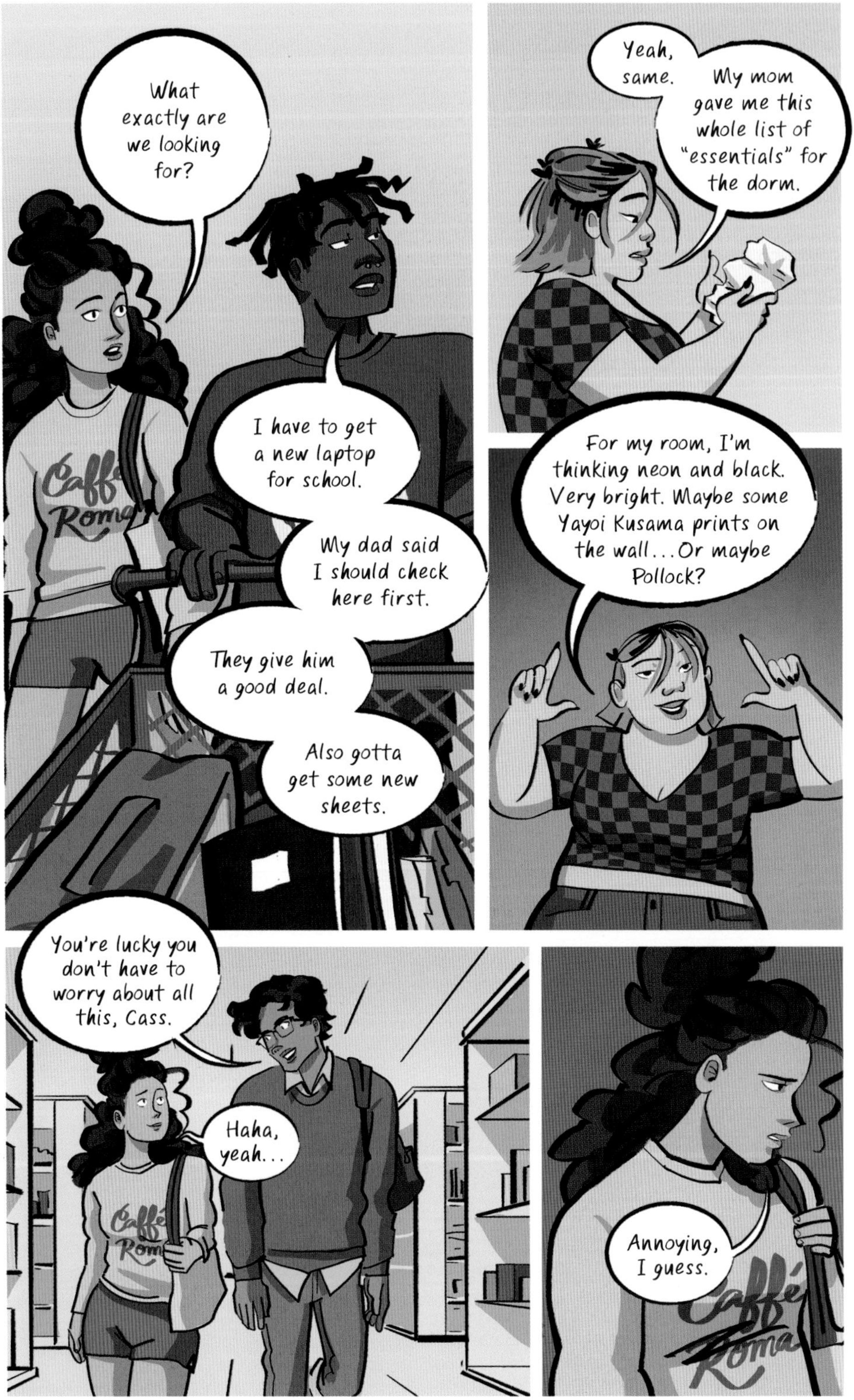
What exactly are we looking for?
I have to get a new laptop for school.
My dad said I should check here first.
They give him a good deal.
Also gotta get some new sheets.
Yeah, same.
My mom gave me this whole list of "essentials" for the dorm.
For my room, I'm thinking neon and black. Very bright. Maybe some Yayoi Kusama prints on the wall...Or maybe Pollock?
You're lucky you don't have to worry about all this, Cass.
Haha, yeah...
Annoying, I guess.

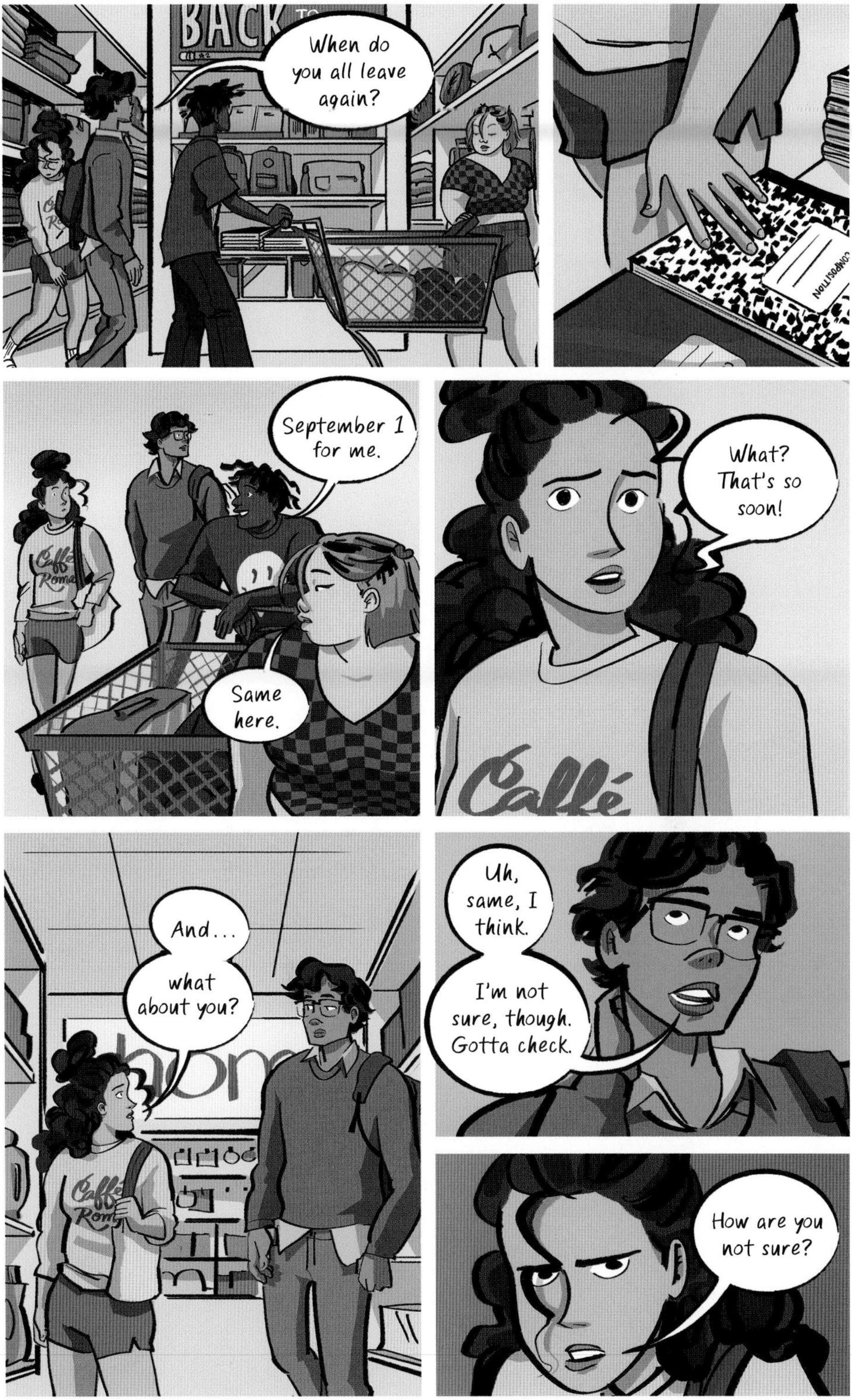
BACK TO
When do you all leave again?
COMPOSITION
September 1 for me.
Same here.
What? That's so soon!
Caffé
And...
what about you?
Uh, same, I think.
I'm not sure, though. Gotta check.
How are you not sure?

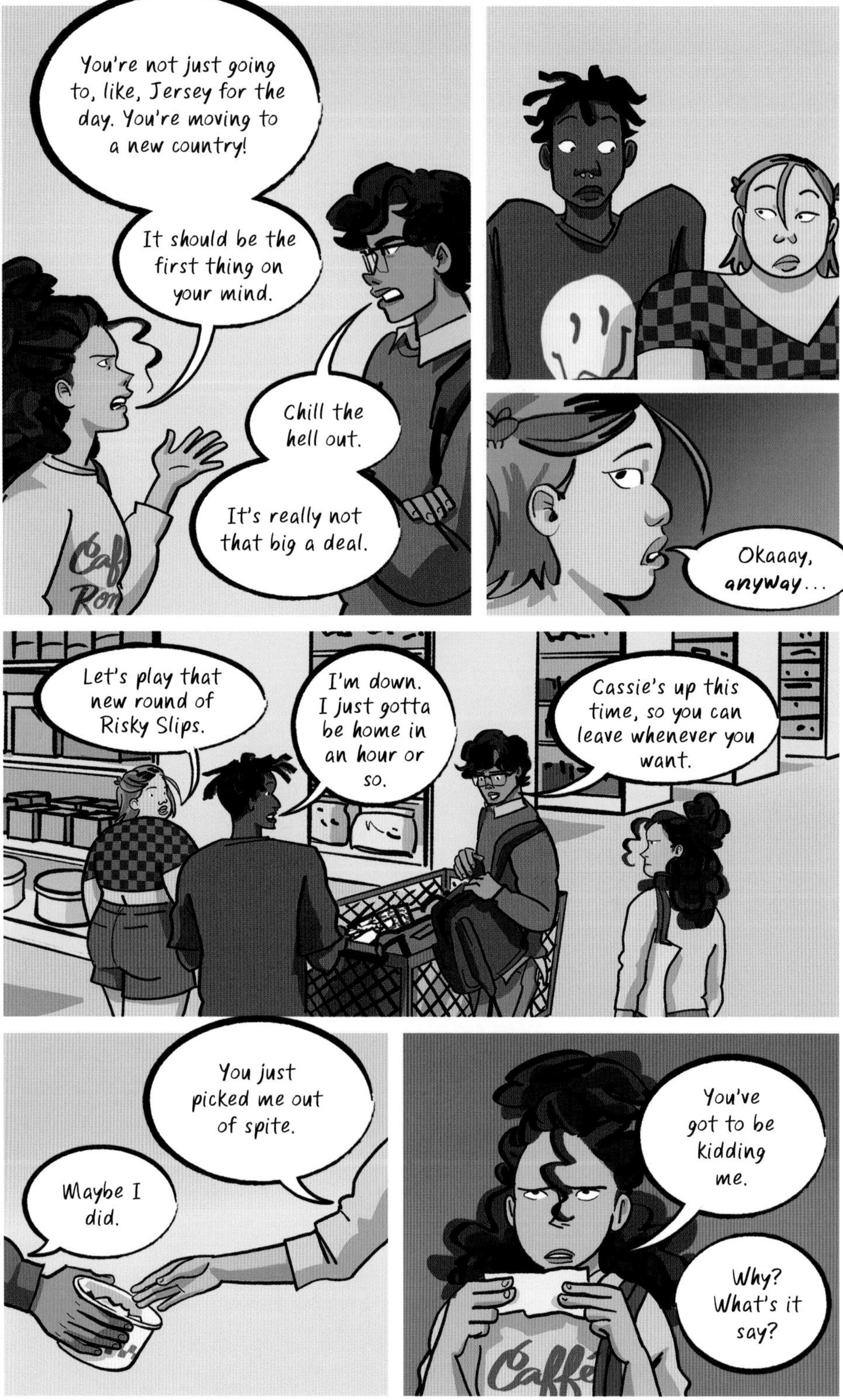
You're not just going to, like, Jersey for the day. You're moving to a new country!
It should be the first thing on your mind.
Chill the hell out.
It's really not that big a deal.
Caff
Ron
Okaaay, **anyway**...
Let's play that new round of Risky Slips.
I'm down. I just gotta be home in an hour or so.
Cassie's up this time, so you can leave whenever you want.
You just picked me out of spite.
Maybe I did.
You've got to be kidding me.
Why? What's it say?
Caffé

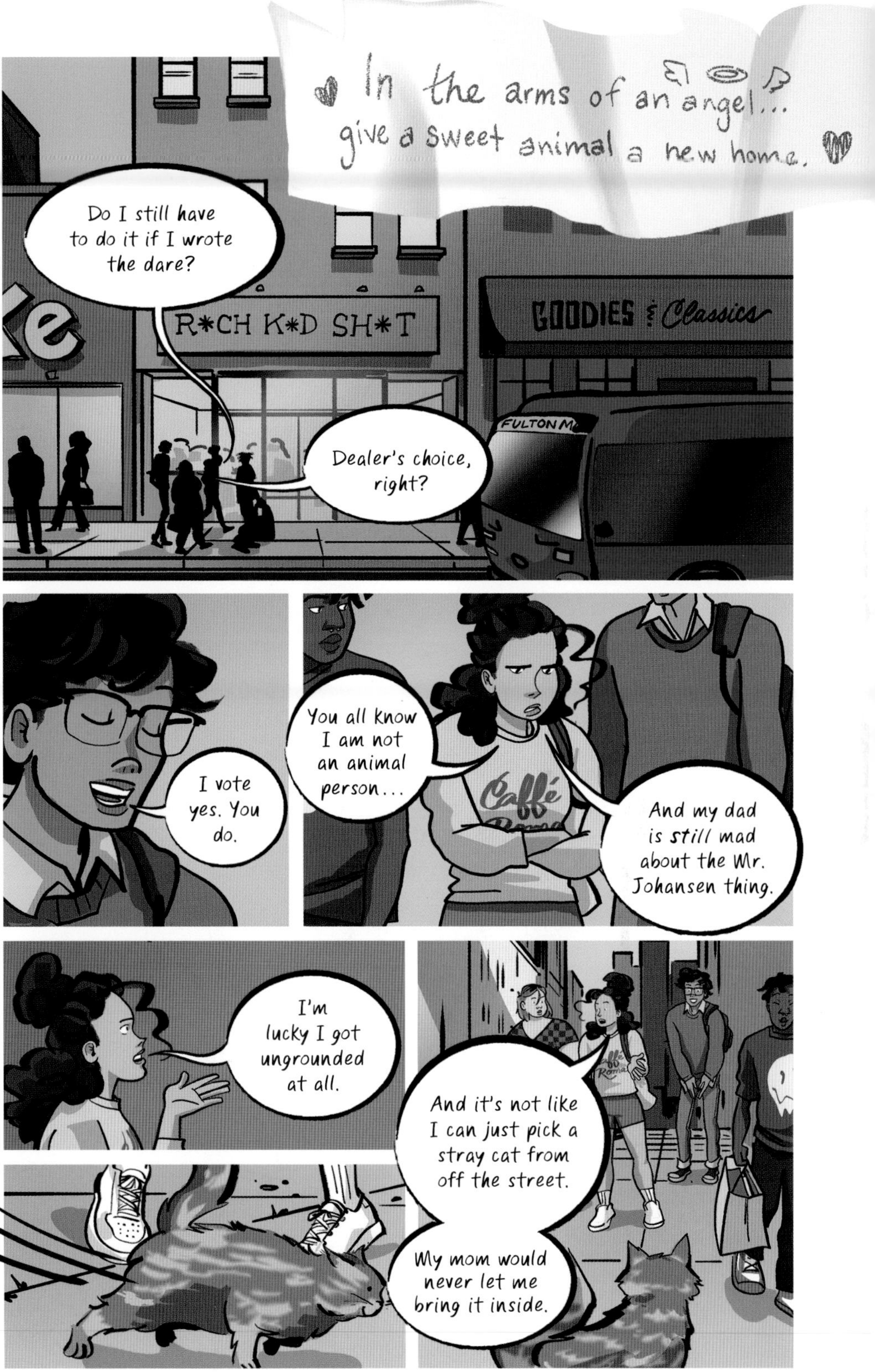
In the arms of an angel... give a sweet animal a new home.
Do I still have to do it if I wrote the dare?
R*CH K*D SH*T
GOODIES & Classics
FULTON M
Dealer's choice, right?
I vote yes. You do.
You all know I am not an animal person...
Caffé
And my dad is still mad about the Mr. Johansen thing.
I'm lucky I got ungrounded at all.
And it's not like I can just pick a stray cat from off the street.
My mom would never let me bring it inside.

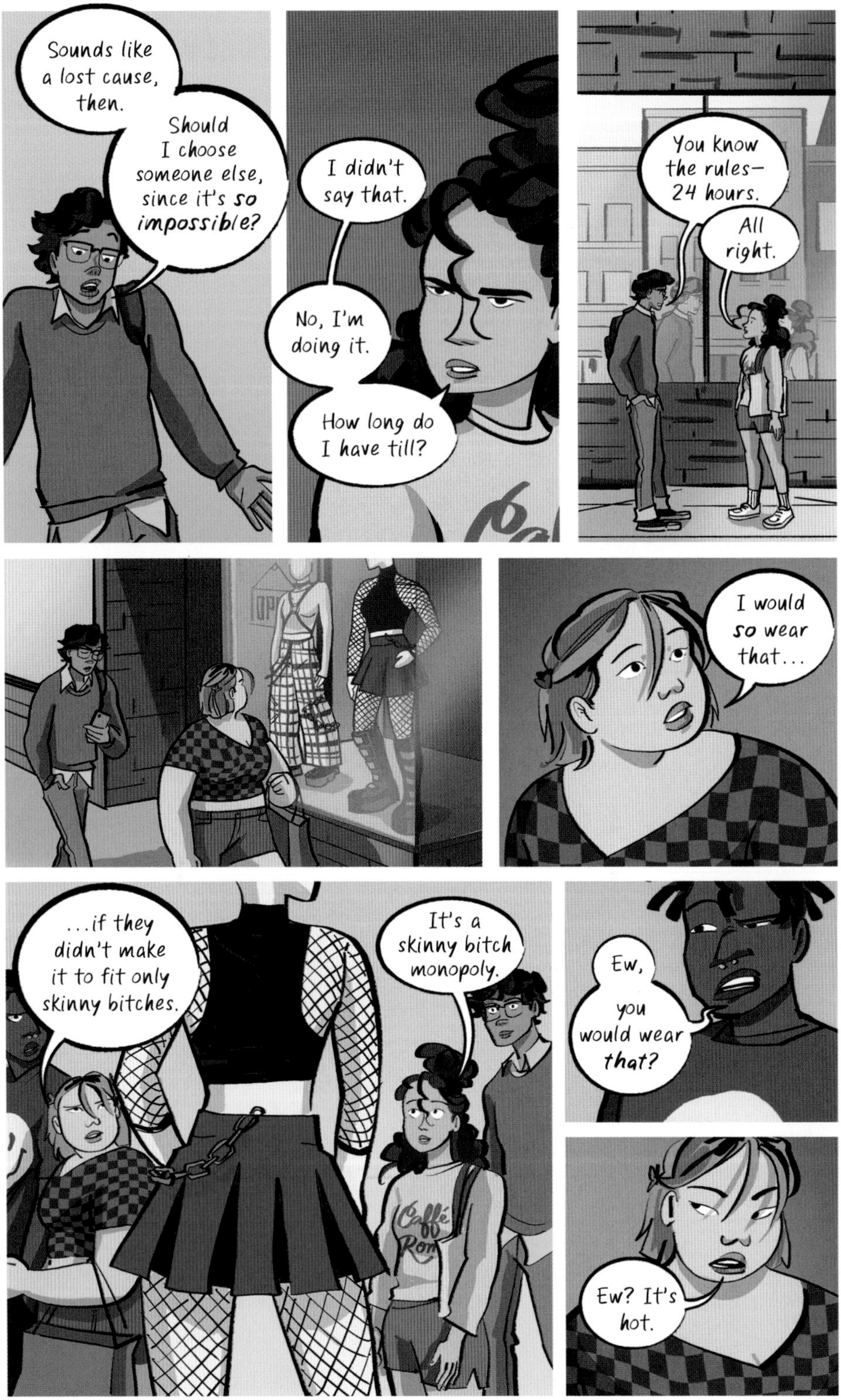
Sounds like a lost cause, then.
Should I choose someone else, since it's so impossible?
I didn't say that.
No, I'm doing it.
How long do I have till?
You know the rules—24 hours.
All right.
I would so wear that...
...if they didn't make it to fit only skinny bitches.
It's a skinny bitch monopoly.
Ew, you would wear that?
Ew? It's hot.

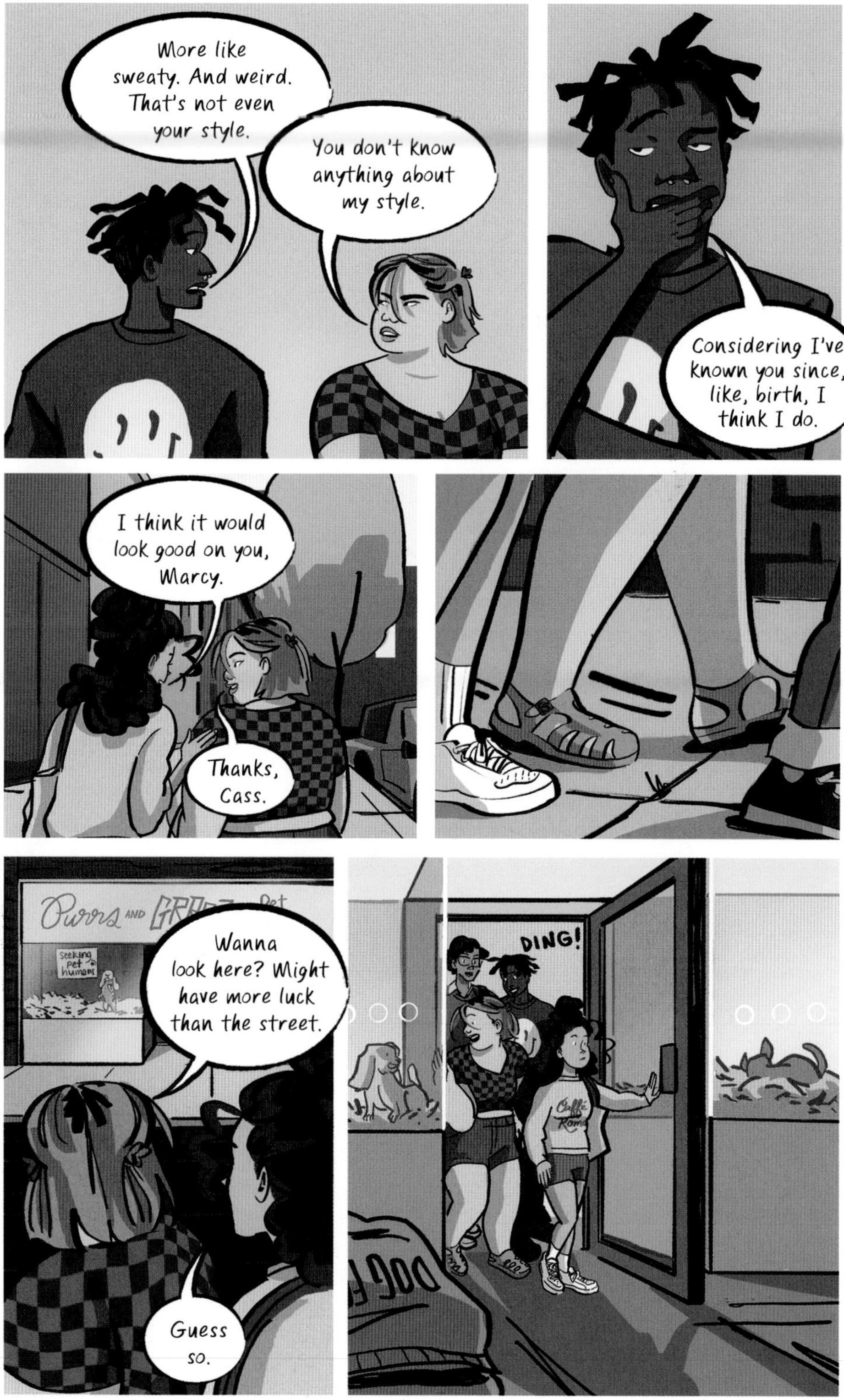
More like sweaty. And weird. That's not even your style.
You don't know anything about my style.
Considering I've known you since, like, birth, I think I do.
I think it would look good on you, Marcy.
Thanks, Cass.
seeking pet humans
Wanna look here? Might have more luck than the street.
Guess so.
DING!

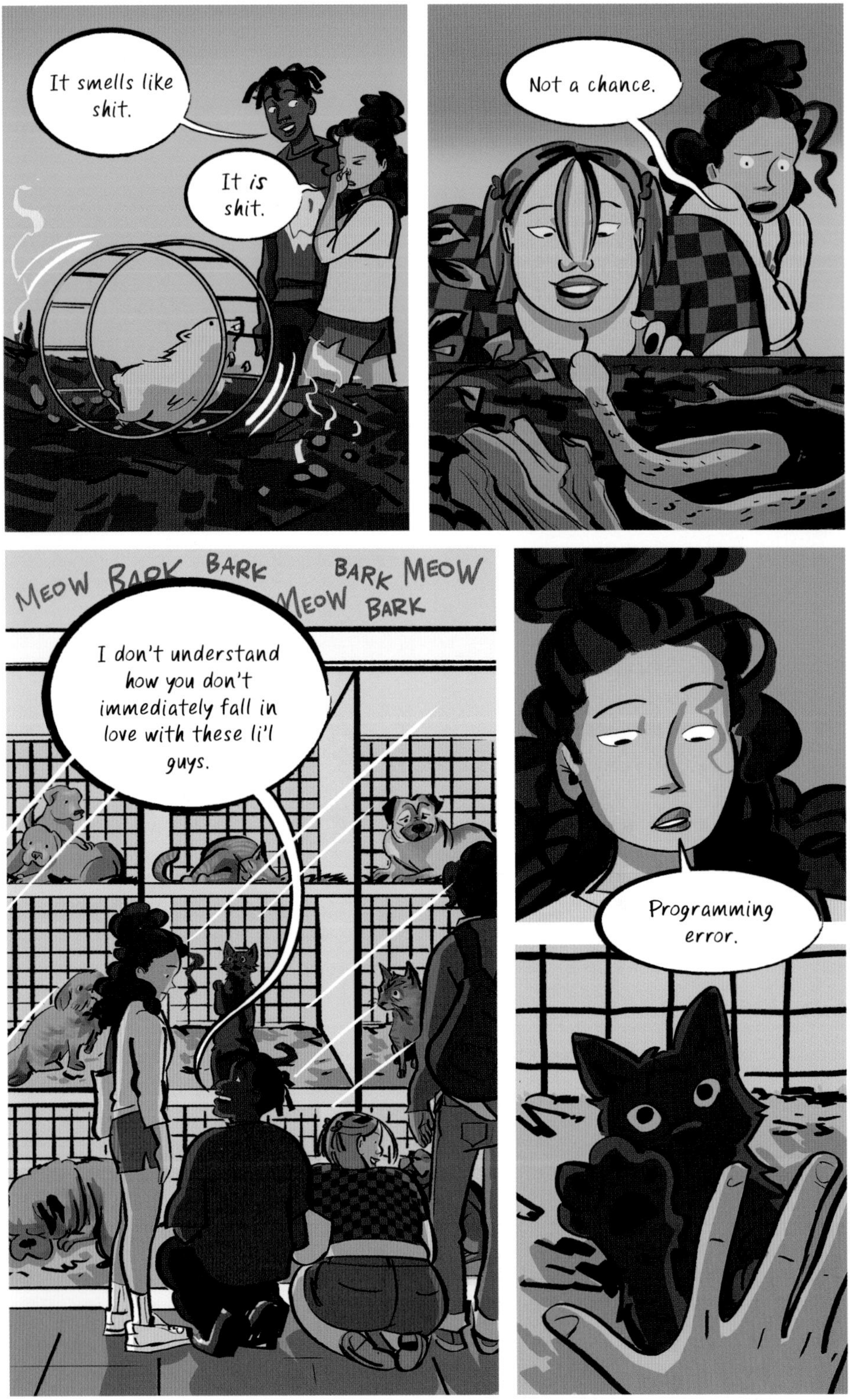
It smells like shit.
It *is* shit.
Not a chance.
MEOW BARK BARK BARK MEOW MEOW BARK
I don't understand how you don't immediately fall in love with these li'l guys.
Programming error.

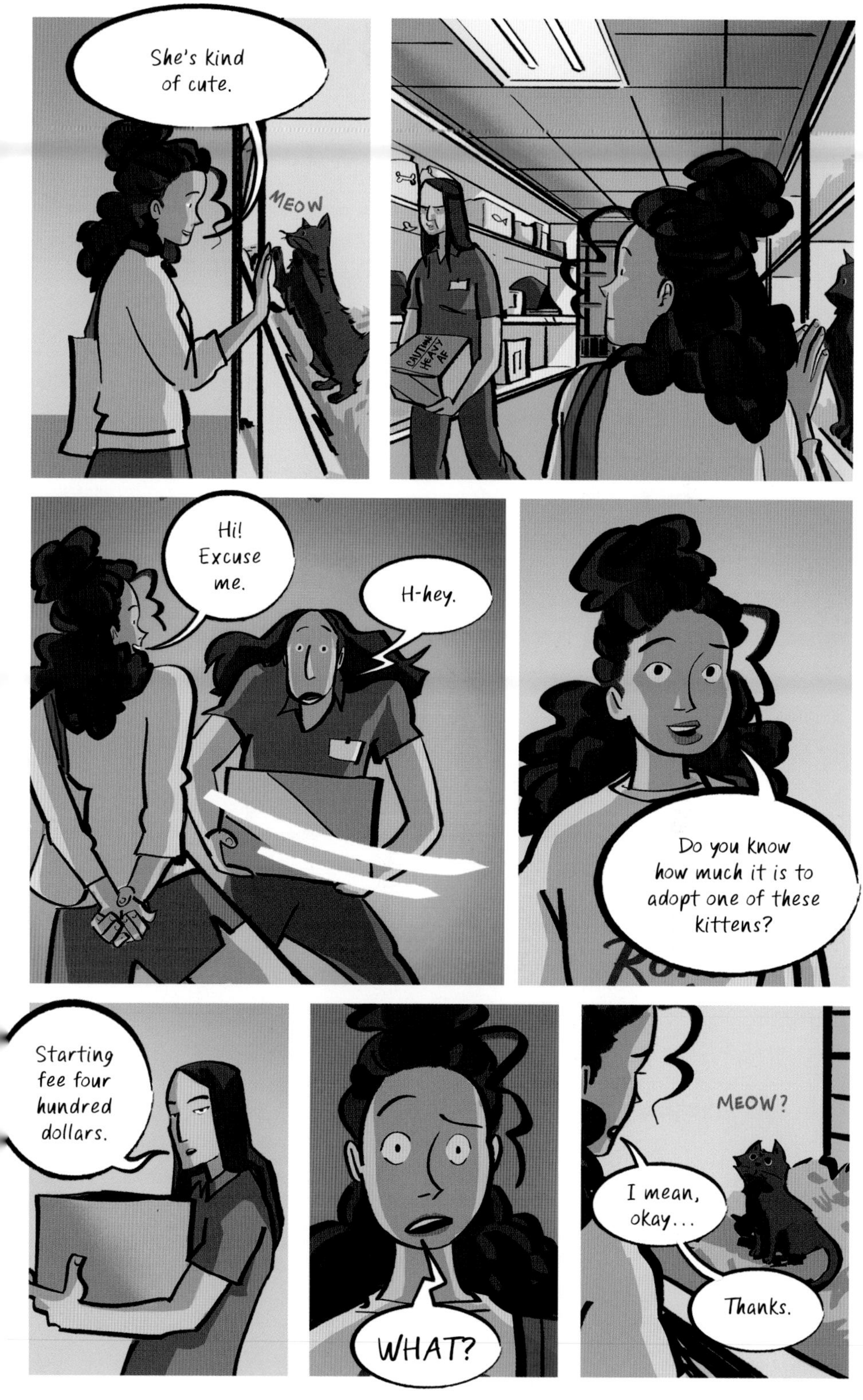
She's kind of cute.
MEOW
CAUTION HEAVY AF
Hi! Excuse me.
H-hey.
Do you know how much it is to adopt one of these kittens?
Starting fee four hundred dollars.
WHAT?
MEOW?
I mean, okay...
Thanks.

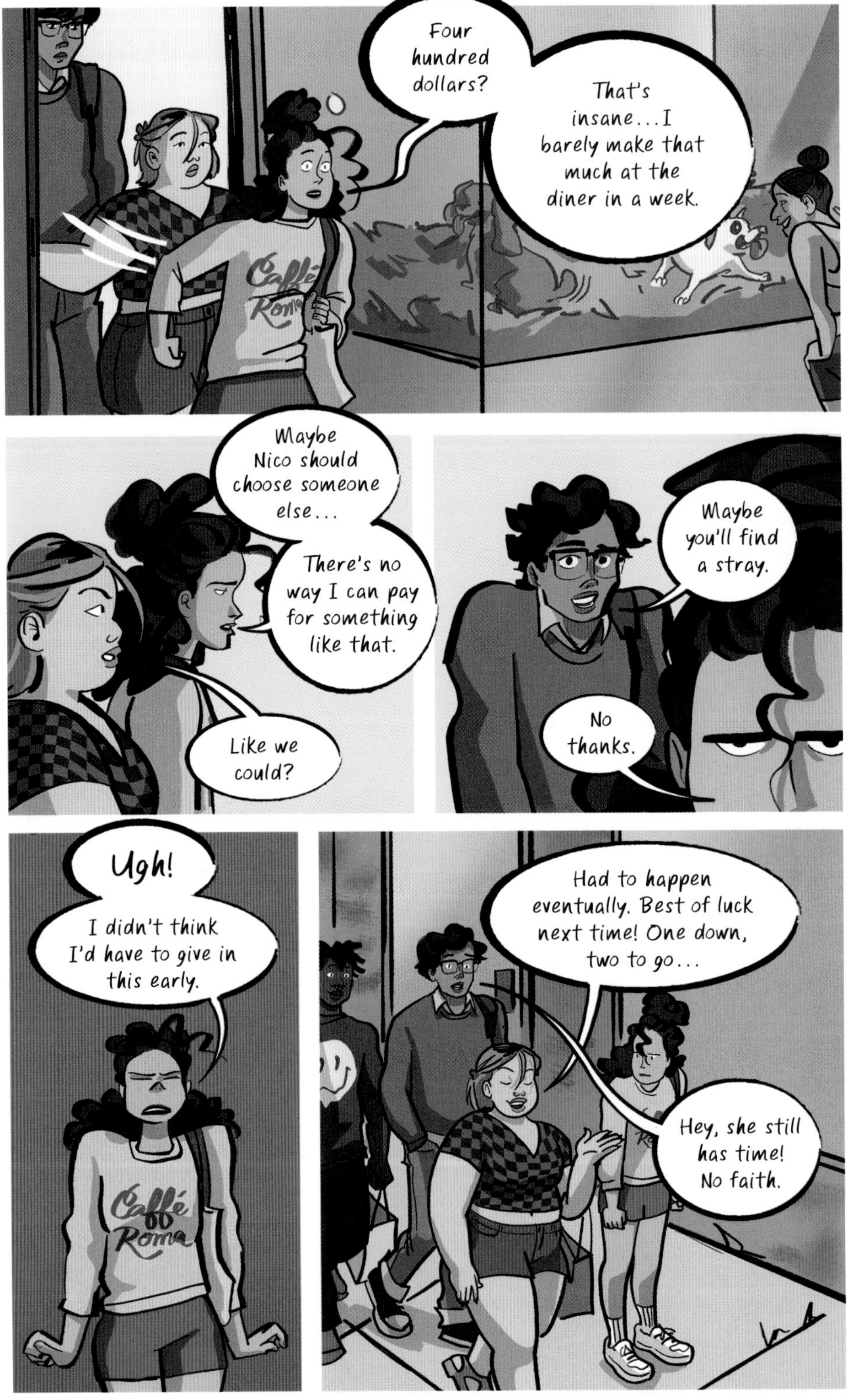
Four hundred dollars?
That's insane...I barely make that much at the diner in a week.
Maybe Nico should choose someone else...
There's no way I can pay for something like that.
Like we could?
Maybe you'll find a stray.
No thanks.
Ugh!
I didn't think I'd have to give in this early.
Had to happen eventually. Best of luck next time! One down, two to go...
Hey, she still has time! No faith.

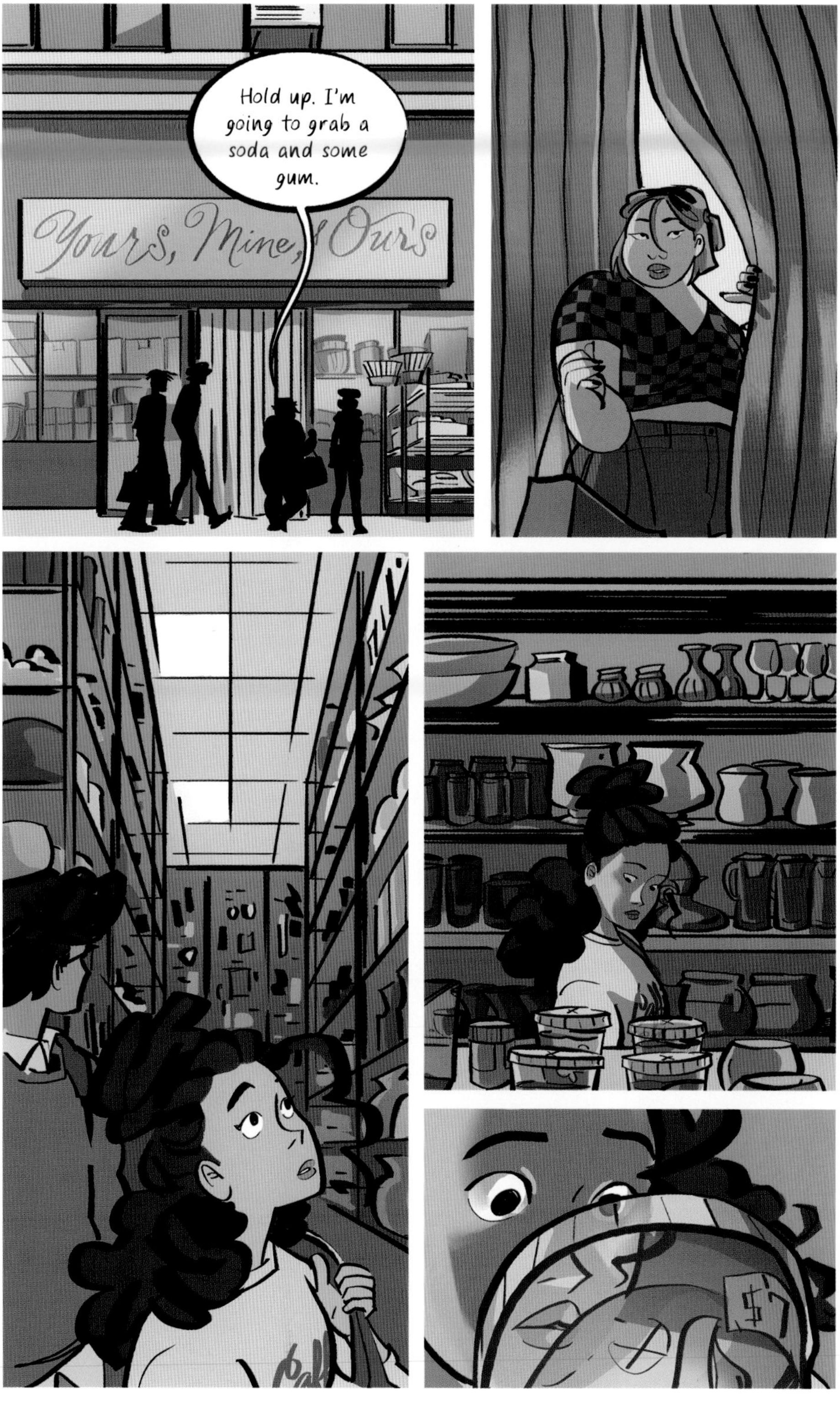
Hold up. I'm going to grab a soda and some gum.
Yours, Mine, & Ours
$7

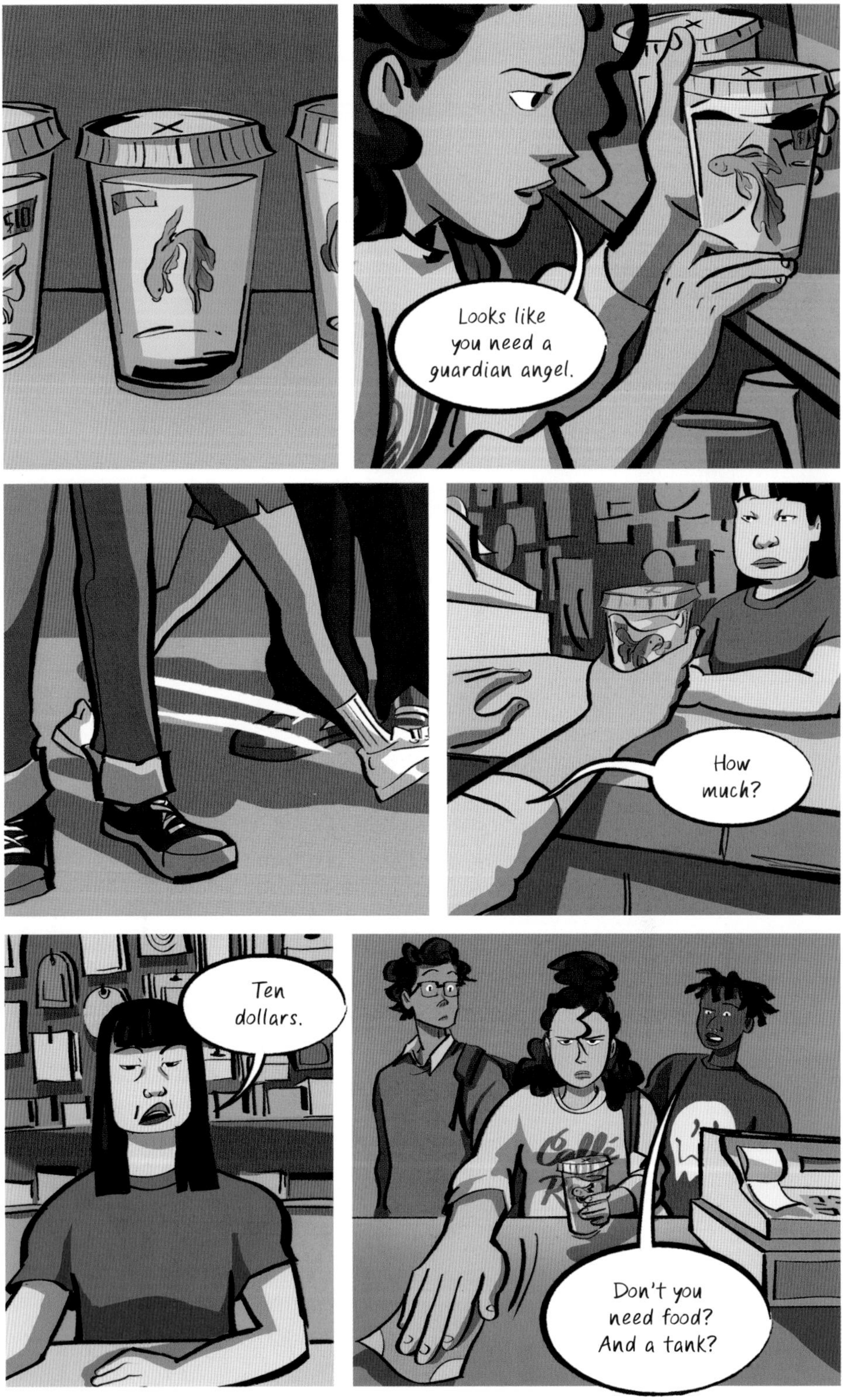
Looks like you need a guardian angel.
How much?
Ten dollars.
Don't you need food? And a tank?

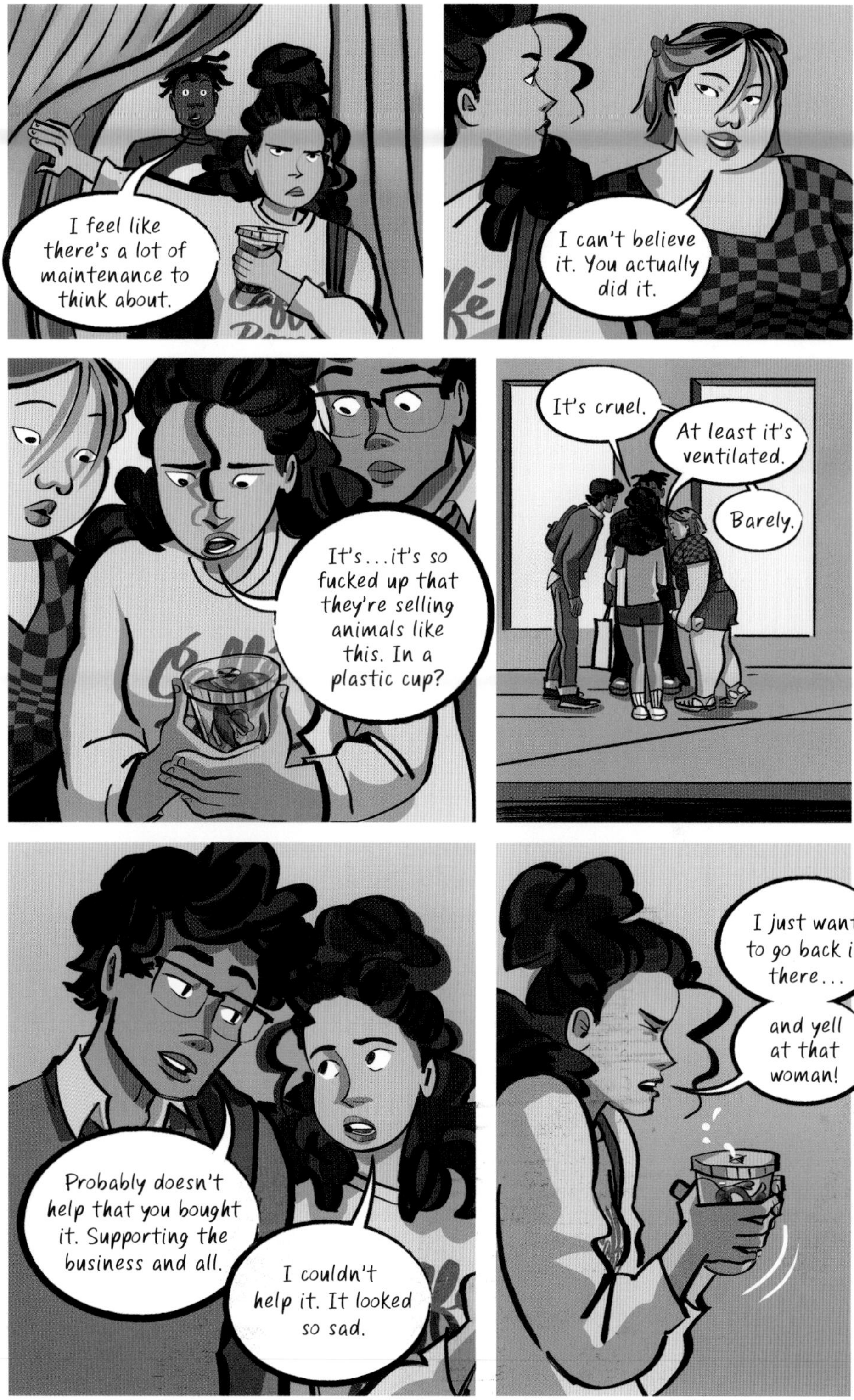
I feel like there's a lot of maintenance to think about.
I can't believe it. You actually did it.
It's...it's so fucked up that they're selling animals like this. In a plastic cup?
It's cruel.
At least it's ventilated.
Barely.
Probably doesn't help that you bought it. Supporting the business and all.
I couldn't help it. It looked so sad.
I just want to go back in there...
and yell at that woman!

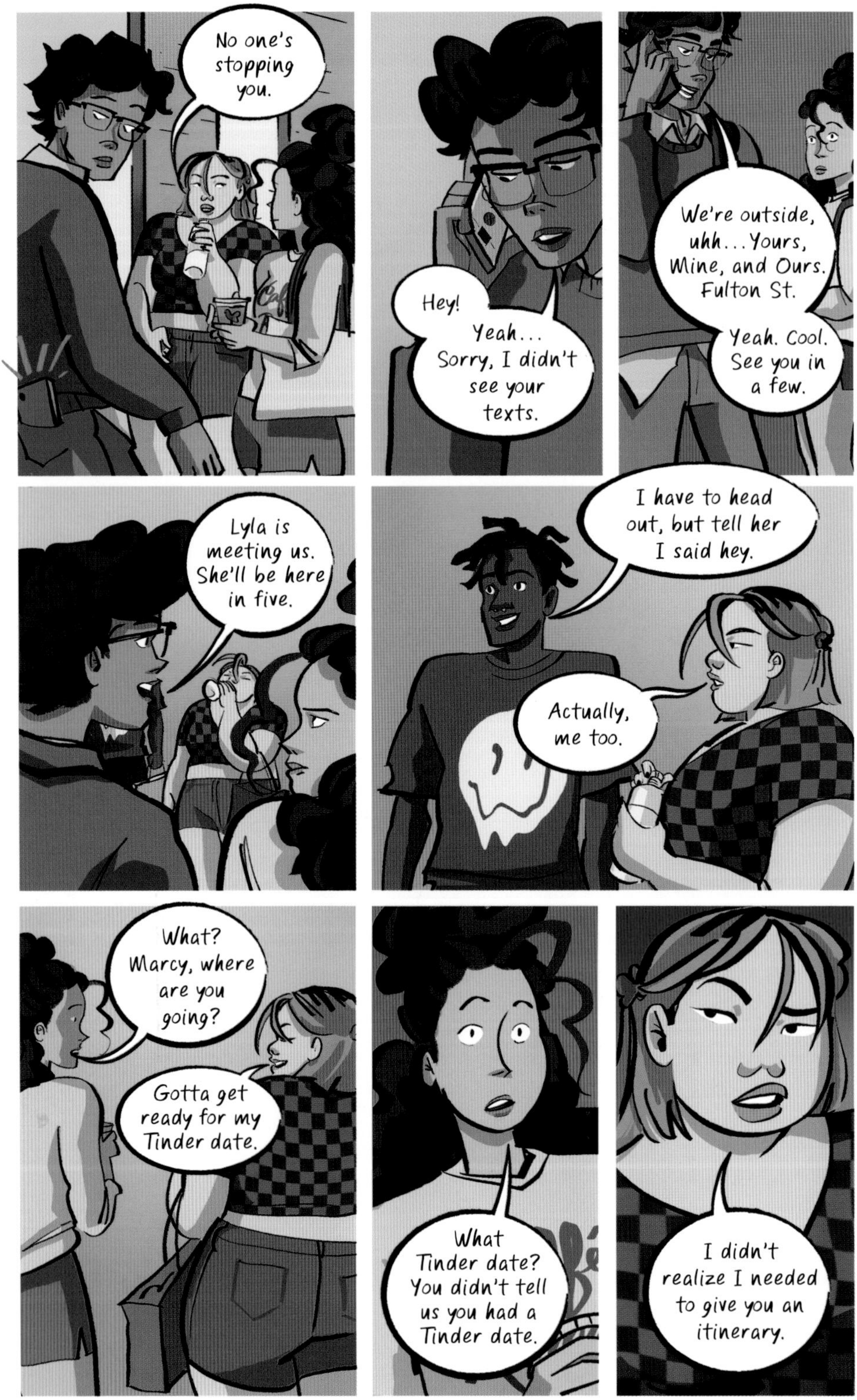
No one's stopping you.
Hey!
Yeah... Sorry, I didn't see your texts.
We're outside, uhh...Yours, Mine, and Ours. Fulton St.
Yeah. Cool. See you in a few.
Lyla is meeting us. She'll be here in five.
I have to head out, but tell her I said hey.
Actually, me too.
What? Marcy, where are you going?
Gotta get ready for my Tinder date.
What Tinder date? You didn't tell us you had a Tinder date.
I didn't realize I needed to give you an itinerary.

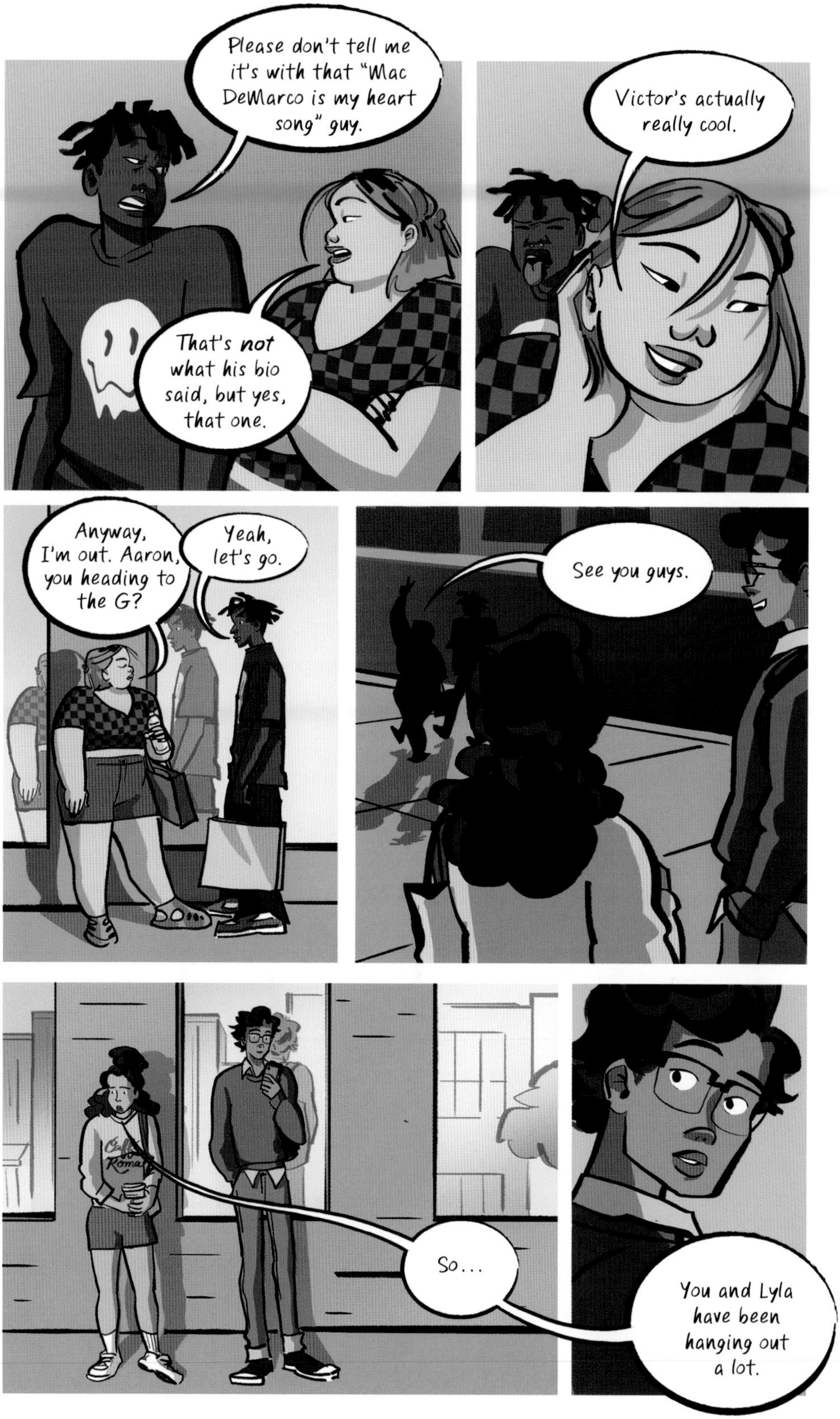
Please don't tell me it's with that "Mac DeMarco is my heart song" guy.
That's not what his bio said, but yes, that one.
Victor's actually really cool.
Anyway, I'm out. Aaron, you heading to the G?
Yeah, let's go.
See you guys.
So...
You and Lyla have been hanging out a lot.

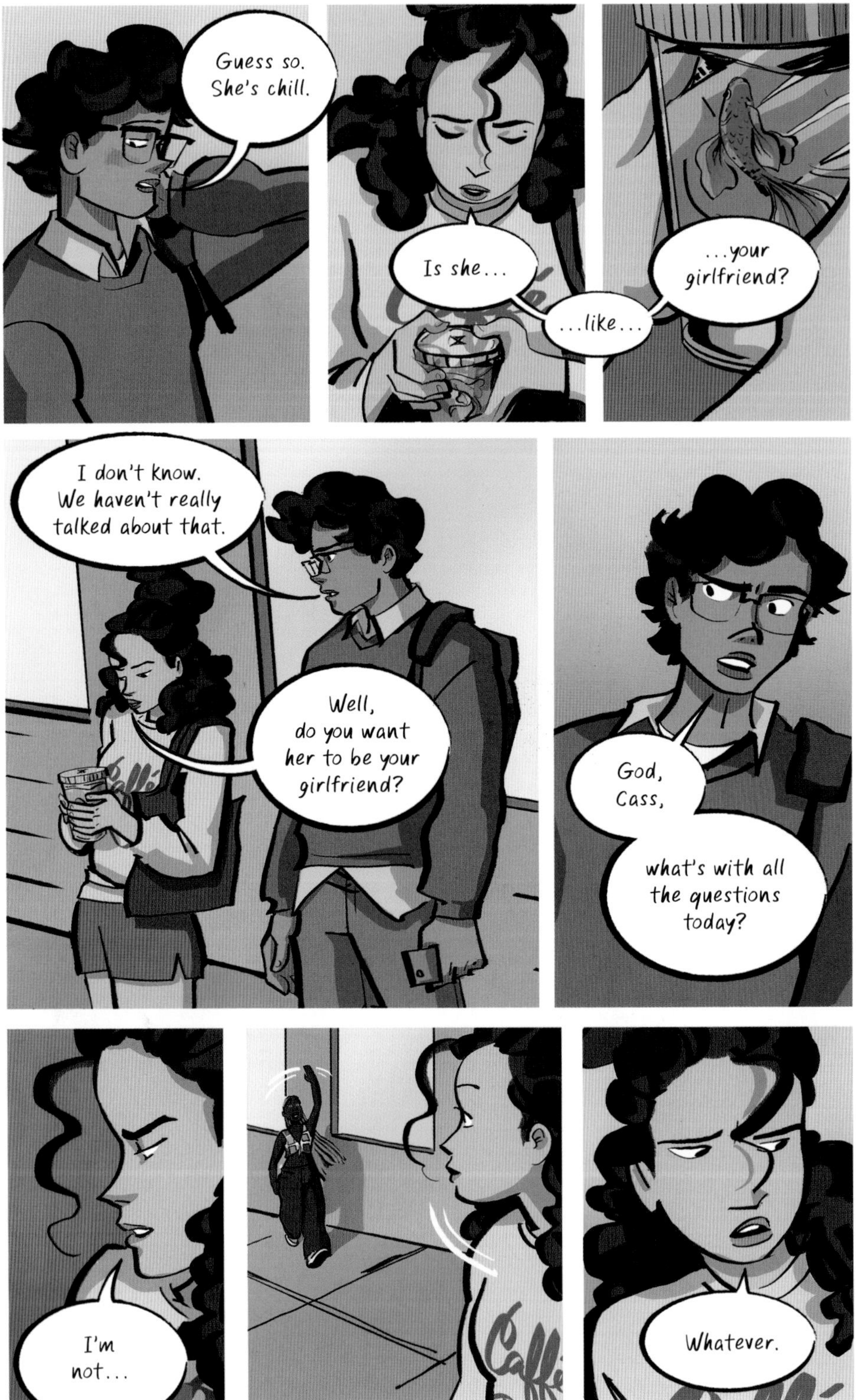
Guess so. She's chill.
Is she...
...like...
...your girlfriend?
I don't know. We haven't really talked about that.
Well, do you want her to be your girlfriend?
God, Cass,
what's with all the questions today?
I'm not...
Whatever.

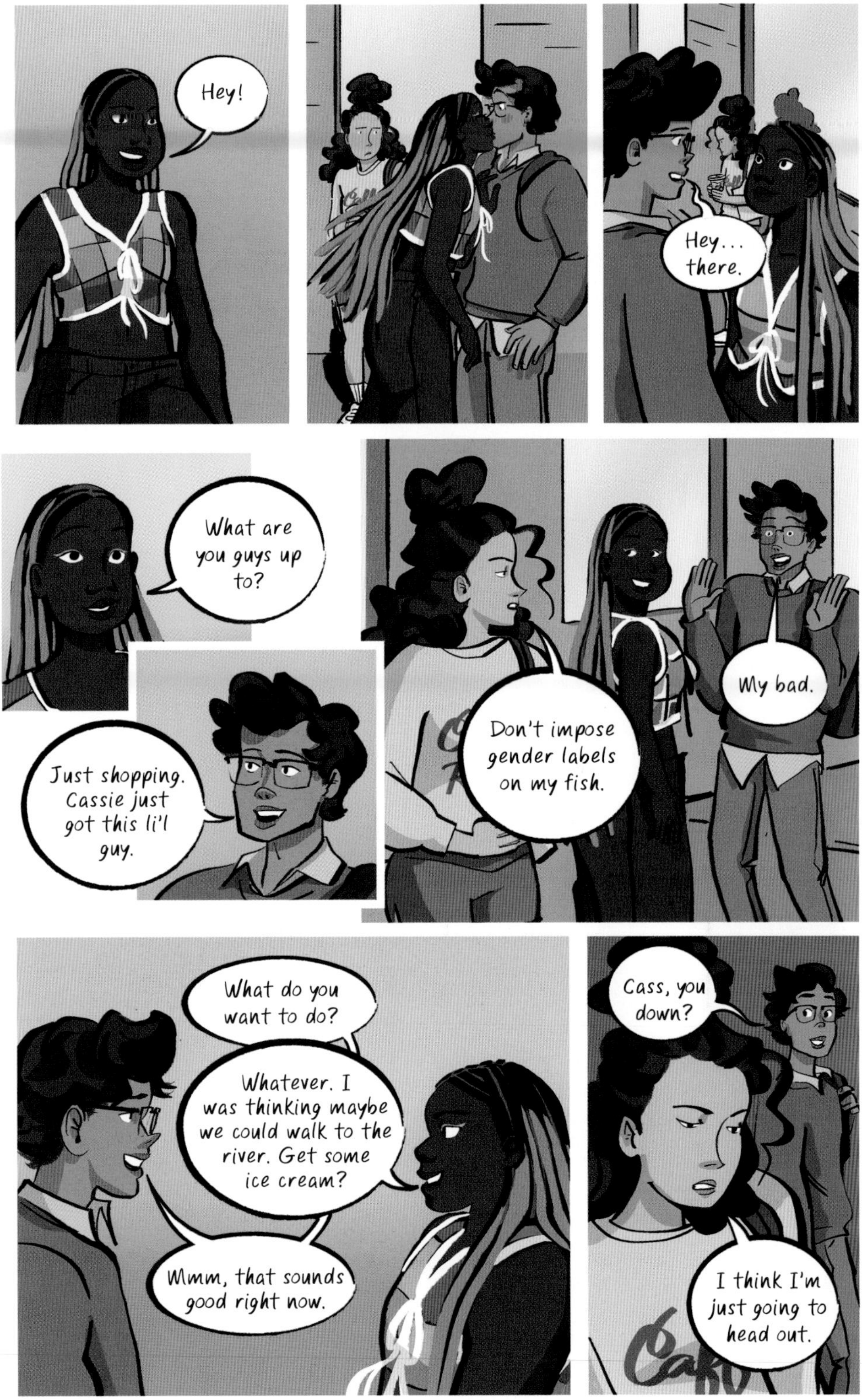
Hey!
Hey... there.
What are you guys up to?
Just shopping. Cassie just got this li'l guy.
Don't impose gender labels on my fish.
My bad.
What do you want to do?
Whatever. I was thinking maybe we could walk to the river. Get some ice cream?
Mmm, that sounds good right now.
Cass, you down?
I think I'm just going to head out.

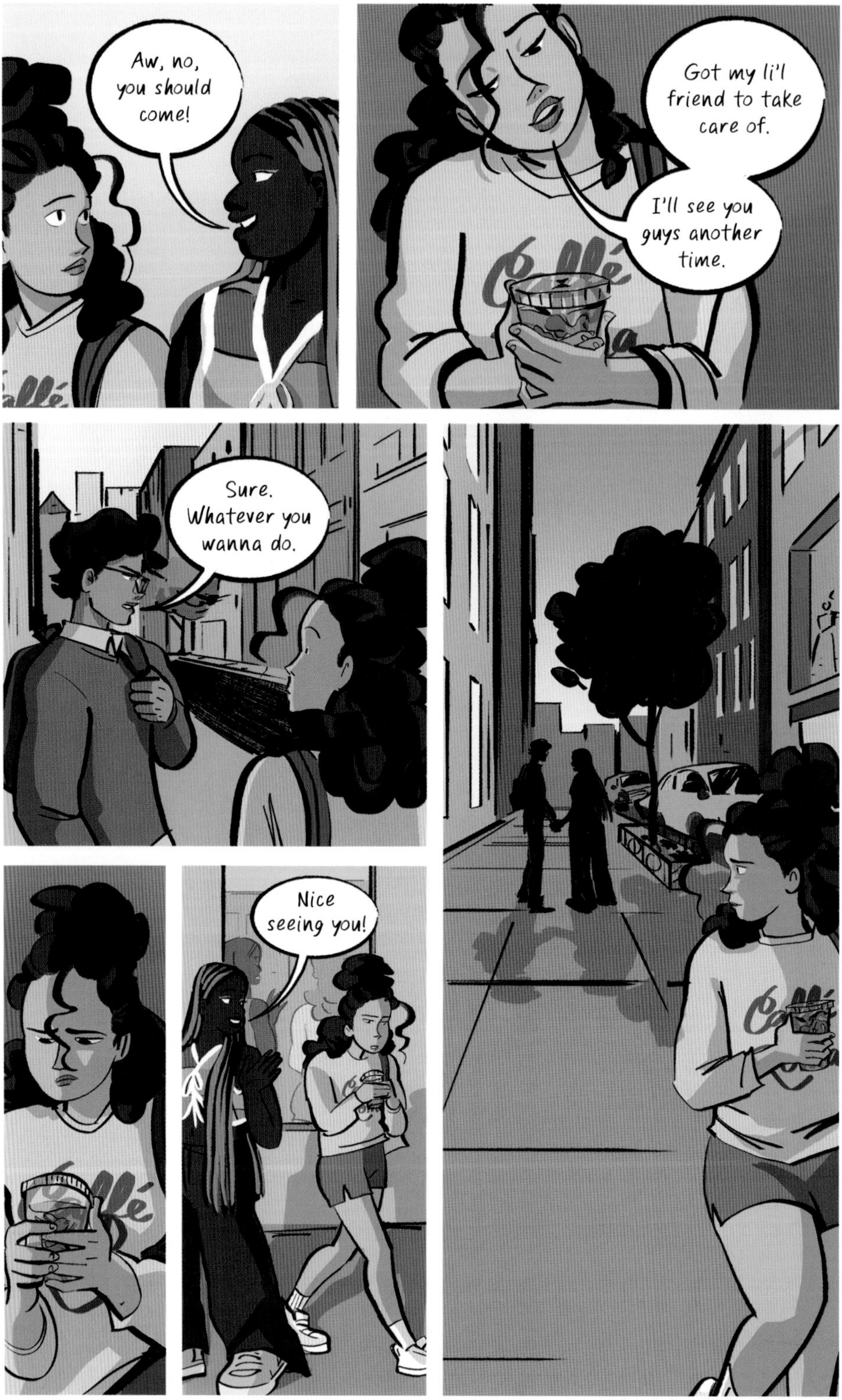
Aw, no, you should come!
Got my li'l friend to take care of.
I'll see you guys another time.
Sure. Whatever you wanna do.
Nice seeing you!

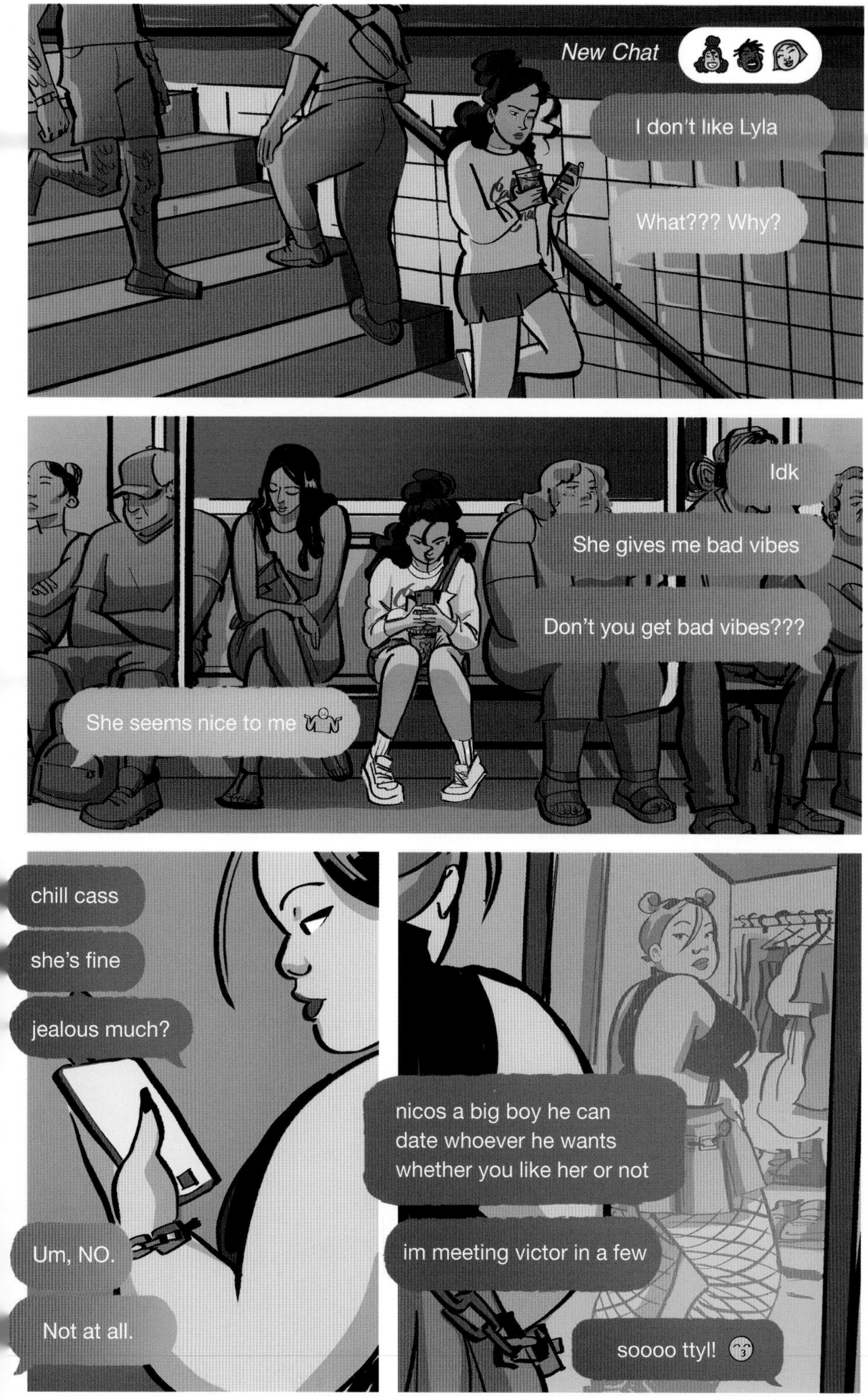
New Chat
I don't like Lyla
What??? Why?
Idk
She gives me bad vibes
Don't you get bad vibes???
She seems nice to me
chill cass
she's fine
jealous much?
Um, NO.
Not at all.
nicos a big boy he can date whoever he wants whether you like her or not
im meeting victor in a few
soooo ttyl!

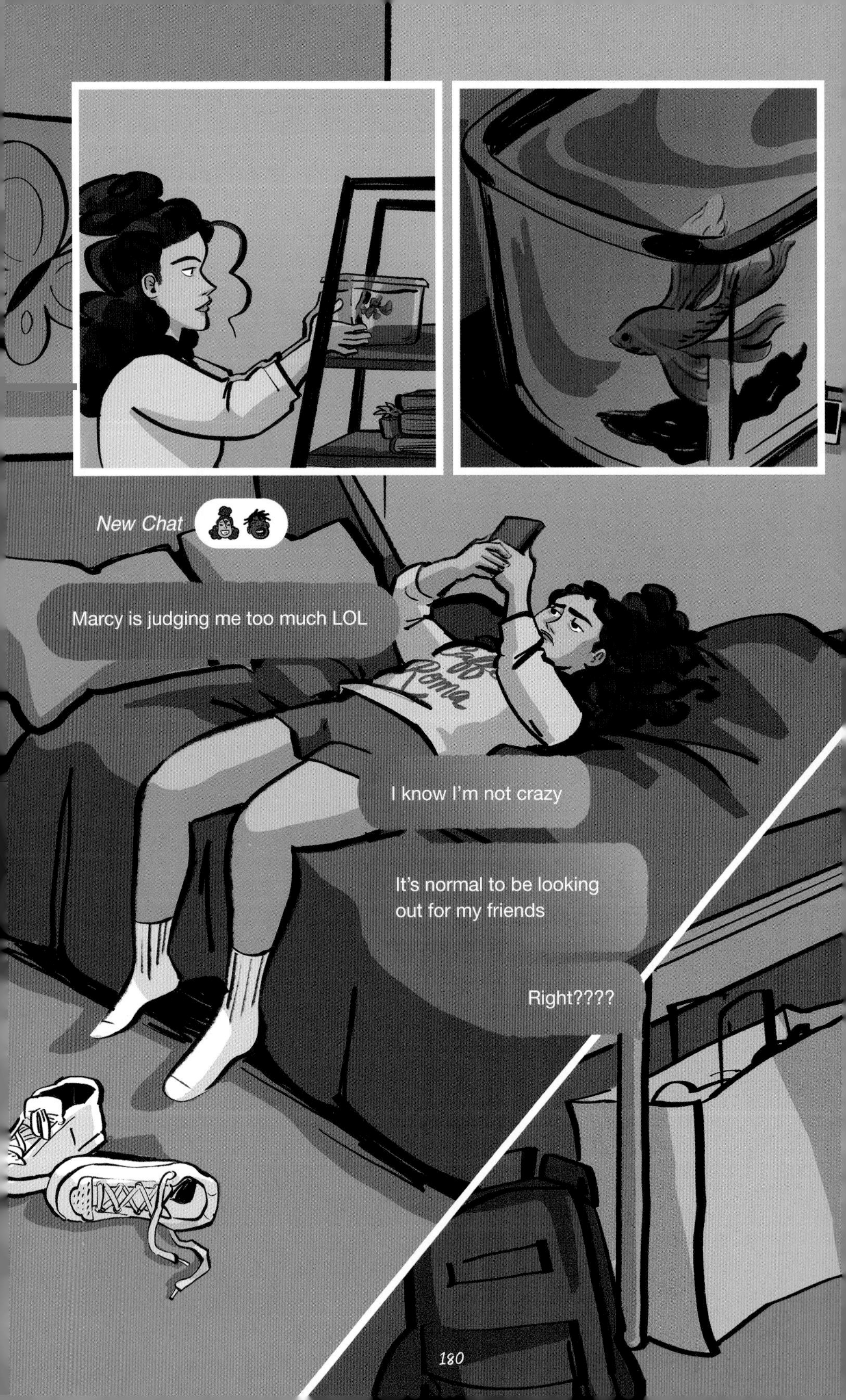
New Chat
Marcy is judging me too much LOL
I know I'm not crazy
It's normal to be looking out for my friends
Right????
Caffè Roma

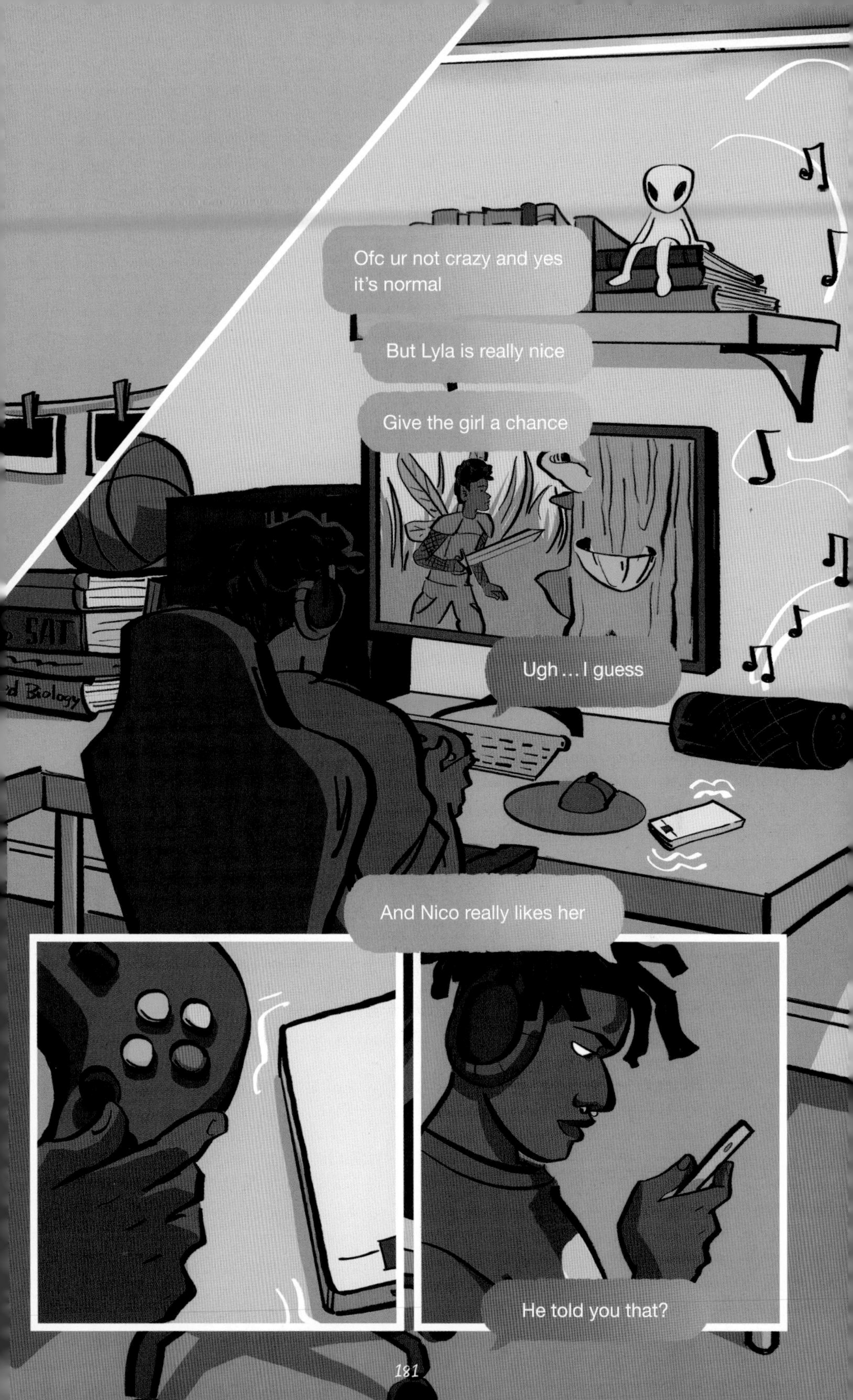
Ofc ur not crazy and yes it's normal
But Lyla is really nice
Give the girl a chance
Ugh . . . I guess
And Nico really likes her
He told you that?

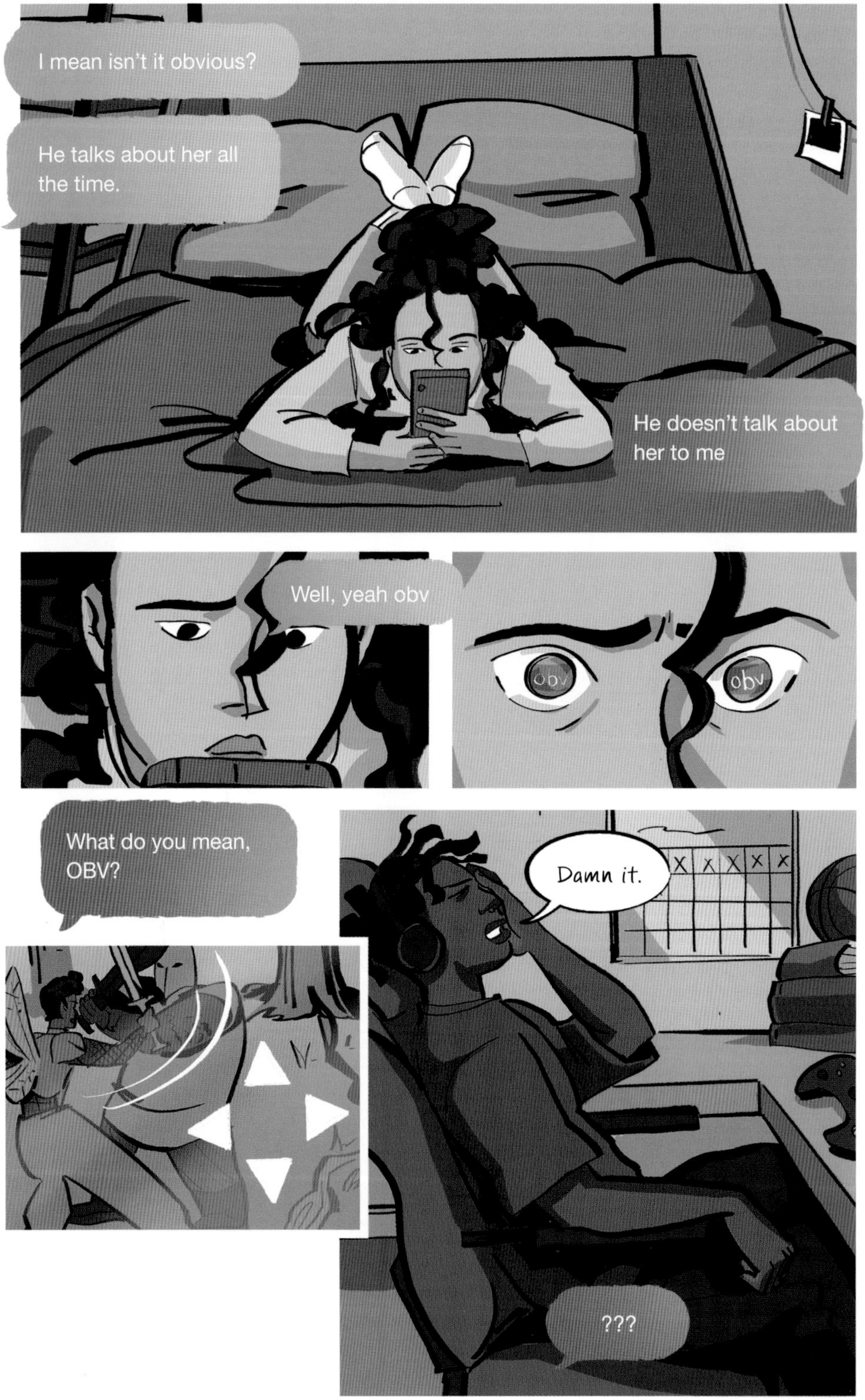
I mean isn't it obvious?
He talks about her all the time.
He doesn't talk about her to me
Well, yeah obv
obv
obv
What do you mean, OBV?
Damn it.
???

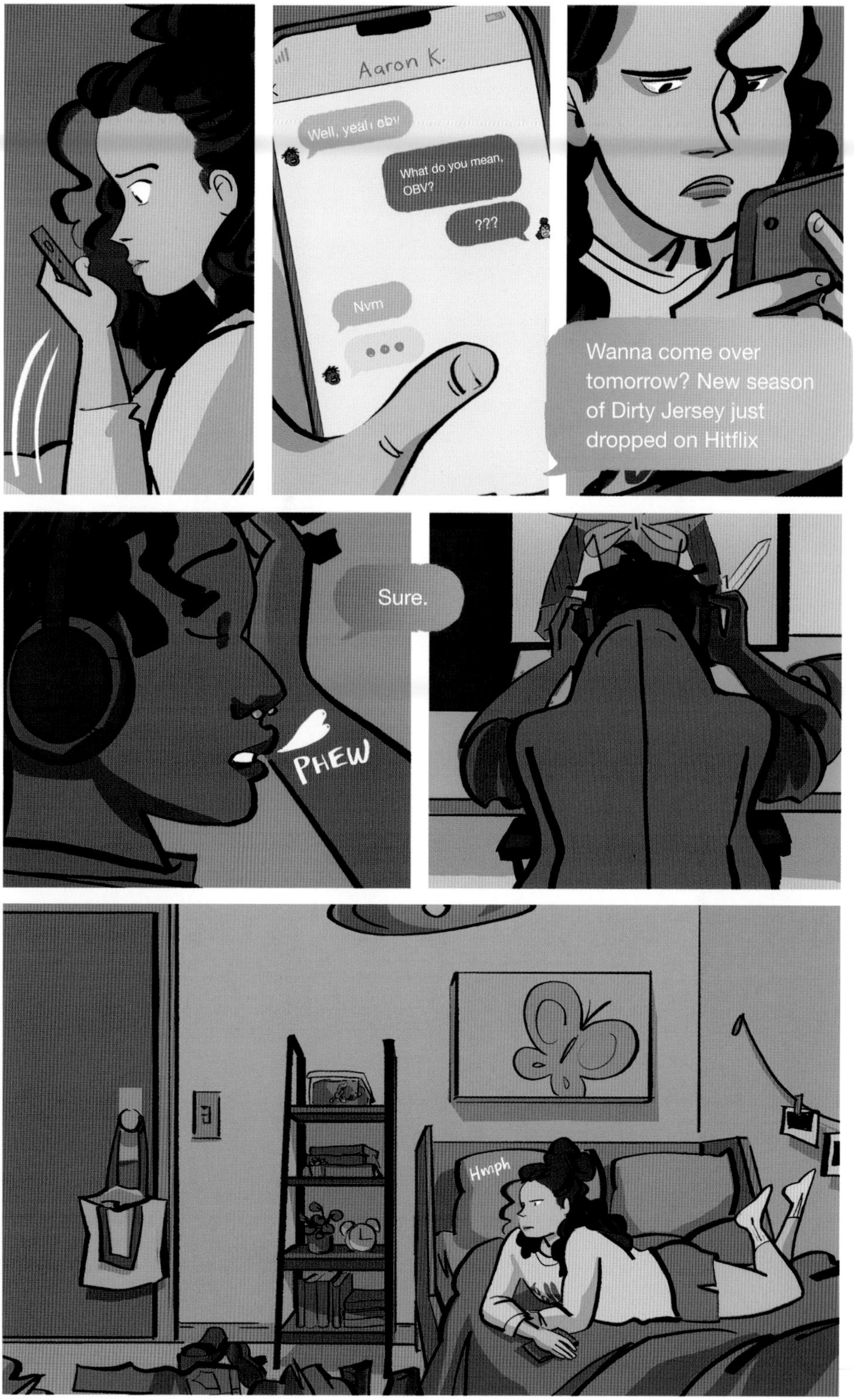
Aaron K.
Well, yeah obv
What do you mean, OBV?
???
Nvm
Wanna come over tomorrow? New season of Dirty Jersey just dropped on Hitflix
Sure.
PHEW
Hmph

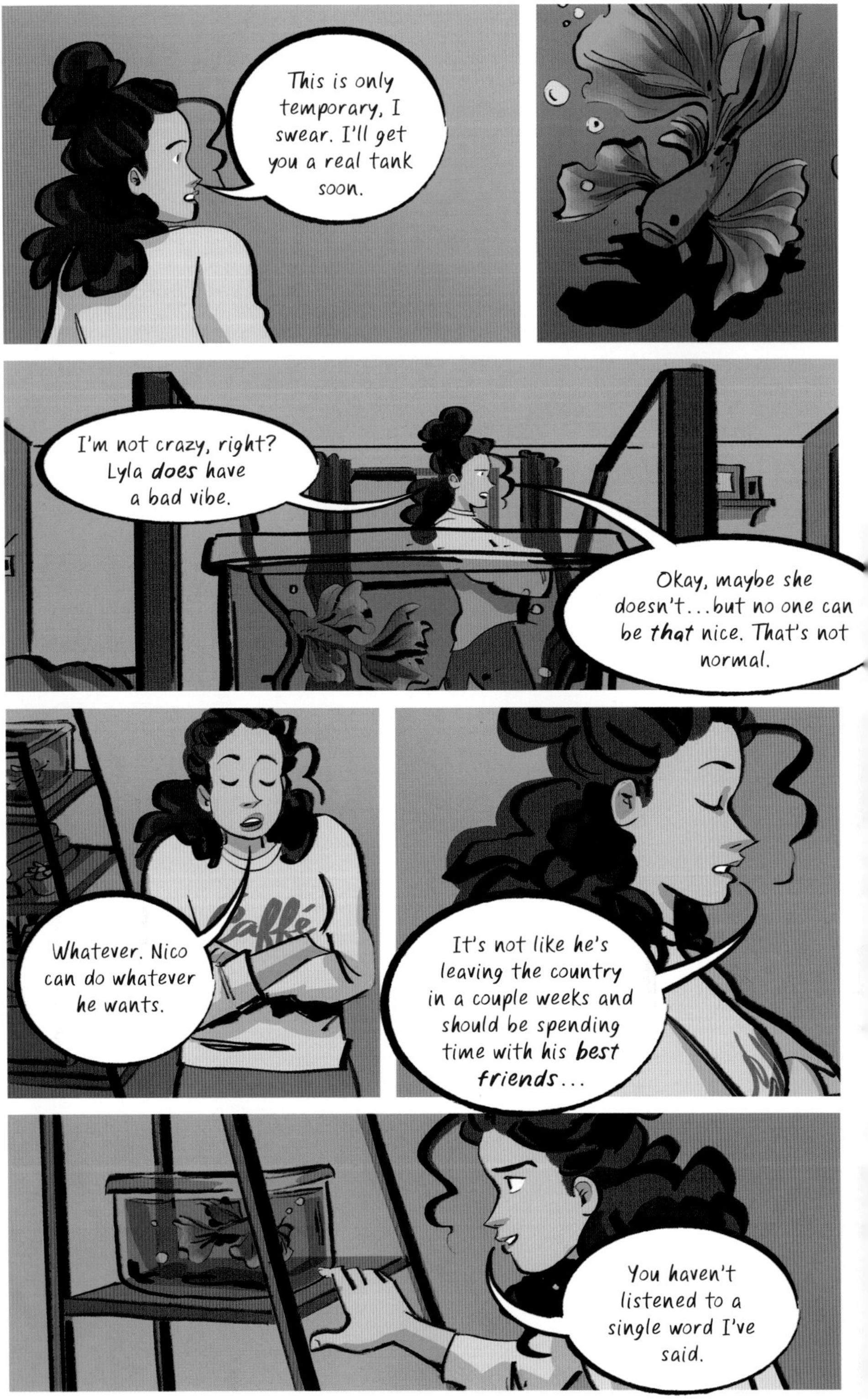
This is only temporary, I swear. I'll get you a real tank soon.
I'm not crazy, right? Lyla **does** have a bad vibe.
Okay, maybe she doesn't...but no one can be **that** nice. That's not normal.
Whatever. Nico can do whatever he wants.
It's not like he's leaving the country in a couple weeks and should be spending time with his **best friends**...
You haven't listened to a single word I've said.

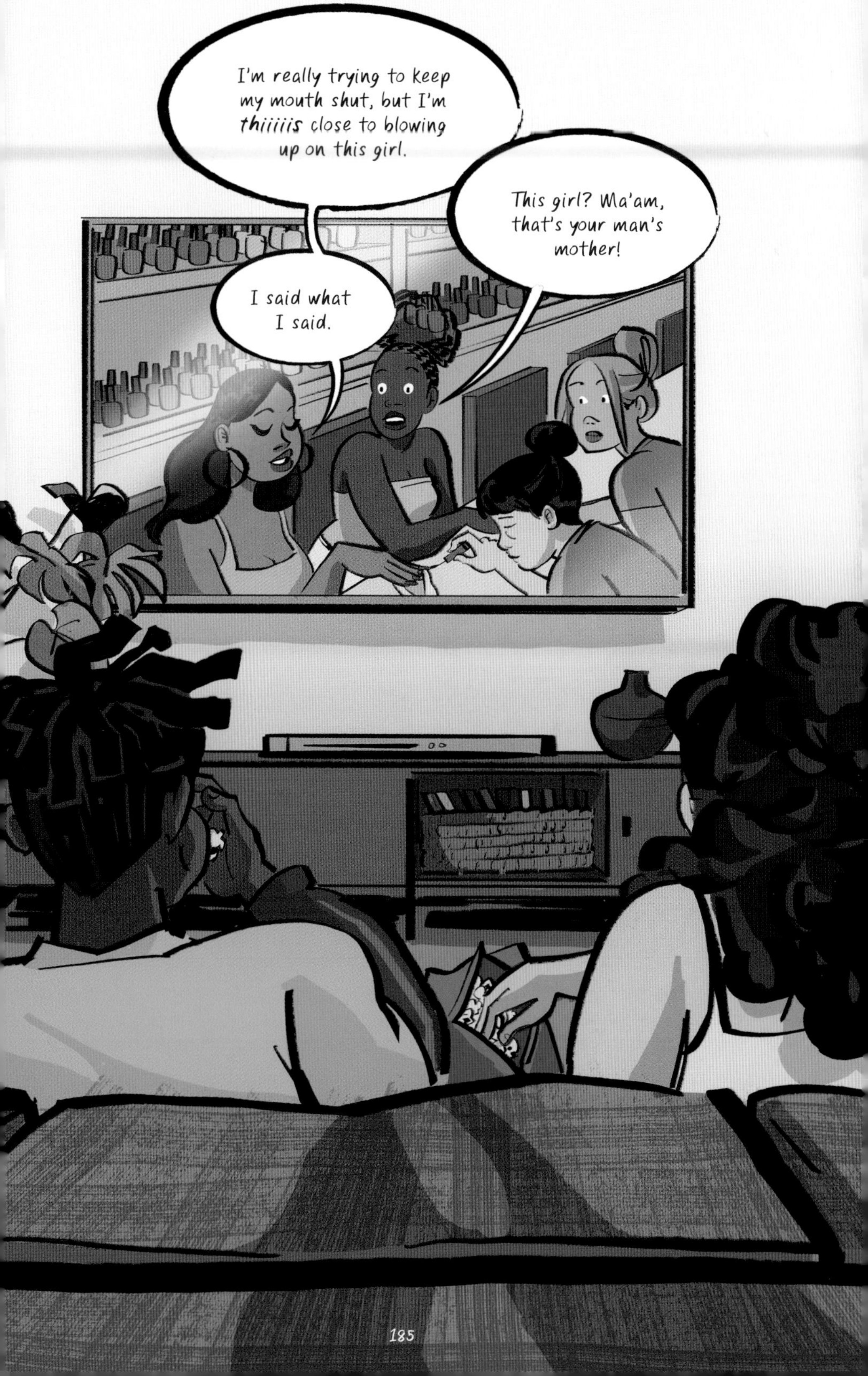
I'm really trying to keep my mouth shut, but I'm *thiiiiis* close to blowing up on this girl.
I said what I said.
This girl? Ma'am, that's your man's mother!

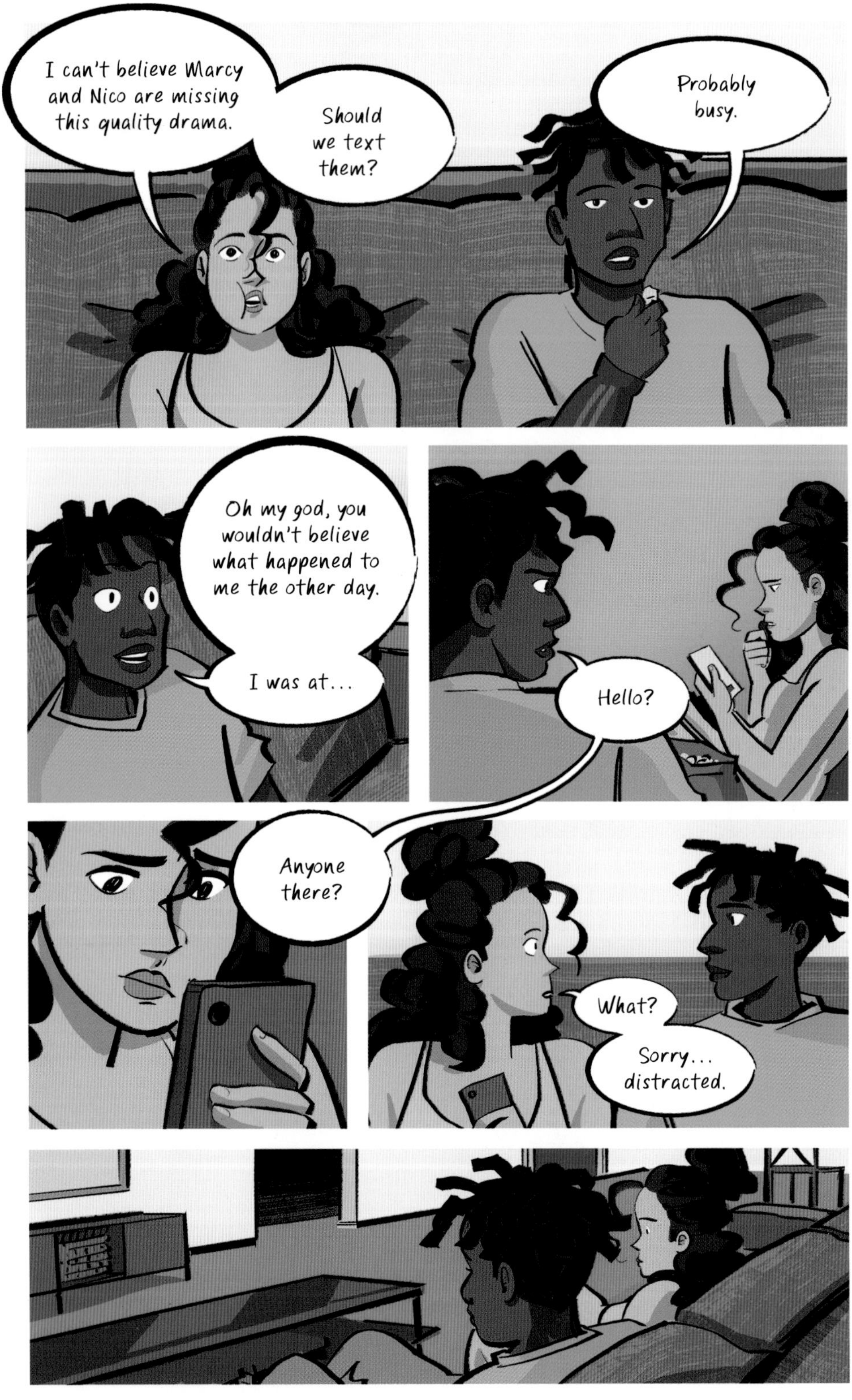
I can't believe Marcy and Nico are missing this quality drama.
Should we text them?
Probably busy.
Oh my god, you wouldn't believe what happened to me the other day.
I was at...
Hello?
Anyone there?
What?
Sorry... distracted.

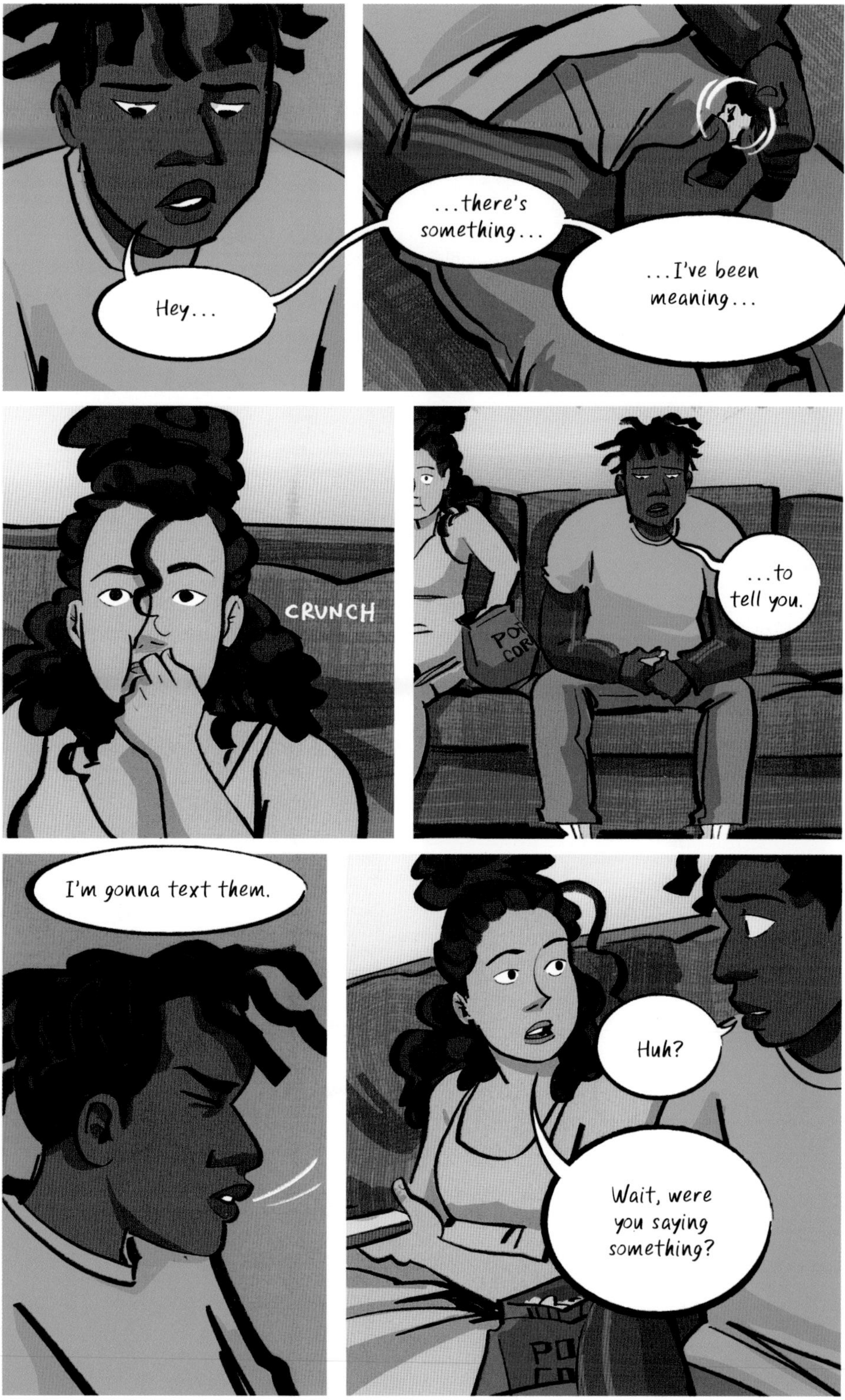
Hey...
...there's something...
...I've been meaning...
CRUNCH
...to tell you.
POP CORN
I'm gonna text them.
Huh?
Wait, were you saying something?

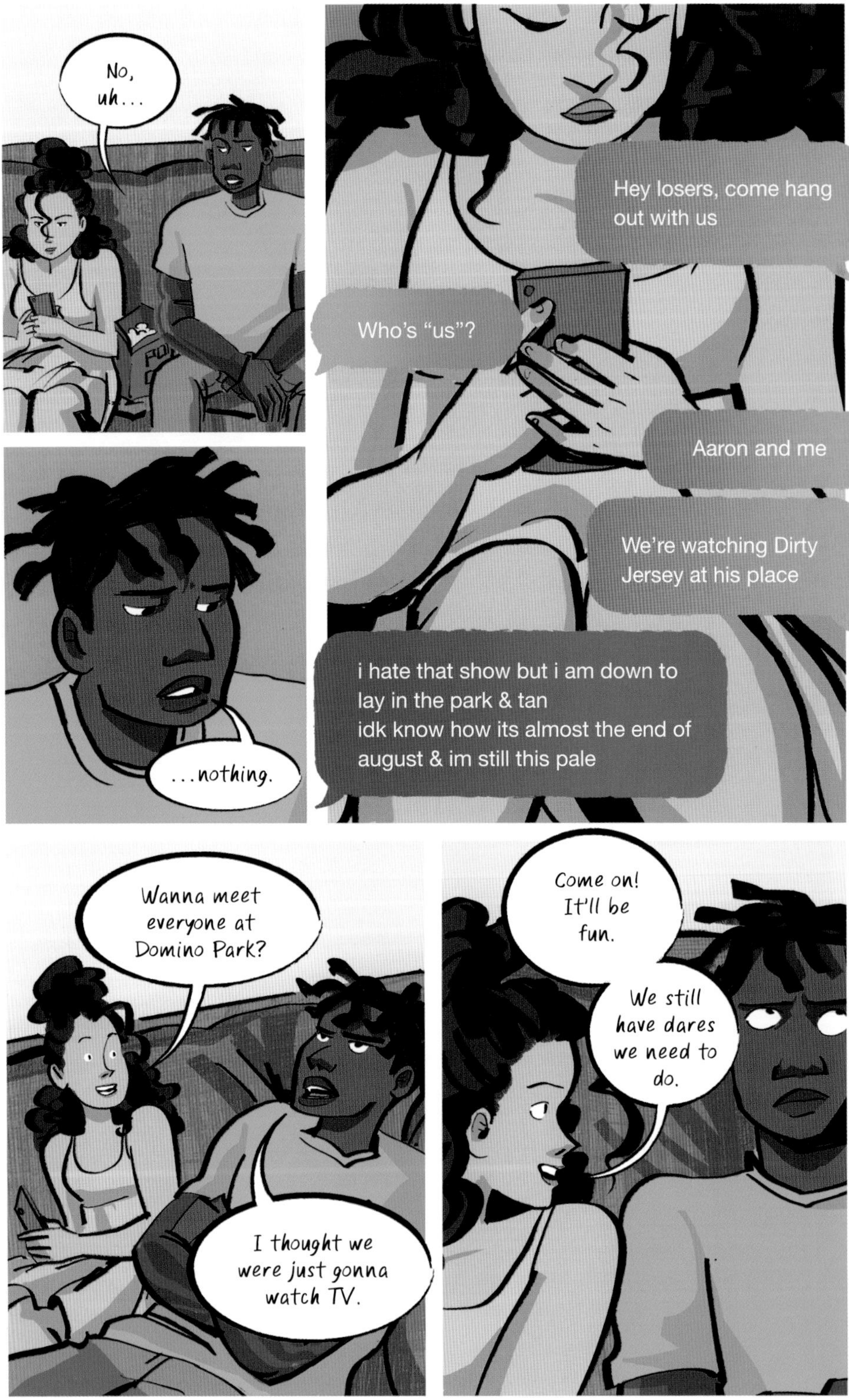
No, uh...
Hey losers, come hang out with us
Who's "us"?
Aaron and me
We're watching Dirty Jersey at his place
...nothing.
i hate that show but i am down to lay in the park & tan
idk know how its almost the end of august & im still this pale
Wanna meet everyone at Domino Park?
I thought we were just gonna watch TV.
Come on! It'll be fun.
We still have dares we need to do.

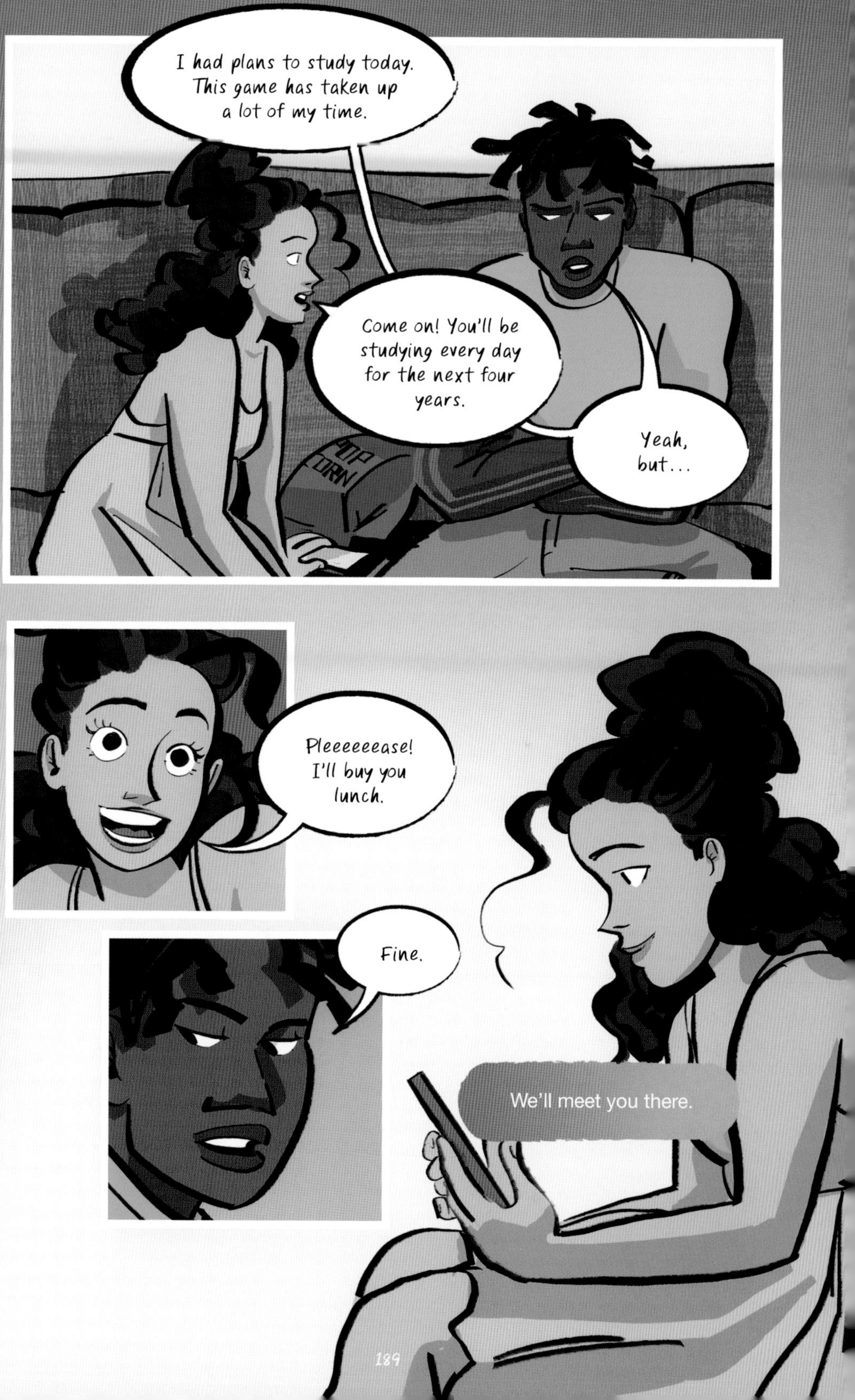
I had plans to study today. This game has taken up a lot of my time.
Come on! You'll be studying every day for the next four years.
Yeah, but...
Pleeeeeease! I'll buy you lunch.
Fine.
We'll meet you there.

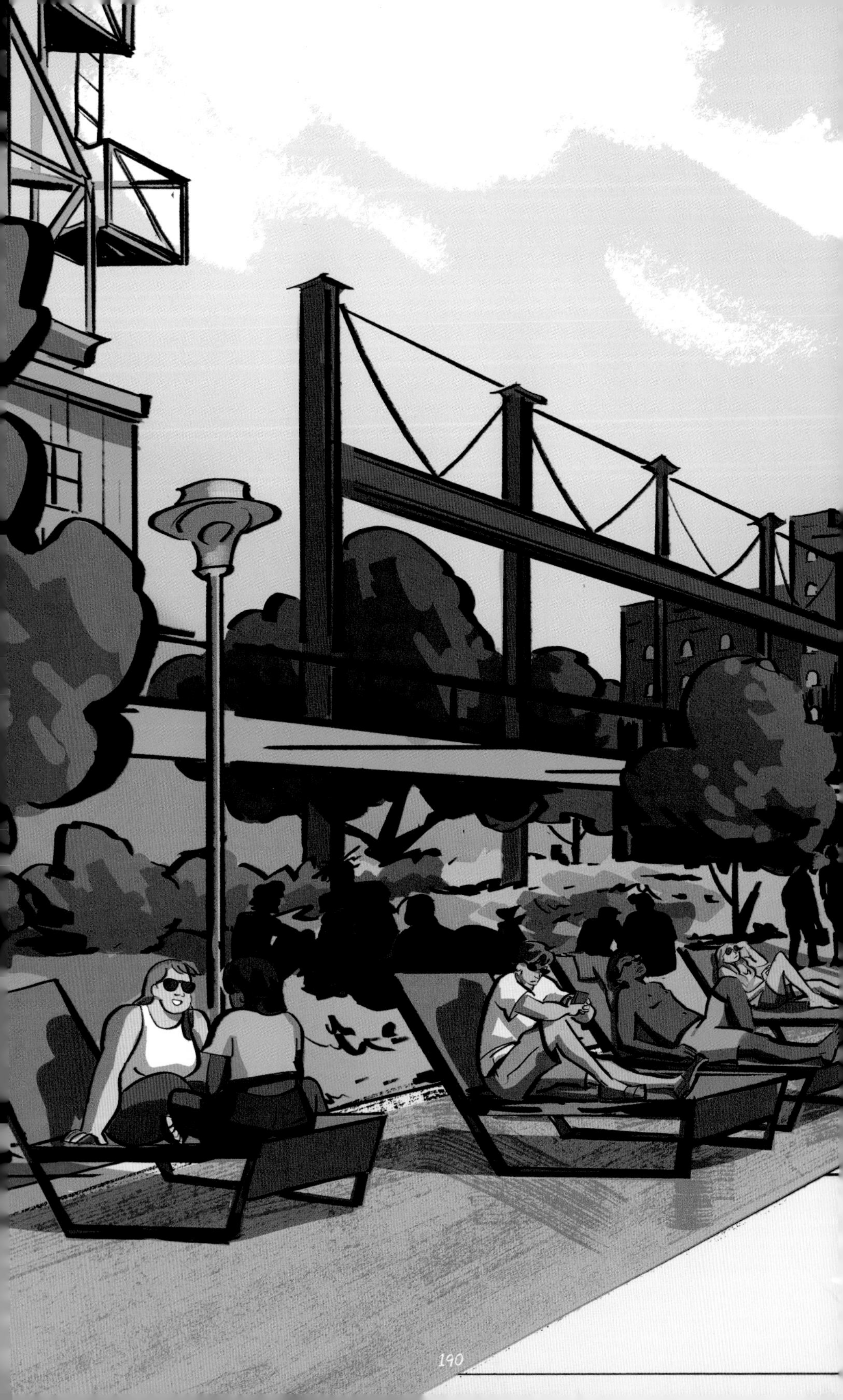

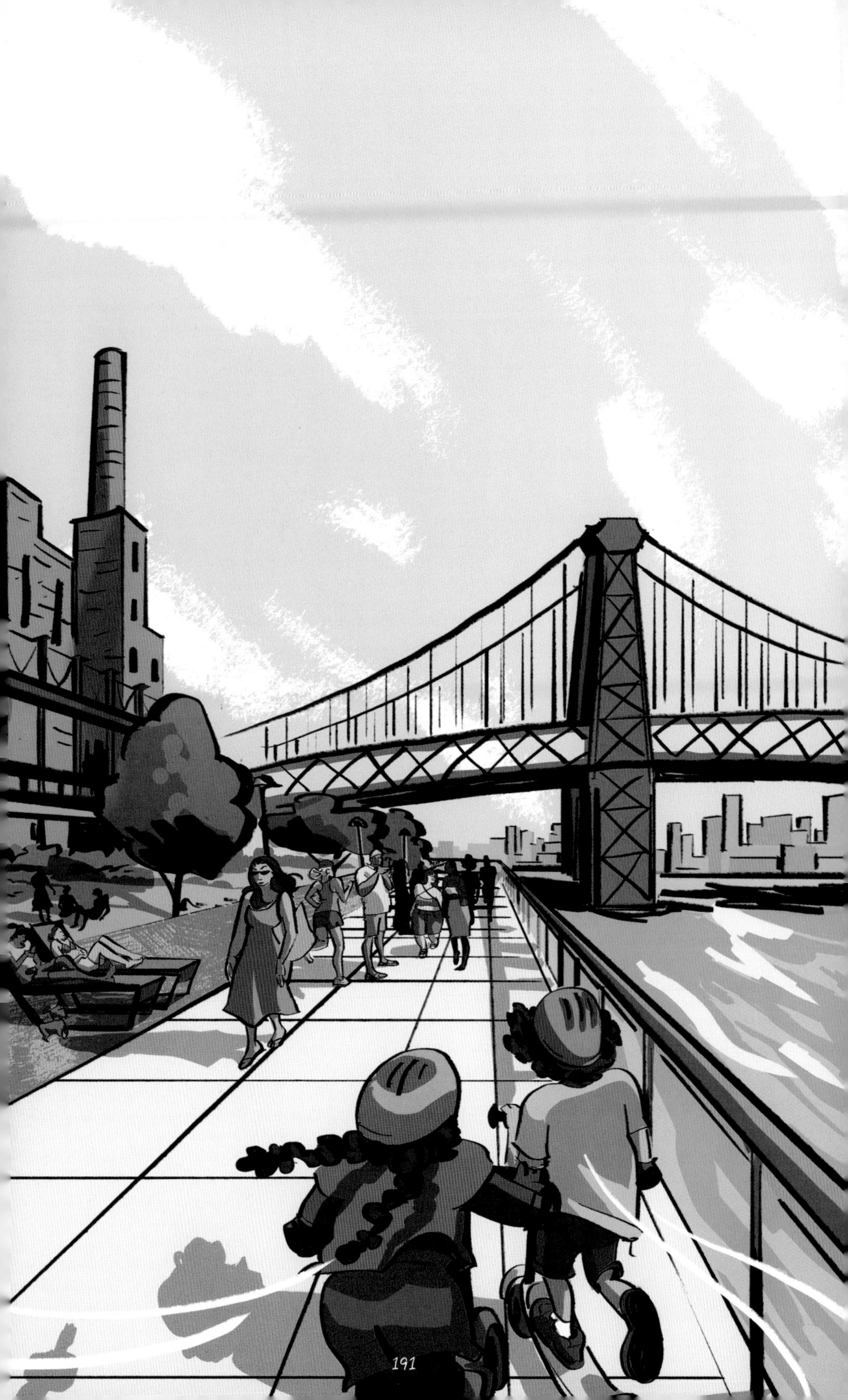

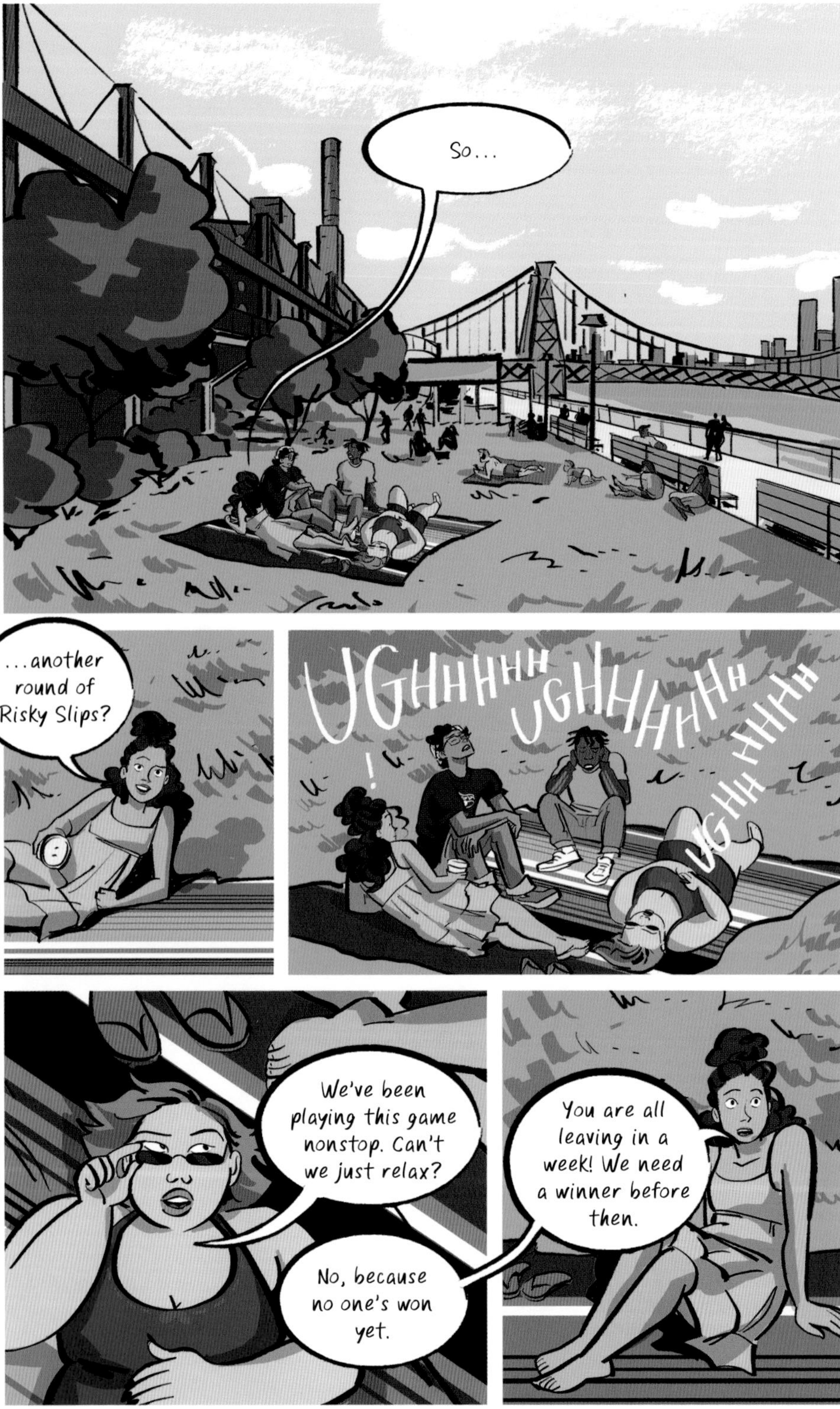
So...
...another round of Risky Slips?
UGHHHHH
UGHHHHHH
UGHHHHHH
!
We've been playing this game nonstop. Can't we just relax?
No, because no one's won yet.
You are all leaving in a week! We need a winner before then.

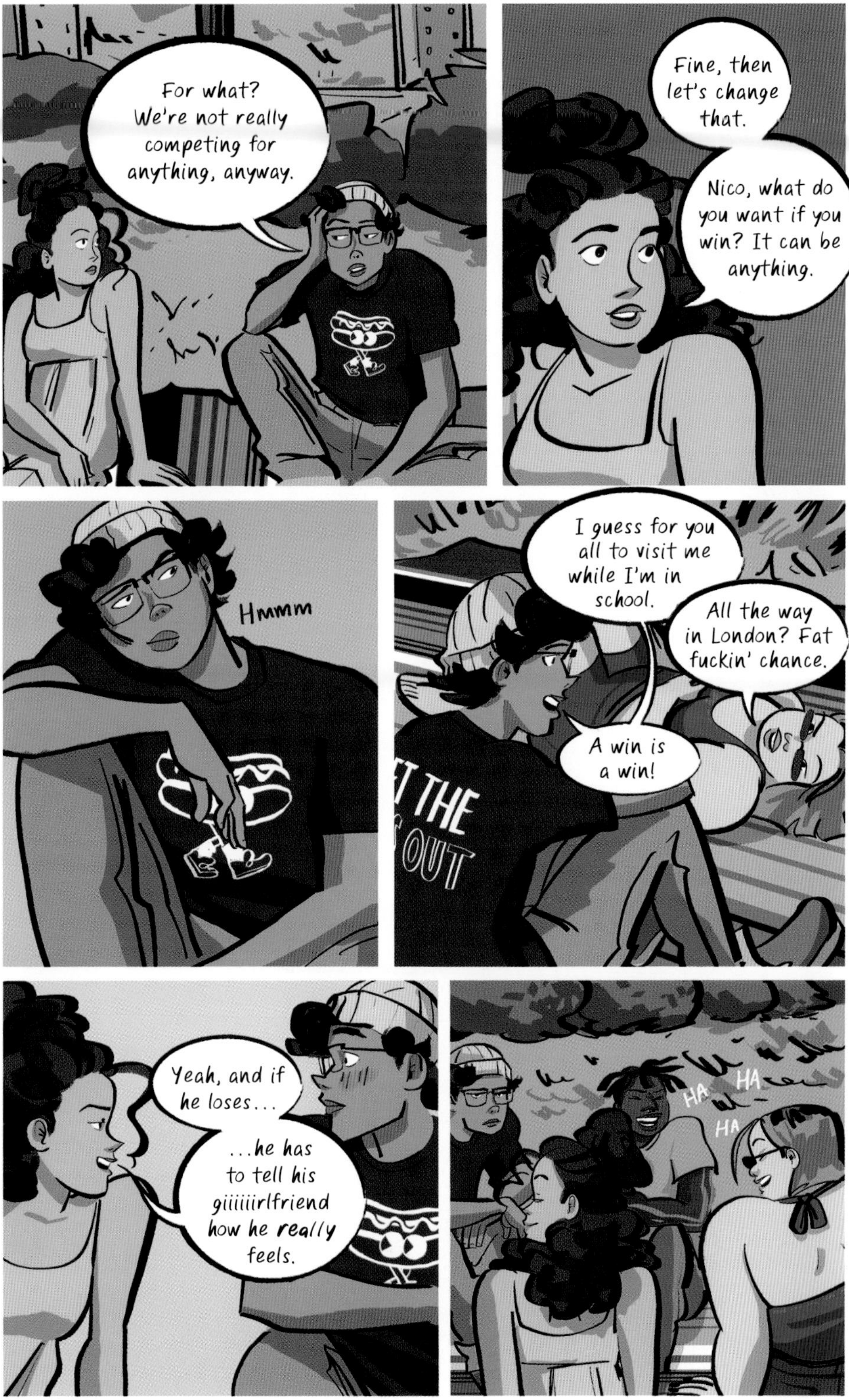

For what? We're not really competing for anything, anyway.
Fine, then let's change that.
Nico, what do you want if you win? It can be anything.
Hmmm
I guess for you all to visit me while I'm in school.
All the way in London? Fat fuckin' chance.
A win is a win!
Yeah, and if he loses...
...he has to tell his giiiiiirlfriend how he *really* feels.
HA
HA
HA

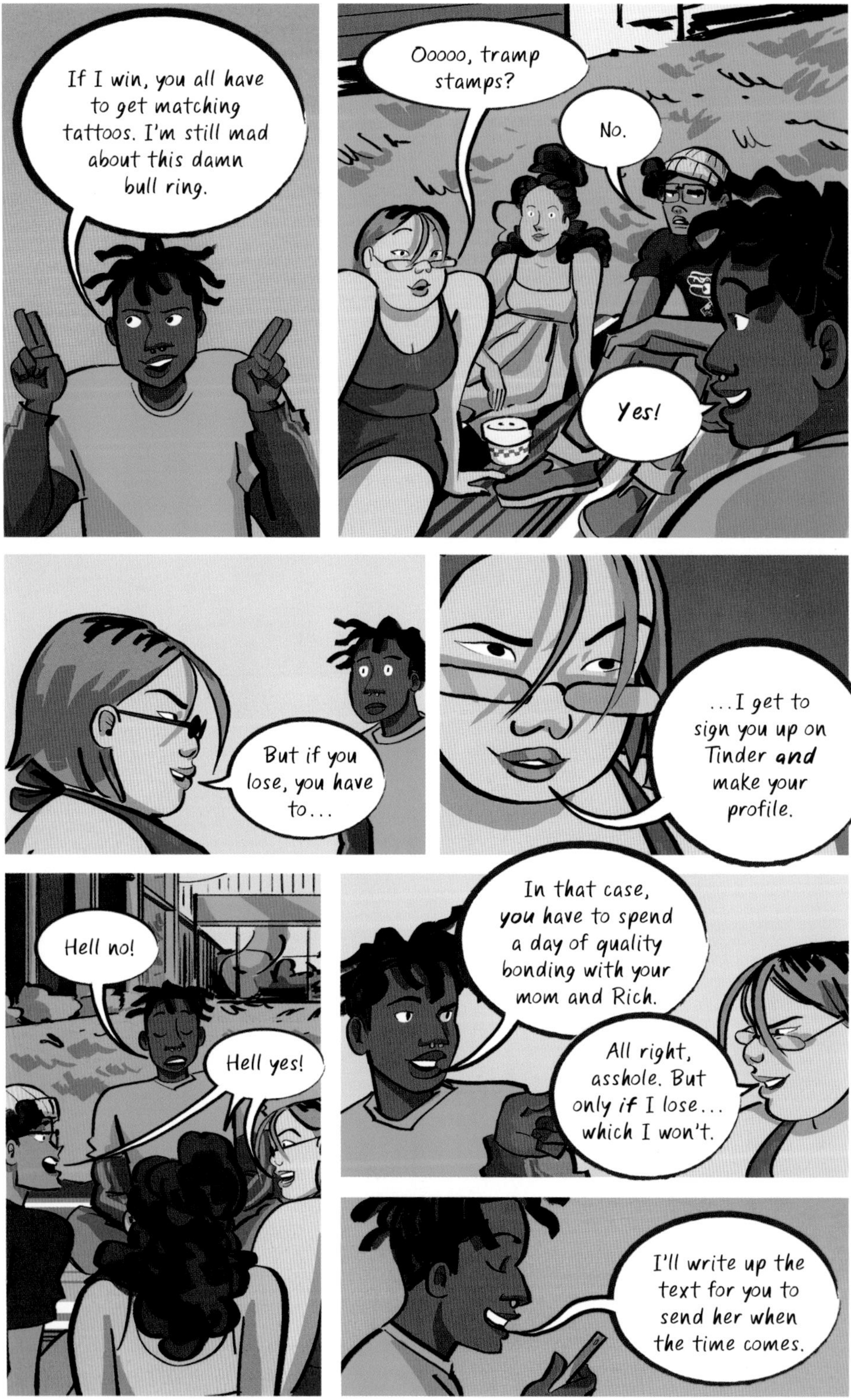
If I win, you all have to get matching tattoos. I'm still mad about this damn bull ring.
Ooooo, tramp stamps?
No.
Yes!
But if you lose, you have to...
...I get to sign you up on Tinder **and** make your profile.
Hell no!
Hell yes!
In that case, **you** have to spend a day of quality bonding with your mom and Rich.
All right, asshole. But only *if* I lose... which I won't.
I'll write up the text for you to send her when the time comes.

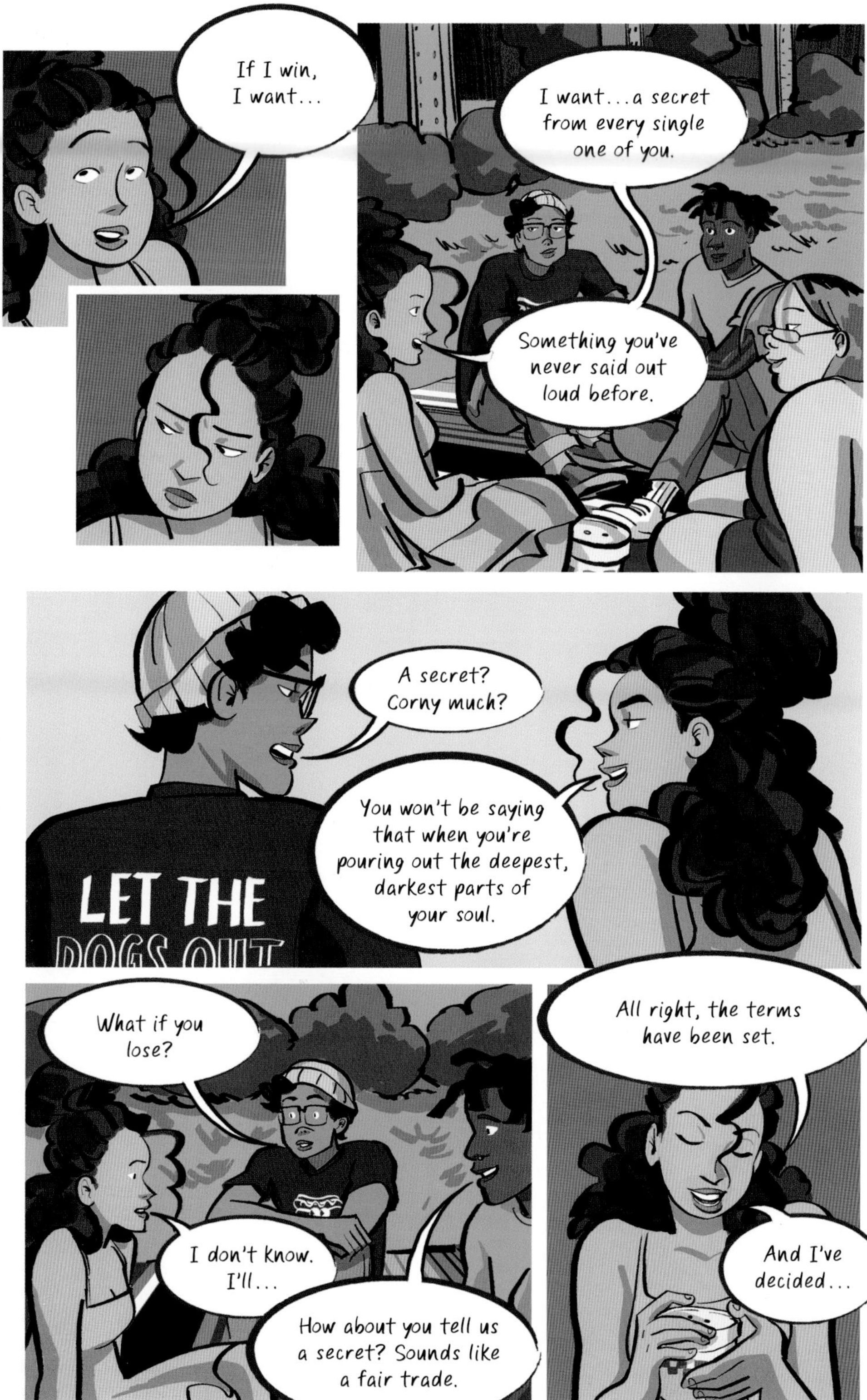
If I win, I want...
I want...a secret from every single one of you.
Something you've never said out loud before.
A secret? Corny much?
You won't be saying that when you're pouring out the deepest, darkest parts of your soul.
LET THE
What if you lose?
I don't know. I'll...
How about you tell us a secret? Sounds like a fair trade.
All right, the terms have been set.
And I've decided...

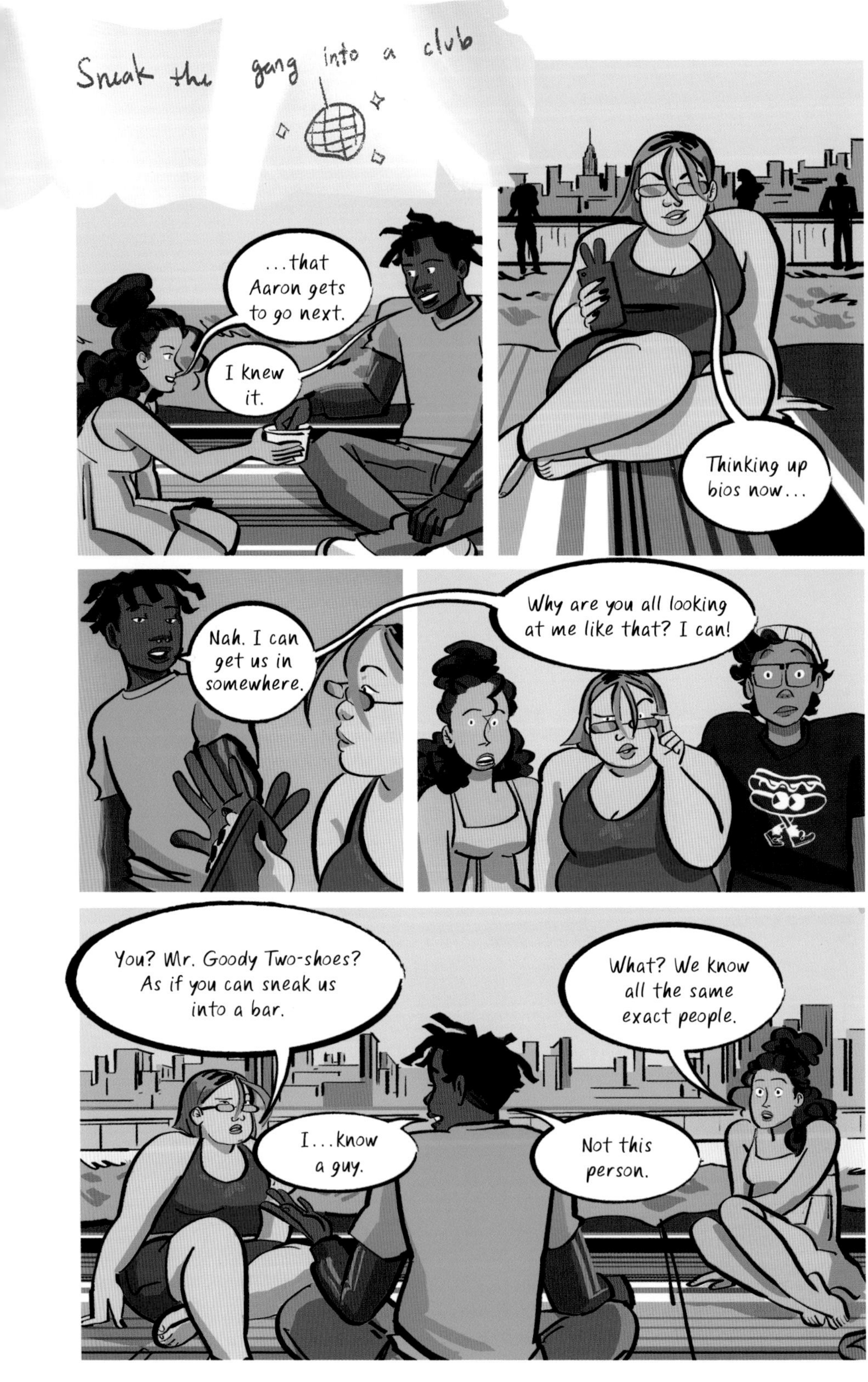
Sneak the gang into a club
...that Aaron gets to go next.
I knew it.
Thinking up bios now...
Nah. I can get us in somewhere.
Why are you all looking at me like that? I can!
You? Mr. Goody Two-shoes? As if you can sneak us into a bar.
What? We know all the same exact people.
I...know a guy.
Not this person.

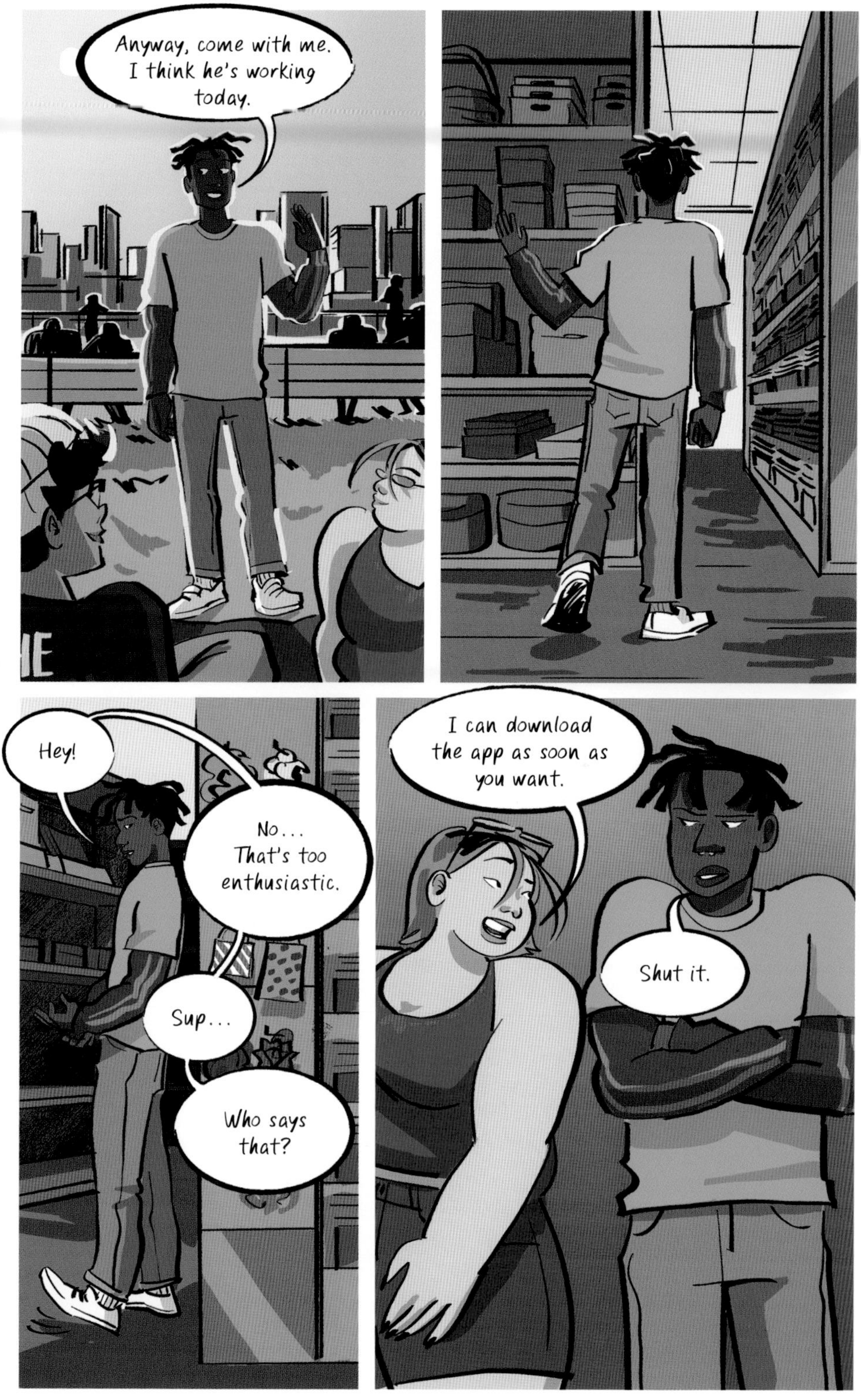
Anyway, come with me. I think he's working today.
Hey!
No... That's too enthusiastic.
Sup...
Who says that?
I can download the app as soon as you want.
Shut it.

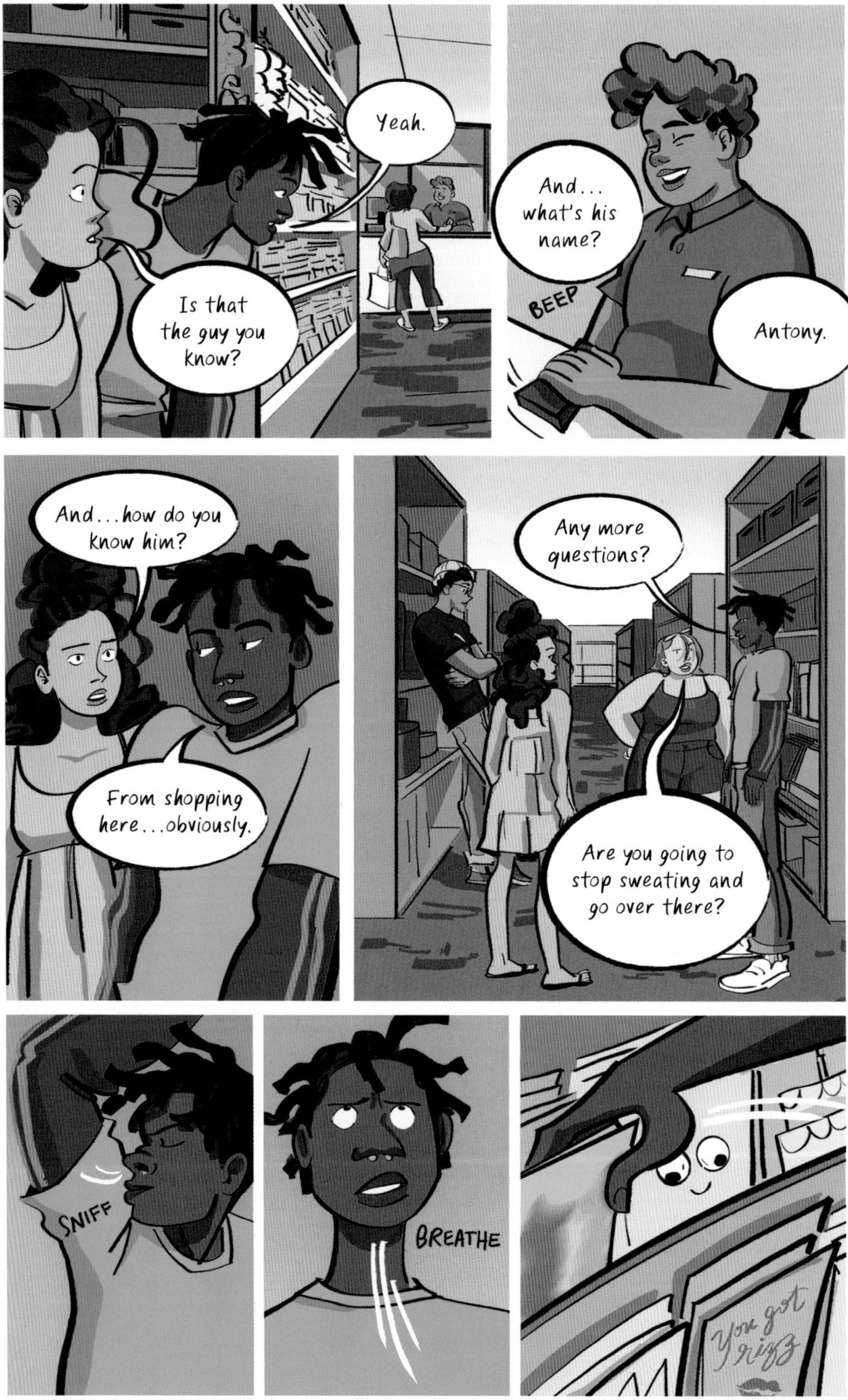
Is that the guy you know?
Yeah.
And... what's his name?
BEEP
Antony.
And...how do you know him?
From shopping here...obviously.
Any more questions?
Are you going to stop sweating and go over there?
SNIFF
BREATHE
You got rizz

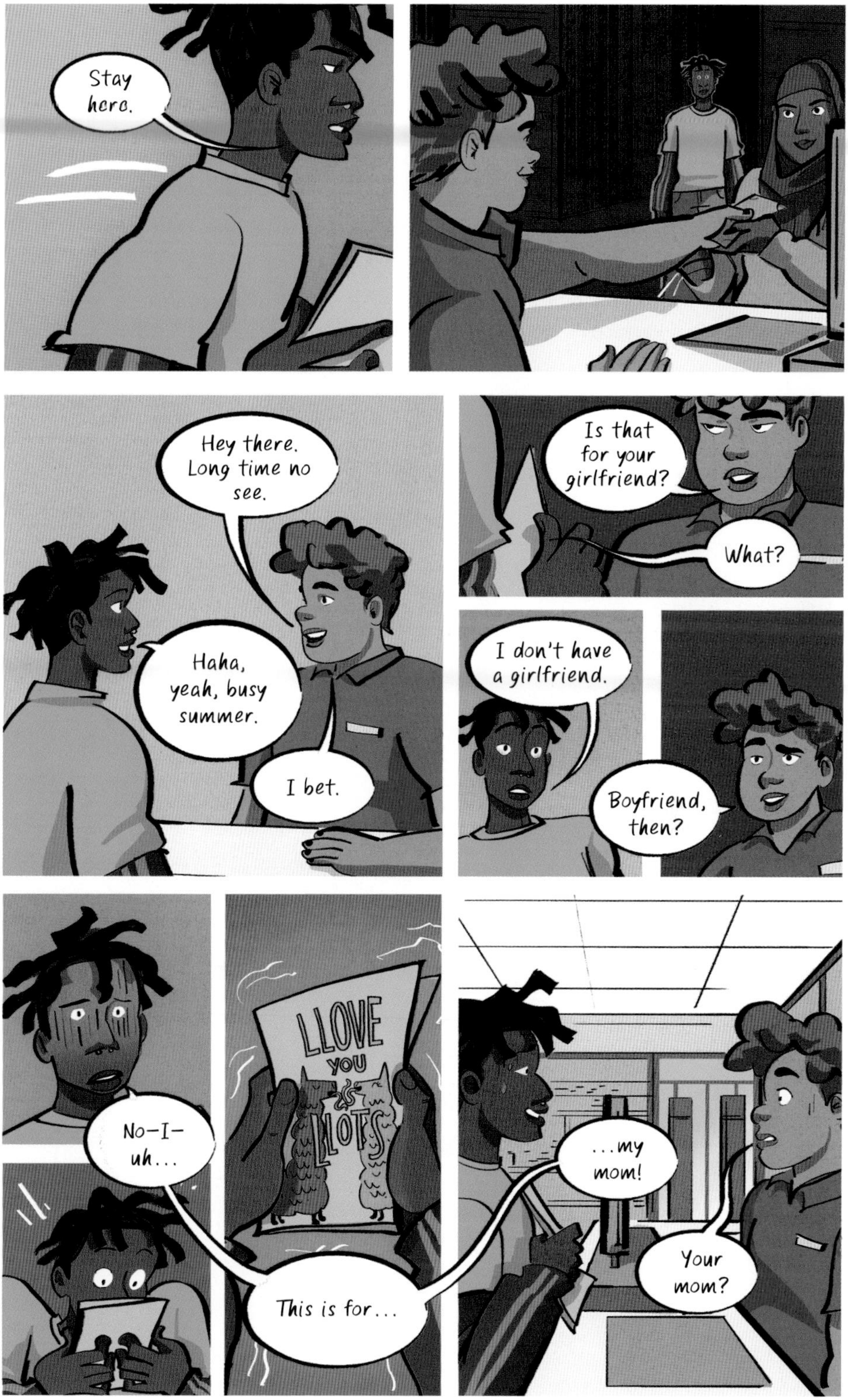
Stay here.
Hey there. Long time no see.
Haha, yeah, busy summer.
I bet.
Is that for your girlfriend?
What?
I don't have a girlfriend.
Boyfriend, then?
No—I— uh...
LLOVE YOU LLOTS
This is for...
...my mom!
Your mom?

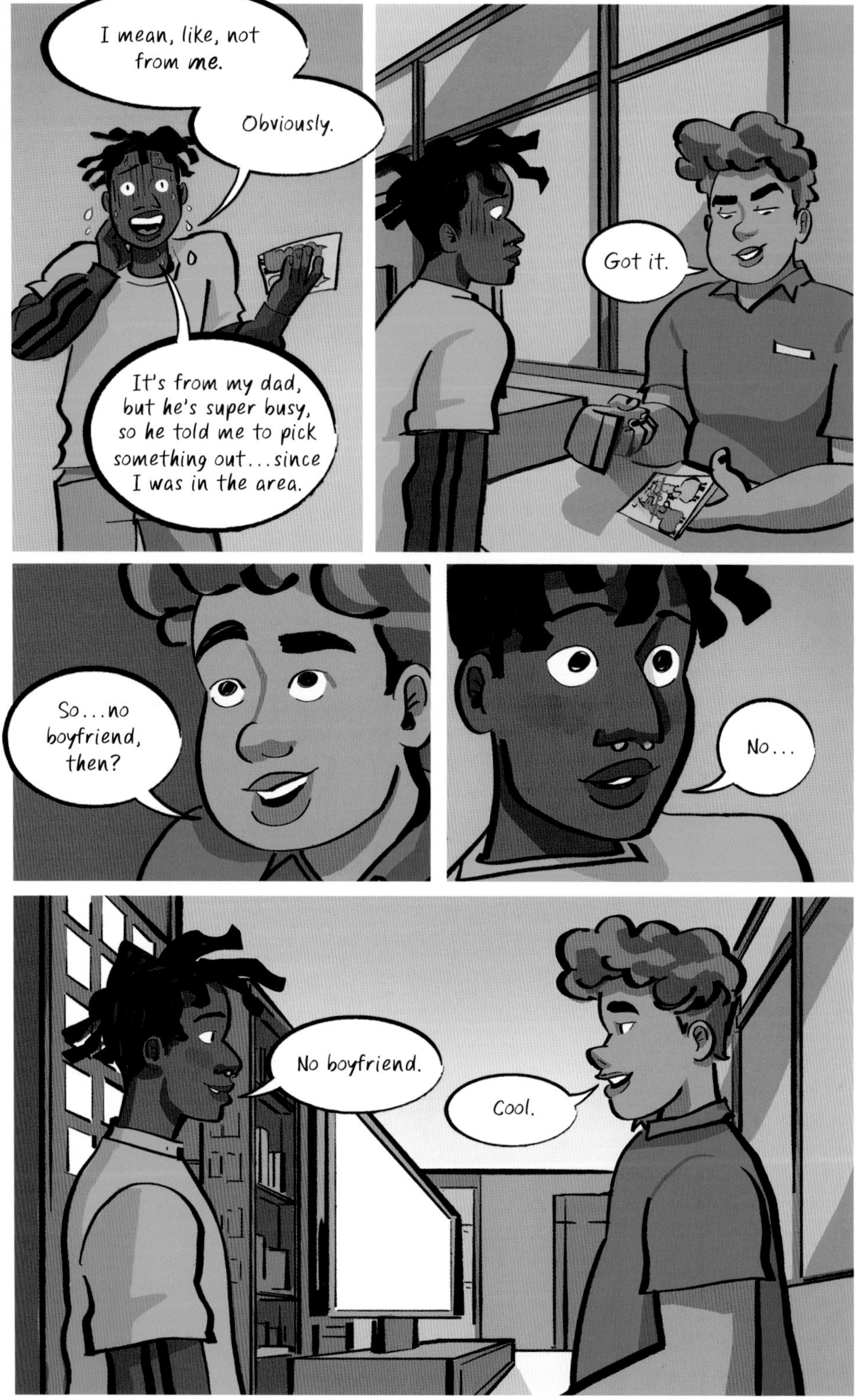
I mean, like, not from me.
Obviously.
It's from my dad, but he's super busy, so he told me to pick something out...since I was in the area.
Got it.
So...no boyfriend, then?
No...
No boyfriend.
Cool.

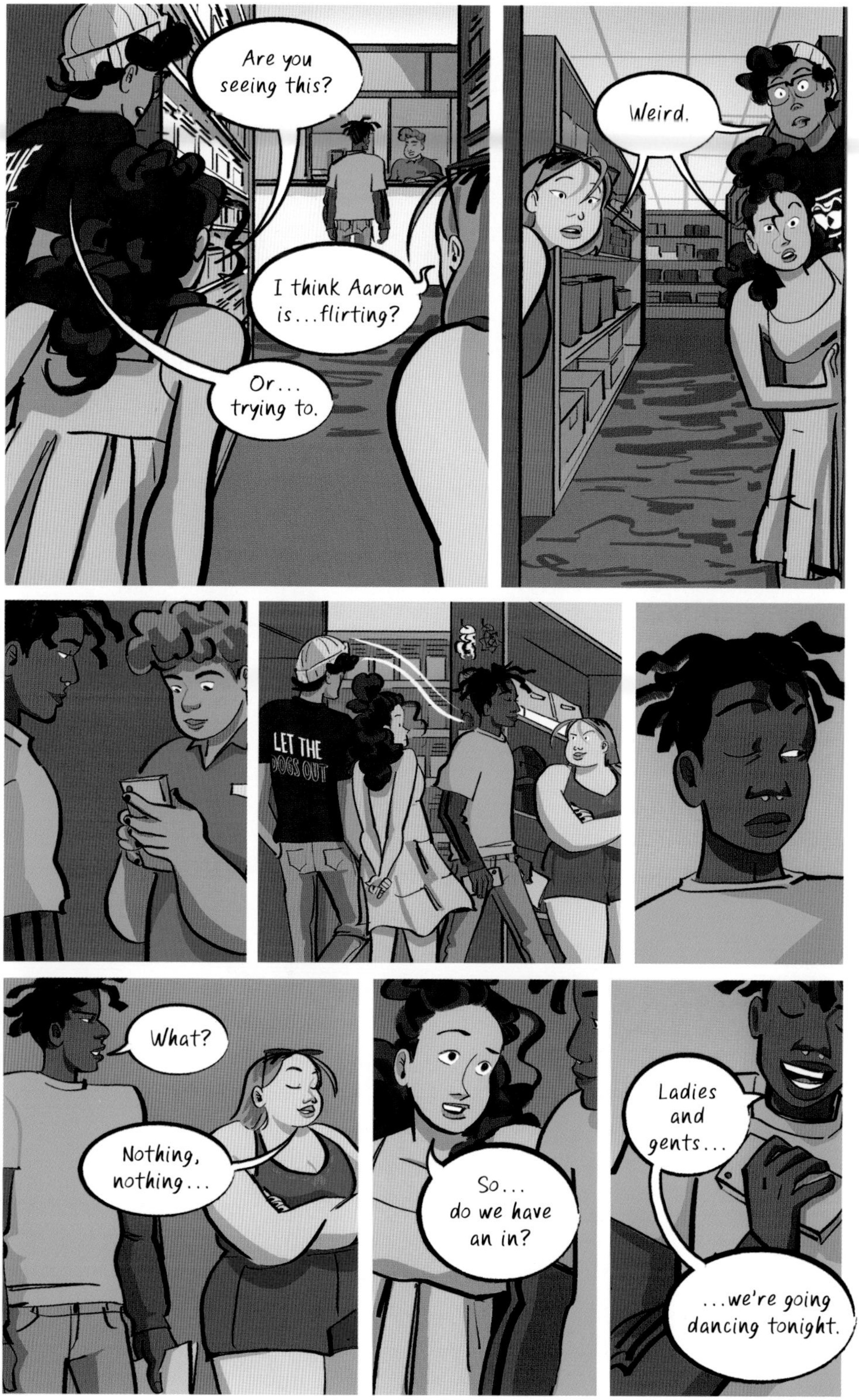
Are you seeing this?
I think Aaron is...flirting?
Or... trying to.
Weird.
LET THE DOGS OUT
What?
Nothing, nothing...
So... do we have an in?
Ladies and gents...
...we're going dancing tonight.

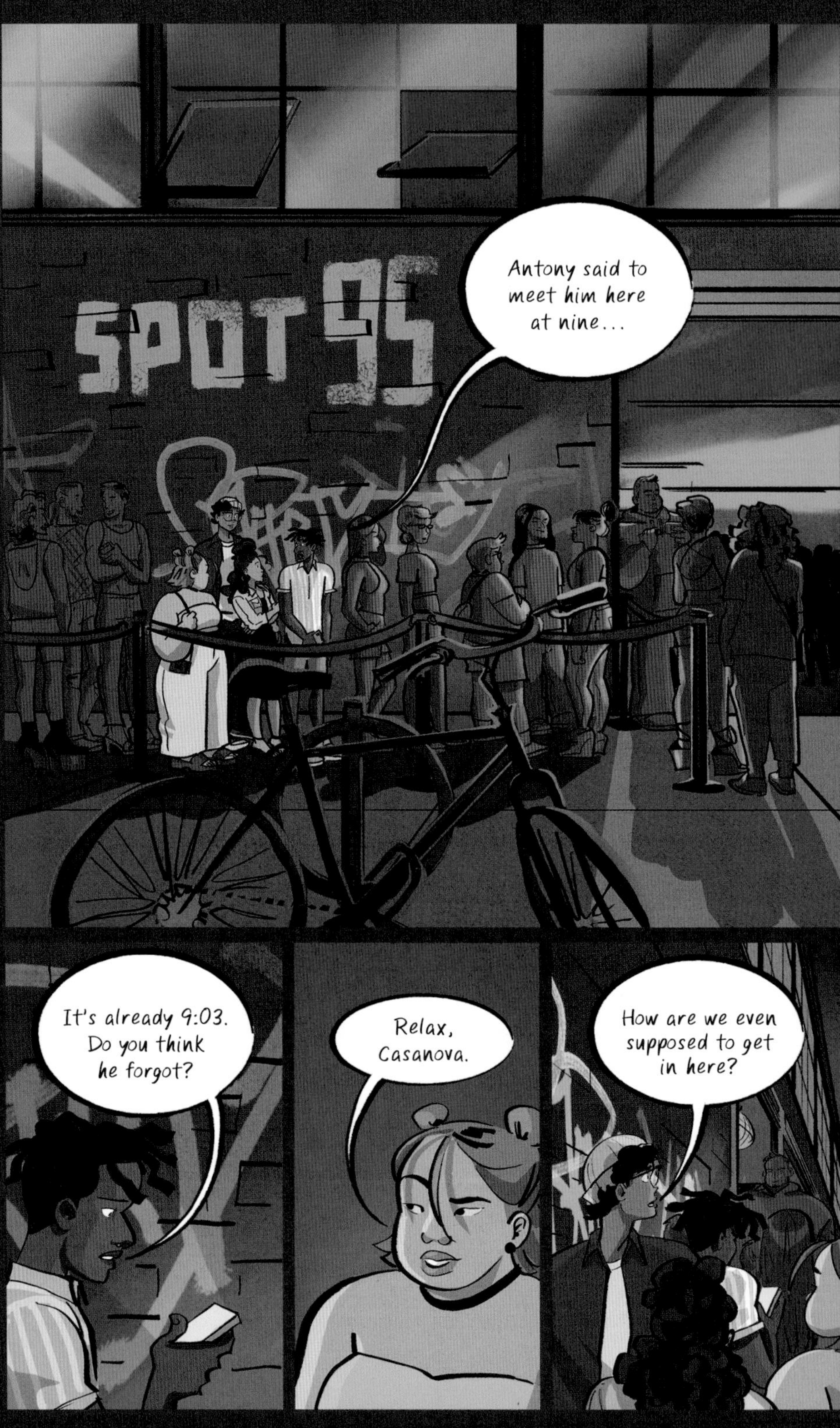
SPOT 95
Antony said to meet him here at nine...
It's already 9:03. Do you think he forgot?
Relax, Casanova.
How are we even supposed to get in here?

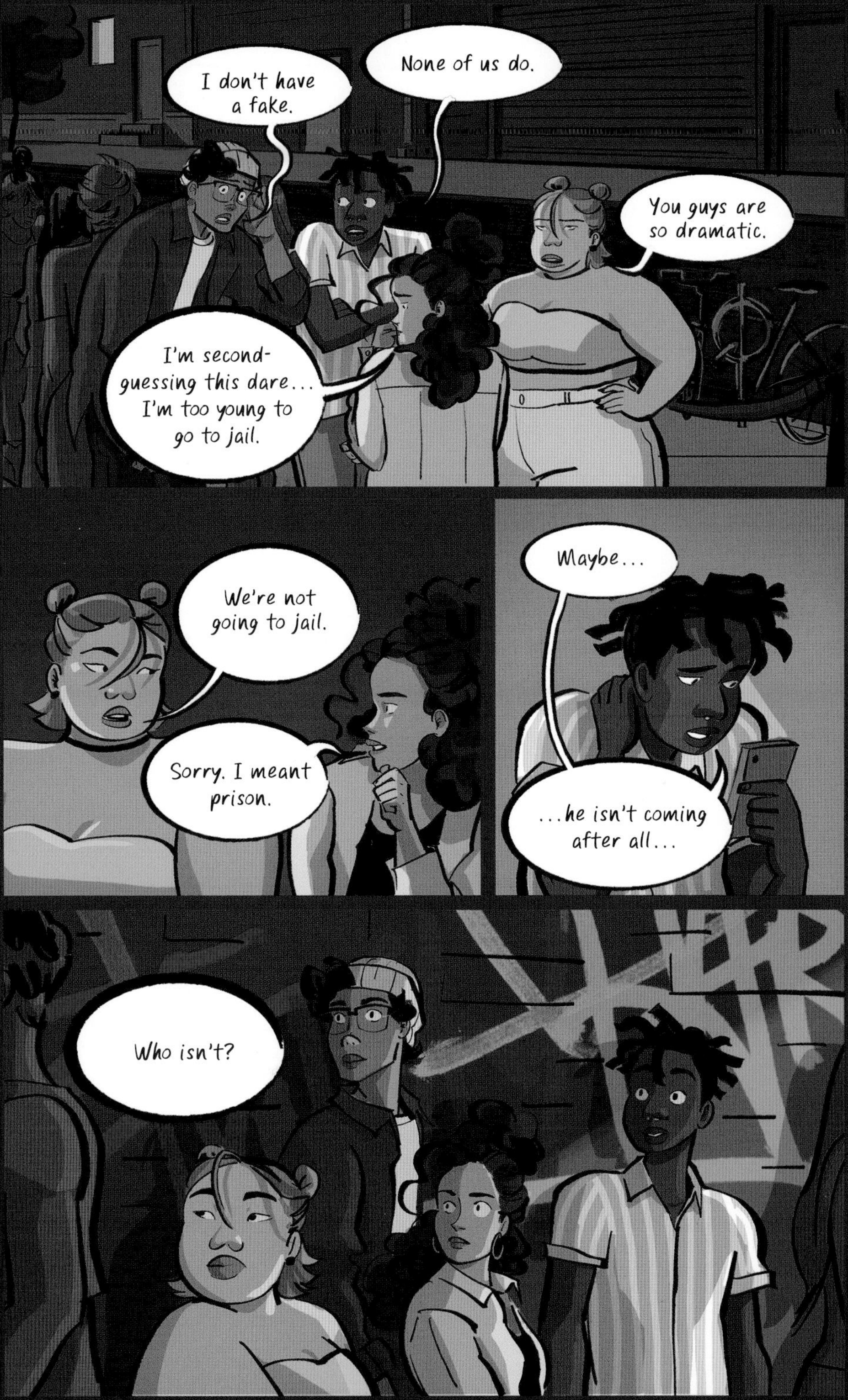
I don't have a fake.
None of us do.
You guys are so dramatic.
I'm second-guessing this dare... I'm too young to go to jail.
We're not going to jail.
Sorry. I meant prison.
Maybe...
...he isn't coming after all...
Who isn't?

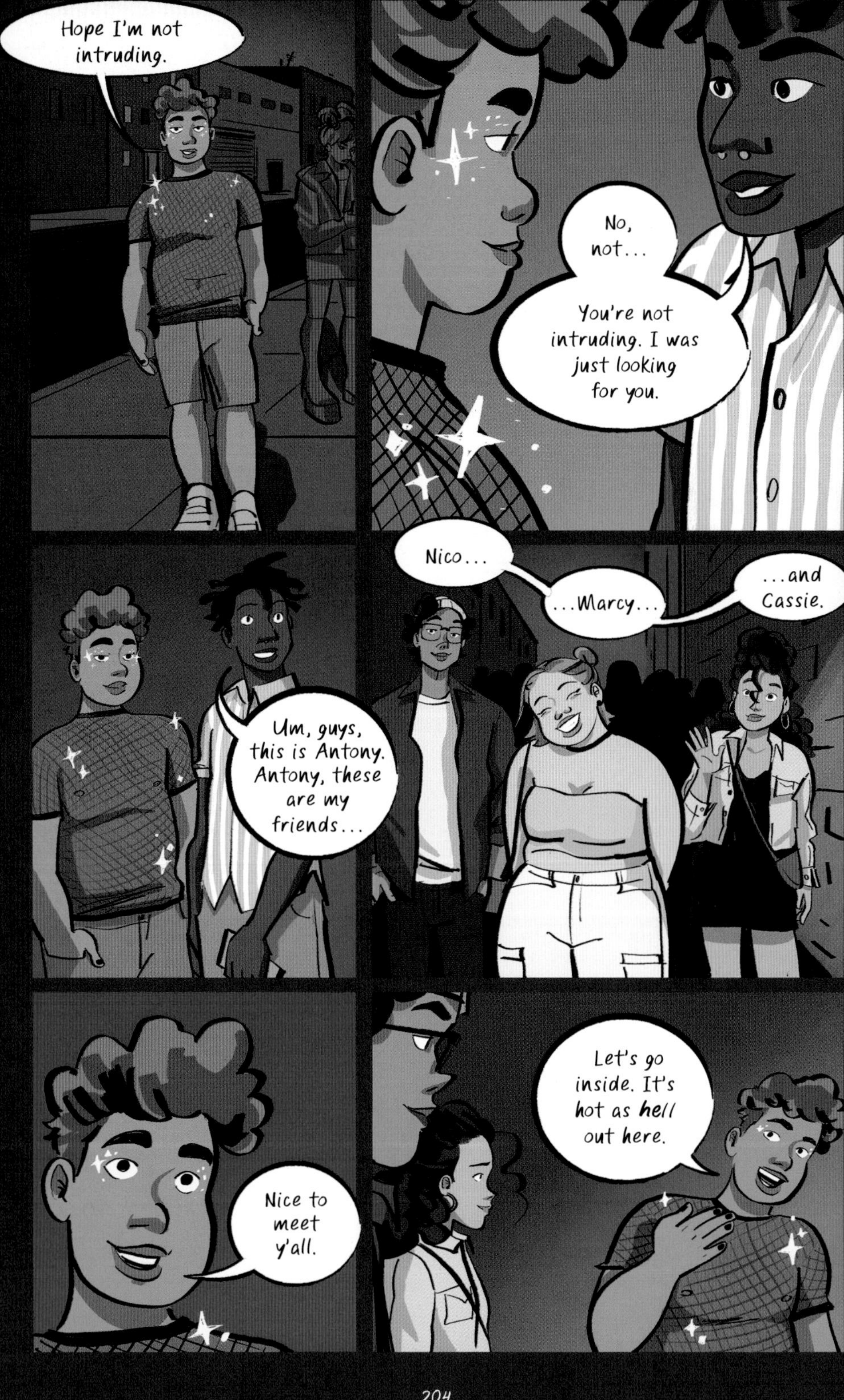
Hope I'm not intruding.
No, not...
You're not intruding. I was just looking for you.
Um, guys, this is Antony. Antony, these are my friends...
Nico...
...Marcy...
...and Cassie.
Nice to meet y'all.
Let's go inside. It's hot as **hell** out here.

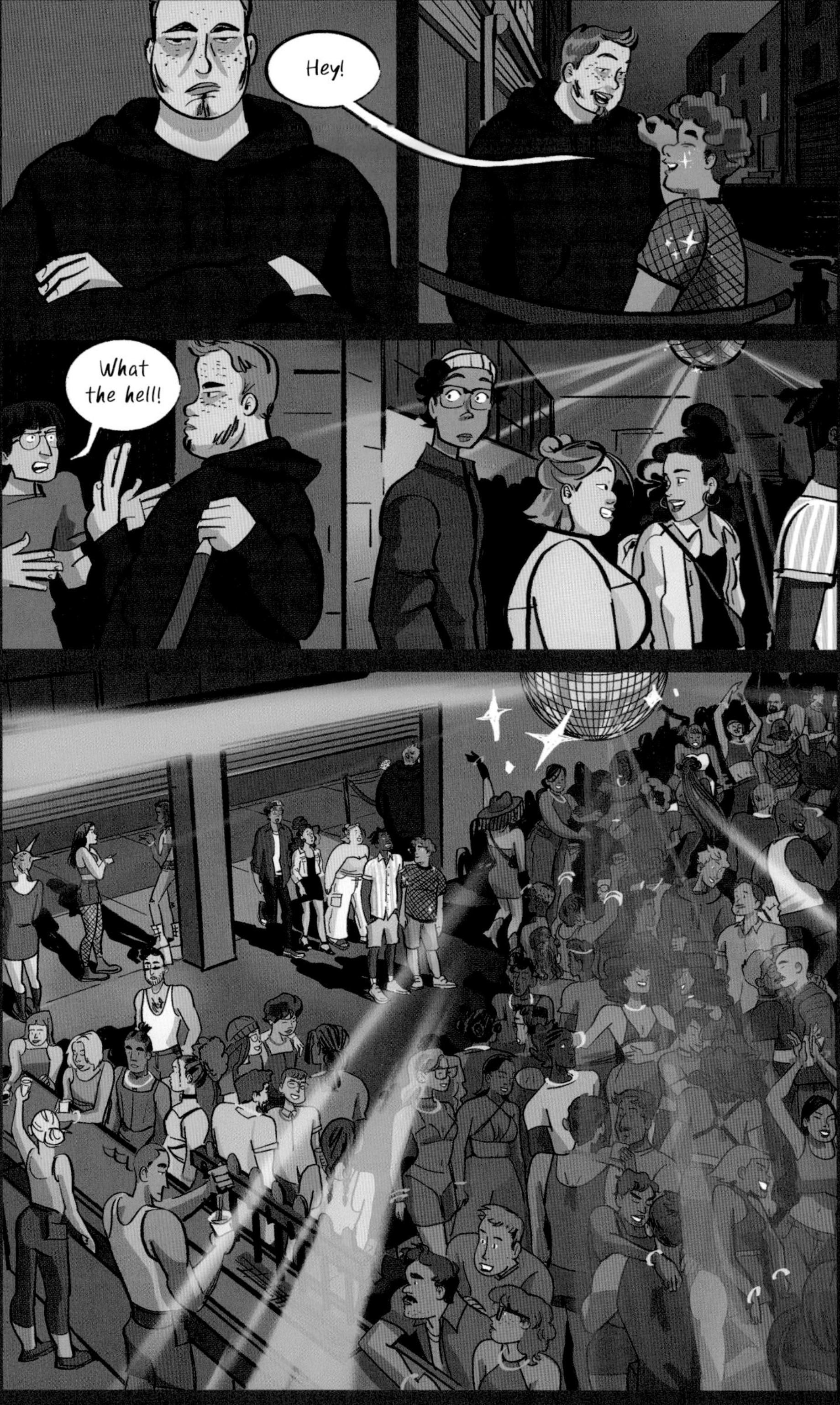
Hey!
What the hell!

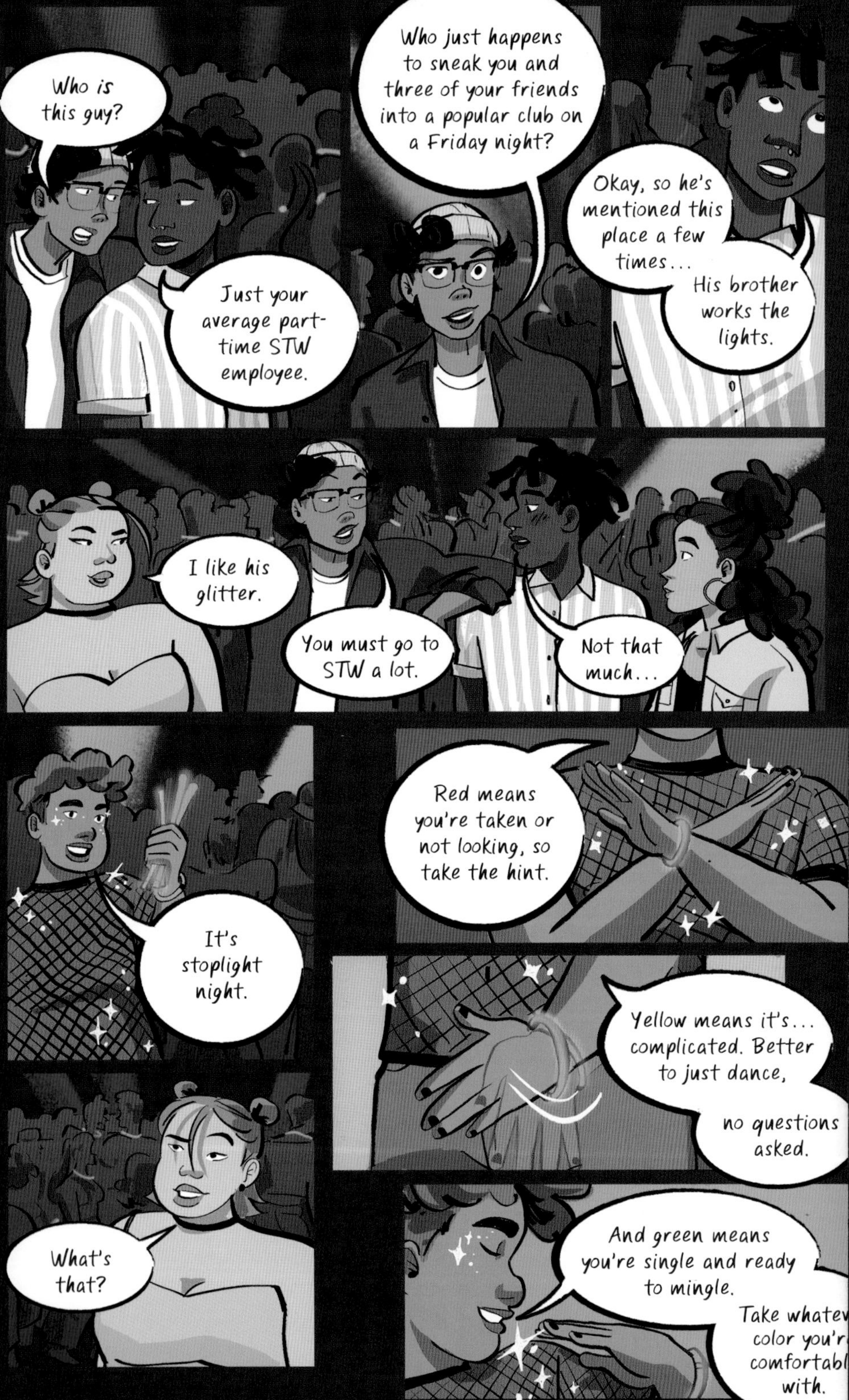
Who is this guy?
Just your average part-time STW employee.
Who just happens to sneak you and three of your friends into a popular club on a Friday night?
Okay, so he's mentioned this place a few times...
His brother works the lights.
I like his glitter.
You must go to STW a lot.
Not that much...
It's stoplight night.
What's that?
Red means you're taken or not looking, so take the hint.
Yellow means it's... complicated. Better to just dance,
no questions asked.
And green means you're single and ready to mingle.
Take whatev
color you'r
comfortabl
with.

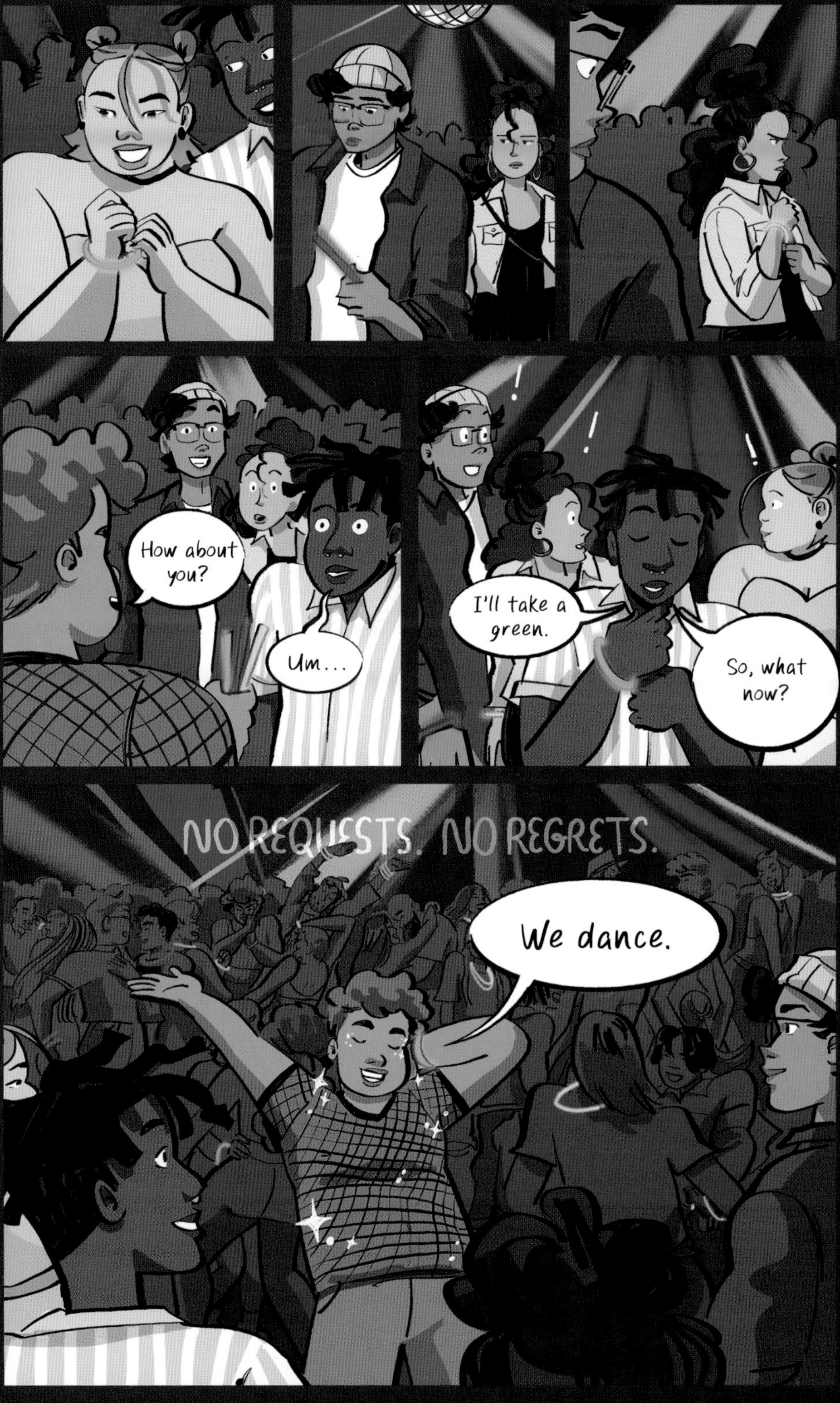
How about you?
Um...
I'll take a green.
So, what now?
NO REQUESTS. NO REGRETS.
We dance.

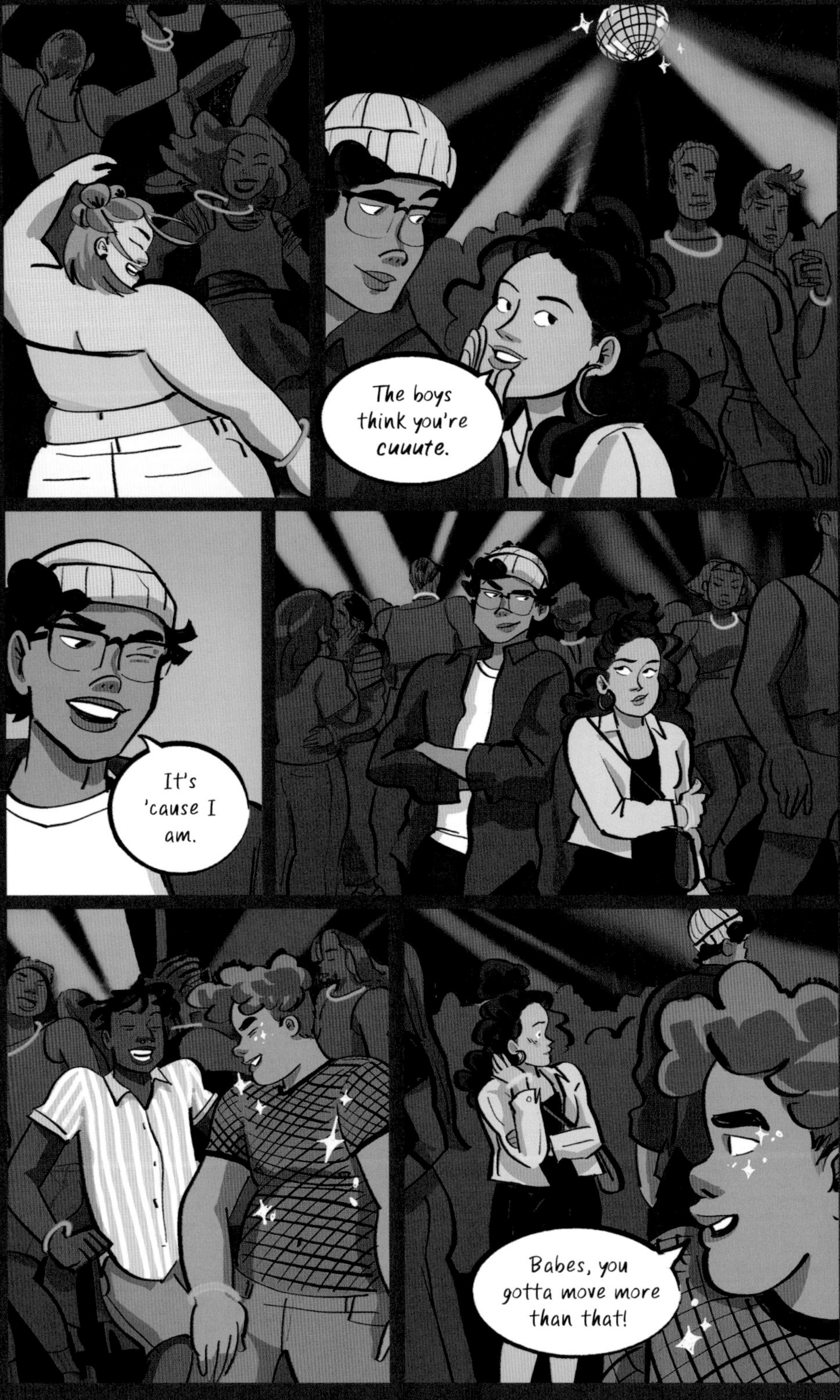
The boys think you're cuuute.
It's 'cause I am.
Babes, you gotta move more than that!

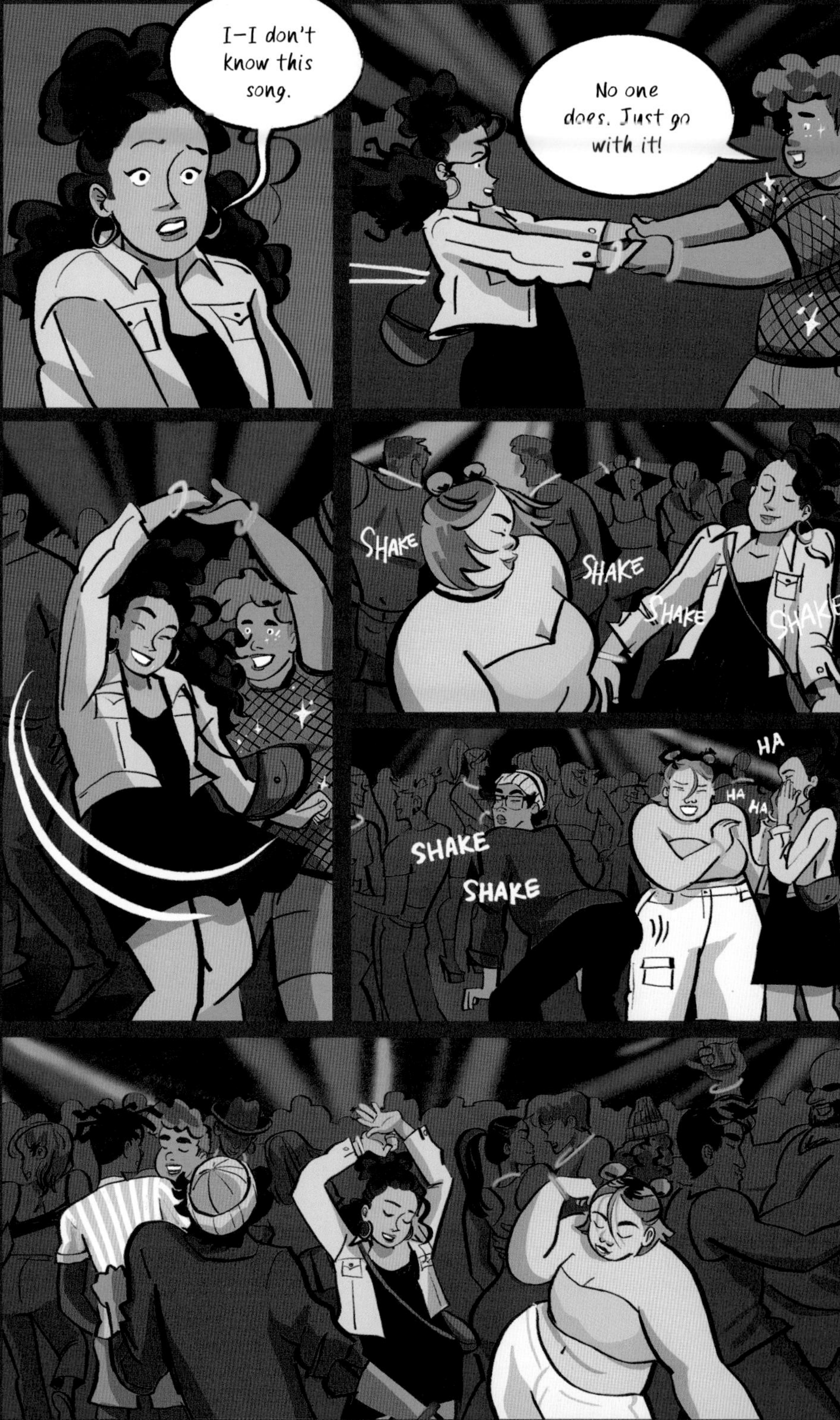
I—I don't know this song.
No one does. Just go with it!
SHAKE
SHAKE
SHAKE
SHAKE
HA
HA
HA
SHAKE
SHAKE

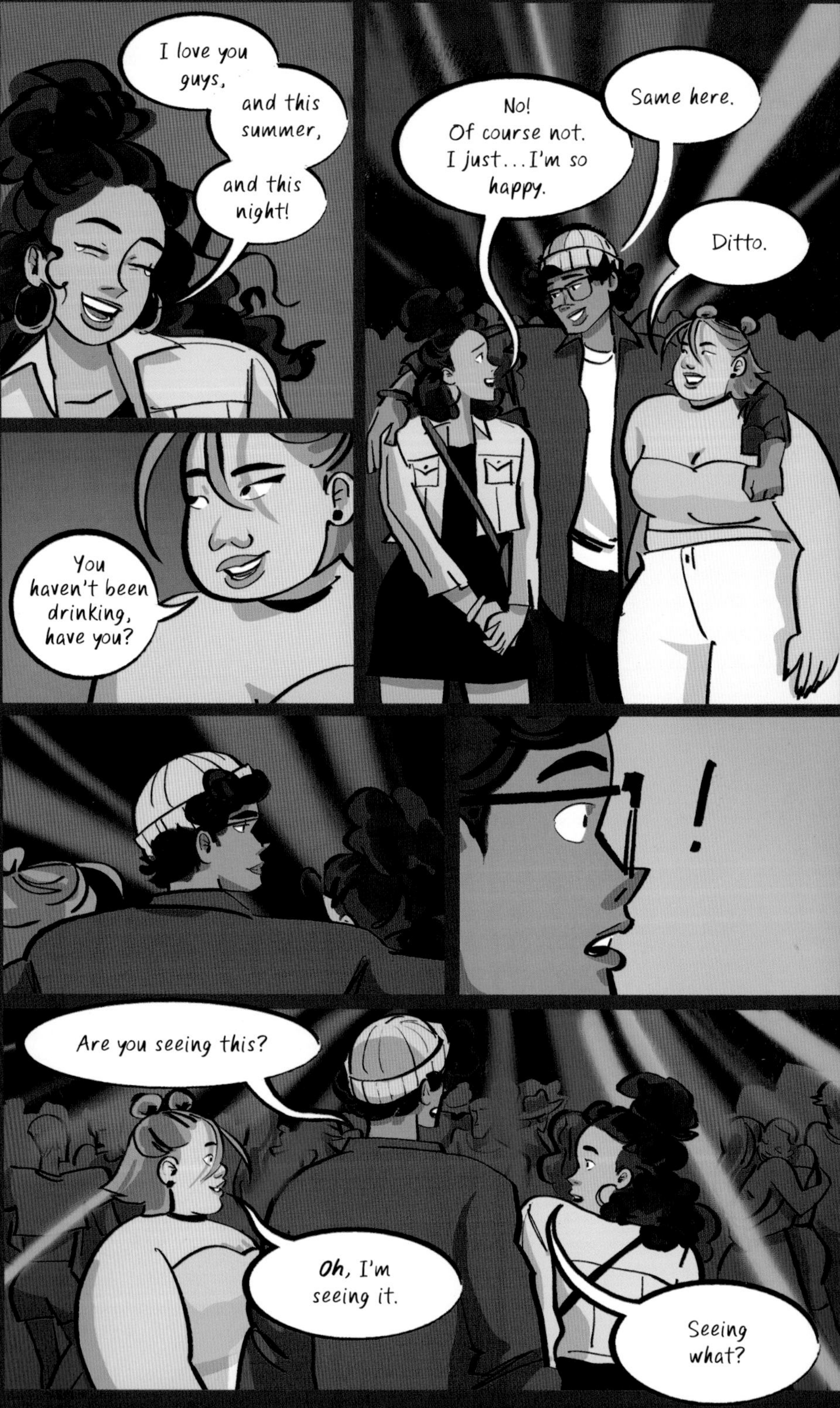
I love you guys,
and this summer,
and this night!
You haven't been drinking, have you?
No! Of course not. I just...I'm so happy.
Same here.
Ditto.
!
Are you seeing this?
Oh, I'm seeing it.
Seeing what?

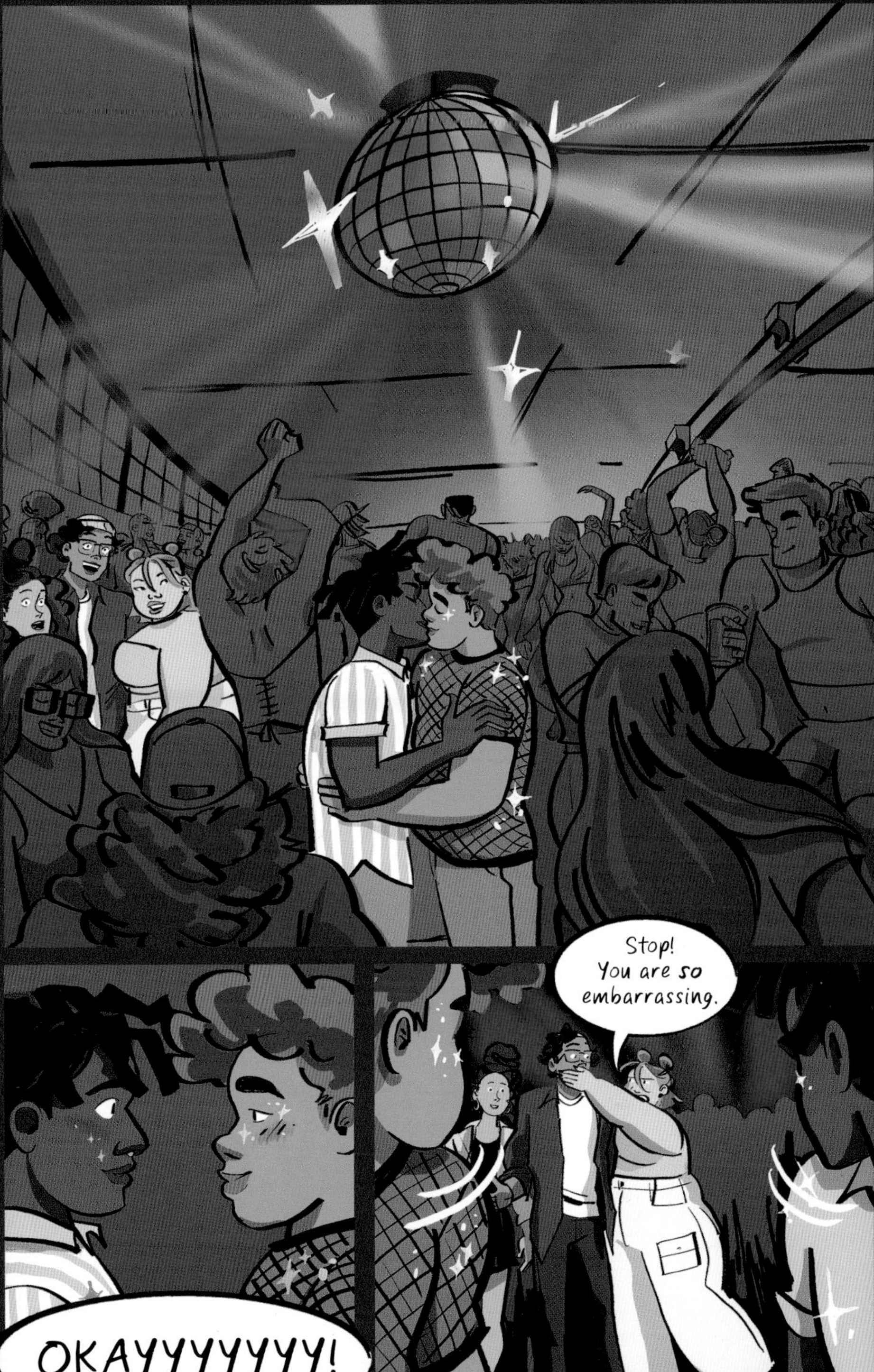
OKAYYYYYYY!
Stop! You are so embarrassing.

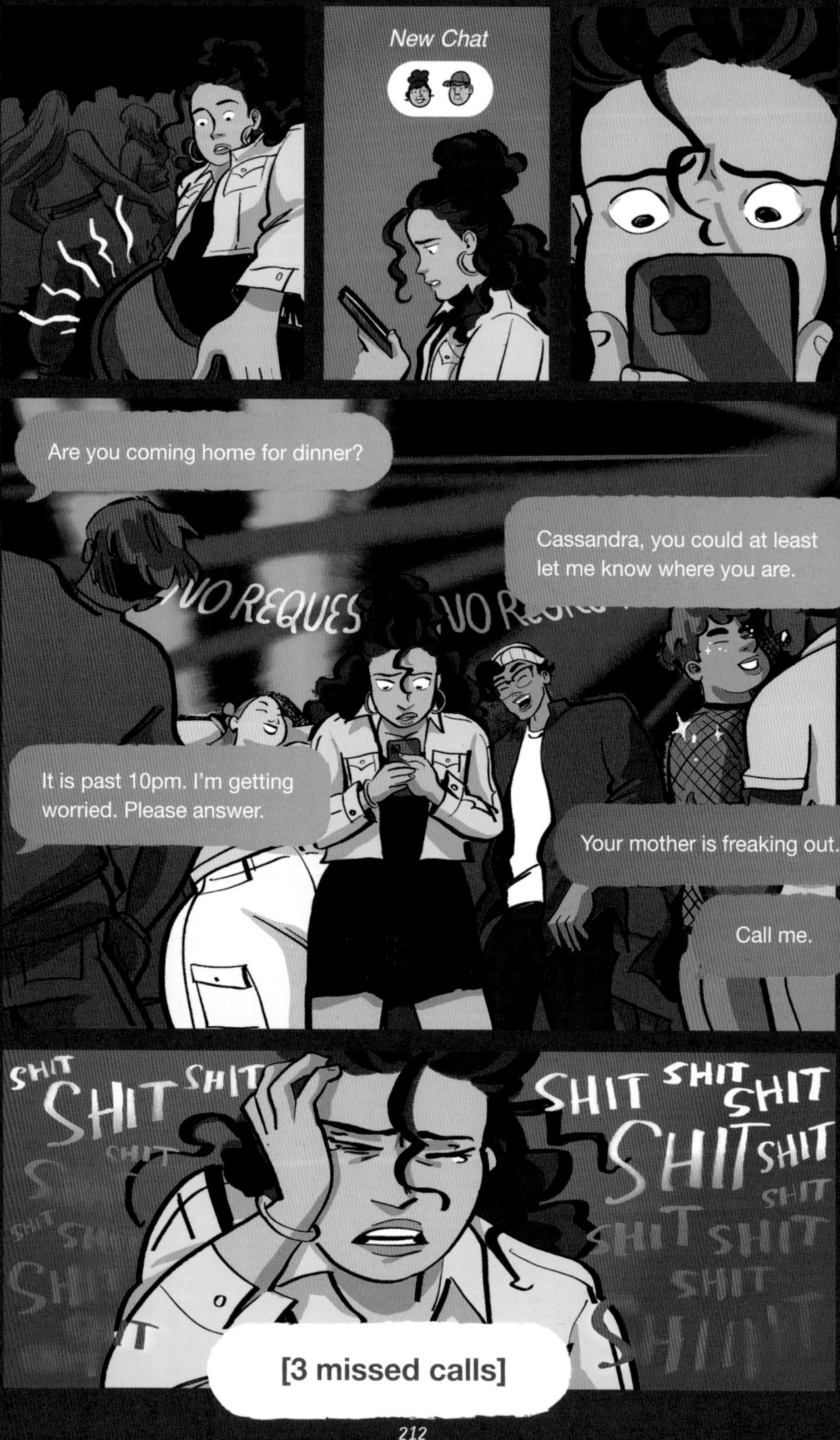
New Chat
Are you coming home for dinner?
Cassandra, you could at least let me know where you are.
It is past 10pm. I'm getting worried. Please answer.
Your mother is freaking out.
Call me.
SHIT SHIT SHIT
SHIT SHIT SHIT SHIT SHIT
[3 missed calls]

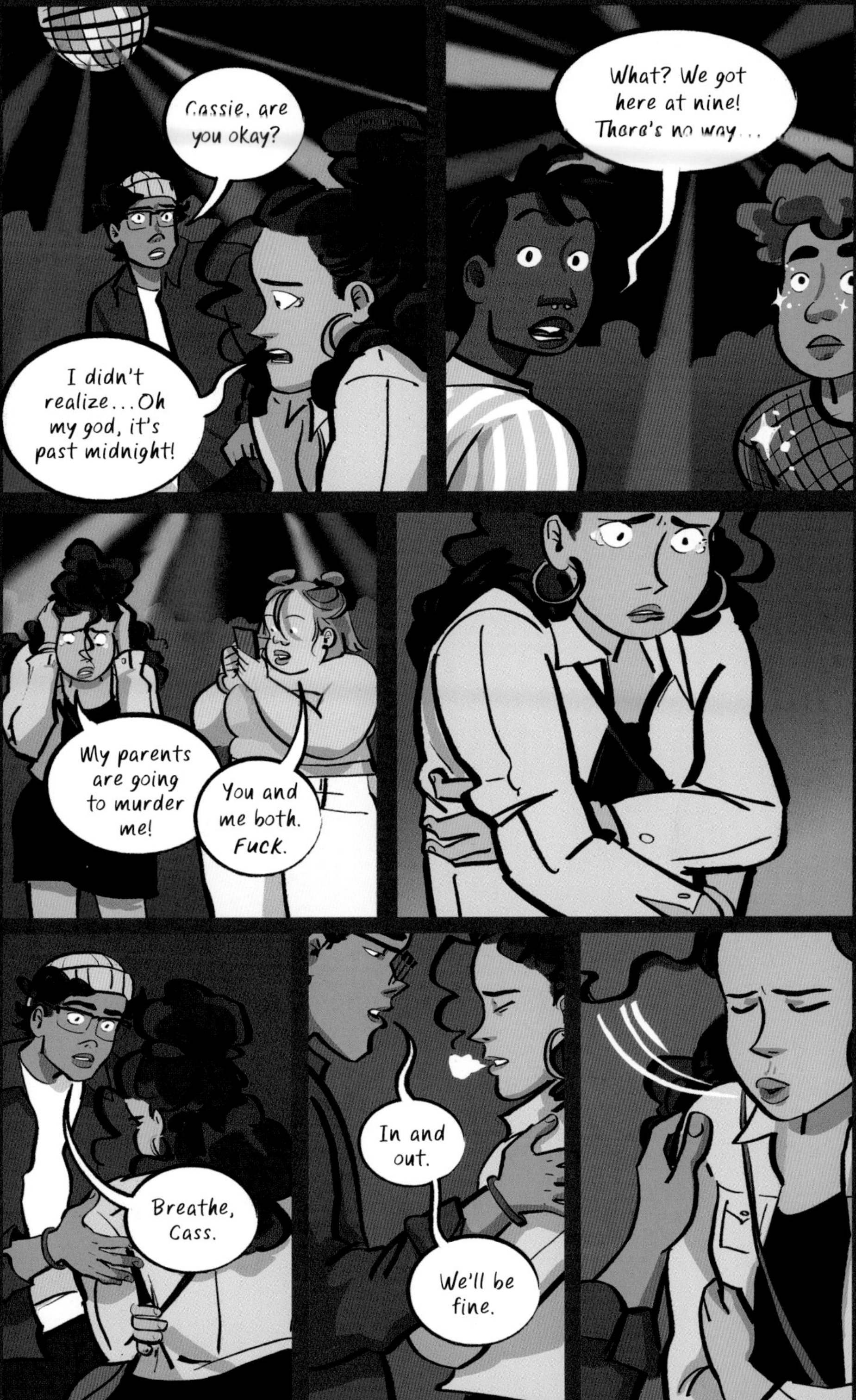
Cassie, are you okay?
I didn't realize...Oh my god, it's past midnight!
What? We got here at nine! There's no way...
My parents are going to murder me!
You and me both. Fuck.
Breathe, Cass.
In and out.
We'll be fine.

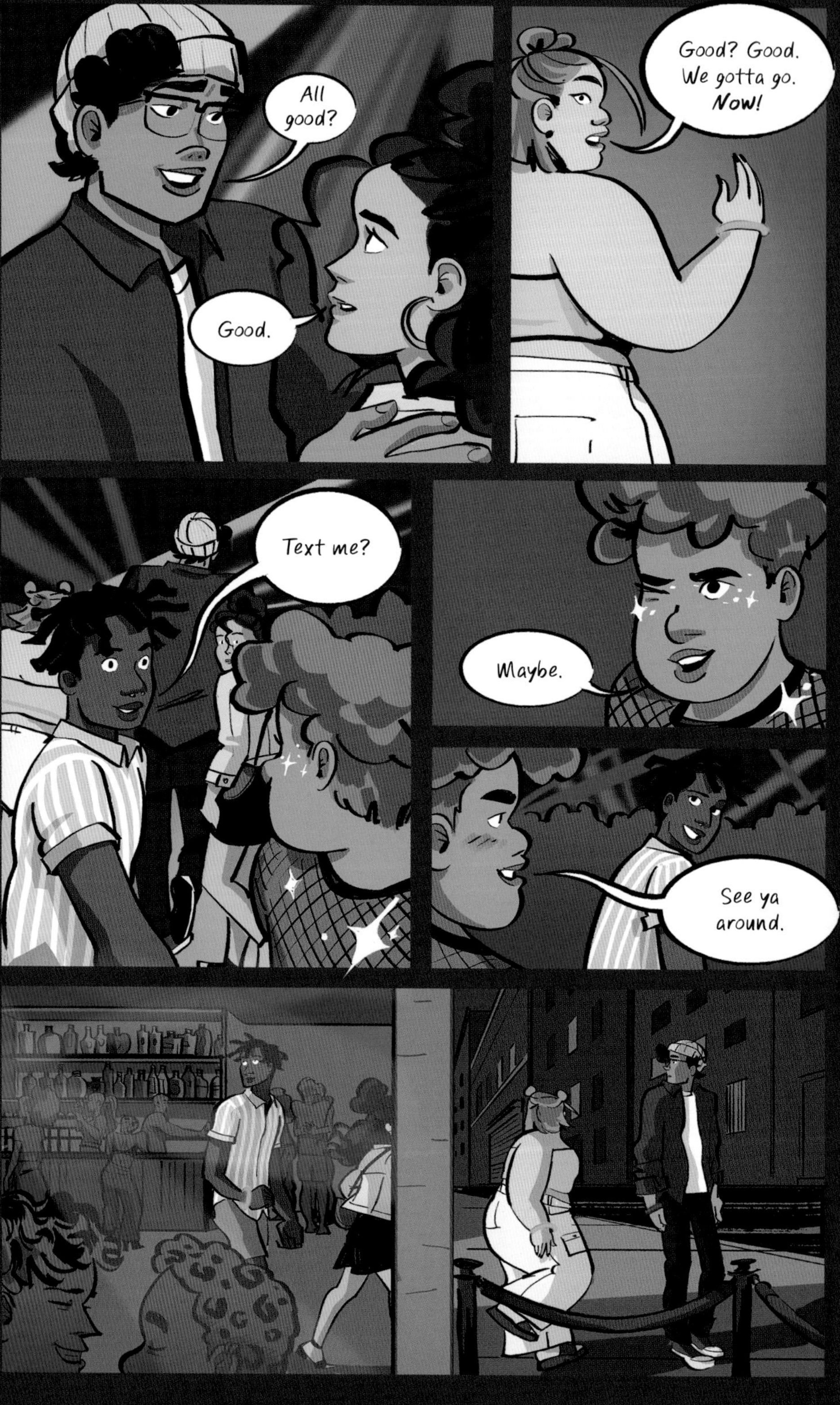
All good?
Good.
Good? Good. We gotta go. Now!
Text me?
Maybe.
See ya around.

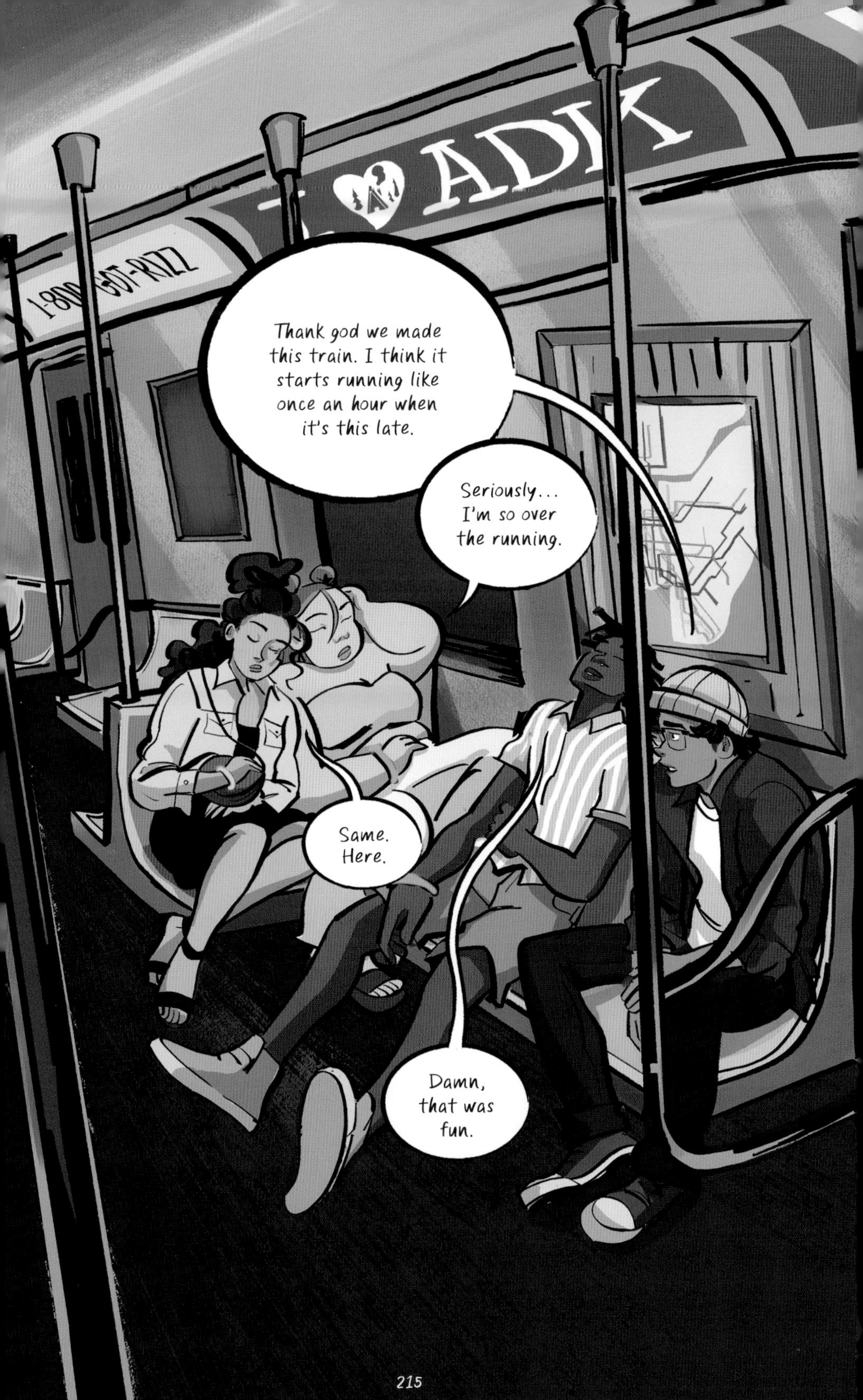
1-800-GOT-RIZZ
I ♥ ADK
Thank god we made this train. I think it starts running like once an hour when it's this late.
Seriously... I'm so over the running.
Same. Here.
Damn, that was fun.

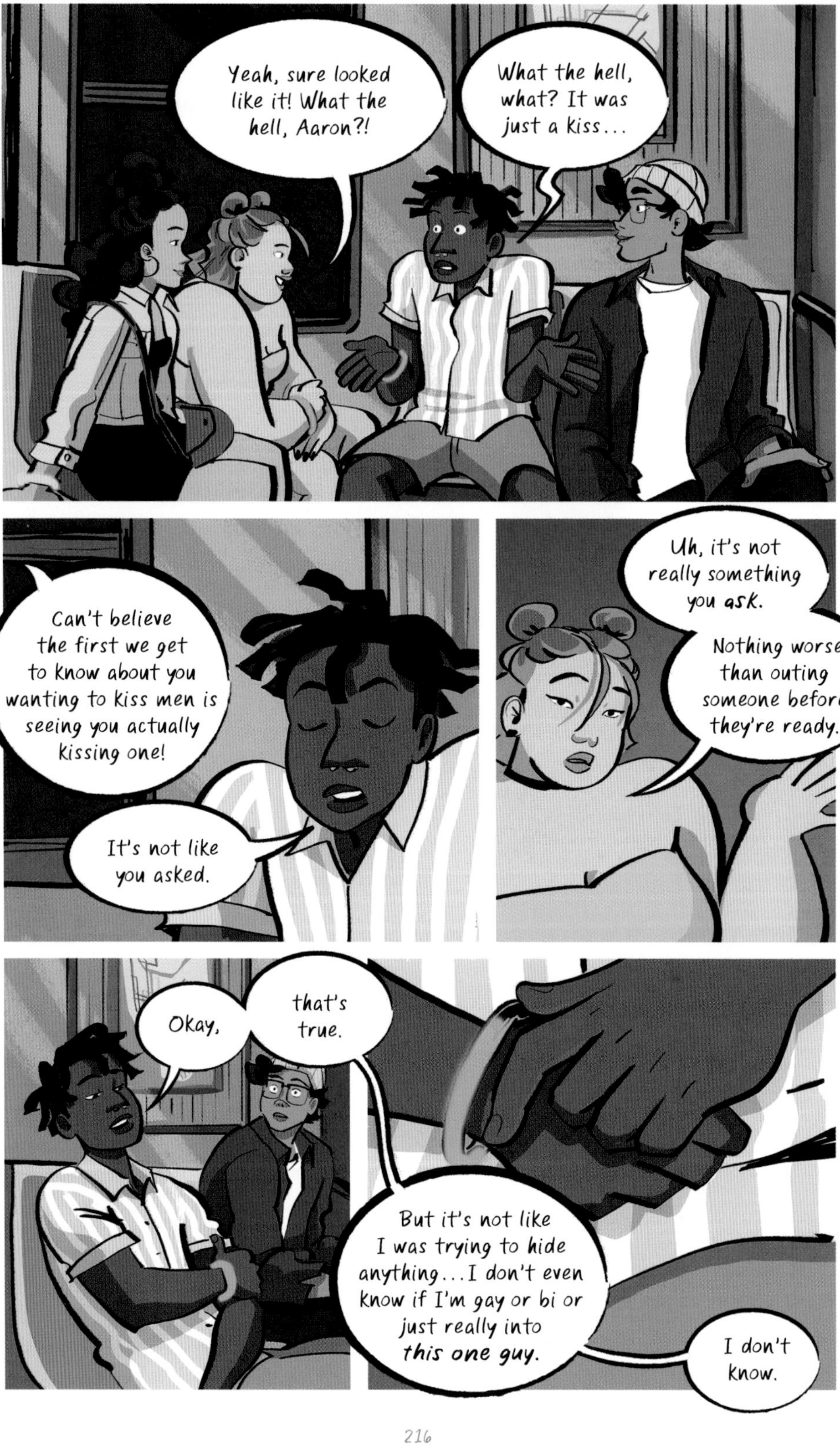
Yeah, sure looked like it! What the hell, Aaron?!
What the hell, what? It was just a kiss...
Can't believe the first we get to know about you wanting to kiss men is seeing you actually kissing one!
It's not like you asked.
Uh, it's not really something you **ask**.
Nothing worse than outing someone before they're ready.
Okay,
that's true.
But it's not like I was trying to hide anything... I don't even know if I'm gay or bi or just really into **this one guy**.
I don't know.

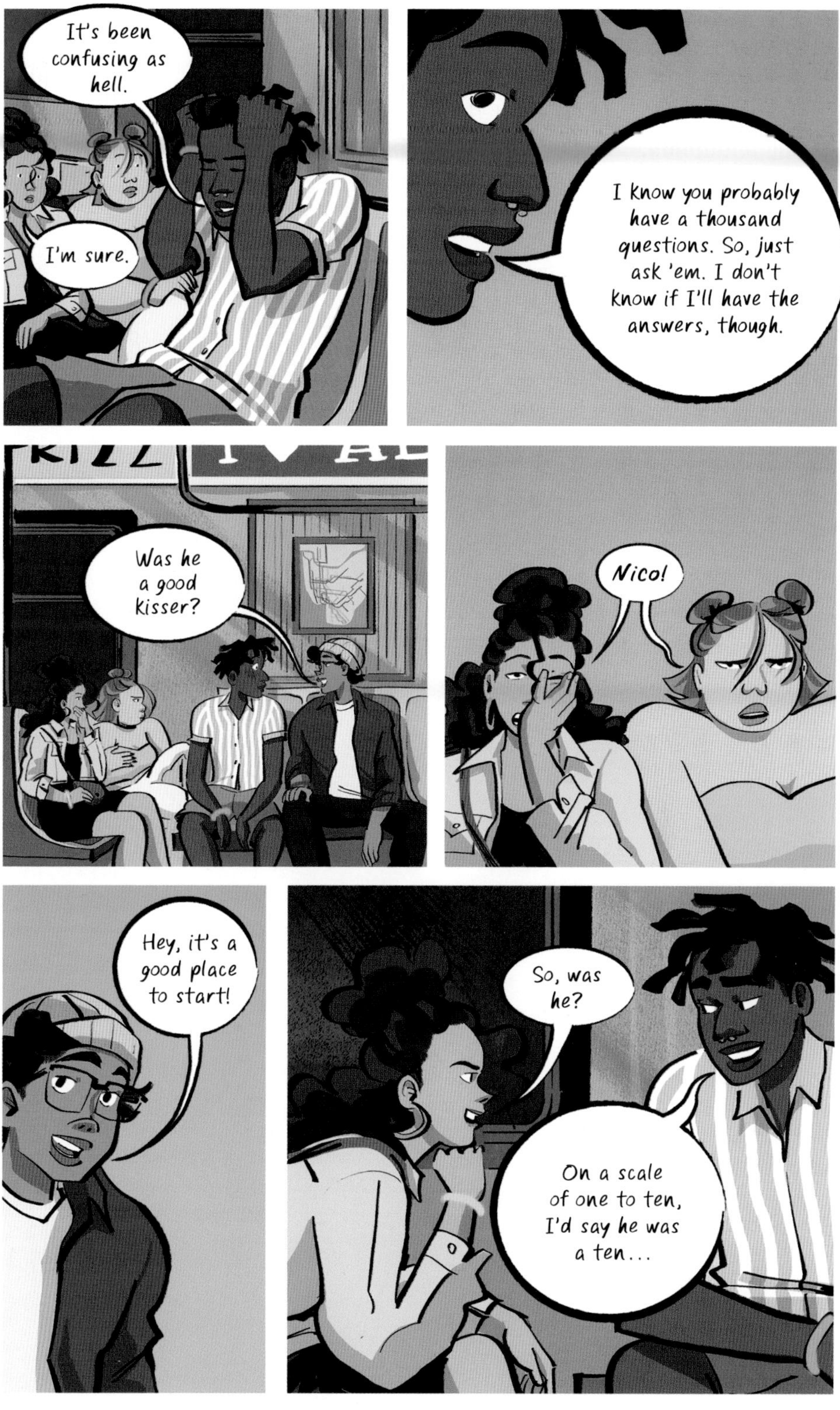
It's been confusing as hell.
I'm sure.
I know you probably have a thousand questions. So, just ask 'em. I don't know if I'll have the answers, though.
Was he a good kisser?
Nico!
Hey, it's a good place to start!
So, was he?
On a scale of one to ten, I'd say he was a ten...

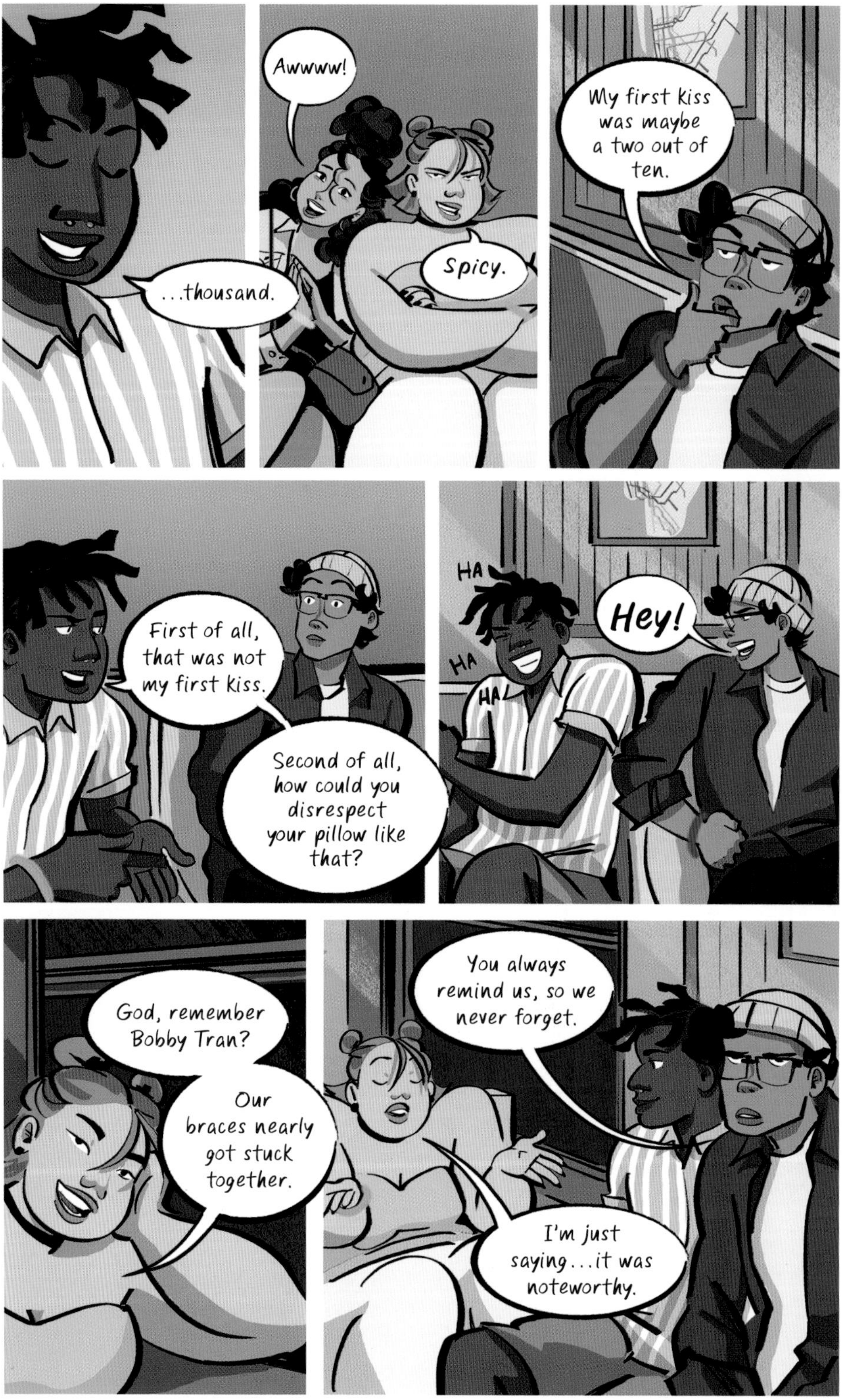
...thousand.
Awwww!
Spicy.
My first kiss was maybe a two out of ten.
First of all, that was not my first kiss.
Second of all, how could you disrespect your pillow like that?
HA
HA
HA
Hey!
God, remember Bobby Tran?
Our braces nearly got stuck together.
You always remind us, so we never forget.
I'm just saying...it was noteworthy.

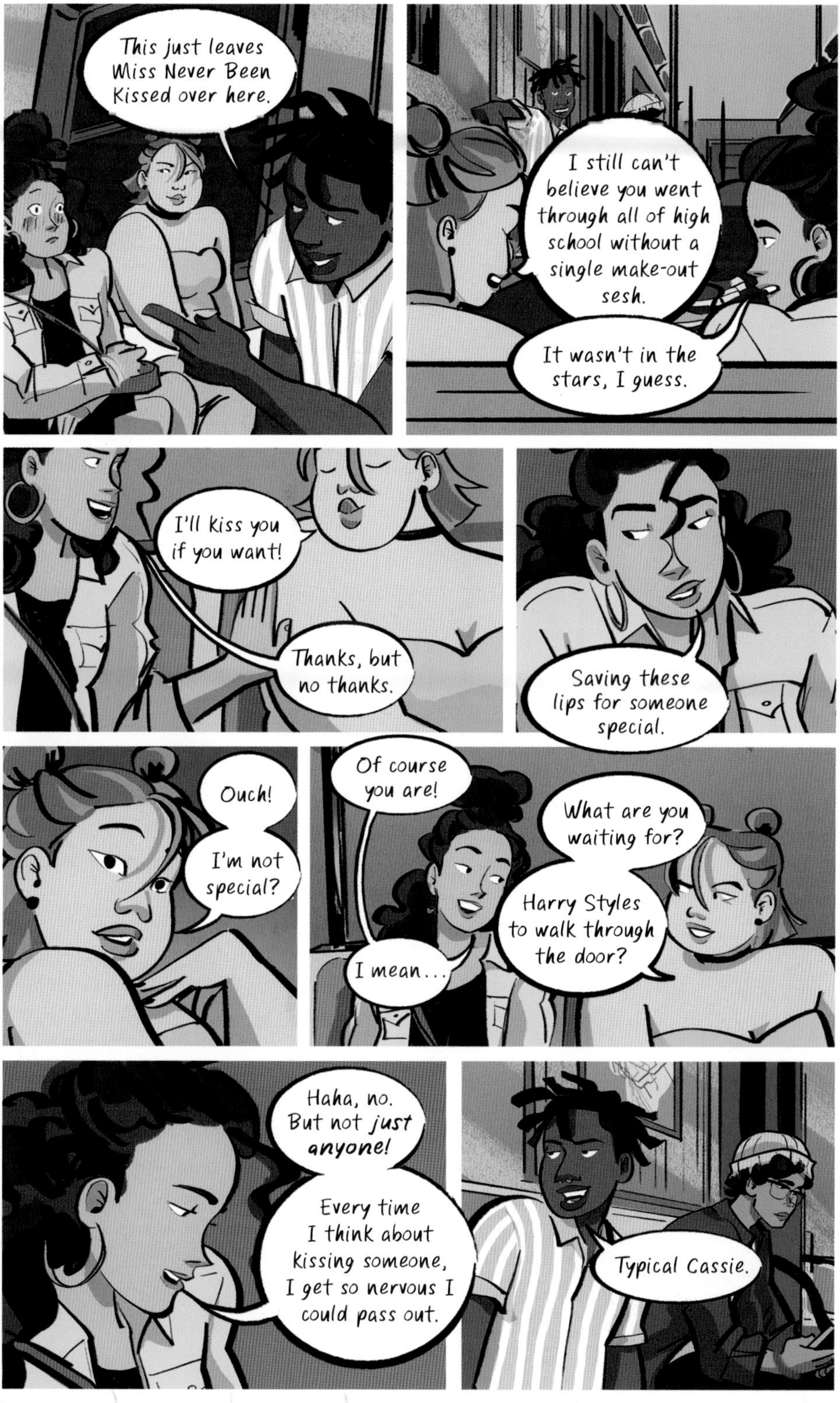
This just leaves Miss Never Been Kissed over here.
I still can't believe you went through all of high school without a single make-out sesh.
It wasn't in the stars, I guess.
I'll kiss you if you want!
Thanks, but no thanks.
Saving these lips for someone special.
Ouch!
I'm not special?
Of course you are!
I mean...
What are you waiting for?
Harry Styles to walk through the door?
Haha, no. But not *just* ***anyone!***
Every time I think about kissing someone, I get so nervous I could pass out.
Typical Cassie.

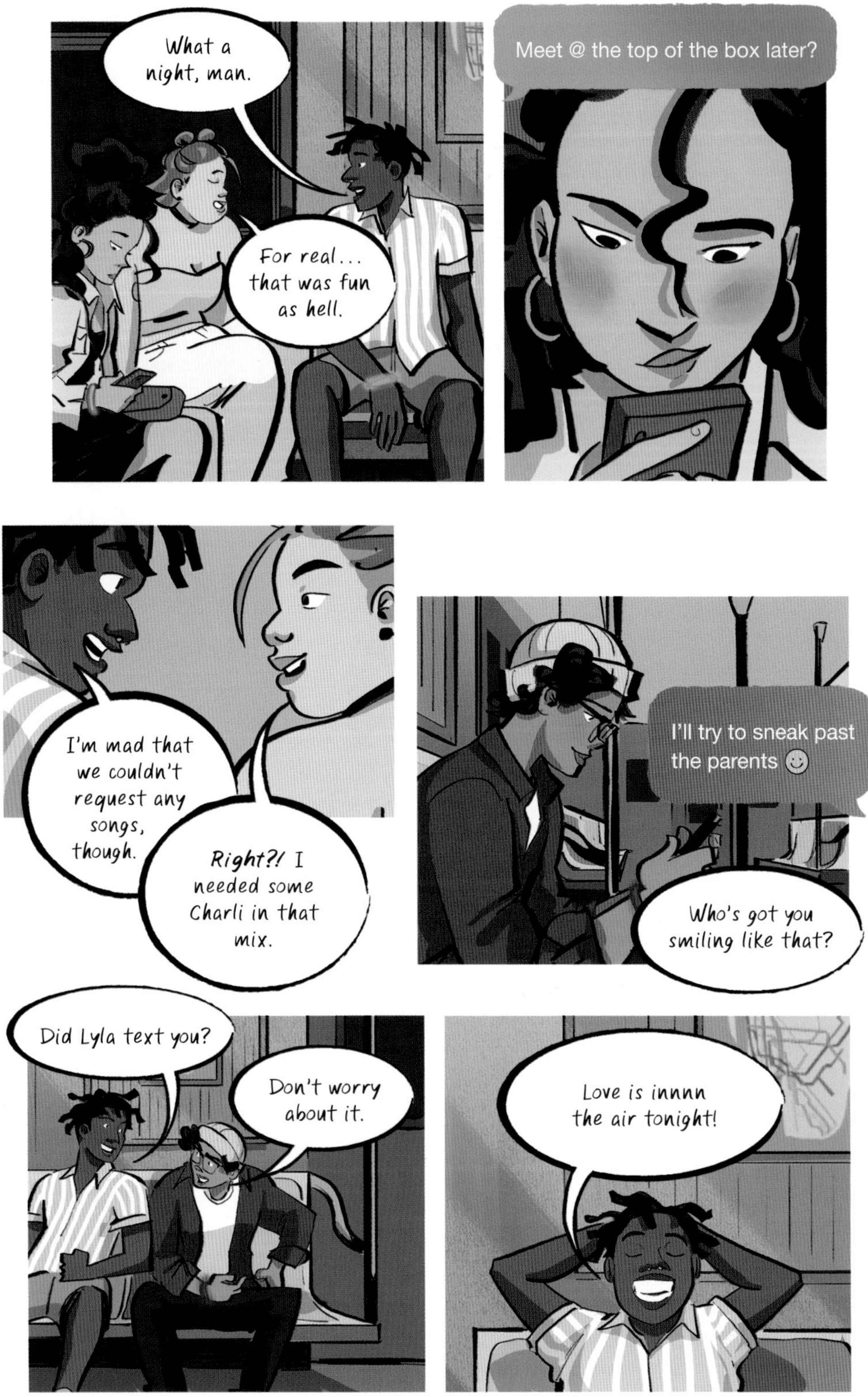
What a night, man.
For real... that was fun as hell.
Meet @ the top of the box later?
I'm mad that we couldn't request any songs, though.
Right?! I needed some Charli in that mix.
I'll try to sneak past the parents ☺
Who's got you smiling like that?
Did Lyla text you?
Don't worry about it.
Love is innnn the air tonight!

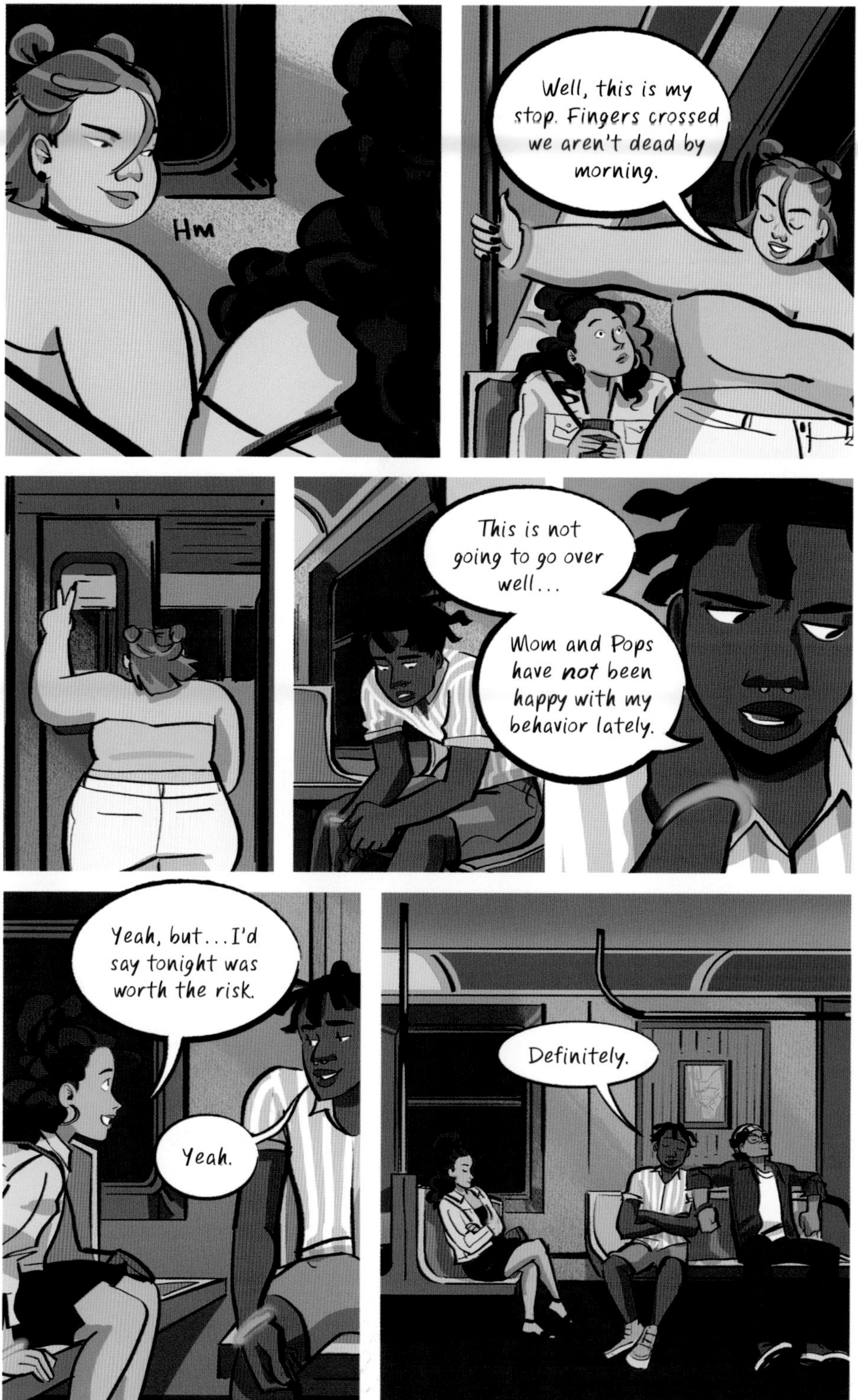
Hm
Well, this is my stop. Fingers crossed we aren't dead by morning.
This is not going to go over well...
Mom and Pops have **not** been happy with my behavior lately.
Yeah, but...I'd say tonight was worth the risk.
Yeah.
Definitely.

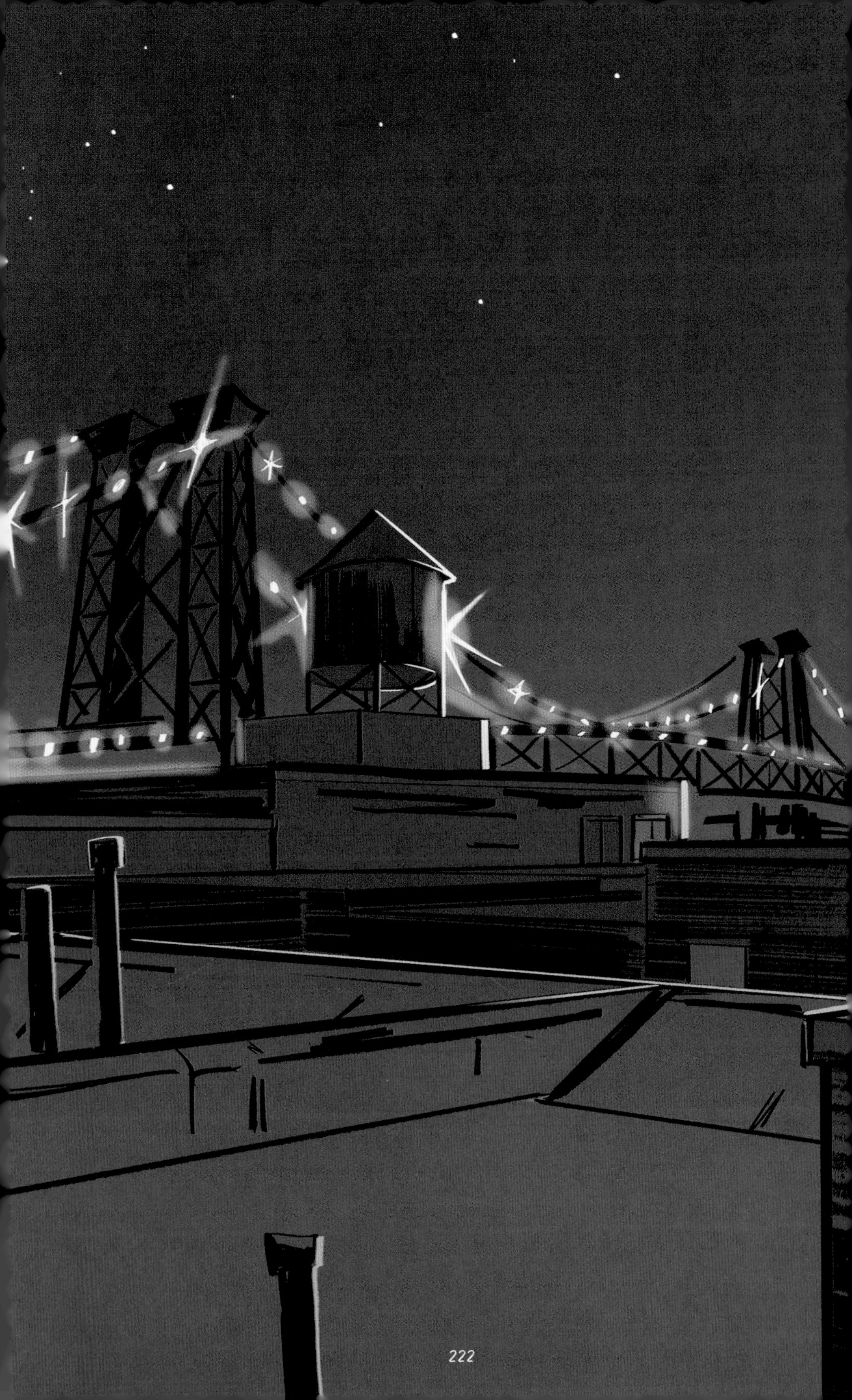

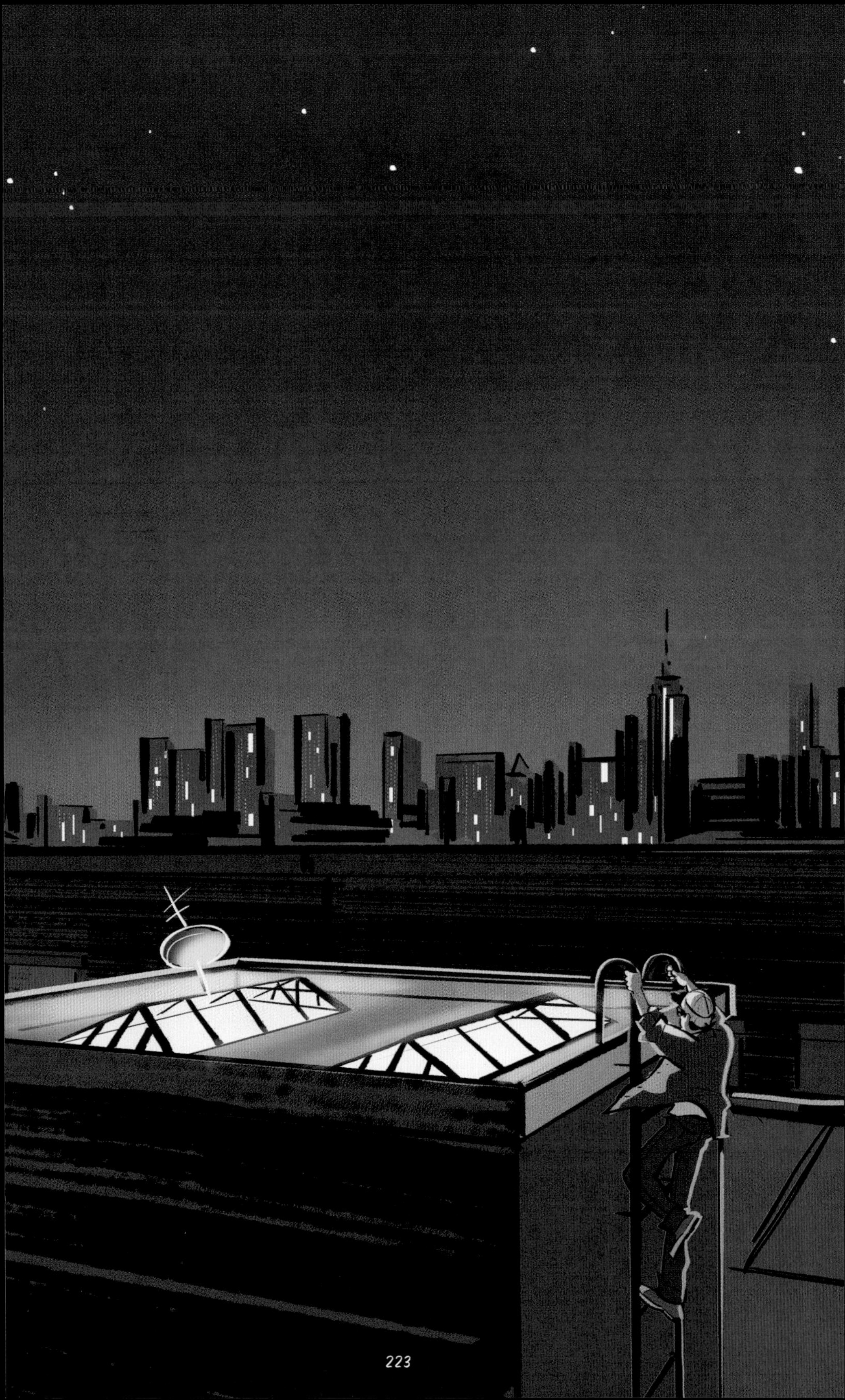

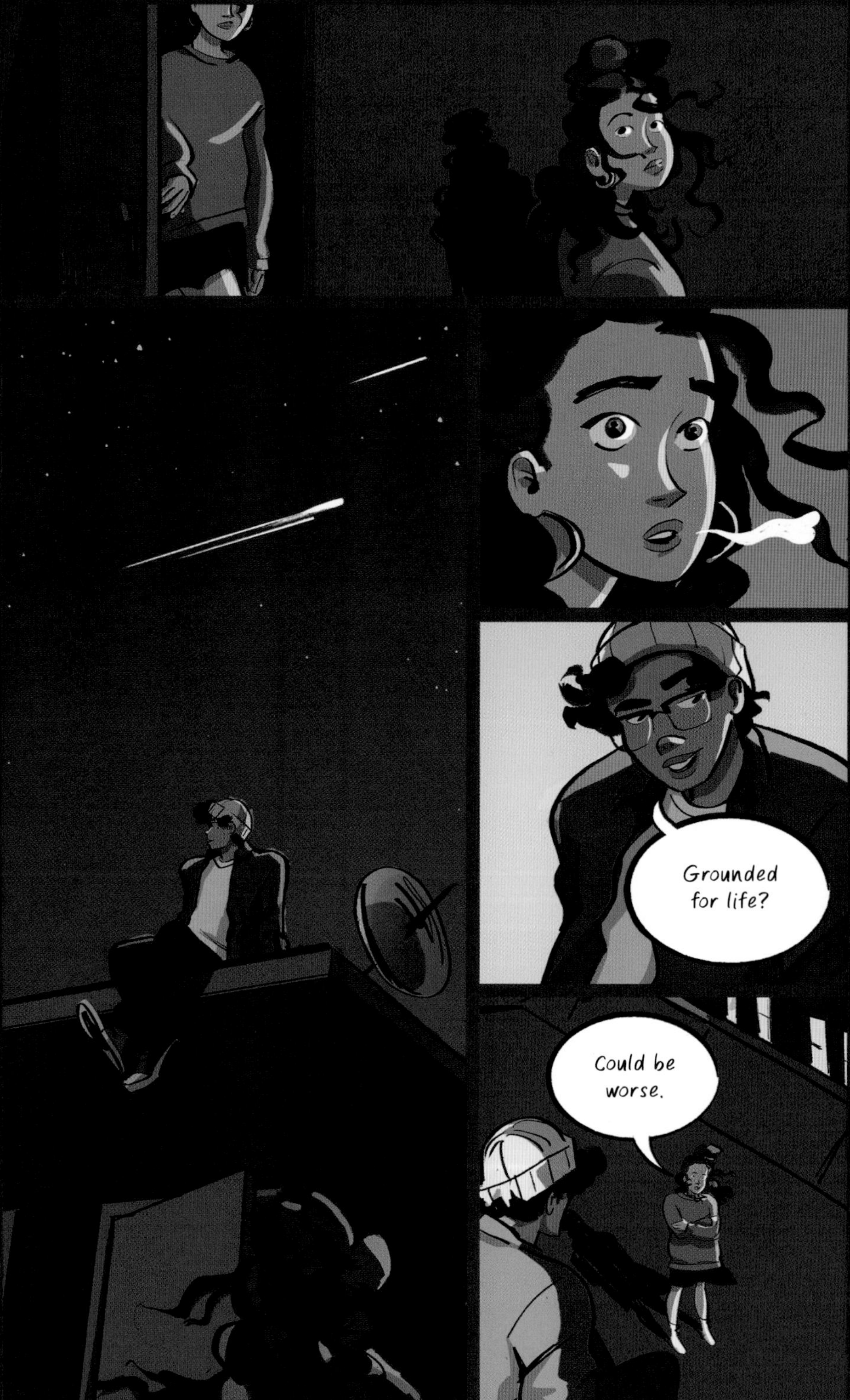
Grounded
for life?
Could be
worse.

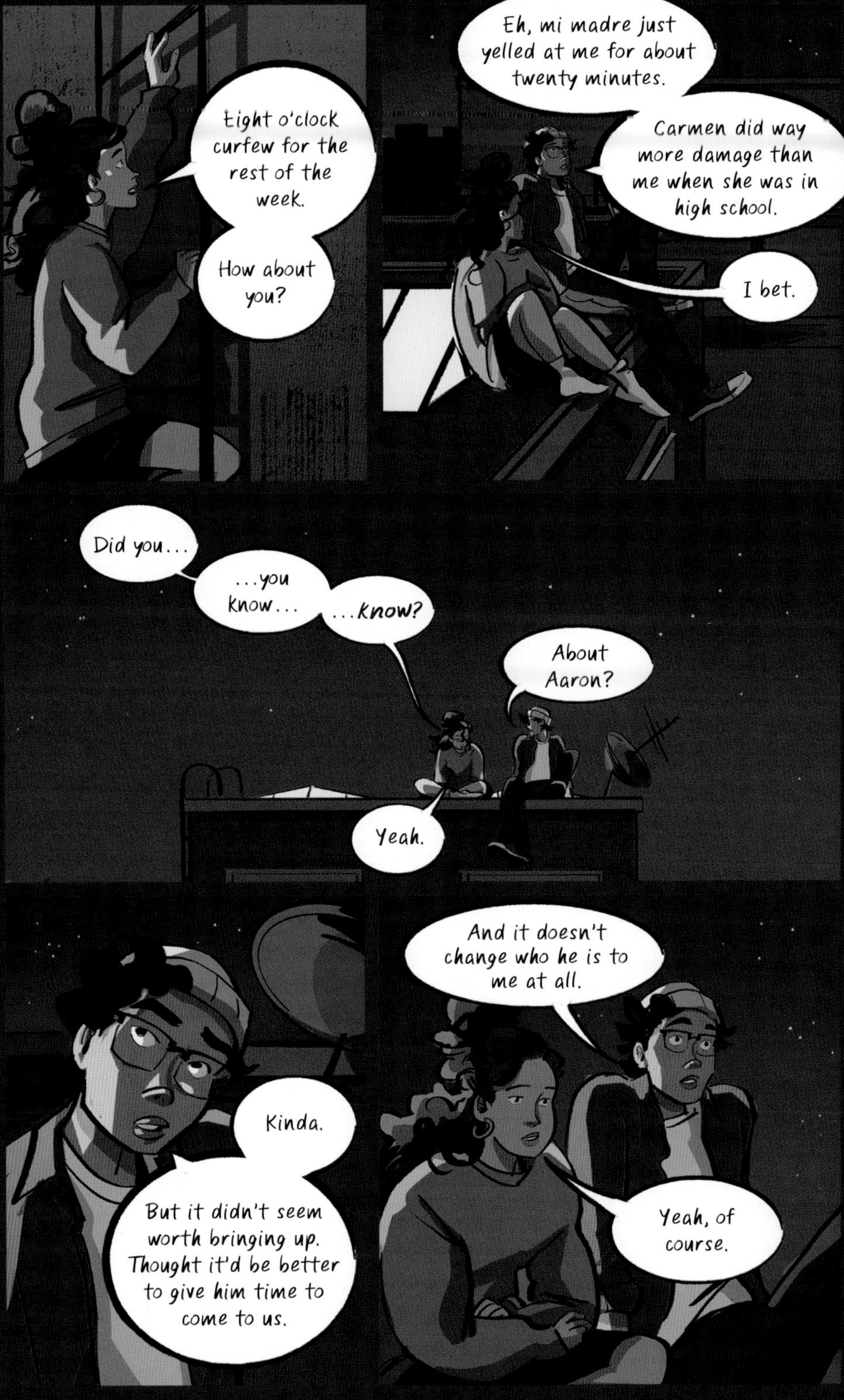
Eight o'clock curfew for the rest of the week.
How about you?
Eh, mi madre just yelled at me for about twenty minutes.
Carmen did way more damage than me when she was in high school.
I bet.
Did you...
...you know...
...know?
About Aaron?
Yeah.
Kinda.
But it didn't seem worth bringing up. Thought it'd be better to give him time to come to us.
And it doesn't change who he is to me at all.
Yeah, of course.

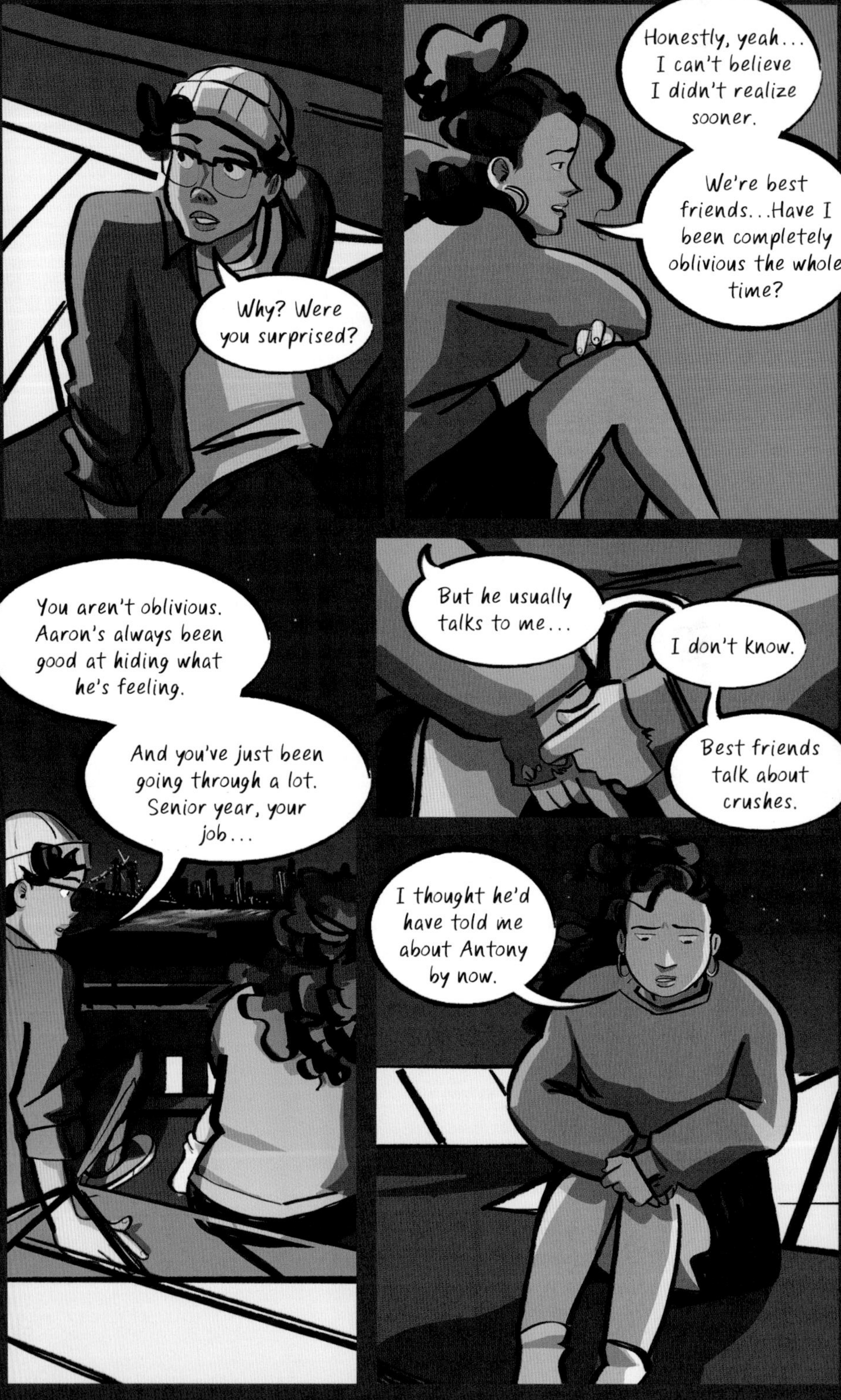
Why? Were you surprised?
Honestly, yeah... I can't believe I didn't realize sooner.
We're best friends...Have I been completely oblivious the whole time?
You aren't oblivious. Aaron's always been good at hiding what he's feeling.
And you've just been going through a lot. Senior year, your job...
But he usually talks to me...
I don't know.
Best friends talk about crushes.
I thought he'd have told me about Antony by now.

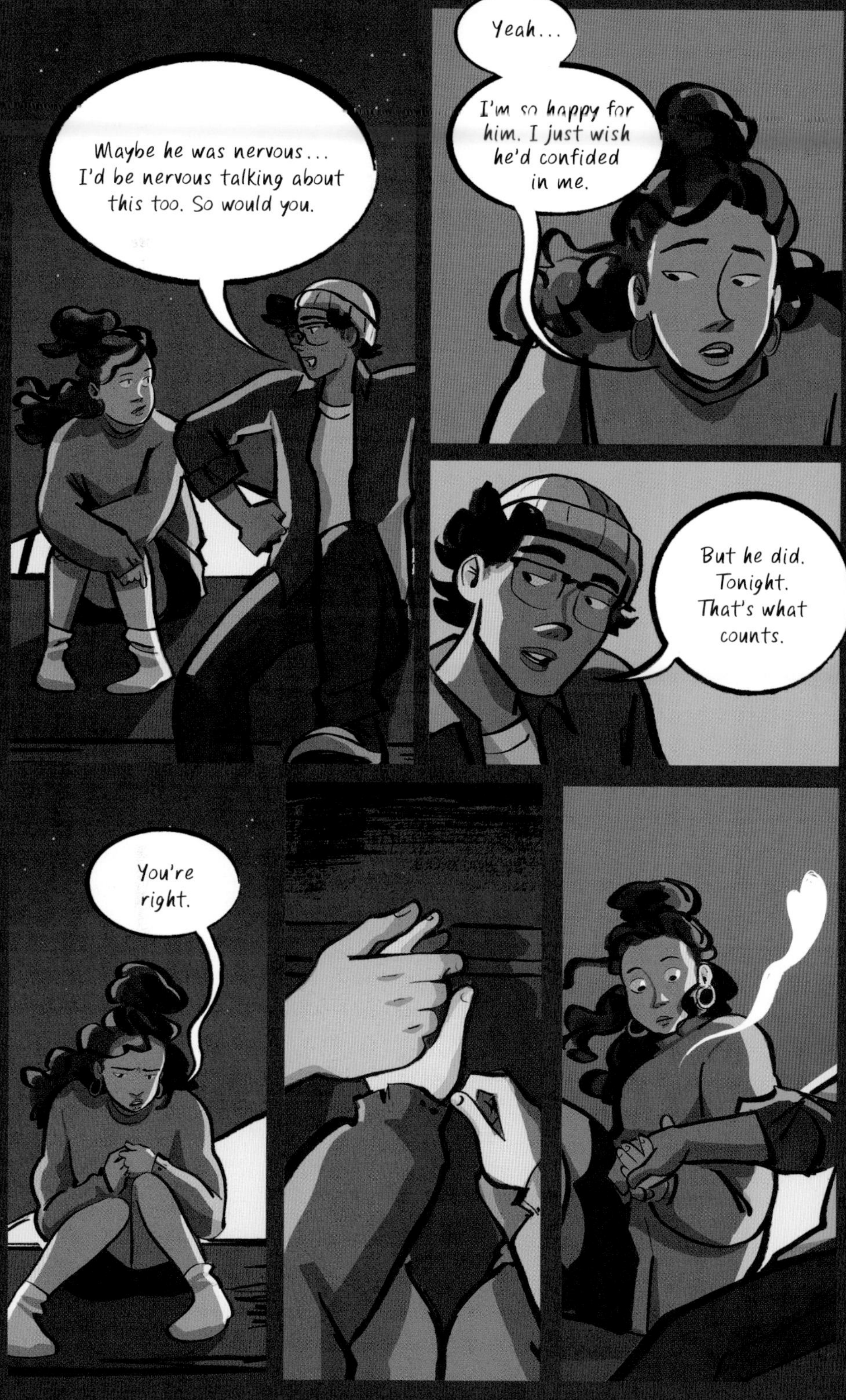
Maybe he was nervous...
I'd be nervous talking about
this too. So would you.
Yeah...
I'm so happy for
him. I just wish
he'd confided
in me.
But he did.
Tonight.
That's what
counts.
You're
right.

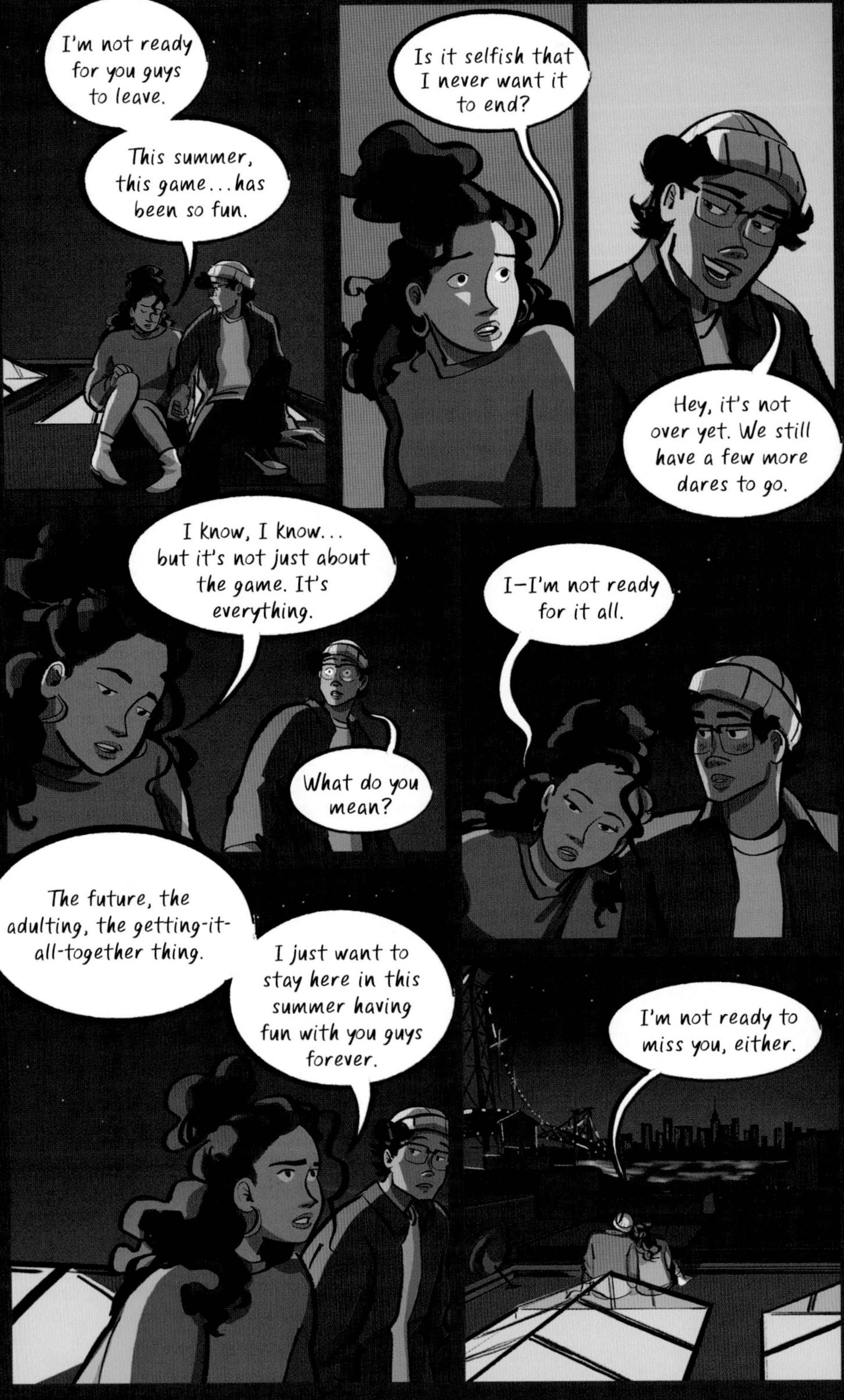
I'm not ready for you guys to leave.
This summer, this game...has been so fun.
Is it selfish that I never want it to end?
Hey, it's not over yet. We still have a few more dares to go.
I know, I know... but it's not just about the game. It's everything.
What do you mean?
I—I'm not ready for it all.
The future, the adulting, the getting-it-all-together thing.
I just want to stay here in this summer having fun with you guys forever.
I'm not ready to miss you, either.

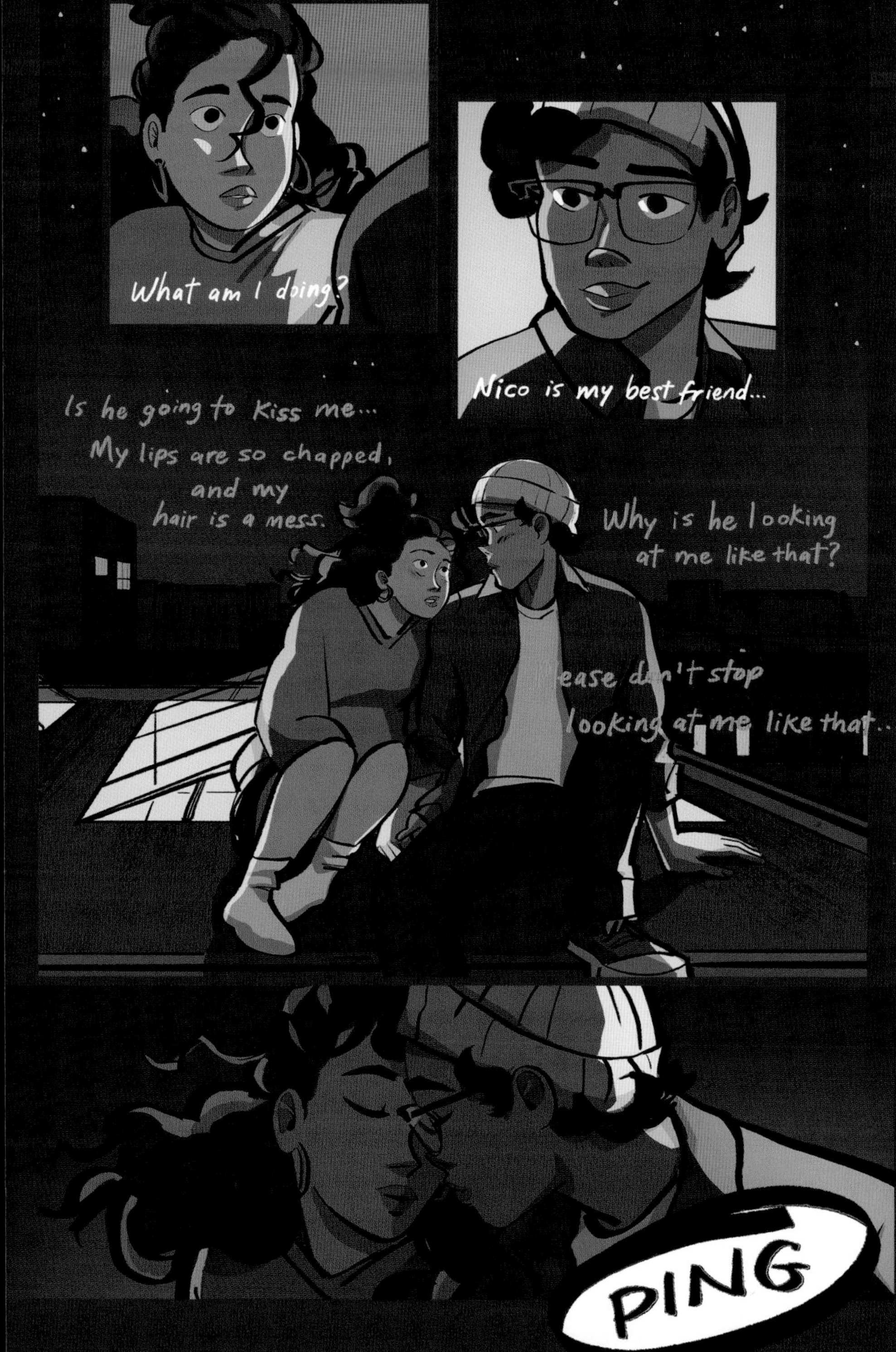
What am I doing?
Nico is my best friend...
Is he going to kiss me...
My lips are so chapped, and my hair is a mess.
Why is he looking at me like that?
Please don't stop looking at me like that...
PING

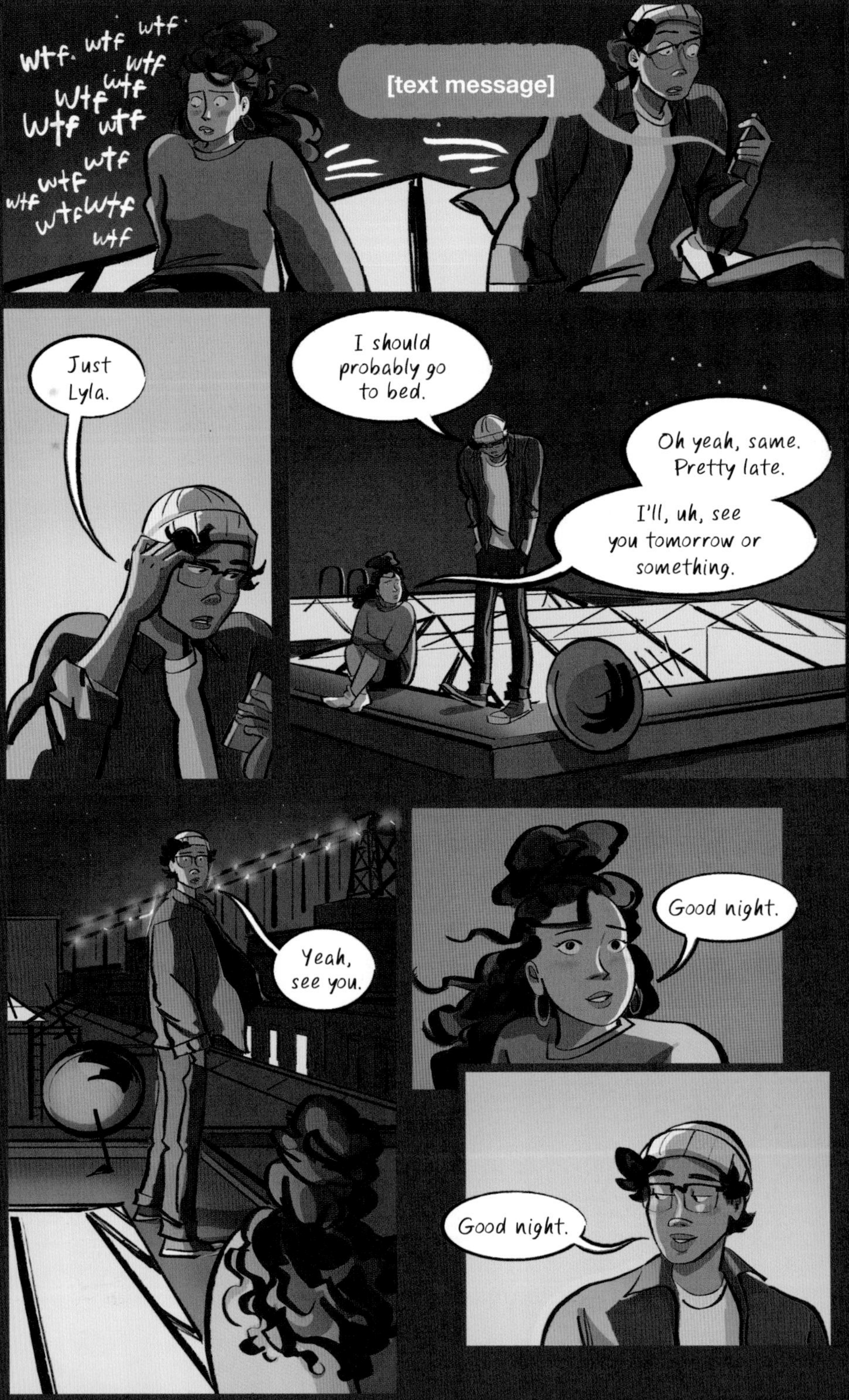

wtf wtf wtf wtf wtf wtf wtf wtf wtf wtf wtf wtf wtf wtf
[text message]
Just Lyla.
I should probably go to bed.
Oh yeah, same. Pretty late.
I'll, uh, see you tomorrow or something.
Yeah, see you.
Good night.
Good night.

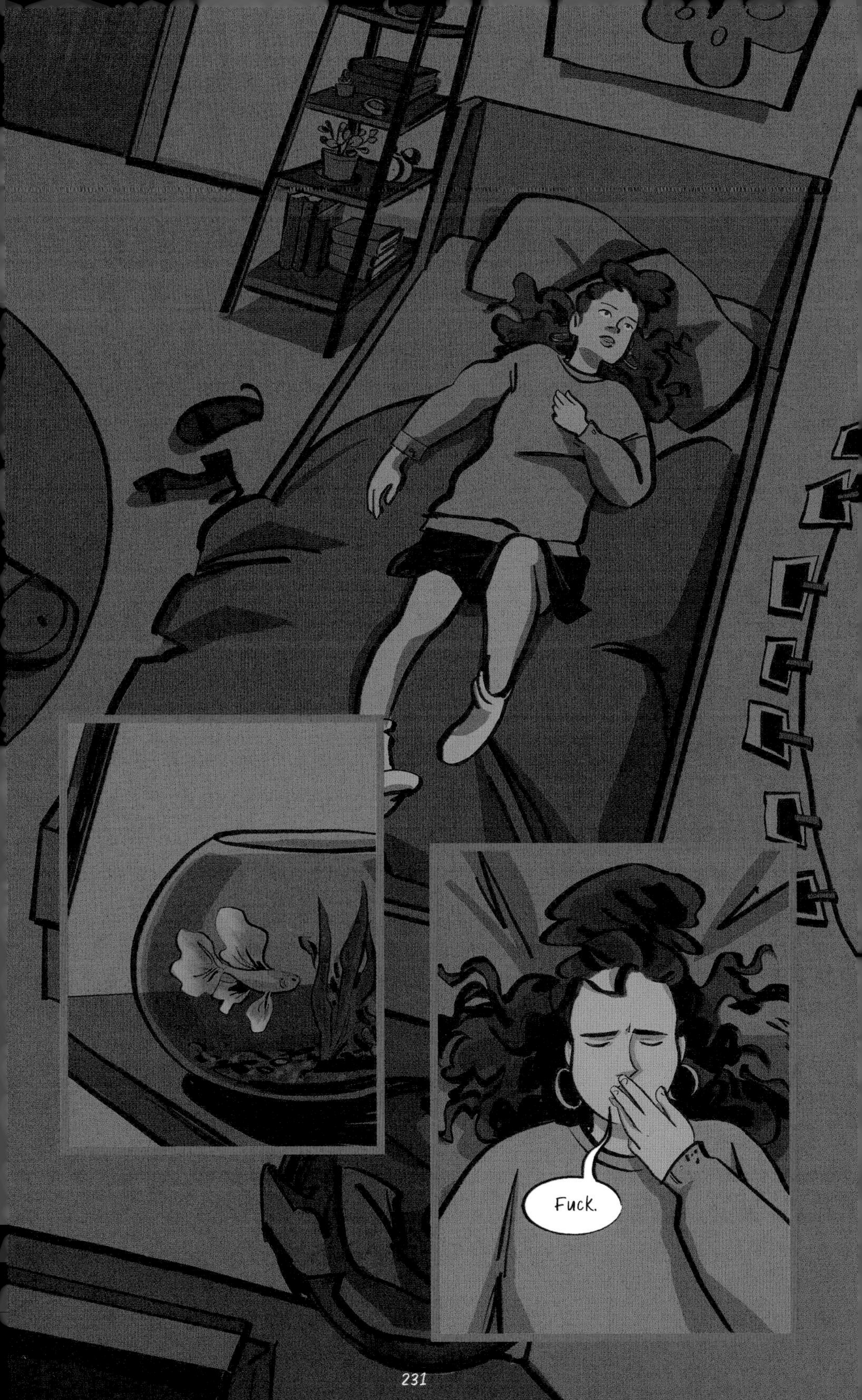
Fuck.

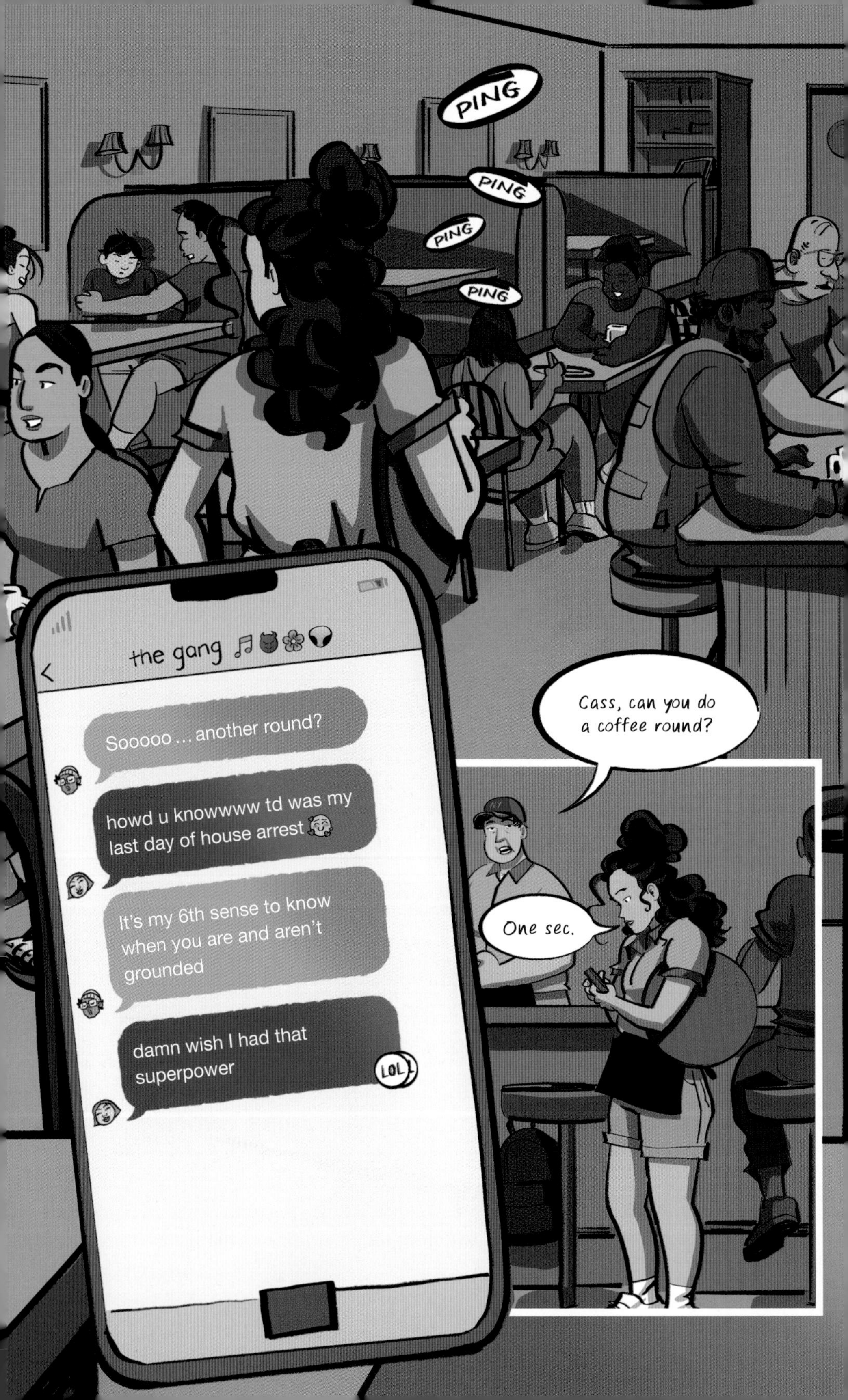
PING
PING
PING
PING
the gang
Sooooo ... another round?
howd u knowwww td was my last day of house arrest
It's my 6th sense to know when you are and aren't grounded
damn wish I had that superpower
LOL
Cass, can you do a coffee round?
One sec.

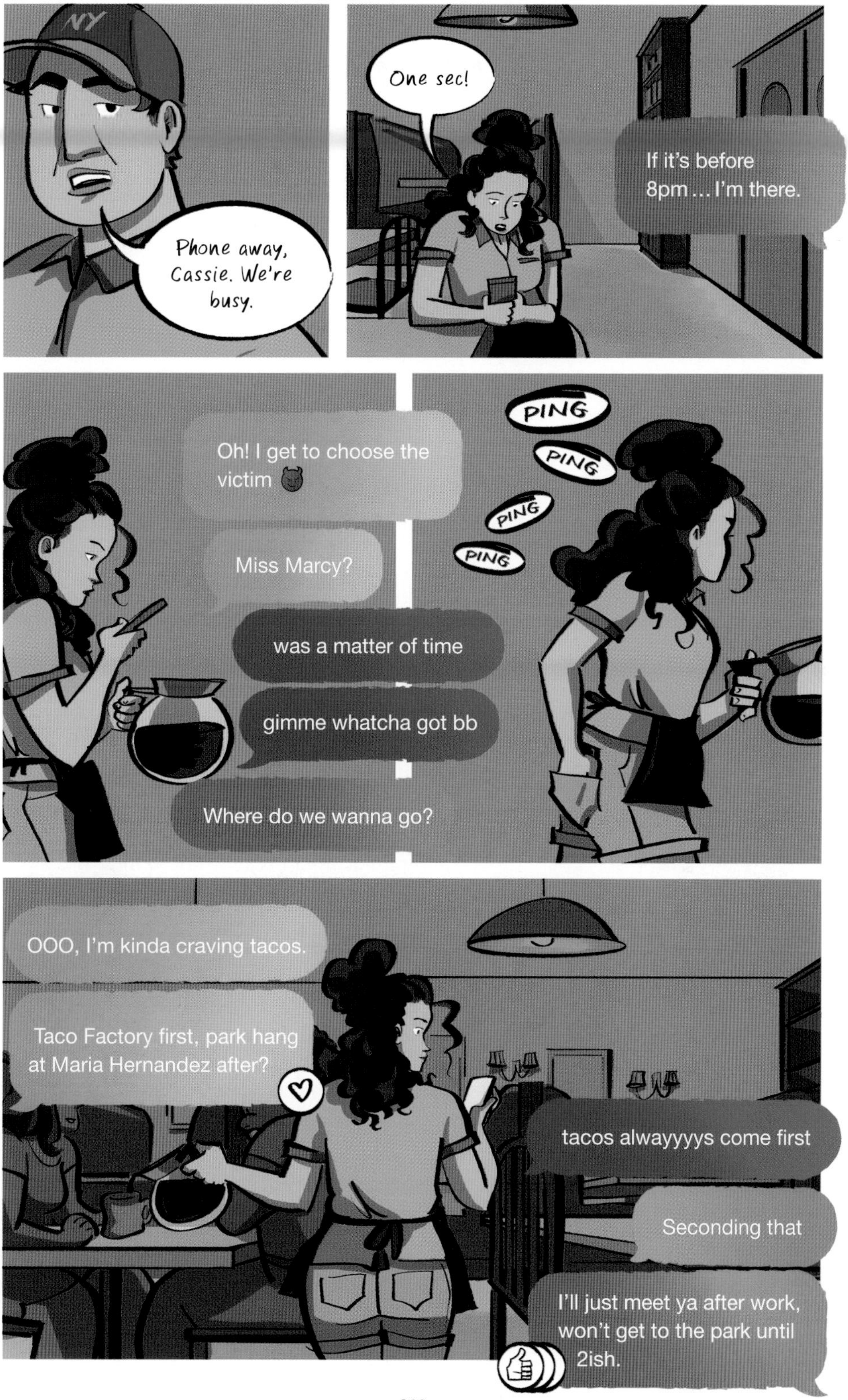
Phone away, Cassie. We're busy.
One sec!
If it's before 8pm … I'm there.
Oh! I get to choose the victim
Miss Marcy?
was a matter of time
gimme whatcha got bb
Where do we wanna go?
PING
PING
PING
PING
OOO, I'm kinda craving tacos.
Taco Factory first, park hang at Maria Hernandez after?
tacos alwayyyys come first
Seconding that
I'll just meet ya after work, won't get to the park until 2ish.

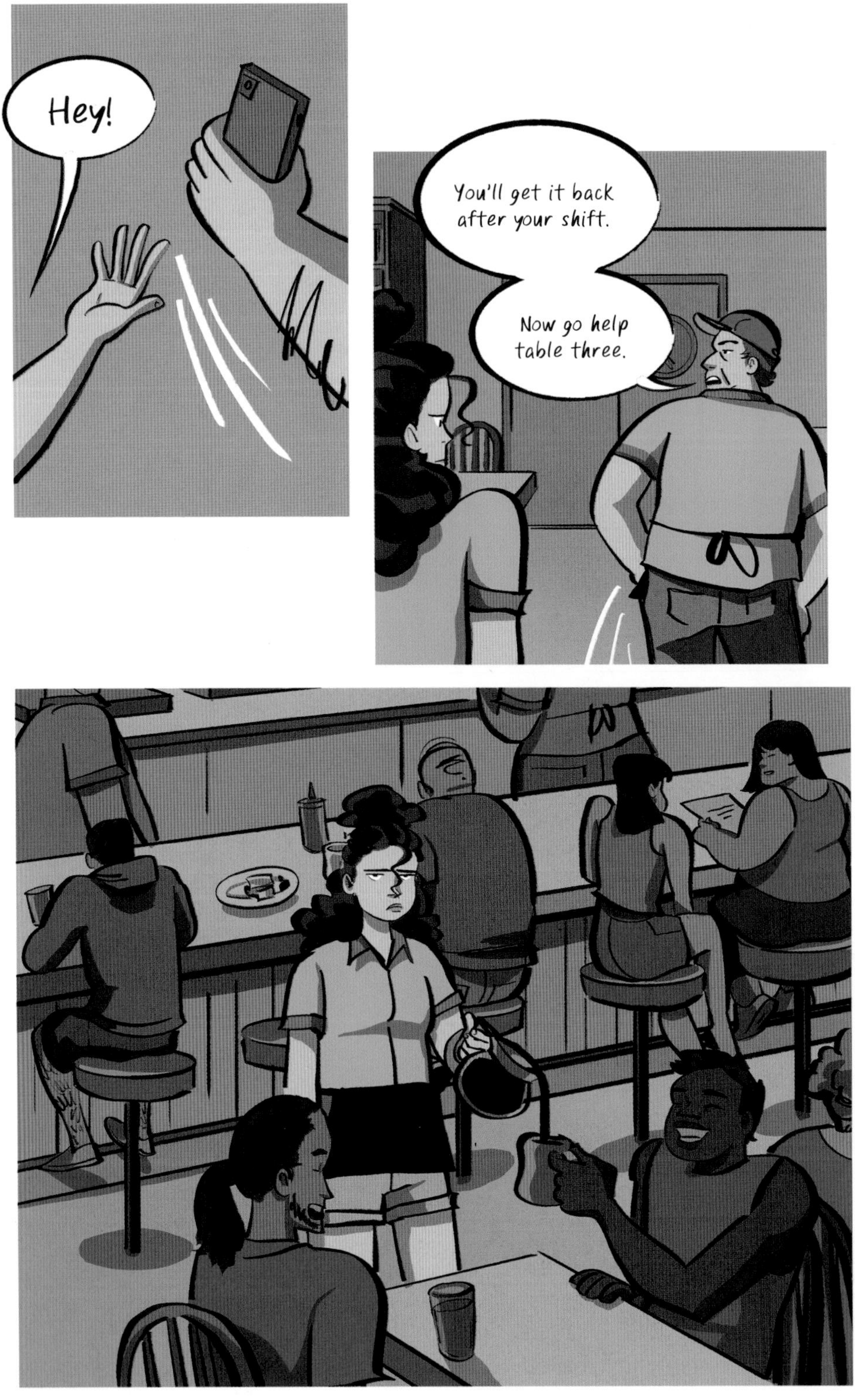
Hey!
You'll get it back after your shift.
Now go help table three.

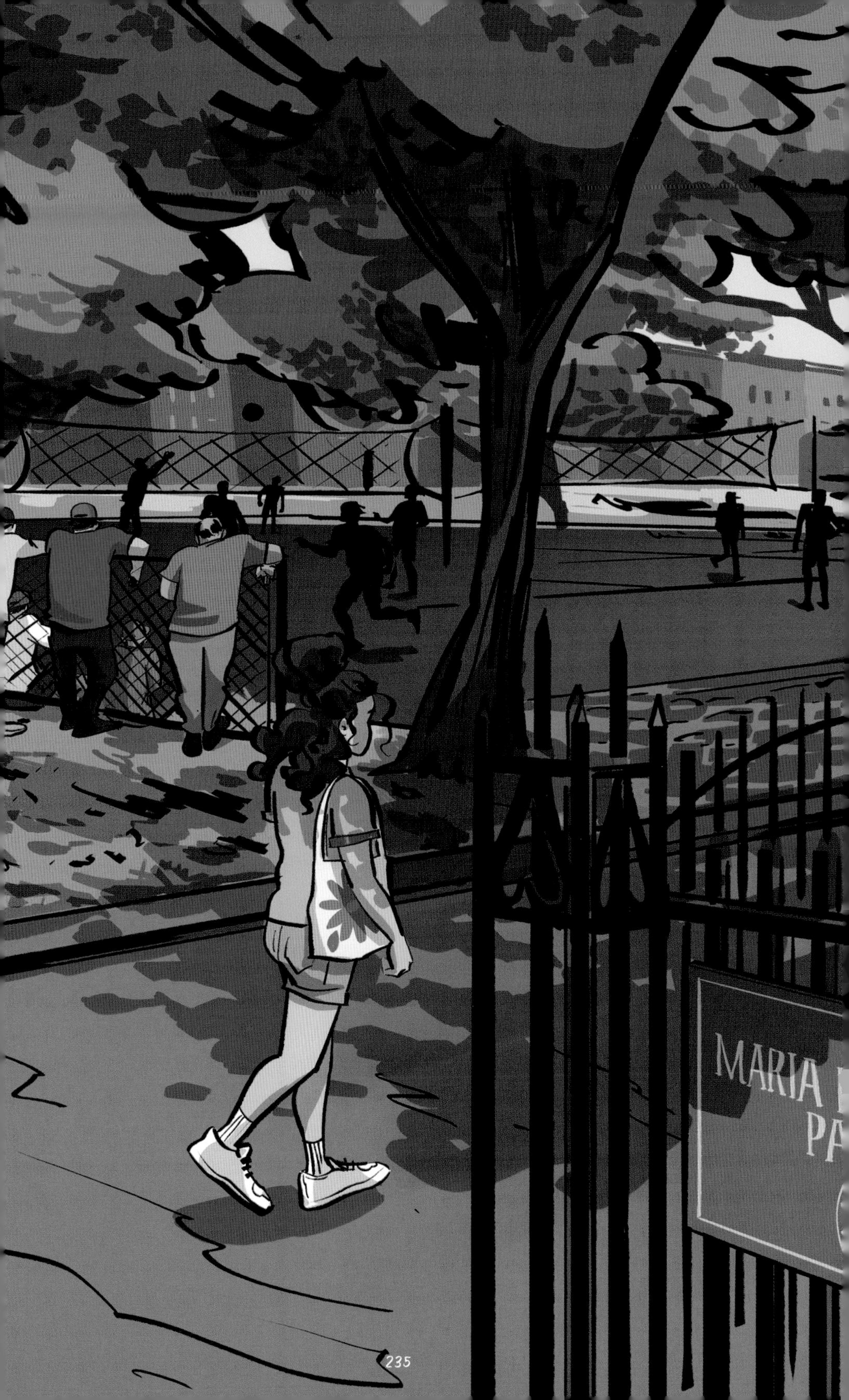
MARIA

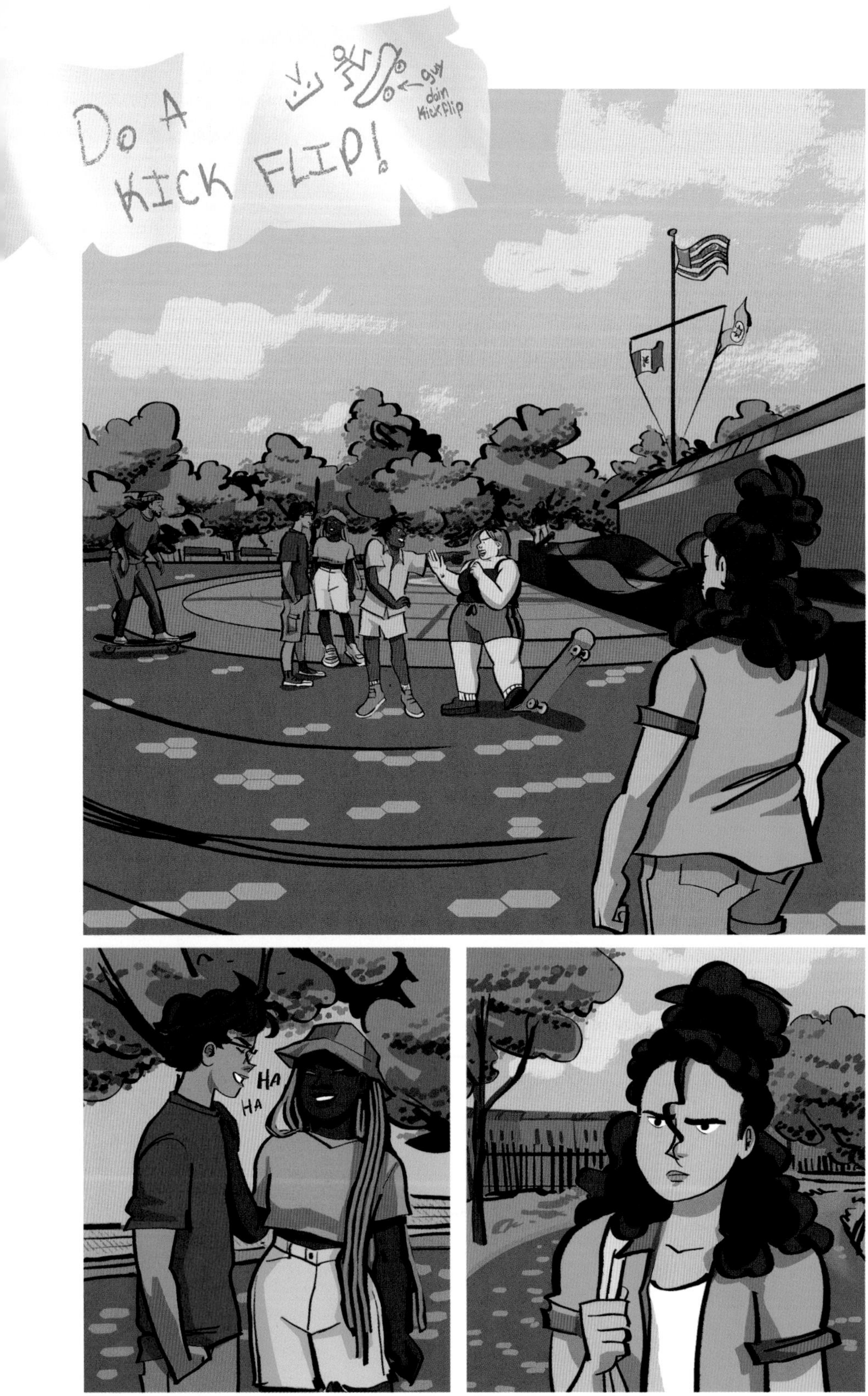
Do A
KICK FLIP!
guy
doin
KickFlip
HA
HA

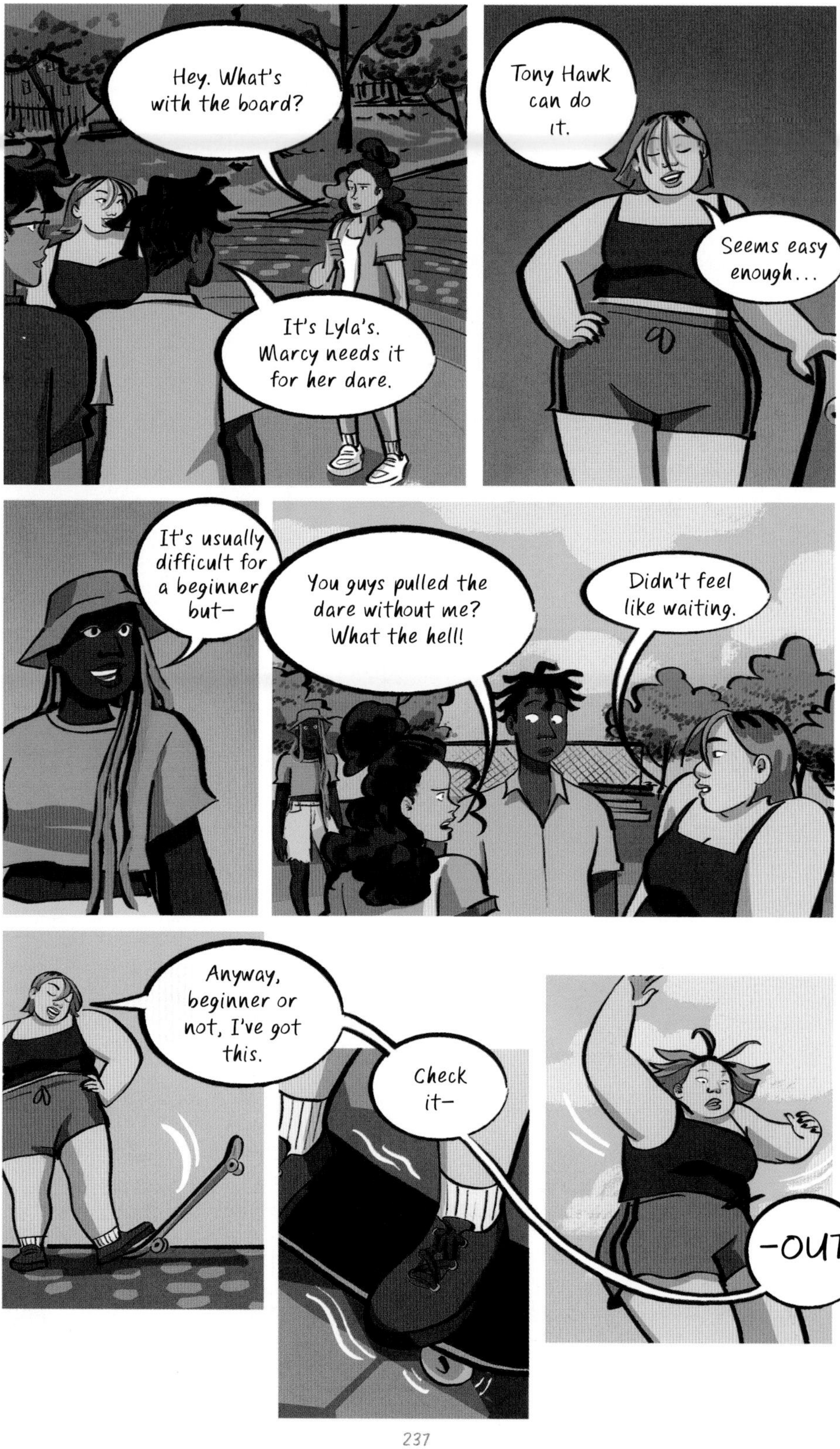
Hey. What's with the board?
It's Lyla's. Marcy needs it for her dare.
Tony Hawk can do it.
Seems easy enough...
It's usually difficult for a beginner but–
You guys pulled the dare without me? What the hell!
Didn't feel like waiting.
Anyway, beginner or not, I've got this.
Check it–
–OUT!

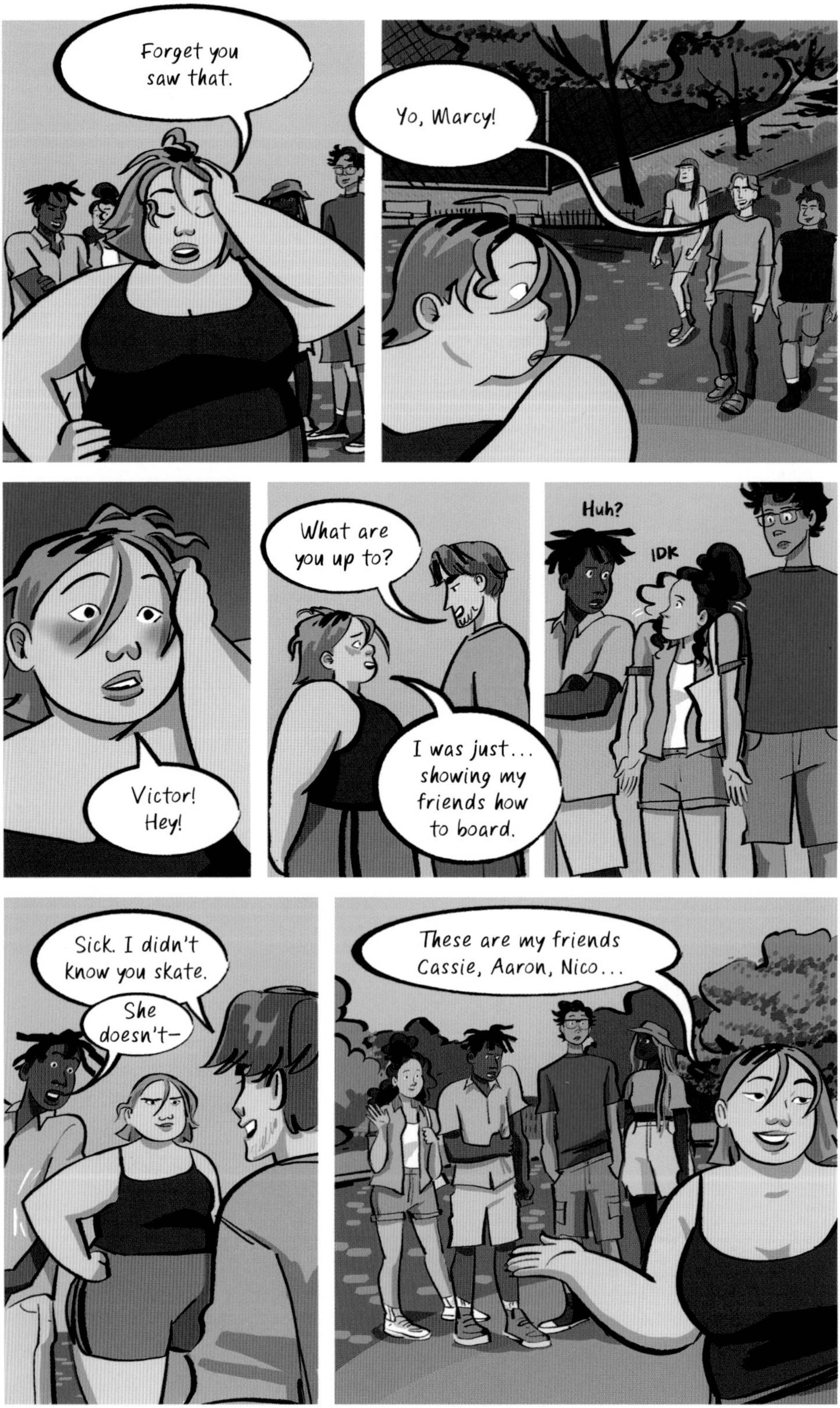
Forget you saw that.
Yo, Marcy!
Victor! Hey!
What are you up to?
I was just... showing my friends how to board.
Huh?
IDK
Sick. I didn't know you skate.
She doesn't–
These are my friends Cassie, Aaron, Nico...

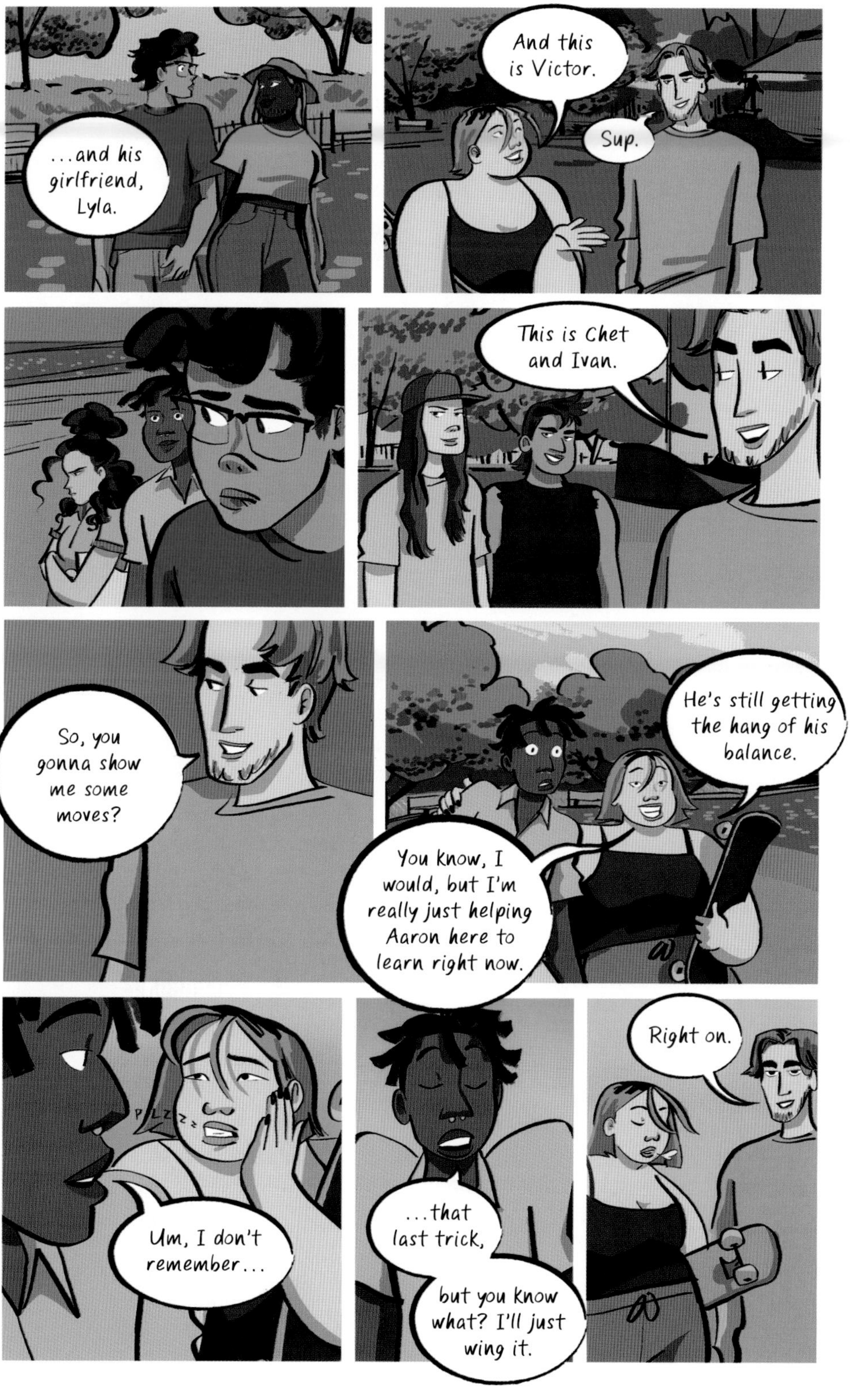
...and his girlfriend, Lyla.
And this is Victor.
Sup.
This is Chet and Ivan.
So, you gonna show me some moves?
He's still getting the hang of his balance.
You know, I would, but I'm really just helping Aaron here to learn right now.
PLZ
Um, I don't remember...
...that last trick,
but you know what? I'll just wing it.
Right on.

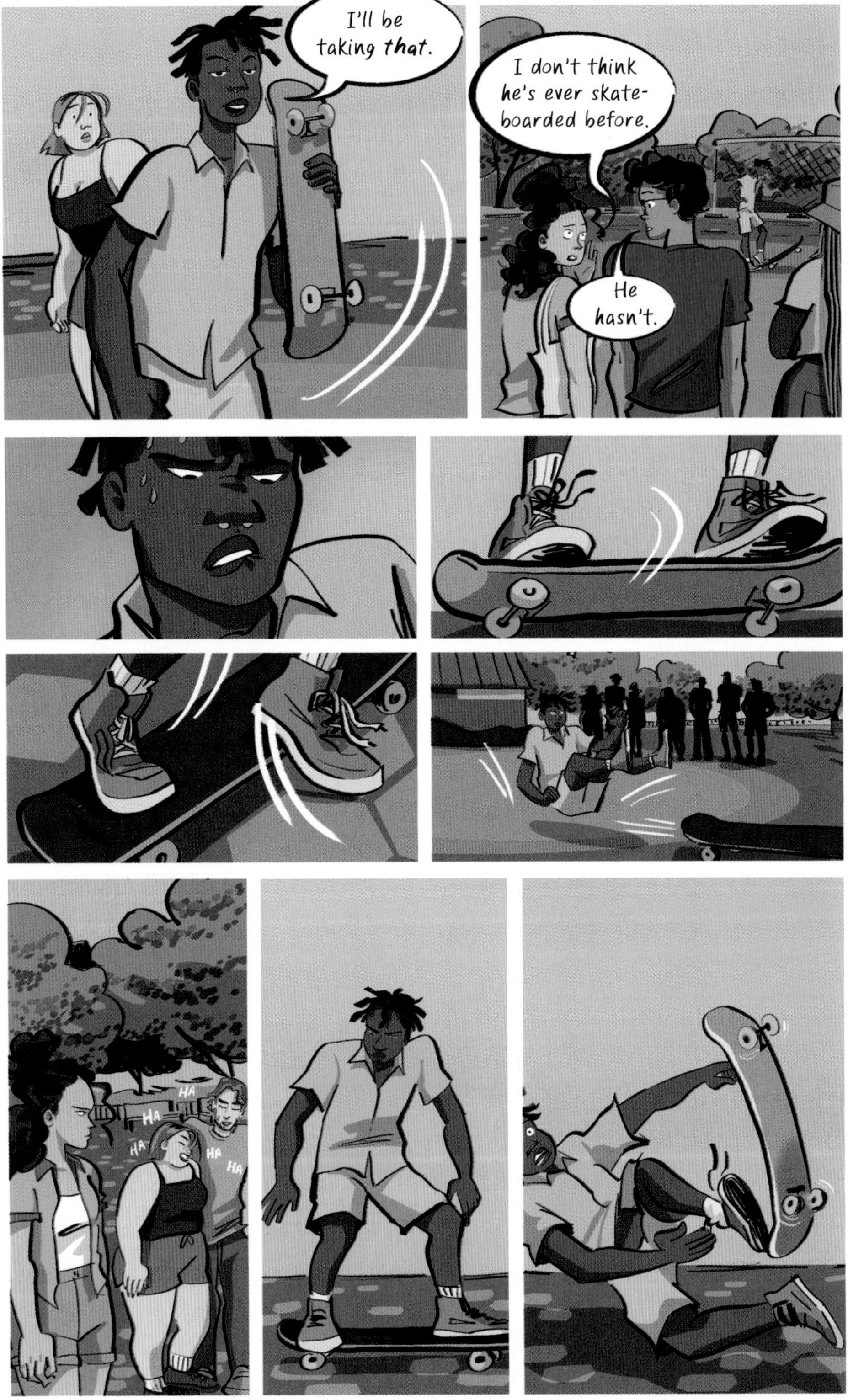
I'll be taking *that*.
I don't think he's ever skateboarded before.
He hasn't.
HA
HA
HA
HA
HA
HA

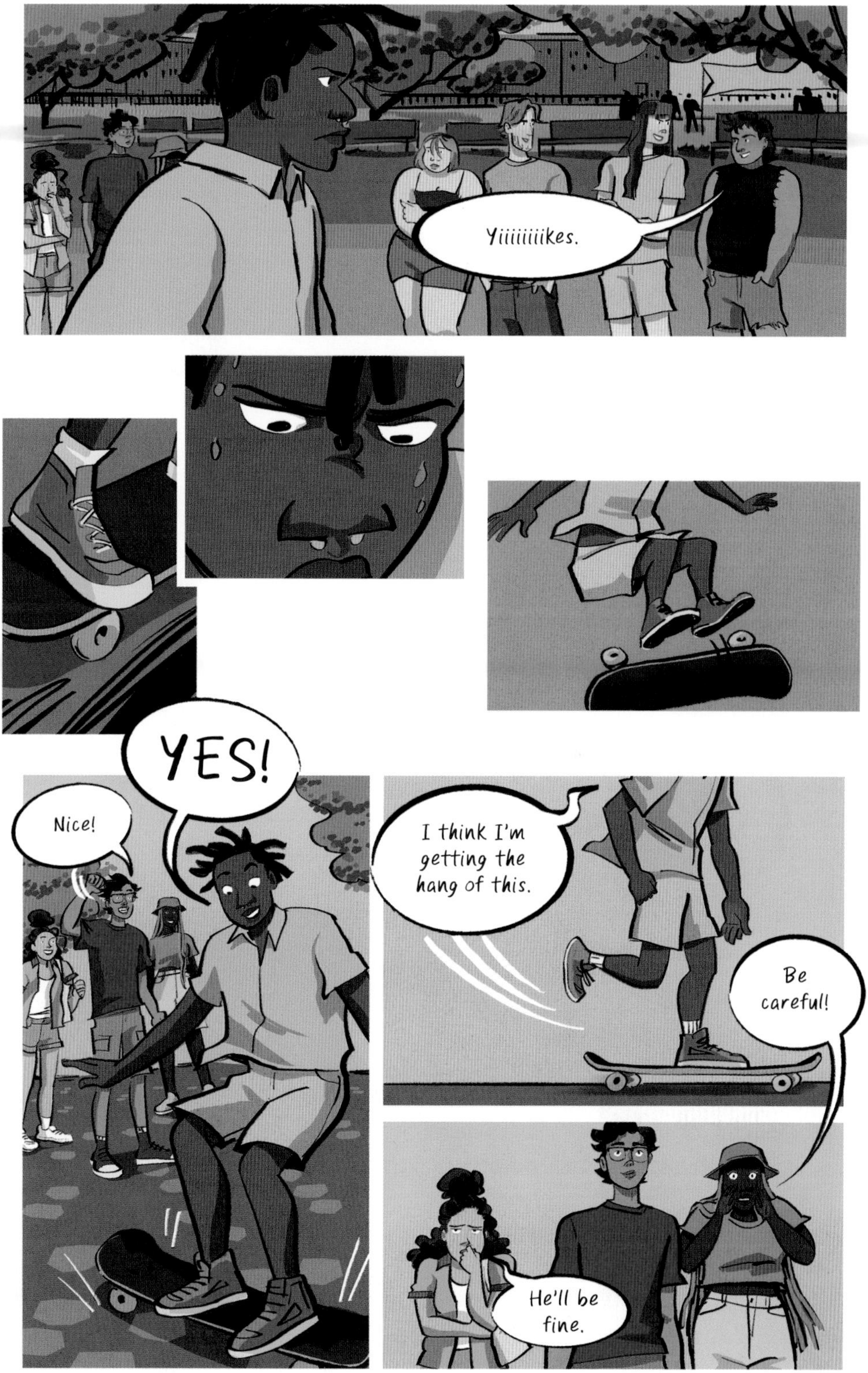
Yiiiiiiiikes.
YES!
Nice!
I think I'm getting the hang of this.
Be careful!
He'll be fine.

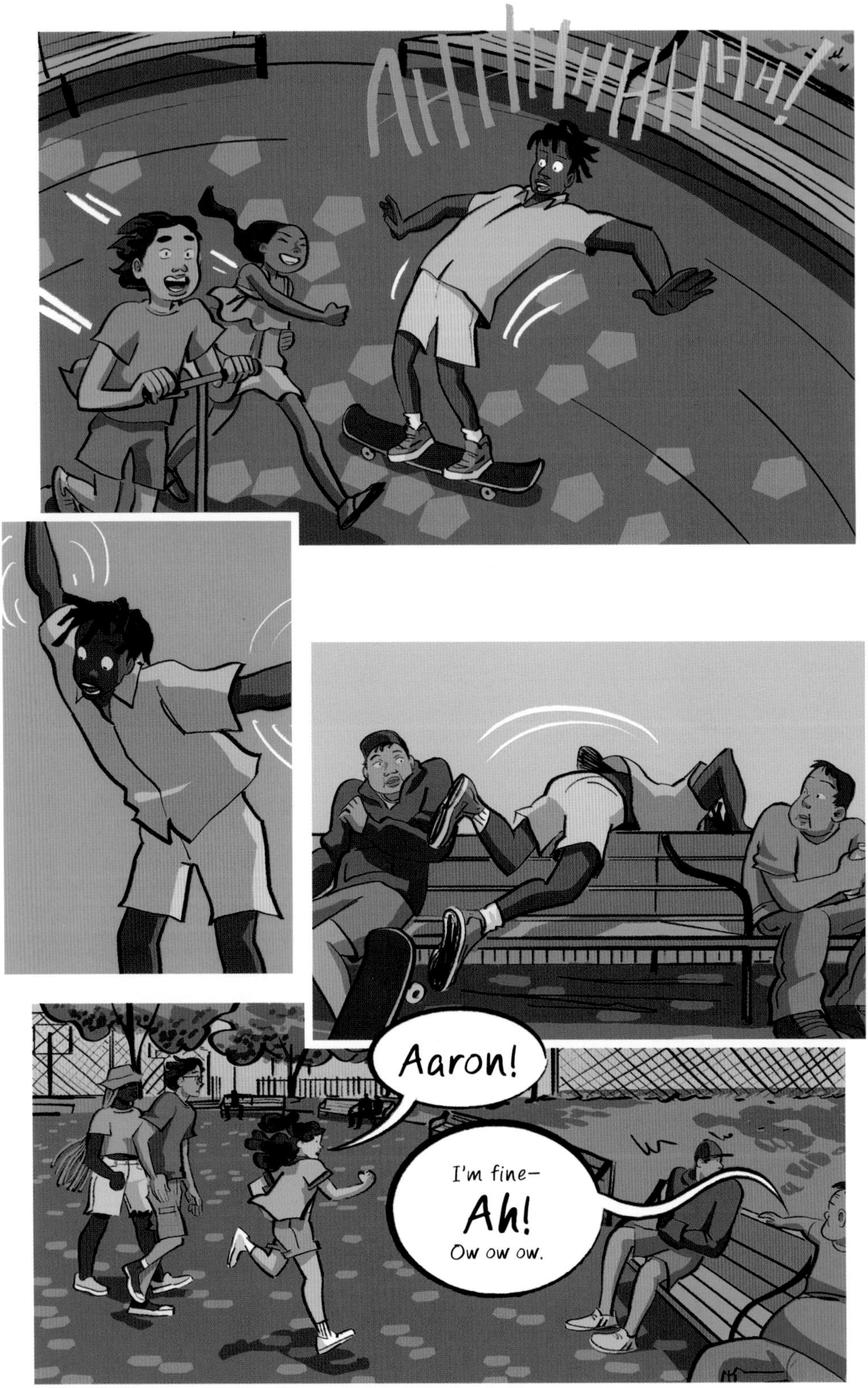
AHHHHHHHH!
Aaron!
I'm fine—
Ah!
Ow ow ow.

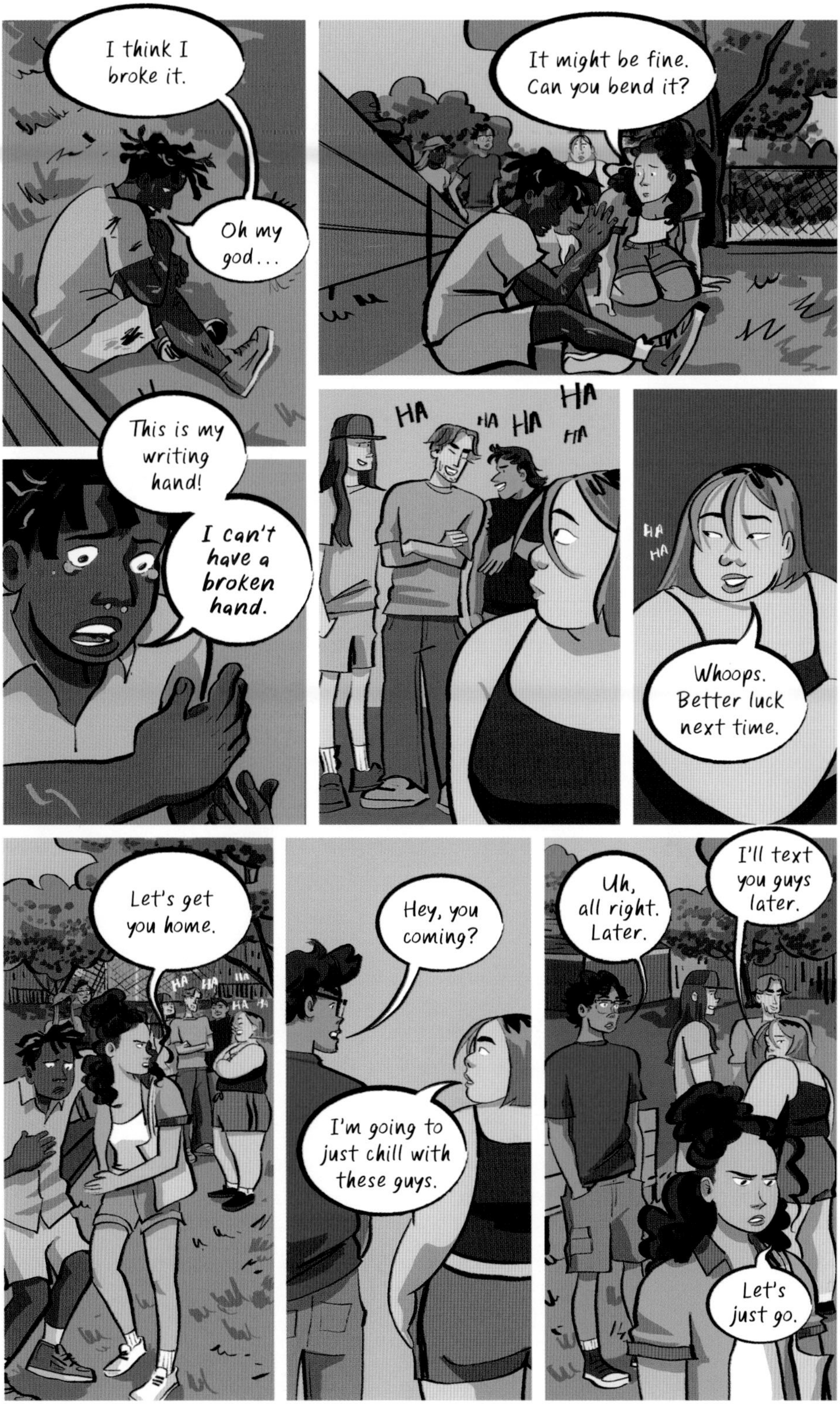
I think I broke it.
Oh my god...
It might be fine. Can you bend it?
This is my writing hand!
I can't have a broken hand.
HA
HA
HA
HA
HA
HA HA
Whoops. Better luck next time.
Let's get you home.
HA HA HA
HA HA
Hey, you coming?
I'm going to just chill with these guys.
Uh, all right. Later.
I'll text you guys later.
Let's just go.

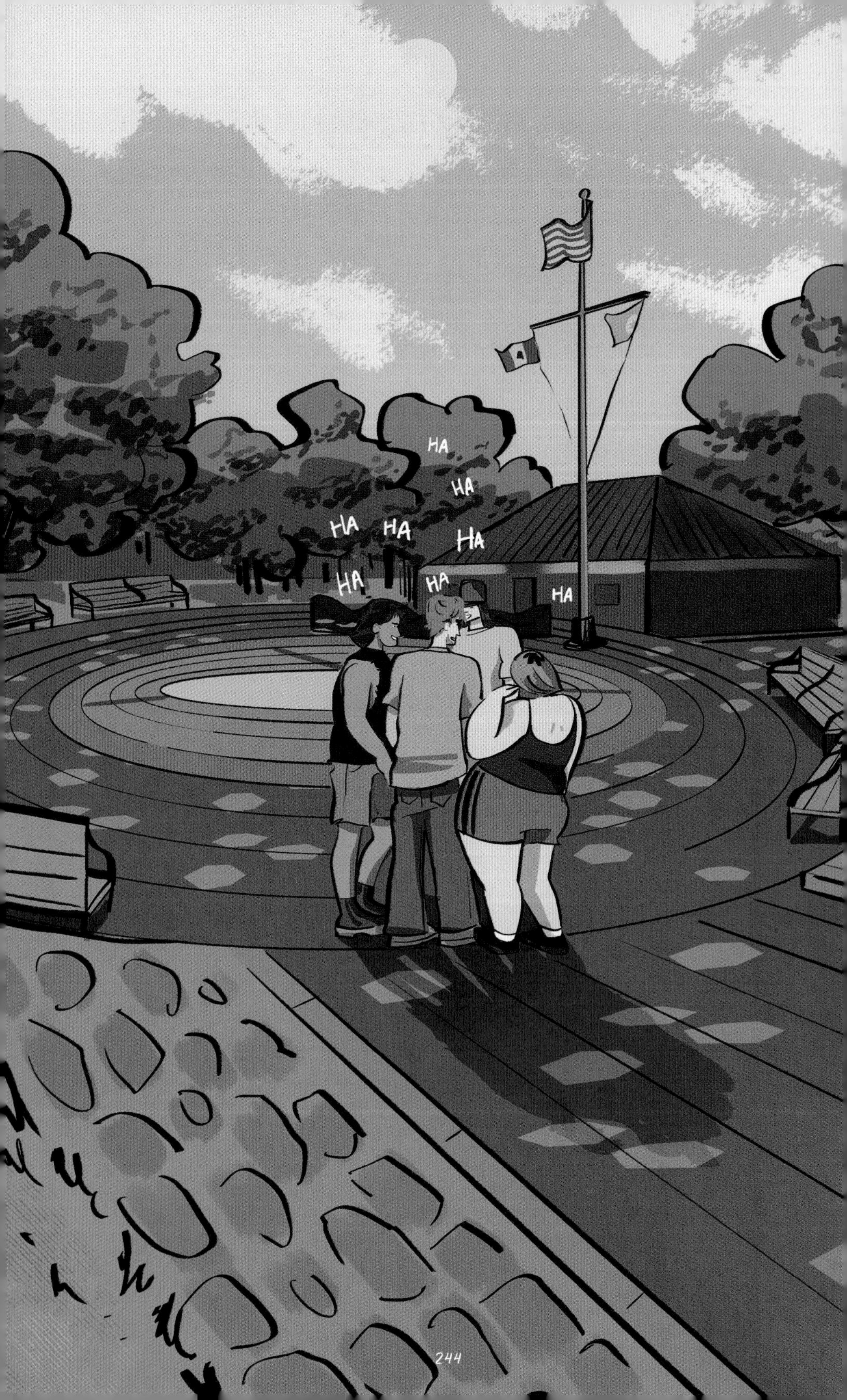
HA
HA
HA
HA
HA
HA
HA
HA

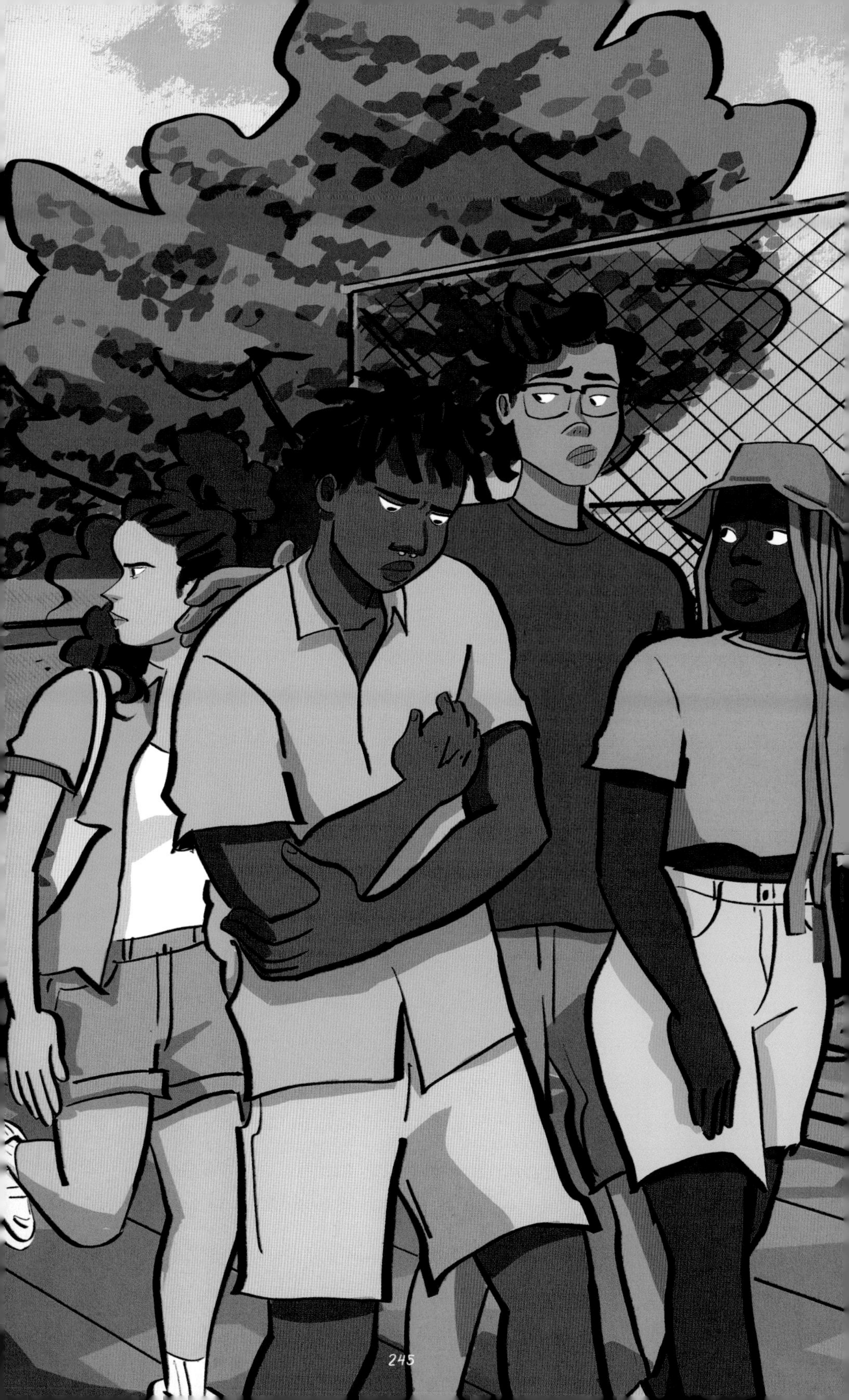

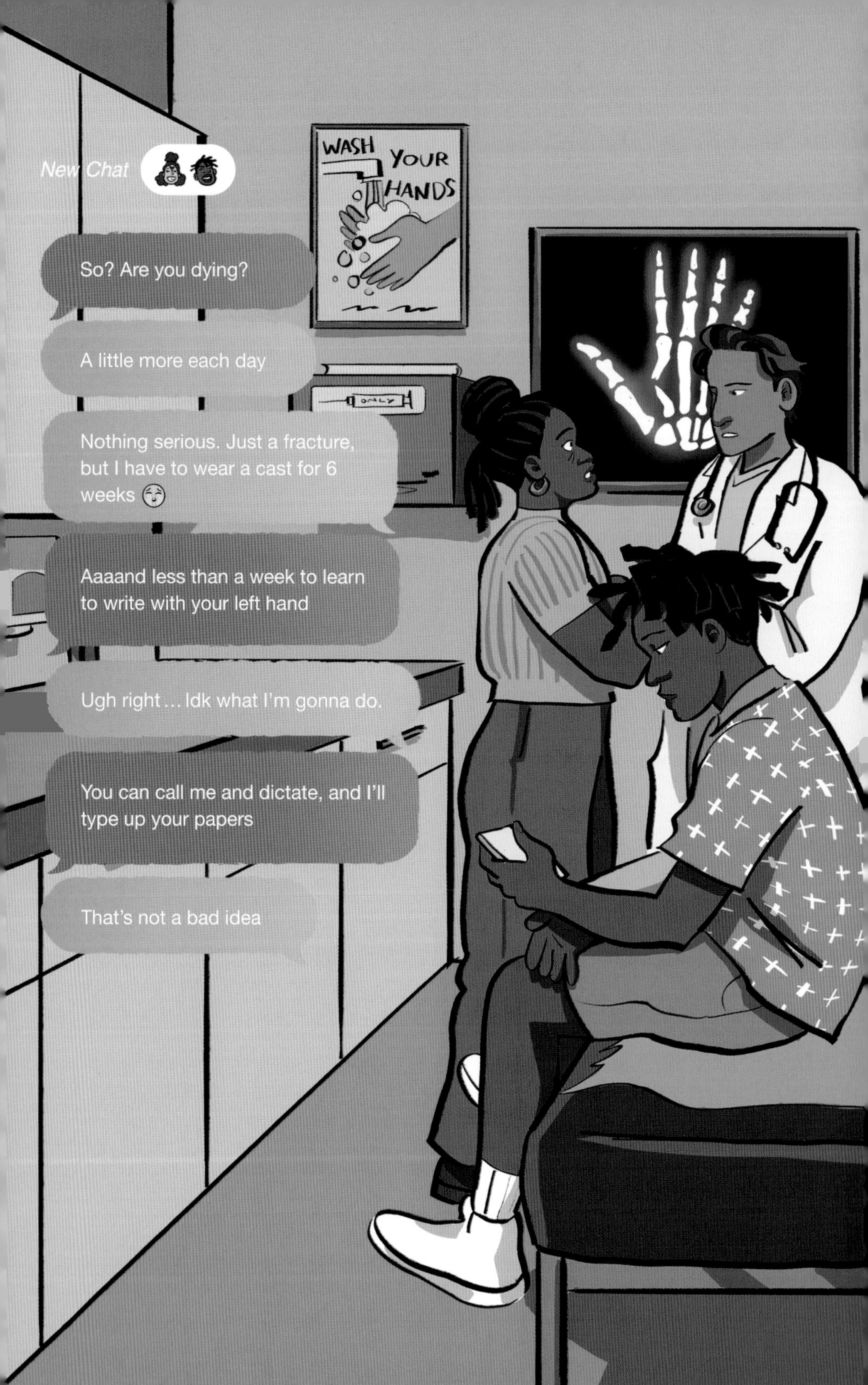
New Chat
WASH YOUR HANDS
So? Are you dying?
A little more each day
Nothing serious. Just a fracture, but I have to wear a cast for 6 weeks 😲
Aaaand less than a week to learn to write with your left hand
Ugh right… Idk what I'm gonna do.
You can call me and dictate, and I'll type up your papers
That's not a bad idea

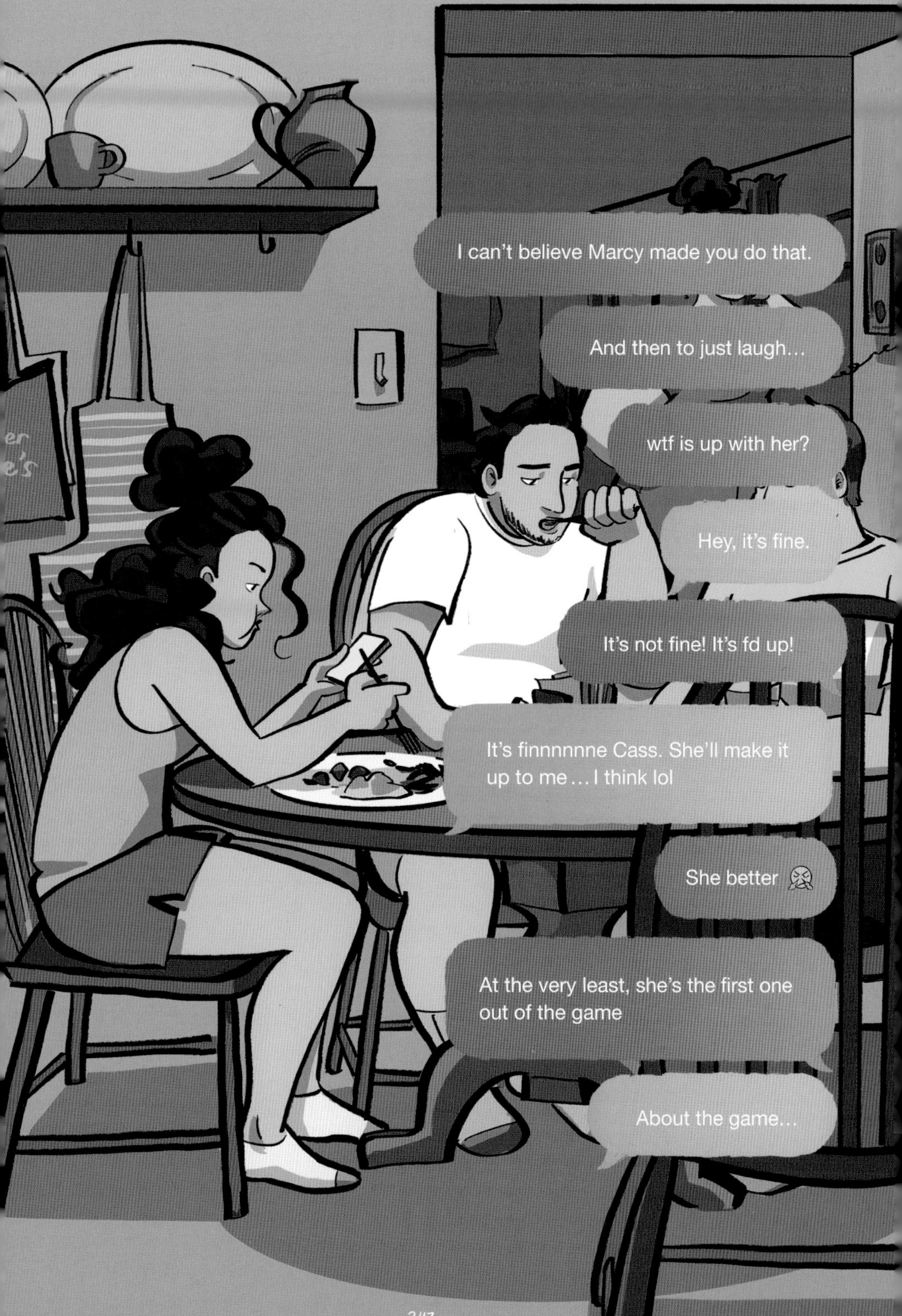

I can't believe Marcy made you do that.
And then to just laugh...
wtf is up with her?
Hey, it's fine.
It's not fine! It's fd up!
It's finnnnnne Cass. She'll make it up to me... I think lol
She better
At the very least, she's the first one out of the game
About the game...

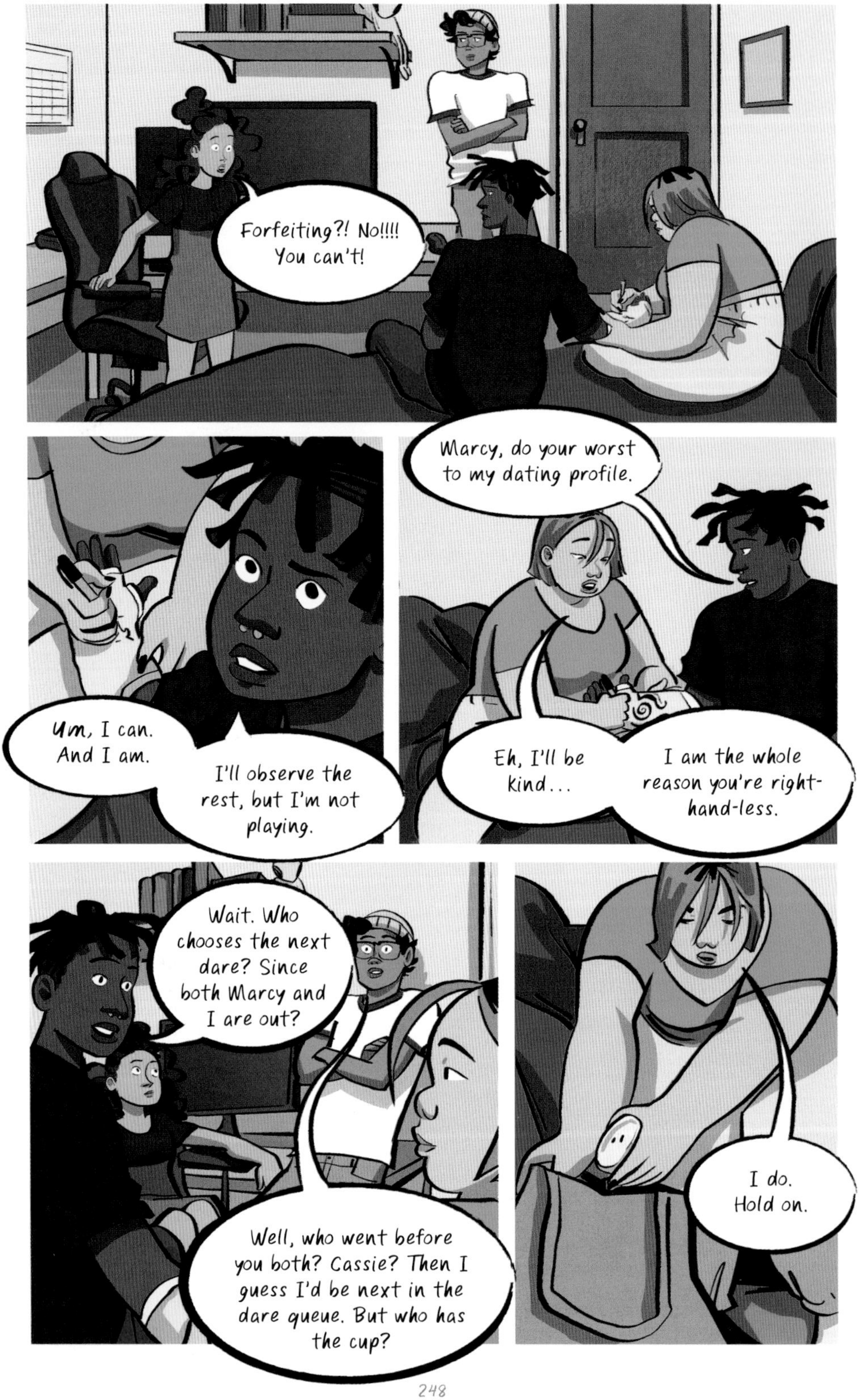
Forfeiting?! No!!!! You can't!
Um, I can. And I am.
I'll observe the rest, but I'm not playing.
Marcy, do your worst to my dating profile.
Eh, I'll be kind...
I am the whole reason you're right-hand-less.
Wait. Who chooses the next dare? Since both Marcy and I are out?
Well, who went before you both? Cassie? Then I guess I'd be next in the dare queue. But who has the cup?
I do. Hold on.

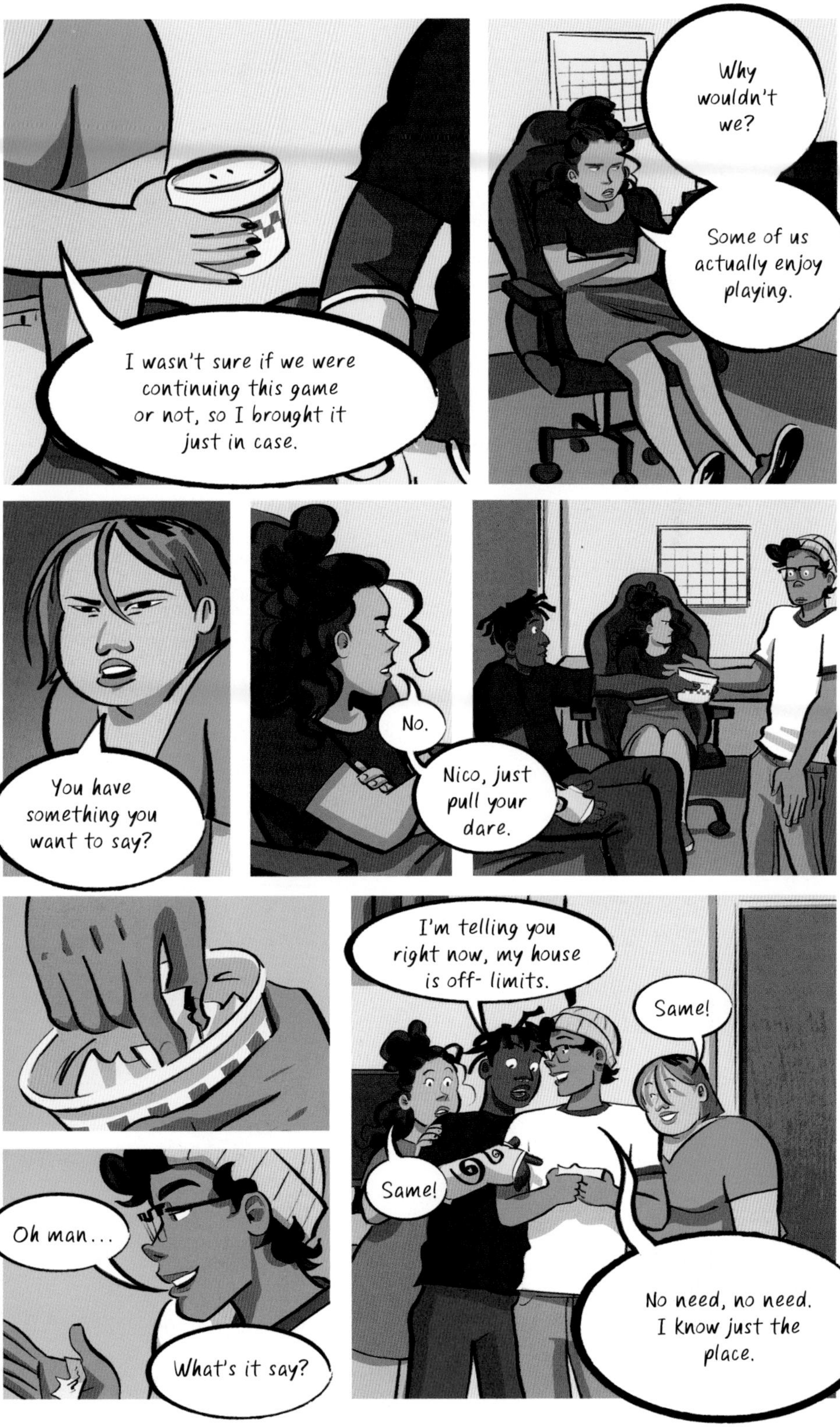
I wasn't sure if we were continuing this game or not, so I brought it just in case.
Why wouldn't we?
Some of us actually enjoy playing.
You have something you want to say?
No.
Nico, just pull your dare.
Oh man...
What's it say?
I'm telling you right now, my house is off- limits.
Same!
Same!
No need, no need. I know just the place.

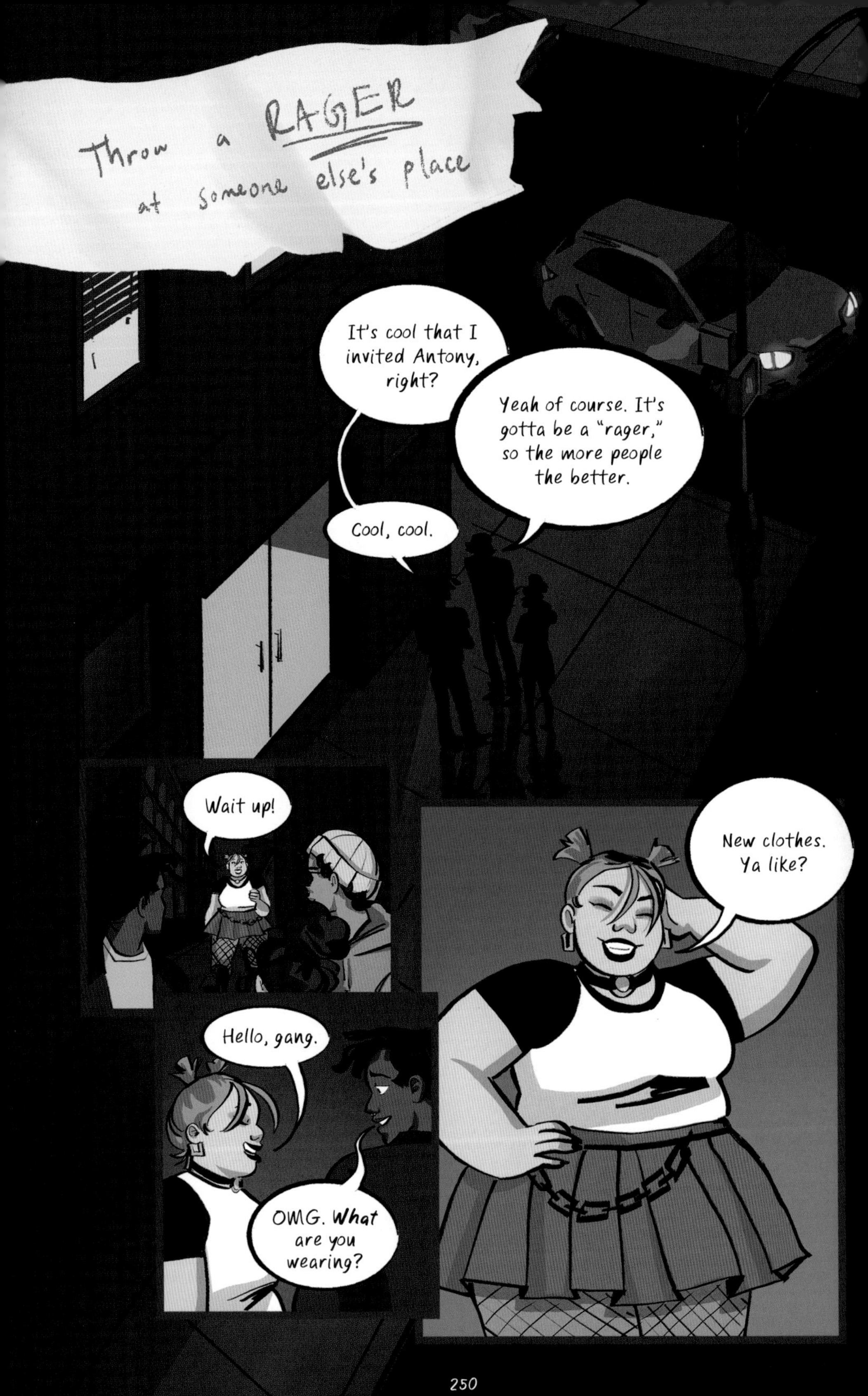
Throw a RAGER at someone else's place
It's cool that I invited Antony, right?
Yeah of course. It's gotta be a "rager," so the more people the better.
Cool, cool.
Wait up!
Hello, gang.
OMG. What are you wearing?
New clothes. Ya like?

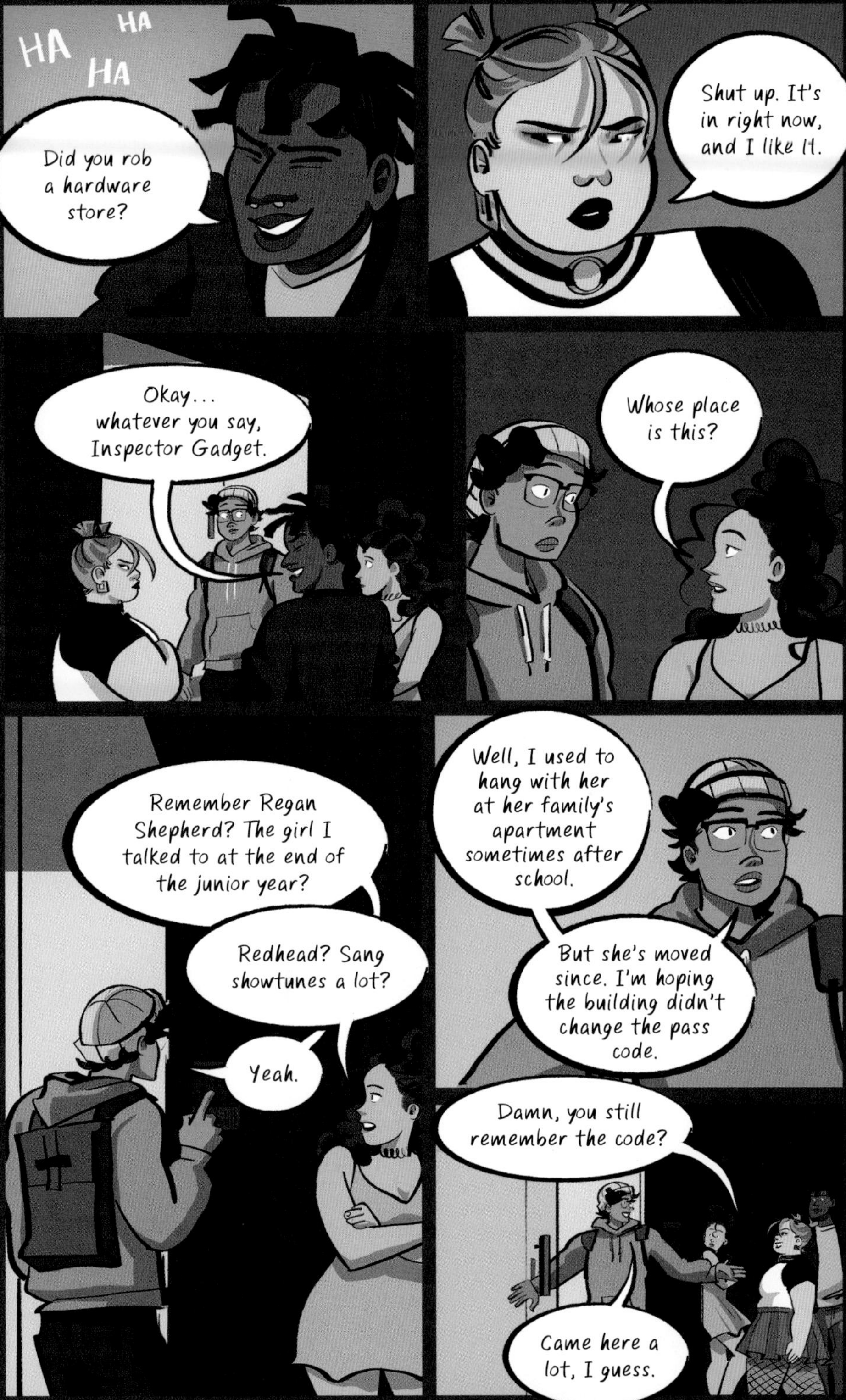
HA HA HA
Did you rob a hardware store?
Shut up. It's in right now, and I like it.
Okay... whatever you say, Inspector Gadget.
Whose place is this?
Remember Regan Shepherd? The girl I talked to at the end of the junior year?
Redhead? Sang showtunes a lot?
Yeah.
Well, I used to hang with her at her family's apartment sometimes after school.
But she's moved since. I'm hoping the building didn't change the pass code.
Damn, you still remember the code?
Came here a lot, I guess.

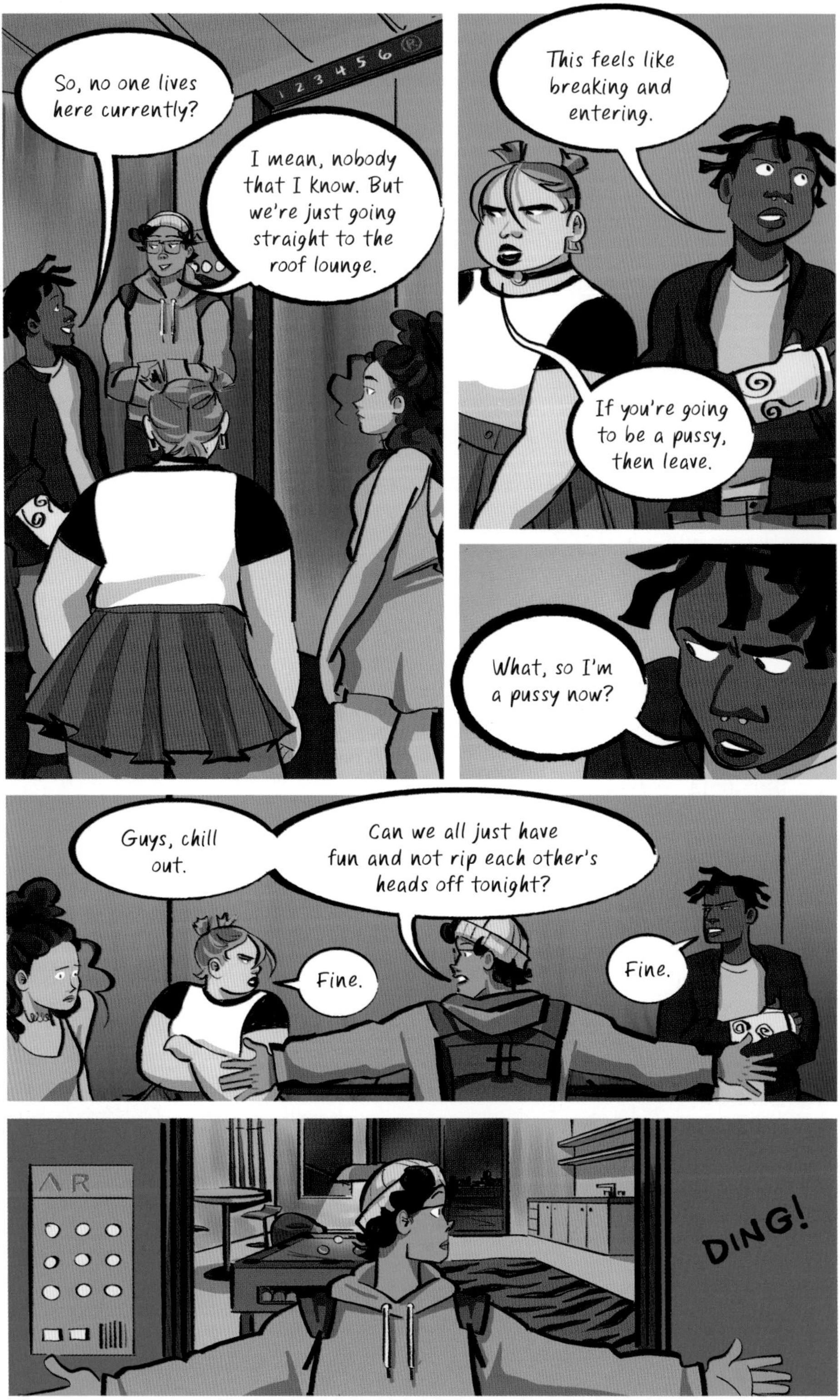

1 2 3 4 5 6 R
So, no one lives here currently?
I mean, nobody that I know. But we're just going straight to the roof lounge.
This feels like breaking and entering.
If you're going to be a pussy, then leave.
What, so I'm a pussy now?
Guys, chill out.
Can we all just have fun and not rip each other's heads off tonight?
Fine.
Fine.
AR
DING!

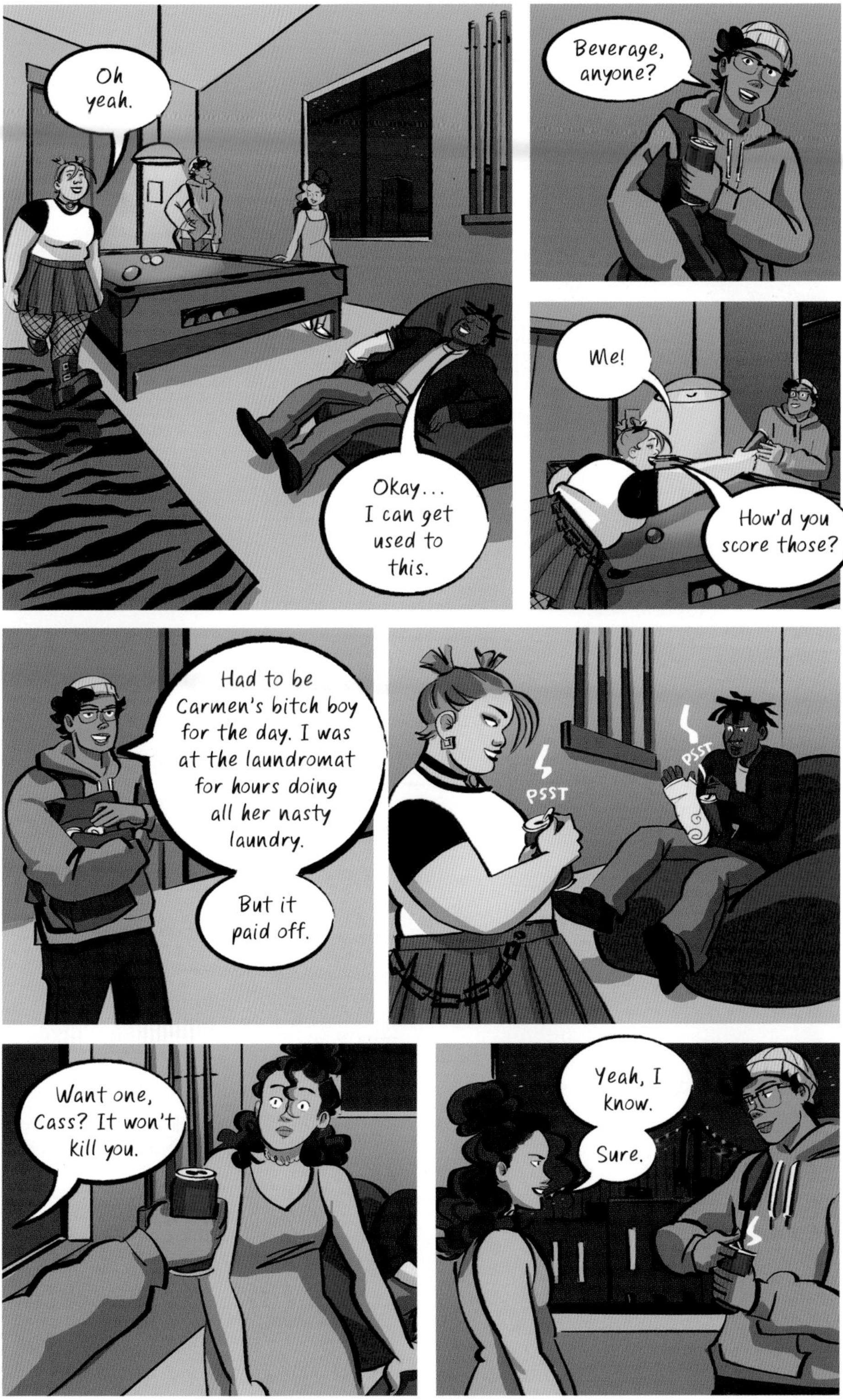
Oh yeah.
Okay... I can get used to this.
Beverage, anyone?
Me!
How'd you score those?
Had to be Carmen's bitch boy for the day. I was at the laundromat for hours doing all her nasty laundry.
But it paid off.
PSST
PSST
Want one, Cass? It won't kill you.
Yeah, I know.
Sure.

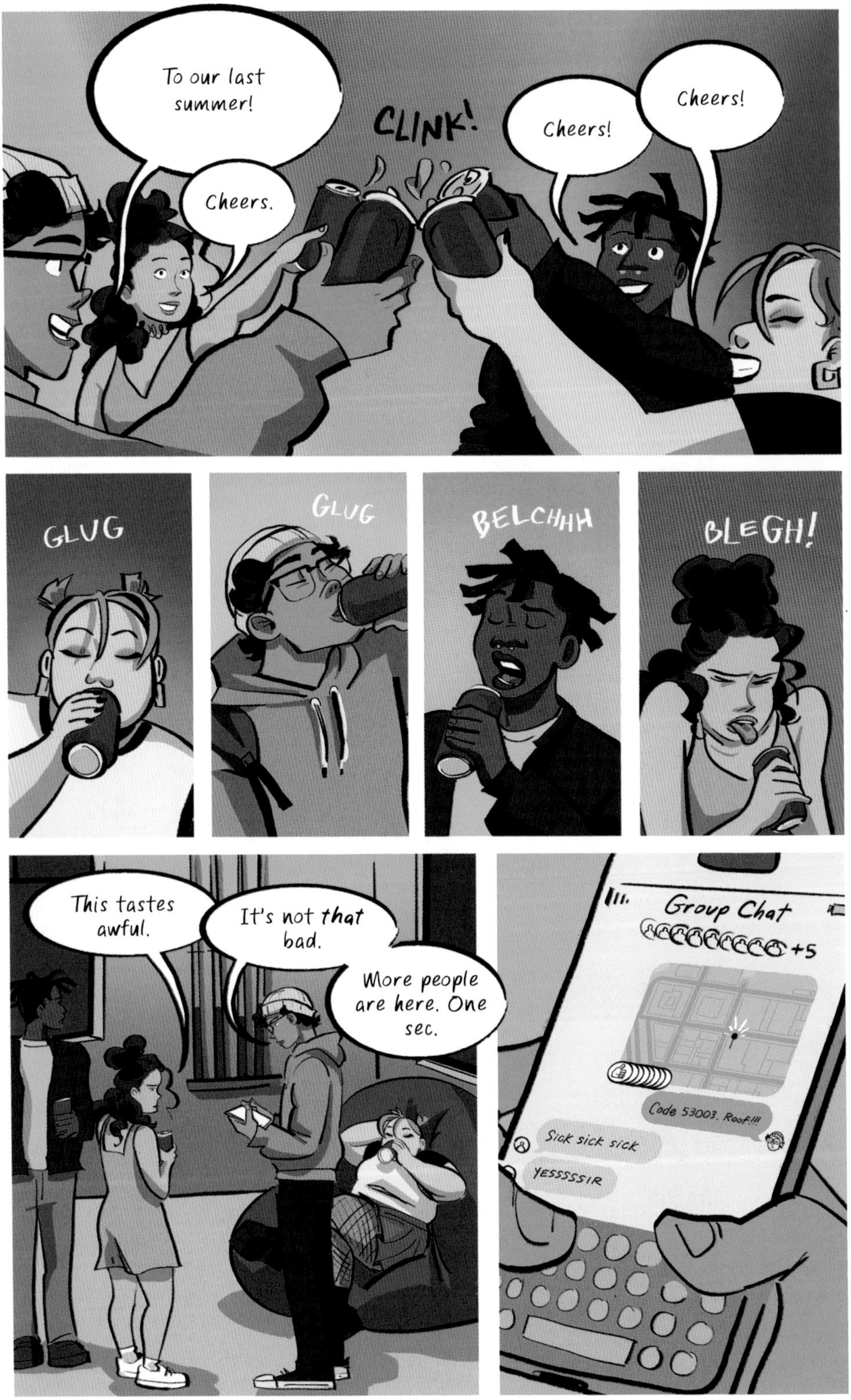
To our last summer!
Cheers.
CLINK!
Cheers!
Cheers!
GLUG
GLUG
BELCHHH
BLEGH!
This tastes awful.
It's not *that* bad.
More people are here. One sec.
Group Chat
+5
Code 53003. Roof!!!
Sick sick sick
YESSSSSIR

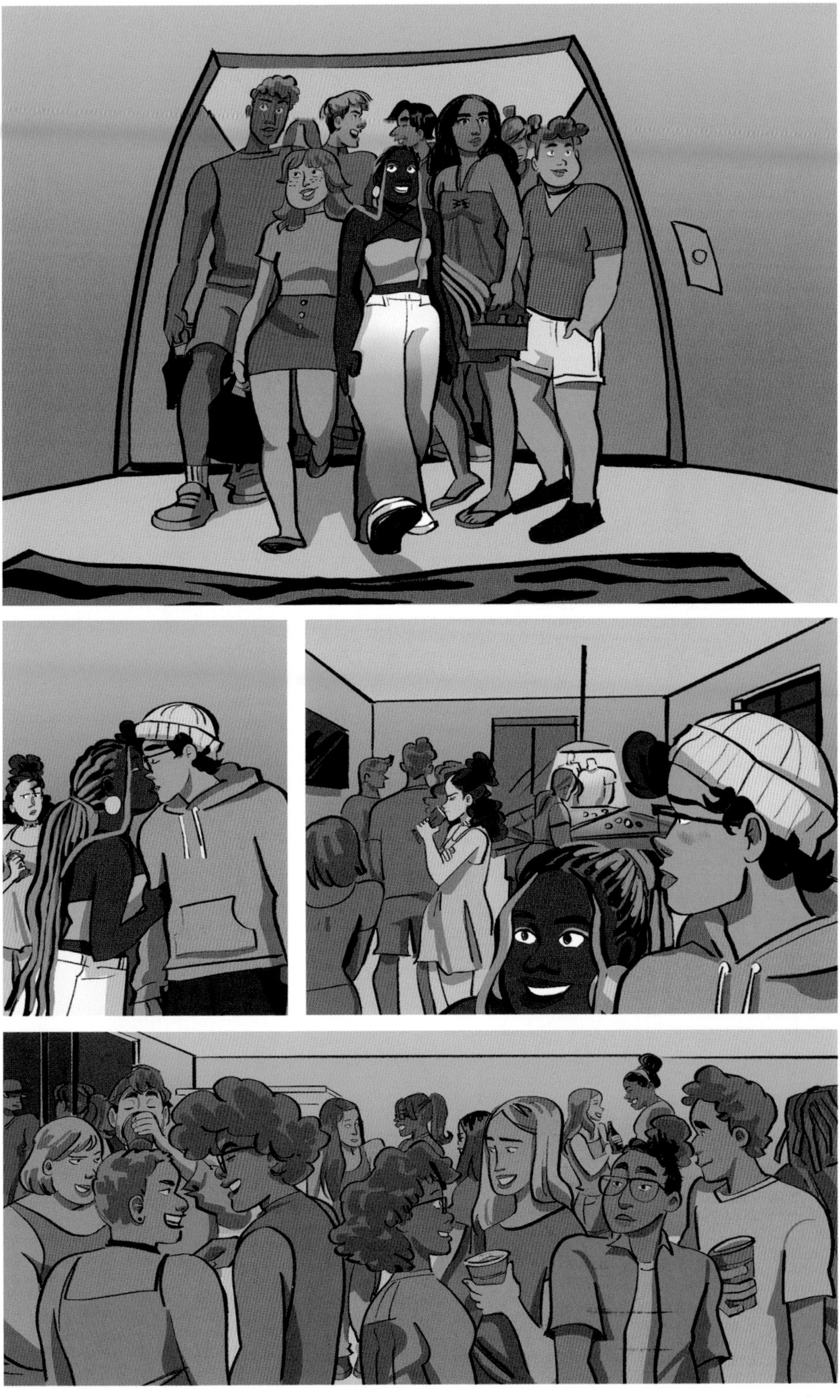

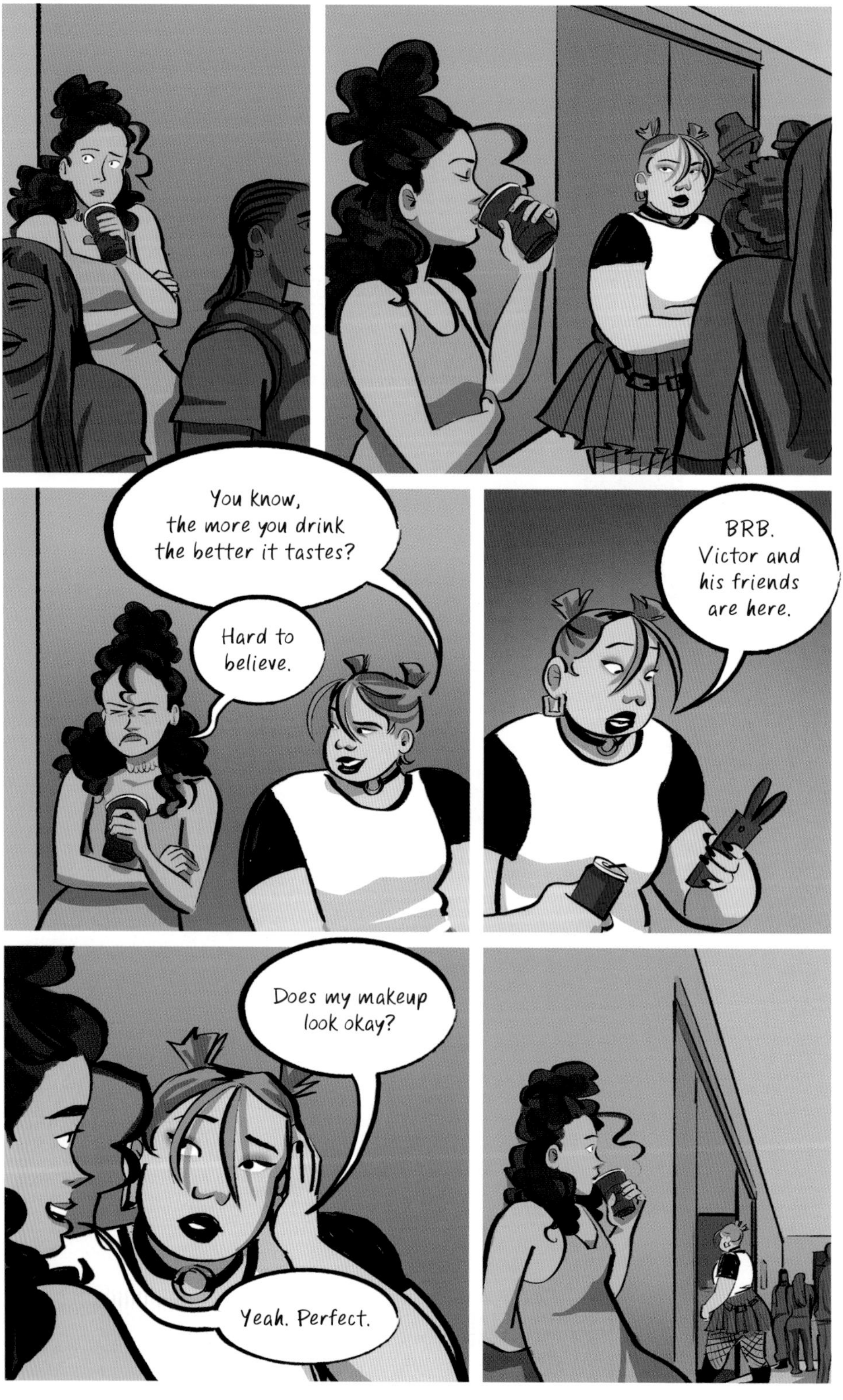
You know, the more you drink the better it tastes?
Hard to believe.
BRB. Victor and his friends are here.
Does my makeup look okay?
Yeah. Perfect.

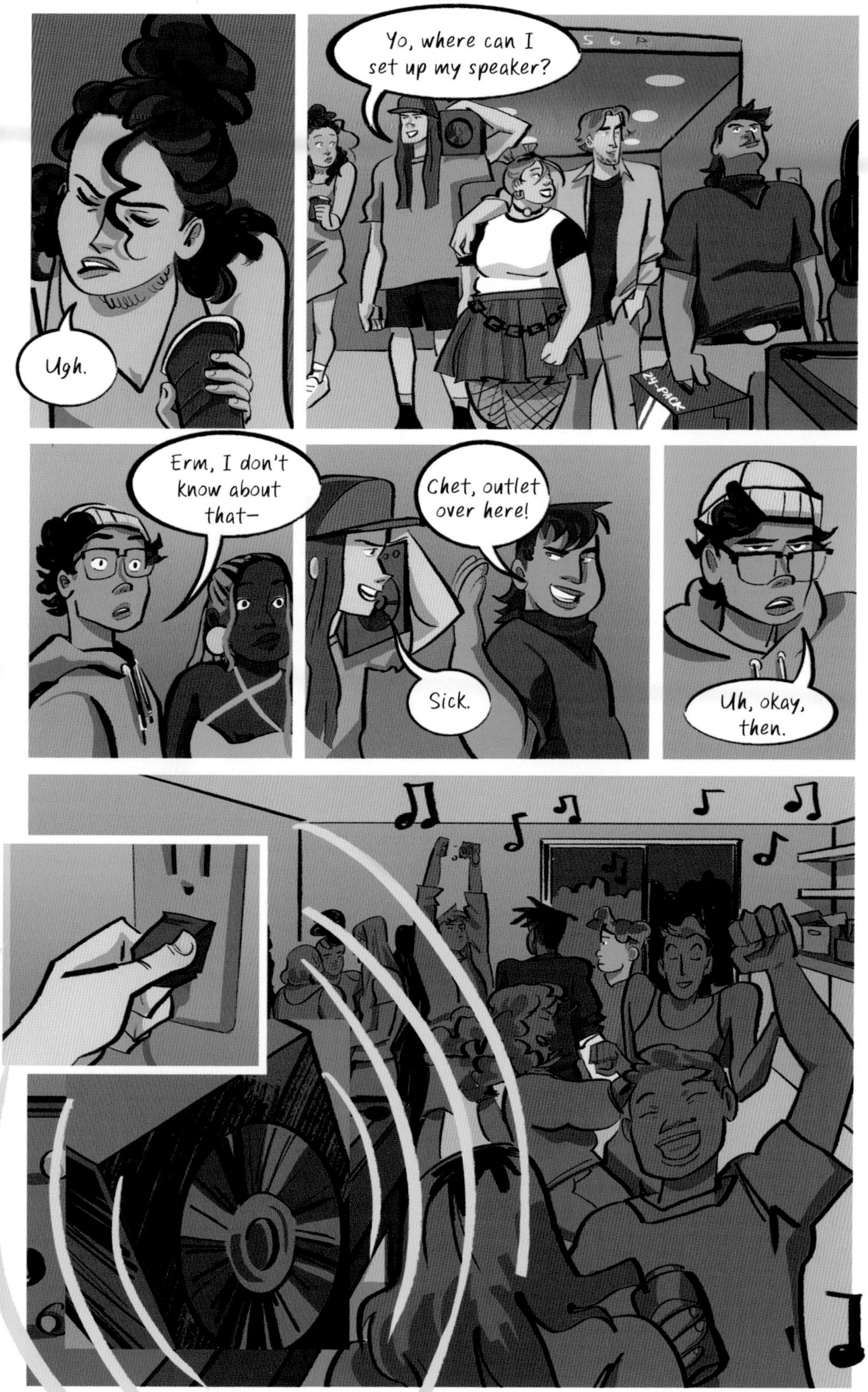
Yo, where can I set up my speaker?
Ugh.
Erm, I don't know about that—
Chet, outlet over here!
Sick.
Uh, okay, then.
24-PACK

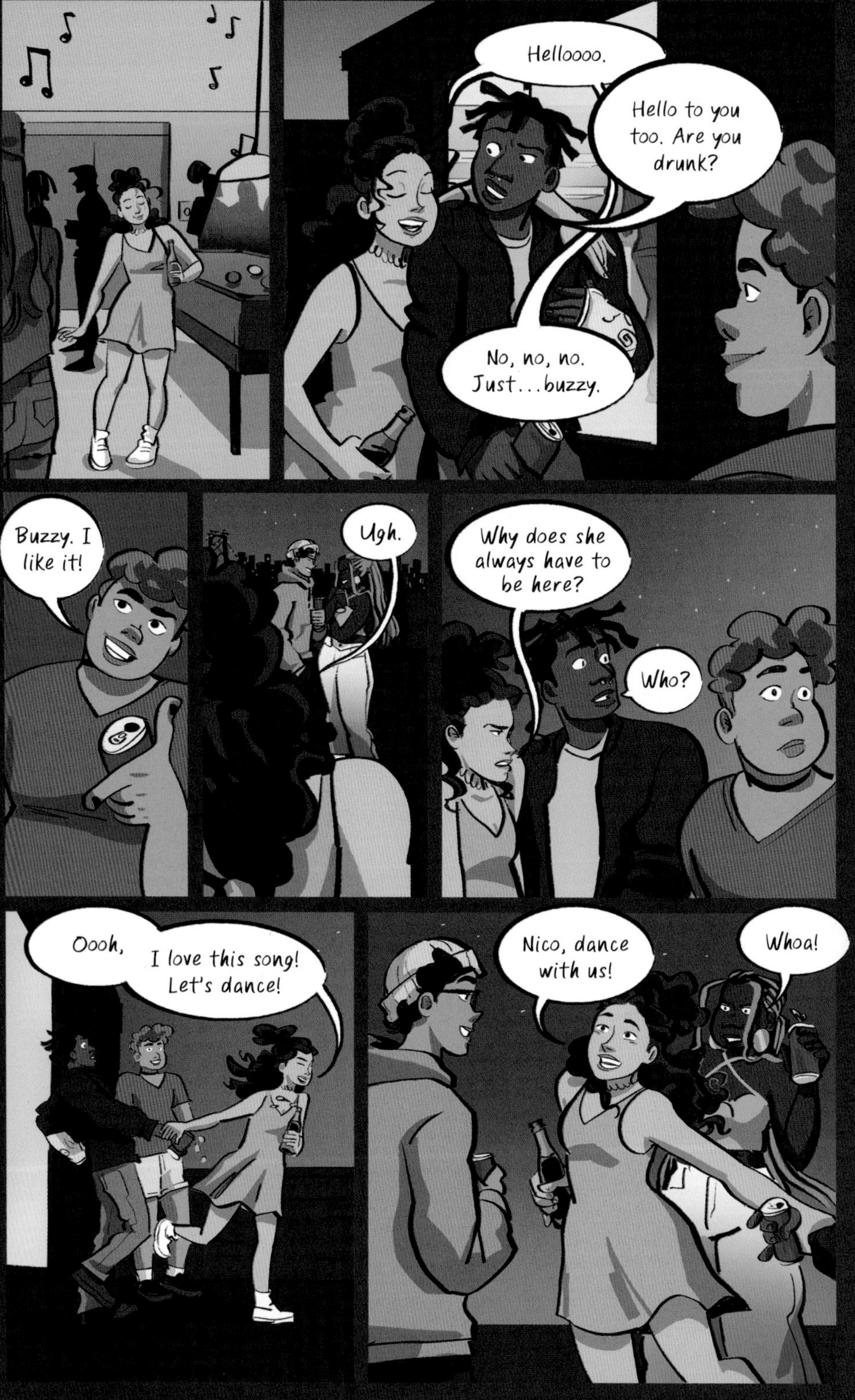

Helloooo.
Hello to you too. Are you drunk?
No, no, no. Just... buzzy.
Buzzy. I like it!
Ugh.
Why does she always have to be here?
Who?
Oooh,
I love this song! Let's dance!
Nico, dance with us!
Whoa!

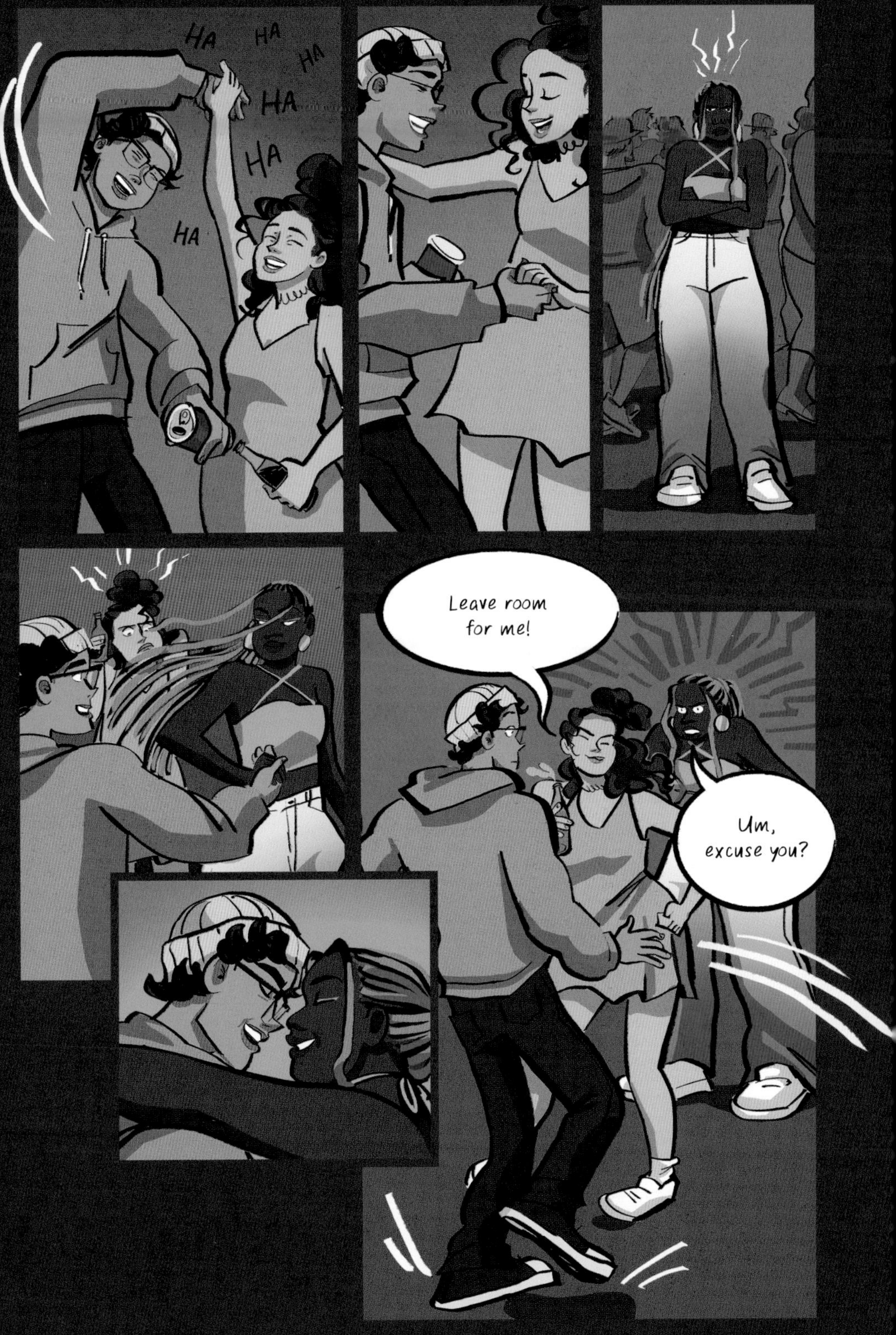
HA
HA
HA
HA
HA
HA
Leave room for me!
Um, excuse you?

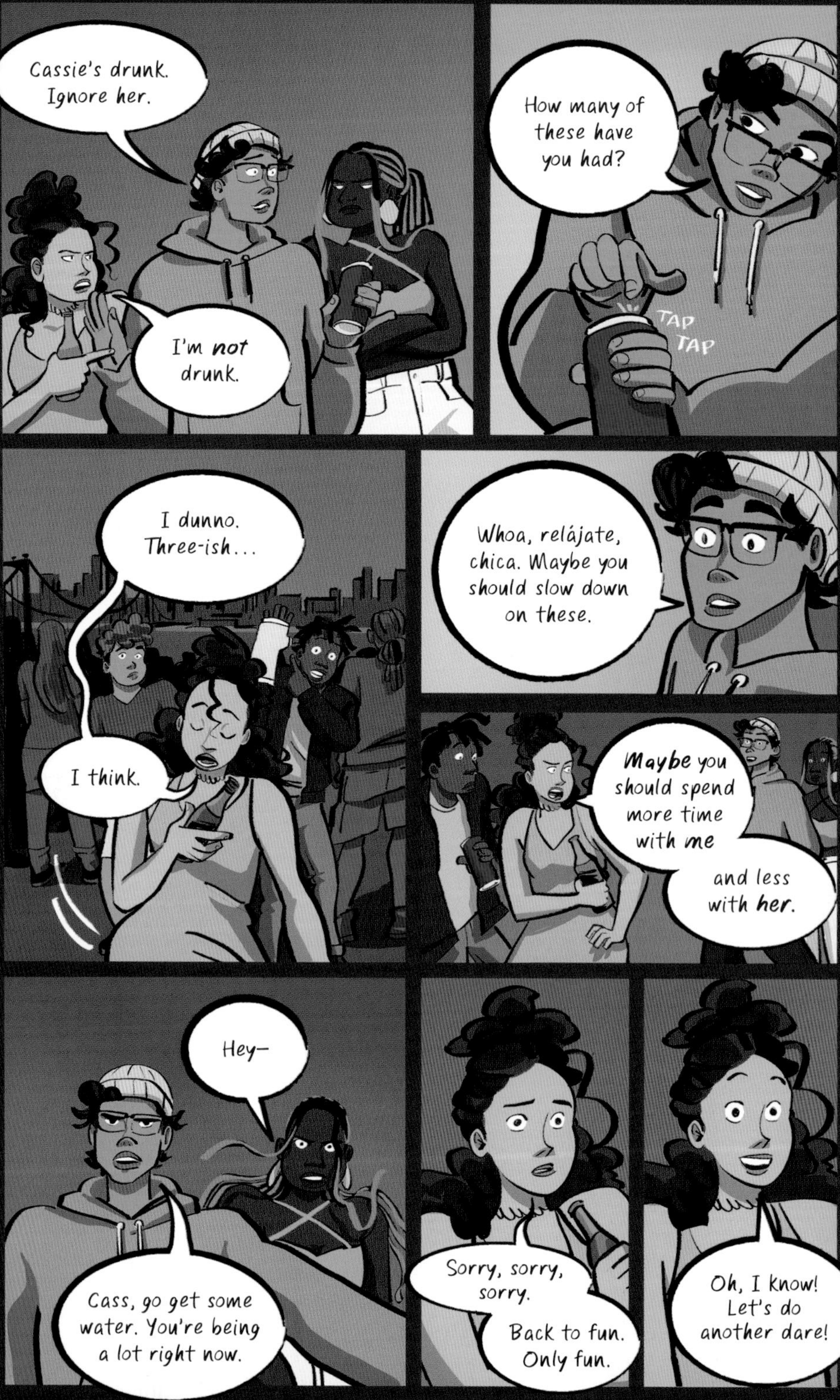
Cassie's drunk. Ignore her.
I'm **not** drunk.
How many of these have you had?
TAP TAP
I dunno. Three-ish...
I think.
Whoa, relájate, chica. Maybe you should slow down on these.
Maybe you should spend more time with **me**
and less with **her**.
Hey—
Cass, go get some water. You're being a lot right now.
Sorry, sorry, sorry.
Back to fun. Only fun.
Oh, I know! Let's do another dare!

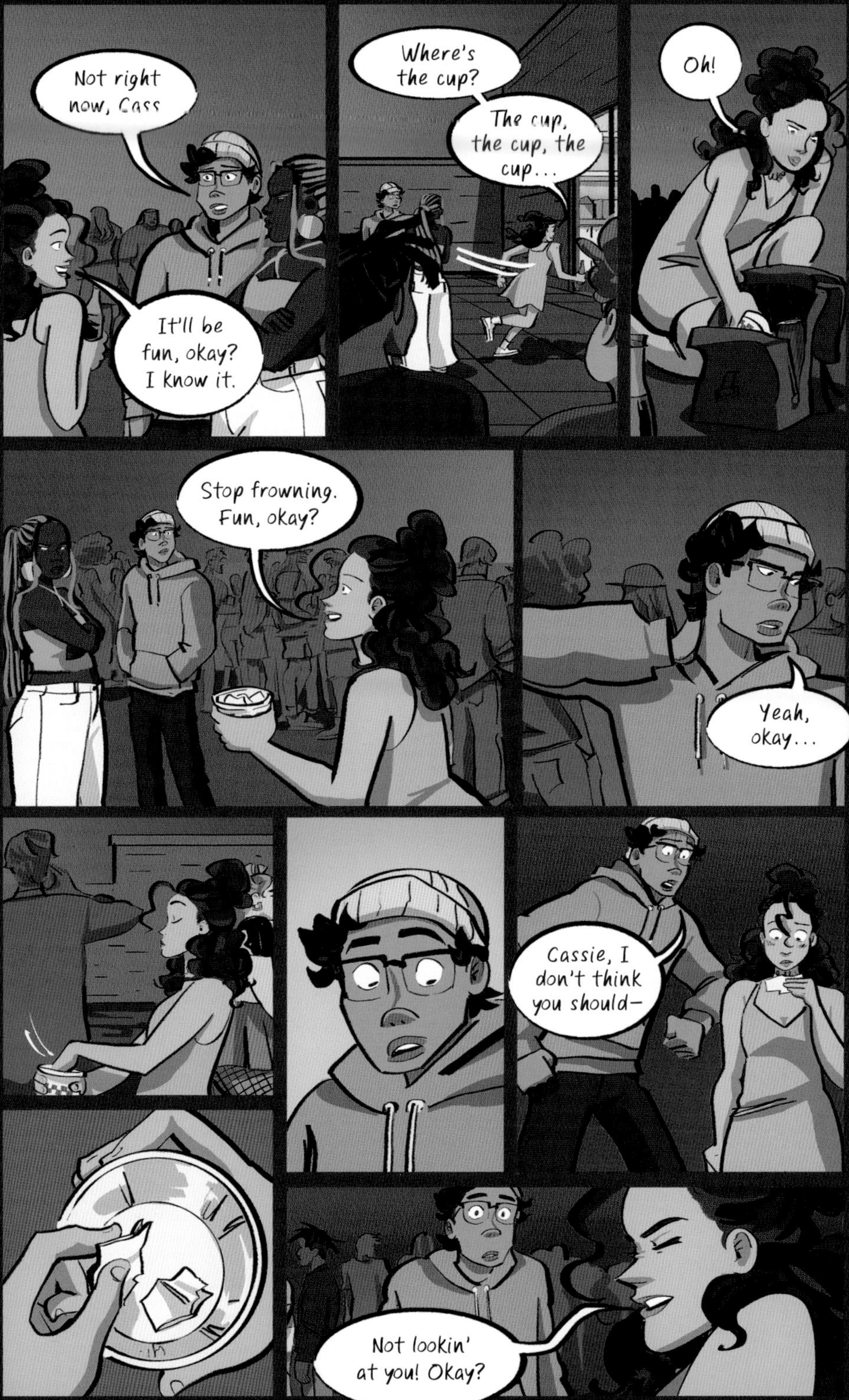

Not right now, Cass
It'll be fun, okay? I know it.
Where's the cup?
The cup, the cup, the cup...
Oh!
Stop frowning. Fun, okay?
Yeah, okay...
Cassie, I don't think you should–
Not lookin' at you! Okay?

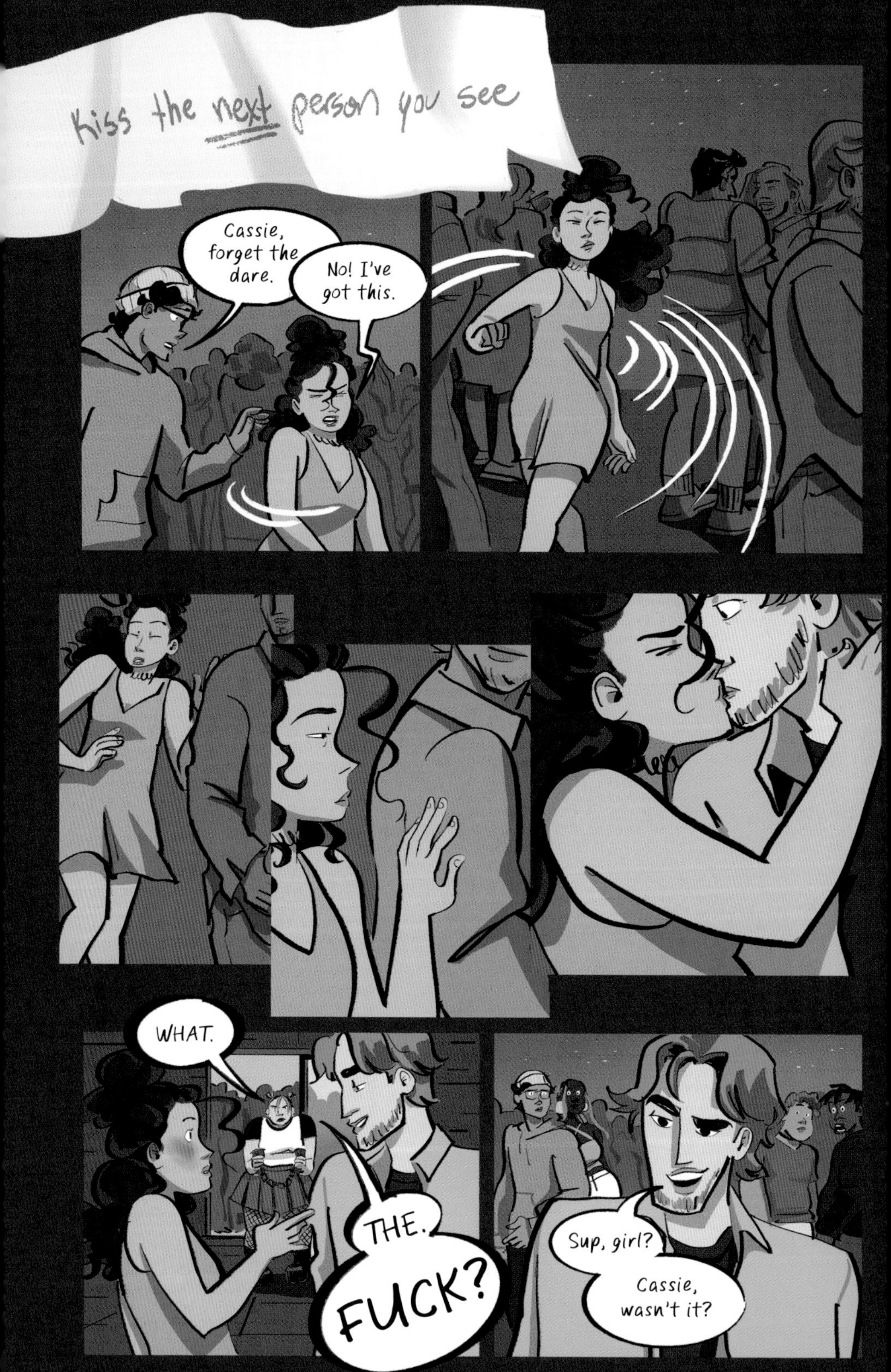
kiss the next person you see
Cassie, forget the dare.
No! I've got this.
WHAT.
THE. FUCK?
Sup, girl?
Cassie, wasn't it?

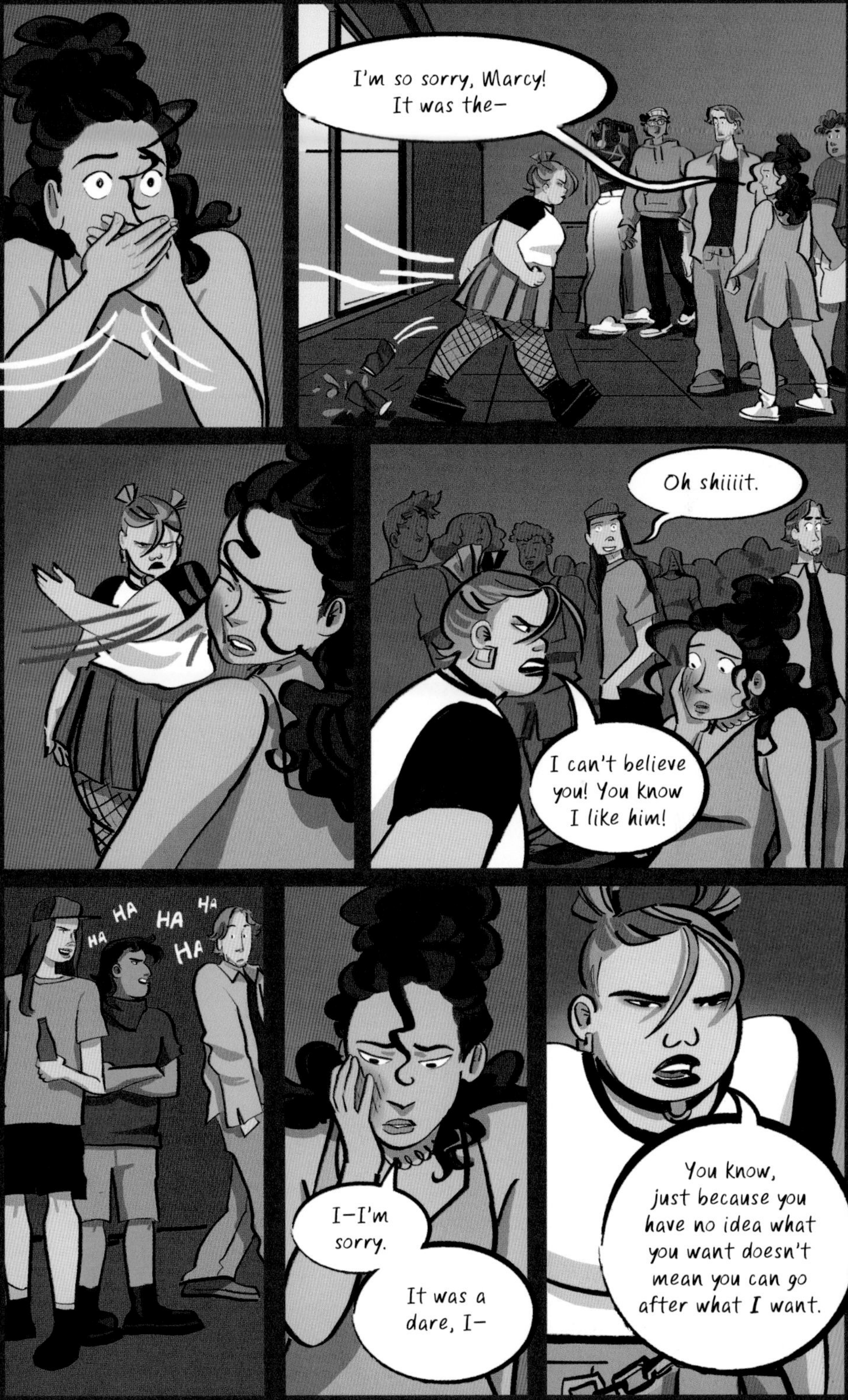
I'm so sorry, Marcy! It was the—
Oh shiiiit.
I can't believe you! You know I like him!
HA HA HA HA HA
I—I'm sorry.
It was a dare, I—
You know, just because you have no idea what you want doesn't mean you can go after what I want.

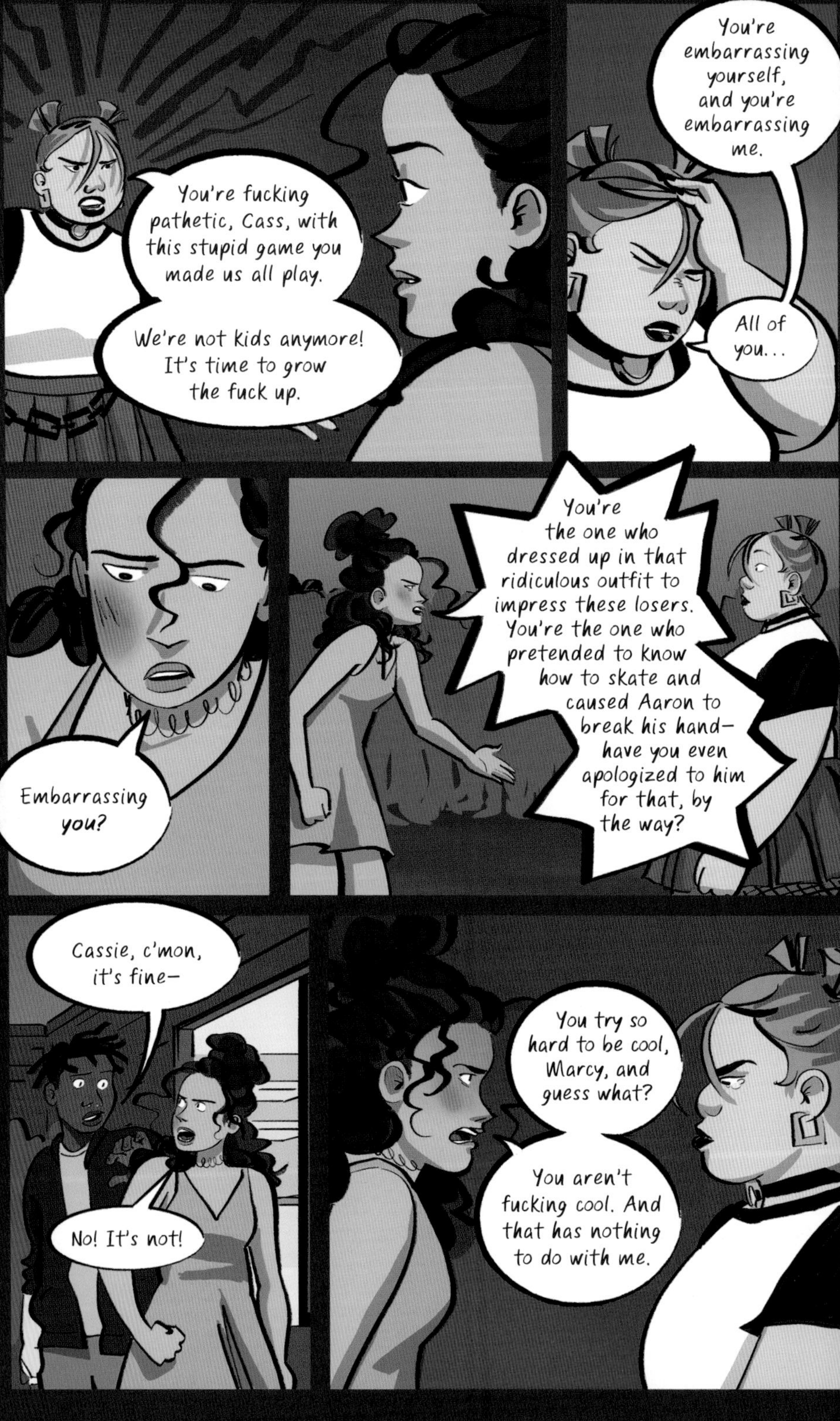
You're fucking pathetic, Cass, with this stupid game you made us all play.
We're not kids anymore! It's time to grow the fuck up.
You're embarrassing yourself, and you're embarrassing me.
All of you...
Embarrassing *you?*
You're the one who dressed up in that ridiculous outfit to impress these losers. You're the one who pretended to know how to skate and caused Aaron to break his hand—have you even apologized to him for that, by the way?
Cassie, c'mon, it's fine—
No! It's not!
You try so hard to be cool, Marcy, and guess what?
You aren't fucking cool. And that has nothing to do with me.

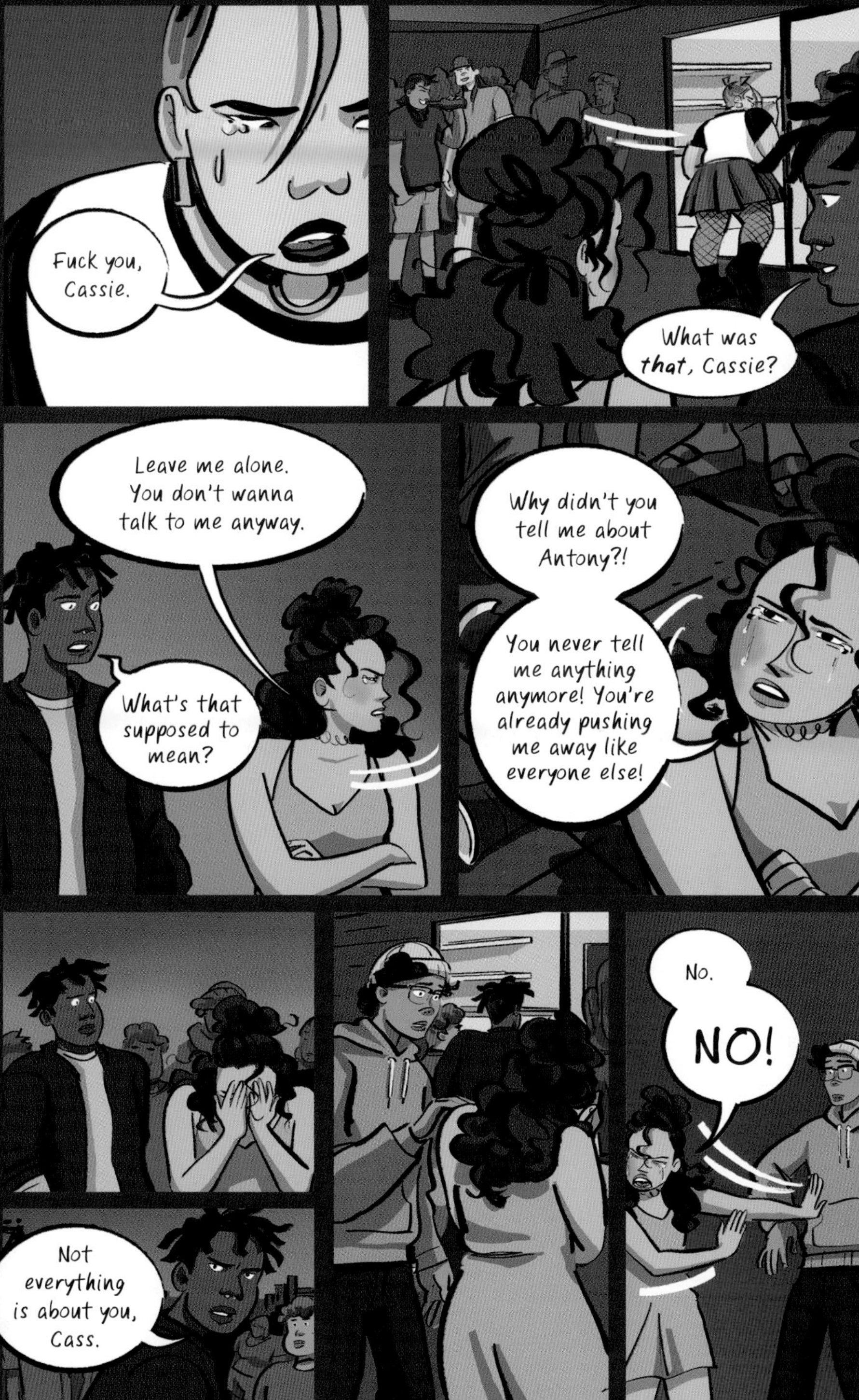

Fuck you, Cassie.
What was that, Cassie?
Leave me alone. You don't wanna talk to me anyway.
What's that supposed to mean?
Why didn't you tell me about Antony?!
You never tell me anything anymore! You're already pushing me away like everyone else!
Not everything is about you, Cass.
No.
NO!

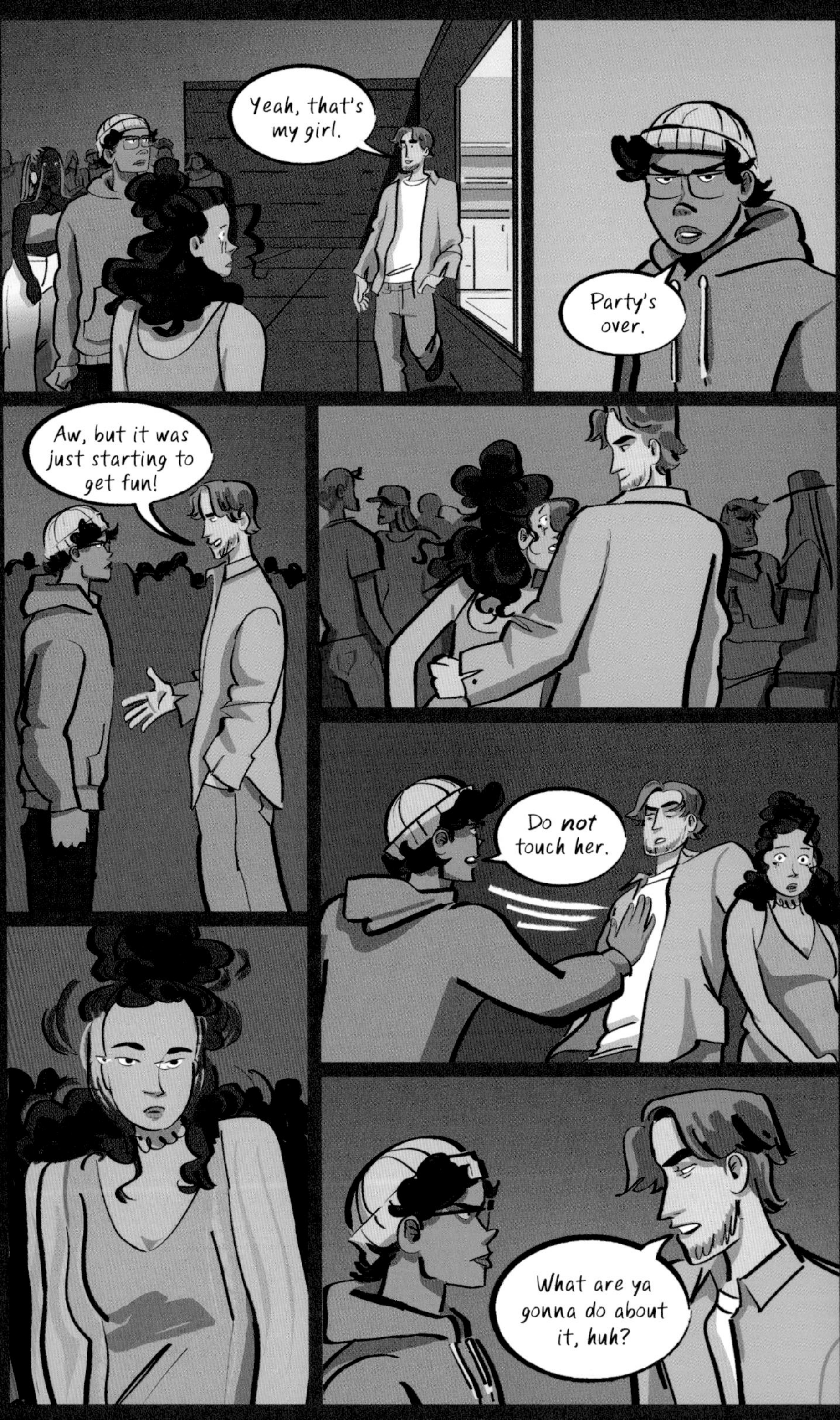
Yeah, that's my girl.
Party's over.
Aw, but it was just starting to get fun!
Do **not** touch her.
What are ya gonna do about it, **huh**?

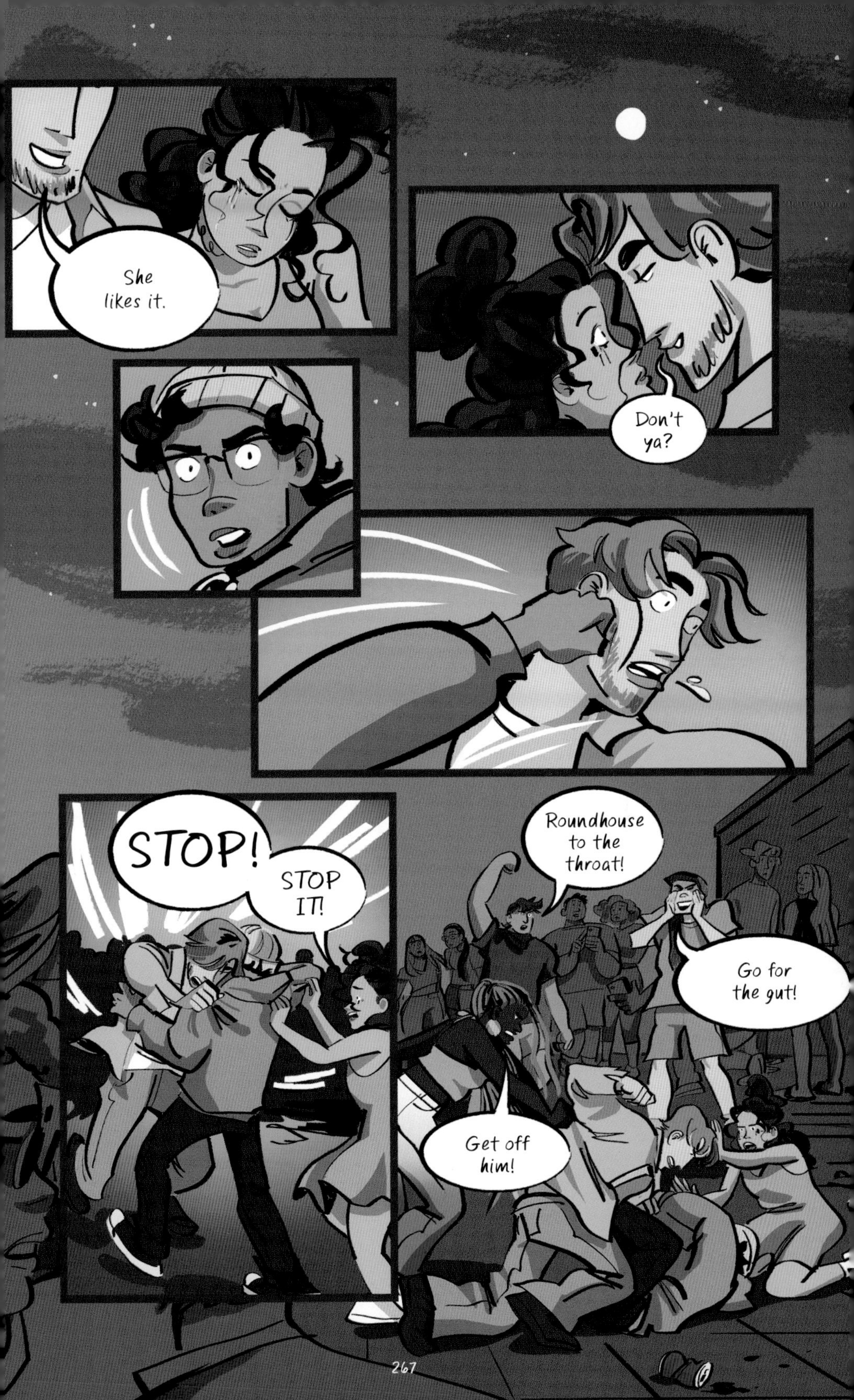
She likes it.
Don't ya?
STOP!
STOP IT!
Roundhouse to the throat!
Go for the gut!
Get off him!

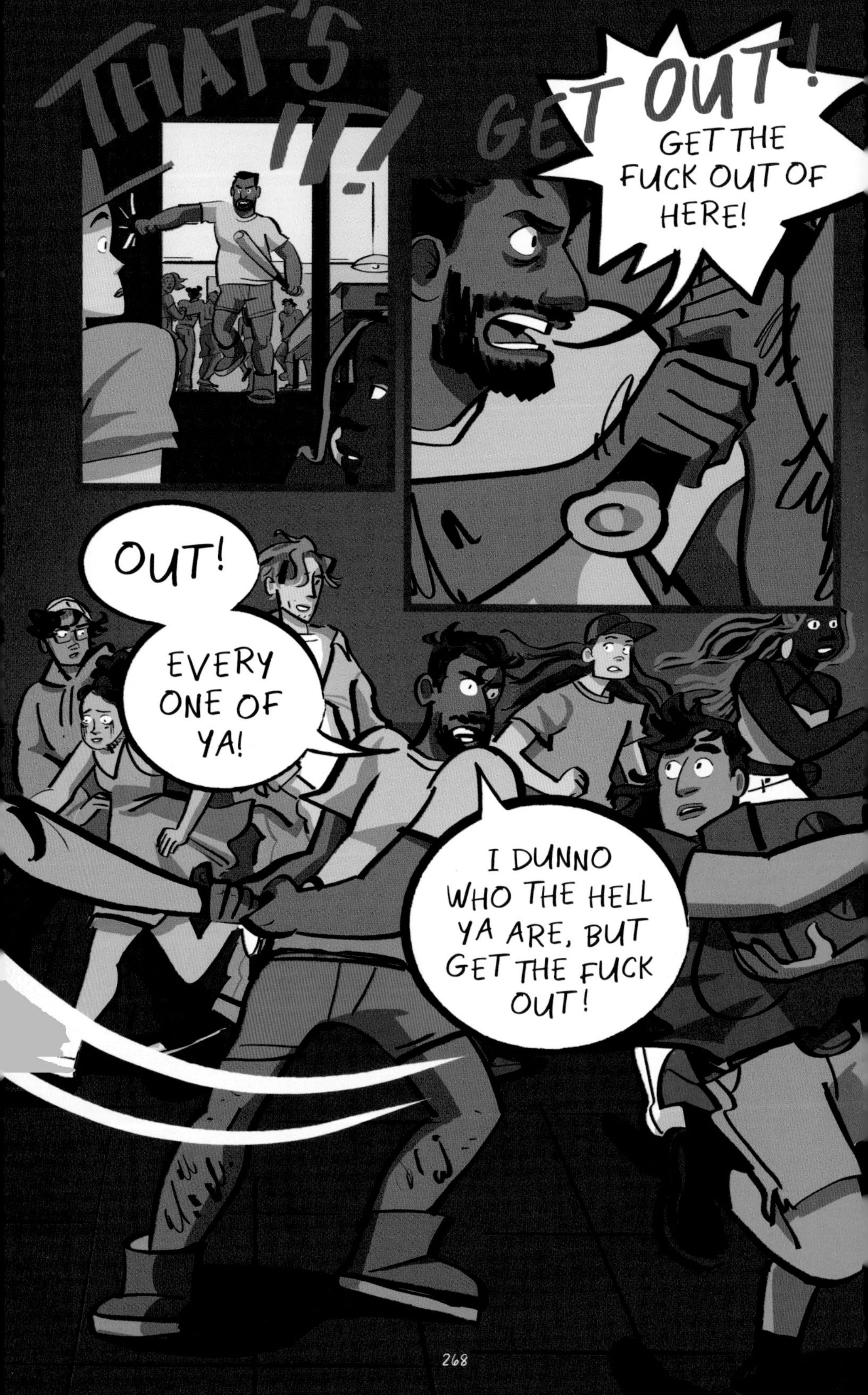
THAT'S IT!
GET OUT!
GET THE FUCK OUT OF HERE!
OUT!
EVERY ONE OF YA!
I DUNNO WHO THE HELL YA ARE, BUT GET THE FUCK OUT!

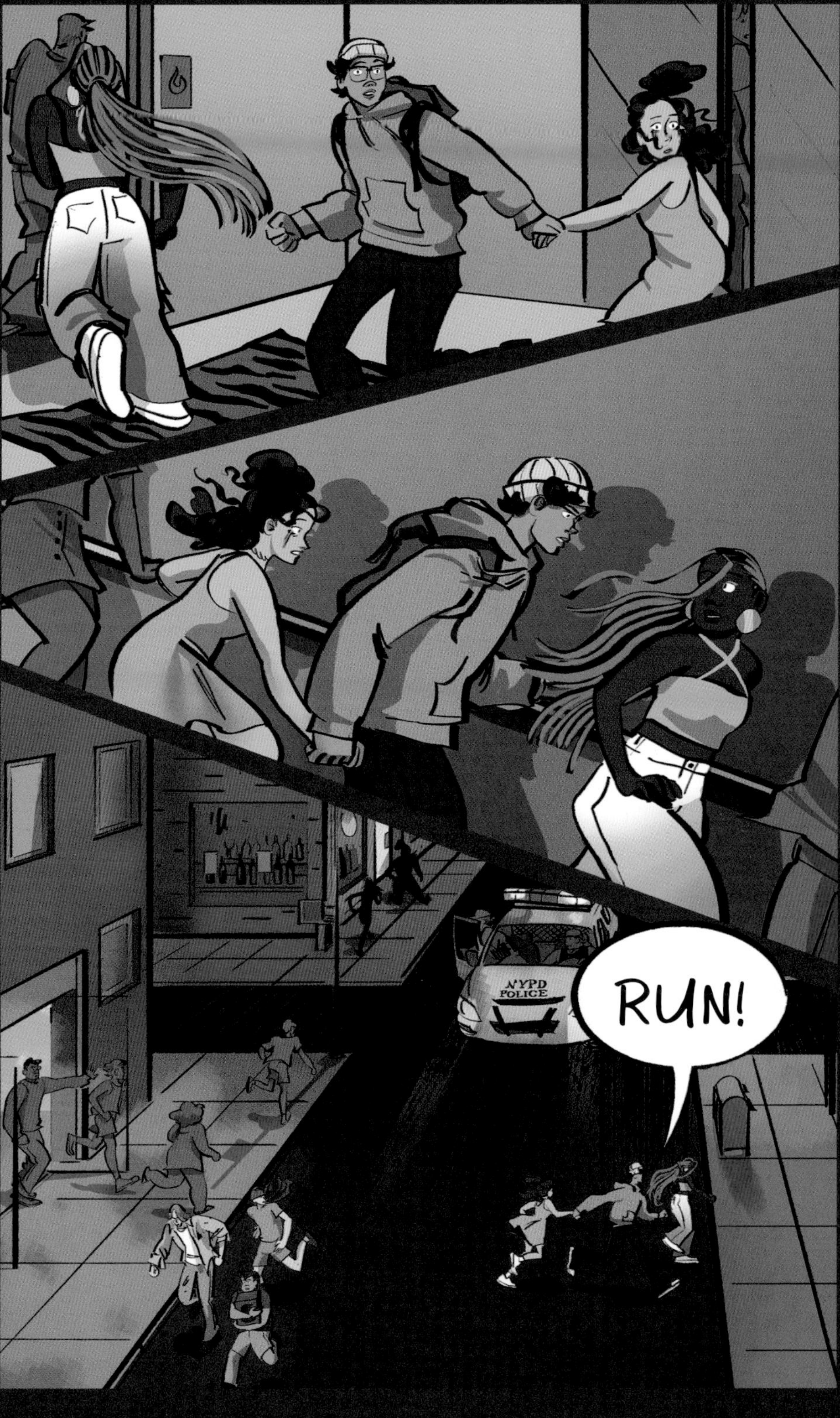
NYPD
POLICE
RUN!

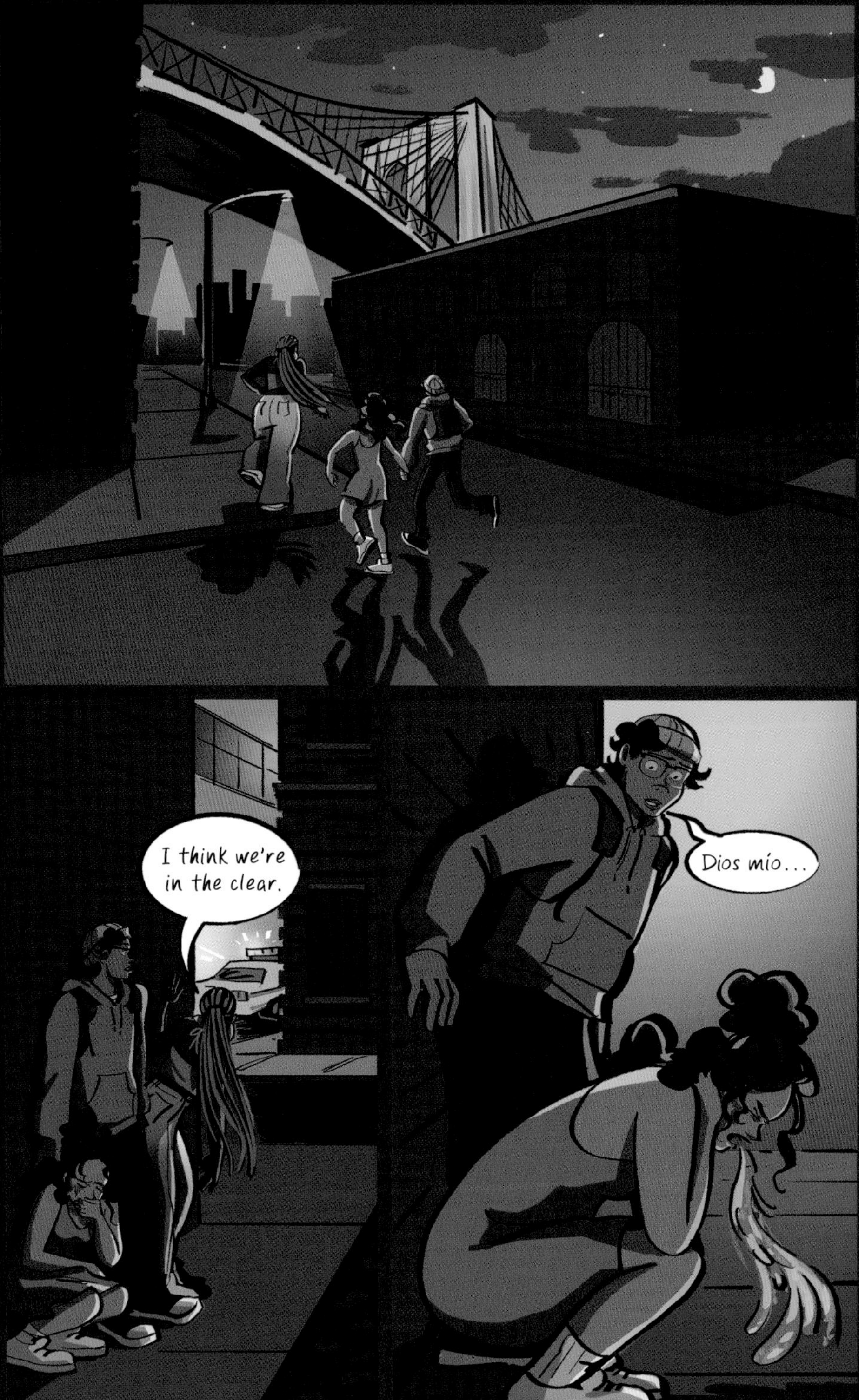
I think we're in the clear.
Dios mío...

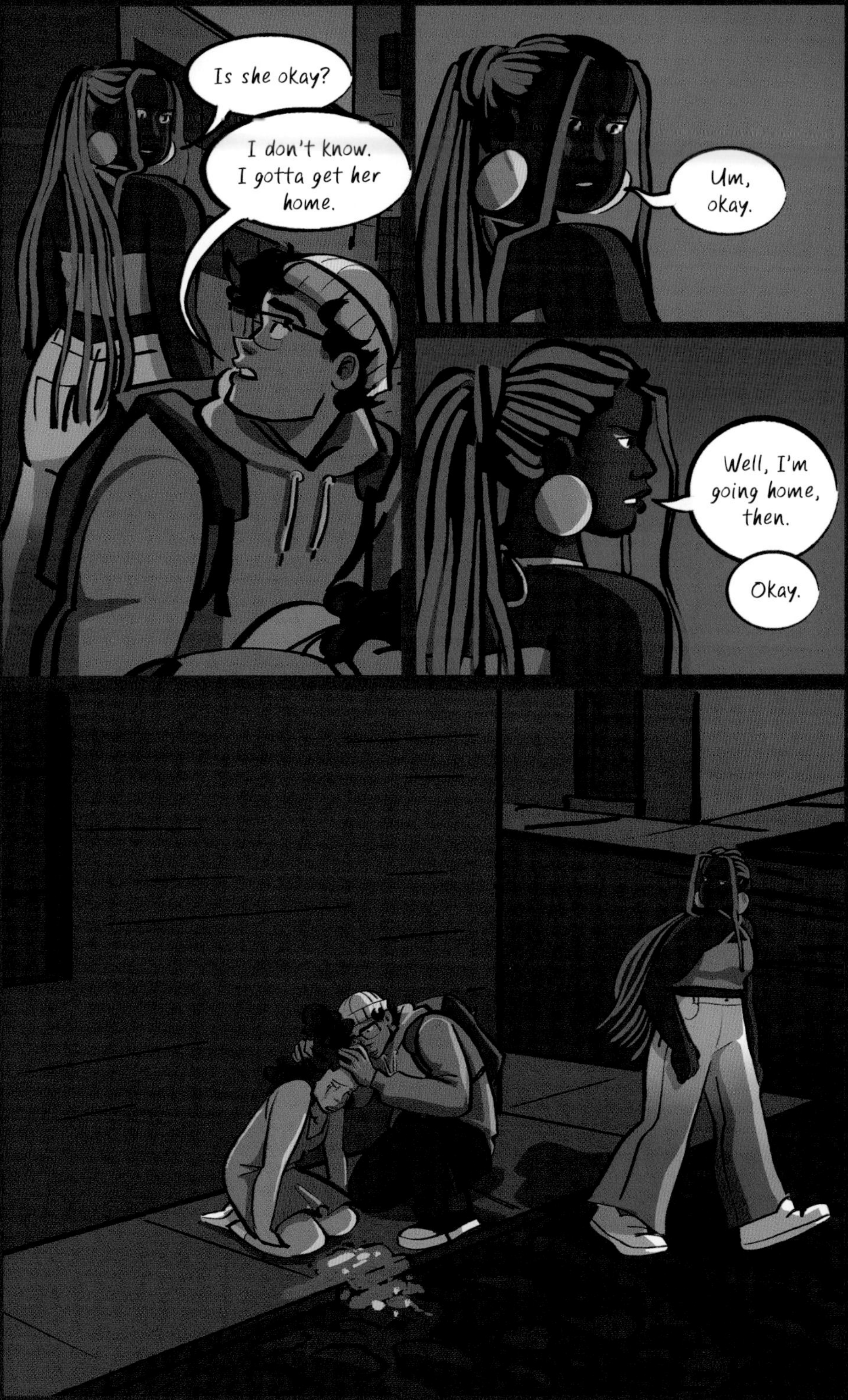
Is she okay?
I don't know. I gotta get her home.
Um, okay.
Well, I'm going home, then.
Okay.

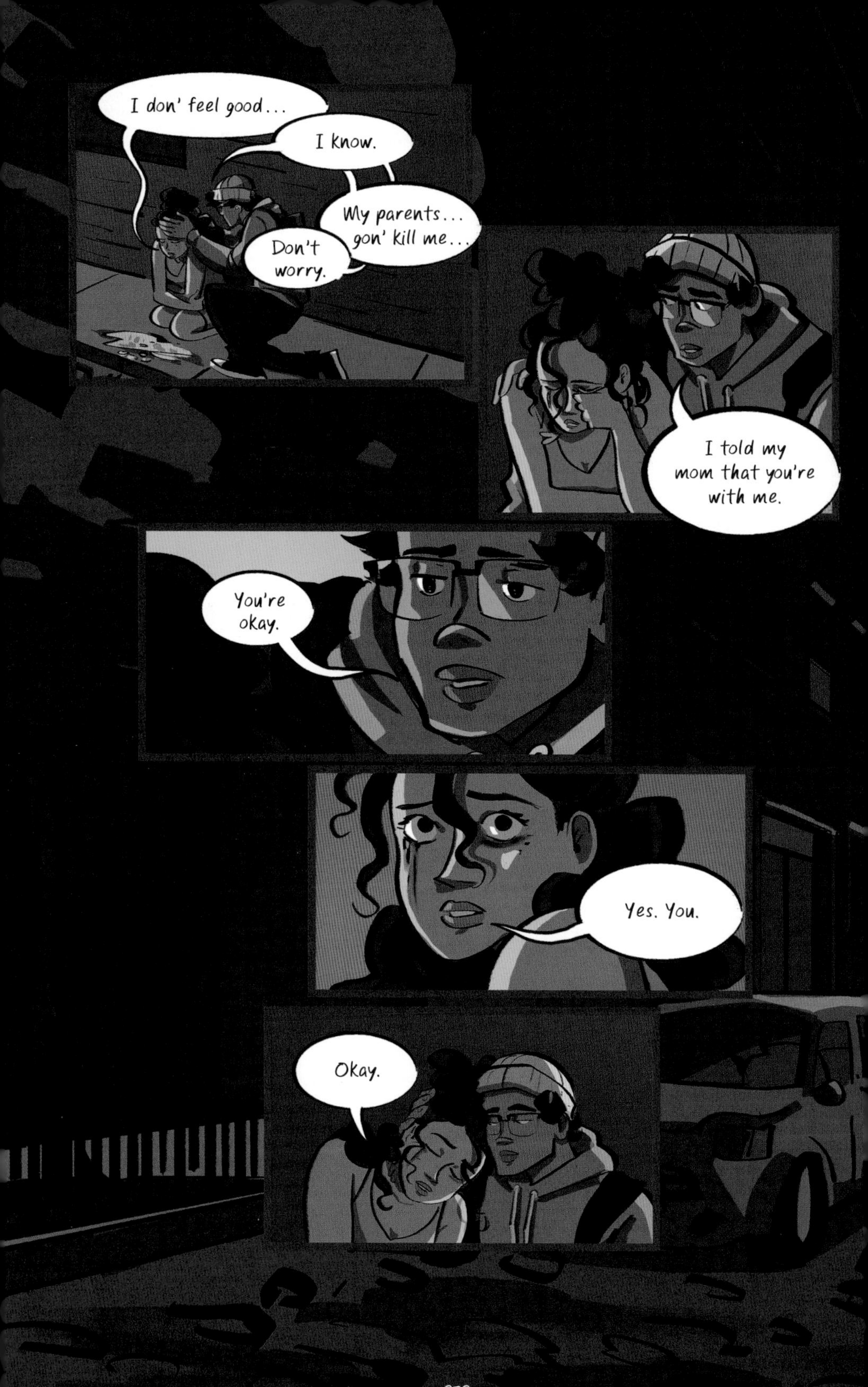
I don' feel good...
I know.
My parents... gon' kill me...
Don't worry.
I told my mom that you're with me.
You're okay.
Yes. You.
Okay.

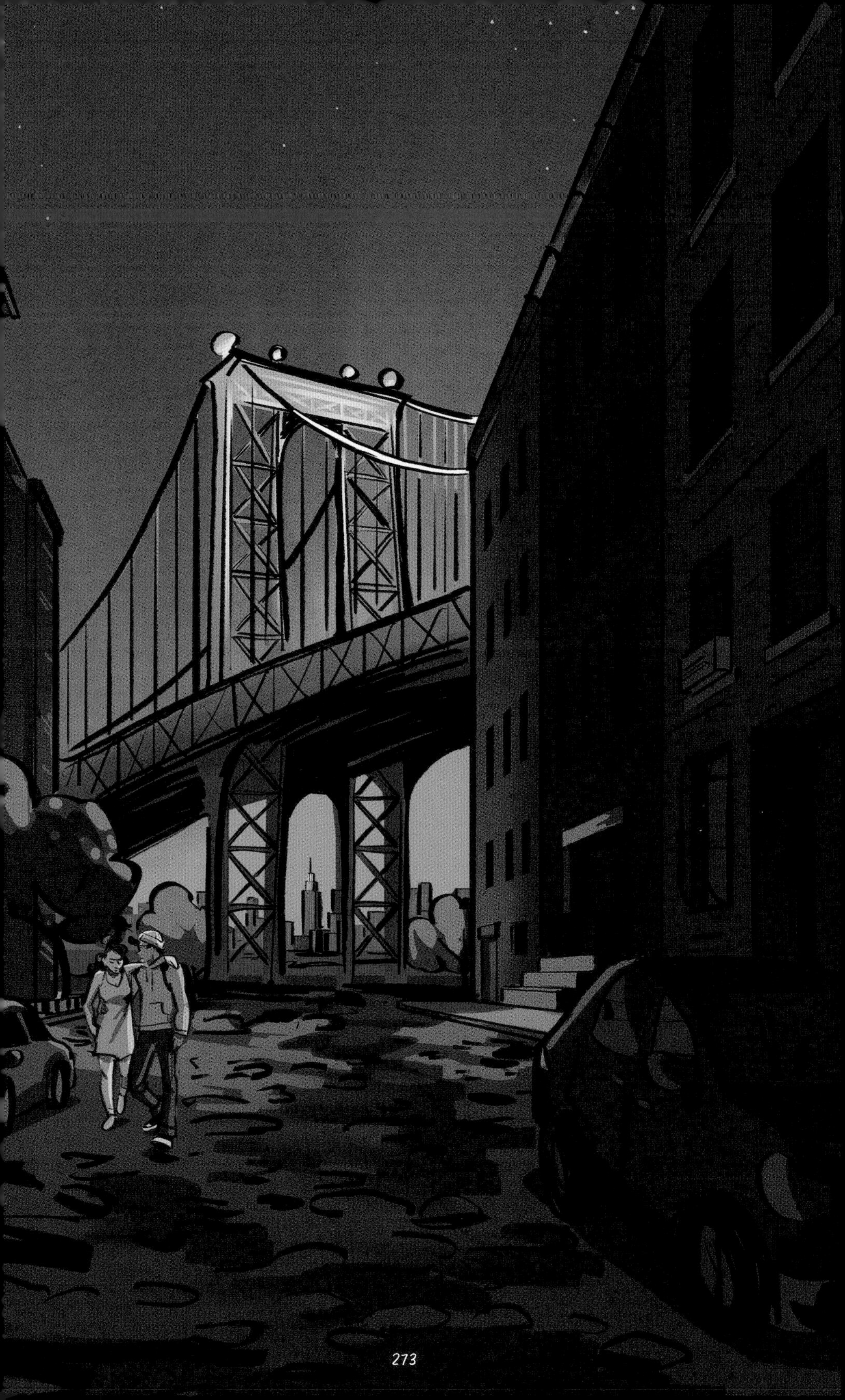

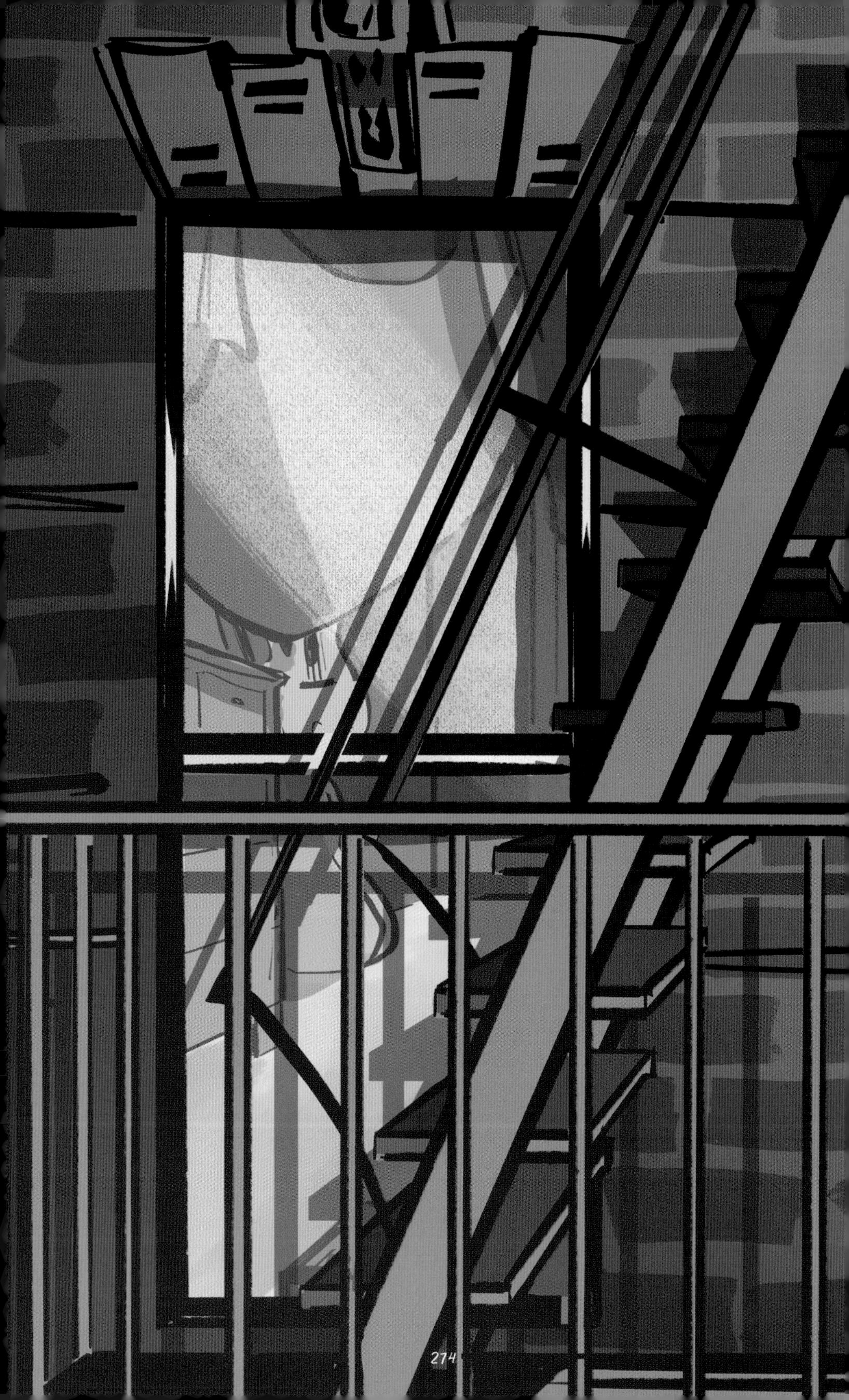

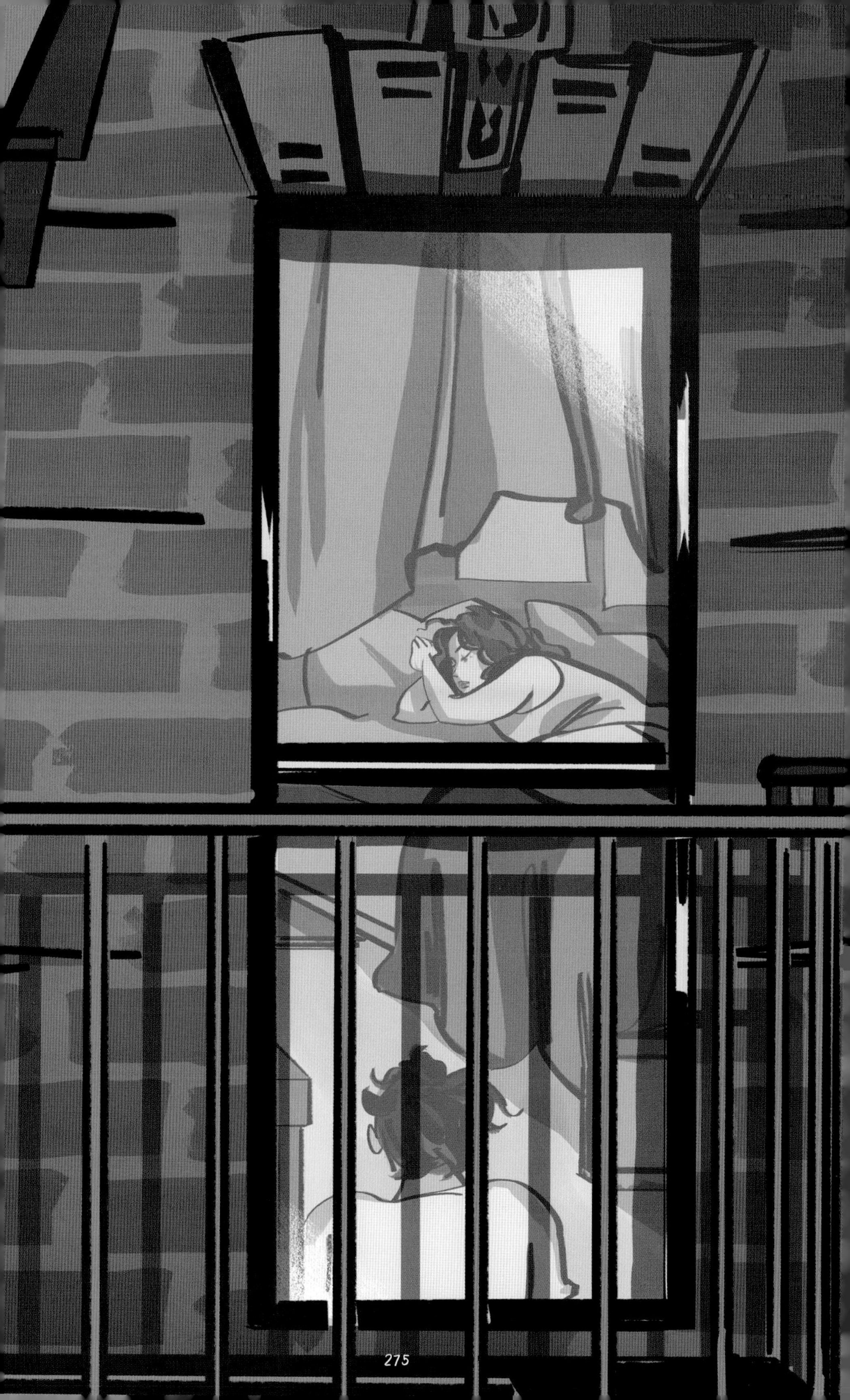

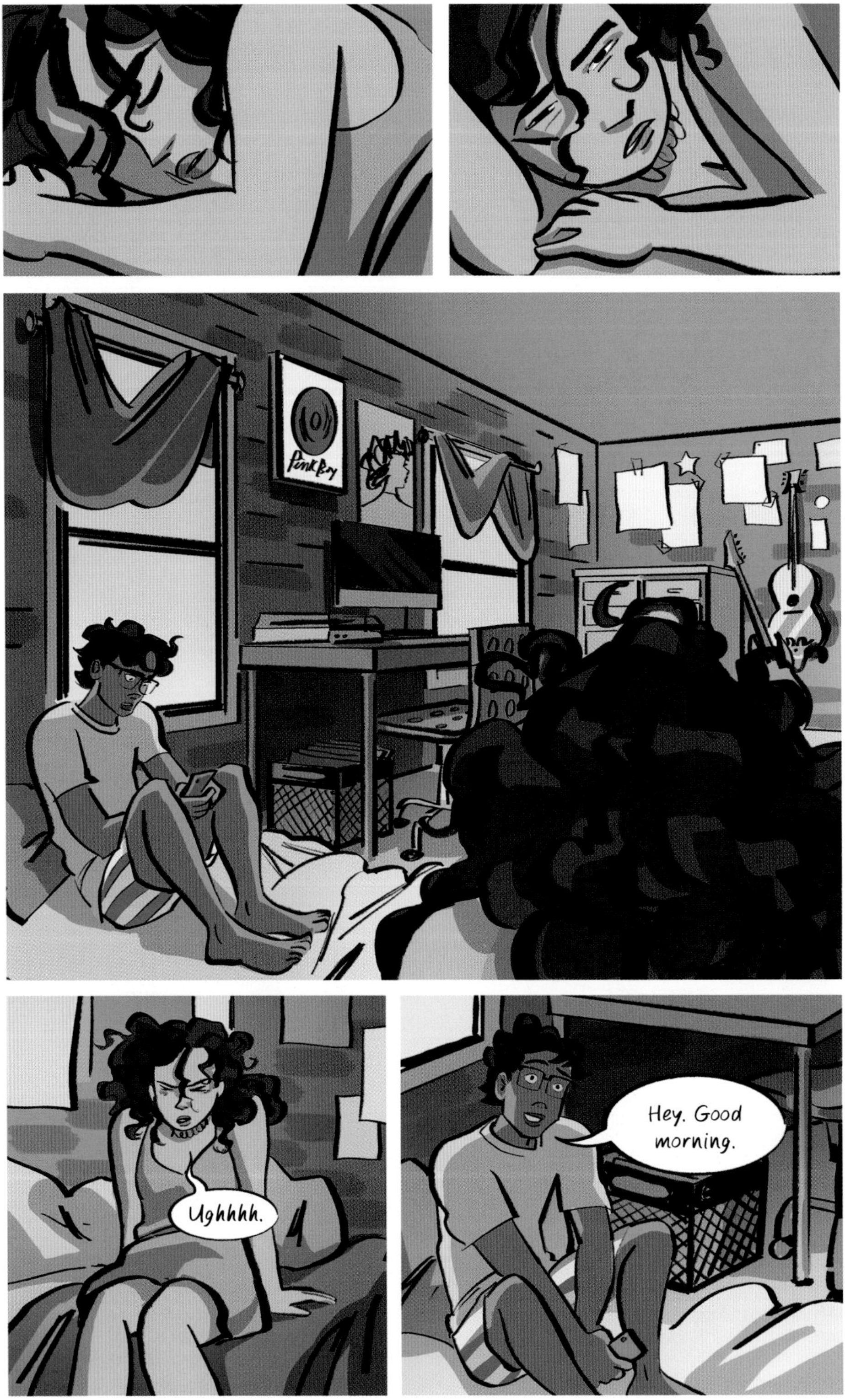

Pink Boy
Ughhhh.
Hey. Good morning.

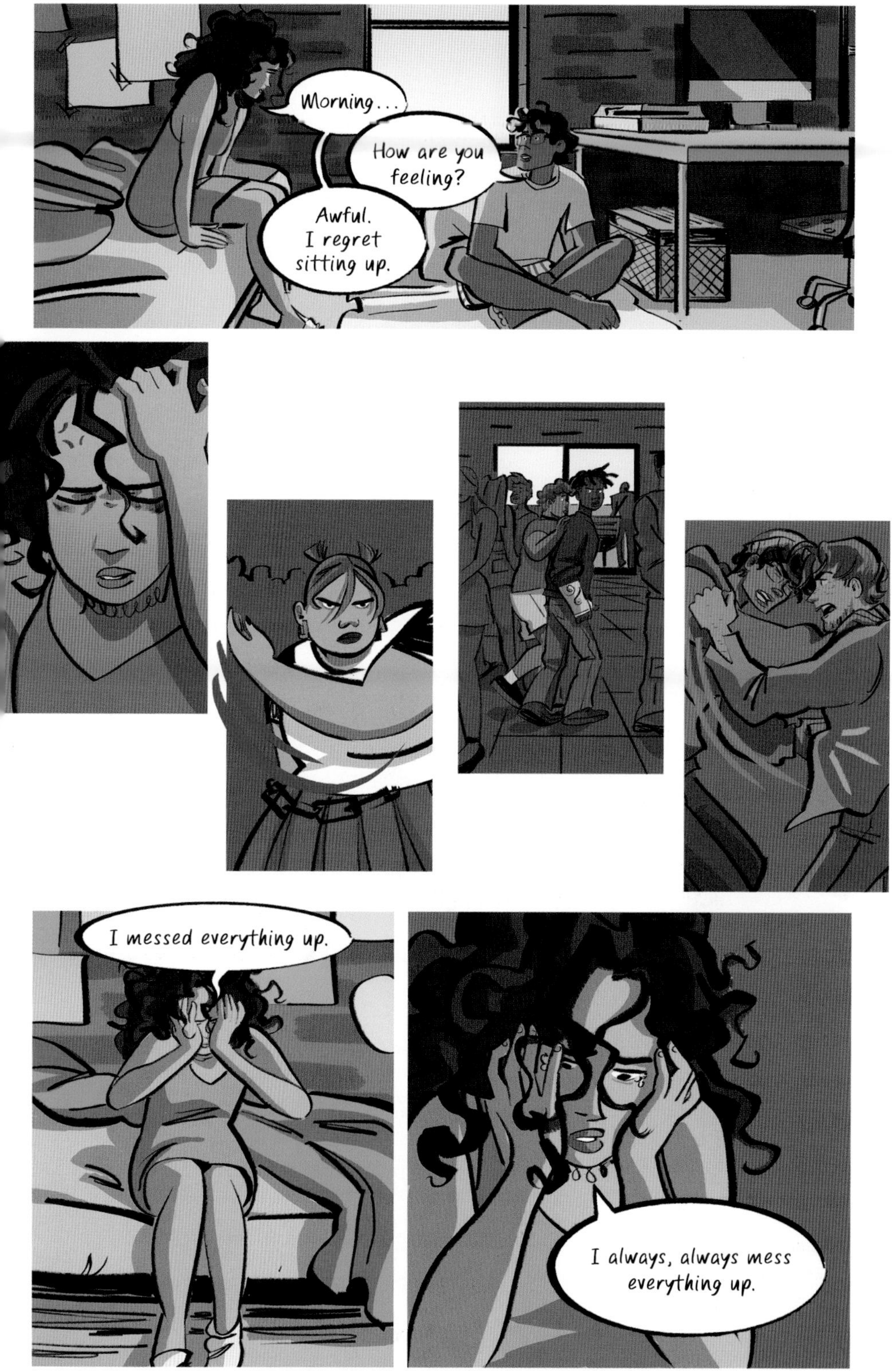
Morning...
How are you feeling?
Awful. I regret sitting up.
I messed everything up.
I always, always mess everything up.

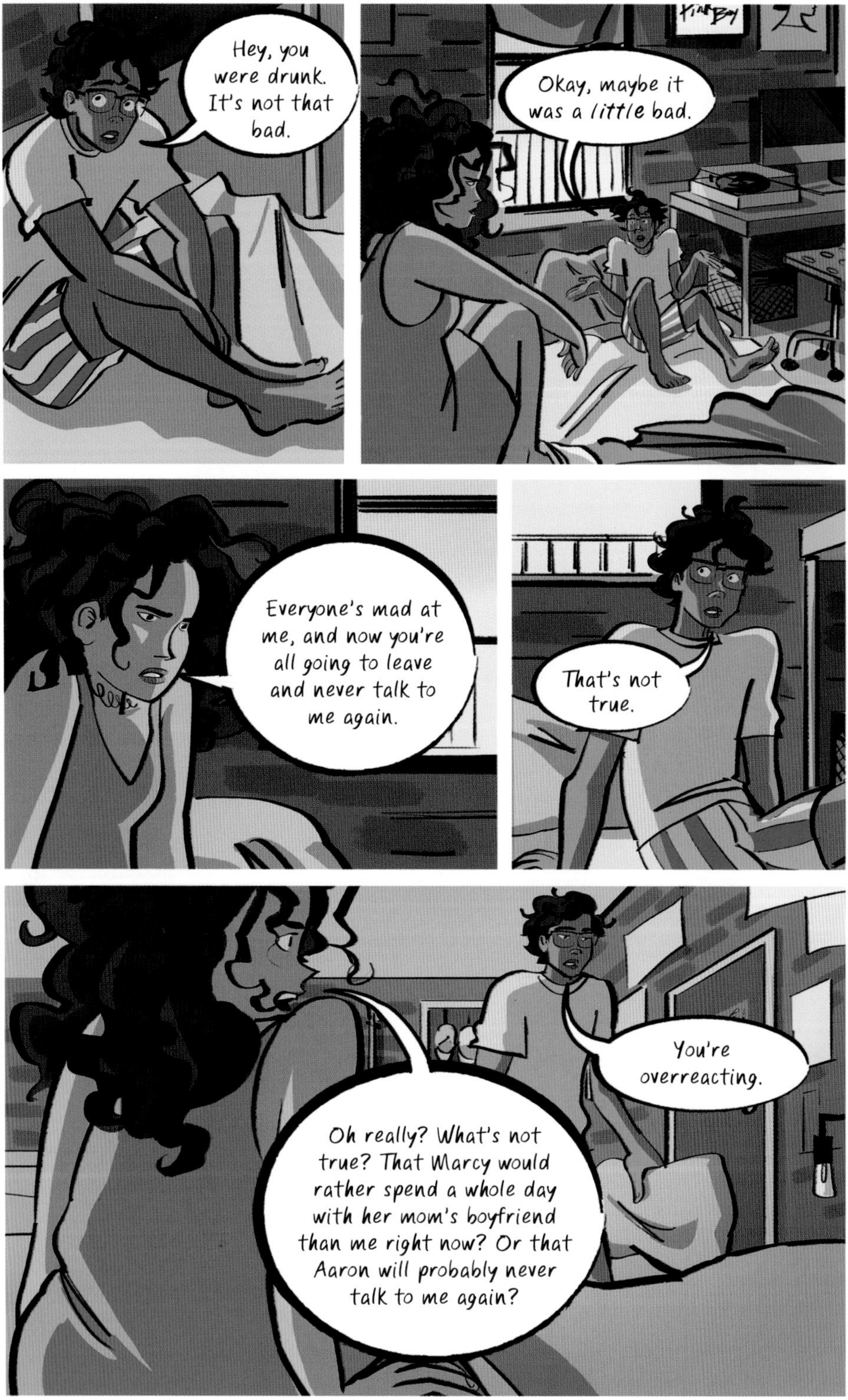
Hey, you were drunk. It's not that bad.
Okay, maybe it was a *little* bad.
Everyone's mad at me, and now you're all going to leave and never talk to me again.
That's not true.
You're overreacting.
Oh really? What's not true? That Marcy would rather spend a whole day with her mom's boyfriend than me right now? Or that Aaron will probably never talk to me again?

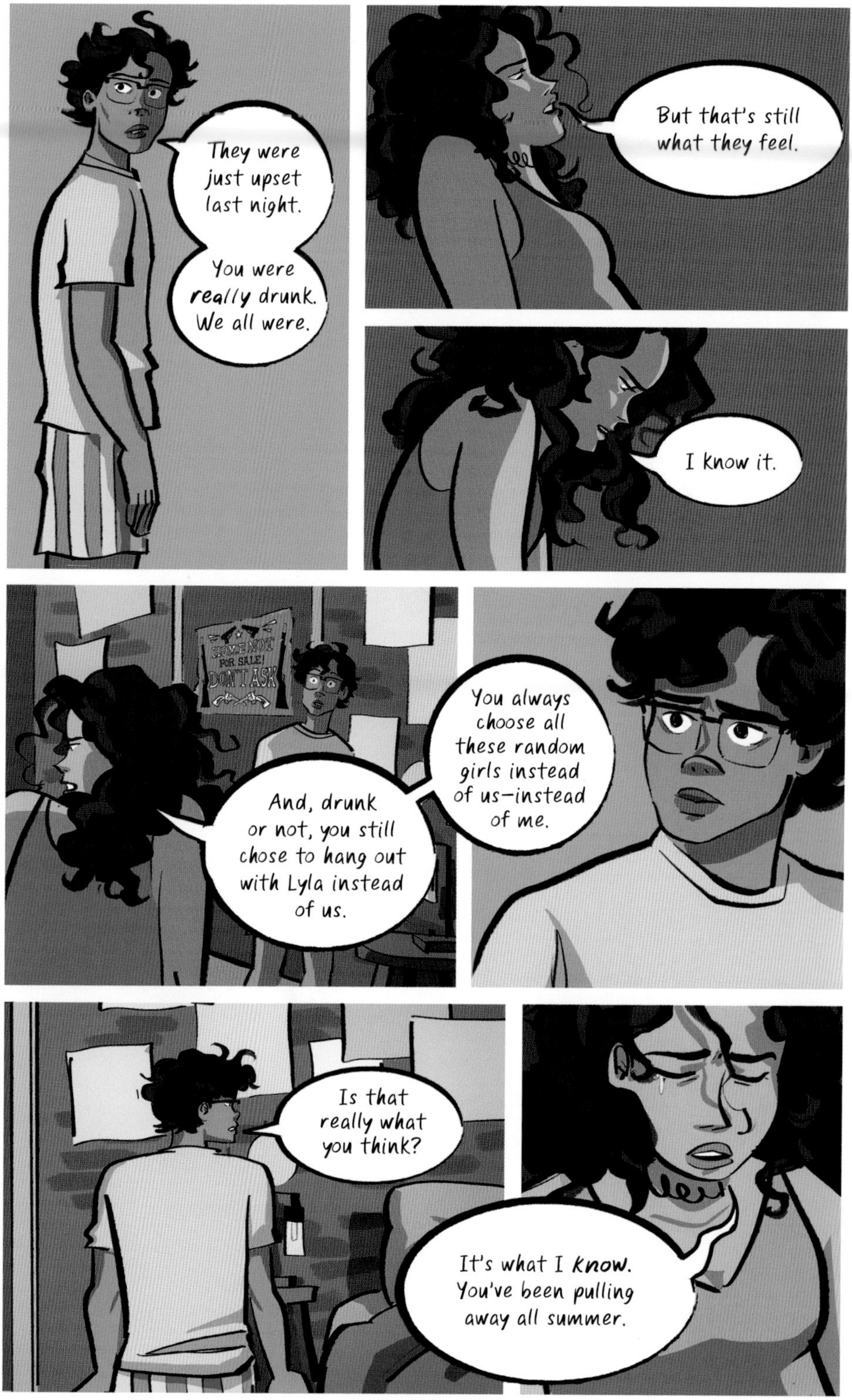
They were just upset last night.
You were *really* drunk. We all were.
But that's still what they feel.
I know it.
HOME NOT FOR SALE! DON'T ASK
And, drunk or not, you still chose to hang out with Lyla instead of us.
You always choose all these random girls instead of us—instead of me.
Is that really what you think?
It's what I **know**. You've been pulling away all summer.

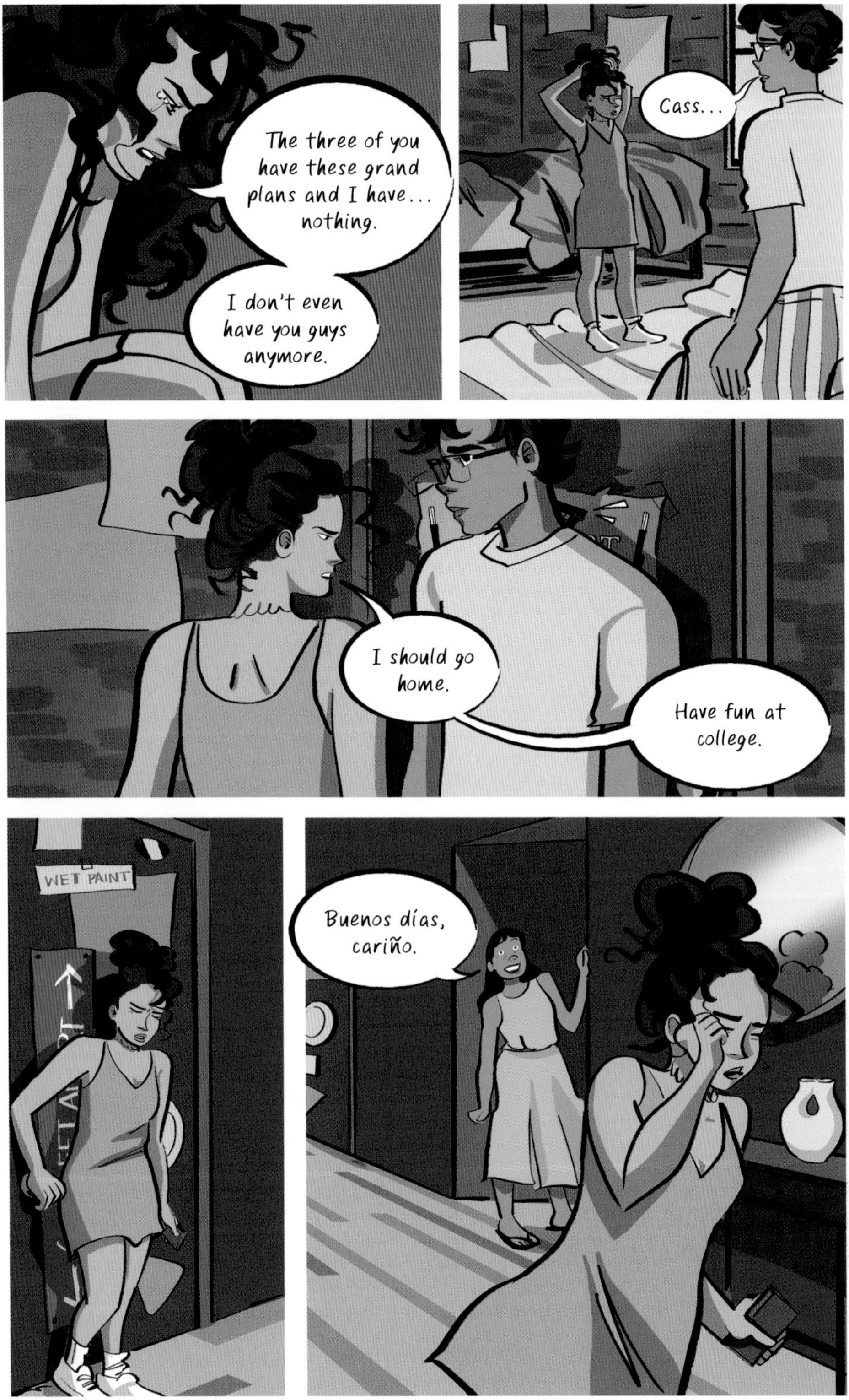
The three of you have these grand plans and I have... nothing.
I don't even have you guys anymore.
Cass...
I should go home.
Have fun at college.
WET PAINT
Buenos días, cariño.

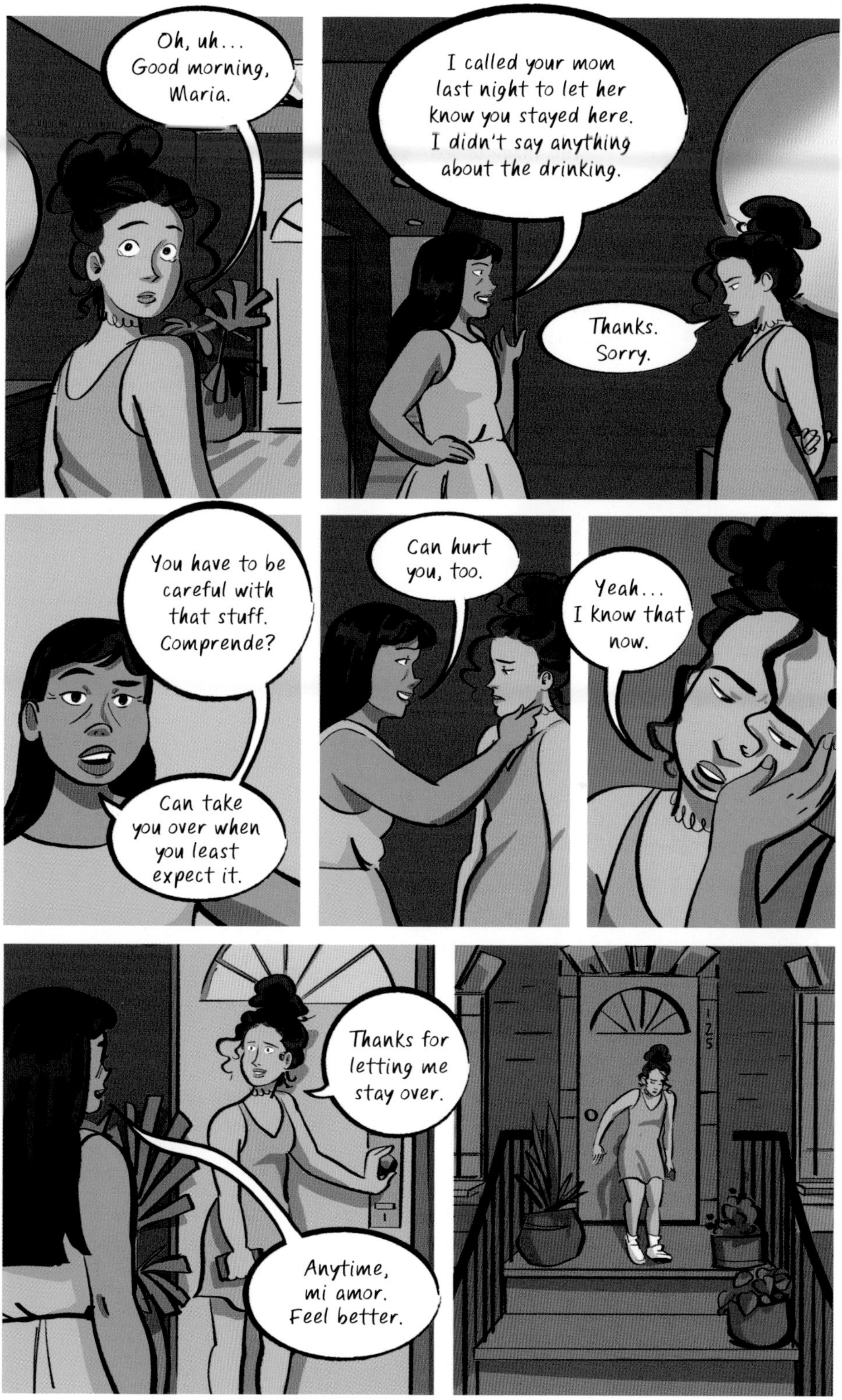
Oh, uh...
Good morning, Maria.
I called your mom last night to let her know you stayed here. I didn't say anything about the drinking.
Thanks. Sorry.
You have to be careful with that stuff. Comprende?
Can take you over when you least expect it.
Can hurt you, too.
Yeah... I know that now.
Thanks for letting me stay over.
Anytime, mi amor. Feel better.
125

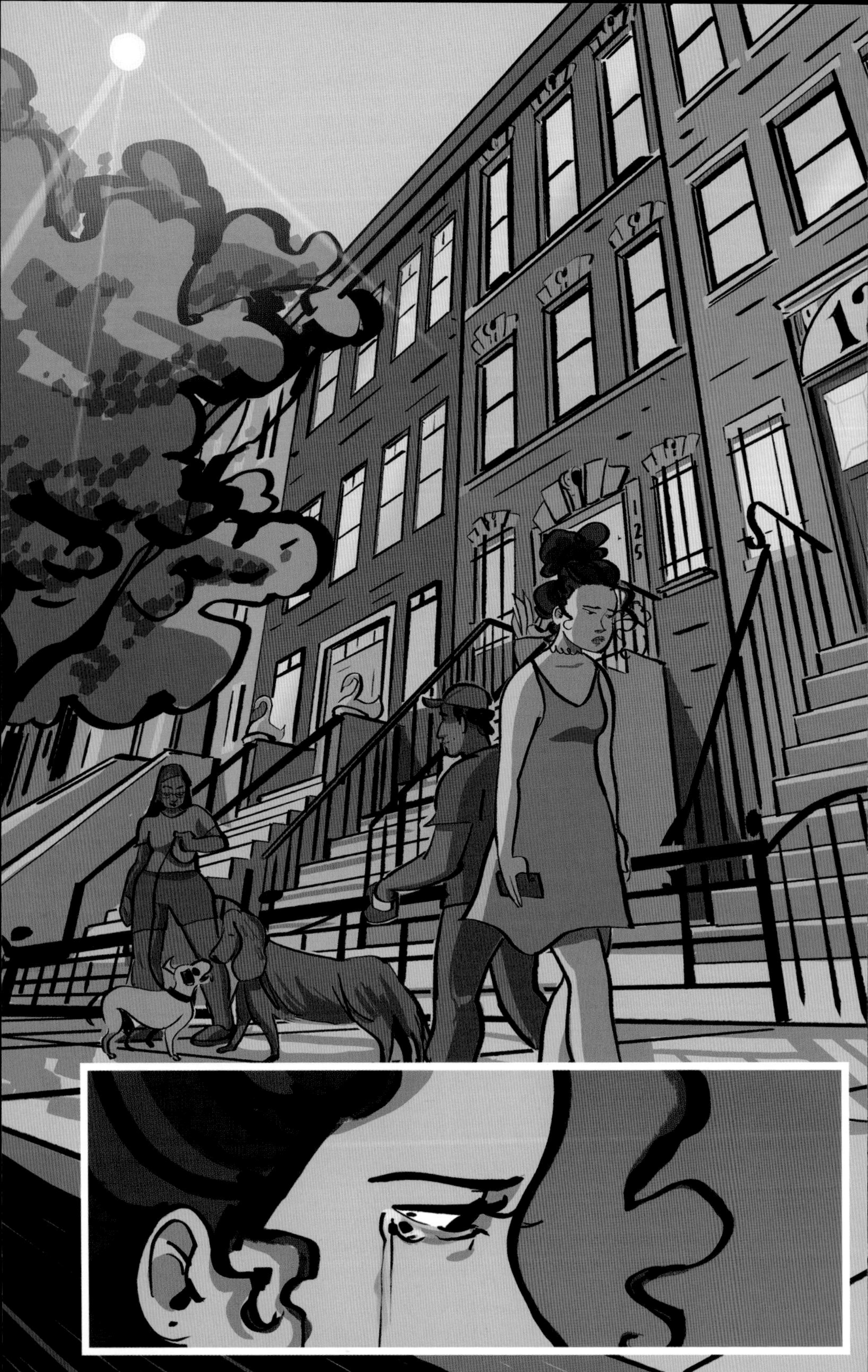
125

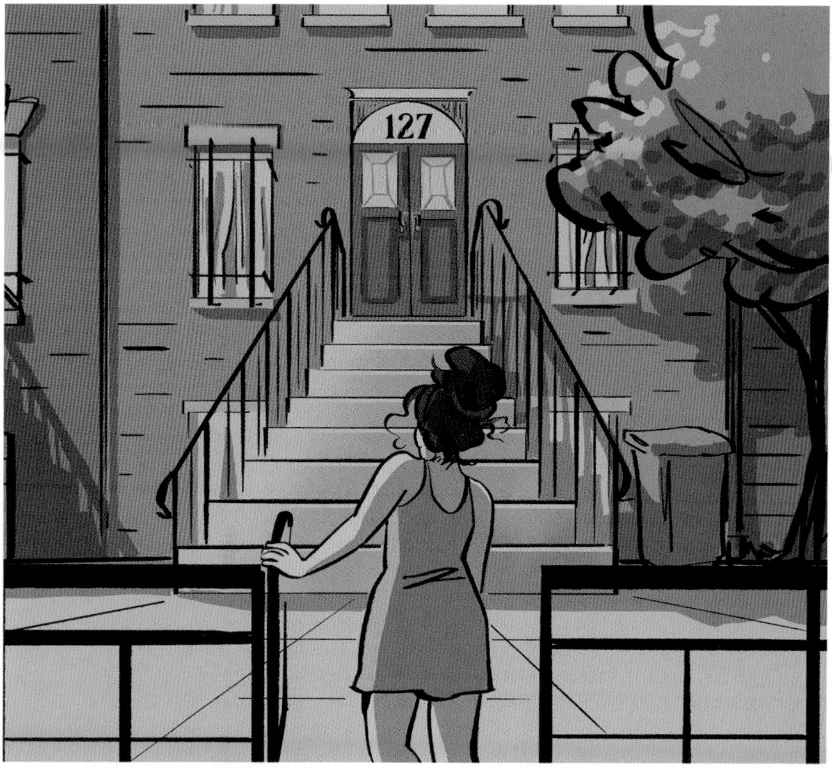
127

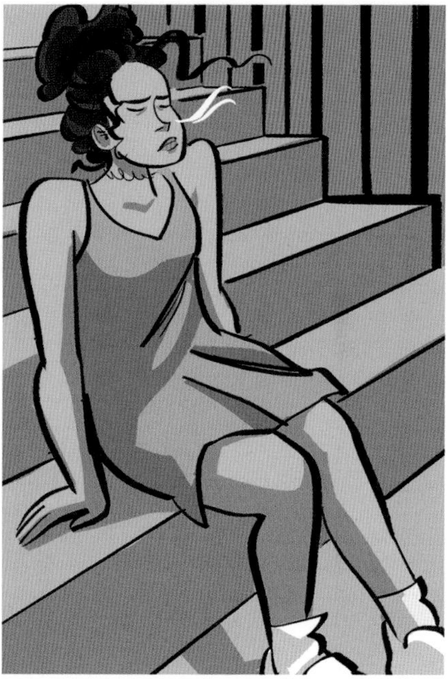

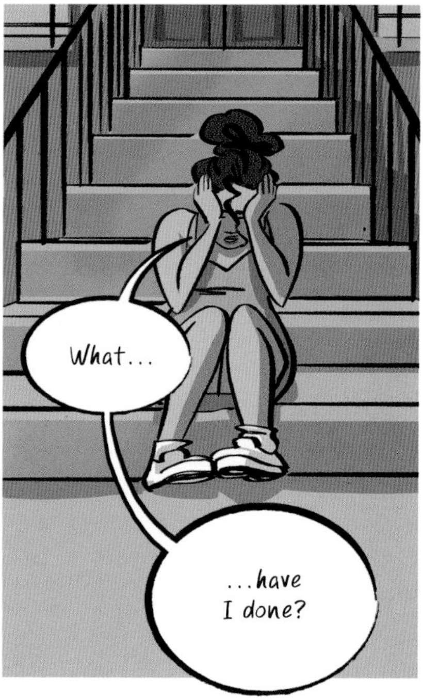
What...
...have I done?

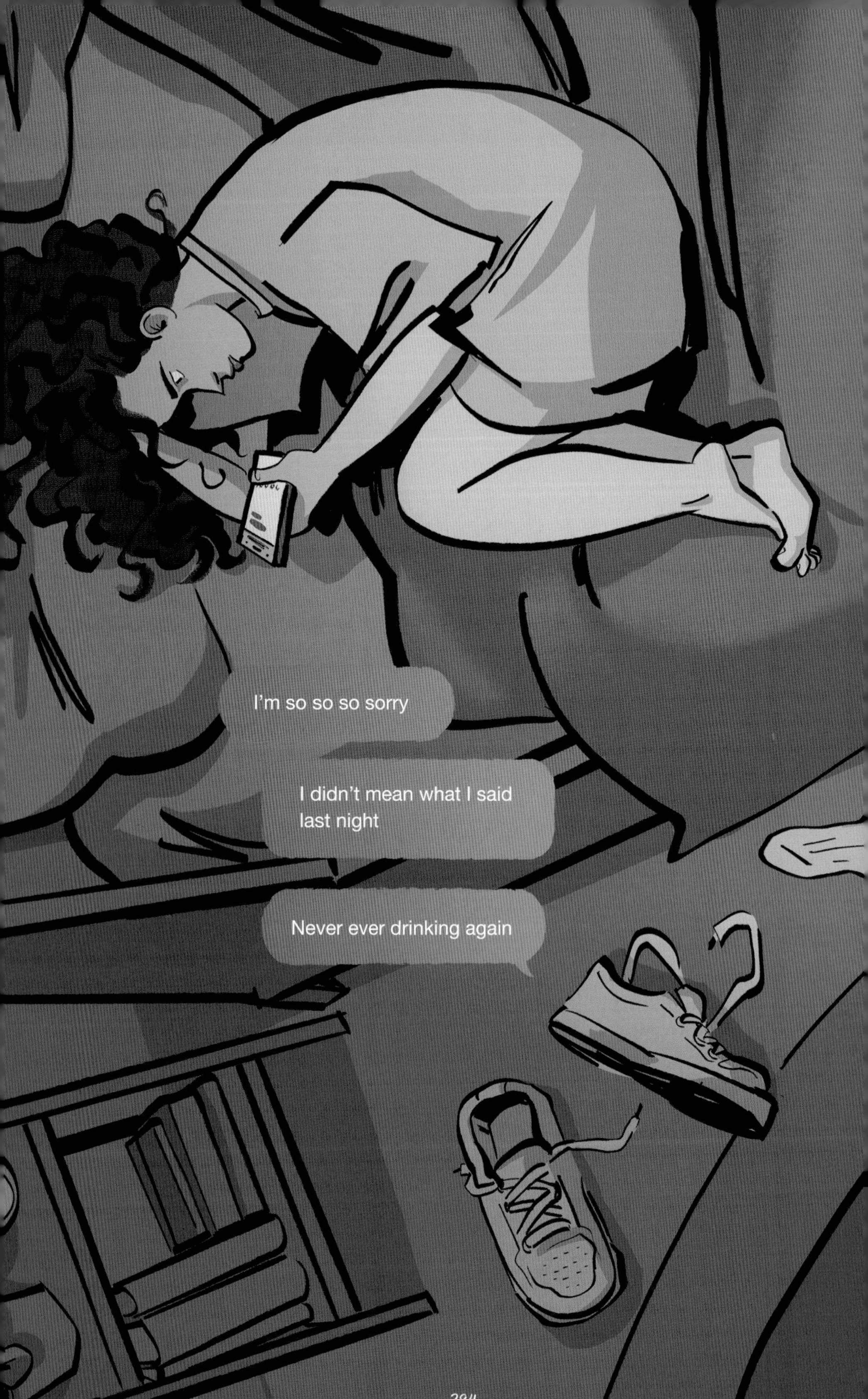
I'm so so so sorry
I didn't mean what I said last night
Never ever drinking again

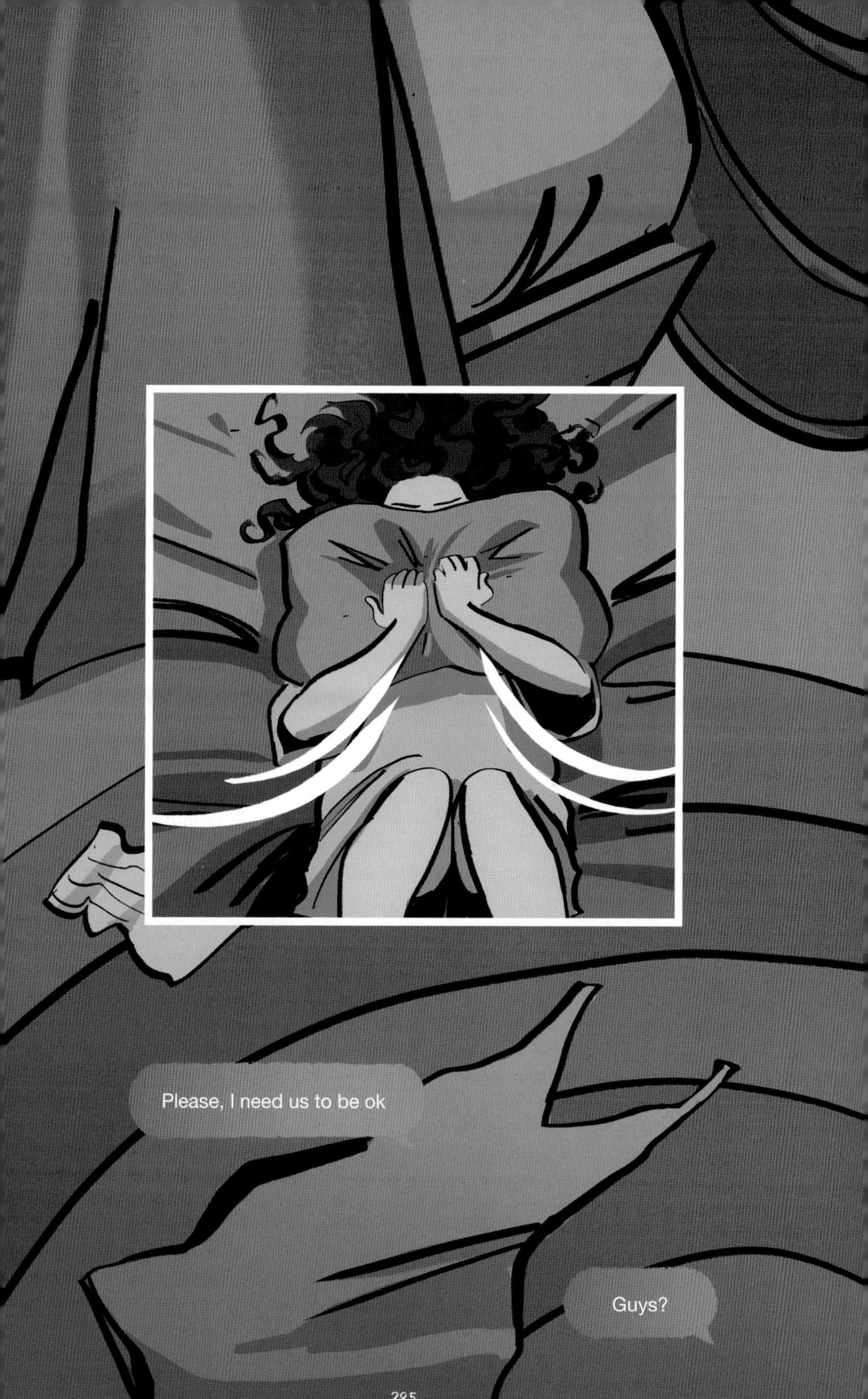
Please, I need us to be ok
Guys?

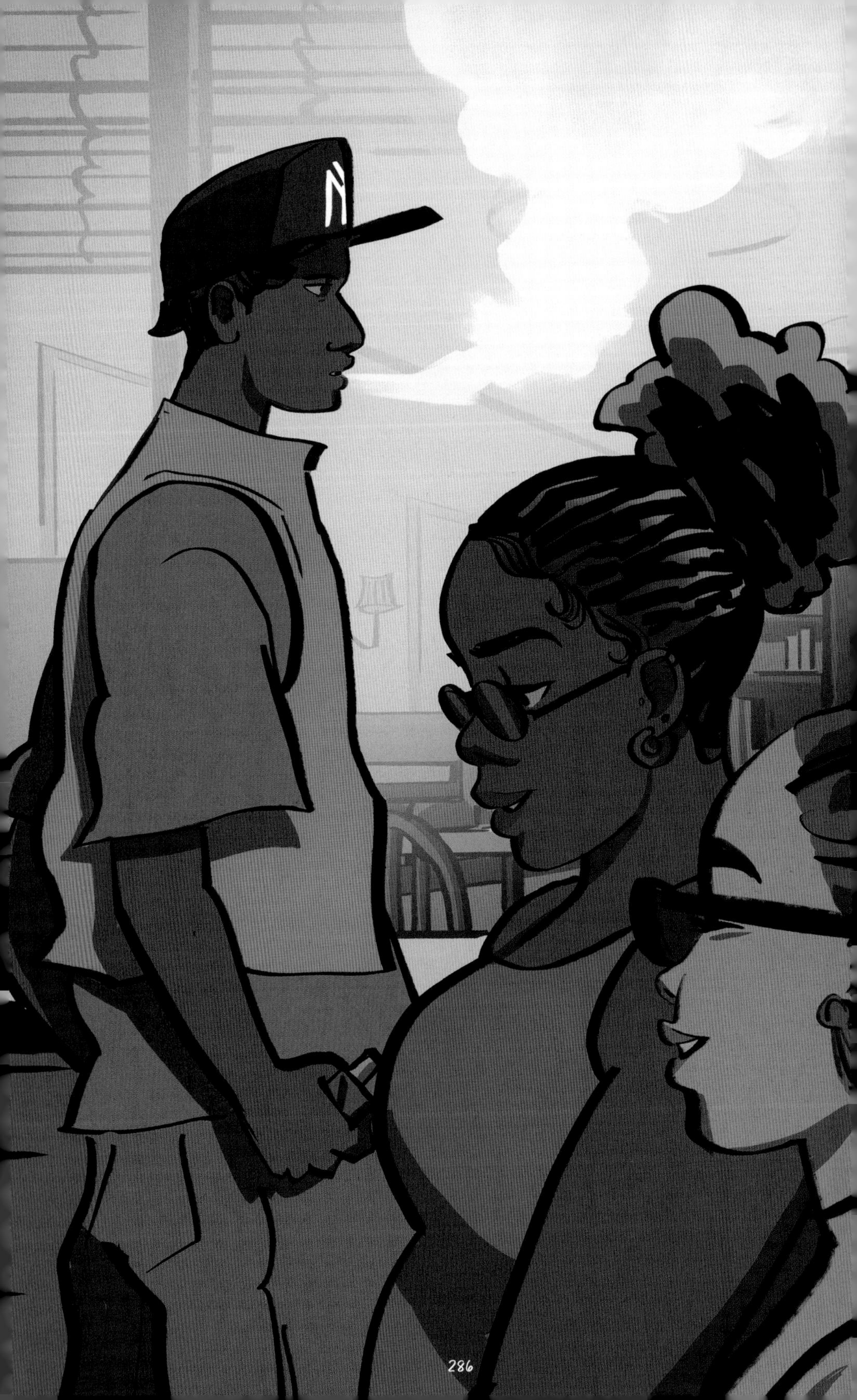

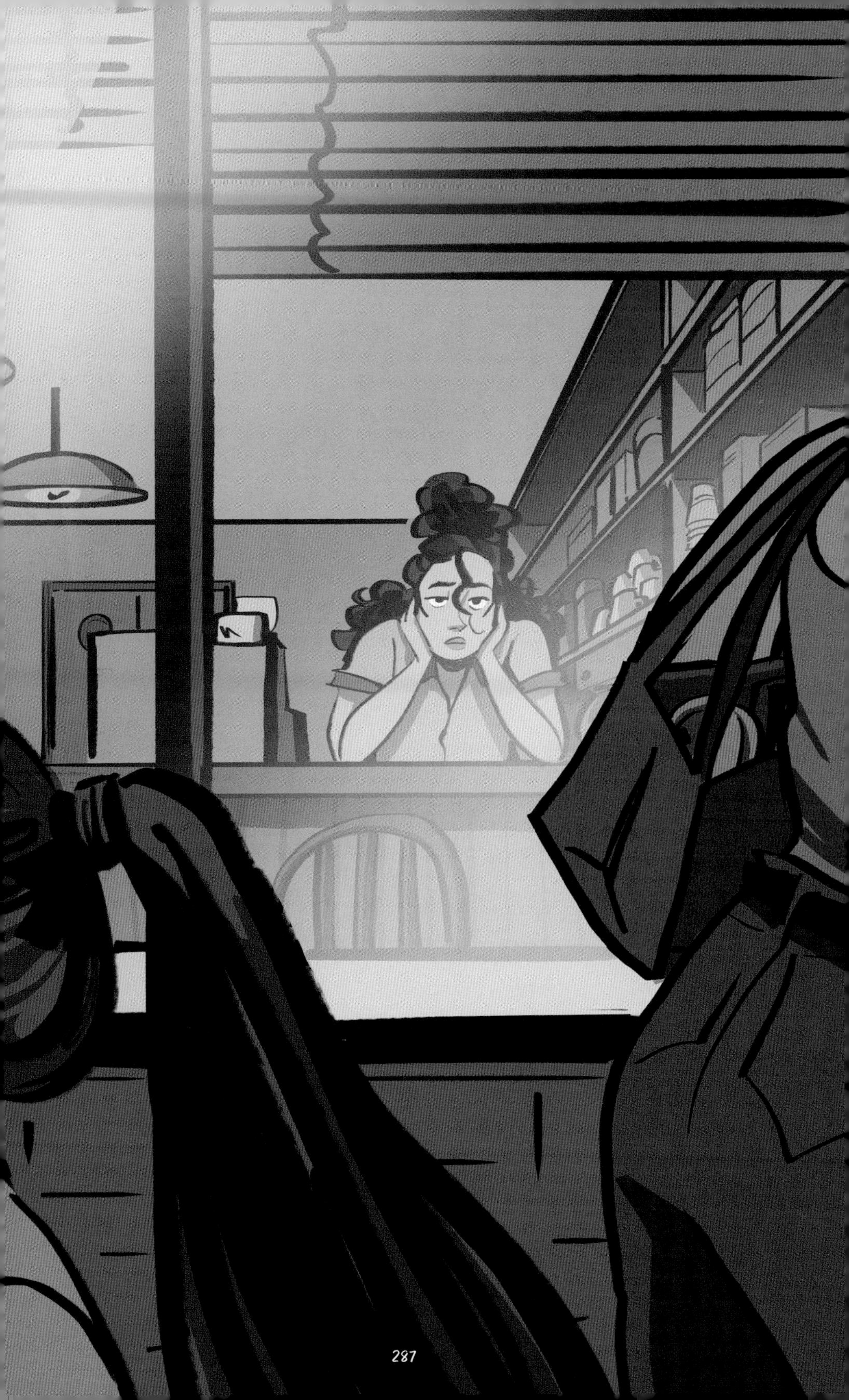

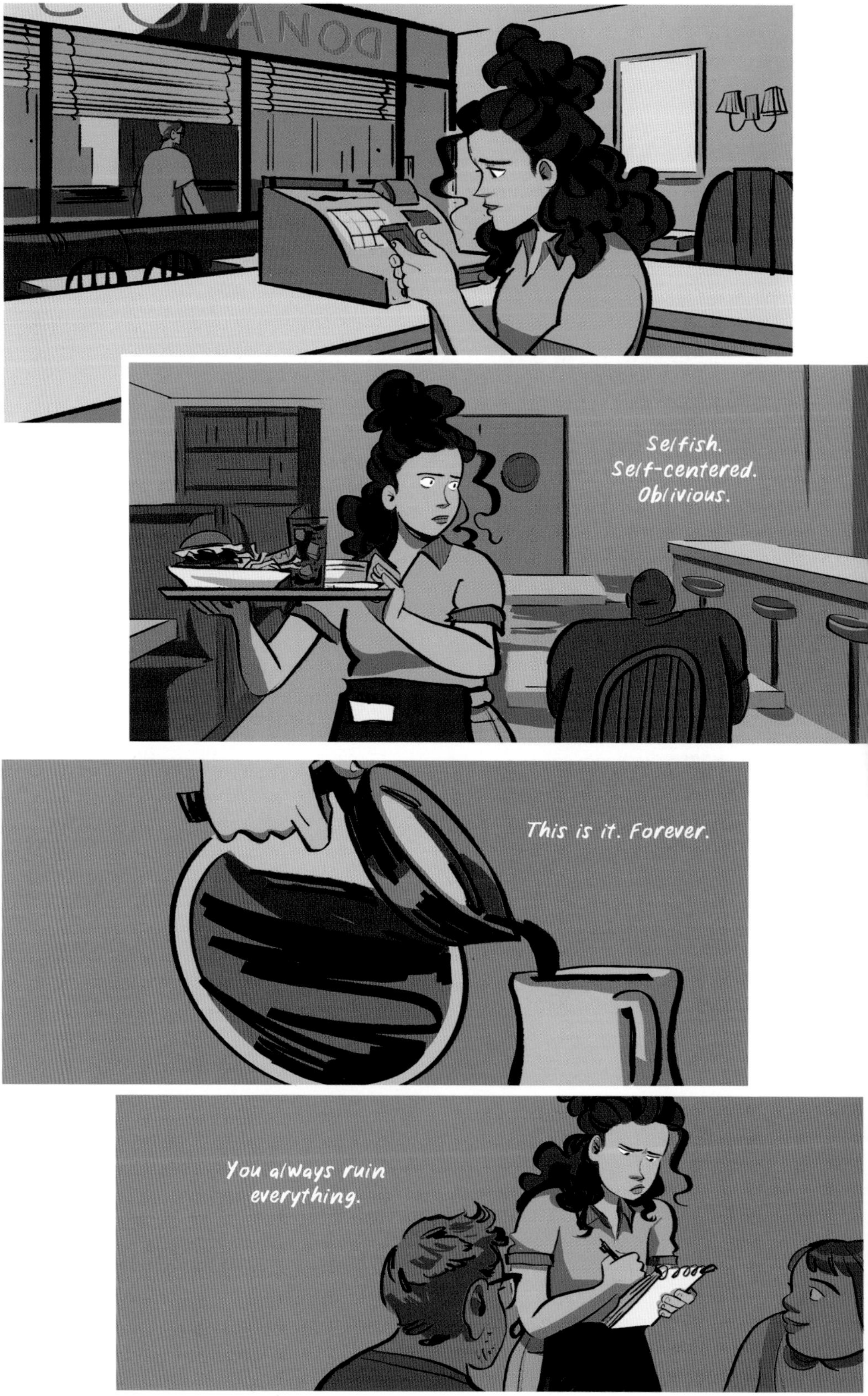
Selfish.
Self-centered.
Oblivious.
This is it. Forever.
You always ruin everything.

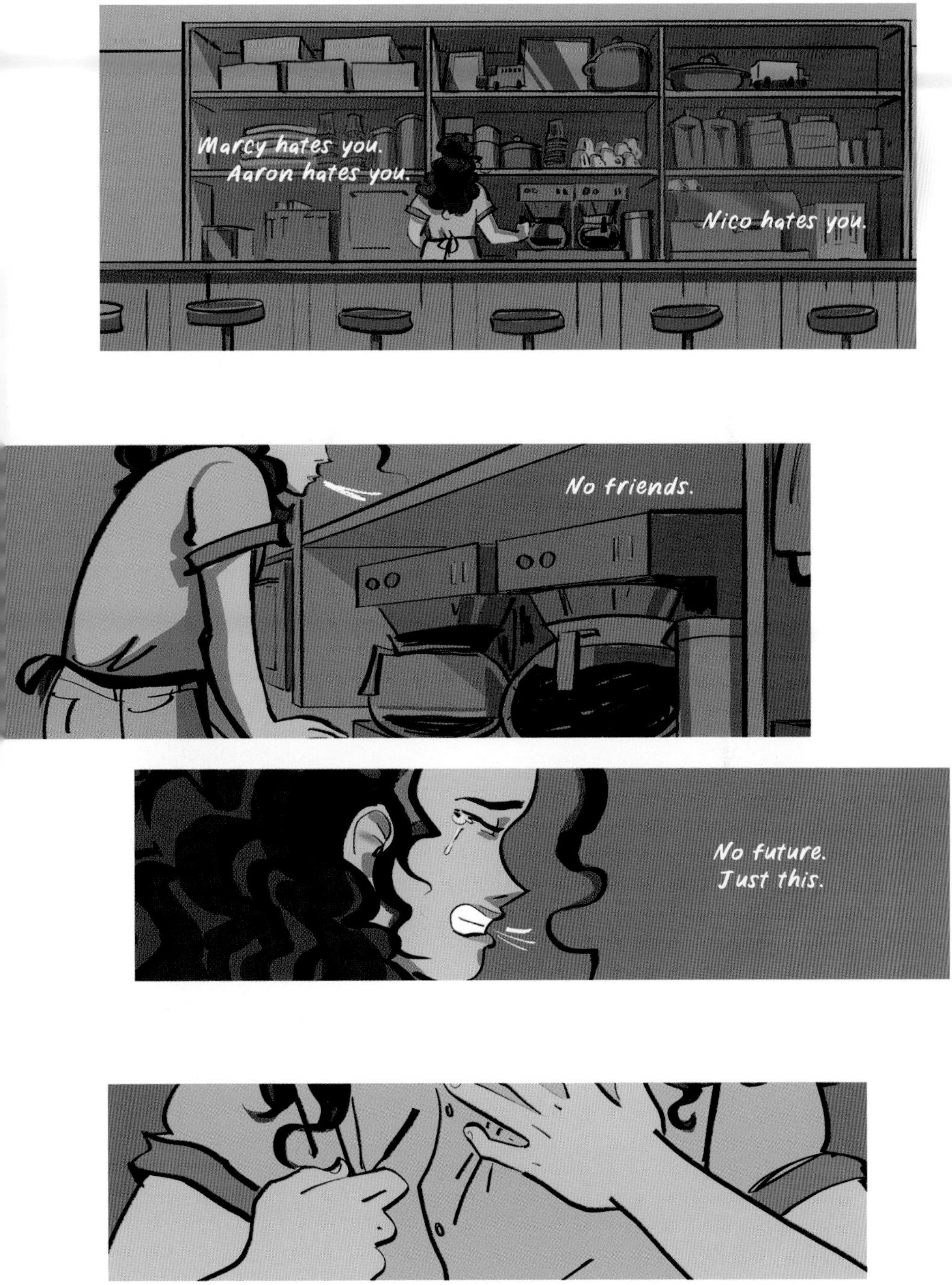
Marcy hates you.
Aaron hates you.
Nico hates you.
No friends.
No future.
Just this.

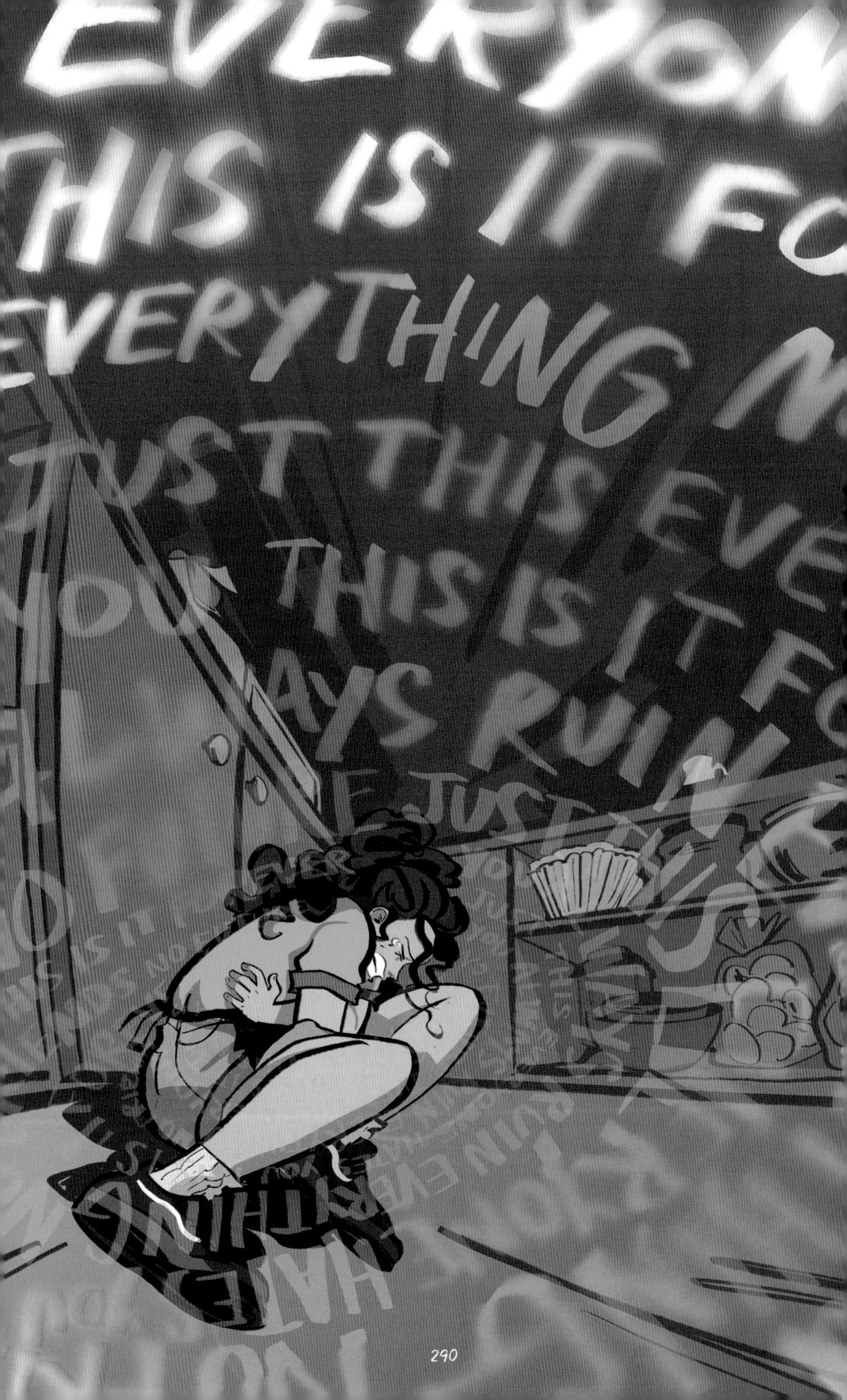
EVERYON
THIS IS IT FO
EVERYTHING N
JUST THIS EVE
THIS IS IT FO
AYS RUI
E JUST

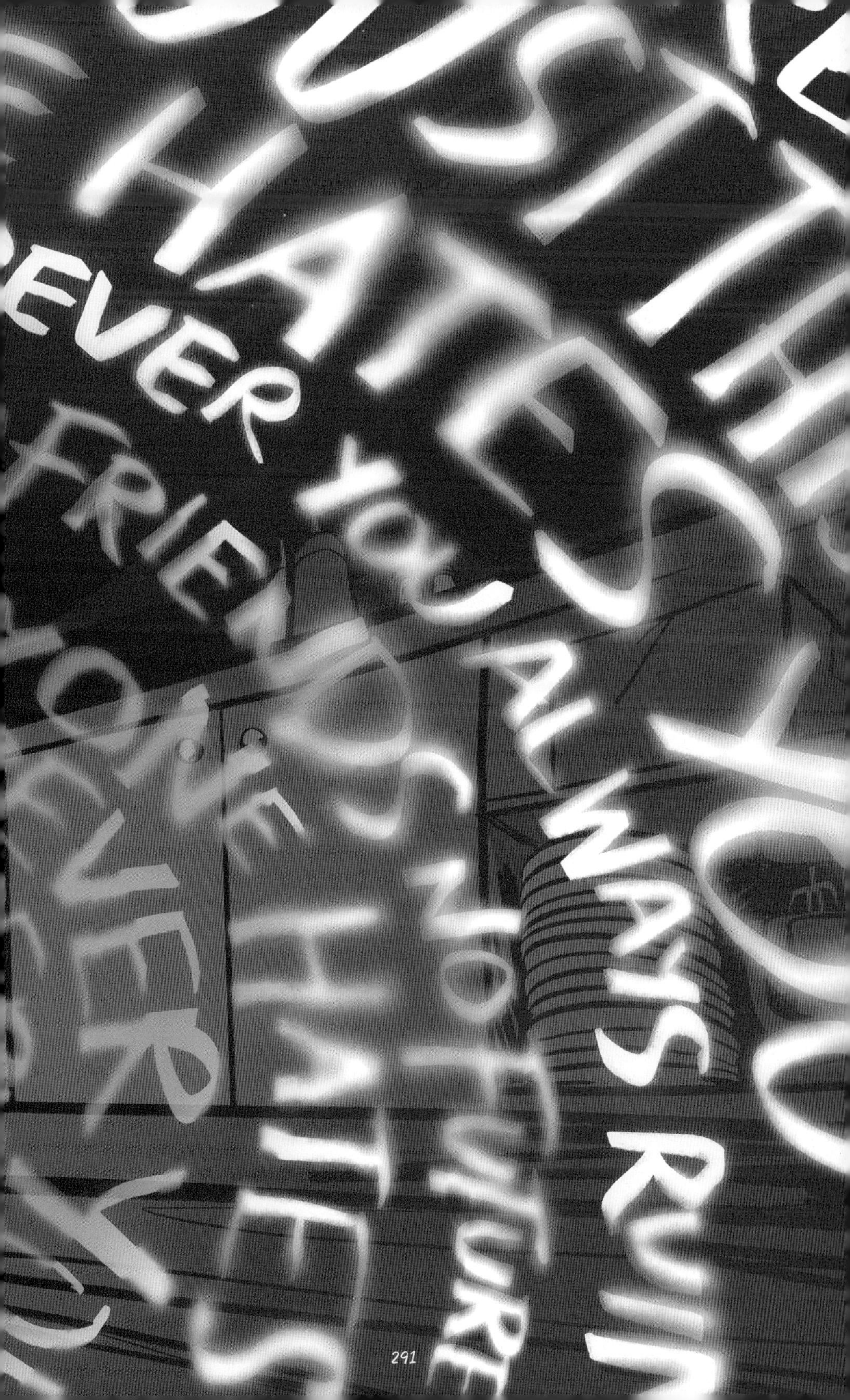
EVER
YOU
ALWAYS

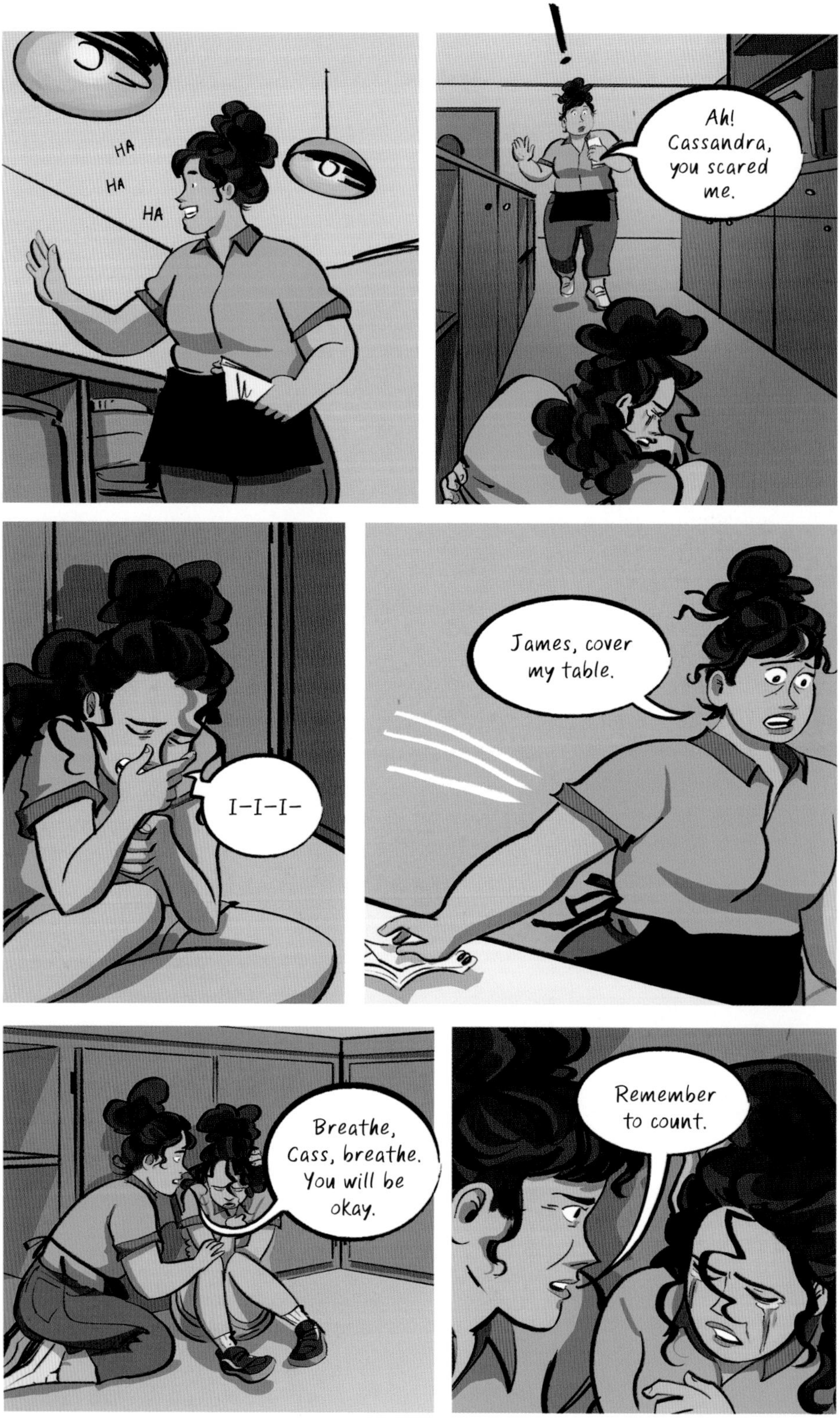
HA
HA
HA
!
Ah! Cassandra, you scared me.
I-I-I-
James, cover my table.
Breathe, Cass, breathe. You will be okay.
Remember to count.

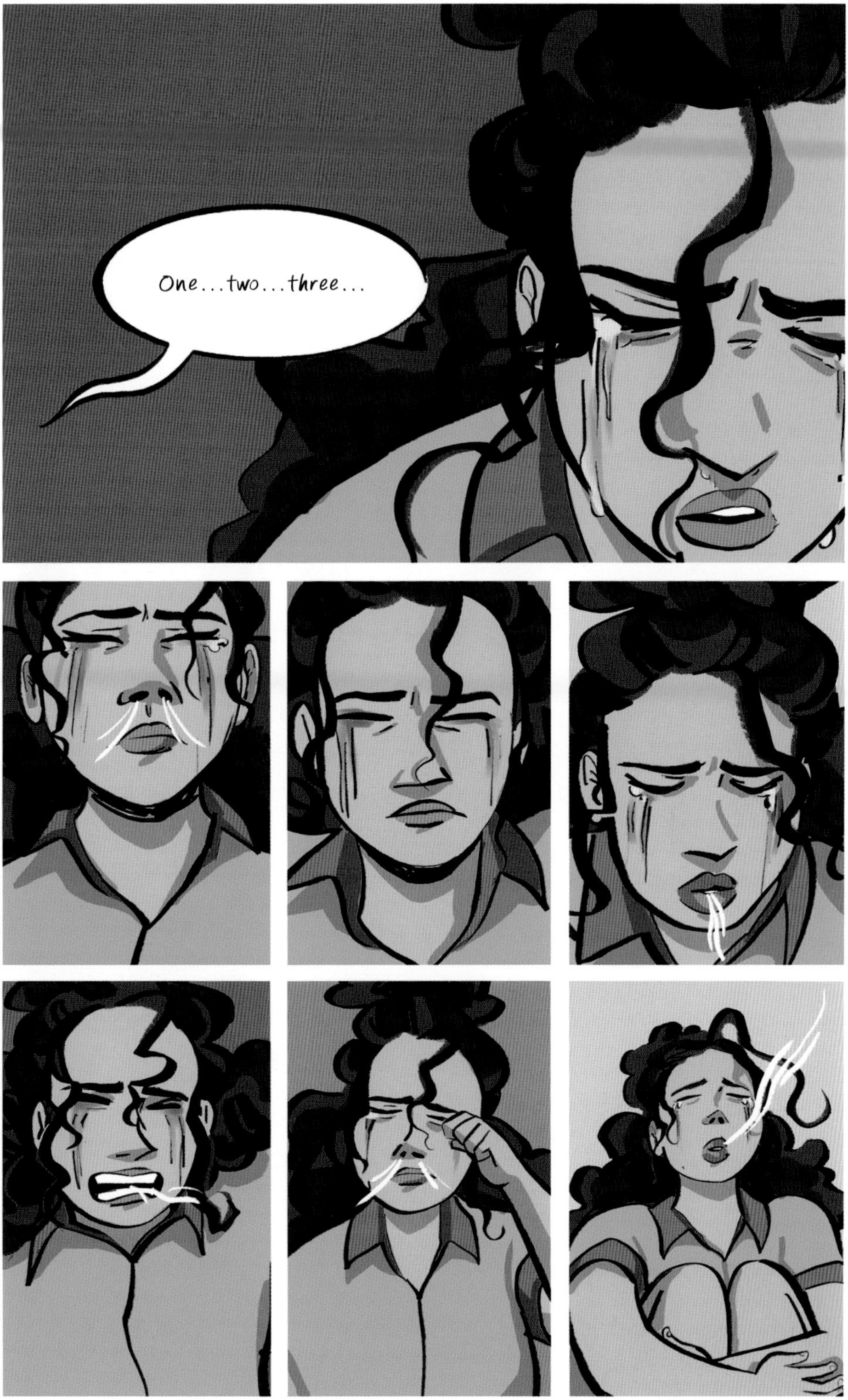
One...two...three...

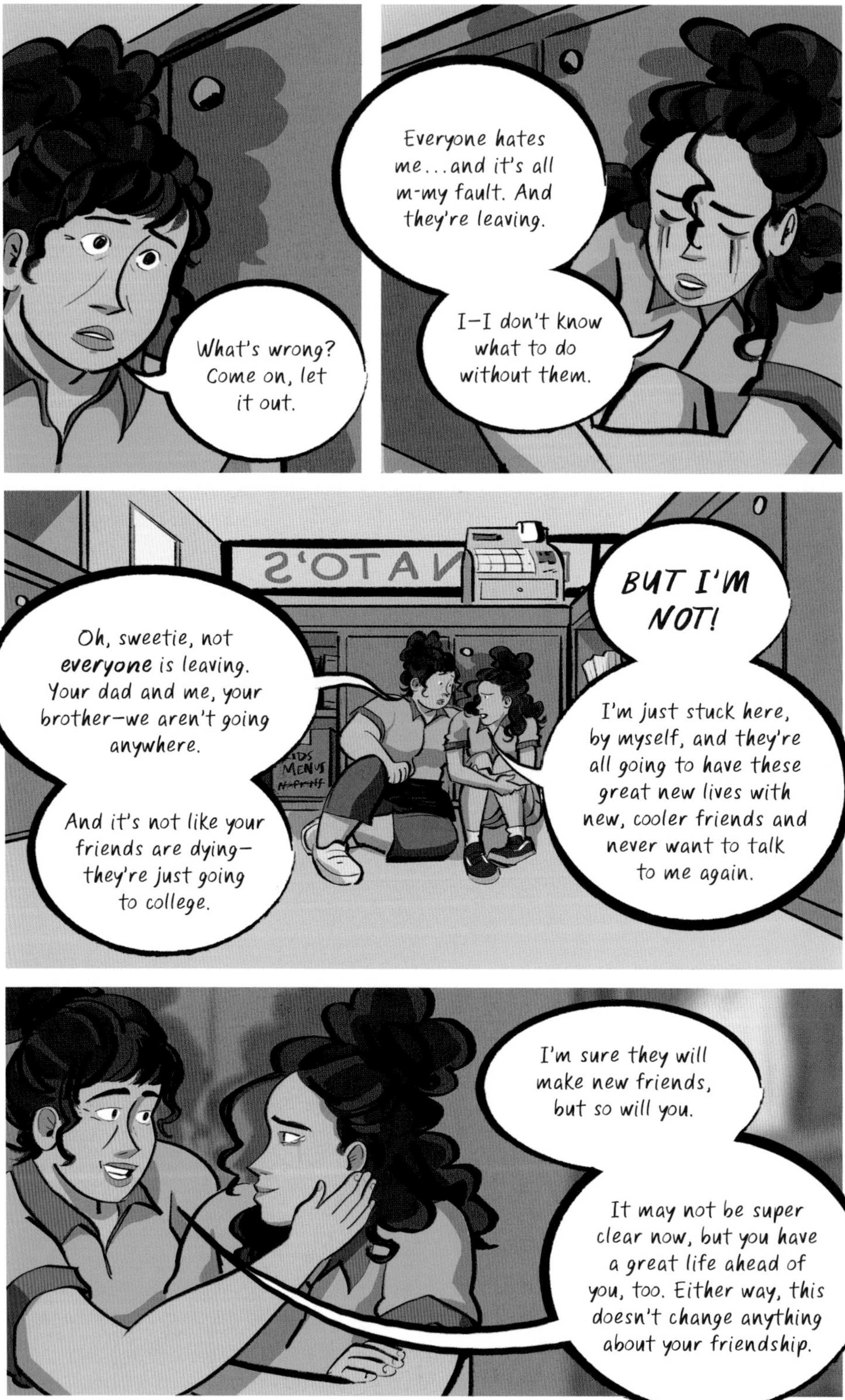
What's wrong? Come on, let it out.
Everyone hates me...and it's all m-my fault. And they're leaving.
I—I don't know what to do without them.
Oh, sweetie, not **everyone** is leaving. Your dad and me, your brother—we aren't going anywhere.
And it's not like your friends are dying—they're just going to college.
BUT I'M NOT!
I'm just stuck here, by myself, and they're all going to have these great new lives with new, cooler friends and never want to talk to me again.
I'm sure they will make new friends, but so will you.
It may not be super clear now, but you have a great life ahead of you, too. Either way, this doesn't change anything about your friendship.

I'm scared.

I have no idea...

No idea what to do at all.

Here's a secret: no one has any idea what to do. Not me, not your dad, and especially not an eighteen-year-old girl. Don't be so hard on yourself.

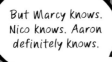

But Marcy knows. Nico knows. Aaron definitely knows.

I bet they're all still figuring themselves out too. Just like you but in different ways.

They are all so...sure of themselves.

Well, yeah...

But they know what they want to do. What to major in and where to go.

I don't know...

...anything.

Cassandra...

...you need to stop comparing yourself to everyone else. You are so smart and so beautiful. You're funny and caring and loving...

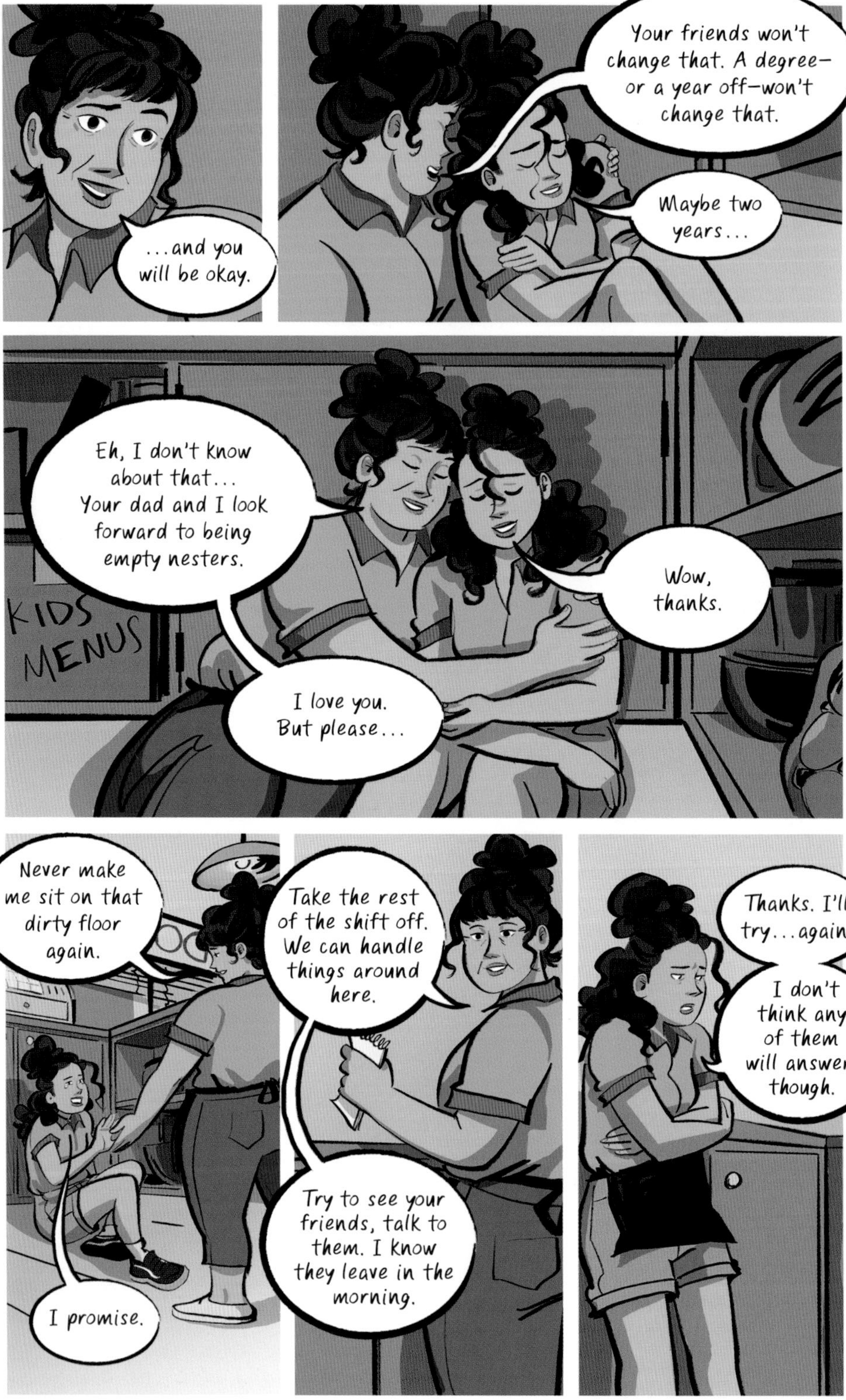
...and you will be okay.
Your friends won't change that. A degree—or a year off—won't change that.
Maybe two years...
Eh, I don't know about that... Your dad and I look forward to being empty nesters.
Wow, thanks.
KIDS MENUS
I love you. But please...
Never make me sit on that dirty floor again.
I promise.
Take the rest of the shift off. We can handle things around here.
Try to see your friends, talk to them. I know they leave in the morning.
Thanks. I'll try...again.
I don't think any of them will answer, though.

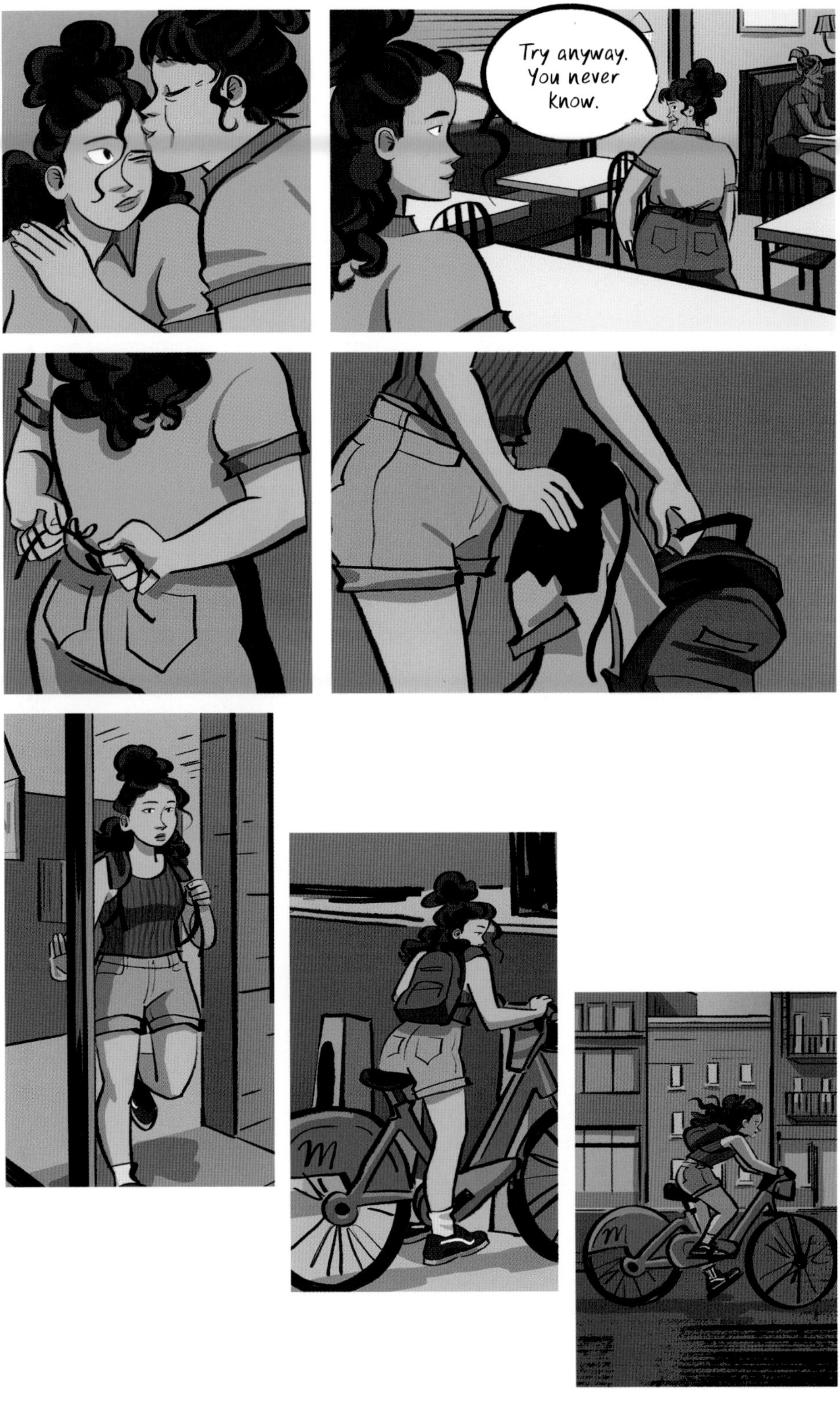
Try anyway. You never know.

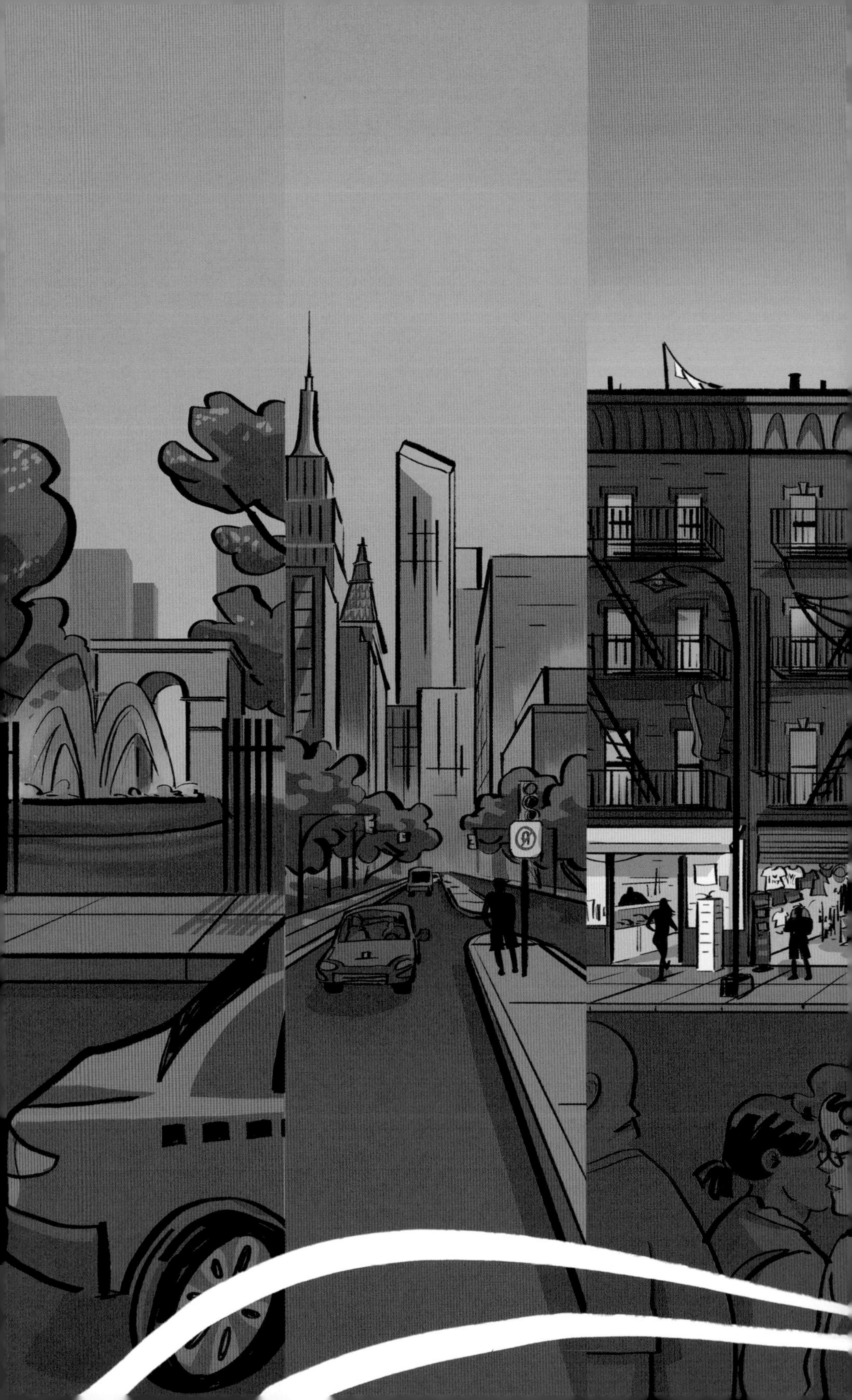

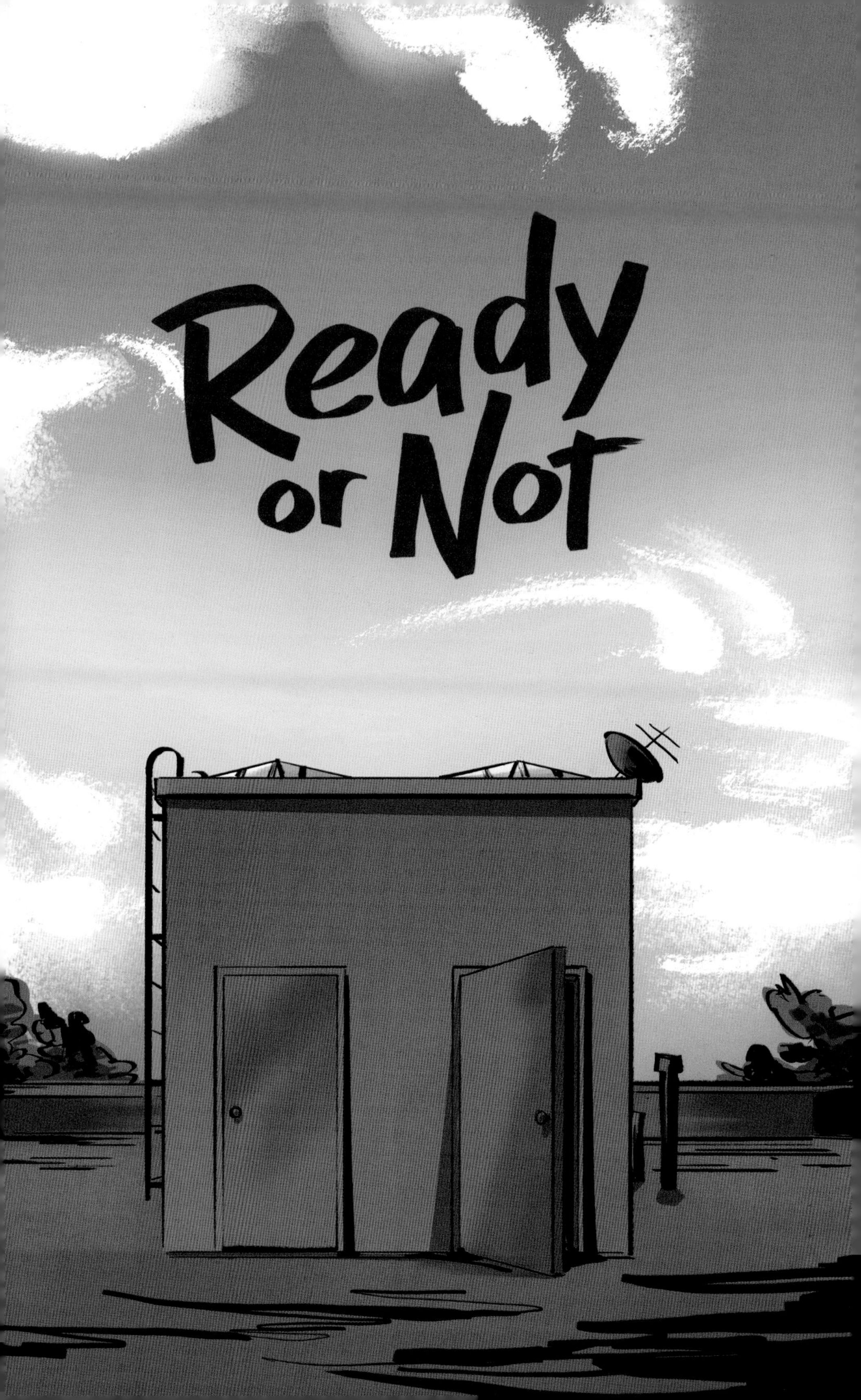
Ready
or Not

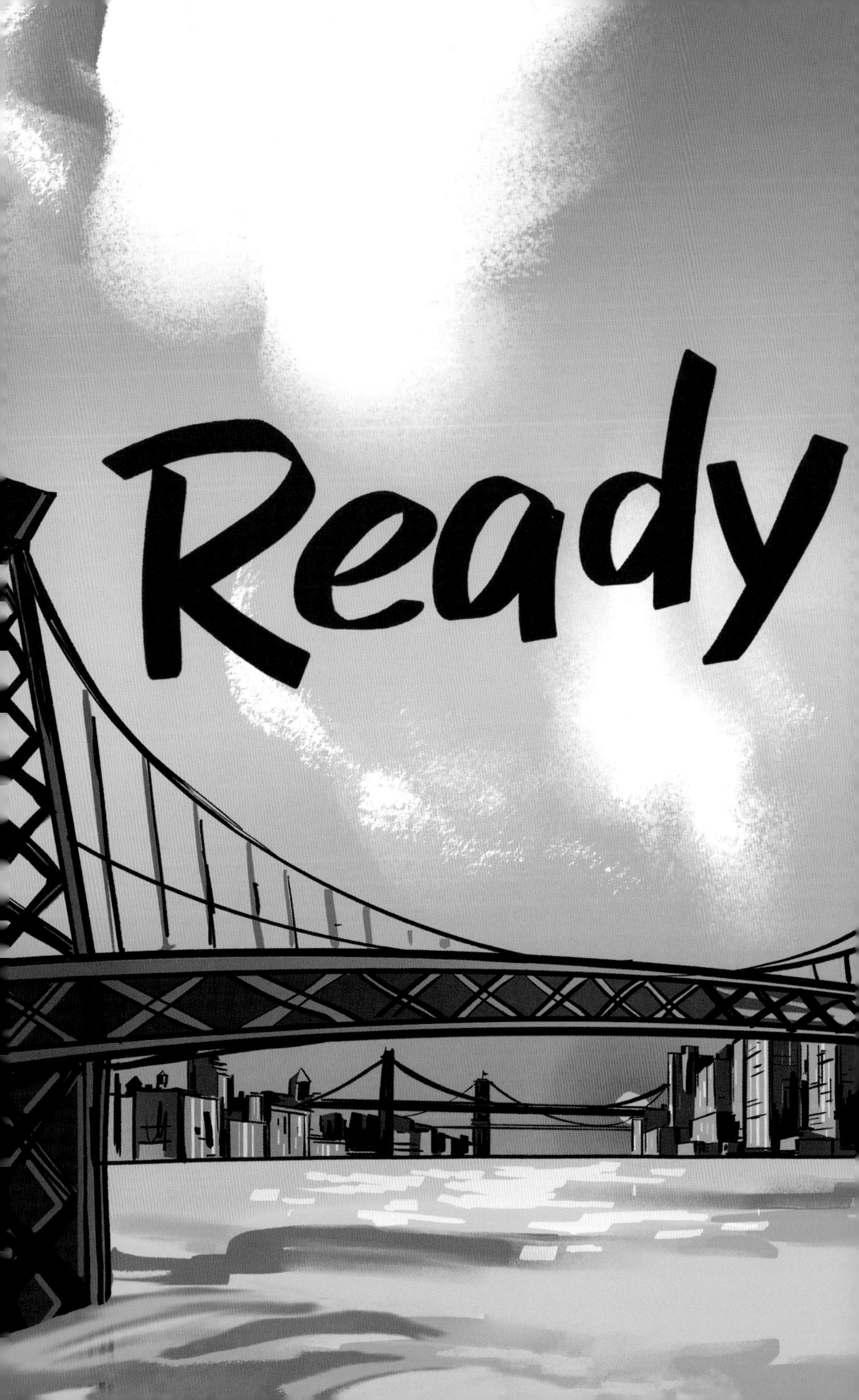
Ready

or Not

Andi Porretta

Flats by Matt Aytch Taylor

A̴ atheneum   New York   London   Toronto   Sydney   New Delhi

An imprint of Simon & Schuster Children's Publishing Division
1230 Avenue of the Americas, New York, New York 10020

Atheneum logo is a trademark of Simon & Schuster, LLC.
Simon & Schuster: Celebrating 100 Years of Publishing in 2024
For information about special discounts for bulk purchases, please contact Simon & Schuster
Special Sales at 1-866-506-1949 or business@simonandschuster.com.
The Simon & Schuster Speakers Bureau can bring authors to your live event.
For more information or to book an event, contact the Simon & Schuster Speakers Bureau at
1-866-248-3049 or visit our website at www.simonspeakers.com.

The text for this book was set in AndiPorrettaV2.
The illustrations for this book were rendered digitally.

Manufactured in China
First Edition
2 4 6 8 10 9 7 5 3 1
CIP data for this book is available from the Library of Congress.
ISBN 9781665907026 (pbk)
ISBN 9781665907033 (hc)
ISBN 9781665907040 (ebook)

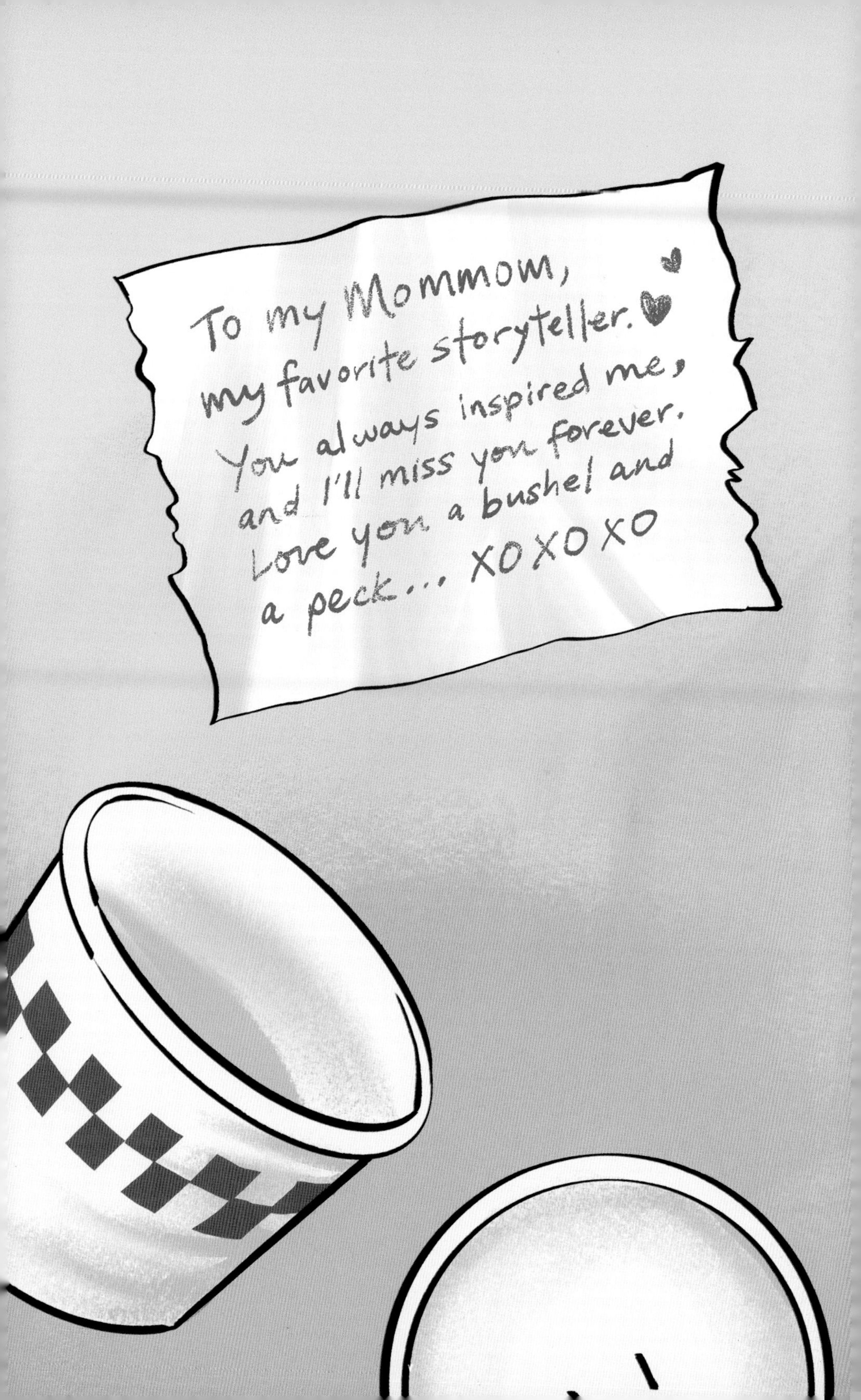
To my Mommom,
my favorite storyteller.
You always inspired me,
and I'll miss you forever.
Love you a bushel and
a peck... XOXOXO

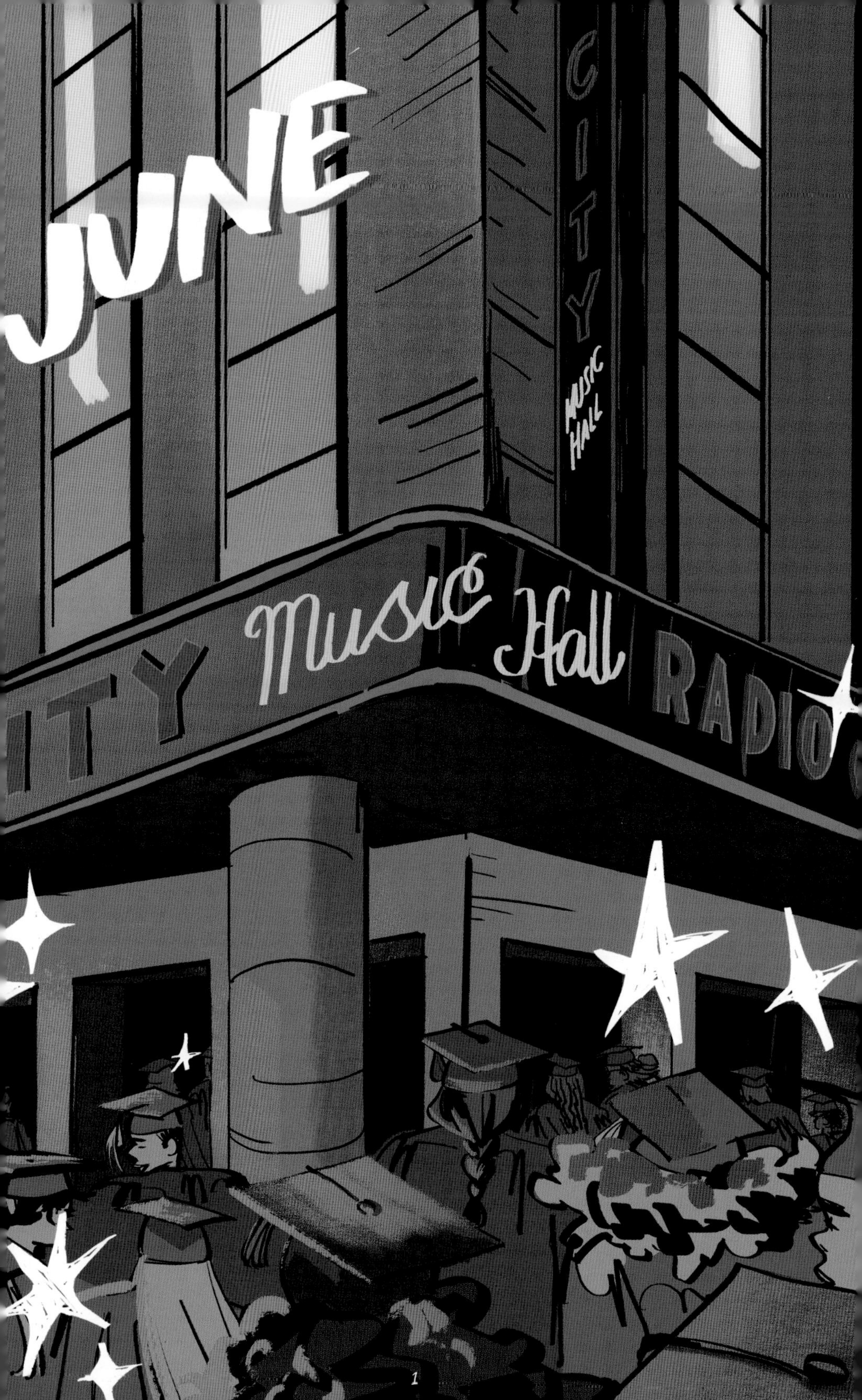

JUNE
CITY
MUSIC HALL
ITY Music Hall RADIO

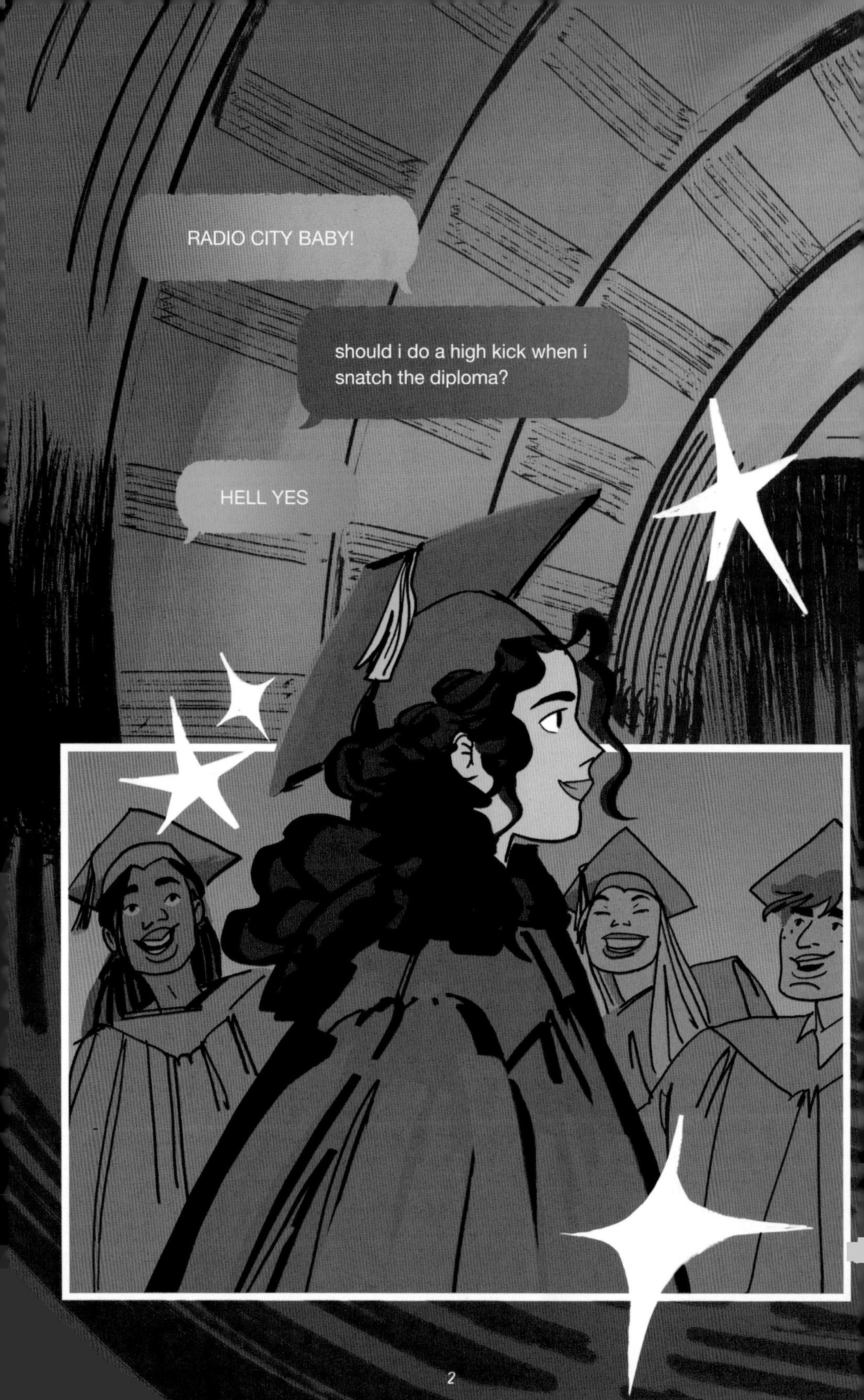
RADIO CITY BABY!
should i do a high kick when i snatch the diploma?
HELL YES

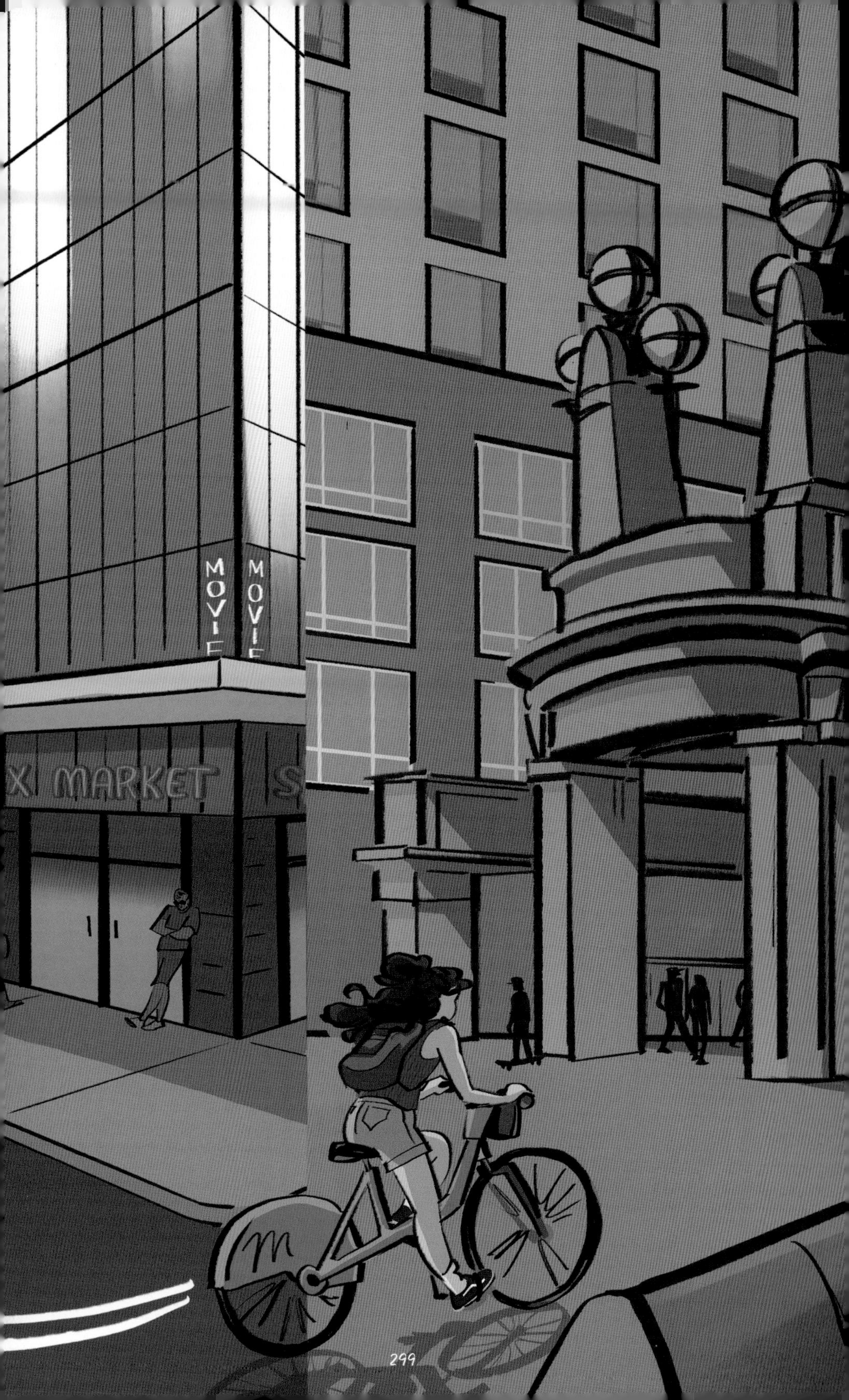
MOVI
MOVI
MARKET

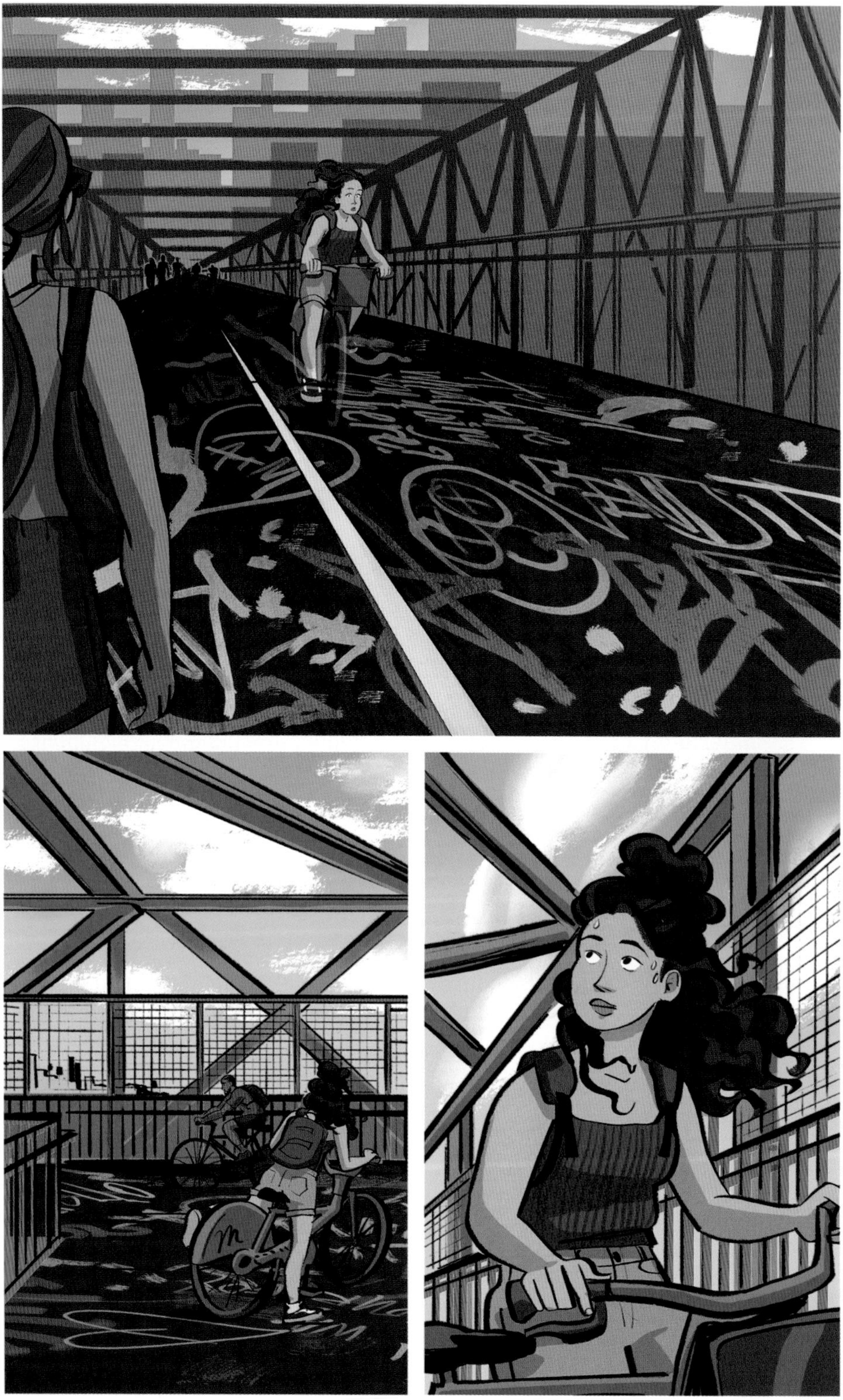

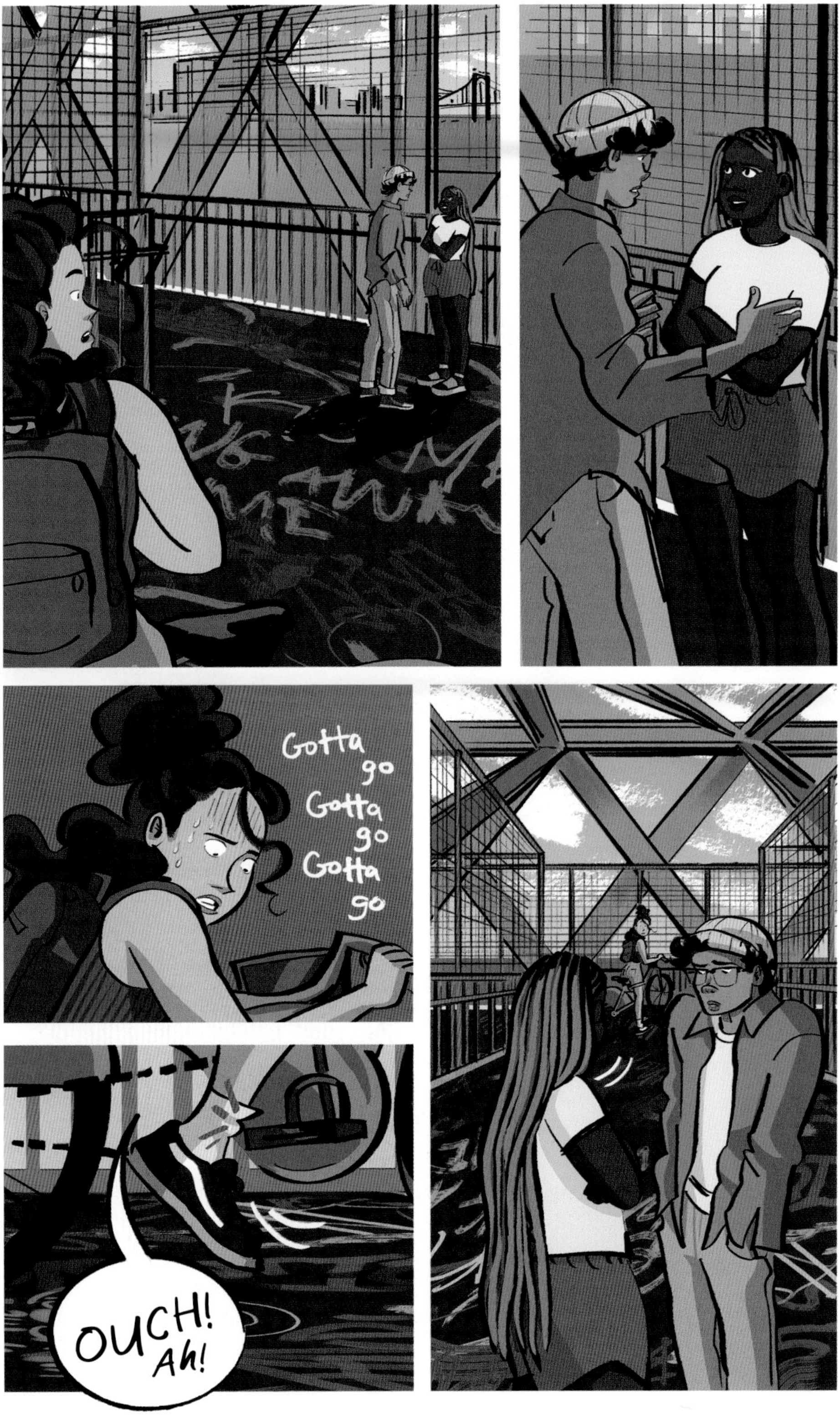
Gotta go Gotta go Gotta go
OUCH! Ah!

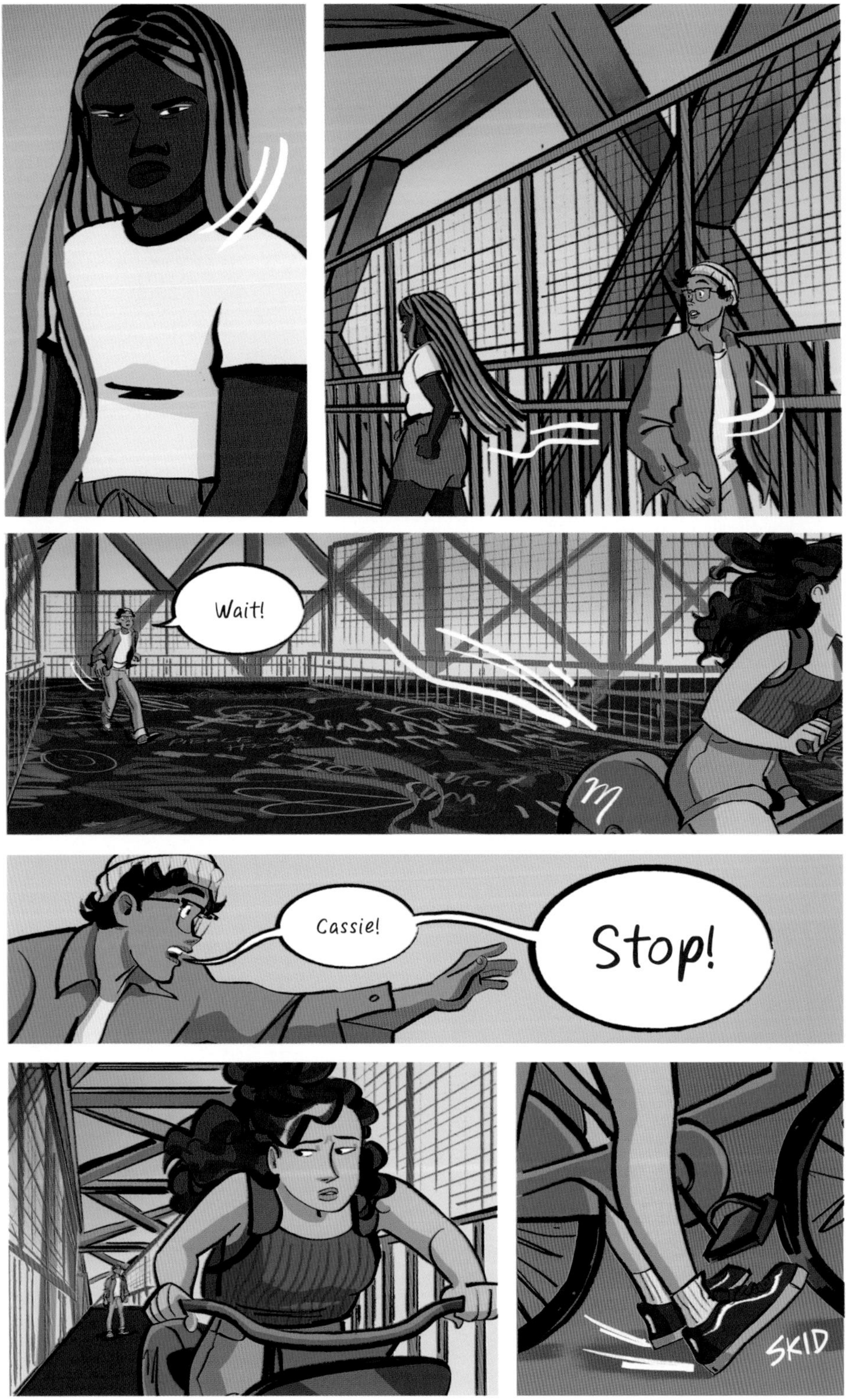
Wait!
Cassie!
Stop!
SKID

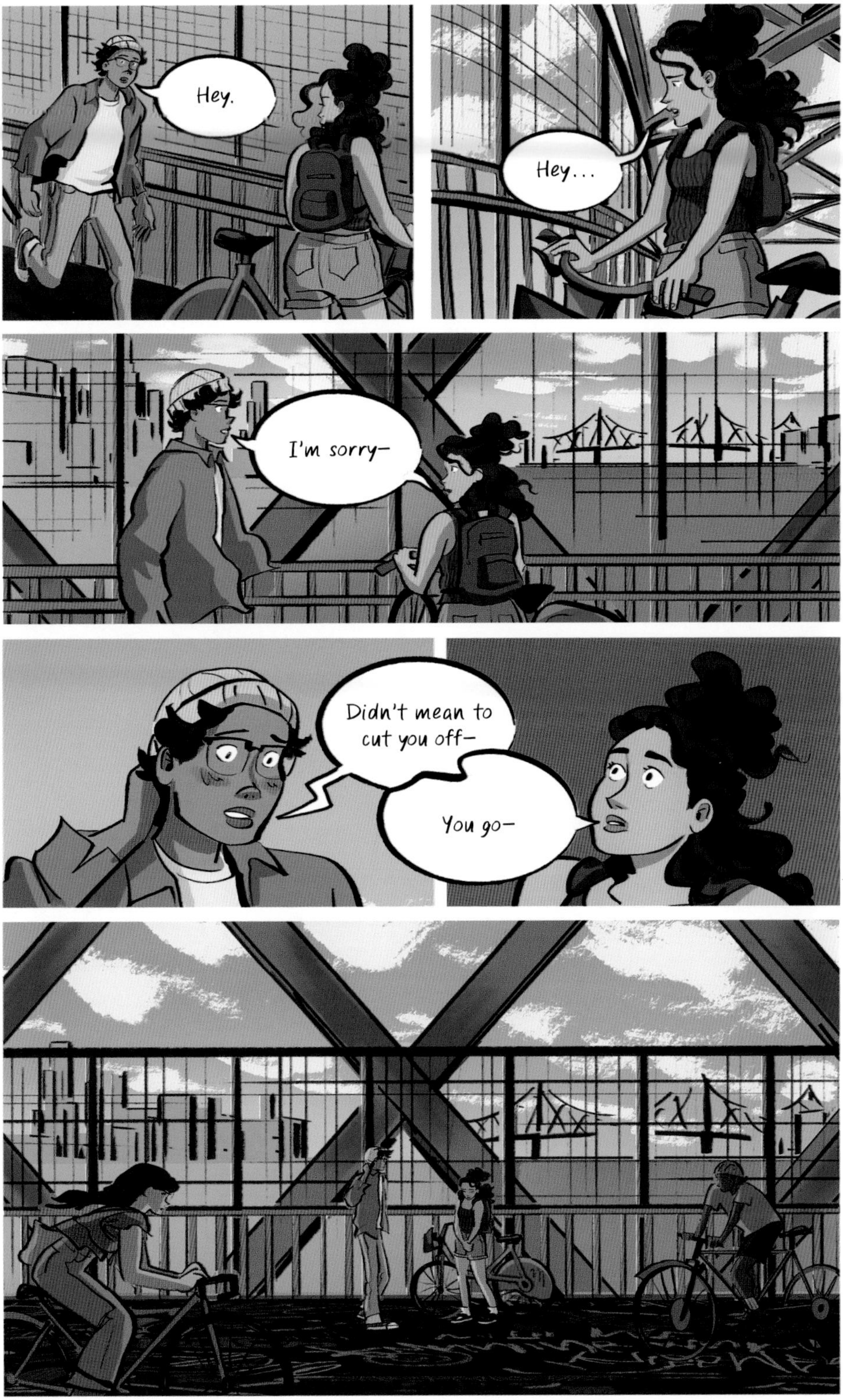
Hey.
Hey...
I'm sorry–
Didn't mean to cut you off–
You go–

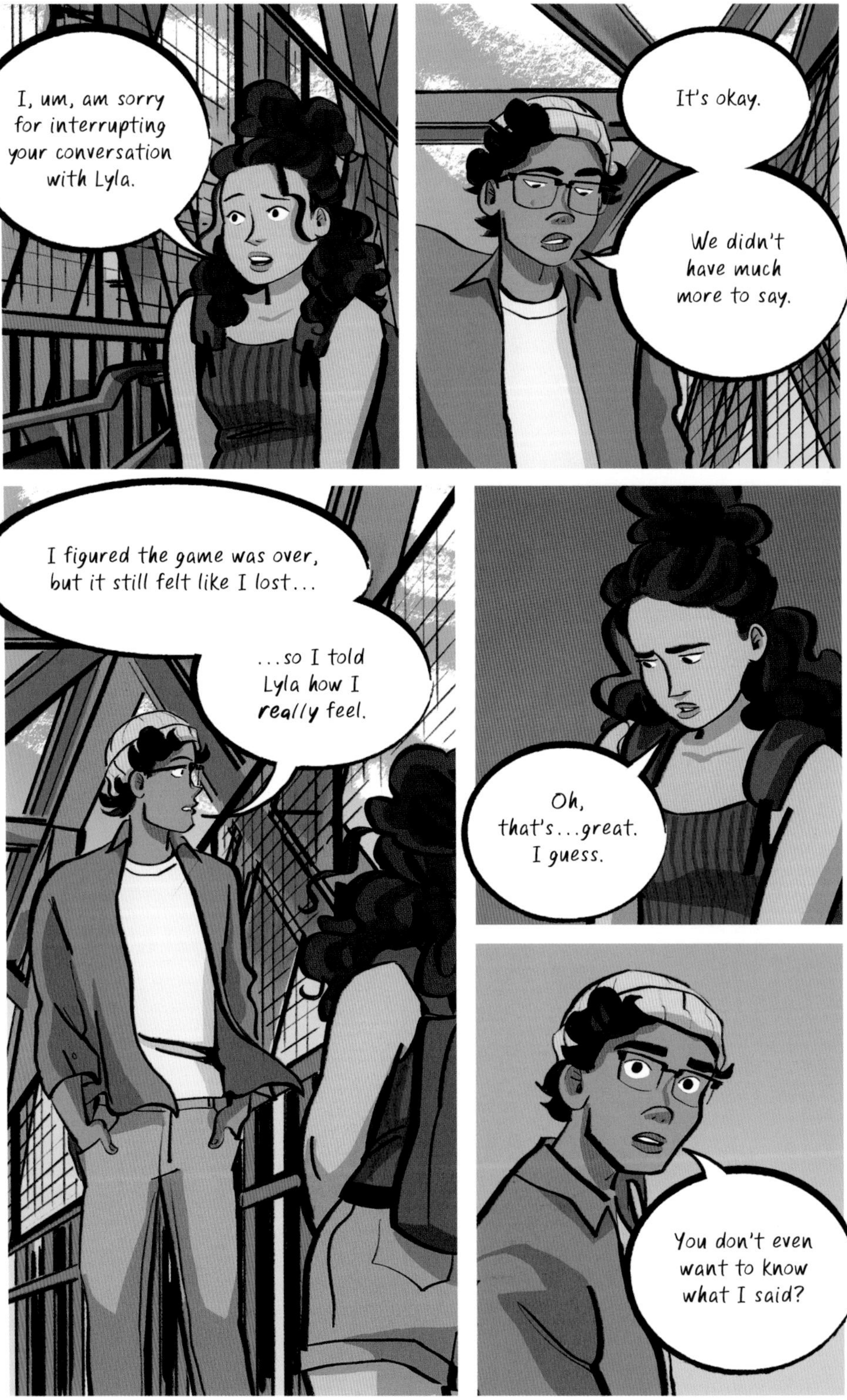
I, um, am sorry for interrupting your conversation with Lyla.
It's okay.
We didn't have much more to say.
I figured the game was over, but it still felt like I lost...
...so I told Lyla how I *really* feel.
Oh, that's...great. I guess.
You don't even want to know what I said?

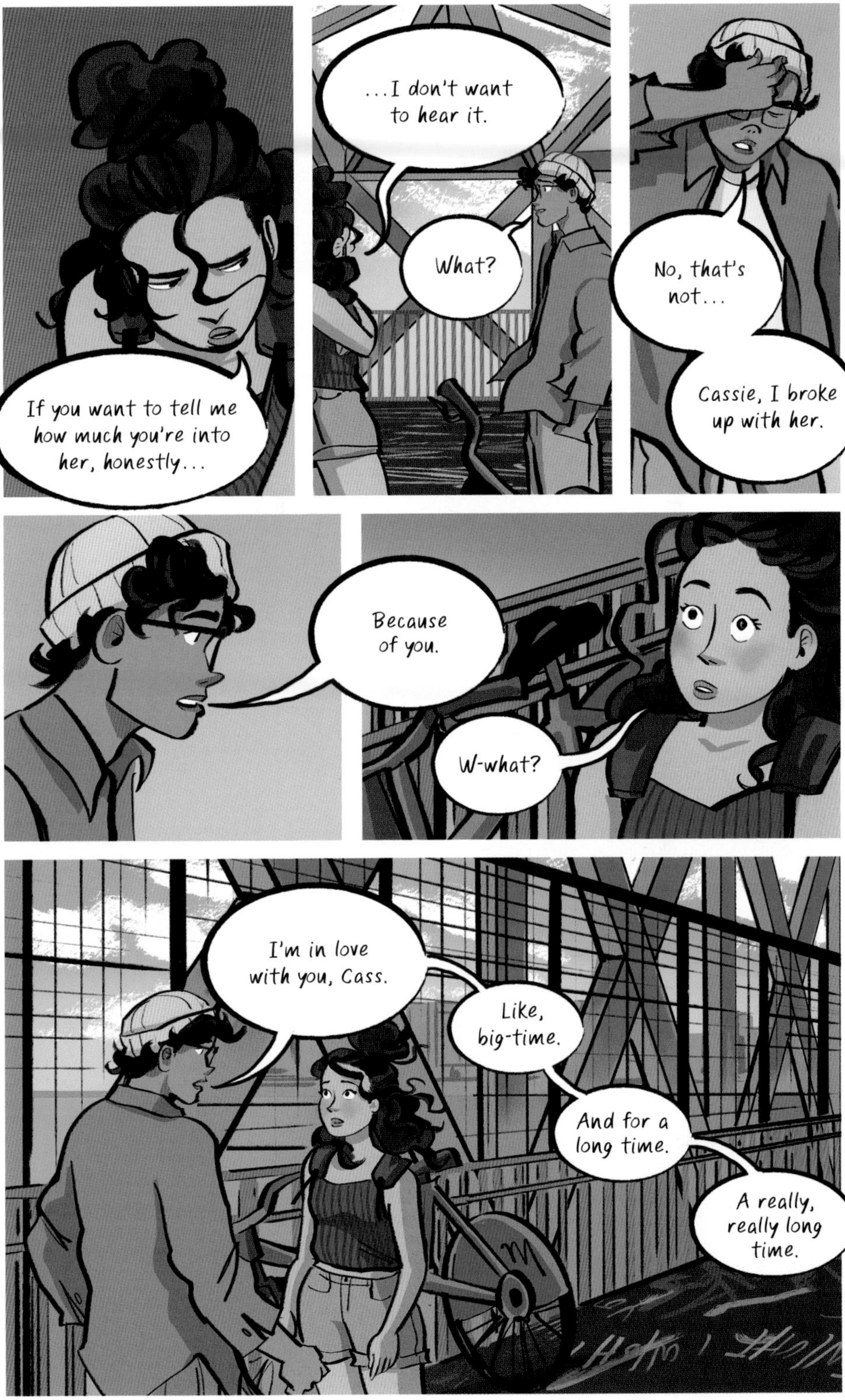
If you want to tell me how much you're into her, honestly...
...I don't want to hear it.
What?
No, that's not...
Cassie, I broke up with her.
Because of you.
W-what?
I'm in love with you, Cass.
Like, big-time.
And for a long time.
A really, really long time.

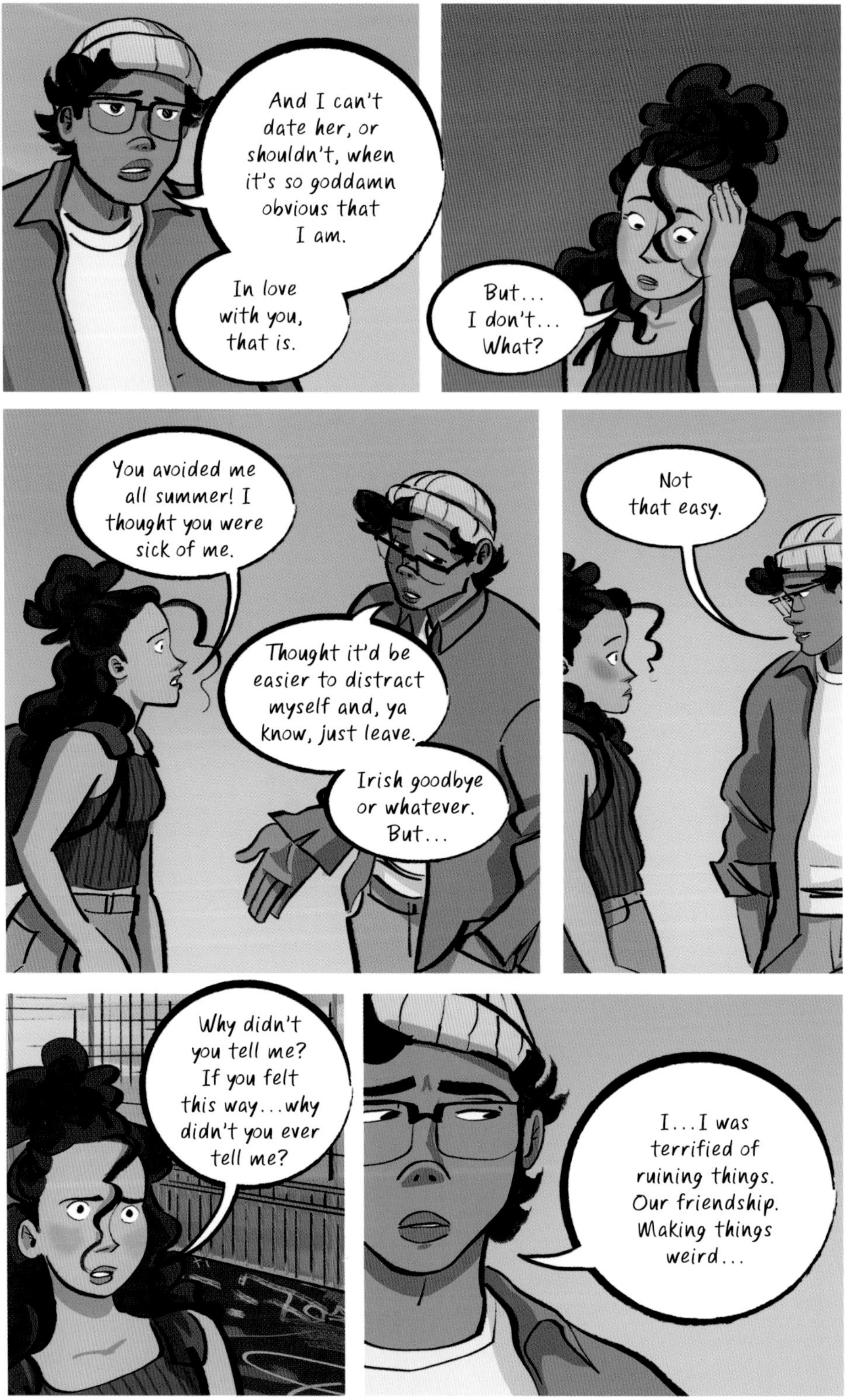
And I can't date her, or shouldn't, when it's so goddamn obvious that I am.
In love with you, that is.
But... I don't... What?
You avoided me all summer! I thought you were sick of me.
Thought it'd be easier to distract myself and, ya know, just leave.
Irish goodbye or whatever. But...
Not that easy.
Why didn't you tell me? If you felt this way...why didn't you ever tell me?
I...I was terrified of ruining things. Our friendship. Making things weird...

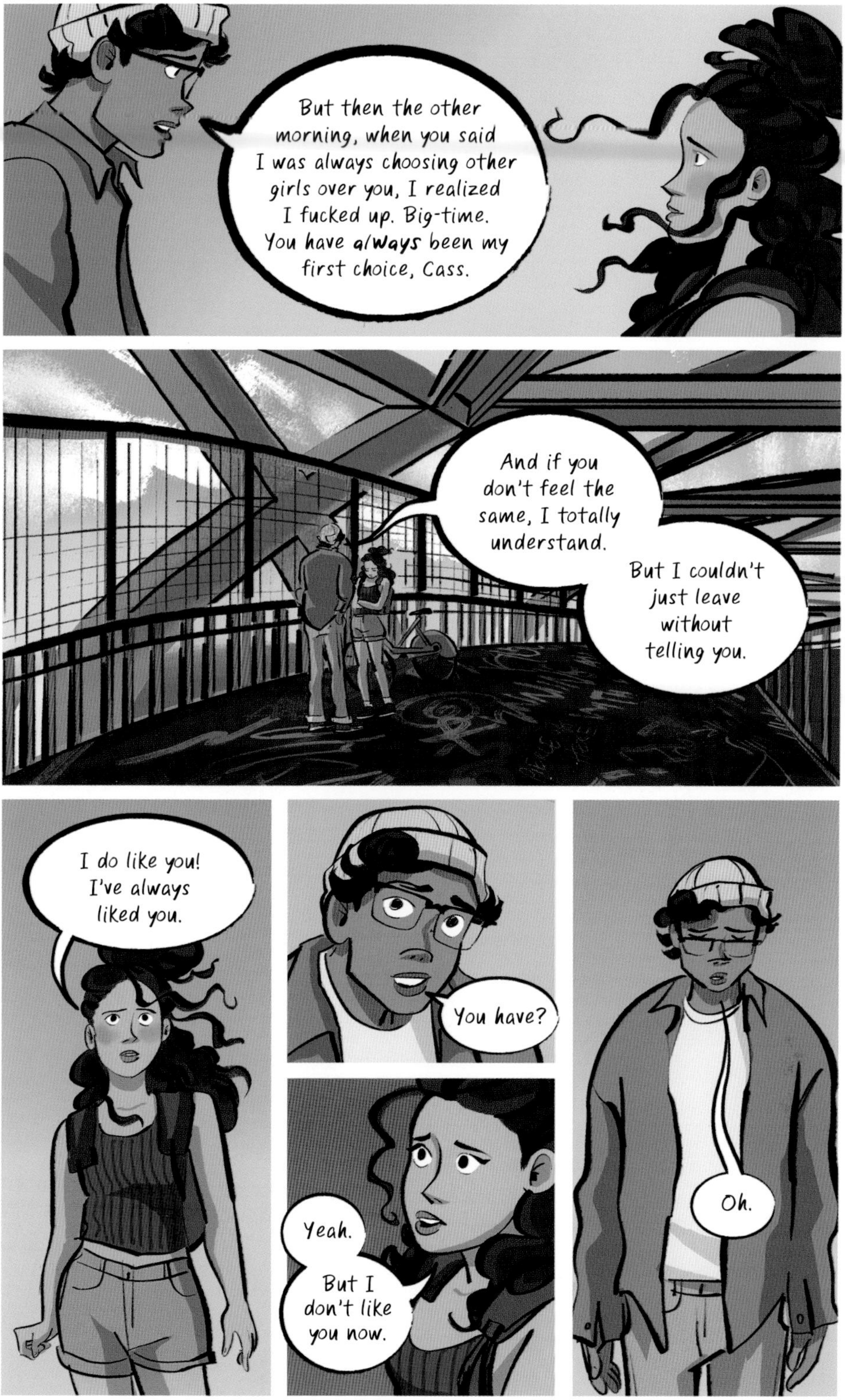
But then the other morning, when you said I was always choosing other girls over you, I realized I fucked up. Big-time. You have **always** been my first choice, Cass.
And if you don't feel the same, I totally understand.
But I couldn't just leave without telling you.
I do like you! I've always liked you.
You have?
Oh.
Yeah.
But I don't like you now.

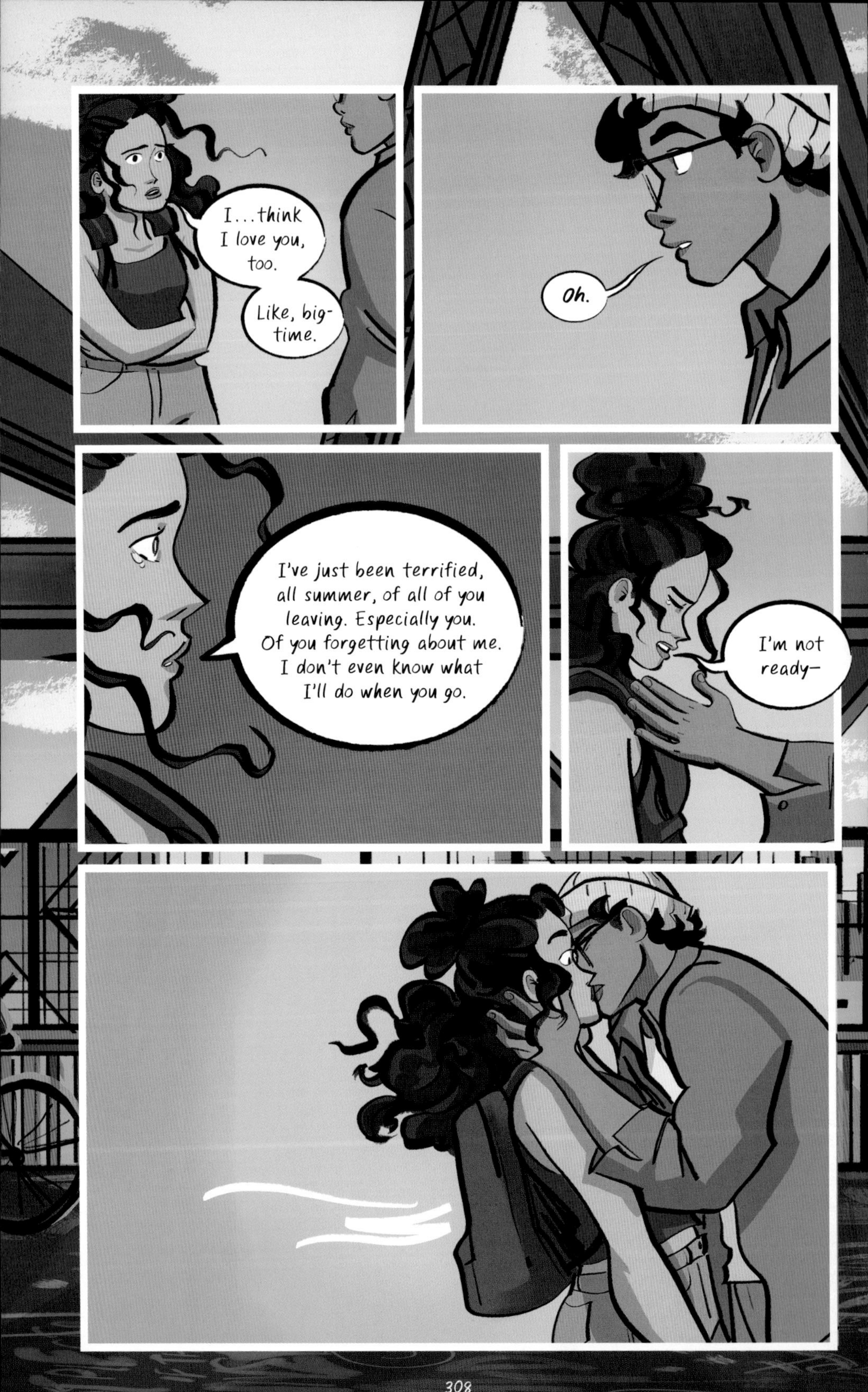
I...think I love you, too.
Like, big-time.
Oh.
I've just been terrified, all summer, of all of you leaving. Especially you. Of you forgetting about me. I don't even know what I'll do when you go.
I'm not ready–

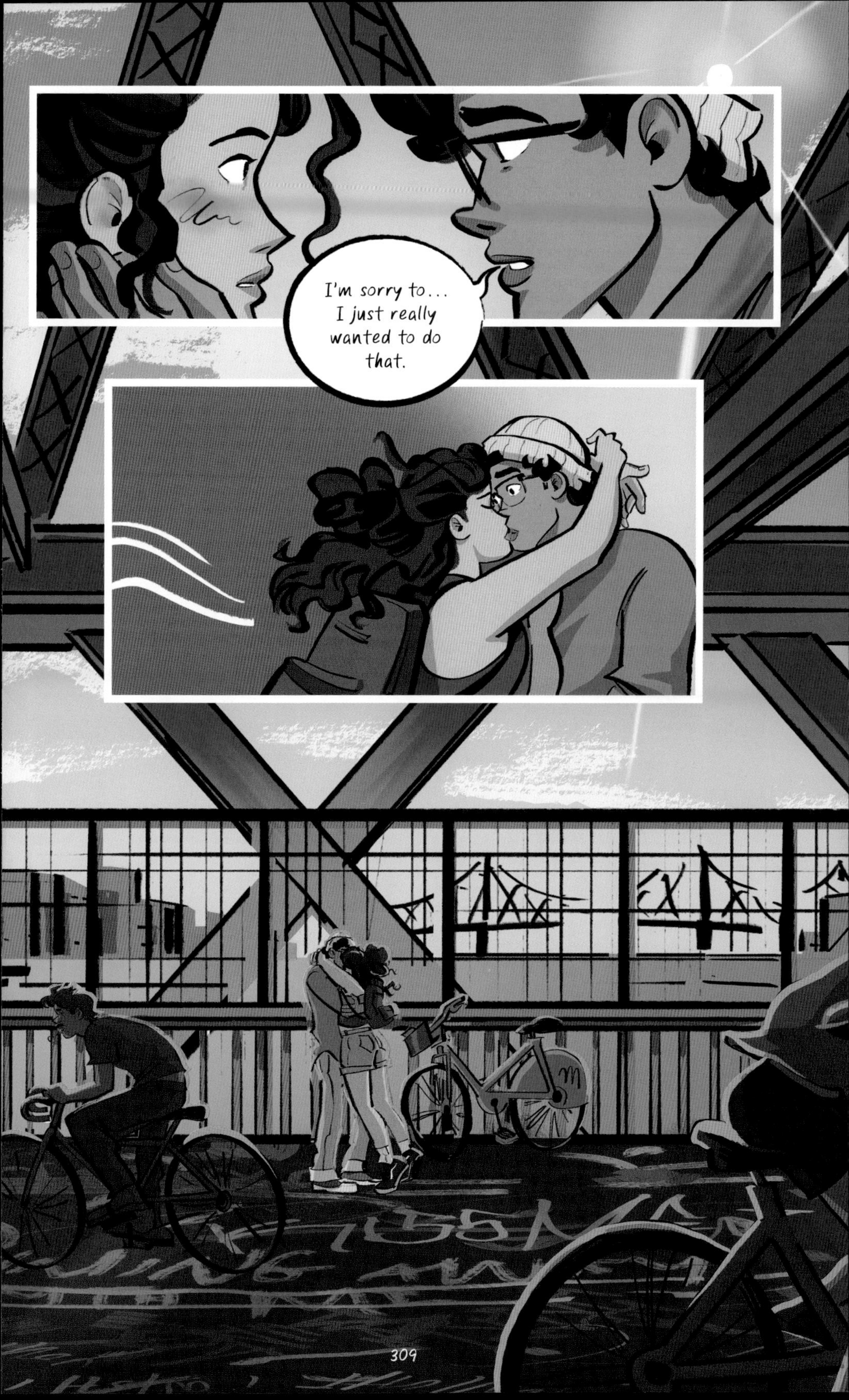
I'm sorry to...
I just really
wanted to do
that.

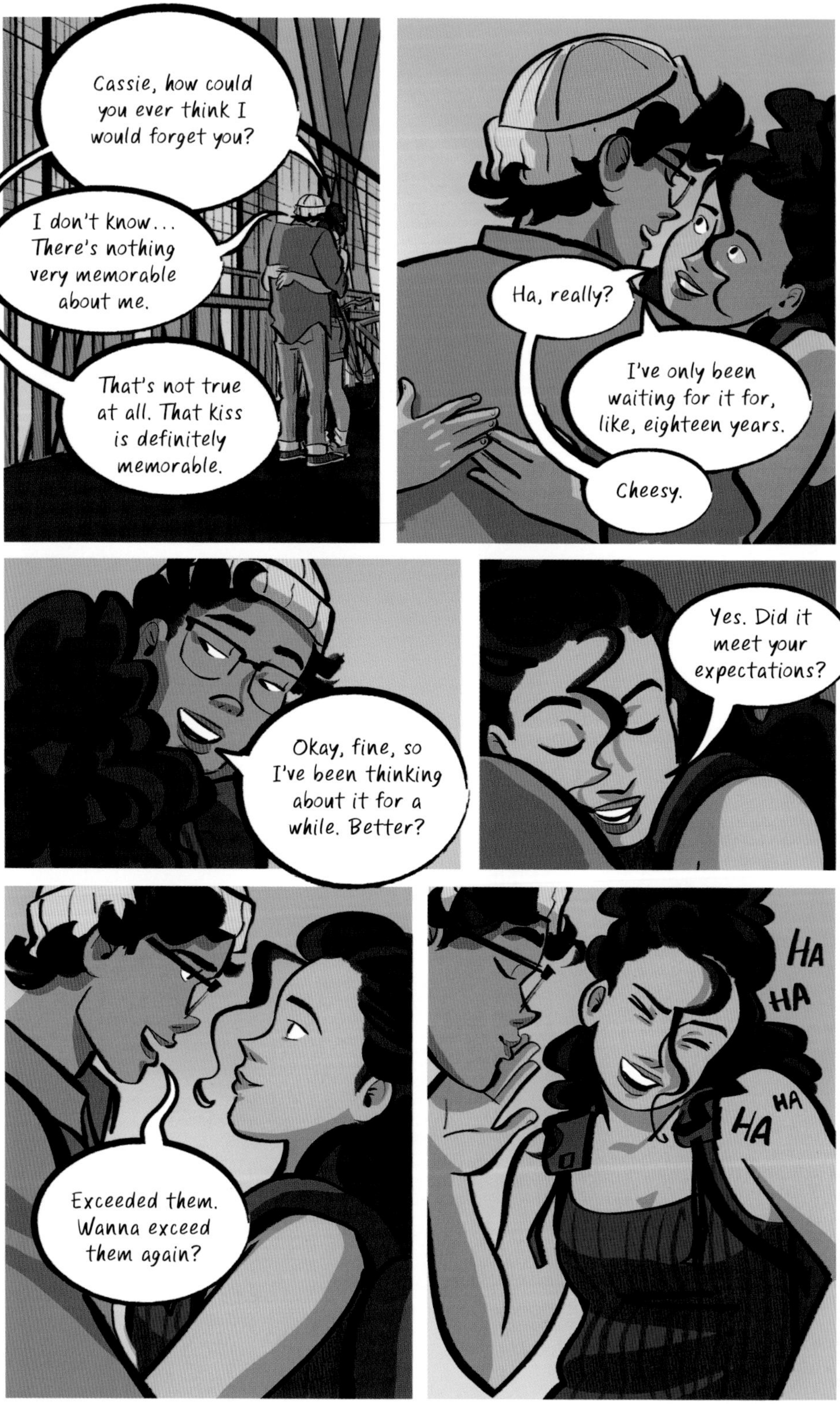
Cassie, how could you ever think I would forget you?
I don't know... There's nothing very memorable about me.
That's not true at all. That kiss is definitely memorable.
Ha, really?
I've only been waiting for it for, like, eighteen years.
Cheesy.
Okay, fine, so I've been thinking about it for a while. Better?
Yes. Did it meet your expectations?
Exceeded them. Wanna exceed them again?
HA
HA
HA
HA

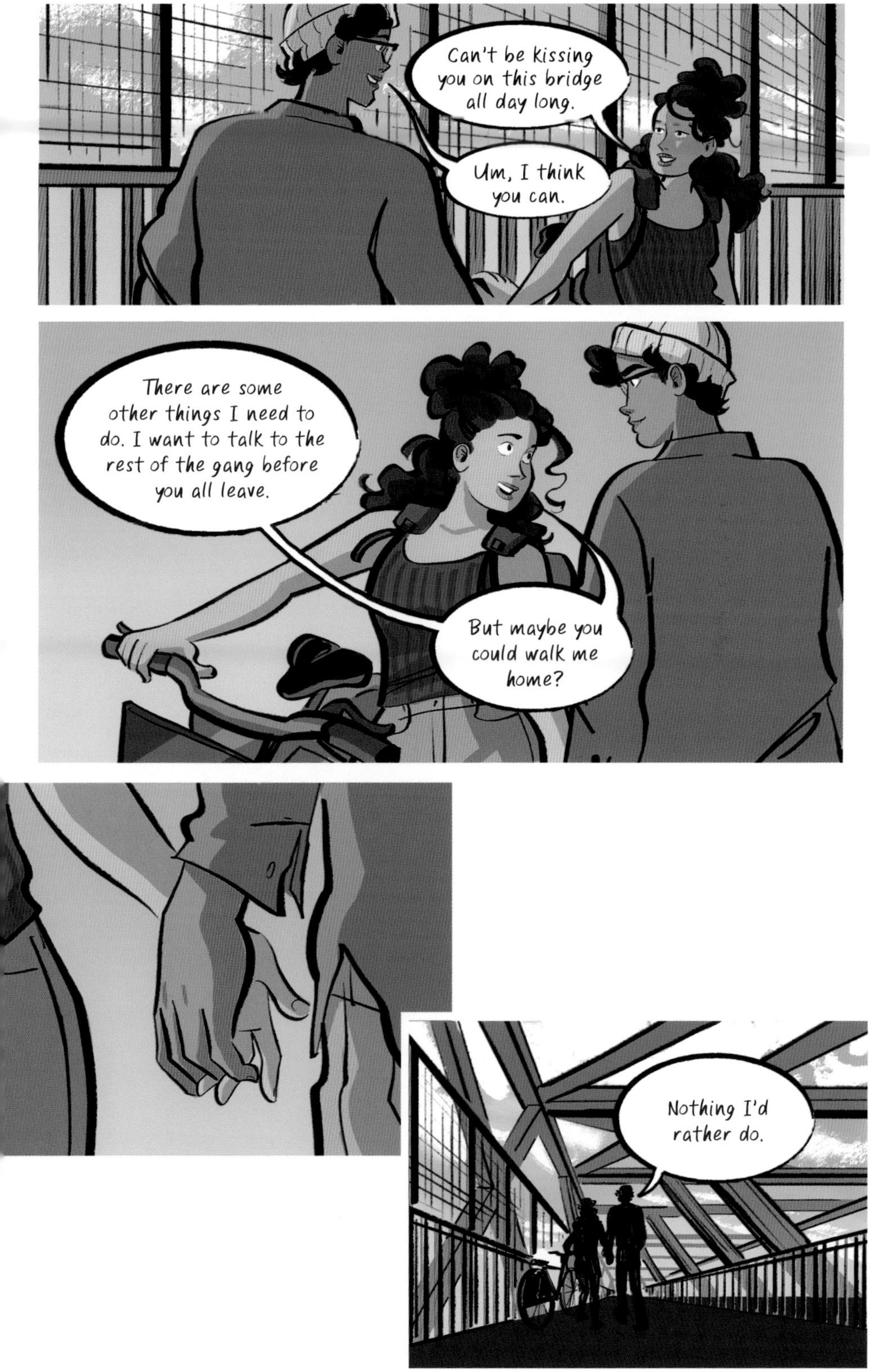
Can't be kissing you on this bridge all day long.
Um, I think you can.
There are some other things I need to do. I want to talk to the rest of the gang before you all leave.
But maybe you could walk me home?
Nothing I'd rather do.

the gang
If you don't all hate me (and I'm really hoping you don't), meet me on my roof @ 7. I have some things I want to say.
Sober?
100%
Just checking. I'll be there.
Me too

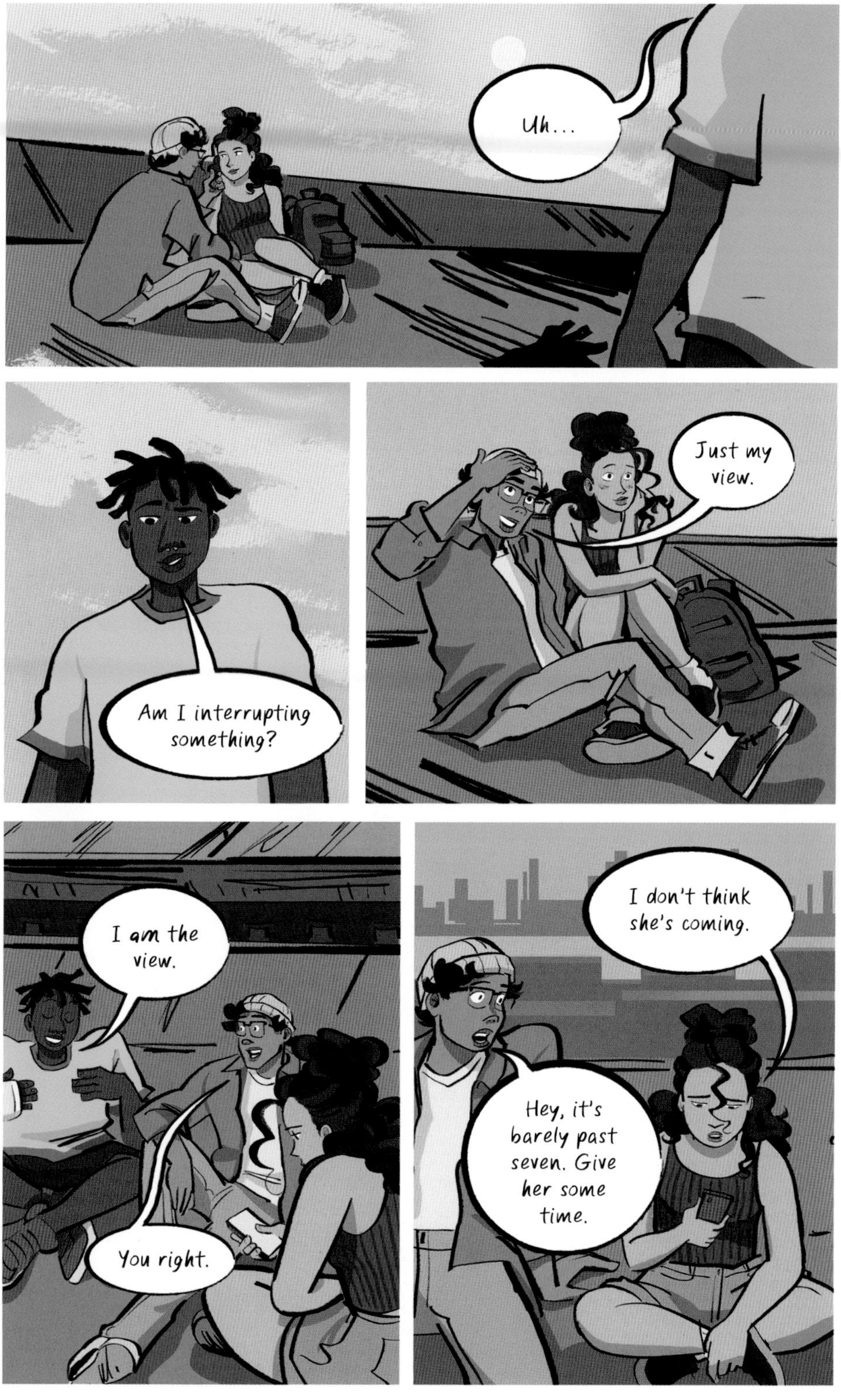
Uh...
Am I interrupting something?
Just my view.
I am the view.
You right.
I don't think she's coming.
Hey, it's barely past seven. Give her some time.

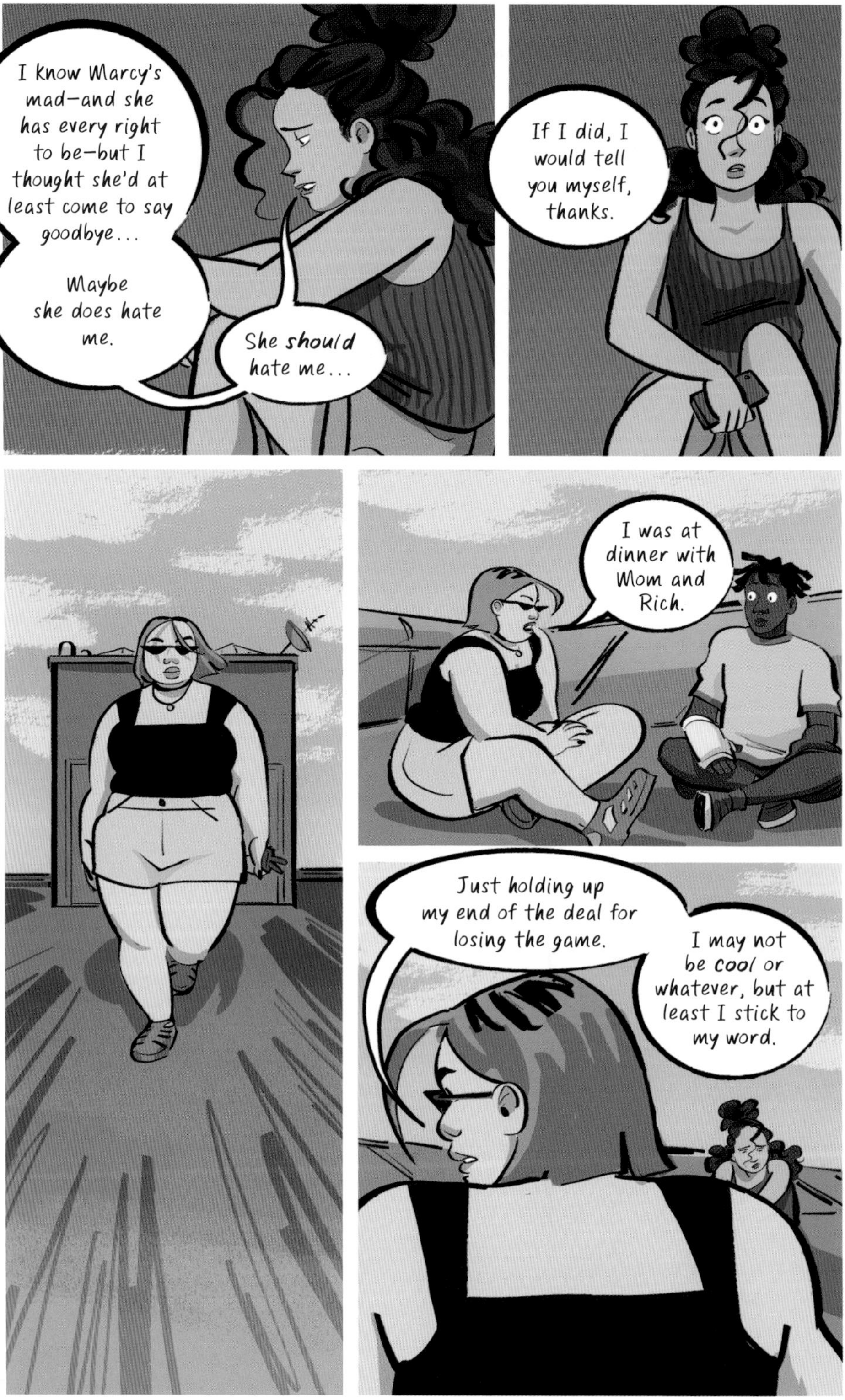

I know Marcy's mad—and she has every right to be—but I thought she'd at least come to say goodbye...
Maybe she does hate me.
She **should** hate me...
If I did, I would tell you myself, thanks.
I was at dinner with Mom and Rich.
Just holding up my end of the deal for losing the game.
I may not be **cool** or whatever, but at least I stick to my word.

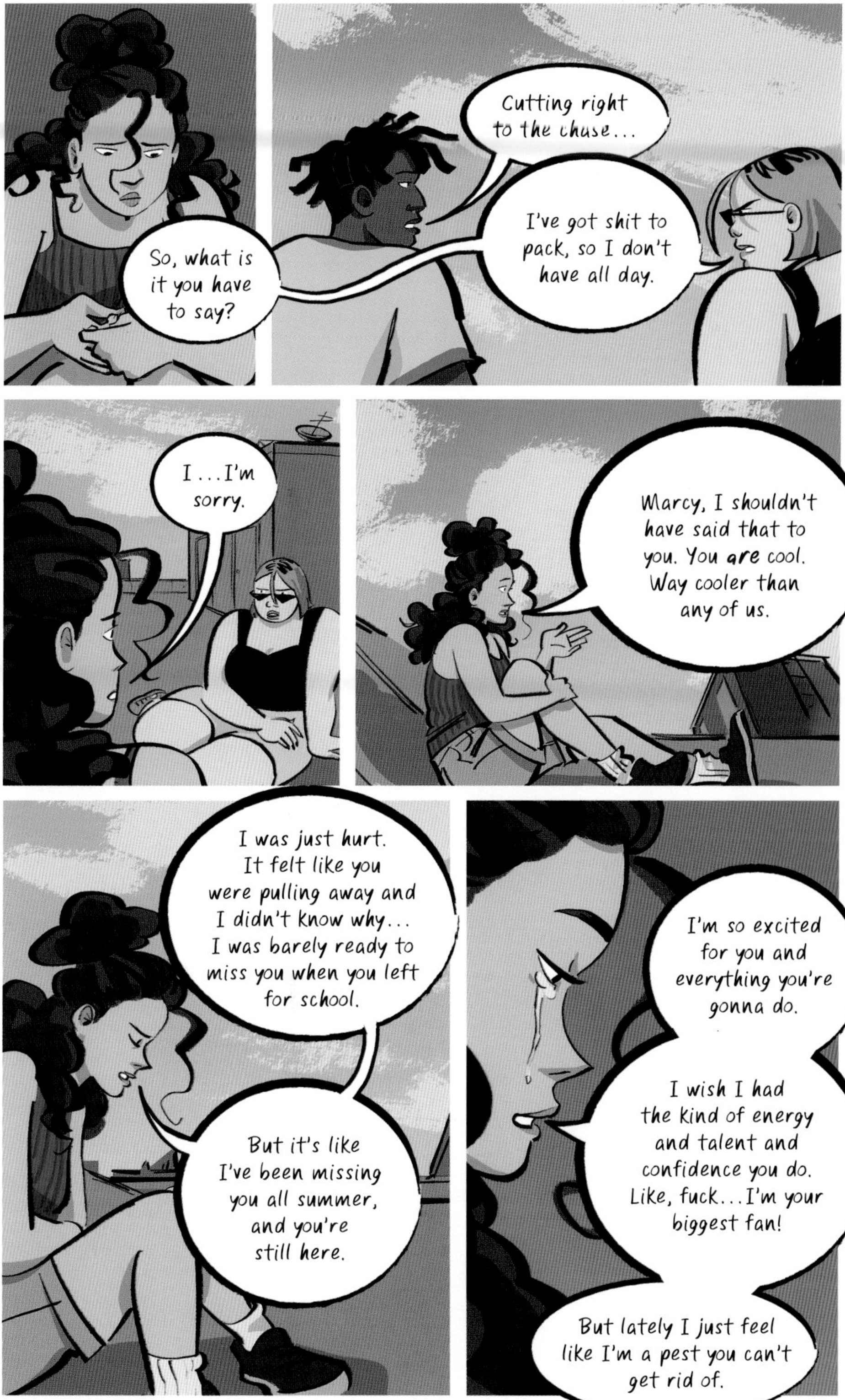

So, what is it you have to say?
Cutting right to the chase...
I've got shit to pack, so I don't have all day.
I...I'm sorry.
Marcy, I shouldn't have said that to you. You *are* cool. Way cooler than any of us.
I was just *hurt*. It felt like you were pulling away and I didn't know why... I was barely ready to miss you when you left for school.
But it's like I've been missing you all summer, and you're still *here*.
I'm so excited for you and everything you're gonna do.
I wish I had the kind of energy and talent and confidence you do. Like, fuck...I'm your biggest fan!
But lately I just feel like I'm a pest you can't get rid of.

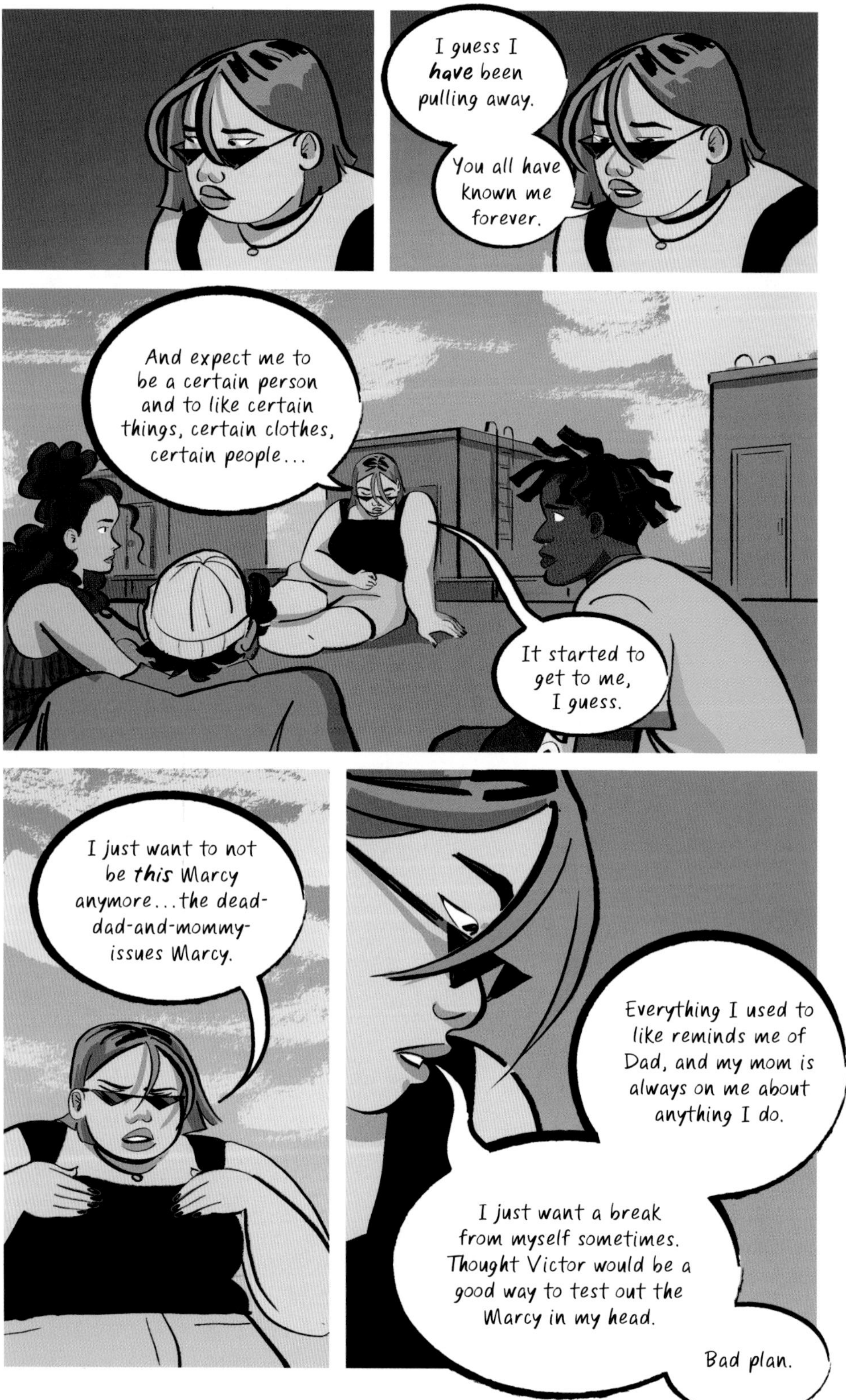
I guess I **have** been pulling away.
You all have known me forever.
And expect me to be a certain person and to like certain things, certain clothes, certain people...
It started to get to me, I guess.
I just want to not be **this** Marcy anymore...the dead-dad-and-mommy-issues Marcy.
Everything I used to like reminds me of Dad, and my mom is always on me about anything I do.
I just want a break from myself sometimes. Thought Victor would be a good way to test out the Marcy in my head.
Bad plan.

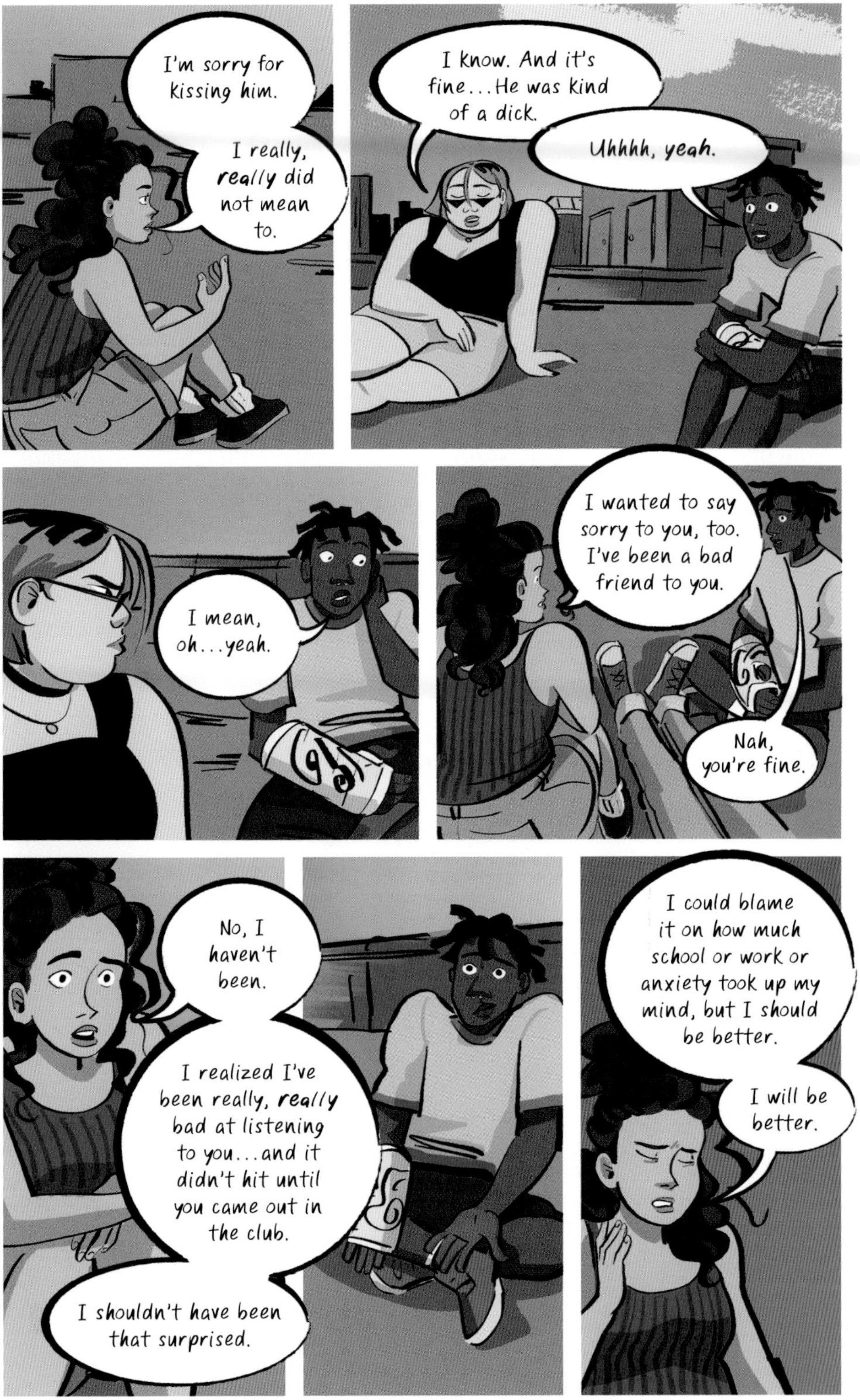
I'm sorry for kissing him.
I really, ***really*** did not mean to.
I know. And it's fine...He was kind of a dick.
Uhhhh, yeah.
I mean, oh...yeah.
I wanted to say sorry to you, too. I've been a bad friend to you.
Nah, you're fine.
No, I haven't been.
I realized I've been really, ***really*** bad at listening to you...and it didn't hit until you came out in the club.
I shouldn't have been that surprised.
I could blame it on how much school or work or anxiety took up my mind, but I should be better.
I will be better.

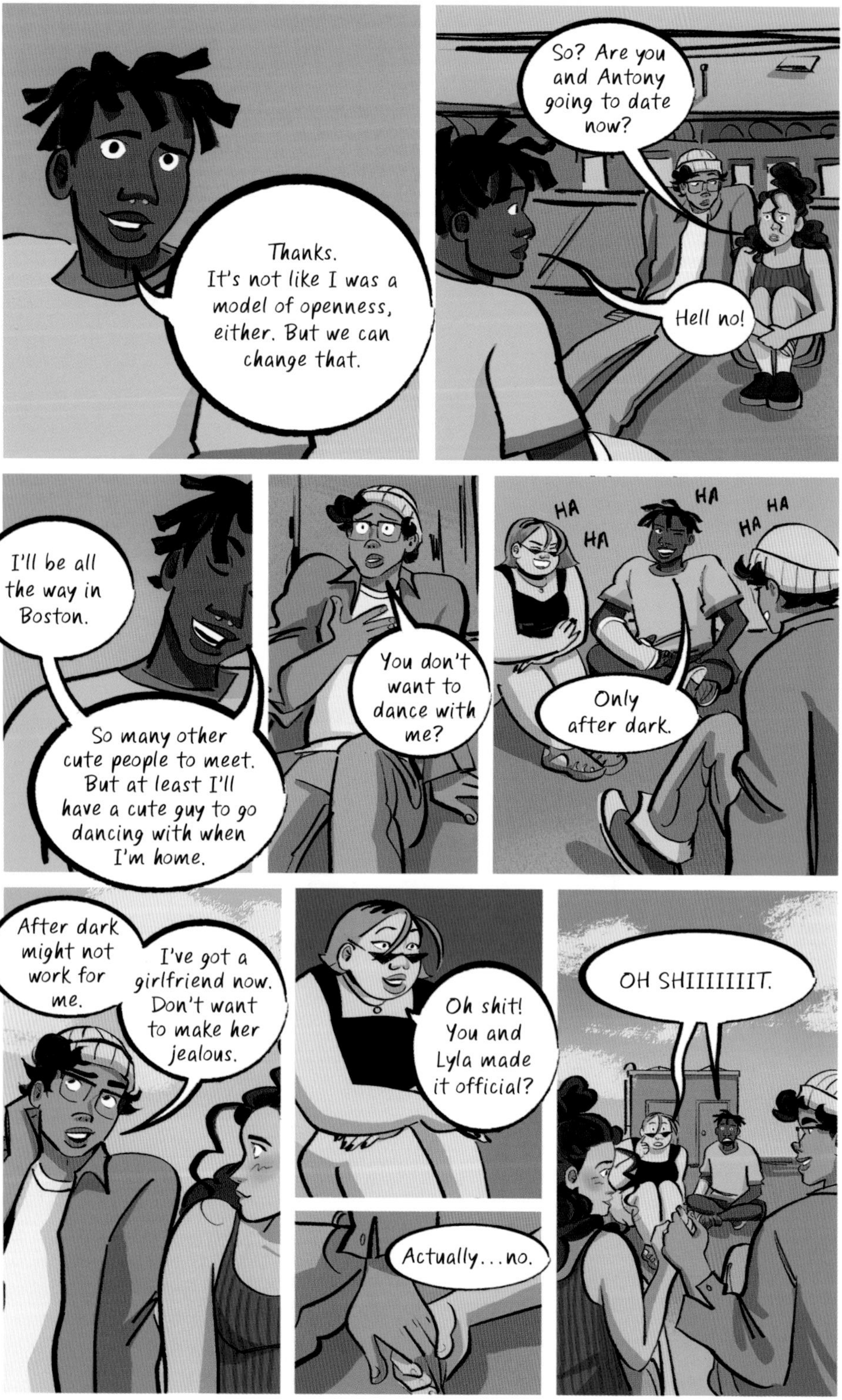
Thanks.
It's not like I was a model of openness, either. But we can change that.
So? Are you and Antony going to date now?
Hell no!
I'll be all the way in Boston.
So many other cute people to meet. But at least I'll have a cute guy to go dancing with when I'm home.
You don't want to dance with me?
HA
HA
HA
HA
HA
Only after dark.
After dark might not work for me.
I've got a girlfriend now. Don't want to make her jealous.
Oh shit! You and Lyla made it official?
Actually...no.
OH SHIIIIIIIT.

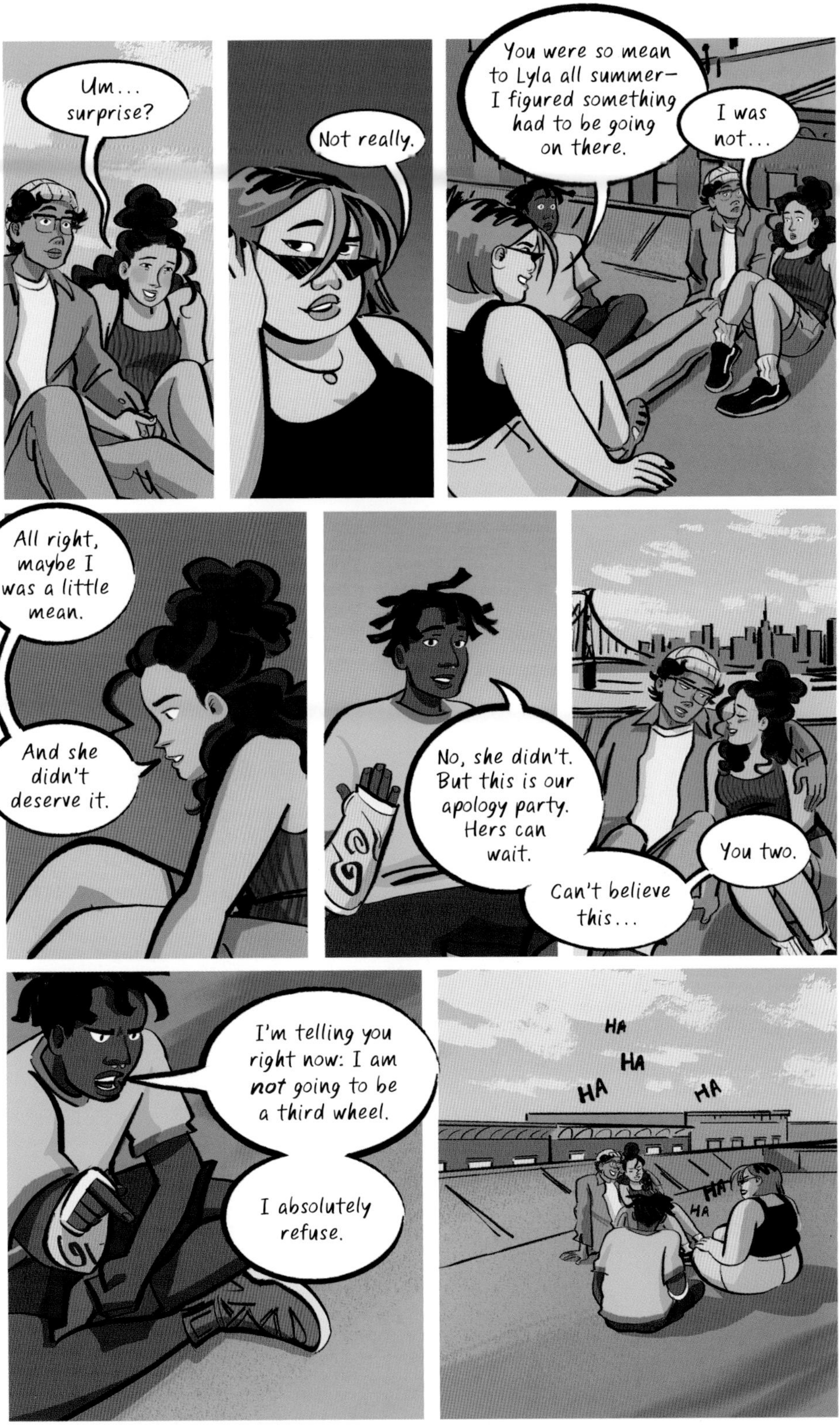
Um... surprise?
Not really.
You were so mean to Lyla all summer— I figured something had to be going on there.
I was not...
All right, maybe I was a little mean.
And she didn't deserve it.
No, she didn't. But this is our apology party. Hers can wait.
You two.
Can't believe this...
I'm telling you right now: I am *not* going to be a third wheel.
I absolutely refuse.
HA
HA
HA
HA
HA
HA

So, what now?

You won the game, Cassie. I guess we all owe you a secret.

I feel like you all spilled enough of your souls for a day.

Can I make one request, though?

After today, I know we're all going to change. We already are.

Changing. I always thought we'd have the kind of friendship that our parents have. Always together, always having each other around, forever.

But...we aren't them.

God, I hope not. I'm trying not to be my mom as much as possible.

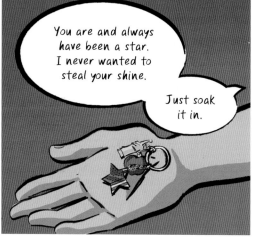

You are and always have been a star. I never wanted to steal your shine.

Just soak it in.

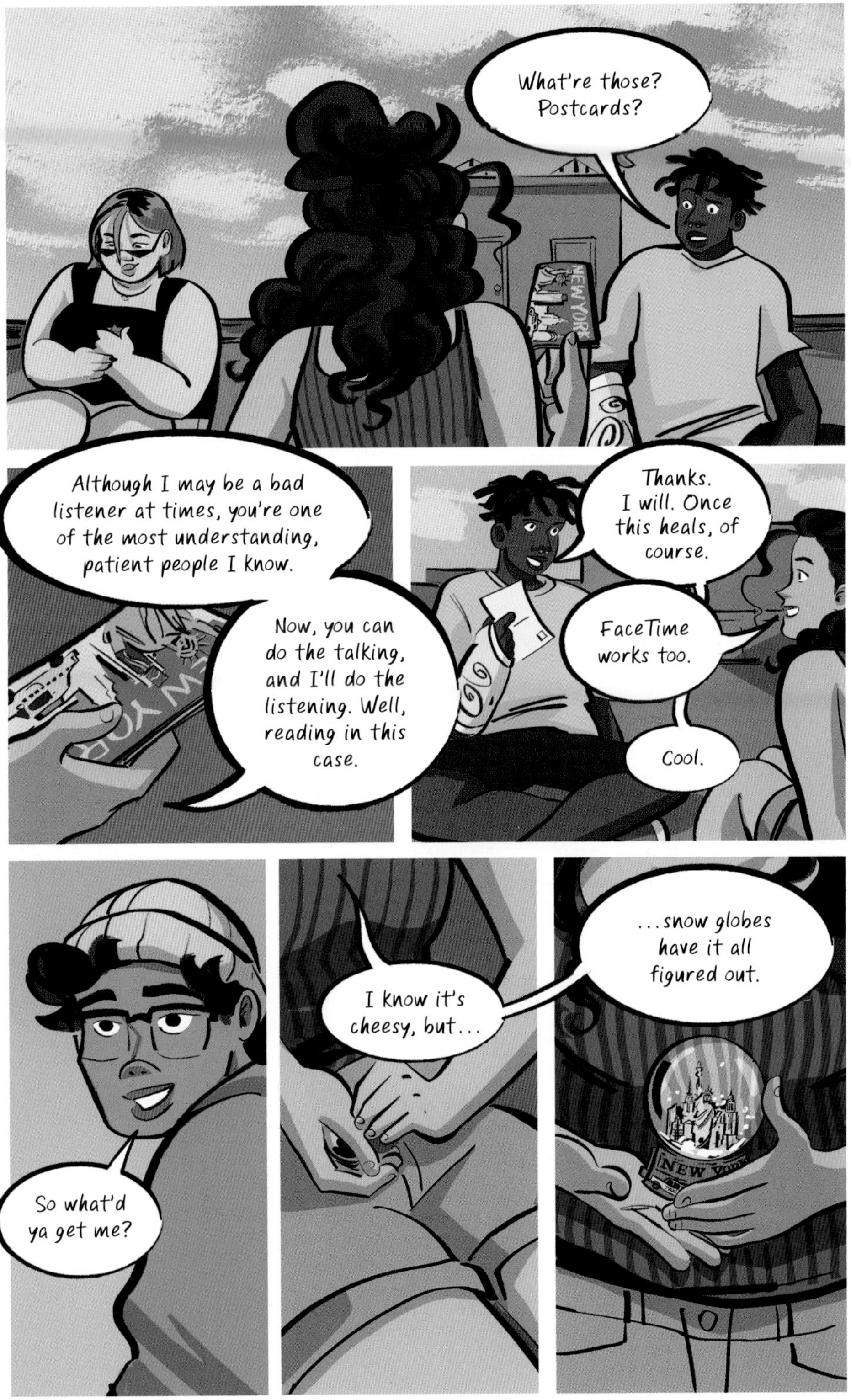
What're those? Postcards?
NEW YORK
Although I may be a bad listener at times, you're one of the most understanding, patient people I know.
Now, you can do the talking, and I'll do the listening. Well, reading in this case.
Thanks. I will. Once this heals, of course.
FaceTime works too.
Cool.
So what'd ya get me?
I know it's cheesy, but...
...snow globes have it all figured out.
NEW YORK

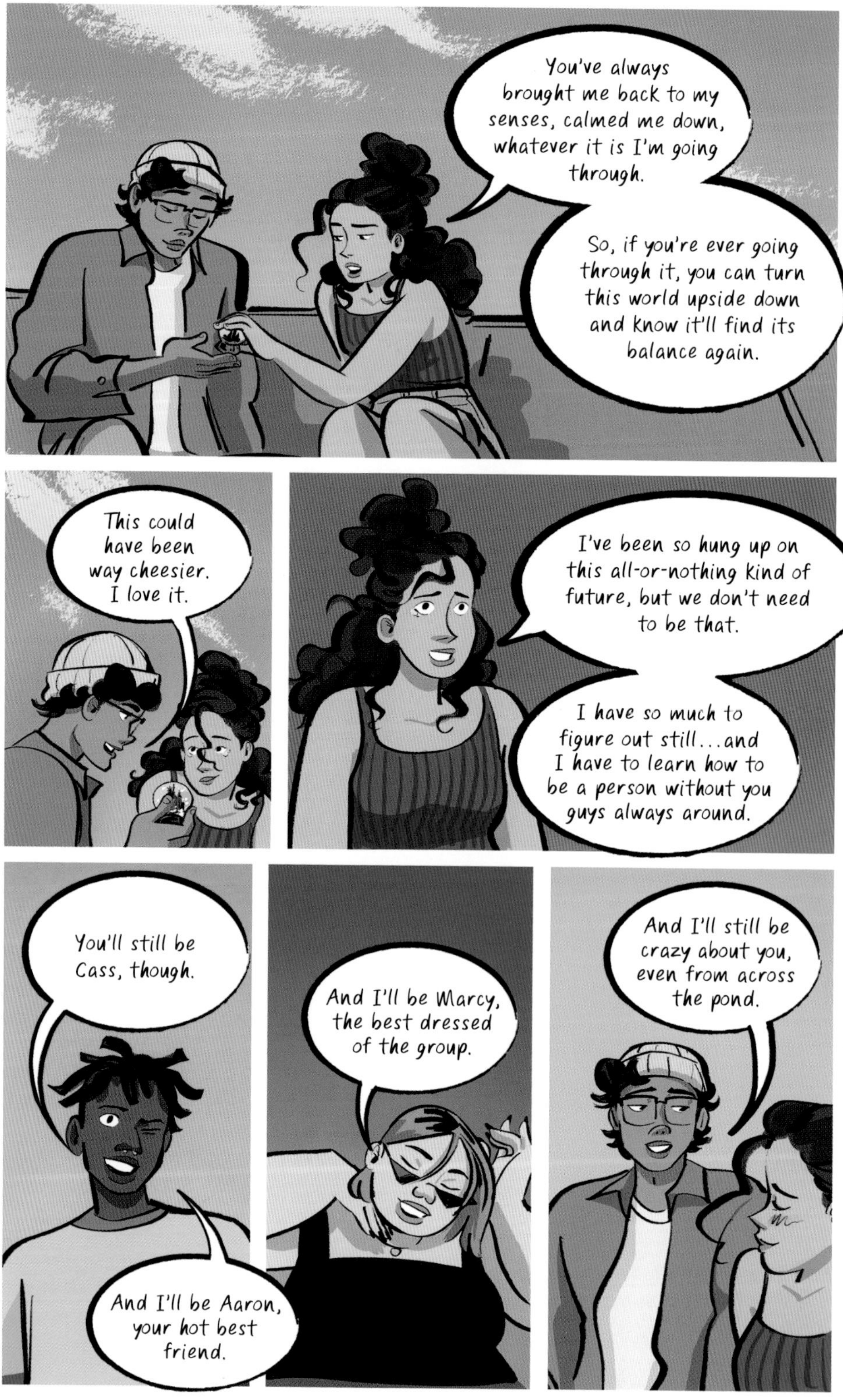
You've always brought me back to my senses, calmed me down, whatever it is I'm going through.
So, if you're ever going through it, you can turn this world upside down and know it'll find its balance again.
This could have been way cheesier. I love it.
I've been so hung up on this all-or-nothing kind of future, but we don't need to be that.
I have so much to figure out still...and I have to learn how to be a person without you guys always around.
You'll still be Cass, though.
And I'll be Aaron, your hot best friend.
And I'll be Marcy, the best dressed of the group.
And I'll still be crazy about you, even from across the pond.

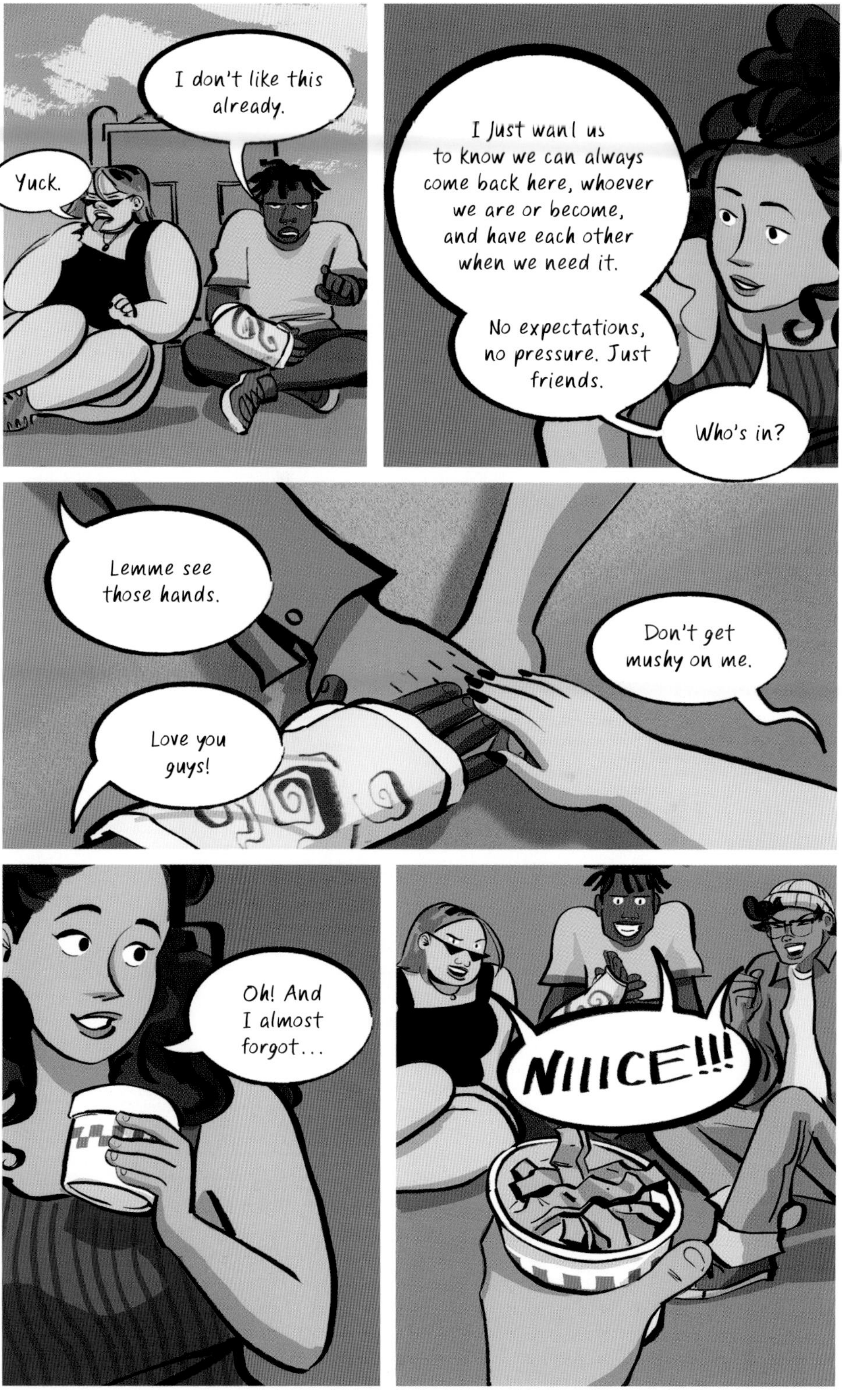

I don't like this already.
Yuck.
I just want us to know we can always come back here, whoever we are or become, and have each other when we need it.
No expectations, no pressure. Just friends.
Who's in?
Lemme see those hands.
Don't get mushy on me.
Love you guys!
Oh! And I almost forgot...
NIIICE!!!

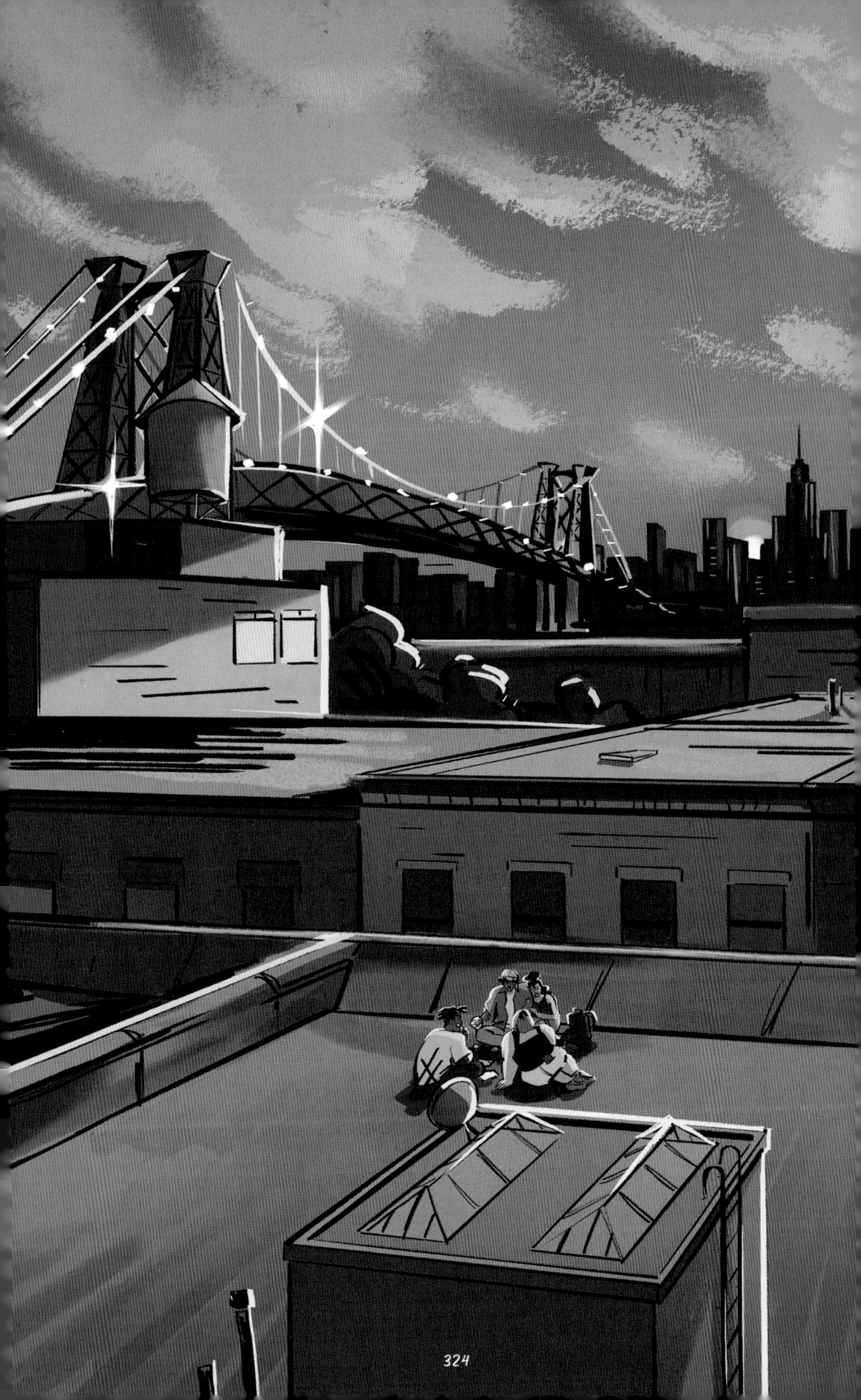

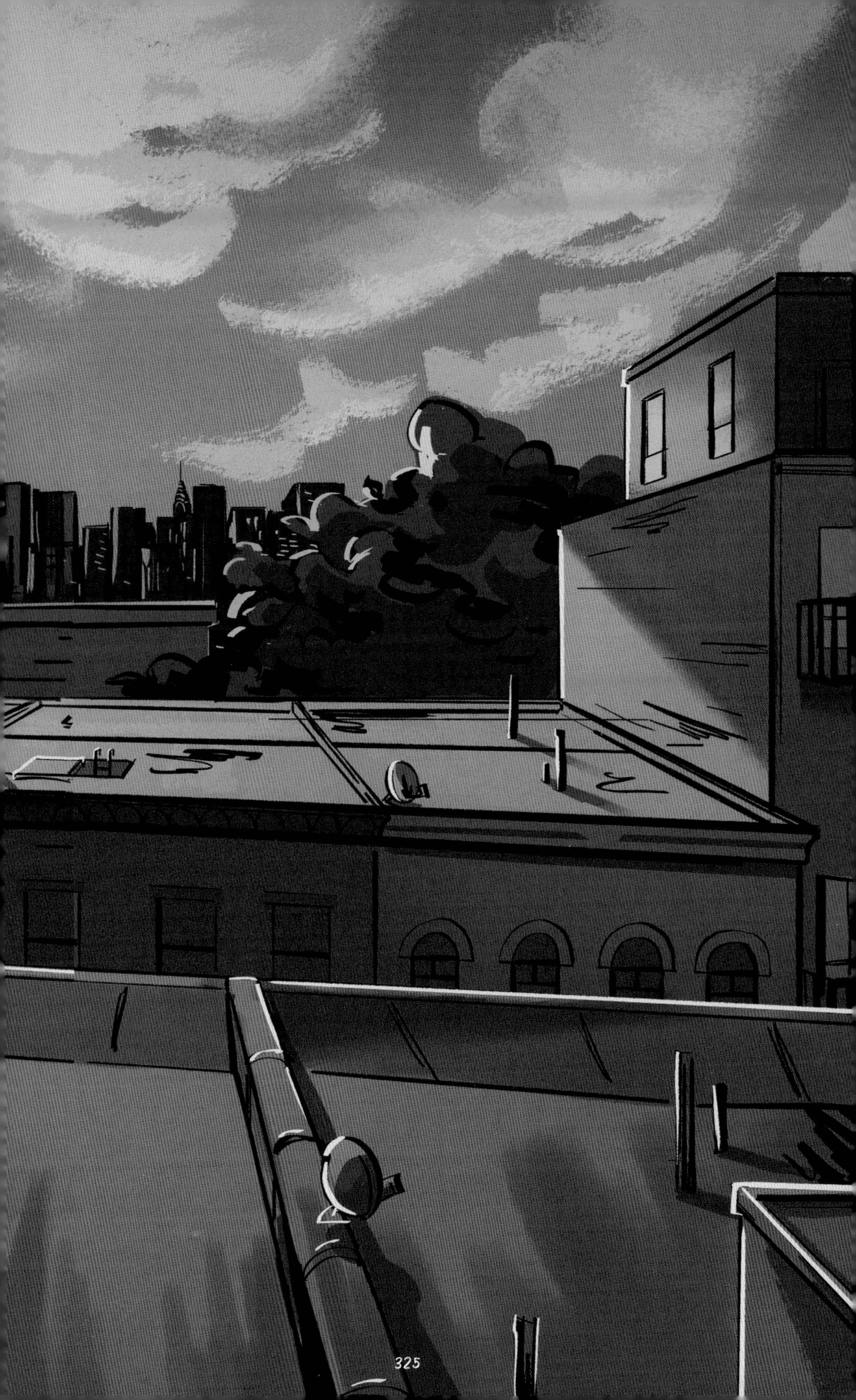

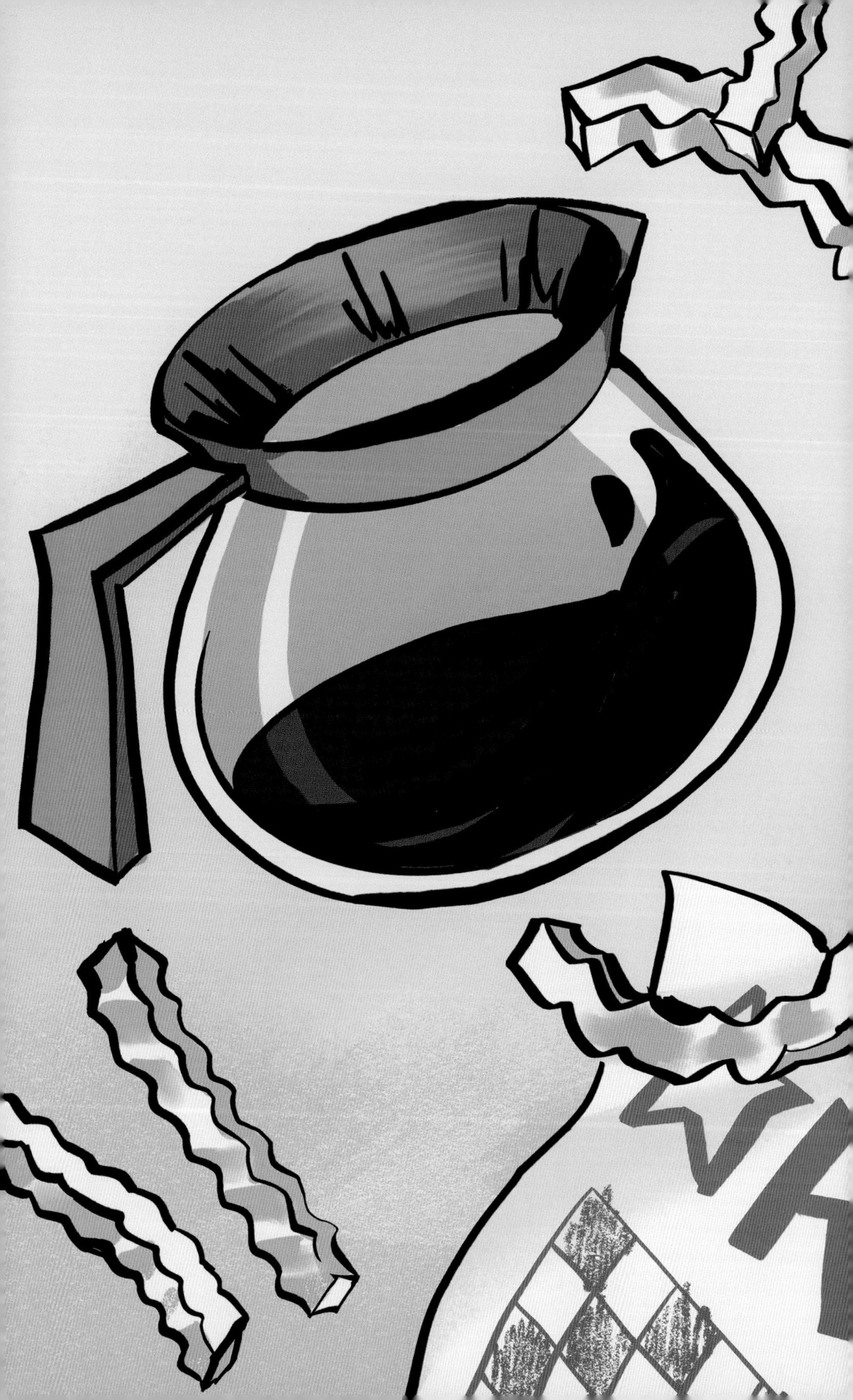

Acknowledgments

Well, kids . . . we did it. And there are a lot of people I need to thank, so sit down and buckle the fuck up.

Thank you to my lovely agent, Natascha Morris, and the unstoppable team at Atheneum. Thank you, Nat, for seeing the stories hidden in my sketches and helping me shape my vision for the page. I'm lucky to have had not only one but *two* powerhouse editors: thank you, Alex Borbolla, for seeing the potential in me and my story, and to Feather Flores, for driving this book through the finish line. Both of you have guided me and offered so much brilliance to *Ready or Not*, and I'm forever indebted. And don't get me staaaaarted on Karyn Lee, my art director and designer. When I tell you I'm your #1 fan for life, my hand is *on the Bible*. I am in awe of everything you've done over the past four years to make this book shine—and keep me sane while you're at it. Thank you to Mr. Lee for offering several thorough Chinese translations at the last minute (you're a real one). Thank you to my flatter, Matt Aytch Taylor, for expertly laying the color groundwork on this behemoth of a book. I'm honored to have your marks on these pages, and I can guarantee my hand would have fallen off without your help. Thank you to my managing editor, Jeannie Ng, and production manager, Elizabeth Blake-Linn, for all the attention and care you've given to my not-so-little graphic novel.

Thank you to my professors: Floyd Hughes, Kelly Donato, Pat Cummings, and Tim O'Brien. Your wisdom and tough love have gotten me this far. Floyd, your vast knowledge of comics and love of inkwork was pivotal to me during my studies, and you made me feel confident pursuing this medium of storytelling. Kelly, you saw more potential in my projects than I could see for myself, and I've been pushing myself to do better and better ever since taking your class. Maybe that's why I made this book 336 pages long. . . .

Pat, the advice and knowledge you've offered me spans volumes. Without you, I don't think I'd have had the courage to author my own book. Tim, you remind me to stay genuine, silly, and always wink with my illustrations. Thank you for being such a wonderful mentor and friend over the years. I have no idea where my art or career would be without all your voices chirping in my ear, and I wouldn't want it any other way.

Thank you to my dearest friends for . . . everything. My friends are my whole damn world. I am blessed beyond belief to have the funniest, coolest, hottest, most supportive and encouraging people in my corner. Thank you to *my* gang—Hollie McGill and Sarah Tarczewski—for forming a friendship and a group chat that has lasted the test of time. Thank you to Kerianne Kerrigan, for lifting my spirits everyday of this project and making me laugh uncontrollably all the while. Thank you to Katie Dermody, for venturing around the city with me in the wind and rain to collect location references. Thank you to Joshua Lieberman, for interpreting my dialogue and helping my characters speak Spanish more authentically. Thank you to Zoe Byun, Setshi Ford, Elyse Morales, and Logan Murray, for lending your doodles and handwriting to the Risky Slips. And thank you to the others whose chicken scratch didn't make the cut but whose humor, love, and rooftop memories are embedded in these pages: Berry Soto-Vega, Miakoda Plude, Pierce Reid, Meghan Rutzebeck, Kendall Odermatt . . . The list goes on and on and on.

Thank you to my boyfriend and big-time love, Marco LoBosco, for being my steadying force through the intense deadlines, ugly tears, and endless brainstorming. As my go-to (and favorite) New Yorker, your city knowledge and fact-checking were invaluable. Thank you for making me take the breaks I desperately needed. I love you to bits, babe.

Thank you to my big, boisterous Molchen and Porretta family, for being my personal cheer squad—starting with the matriarch and my biggest fan, Marie Molchen. Thank you for teaching me perseverance, patience, and kindness. And, of course, how to tell a good, long story. I wish you could be here to hold this finished book and show it off to every friend or stranger who passes by, but I'll just have to do it for you. I know it's what you'd want.

Thank you to Nick and Laura, my favorite people in the world, even when we bicker. I'm so lucky to be your sister, and I can't wait to get your brutally honest opinions on this book of mine. Thank you to my Daddio, for always believing in me no matter the challenge and (repeatedly) driving to Target when I was on deadline and left my Apple Pencil in another state. And to my mom, for being my loudest cheerleader and brightest lighthouse. You always put me on the right path, even if I don't realize it right away. I love you all so, so much.

And thank you, reader, for picking this one up and giving it a read. I'm grateful to share this first story with you, and I hope you can relate and resonate with Cassie, Aaron, Marcy, and Nico. They all hold a piece of something very close to my heart, and . . . it's not French fries.

Thank you, everyone. It's been a wild one.

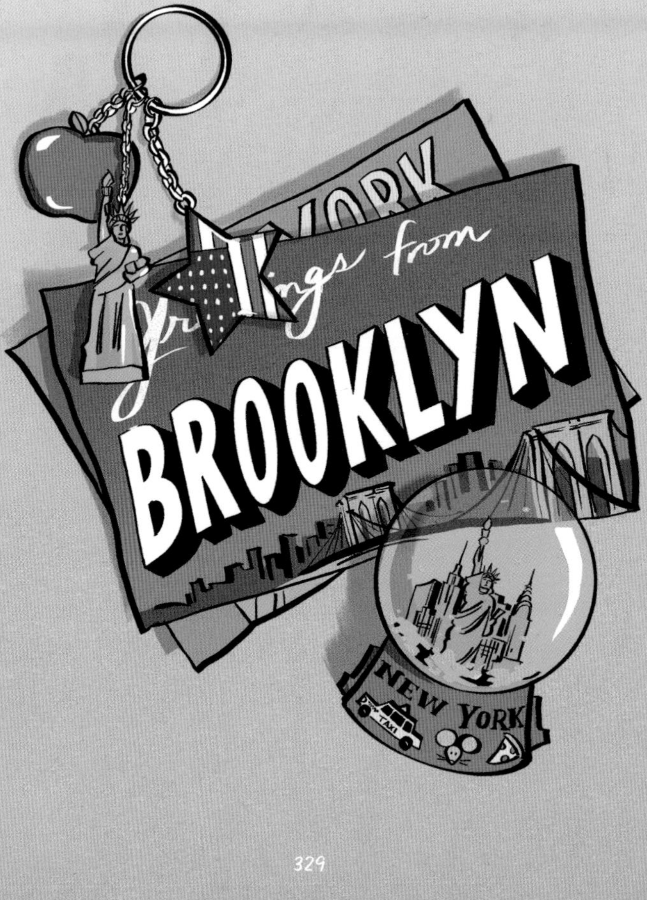
from
BROOKLYN
NEW YORK
TAXI